KU-286-449

Susanna Gregory was a police officer in Leeds before taking up an academic career. She has served as an environmental consultant, worked seventeen field seasons in the polar regions, and has taught comparative anatomy and biological anthropology.

She is the creator of the Matthew Bartholomew series of mysteries set in medieval Cambridge and the Thomas Chaloner adventures in Restoration London, and now lives in Wales with her husband, who is also a writer.

SUSANNA GREGORY

THE SANCTUARY MURDERS

THE TWENTY-FOURTH CHRONICLE OF
MATTHEW BARTHOLOMEW

SPHERE

First published in Great Britain in 2019 by Sphere
This paperback edition published in 2020 by Sphere

1 3 5 7 9 10 8 6 4 2

Copyright © Susanna Gregory 2019

The moral right of the author has been asserted.

A CIP catalogue record for this book
is available from the British Library.

ISBN 978-0-7515-6266-8

Typeset in ITC New Baskerville by Palimpsest Book Production Limited,
Falkirk, Stirlingshire
Printed and bound in Great Britain by Clays Ltd, Elcograf S.p.A

Papers used by Sphere are from well-managed forests
and other responsible sources.

MIX
Paper from
responsible sources
FSC® C104740

Sphere
An imprint of
Little, Brown Book Group
Carmelite House
50 Victoria Embankment
London EC4Y 0DZ

An Hachette UK Company
www.hachette.co.uk

www.littlebrown.co.uk

In loving memory of
Ethel, Audrey, Gertie, Food (Ada), Dusty,
Florrie, Sybil, Olive and Ma
and for
Hen, Hulda, Molly, Mabel, Hazel and Harriet

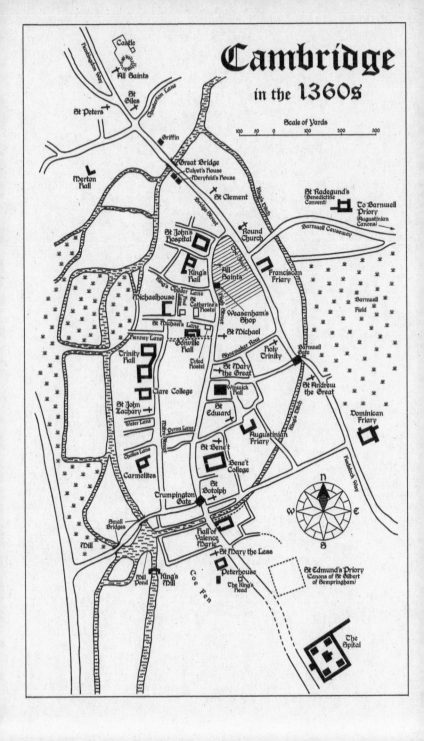

PROLOGUE

Sussex, March 1360

Robert Arnold, Mayor of Winchelsea, had many flaws, but chief among them was an inappropriate fondness for other men's wives. His current lover was Herluva Dover, the miller's woman. She had agreed to meet him at a secluded spot near the sea – on a little hill that afforded excellent views in all directions, thus reducing the chances of them being caught.

Herluva was plump and buck-toothed, so Arnold was not sure why she had caught his fancy. Perhaps it was to spite her husband, Valentine Dover, whom he detested. Or maybe he was just running out of suitable prey and Herluva was the best of those who had not yet succumbed to his silver tongue and roving hands.

Although there was a little hut on the hill, Arnold had chosen to entertain Herluva outside that day. It was a beautiful morning, unseasonably warm, and the scent of approaching spring was in the air. The heather on which they lay was fragrant with new growth, while the sea was calm and almost impossibly blue. A solitary gull cried overhead, but their hideaway was otherwise silent. Arnold sighed contentedly, savouring both the tranquillity and the giddy prospect of what Herluva was about to provide.

Then she spoiled it all by sitting up and blurting, 'What is that? Look, Rob! A whole host of boats aiming for the river—'

'The grocers' ships,' interrupted Arnold, leaning over to plunge his face into her ample bosom. It smelled of flour and sweat – a not unpleasing combination, he

1

thought serenely. His next words were rather muffled. 'They are due back any—'

'I know the grocers' ships.' Herluva shoved him away and scrambled to her feet. 'These are different. *Look* at them, Rob.'

Frustrated and irked in equal measure, Arnold stood. Then gaped in horror at what he saw: a great fleet aimed directly at Winchelsea. His stomach lurched. It had been more than a year since the French had last come a-raiding, and he had confidently informed his burgesses that it would never happen again – that King Edward's immediate and ruthless reprisals in France meant the enemy would never dare attempt a repeat performance.

He recalled with sickening clarity what had happened the last time. Then, the invasion had been on a Sunday, when Winchelsea folk had been at their devotions. The raiders had locked the doors and set the church alight, and anyone who managed to escape the inferno was hacked to pieces outside. The slaughter had been terrible.

'Stop them, Rob,' gulped Herluva. 'Please! My children are down there!'

But Arnold was paralysed with fear as memories of the previous attack overwhelmed him – the screams of those roasted alive in the church, the demented howls of the attackers as they tore through the town, killing and looting. He dropped to his knees in the heather, shaking uncontrollably. He had never seen so many boats in one place – there were far more than last time – and he knew every one would be bursting with French marauders, all intent on murder, rape and pillage.

'Rob!' screeched Herluva. 'For God's sake, *do something*!'

Arnold pulled himself together. 'Sound the tocsin bell,' he ordered shakily. 'Then take your little ones to the marshes. They will be safe there. Hurry, woman!'

'What about you?' she demanded suspiciously. 'What will you be doing?'

'I have a plan to send them packing,' he snapped, looking out to sea so she would not see the lie in his eyes. 'Now go! Quickly, before it is too late.'

He watched her scamper away, but made no move to follow. By the time either of them reached the town, it would be far too late to organise any kind of defence. Besides, he knew what happened to those who challenged raiders, so why squander his life for no purpose? It would be better to hide until the attack was over, then take command once the enemy had gone. It was then that a man with good organisational skills would be most useful – arranging for the dead to be buried, the wounded tended, and damaged properties repaired.

He crouched in the heather and watched the ugly, high-prowed vessels reach the mouth of the river, where they furled their sails and rowed towards the town. On a gentle breeze, he heard the first frantic clang of bells, followed by distant howls of alarm as the residents of Winchelsea realised what was about to happen. He could picture the scene – people racing in all directions, rushing to barricade themselves inside their houses, rounding up missing children, loading carts in the wild hope of escape.

Like the last time, the French could not have picked a better occasion to attack. It was market day, so wares would be laid out for the taking, while half the town was in church, listening to a special Lenten sermon by the priest. Arnold's eyes narrowed. Was it possible that they had been told when to come by spies?

France was not only at war with England, but with herself, and two years before, a small group of displaced Frenchmen had taken up residence in Winchelsea. They were tolerated because they were generous to local charities, never did anything to offend, and regularly professed a love of all things English. But were they decent, honest folk eager to adapt to their new lives, or were they vipers in the nest? Perhaps *they* had sent messages home, saying when

3

Winchelsea would be most vulnerable. Arnold had suggested as much after the last raid, but the miller, Val Dover, had dismissed the accusation as false and mean-spirited.

Arnold allowed himself a small, grim smile of satisfaction. But who had been right? *He* had, and the current raid was the price of Dover's reckless support of strangers. He decided that as soon as the crisis was over, he would announce his suspicions again, and this time the foreigners would pay for their treachery with their lives.

He watched the first enemy ship reach the pier. Armed figures swarmed off it. A few brave townsmen raced to repel them – two invaders went down under a hail of kicks and punches – but a second boat joined the first, then a third, a fourth, a fifth, until the tide was impossible to stem. Then it was the defenders who were overwhelmed by sheer force of numbers. In the river, ships jostled and collided as their captains struggled to find a place to land their howling, blood-crazed passengers. Then came the first wisps of smoke.

Unable to watch more, Arnold went inside the little hut and closed the door.

Hours later, when the sun had set and the shadows faded into darkness, Arnold started to walk home. He arrived to sights even worse than he had feared. The dead littered the streets, and the dying wept, cursed and begged for help as he picked his way through them. He coughed as smoke billowed from the inferno that was the guildhall, and its heat seared his face. Then someone grabbed his arm. He yelped in terror, then recognised the soot-stained, bloodied face of his old rival Val Dover.

'You told us we were safe,' the miller rasped accusingly. 'We believed you. It was—'

'It is not my fault,' snapped Arnold, wrenching free. 'Blame the spies who told the French that I was in Rye today, thus leaving no one to mount a proper defence.

They are the ones responsible for this outrage, not me. I was appalled when I came home to find—'

'You? Mount a defence?' sneered Dover. 'And what is this about spies? I hope you do not aim to accuse our settlers again. They are our friends.'

At that moment, a gaggle of invaders swaggered past – stragglers, drunk on stolen wine, who were in no hurry to follow their compatriots back to France while there was still plunder to be had. Yelling for Arnold to follow, Dover plunged among them, cudgel flailing furiously. Two stalwart defenders could have defeated them with ease, but Arnold was too frightened to help, and only watched uselessly from the shadows.

When Dover was dead and his killers had lurched away, Arnold hid, vowing not to emerge again until the last enemy ship had sailed away. While he waited, he became increasingly convinced that someone *had* sent word to the French, telling them when to come. He scowled into the darkness. It *was* the settlers – their gratitude for Winchelsea's friendship was a ruse, and they had betrayed their hosts at the first opportunity. Well, *he* would not sit back while they profited from their treachery – he would round them up and hang them all.

But what if Dover was right, and they were innocent? His heart hardened. Then that was too bad. He needed a way to deflect the accusations of cowardice he knew would be coming his way, and the settlers would provide it. His mind made up, he hunkered down until it was safe enough to show his face.

Cambridge, late April 1360

'The French are coming!'

Isnard the bargeman's frantic howl attracted a sizeable audience, and folk listened agog as he gasped out his report. Then they hurried away to tell their friends and families, adding their own embellishments to the story as they did so. By the time the news reached the castle, Sheriff Tulyet was startled to hear that a vast enemy horde was marching along the Trumpington road, and would be sacking Cambridge within the hour.

'They landed on the coast and headed straight for us, sir,' declared Sergeant Orwel, delighted by the prospect of a skirmish; he had fought at Poitiers and hated Frenchmen with a passion. 'They heard about the great riches held by the University, see, and aim to carry it all home with them. We must prepare for battle at once.'

Although small in stature, with elfin features and a boyish beard, Tulyet was one of the strongest, ablest and most astute royal officials in the country. Unlike his sergeant, he understood how quickly rumours blossomed beyond all truth, and was disinclined to fly into action over a tale that was patently absurd – particularly as he knew exactly how Isnard had reached the conclusions he was currently bawling around the town.

'I had a letter from the King this morning,' he explained. 'Rashly, I left it on the table while I went to Mass, and I came home to find my clerk reading it out to the servants. Unfortunately, Isnard happened to hear – he was there delivering firewood – and he seems to have interpreted His Majesty's words rather liberally.'

Orwel frowned his mystification. 'What do you mean, sir?'

'The first part of the letter described how several thousand Frenchmen attacked Winchelsea last month,' began Tulyet.

Orwel nodded. 'And slaughtered every single citizen. It was an outrage!'

'It was an outrage,' agreed Tulyet soberly. 'And although many people *were* killed, far more survived. In the next part of the letter, the King wrote that the marauders went home so loaded with plunder that it may encourage them to come back for more. Somehow, Isnard took this to mean that they *will* return and that Cambridge is the target.'

'And it is not?' asked Orwel, disappointed to learn he was to be cheated of a battle that day. 'Why did the King write to you then?'

'As part of a country-wide call to arms. We are to gather every able-bodied man aged between sixteen and sixty, and train them in hand-to-hand combat and archery. Then if the French do mount a major invasion, he will have competent troops ready to fight them off.'

'A major invasion?' echoed Orwel eagerly. 'So we might see the French at our gates yet? We are easy to reach from the sea – you just sail a boat up the river.'

'Yes,' acknowledged Tulyet, 'but the enemy will opt for easier targets first, and if they do, we shall march there to fight them. Personally, I cannot see it happening, but the King is wise to take precautions.'

Orwel was dismayed by the Sheriff's predictions, but tried to look on the bright side. 'I suppose training new troops might be fun. Does the order apply to the University as well? Most of them are between sixteen and sixty.'

Tulyet nodded. 'Which means we shall have a lot of armed scholars and armed townsfolk in close proximity to each other, which is never a good thing. Let us hope Brother Michael and I will be able to keep the peace.'

'Why bother?' asked Orwel, scowling. 'Most of them University bastards are French – I hear them blathering in that foul tongue all the time. Fighting them would be a good way to hone our battle skills *and* deal a blow to the enemy at the same time.'

'Most scholars are English,' countered Tulyet sharply. 'They speak French because . . . it is the language they use at home.'

It was actually the language of the ruling elite, while

those of lower birth tended to stick to the vernacular. Tulyet just managed to stop himself from saying so, unwilling for Orwel to repeat his words to the garrison. Soldiers already resented scholars' assumed superiority, and reminding them of it would not be a good idea.

Orwel continued to glower. 'They live in England, so they should learn English. I do not hold with talking foreign.'

'No,' said Tulyet drily. 'I can see that.'

Orwel regarded him rather challengingly. 'Will you tell Brother Michael to stop them from strutting around in packs, pretending they are better than us? Because they are not. And if the French do invade and the University rushes to fight at their side, we shall beat them soundly. No scholar is a match for me and the lads.'

'Underestimate them at your peril,' warned Tulyet. 'Some trained as knights, while others are skilled swordsmen. They are a formidable force, which is why the King has included them in his call to arms.'

'*We* have knights,' Orwel pointed out stoutly. 'And all of them are better warriors than any French-babbling scholar.'

Tulyet saw he was wasting his time trying to reason with such rigidly held convictions, and only hoped the belligerent sergeant could be trusted not to provoke a fight. Relations between the University and the town were uneasy at best, and it took very little to spark a brawl. A taunting insult from a soldier to a student would certainly ignite trouble.

'We shall have two more knights by the end of the week,' he said, to change the subject. 'The King is sending them to help us drill our new recruits. Sir Leger and Sir Norbert, both veterans of the French wars.'

Orwel was delighted by the news, although Tulyet was full of trepidation. He knew exactly what the newcomers would be like – vicious, hard-bitten warriors whose

8

experiences on the battlefield would have left them with a deep and unbending hatred of all things French. The townsfolk would follow their example, and friction would follow for certain. He heartily wished the King had sent them to some other town.

At that moment, there was a commotion by the gate – Isnard was trying to force his way past the guards. As the felonious bargeman never entered the castle willingly, Tulyet knew there must be a very good reason as to why he was keen to do it now. He indicated that Isnard should be allowed inside.

'I came out of the goodness of my heart,' declared Isnard, all bristling indignation as he brushed himself down. 'But if you do not want to hear my news, I shall go home.'

'My apologies, Isnard,' said Tulyet mildly. 'Now, what did you want to tell me?'

'That there has been a murder,' reported Isnard gleefully. 'Of a *French* scholar named Baldwin de Paris. He was a member of King's Hall, a place that is well known for harbouring foreigners, traitors and spies.'

'And so it begins,' sighed Tulyet wearily.

CHAPTER 1

Cambridge, early May 1360

It was noon, and the bell had just rung to tell the scholars of Michaelhouse that it was time for their midday meal. The masters drew their discourses to a close, and the servants came to turn the hall from lecture room to refectory, carrying trestle tables from the stack near the hearth and setting benches next to them.

Most Fellows were only too happy to stop mid-sentence and rub their hands in gluttonous anticipation, but one always needed a nudge to make him finish. This was Doctor Matthew Bartholomew, who felt there was never enough time in the day to teach his budding physicians all they needed to know. He was regarded as something of a slave driver by his pupils, although he genuinely failed to understand why.

'Enough, Matt!' snapped Brother Michael, tapping his friend sharply on the shoulder when the first two more polite warnings went unheeded.

Michael was a portly Benedictine and a theologian of some repute. He was also the University's Senior Proctor, and had recently been elected Master of Michaelhouse – although what had actually happened was that he had announced he was taking over and none of the other Fellows had liked to argue.

Under Michael's auspices, College meals had improved dramatically. Gone was the miserable fare of his predecessors, and in its place was good red meat, plenty of bread and imported treats like raisins. He considered food a divine blessing, and was not about to deprive himself or the scholars under his care of God's gracious bounty.

As he dragged his mind away from teaching, Bartholomew was astonished that it was midday already. He had been explaining a particularly complicated passage in Galen's *De semine*, and as semen held a special fascination for most of the young lads under his tutelage, they had not minded running over time for once.

'Are you sure it is noon, Brother?' he asked, startled. 'I only started an hour ago.'

'*Four* hours ago,' corrected Michael. 'I appreciate that you have much to cover before you leave us for a life of wedded bliss in ten weeks, but you should remember that even your lively lads have their limits. They look dazed to me.'

'Transfixed,' corrected Bartholomew, although it occurred to him that while *De semine* might have captured their prurient imaginations, he was less sure that his analysis of purgative medicines, which had taken up the earlier part of the morning, had held their attention quite so securely. Indeed, he was fairly sure a couple had dozed off.

'Well, you can continue to dazzle them this afternoon,' said Michael, drawing him to one side of the hall, out of the servants' way. 'But make the most of it, because tomorrow morning will be wasted.'

Bartholomew frowned. 'Will it? Why?'

Michael scowled. 'Because William is scheduled to preach on the nominalism–realism debate. You *know* this, Matt – we have been discussing ways to prevent it for weeks. But my predecessor agreed to let him do it, and William refuses to let me cancel.'

Father William was the College's Franciscan friar. He was bigoted, stupid, fanatical and a disgrace to the University in more ways than his colleagues could count. Unfortunately, he had been a Fellow for so long that it was impossible to get rid of him, as the statutes did not list dogmatism and unintelligence among the crimes for which an offender could be sent packing.

'You should have tried harder,' grumbled Bartholomew, hating the thought of losing an entire morning to the ramblings of a man who knew even less about the subject than he did.

The dispute between nominalists and realists was deeply contentious, although Bartholomew failed to understand why it evinced such fierce passions. It was a metaphysical matter, revolving around the question of whether properties – called universals – exist in reality or just in the mind or speech. Even those who did not really understand it felt compelled to make a stand, with the result that a lot of rubbish was being spouted. William was a worse offender than most.

'"Tried harder"?' asked Michael crossly. 'How, when William threatened to sue me for breach of contract if I stood in his way? Yet I shall be glad of a morning away from the lecture hall. I have a lot to do now that I am Master of Michaelhouse *and* Senior Proctor.'

'You mean like hunting whoever murdered Paris the Plagiarist?'

Paris, an elderly French priest, had caused a major scandal the previous term, when he had stolen another scholar's work and passed it off as his own. In academic circles, this was considered the most heinous of crimes, and had brought great shame to King's Hall, where Paris had been a Fellow. Someone had stabbed him ten days before, but Michael was no nearer to finding the killer now than he had been when it had first happened.

'I suspect the culprit acted in a drunken rage,' the monk confided. 'He was no doubt sorry afterwards, and aims to get away with his crime by keeping his head down. I shall not give up, of course, but the trail is stone cold.'

'You have no leads at all?'

'There are no clues and no witnesses. It was a random act of violence.'

'Not random,' said Bartholomew, who had been particularly repelled by what Paris had done. Academic integrity was important to him, and he thought Paris had committed an unpardonable offence. 'I imagine he was killed for being a fraud, a liar and a cheat.'

'His killer may be someone who feels like you,' acknowledged Michael. 'But *I* think he was struck down because he was French.'

Bartholomew blinked. 'You consider being French worse than stealing ideas?'

'Most townsmen do. The Winchelsea massacre ignited much anti-French fervour, as you know. The last few days have seen the rise of a ridiculous but popular belief that anyone with even remote connections to France will applaud what happened in Sussex.'

Bartholomew grimaced, aware of how quickly decent people could turn into a mob with unpalatable opinions. 'Of course, our own army is no better. I saw them run amok in Normandy once, and it was an ugly sight.'

'Hush!' warned Michael sharply. 'Say *nothing* that might be considered pro-French, not even here among friends. Emotions run too high, and folk are eager to roust out anyone they deem to be a traitor.'

'No one can accuse me of being unpatriotic,' grumbled Bartholomew. 'Not when I shall squander an entire evening practising archery tonight – time that would have been much better spent teaching.'

'It would,' agreed Michael. 'But shooting a few arrows will not save you from the prejudices of the ignorant.'

Reluctantly, Bartholomew conceded that the monk was right. 'Townsfolk glare at me when I go out, even ones I have known for years. I am glad Matilde and Edith are away.'

Matilde, the woman he was going to marry, had gone

to fetch an elderly aunt to their wedding, and had taken his sister with her for company.

'I wish I was with them,' sighed Michael. 'Of course, that would leave Chancellor de Wetherset unsupervised. I like the man, but he should let *me* decide what is best for the University, and it is a wretched nuisance when he tries to govern for himself.'

Bartholomew smothered a smile. Over the years, Michael had manipulated the post of Senior Proctor to the point where he, not the Chancellor, wielded the real power in the University. The last two incumbents had been his puppets, implementing the policies he devised and following his edicts. But the current holder, Richard de Wetherset, bucked under Michael's heavy hand.

'He ran the University well enough when he was Chancellor before,' Bartholomew said, not surprised that de Wetherset had his own ideas about what the office entailed.

'Yes, but times have changed since then, and I do not want him undoing all the good I have done. For example, he disapproves of me compromising when dealing with the town – he thinks we should best them every time, to show them who is in charge. He believes the only way forward is to fight until we are the undisputed rulers.'

'And have sawdust in our flour, spit in our beer, and candles that smoke?'

'Quite! Of course, none of it would be a problem if Suttone was still in post. Why did he not talk to me before resigning as Chancellor? I would have convinced him to stay, and then there would be no great rift opening between us and the town.'

'Depose de Wetherset,' shrugged Bartholomew. 'You have dismissed awkward officials in the past, so I am sure you can do it again.'

'It is tempting, but no,' said Michael. 'Not least because it would mean another election, and I am tired of fixing those. De Wetherset is not a bad man or a stupid one. We worked well together in the past, and I am sure we can do it again. He just needs a few weeks to adjust to my way of doing things.'

While the servants toted steaming pots and platters from the kitchens, Bartholomew looked around the place that had been his home for so many years – something he had taken to doing a lot since Matilde had agreed to be his wife. Scholars were not permitted to marry, so he would have to resign his Fellowship when he wed her at the end of term. He loved her, but even so, he was dreading the day when he would walk out of Michaelhouse for the last time.

The College comprised a quadrangle of buildings around a muddy courtyard, with the hall and the Fellows' room – called the conclave – at one end, and two accommodation blocks jutting from them at right angles. The square was completed by a high wall abutting the lane, along which stood a gate, stables, sheds and storerooms. It had grounds that ran down to the river, and included an orchard, vegetable plots and a private pier.

Michaelhouse had never been wealthy, and bad luck and a series of unfortunate investments had resulted in it teetering on the verge of collapse more times than Bartholomew could remember. However, now Michael was Master, things had changed. New benefactors were eager to support a foundation with him at its helm, and his 'election' had attracted not just generous donations, but powerful supporters at Court, which combined to ensure the College a much more stable and prosperous future.

He had also appointed two new Fellows. The first was Bartholomew's student John Aungel – young, energetic and eager to step into his master's shoes. The second was Will Theophilis, a canon lawyer who had compiled a popular timetable of scripture readings entitled *Calendarium cum tribus cyclis*. Theophilis was ambitious, so Michael had also made him his Junior Proctor, which he promised would lead to even loftier posts in the future.

Michael had raised the College's academic standing as well. He had written several sermons that were very well regarded in theological circles, while Bartholomew had finally published the massive treatise on fevers that he had been compiling for the past decade – a work that would spark considerable controversy if anyone ever read it. No one had attempted it yet, and the only comments he had received so far pertained to how much space it took up on a bookshelf.

But these were eclipsed by a stunning theosophical work produced by John Clippesby, a gentle Dominican who talked to animals and claimed they answered back. Michael had wasted no time in promoting it, and the College now basked in its reflected glory.

Clippesby's thesis took the form of a conversation between two hens – one a nominalist, the other a realist. Although an eccentric way of presenting an argument, his logic was impeccable and the philosophy ground-breaking without being heretical. The whole University was gripped by the 'Chicken Debate', which was considered to be the most significant work to have emerged from Cambridge since the plague.

The two new Fellows filled the seats at the high table once occupied by Master Langelee and Chancellor Suttone. Master Langelee had gone to fight in France, where he was far more comfortable with a sword in his hand than he had ever been with a pen; Suttone had resigned the Chancellorship and disappeared to his native Lincolnshire. Bartholomew missed them both, and had liked the College more when they were there. Or was he just getting old and resistant to change?

'Do you think Michael will excuse me tomorrow, Matt?'

The voice that broke into his thoughts belonged to Clippesby, who cradled a sleeping duck in his arms. The Dominican was slightly built with dark, spiky hair and a sweet, if somewhat other-worldly, smile.

'Tomorrow?' asked Bartholomew blankly.

'Father William's lecture,' explained Clippesby. 'He will attempt to explain why he thinks realism is better than nominalism, and I do not think I can bear it.'

One of William's many unattractive traits was his passionate dislike of anyone from a rival Order. He particularly detested Dominicans, and was deeply jealous of Clippesby's recent academic success. His determination to ridicule the Chicken Debate was why he had refused to let Michael cancel his lecture – he believed he could demolish Clippesby's ideas, although he was wholly incapable of succeeding, and would likely be intellectually savaged in the process. Bartholomew was not surprised the kindly Clippesby was loath to watch.

'I am sure Michael will understand if you slip away,' he said. 'I hope to miss it, too – with any luck, a patient will summon me.'

Clippesby wagged a cautionary finger. 'Be careful what you wish for. It might come true.'

'What might come true?' asked Theophilis, coming to join them.

The new Junior Proctor had long black hair parted in the middle, and a soft voice that had a distinctly sinister timbre. Bartholomew had disliked him on sight, which was unusual, as he tended to find something to admire in the most deplorable of rogues. He considered Theophilis sly, smug and untrustworthy, although Michael often remarked how glad he was that the canon lawyer had agreed to be his deputy.

'We were discussing wishes,' explained Clippesby, laying an affectionate hand on the duck's back. 'Ada here expressed a desire for a large dish of grain, but when one appeared, greed made her ill. Now she is sleeping off her excesses.'

'Goodness!' murmured Theophilis, regarding the bird askance. 'Perhaps she should have enrolled at King's Hall instead – that is the College noted for overindulgence, not ours. Incidentally, have you thought about the questions I raised last night – the ones about Scotist realism and the problem of universals?'

He often asked the Dominican's opinion on philosophical matters, although he demonstrated a polite interest in the answer only as long as Clippesby was within earshot; once the Dominican was away, he mocked his eccentric ways. This duplicity was another reason why Bartholomew had taken against him.

'Things have a common nature indeed!' he scoffed when Clippesby had gone. 'What nonsense! He should be locked up, where he can do no harm.'

'If you really think that,' said Bartholomew icily, 'why do you spend so much time with him?'

Theophilis shrugged. 'It amuses me. Besides, there is no harm in making friends, even with lunatics. But speaking of friends, I have been invited to St Radegund's Priory tomorrow, to hear a nun pontificate on sainthood. I have permission to bring a guest, so would you care to join me? It will allow you to escape William's tirade.'

Bartholomew flailed around for an excuse to decline, as even listening to William was preferable to a jaunt with Theophilis. 'I may have patients to attend,' he hedged. 'You will be better off asking someone else.'

'Perhaps another time, then,' said Theophilis, all amiability.

Bartholomew hoped not.

A short while later, the bell rang to announce that the food was ready to be served. The students aimed for the body of the hall, while Michael and his five Fellows stepped on to the dais – the raised platform near the hearth where the 'high table' stood. The Master's chair occupied pride of place in the middle, with benches for Bartholomew, Clippesby and Aungel on his right, and William and Theophilis to his left.

Michael waited until everyone had reached his allotted place, then intoned a Grace. It was neither too short nor too long, and each word was beautifully enunciated, so that even William, whose grasp of Latin was questionable, could follow. As Michael spoke, Bartholomew reflected on the other Masters he had known during his tenure – dear old Kenyngham, who had been overly wordy; the smarmy Wilson cousins; and Langelee, whose Graces had been brief to the point of irreverence. Michael did everything better than any of them, and he wondered why he and his colleagues had not elected him sooner.

When the monk finished, everyone sat and the servants brought the food from behind the serving screen. There was bread – not white, but not rye bulked out with sawdust either – and a stew containing a good deal of meat and no vegetables, just as Michael liked it. As a sop to Bartholomew's insistence on a balanced diet, there was also a small dish of peas.

Meals were meant to be eaten in silence, with no sound other than the Bible Scholar's drone, but Michael considered this a foolish rule. Students spent much of the day listening to their teachers, so it was unreasonable to expect them to stay quiet during meals as well. A few were monks or friars, used to such discipline, but most were not, and needed to make some noise. Moreover, many were eager to discuss what they had learned that day, and Michael hated to stifle intelligent conversation.

The students were not the only ones who appreciated the opportunity to talk. So did Bartholomew, because it allowed him to collar Aungel and issue yet more instructions about how the medical students were to be taught

19

after he left. He was about to launch into a monologue regarding how to approach the tricky subject of surgery – physicians were supposed to leave it to barbers, but he liked to dabble and encouraged his pupils to do likewise – when his attention was caught by what Theophilis was saying in his slyly whispering voice.

'The Chancellor granted the stationer special licence to produce more copies of the Chicken Debate this morning. All profits are to go to the University Chest.'

Michael gaped his shock. 'But de Wetherset cannot decide how and when that treatise is published, and he certainly cannot pocket the proceeds for the University! They belong to Clippesby – and, by extension, to Michaelhouse.'

'He told me that Clippesby had agreed to it,' explained Theophilis. 'The Vice-Chancellor arranged it with him, apparently.'

He glanced at the Dominican, who was feeding wet bread to the two hens he had contrived to smuggle into the hall. As a relative newcomer, Theophilis still found Clippesby's idiosyncrasies disconcerting. The other Fellows were used to animals and birds joining them for dinner, although Bartholomew had banned rats in the interests of hygiene and cows in the interests of safety.

'Well, Clippesby?' demanded Michael angrily. 'Did you treat with Vice-Chancellor Heltisle behind my back?'

Heltisle was the first ever to hold the office of Vice-Chancellor, a post de Wetherset had created on the grounds that the University was now too big for one man to run. De Wetherset was right: it had doubled in size over the last decade, and involved considerably more work. Appointing a deputy also meant that Michael could not swamp him with a lot of mundane administration, as he had done with his puppet predecessors – a ploy to keep them too busy to notice what he was doing in their names. De Wetherset passed such chores to Heltisle, leaving him free to monitor exactly what the monk was up to.

Clippesby nodded happily. 'He told me that the money would be used to build a shelter for homeless dogs. How could I refuse?'

Michael's expression hardened. 'Your dogs will not see a penny, and you are a fool to think otherwise. Heltisle loathes Michaelhouse, because we are older and more venerable than his own upstart College. He will do anything to harm us.'

Clippesby smiled serenely. 'I know, which is why I added a clause to the contract. It states that unless the kennel is built within a week, he will be personally liable to pay me twice the sum raised from selling the treatise.'

The other Fellows gazed at him in astonishment. Clippesby was notoriously ingenuous, and was usually the victim of that sort of tactic, not the perpetrator.

'And Heltisle signed it?' asked Michael, the first to find his tongue.

Clippesby continued to beam. 'I do not think he noticed the addendum when he put pen to parchment. He was more interested in convincing me that it was the right thing to do.'

Michael laughed. 'Clippesby, you never cease to amaze me! Heltisle will be livid.'

'Very probably,' acknowledged Clippesby. 'But the dogs will be pleased, and that is much more important.'

'I hope you do not expect me, as Junior Proctor, to draw Heltisle's attention to this clause when the week is up,' said Theophilis uneasily.

'I shall reserve that pleasure for myself,' said Michael, eyes gleaming in anticipation.

For the rest of the meal, the monk made plans for the unexpected windfall – the gutters on the kitchens needed replacing, and he wanted glass in the conclave windows before winter.

While Michael devised ways to spend Clippesby's money, Bartholomew studied Theophilis. Because Michael had given him his Fellowship and started him on the road to a successful academic career, Theophilis claimed he was in the monk's debt. In order to repay the favour shown, he had offered to spy on the Chancellor and the Vice-Chancellor on Michael's behalf. It was distasteful, and Bartholomew wondered yet again if Michael was right to trust him.

'Heltisle will not have fallen for your ruse,' warned Father William, a burly, rough-looking man with a greasy halo of hair around an untidy tonsure. His habit had once been grey, but was now so filthy that Bartholomew considered it a health hazard. 'He will have added some clause of his own – one that will make us the losers.'

'He did not,' Clippesby assured him. 'I watched him very closely, as did the robin, four spiders and a chicken.'

'Which chicken?' demanded William, eyeing the pair that pecked around Clippesby's feet. 'Because if it is the bird that expounded all that nominalist nonsense, then I submit that its testimony cannot be trusted.'

'*She*, not it,' corrected Clippesby with one of the grins that made most people assume he was not in his right mind. He bent to stroke one of the hens. 'Gertrude is a very sound theologian. But as it happens, it was her sister Ma who helped me to hoodwink Heltisle.'

This was too much for William. 'How can a debate between two fowls be taken seriously?' he scoffed. 'It is heresy in its most insidious form. You should be ex-communicated!'

Clippesby was a firm favourite among the students, far more so than William, so there was an instant angry growl from the body of the hall. Aungel, so recently a student himself, rushed to the Dominican's defence.

'Many Greek and Roman philosophers used imaginary conversations between animals as a vehicle to expound their theories,' he pointed out sharply. 'It is a perfectly acceptable literary device.'

'But those discussions were between *noble* beasts,' argued William. 'Like lions or goats. But Clippesby chose to use hens.' He virtually spat the last word.

'Goats?' blurted Theophilis. 'I hardly think *they* can be described as noble.'

'What is wrong with hens?' demanded Clippesby at the same time.

'They are female,' replied William loftily. 'And it is a fact of nature that those are always less intelligent than us males.' He jabbed a grubby finger at Gertrude. 'And do not claim otherwise, because I saw *her* eating worms the other day, which is hardly clever.'

'But *you* eat worms, Father,' said Clippesby guilelessly. 'There is one in your mouth right now, in fact – it was among the peas.'

There followed an unedifying scene during which William spat, the chickens raced to examine what was expelled, Clippesby struggled to stop them, and the students howled with laughter. Aungel joined in, while Theophilis watched in tight-lipped disapproval. Michael could have ended the spectacle with a single word, but he let it run its course, feeling it served William right.

'How do you like University life, Theophilis?' asked Bartholomew, once the commotion had died down and everyone was eating again, although no one was very interested in the peas. 'Are you happy here?'

'Yes – I enjoy teaching, while spying on the Chancellor and his deputy for Michael is pleasingly challenging. However, the tension between scholars and the town is worrisome.'

'Relations are strained at the moment,' acknowledged Bartholomew. 'But the hostility will subside. It always does.'

'Perhaps it has in the past, but that was when Michael was in charge,' said Theophilis, pursing his lips. 'Now we have de Wetherset, who has a mind and opinions of his own. For example, Michael wanted to pass an edict forbidding scholars from speaking French on the streets, but de Wetherset blocked it, which was stupid.'

Bartholomew agreed. 'It would have removed one cause for resentment. However, in de Wetherset's defence, there are a lot of scholars who do not know English – and tradesmen will not understand them if they speak Latin. I understand his reservations.'

Theophilis lowered his voice. 'De Wetherset wants to rule alone, like he did the last time he was Chancellor. He chips away at Michael's authority constantly, so that Michael grows weaker every day. Moreover, Heltisle supports him in all he does, which is why de Wetherset created the post of Vice-Chancellor, of course – for an ally against Michael.'

'De Wetherset will never best our Master,' said Bartholomew confidently. 'So it does not matter if he has Heltisle to support him or not – Heltisle is irrelevant.'

'I hope you are right, because if not, de Wetherset will take us to war with the town, and I fear—' Theophilis broke off when a soldier from the castle hurried in and a student conducted him towards the high table.

'You are needed at the market square,' the man told Bartholomew breathlessly. 'Bonet the spicer has been murdered, and the Sheriff wants your opinion about it.'

It was not far from the College to the market square, where Jean Bonet occupied a handsome house overlooking the stall where he sold his costly wares. He had lived in Cambridge for many years, but his nationality had only become a problem since the Winchelsea massacre and the King's call to arms. He lived alone, and was reputed to be fabulously wealthy.

Bartholomew arrived at the spicer's home to find three men waiting for him. One was Sheriff Tulyet, who owed at least part of his shrieval success to the good working relationship he had developed with Michael. He had been horrified when Suttone had resigned, lest the new Chancellor proved to be less amenable. He was right to be concerned: relations had grown chilly with de Wetherset at the helm, despite Michael's efforts to keep matters on an even keel.

Tulyet was dwarfed by the two knights who were with him. They were Sir Norbert and Sir Leger, sent by the King to oversee the town's military training. The pair were much of an ilk – warriors who had honed their trade in France, with the scars to prove it. Sir Norbert was larger and sported an oily black mane that cascaded over his shoulders. He was a dim-witted brute, never happy unless he was fighting. His friend Leger was fair-headed and a little shorter, but far more dangerous, because he possessed brains to go with his brawn.

'You took your time,' Norbert growled when Bartholomew walked in. 'No doubt you would have been faster if it had been a scholar who asked you to come.'

'Perhaps he just does not want to help us solve the murder of a Frenchie,' shrugged Leger slyly. 'Who can blame him?'

'I came as quickly as I could,' objected Bartholomew. He did not care what the two knights thought, but Dick Tulyet was his friend, and he did not want him to think he had dallied.

Tulyet indicated the body on the floor. 'We believe this happened last night – the alarm was raised when no one opened his shop this morning. Clearly, he has been stabbed, but can you tell us anything that might help us find out who did it?'

Bartholomew was sorry the spicer had come to such an end. There had been no harm in him, and he had been careful to keep a low profile once the town – and the University, for that matter – had decided that anyone even remotely foreign should be treated with suspicion and contempt. He was on the floor of his solar, and had been trying to run away when his attacker had struck – the wound was in his back, and his arms were thrown out in front of him. Bartholomew glanced around carefully, reading the clues in what he could see.

'The killer came while Bonet was eating his supper,' he began. 'There is no sign that the door was forced, so I suspect he answered it in the belief that whoever was calling was friendly.'

'He was clearly no warrior then,' said Norbert in smug disdain. 'Or he would have known to consider any visitor a potential threat.'

'No, he was not a warrior,' said Bartholomew coolly. 'And I cannot imagine why anyone would kill a peaceable old man. However, I can tell you that the culprit is a coward of the most contemptible kind – the same kind of vermin who has no problem slaughtering unarmed women and children in French villages.'

Tulyet stepped between him and the knights when hands went to the hilts of swords.

'What can you tell us about the wound, Matt?' he asked quickly, to defuse the situation before there was trouble. 'Was it caused by a knife from the dinner table?'

Bartholomew shook his head. 'Bonet was killed by a blade with two sharp edges – a dagger, rather than a knife.' He nodded to a bloody imprint on the floor. 'It lay there for some time after the murder, which probably means the killer left it behind when he fled the scene of the crime. Who found the body?'

Tulyet sighed. 'Half the population of Cambridge – they burst in en masse when it became clear that something was amiss. My sergeant did his best to keep order, but

Bonet was French, so his home was considered fair game for looters. His servants say all manner of goods are missing, and the murder weapon must be among them.'

'You will never find it then,' said Norbert, giving the impression that his sympathies lay firmly with the English thieves rather than the French victim. 'The culprit will know better than to sell it here, so you should consider it gone permanently.'

'We have asked for witnesses,' added Leger quickly, seeing Tulyet's disapproving scowl. 'But no one saw a thing – or at least, nothing they are willing to admit.'

'Because Bonet was a Frenchie.' Norbert was about to spit when he caught Tulyet's eye and thought better of it. 'Cambridge folk think as I do – that the world is a better place without so many of them in it.'

'Then go outside and ask again,' ordered Tulyet sharply. 'Because Bonet was not just some "Frenchie" – he was a burgess who lived among us for years. I want his killer caught and hanged.'

'Even if a scholar did it?' asked Leger deviously, and smirked. 'The Chancellor will not approve of you executing his people. It will likely spark a riot.'

It was not a discussion Tulyet was about to have with them. He glared until they mumbled acknowledgement of his orders and slouched out. Bartholomew breathed a sigh of relief. The solar was spacious, but Leger and Norbert overfilled it with their belligerently menacing presence.

'They might be good at teaching archery,' he told Tulyet, 'but they are always trying to pick quarrels with scholars, and one day they will succeed. Then we will have a bloodbath.'

'I know,' sighed Tulyet. 'But Leger is clever – he makes sure all their aggression is couched in terms of patriotic zeal, thus making it difficult for me to berate them. They are a problem I could do without, especially as de

Wetherset seems intent on destroying all that Michael and I have built.'

'Perhaps the situation will improve when the horror of Winchelsea fades in everyone's mind,' said Bartholomew, sorry to see the lines of strain in his friend's face. 'We cannot hate France and all things French for ever.'

'I think you will find we can,' said Tulyet wryly, 'so do not expect a lessening of hostilities anytime soon. But tell me more about poor old Bonet. You say he was killed with a dagger. So was Paris the Plagiarist. Do we have a common culprit?'

'I cannot say for certain, but it seems likely, given that both were French. Will it serve to unite town and University, do you think? We have lost a scholar and you a burgess.'

'Unfortunately, what Norbert said is true: most towns-folk *do* think the world is a better place with fewer Frenchmen in it. Ergo, I do not see us joining you on Bonet's behalf, or your scholars standing with us to catch Paris's killer.'

Unhappily, Bartholomew suspected he was right.

CHAPTER 2

'Two weeks,' grumbled Michael the following morning. The scholars had attended Mass, broken their fast and then the Fellows had repaired to the comfortable room adjoining the hall that provided them with a refuge from students. 'You and I were in Suffolk for *two weeks* over the Easter vacation, and we returned to find our entire world turned upside down!'

He was talking to Bartholomew, who sat by the fire with him. Three other Fellows were also in the room: William was by the window, practising the lecture he was to give that day; Clippesby was on the floor, conversing with an assortment of poultry; and Aungel was at the table reading an ostentatiously large medical tome, one specifically chosen to show his colleagues that he took his new teaching duties seriously. The last Fellow, Theophilis, had gone to St Mary the Great to spy on the Chancellor for Michael.

Bartholomew cast his mind back to the tumultuous fortnight that he and the monk had spent in Clare, where they had learned that Cambridge was not the only town plagued by murderers and people with grudges. It had only been a month ago, but felt longer, because both had been so busy since – Michael with his new responsibilities as Master, and Bartholomew determined to make the most of his last term in academia.

'Not all the changes have been bad,' he said. 'You have made improvements—'

'Yes, yes,' interrupted Michael impatiently. 'There is no question that I am a fine Master, and if I ousted William we would easily be the best College in the University.

However, I was referring to Chancellor Suttone and his inexcusable flight. How *could* he abandon us without so much as a backward glance?'

'We should have predicted that his terror of the plague might override his sense of duty. He was obsessed with the possibility of a second outbreak.'

Michael glared into the flames. 'He still should have spoken to me before resigning. When I think of all the trouble I took to get him in post . . .'

'I imagine he went then precisely *because* you were away – if he had waited, you would have talked him out of it. He never could stand up to you.'

Michael continued to scowl. 'I shall never forgive him. And it is not as if the Death *is* poised to return. There have been no rumours of it, like there were the last time.'

'Actually, there have,' countered Bartholomew soberly. 'In the Italian—'

'No,' interrupted Michael. 'I will not allow it to sweep among us. Not again.'

Bartholomew raised his eyebrows. 'And how will you stop it exactly? Or have you set your ambitions on more lofty roles than mere bishoprics or abbacies, and aim to play God?'

Michael glared at him. 'I was thinking that you and I have the authority to impose sensible anti-plague measures this time – setting up hospitals, separating the sick from the healthy, and burning infected clothing. Working together, we could defeat it.'

Bartholomew knew it was not that simple. 'It would be—'

'Of course, it is Heltisle's fault that we have de Wetherset as Chancellor,' interrupted Michael, more interested in University politics than a disease that might never materialise. '*He* was the one who forced an election the moment Suttone slunk away. Everyone else wanted to wait until I got back.'

'He must have been within his rights to do it,' Bartholomew pointed out. 'Or you would have contested the result.'

'Being legal does not make it acceptable,' sniffed Michael. 'And as Senior Proctor, I should have been here. I imagine Heltisle wanted the post himself, but when he realised no one would vote for him, he encouraged de Wetherset to stand instead. Then he demanded a reward, so de Wetherset created the post of Vice-Chancellor for him.'

Bartholomew had known Heltisle, who was also the Master of Bene't College, for years, and had always disliked him. He was arrogant, dangerously ambitious, and made no secret of his disdain for the way Bartholomew practised and taught medicine. Their mutual antipathy meant they avoided each other whenever possible, as encounters invariably ended in a spat. Unfortunately, Heltisle's new position meant Bartholomew was now obliged to deal with him more often than was pleasant.

'It is a pity he and de Wetherset are friends,' he mused. 'De Wetherset was a lot nicer before poisonous old Heltisle started whispering in his ear.'

'Heltisle is poisonous,' agreed Michael. 'Fortunately, he is not clever enough to be dangerous. The man who *is* dangerous is Commissary Aynton. *Commissary* Aynton! Yet another sinecure created without my permission!'

Bartholomew blinked. Calling Aynton dangerous was akin to saying the same about a mouse, and any teeth the new Commissary might possess were far too small to cause trouble. Indeed, Bartholomew was sorry that the bumbling, well-meaning Aynton had allowed himself to be dragged into the perfidious world of University politics in the first place, as strong, confident men like Michael, Heltisle and de Wetherset were sure to mangle him.

'There is no harm in Aynton,' he argued. 'Besides, he has no real power – it is Heltisle who will rule if de

Wetherset is ill or absent. All the Commissary does is sign documents.'

'Quite!' said Michael between gritted teeth. '*Sign documents*. And what do these documents entail? Agreements pertaining to money, benefactions or property; the appointment of officials; the giving of degrees; and the granting of licences to travel, preach or establish new hostels. All were matters handled by me until *he* came along.'

Bartholomew was astonished. 'You let de Wetherset take those privileges away from you and give them to someone else?'

Michael's scowl deepened. 'I did not "let" him do anything – I returned from Suffolk to find it had already happened. I shall take it back, of course, but not yet. I will wait until Aynton makes some catastrophic blunder, then step in and save the day.'

'*If* he makes a catastrophic blunder. He is not a fool.'

'No, which is why I say he is dangerous. I call the three of them – de Wetherset, Heltisle and Aynton – the triumvirate. I am sure their ultimate goal is to oust me completely. Fortunately, I have a secret weapon: Theophilis is an excellent spy and wholly loyal to me. The triumvirate have no idea that he tells me everything they do or say.'

'I hope you are right about him,' said Bartholomew. 'Because he makes me uneasy.'

Michael dismissed the physician's concerns with an impatient wave of a hand. 'He owes all he has to me – his Fellowship, his appointment as Junior Proctor, and a nice little benefice in York that pays him a handsome stipend for doing nothing.'

'We have met colleagues who bite the hand that feeds them before,' warned Bartholomew, thinking there had been rather too many of them over the years.

'Theophilis is not a viper,' declared Michael confidently. 'Besides, I have promised to make him Chancellor in time – which will not be in the too-distant future if de Wetherset continues to heed the dubious advice of Heltisle and Aynton over sensible suggestions from me. But enough of this. Tell me about Bonet. Dick says he was killed by the same culprit as Paris.'

'Probably, although we cannot say for certain without more evidence. Why? Will you explore his death as well as Paris's?'

Michael nodded. 'The town will not approve, of course, just as scholars will resent Dick looking into Paris. All I hope is that one of us finds the killer before there is trouble over it.'

A short while later, Bartholomew returned to his room, which he shared with four medical students. They were rolling up their mattresses and stowing them under the bed when he arrived, and he reflected that this was something else that had changed since Michael had become Master. Before, a dozen lads had been crammed in with him, which meant no one had slept very well. One of the monk's first undertakings had been to convert the stables into a spacious dormitory, so conditions were far less crowded for everyone. Matters would improve further still when the new wing was built. This would be funded by the new benefactors he had secured – three wealthy burgesses, the Earl of Suffolk, four knights and a host of alumni who remembered their College days with great fondness.

'Do we really have to listen to Father William this morning?' asked Islaye, one of Bartholomew's senior students. He was a gentle lad, too easily upset by patients' suffering to make a good physician. 'I would rather study.'

'We can do that while he is ranting,' said his crony Mallett, who was not sympathetic to suffering at all, and saw medicine purely as a way to earn lots of money. 'He will not notice.'

'Sit at the back then,' advised Michael, overhearing as he walked in. He sat so heavily on a chair that there was a crack and Bartholomew was sure the legs bowed. 'If he suspects you are not listening, he will fine you.'

The students gulped their alarm at this notion, and hurried away to discuss tactics that would avoid such a calamity. Through the window, Bartholomew saw William walking towards the hall, carrying an enormous sheaf of notes that suggested he might still be holding forth at midnight.

At that moment, Cynric, Bartholomew's book-bearer, arrived. The Welshman had been with him for years, and although he rarely did much in the way of carrying tomes, he was a useful man to have around. He acted not only as a servant, but as bodyguard, warrior, burglar and spy, as the occasion demanded. He had saved Bartholomew's life more times than the physician cared to remember, and was a loyal friend. He was also deeply superstitious, and his hat and cloak were loaded down with talismans, charms and amulets.

'Does a patient need me?' asked Bartholomew, hopeful for an excuse to go out.

Cynric nodded. 'Chancellor de Wetherset – the fat pork he ate for breakfast has given him a griping in the guts. I know a couple of spells that will sort him out. Shall I—'

'No,' gulped Bartholomew, suspecting Cynric meant the Chancellor harm. The book-bearer had been affronted when de Wetherset had replaced Suttone with what he considered to be indecent haste, and had offered several times to help Michael oust him. 'I am coming. Where is he? At his home in Tyled Hostel?'

The University had eight Colleges and dozens of hostels. The difference between them was that Colleges had endowments to provide their occupants with a regular and reliable income, so were financially stable, whereas hostels tended to be poor, shabby and short-lived. Tyled

34

Hostel was an exception to the rule, and was both old and relatively affluent. It stood on the corner of St Michael's Lane and the high street, and had, as its name suggested, a roof with tiles rather than the more usual thatch. It had six masters and two dozen students, and was currently enjoying the distinction of being home not only to the Chancellor, but to the Commissary as well – de Wetherset and Aynton both lived there.

'He is in St Mary the Great.' Cynric turned to Michael. 'He wants you as well, Brother. The cheek of it, summoning you like a lackey! Shall I tell him to—'

'Now, now, Cynric,' tutted Michael. 'I am sure he meant no offence.'

'Are you?' muttered Cynric sourly. 'Because I am not.'

'Besides, it will allow me to miss William's lecture,' Michael went on. 'There is nothing worse than listening to a man who has no idea what he is talking about. I do enough of that when Heltisle and Aynton regale me with their opinions about University affairs.'

He and Bartholomew began to walk across the yard, where a dozen chickens – including Clippesby's two philosophers – pecked. They met Theophilis on the way. The Junior Proctor handed Michael the Chancellor's morning correspondence with a flourish.

'I took the liberty of briefing the beadles, too,' he said gushingly. 'To save you the trouble. Your time is too precious for such menial tasks.'

Beadles were the small army of men who kept order among the scholars.

'Thank you,' said Michael, scanning the letters quickly and deciding that none held anything important. 'You had better go to the hall now. William will start in a moment.'

The Junior Proctor regarded him in dismay. 'You expect *me* to be there? I assumed you would spare me such horrors.'

'I wish I could,' said Michael apologetically. 'But someone needs to supervise. Matt and I are summoned to St Mary the Great, Clippesby has a prior appointment with a pig, and Aungel is too junior. You are the only Fellow left.'

'But I was going to St Radegund's Priory,' objected Theophilis. 'One of the nuns is going to preach about sainthood, and I invited Aynton to accompany me. He will be disappointed if I tell him that we cannot go.'

'Then I am afraid he must bear it as well as he can,' said Michael, unmoved, 'because you are needed here. Now, remember – seat all the Dominicans at the back, where they cannot hit the speaker, and separate the Franciscans from the Carmelites. Keep your wits about you at all times, and be ready to intervene if the situation looks set to turn violent.'

'You think a lecture on theology will end in fisticuffs?' gulped Theophilis, alarmed.

'Only a man who has never heard William sounding off would ask *that* question,' muttered Michael as he walked away.

Although it was May, the weather was unseasonably warm. Unusually, there had been no snow or frost after January, and the first signs of spring had started to appear before February was out. By April, the countryside had exploded into leaf. Farmers boasted that they were more than a month ahead of schedule, and predicted bumper harvests. It was so mild that even the short walk from the College was enough to work up a sweat, and Michael mopped his face with the piece of silk that he kept for the purpose.

Cambridge was attractive if one did not look too closely. It boasted more than a dozen churches, each a jewel in its own right, and a wealth of priories, as most of the main religious Orders were represented – Franciscans,

Dominicans, Carmelites, Austins and Gilbertines. And then there were the eight Colleges, ranging from the palatial fortress that was King's Hall to little Peterhouse, the oldest and most picturesque.

There were also two hospitals. One was St John's, a venerable establishment that accommodated some of the town's elderly infirm. The other was a new foundation on the Trumpington road named the Hospital of St Anthony and St Eloy, although everyone usually just called it 'the Spital'. It was to have housed lepers, but incidence of that particular disease had declined over the last century, so it had opened its doors to lunatics instead.

The high street was pretty in the early summer sunlight, the plasterwork on its houses glowing gold, pink, blue and cream. There was a busy clatter as carts rattled to and from the market square, interspersed with the cries of vendors hawking their wares. Above it all rose the clang of bells, from the rich bass of St Mary the Great to the tinny jangle of St Botolph, calling the faithful to prayer.

Despite the beauty, Bartholomew sensed a darkly menacing atmosphere. So far, the heightened tension between town and University had been confined to words and the occasional scuffle, although everyone knew it would not be long before there was a full-scale brawl. The College that bore the brunt of the town's hostility was King's Hall – massive, ostentatiously wealthy, and home to the sons of nobles or those destined to be courtiers or royal clerks. By contrast, Michaelhouse was popular because Bartholomew treated the town's poor free of charge, while Michael ran the choir, a group of supremely untalented individuals who came for the free bread and ale after practices.

'I hope there will be no trouble while the nuns are here,' the monk said, watching a group of apprentices make obscene gestures at two Gonville Hall men, who had rashly elected to don tunics that were currently fashionable in France. 'I hope to secure a couple of abbesses as benefactors, so I shall be vexed if they witness any unseemly behaviour.'

Bartholomew regarded him blankly. 'What nuns?'

Michael shot him a weary glance. 'The ones who are here for the *conloquium*. Do not pretend to be ignorant, because I have spoken of little else since the Bishop's letter came.'

'Our Bishop?' asked Bartholomew, vaguely recalling that a missive had arrived, although it had been some weeks back, so he thought he could be forgiven for having forgotten. Moreover, Michael had been the prelate's emissary for years, keeping him informed of what was happening in the University, and the Bishop was always writing to thank him. As a result, letters bearing the episcopal seal were nothing out of the ordinary.

'Of course our Bishop,' said Michael crossly. 'Surely you cannot think I would arrange such an event for another one?'

Gradually, Bartholomew remembered what Michael had told him about the *conloquium*. It was a once-in-a-decade event, when leading Benedictine nuns gathered for lectures, discussions and religious instruction. He recalled being surprised that Michael had agreed to let it happen in Cambridge, given that he had his hands so full already. He said as much again.

'I did it because the Bishop is on the verge of recommending me to the Pope as his successor,' explained Michael. 'I cannot afford to lose his goodwill by refusing to let a few nuns get together, not after all my dedicated grovelling these last ten years.'

'I suppose not,' said Bartholomew, amused by the naked ambition. 'But if I recall aright, the *conloquium* was supposed to be in Lyminster Priory this time around.'

'It was, but Lyminster is near the coast, and the King

felt it would represent too great a temptation for French raiders. He is right: not only would there be rich pickings for looters, but high-ranking delegates could be kidnapped and held to ransom.'

'Would the Dauphin risk such an assault? We have his father in the Tower of London – a father who will forfeit his head if the son attacks us again.'

'You can never trust the French to see sense, Matt. *Our* King certainly does not, or he would not have issued the call to arms. Anyway, His Majesty wanted the *conloquium* held inland, so our Bishop recommended St Radegund's. I agreed to organise everything, and the delegates began arriving a fortnight ago. It has gone well, and will end in just over a week.'

'St Radegund's,' mused Bartholomew. 'Was there nowhere more suitable to hold it?'

He phrased the question carefully, because that particular foundation had been the subject of several episcopal visitations, after which even the worldly Bishop had declared himself shocked by what went on there. The present incumbent was irreproachable, but the convent's reputation remained tarnished even so. Ergo, it was not a place *he* would have chosen for a gathering of the country's female religious elite.

'It has a large dormitory, a refectory big enough for everyone to eat together, and a huge chapel for their devotions. The Bishop was right to suggest it – it is the perfect venue.'

As the monk had elected not to understand his meaning, Bartholomew let the matter of the foundation's dubious past drop. 'How many nuns are here?' he asked instead.

'Two hundred or so – the heads of about fifty houses and their retinues. St Radegund's cannot accommodate them all comfortably, so I put ten in the Gilbertines' guesthouse and twenty in the Spital. The lunatics were not very pleased to learn they were to have company, but it could not be helped.'

'You brought two hundred women here?' asked Bartholomew in disbelief. 'In term time, when we have students in residence?'

He did not need to add more. Women were forbidden to scholars, but it was a stricture few were inclined to follow, especially the younger ones.

'They are nuns, not ladies of the night,' retorted Michael. 'Besides, the delegates have a full schedule of interesting events, so are far too busy for romantic dalliances. The only ones you will see in town are those going to or from their lodgings with the Gilbertines or at the Spital.'

'Yes, but some of these "interesting events" are open to outsiders – Theophilis was invited to a lecture. Moreover, it is unreasonable to expect these women to go home without seeing something of the town.'

'Then I shall encourage them to leave promptly – hopefully *before* they witness anything unedifying, especially the ones I aim to make Michaelhouse benefactors.'

'Good luck with that! Mischief is in the air, and has been ever since we heard about Winchelsea and the King ordered everyone to train to arms. Not to mention the murders of Paris the Plagiarist and now Bonet the spicer.'

'Yes,' acknowledged Michael unhappily. 'There will be a battle sooner or later, despite my efforts to prevent one. All I hope is that these rich – and hopefully generous – nuns do not see it.'

St Mary the Great was the University's centre of power, as all its senior officers worked there. It was a handsome church, occupying a commanding position on the high street, and was the only building in the town that could accommodate every scholar at the same time.

The largest and most impressive room should have

been the Chancellor's, but Michael had appropriated that years before, leaving the University's titular head with a rather poky chamber near the back door. De Wetherset had tried to reclaim it while Michael was in Suffolk, but the beadles were devoted to their Senior Proctor and refused to allow it. Thus Michael's domain remained his own.

Bartholomew glanced through its door as he and Michael hurried past. It was sumptuously decorated, with wool rugs and fine furniture. It had two desks, both set to catch the light from the beautifully glazed windows. The ornate, oaken one was Michael's, piled high with documents bearing the seals of nobles or high-ranking churchmen. The other was Junior Proctor Theophilis's, neat to the point of obsessional.

By contrast, de Wetherset's room was dark, plain and smelled of damp. It was also cramped, as the Vice-Chancellor and Commissary worked there, too – Michael had declined to oust his clerks and secretaries to make room for the newly created officials, claiming that de Wetherset should have considered such practicalities before appointing anyone.

'Ah, here you are,' said de Wetherset, as Michael strutted in without knocking. Bartholomew hovered on the threshold, uncertain whether to follow suit, but the Chancellor beckoned him inside. 'Good.'

He was a solid man of late-to-middle years, whose physical strength was turning to fat. He had iron-grey hair, small eyes, and wore Tyled Hostel's uniform of a dark green academic tabard, which fitted him like a glove. Although he seemed honourable, there was something about him that had always made Bartholomew wary. Perhaps it was the aura of power that emanated from him, or his sharp, sometimes unkind tongue. Regardless, he was not someone the physician would ever consider a friend.

41

He had been Chancellor for years before the stress of the post had forced him to resign. To recover, he had gone on a pilgrimage to Walsingham, and had returned bursting with vitality. He claimed his good health was a miracle, although Bartholomew suspected he had just benefited from fresh air, regular meals and plenty of exercise. He had bought a pilgrim badge when he had reached the shrine, which he always wore pinned proudly on his hat.

As usual, the men he had appointed were with him. Tall, haughty, elegant Vice-Chancellor Heltisle was immaculately clad in a gold-trimmed gipon with his uniform tabard – in Bene't College's royal blue – over the top. His shoes were crafted from soft leather, and he wore a floppy hat that most townsfolk would automatically assume was French. He had always been wealthy, but additional funds had come his way after he had invented a metal pen. These had quickly become status symbols, with scholars scrambling to buy them, even though they were indecently expensive. Matilde had given one to Bartholomew, although he had found it more trouble than it was worth and never used it.

Commissary Aynton was a stooped, gangling man with a benign smile and dreamy eyes, so that Bartholomew sometimes wondered if he was fully aware of what was going on around him. His clothes were expensive, but he wore them badly, so he always looked vaguely disreputable. Bartholomew liked him because he often made discreet donations of medicine for the poor, something Heltisle would never do.

'I am glad to see you, Bartholomew,' said de Wetherset, one hand clasped to his paunch. 'Do you have that remedy for a griping in the guts? I thought I was cured of my delicate innards – this is the first trouble I have suffered since Walsingham.'

'Do not trust *him* to give you relief, de Wetherset,' said

Heltisle nastily. 'You should have sent for Rougham. He is a much better physician, and does not waste time washing his hands with such irritating regularity.'

'Oh, come, Heltisle,' chided Aynton with a pleasant smile. 'Matthew has a rare skill with griping guts, as you know perfectly well. Or were you the only member of your College who did not swallow his remedy after the feast that made everyone vomit?'

Heltisle's red face provided the answer to that question, but he was not a man to recant, so he went on another offensive to mask his discomfiture. 'If you are going to physick him, Bartholomew, hurry up. We are busy, and cannot wait for you all day.'

Bartholomew was tempted to leave there and then, but de Wetherset was looking decidedly unwell, and the physician was not in the habit of abandoning those who needed him. He indicated that de Wetherset was to lie on a bench – the Chancellor probably had indigestion, but it would be remiss not to examine him before prescribing a tonic.

'These nuns, Brother,' said Aynton, watching Bartholomew palpate the Chancellor's ample abdomen. 'Are you sure it was a good idea to bring them here? I have heard alarming stories about what St Radegund's was like in the past.'

'You mean when it was a delightful place to visit?' asked Heltisle with a leer that made Bartholomew dislike him even more. 'As opposed to now, when it is full of women who only want to pray? Of course, you had no right to arrange a *conloquium* here, Brother. It should have been de Wetherset's decision.'

Michael regarded him coolly. 'No, it should not. First, St Radegund's does not come under the University's jurisdiction. Second, de Wetherset was not Chancellor when the Bishop made his request. And third, the Bishop approached me because the delegates are from my own Order.'

Heltisle sniffed. 'Well, do not blame *me* if our students

take advantage of the fact that thousands of nubile young ladies lie within their grasp.'

Michael laughed. 'There are only two hundred, and few are nubile.'

'Nor are they within anyone's grasp,' put in Bartholomew, not liking the notion of someone like Heltisle marching out there in the hope that he would receive the kind of welcome he had evidently enjoyed when standards had been different.

Heltisle rounded on him. 'And you would know, of course. You have no right to be a scholar while you have a woman waiting to wed you.'

'He breaks no statute – not in the University and not in Michaelhouse,' retorted Michael sharply. 'And do not accuse him of enjoying illicit relations, because Matilde is away.' He turned away before Heltisle could argue and addressed de Wetherset, who was sitting up to sip the tonic Bartholomew had poured. 'Why did you send for me, Chancellor?'

'To discuss the call to arms,' explained de Wetherset, some colour returning to his plump cheeks. 'The town has two knights to monitor its training, but we have no one – our scholars just arrive at the butts, loose a few arrows and go home. We need someone who can teach them how to improve.'

'Cynric,' said Aynton, smiling at Bartholomew. 'He is a very good archer, and I am sure you will not mind lending him out. Beadle Meadowman will help.'

'Not Meadowman,' said Michael immediately, loath to lose his favourite henchman when he was needed to prevent brawls.

'Nonsense,' stated Heltisle. 'He and Cynric will oversee matters, and your Junior Proctor can record the name of everyone who attends. Then we can identify those who think they are too important to sully their hands with weapons, and inform them that they are not.'

Michael concealed his irritation at such presumptuousness with a show of indifference. 'Very well. Of course, I shall expect you three to be the first in line, setting a good example.'

'Then you will be disappointed,' declared Heltisle, 'because we have hired proxies – men from the Spital, who are mad and therefore not expected to answer the call themselves.'

'*My* proxy is not a lunatic,' said Aynton hastily. 'He is a scholar from King's Hall – a Fleming, who is exempt on the grounds of being foreign. I dared not hire a madman, lest he forgets whose side he is on and attacks his friends. I do not want that on my conscience!'

Michael raised his eyebrows. 'I hate to break this to you, but the option of hiring proxies is only available to certain priests. You are not—'

'It is available to anyone who makes a suitable donation to the King's war chest,' countered Heltisle smugly. 'Several of my Bene't colleagues will follow my example, although I imagine no one at Michaelhouse can afford it.'

Michael's smile was tight. 'We could, but none of us will, because it reeks of cowardice and elitism. I advise you to reconsider, lest you win the contempt of your fellow scholars.'

'Not to mention the resentment of townsfolk,' put in Bartholomew. 'They will not take kindly to the fact that the wealthy can buy their way out of their military obligations.'

'Who cares what they think?' shrugged Heltisle. 'Our fiscal arrangements with the King are none of their business. Besides, it is inappropriate for high-ranking members of the University to engage in such lowly activities. We have our dignity to consider. It is—'

He was interrupted by Cynric, who appeared silently at the door – so silently that Bartholomew was sure he had been listening. The book-bearer gave no indication as to whether he was pleased or alarmed by the plans being made for his future, and his expression was carefully neutral as he addressed Michael.

'You must come at once, Brother. There is a situation at the Gilbertine Priory.'

'What kind of situation?' demanded Heltisle. 'And please direct your remarks to the Chancellor. He is in charge here, not the Senior Proctor.'

'Of course he is,' said Cynric flatly, and turned back to Michael. 'Apparently, it is ablaze, and as you have lodged some of your nuns there, I thought you should know.'

CHAPTER 3

Bartholomew, Michael and the triumvirate hurried into the high street to gaze at the plume of greasy black smoke that wafted into the air to the south.

'That is not the Gilbertine Priory,' said de Wetherset. 'It is further away.'

'Some farmer, clearing land, probably,' said Heltisle dismissively.

'It is the Spital!' exclaimed Michael in alarm. 'I have nuns lodged there, too – a score of ladies from Lyminster Priory.'

'One convent sent *twenty* delegates?' asked de Wetherset in surprise. 'That is a lot.'

'The largest by a considerable margin,' acknowledged Michael, his face pale. 'And one of them is Magistra Katherine de Lisle.'

'De Lisle?' mused de Wetherset. 'Is she any relation to our Bishop Thomas de Lisle?'

'His older sister,' replied Michael tautly. 'She is scheduled to speak at the *conloquium* today, so hopefully she will have left the Spital already, but—'

'Then go and make sure,' gulped de Wetherset. 'The Bishop will never forgive us if his sister is incinerated at an event organised by an officer of the University.'

Knowing this was true, Michael began to hurry along the high street. Bartholomew fell in at his side, because everything was tinder-dry after the long spell of warm weather, and he wanted to be sure the blaze represented no danger to the town – only fools were unconcerned about fire when most buildings were made of timber and thatch. Cynric followed, and so did the triumvirate.

'We cannot have you telling the Bishop that we skulked here while the Senior Proctor and his Corpse Examiner rescued his beloved sister,' called Heltisle. 'We know the kind of sly politics you two practise.'

A few years before, Bartholomew had objected to the number of bodies he was required to inspect out of the goodness of his heart, so Michael had established the post of Corpse Examiner. The duties entailed determining an official cause of death for any scholar who passed away, or anyone who died on University property. Bartholomew was paid threepence for each body he assessed, all of which was spent on medicine for the poor. However, he wished Michael had chosen a less sinister-sounding title for the work he did.

'Speaking of sly politics, Heltisle,' said the monk coolly, 'I understand you struck a deal with Clippesby over the sale of his treatise.'

Heltisle smirked. 'And there is a contract to prove it – signed with one of my own metal pens, in fact – so do not try to renege. And if you claim he is mentally unfit to make such arrangements, then he should not be in the University. You cannot have it both ways.'

'I cannot wait to see his face when he realises he has been bested by Clippesby,' murmured Michael, walking more quickly to put some distance between them. 'I must find a way to depose him, as he is a dreadful man. Even so, I would sooner have him than Aynton – at least Heltisle does not try to disguise his vileness with cloying amiability.'

'Perhaps I can shoot him while I show scholars how to use a bow,' suggested Cynric. 'An arrow in the posterior will teach him a little humility.'

'Please do not,' begged Bartholomew, afraid he might actually do it. 'He would claim you acted on our orders, and we do not want Michaelhouse sued.'

The plume of smoke seemed no closer when they

reached the Trumpington Gate, where the sentries were gazing at the smudge of black that stained the sky.

'It *is* the Spital,' said a soldier to his cronies, 'which is no bad thing. The place is haunted, and I shall not be sorry to see it go up in flames.'

'He is right,' Cynric told Bartholomew and Michael, as they hurried through the gate. He considered himself an expert on the supernatural, and was always willing to share his views with the less well informed. 'It stands on the site of a pagan temple, see, where human sacrifices were made.'

'It does not!' exclaimed Bartholomew, although he should have known better than to argue with Cynric. The book-bearer's opinions, once formed, were permanent, and there was no changing his mind.

'You do not understand these things, boy,' declared Cynric darkly. 'Building that Spital woke a lot of evil sprites. Indeed, it may even be them who set the place afire.'

'Then let us hope Heltisle has the right of it,' said Michael, 'and it is just a farmer burning brush in order to plant some crops.'

'Regardless,' said Bartholomew, fearing it was not, 'we should hurry.'

Five high-ranking scholars and Cynric, trotting three abreast along the main road south, was enough to attract attention, and folk abandoned what they were doing to trail after them, sure an interesting spectacle was in the offing. They included both scholars and townsfolk, who immediately began to jostle each other. Isnard the bargeman and his cronies were among the worst offenders, and Bartholomew was concerned – with only one leg, Isnard was vulnerable in a scuffle, although he never allowed it to prevent him from joining in.

'I feel like the Piper of Hamelin,' grumbled Michael.

'Followed by rats.' His eyes narrowed. 'And four louts from King's Hall, who have chosen to don clothes that are brazenly French. They have done it purely to antagonise the likes of Isnard.'

'It is working,' said Bartholomew, aware that the bargeman had fixed the haughty quartet with angry eyes. 'I had better send him and his friends home before there is a spat – the King's Hall men have swords.'

For which we have His Majesty to thank, he thought sourly. Scholars were forbidden to bear arms in the town, but this stricture had been suspended by royal decree until the French threat was over. King's Hall, which had always been warlike, was delighted to arm its scholars to the teeth.

Bartholomew knew Isnard and his cronies well, as all were either his patients or members of the Michaelhouse Choir. They had never been particularly patriotic, but the raid on Winchelsea had ignited a nationalistic fervour that verged on the fanatical. It would be forgotten when some other issue caught their attention, but until then, they were affronted by anything they deemed to be even remotely foreign. They met in disreputable taverns, where they nurtured their grievances over large flagons of ale.

'No,' snapped Bartholomew, seeing Isnard prepare to lob a handful of horse manure at the scholars. 'If you make a mess on their fine clothes, they will fight you.'

'Then they should wear English ones,' retorted Isnard sullenly. 'Right, lads?'

There was a growl of agreement, the loudest from a soldier named Pierre Sauvage. It was an unusual name for a man who had never ventured more than three miles outside Cambridge, but his mother had once rented her spare room to an itinerant acrobat from Lyons. Sauvage was so touchy about the possibility of having foreign blood that he was rabidly xenophobic. He told anyone who would listen that he had signed on at the castle purely because he wanted Tulyet to teach him how to kill Frenchmen.

'Too right,' he declared. 'They have no right to strut around looking like the dolphin.'

'He means the Dauphin,' said Isnard, evidently of the opinion that the physician was unable to deduce this for himself. 'Who we hate because it was *his* army what invaded Winchelsea and did all those terrible things. Is that not so, Sauvage?'

Unfortunately, his indignant remarks were overheard by the scholars from King's Hall, who immediately swaggered over. Bartholomew shot an agonised glance at the smoke – he did not have time to prevent quarrels when he should be making sure the blaze represented no threat to the town.

'Sauvage, Sauvage,' mused one. 'I think we might have a Frenchman here, boys. Shall we slit him open and see what is inside?'

'Go home,' ordered Bartholomew, cutting across the outraged response Sauvage began to make. 'All of you. There will be nothing to see at the Spital.'

'No?' demanded the scholar archly. 'Then why are you going there?'

Bartholomew thought fast. 'Because the inmates have contagious diseases for me to treat.'

'Lord!' gulped Isnard. 'I never thought of that. Come on, Sauvage. The Griffin broached a new barrel of ale today, and it would be a pity to let it go sour.'

He swung away on his crutches, and most of his cronies followed. The scholars stood fast, though, so Bartholomew began to describe some of the more alarming ailments he expected to be rife in the Spital, and was relieved when the King's Hall men edged away and began to saunter back the way they had come.

'Follow them,' he told Cynric. 'Make sure they go home

– preferably without goading any more townsfolk into a spat along the way.'

By the time Bartholomew caught up with Michael, the monk and the triumvirate had passed the Gilbertine Priory with its handsome gatehouse and towering walls. Beyond it, the road was in a terrible state. There had been heavy rains the previous month, and carts had churned it into ruts. These had dried like petrified waves when the weather turned warm, so anyone hurrying risked a twisted ankle or worse. Bartholomew and his companions were obliged to slow to a snail's pace, leaving Michael fretting about the nuns.

The Spital stood on what had, until recently, been nothing but scrubland. It comprised five buildings within a perfect walled square. In the centre was a hall that had a large room for communal eating below and a dormitory above. A chapel jutted from its back, placed to catch the rising sun at its altar end. The other buildings were in each of the four corners: a kitchen and accommodation for staff; a substantial guesthouse; the stable block; and a large shed-cum-storeroom.

The Spital's gates were always closed, as not everyone was happy about lepers – or lunatics – living near the town, and the founders were cognisant of security. However, the gates stood open that day, as access was needed to the brook that ran along the side of the road for water. The scholars looked through them to see the blaze was in the shed – a temporary, albeit sturdy, structure used to store building materials. Smoke billowed through its reed-thatched roof, although the fire was so far contained, as there were no leaping flames.

'The nuns are safe,' breathed Michael in relief, seeing a black-robed gaggle near the stables. 'Thank God!'

As everyone inside the Spital was busy with the fire, and no one came to greet them, de Wetherset began to relate its history to Aynton, who was a relative newcomer to the town.

'A man named Henry Tangmer founded it to atone for sins committed by his niece. What was her name, Brother? I cannot recall.'

'Adela,' supplied Michael, who remembered her very well. 'She is dead now, God rest her soul, and we have a leper hospital.'

'I am no physician,' said Aynton, 'but I do know that one does not meet many lepers these days. So why did Tangmer dedicate his wealth to helping them, of all people?'

'Lepers, lunatics, they are all the same,' said Heltisle with a dismissive shrug. 'Folk who cannot be allowed out, lest they infect the rest of us with their deadly miasmas.'

'Lunacy is not contagious,' said Bartholomew, not about to let such an outlandish claim pass unchallenged. 'Nor are many kinds of leprosy.'

'Regardless, the sufferers are still pariahs,' retorted Heltisle, 'so it is good that they are locked away, out of sight and mind.'

'That is a terrible attitude towards—' began Bartholomew hotly.

'I have heard that Tangmer's wife is very good at curing diseases of the mind,' said de Wetherset, cutting across him. 'She uses herbs, fresh air and exercise, by all accounts.'

'Does she?' asked Bartholomew, immediately intrigued.

'Do not tell me that you have never been called out here,' said Heltisle, then smiled superiorly. 'But of course you have not. The inmates may be mad, but they will not want to be tended by a man who loves paupers and who insists on washing his hands at every turn.'

Bartholomew ignored him, knowing this would annoy him far more than any riposte he could devise on the spur of the moment. He asked de Wetherset to tell him more about Mistress Tangmer's unusual therapies, but the Chancellor had had enough of the Spital.

'They have the blaze under control,' he said, watching two servants use fire hooks to haul down patches of smouldering thatch, where they could be doused with water. 'The Bishop's sister is safe and there is no danger to the University. I am going home.'

He, Heltisle and Aynton began to walk back the way they had come, Heltisle grumbling about the wasted effort. Bartholomew and Michael lingered though; Michael wanted to speak to the nuns, while Bartholomew's interest was piqued by the Spital's innovative-sounding treatment of lunacy and he hoped to learn more.

'I asked Tangmer to show me around when I arranged for him to take my nuns,' said Michael. 'But he refused, lest my presence upset his patients.'

'It might,' said Bartholomew. 'However, a fire will be far more distressing. I wonder how the Tangmers will deal with it.'

He watched the people inside, trying to distinguish patients from staff. Most were busy with the fire, although two distinct groups were not: the nuns, and a dozen respectably dressed individuals with children, who stood near the hall. Curiously, there was none of the frantic yelling that usually accompanied such crises, and the whole operation was conducted in almost complete silence. It was peculiarly eerie.

'Of course, the nuns should be at the *conloquium*,' said Michael, watching them crossly. 'Magistra Katherine is due to lecture there shortly, and the other delegates will be wondering what has happened to her.'

Bartholomew frowned. 'I thought you put twenty ladies here. I only count nineteen.'

Michael looked around wildly. 'The Prioress – Joan de Ferraris! *She* is missing!' Then he gave an irritable tut of relief. 'There she is – in the stables. I might have guessed. She has always preferred horses to people.'

He nodded to where a massive woman, who would stand head and shoulders above her sisters, was soothing the animals. She looked rather like a horse herself, with a long face, large teeth and big brown eyes. She had rolled up her sleeves to reveal a pair of brawny forearms.

'She is an excellent rider,' Michael went on, and as he had lofty standards where equestrianism was concerned, Bartholomew supposed she must be skilled indeed. 'And she single-handedly built her priory's stables, which are reputed to be the best in the country. I should love to see them.'

'But is she a good head of house?' asked Bartholomew, aware that riding and stable-building were not especially useful skills for running a convent.

'She is stern but fair, and not afraid to delegate tasks she feels are beyond her. She can also repair roofs, clean gutters and chop wood. Her nuns like her, and Lyminster is a happy, prosperous place, so yes, she is a good leader. But I had better go and pay my respects.'

He and Bartholomew started to walk towards them, but were intercepted by three men – Sheriff Tulyet and his two new knights, who were stationed just inside the gates.

'Tangmer has asked us to keep sightseers out,' explained Tulyet, raising a hand to stop the scholars from going any further. 'He says they frighten his inmates.'

'They do not look overly concerned to me,' said Michael, although Bartholomew was aware of being eyed by the group near the hall. 'They do not look particularly mad either.'

'Insanity is not something you can diagnose at a glance,' said Tulyet. 'At least, that is what Tangmer told me, when I suggested much the same.'

'How dare he use us as free labour,' growled huge, black-haired Sir Norbert. 'We are not servants, to be ordered hither and thither. We are friends of the King.'

'You offered your help,' said Tulyet drily. 'And this is how Tangmer chose to deploy it. It is your own fault for recklessly putting yourself at his disposal.'

'*I* know why he wants everyone kept away,' said fair-headed Sir Leger sourly. 'Because madmen are exempt from the King's call to arms, so are eligible for hire as proxies. Several scholars have already been here, clamouring to buy substitutes, and Tangmer aims to put a stop to it.'

'By "scholars" he means Chancellor de Wetherset and his henchman Heltisle,' put in Norbert, and spat. 'Cowards!'

'Speaking of cowards, have you made any progress with finding whoever dispatched Bonet the spicer?' asked Michael.

'None,' replied Leger. 'The killer left no clues, and there are no witnesses. Ergo, I am not sure we will ever—'

'That man is on fire!' interrupted Tulyet urgently, and stepped aside. 'Your services will be needed, Matt. If Tangmer complains, tell him *I* let you in.'

By the time Bartholomew arrived, the burning man had smothered the flames by rolling in the grass, saving himself from serious injury. One arm was scorched, though, so Bartholomew sat him down and applied a soothing salve. Grateful for his help, the man began to chat, saying he was Tangmer's cousin, Eudo. He was enormous by any standards, larger even than Sir Norbert, and reminded Bartholomew of a bull – powerful, unpredictable and not overly bright.

'Everyone who works here is a Tangmer,' Eudo said. 'Henry and Amphelisa have no children, but his father

56

had six brothers, so he has uncles and cousins galore. Lots of us were eager to come and work for him.'

Bartholomew had been told this before, and remembered that the policy of kin-only staff had caused great resentment in the town – there had been an expectation of employment for locals, and folk were disappointed when none was offered. Worse, the Tangmers declined to socialise outside the Spital, which, along with them refusing visitors, had given rise to rumours that it was haunted and that all its patients were dangerously insane.

'Do you like Cambridge, Eudo?' Bartholomew asked conversationally.

Eudo shook his massive head. 'I used to go there to buy candles – before we started making our own – and there was always some spat between students and apprentices. I think it is a violent little place, so I try to avoid going there.'

'You are not obliged to practise your archery, like the rest of us?'

'Cousin Henry arranged for us to do it here instead, which is much nicer than rubbing shoulders with brawlers.'

When he had finished tending Eudo's burns, Bartholomew started to walk back to the gate, but was intercepted by the founders themselves – Henry and Amphelisa Tangmer.

They were a curious pair. Tangmer was a heavyset, rosy-cheeked man who could have been nothing but an English yeoman. His wife was an elegant lady in a burgundy-coloured robe, who smelled strongly of fragrant oils. To Bartholomew's eye, her facial features and casual grace were unmistakably French, and with sudden, blinding clarity, he understood exactly why they discouraged visitors. It was a sensible precaution in the current climate of intolerance and unease.

'Thank you for helping Eudo,' said Tangmer, stiffly formal. 'But we can manage now. The shed is lost, but it was due to be demolished anyway, so it does not matter. All it means is that we shall have to build our bathhouse a bit sooner than we anticipated.'

'Bathhouse?' asked Bartholomew, immediately interested.

Amphelisa smiled. 'We feel cleanliness is important in a hospital.'

Bartholomew thought so, too, although he was in a distinct minority, as most medical practitioners considered hygiene a waste of time. He opened his mouth to see what else he and Amphelisa might have in common, but Tangmer cut across him.

'The children love to play in the shed, and I imagine one knocked over a candle. But the blaze is under control now, so if there is nothing else . . .'

'I saw children by the hall,' fished Bartholomew. 'Are they patients?'

'No, but we believe madness can be cured faster when the afflicted person is surrounded by his loved ones,' explained Amphelisa. 'We encourage our inmates to bring their families.'

'Does it work?' asked Bartholomew keenly.

Amphelisa was willing to discuss it, but her husband cleared his throat meaningfully, so she made an apologetic face. 'Perhaps we can talk another time, but now I must soothe those who are distressed by the commotion.'

'I can help,' offered Bartholomew. 'A decoction of chamomile and dittany will—'

'We have our own remedies, thank you,' interrupted Tangmer, polite but firm. 'And now, if you will excuse us . . .'

He took Bartholomew's arm and began to propel him towards the gate, but stopped when there was an urgent yell from Eudo, who had returned to help with the fire.

At the same time, a flame burst through the roof in a slender orange tongue.

'Let it burn,' Tangmer called. 'It will save us the bother of knocking it down later.'

Eudo turned a stricken face towards him. 'But I heard something. I think someone is still inside!'

Loath to get in the way while the Spital's people effected a rescue, Bartholomew returned to Michael, Tulyet and the knights. The nuns also kept their distance, other than the mannish Prioress Joan, who abandoned the horses and strode forward to see if she could be of any use. Meanwhile, all the inmates raced towards the shed and began to hammer on it with their fists.

'Stop! Get back!' shouted Tangmer in alarm. 'You will hurt yourselves. Eudo is mistaken – no one is inside. Is that not right, Goda?'

He turned to a woman who stood nearby. She was so small that Bartholomew had assumed she was a child, especially as she wore a bright yellow dress – an unusual colour for an adult – but Michael murmured that she was wife to the vast Eudo, leading the physician to speculate, somewhat voyeurishly, about the difficulties their disparity in size must generate in the marriage bed.

'Of course it is empty,' Goda said irritably. 'The door was ajar, and the fire had not taken hold when I first saw the smoke. Anyone inside would have walked out then.'

'Well, the door is closed now,' said Prioress Joan, peering at it through the smoke. 'So perhaps we had better open it and have a look inside.'

'I ordered it shut after Goda raised the alarm,' explained Tangmer, 'to contain the blaze and make it easier to put out. But I can assure you that no one is—'

'There!' yelled Eudo, cocking his head to one side. 'Voices – a woman's.'

Bartholomew suspected the big man was mistaken, as the fire had been going for some time, belching smoke at a colossal rate. It was unlikely that anyone was still alive inside.

'I heard it, too!' shouted another of the staff, his face tight with horror. 'We have to get her out. Open the door! Quick!'

'*No!*' howled Bartholomew, darting forward to stop him. 'The door is smouldering – open it, and the fire will explode outwards, greedy for air. Is there another way in?'

Tangmer shook his head, his face pale. 'All we can do is to hurl water at the flames until they are extinguished, and hope we are in time. Everyone – remove your shoes and fill them from the stream over the—'

'Shoes will not suffice,' snapped Prioress Joan. 'Sheriff – set the men in a chain between here and the brook. Amphelisa – round up the women and children and send them for buckets. Well? What are you waiting for? *Move!*'

The urgency of the situation had caused her to lapse into French, the first language of most high-born ladies who held positions of authority in the Church. Bartholomew began to translate, sure few Spital folk would understand, but most immediately looked at Tulyet and Amphelisa, suggesting that they had.

'But we do not have more buckets,' gulped Amphelisa. 'We have already used—'

'Then bring pots and pans,' barked Joan. 'Anything that holds water. Master Tangmer – take your elderly lunatics and the smallest brats to the chapel. They are in the way here.'

'If there is no other entrance, we will have to make one,' said Bartholomew urgently. 'At the back, where the fire burns less fiercely.'

'Good thinking,' said Joan. 'Come with me and choose

60

the best place.' She jabbed a thick forefinger at one of the inmates, a dark-haired, wiry man with angry eyes. 'You, bring us an axe. The rest of you, human chain and water *now*!'

She hitched up her habit and strode to the back of the shed, managing a pace that had Bartholomew running to keep up. They arrived to find smoke oozing between the planks that formed the walls. Bartholomew put his hand to one and found it was cool – the flames had not yet reached it. He heard the faintest of moans. Eudo was right: someone *was* inside!

He grabbed a stone and pounded the wall with it, to reassure whoever was inside that help was coming. Joan did likewise, although her blows caused significant dents.

'Where is that lunatic with the axe?' she demanded in agitation. 'Hah! Here he is at last. Where have you been, man? To buy it in town?'

'I did not know where to look,' snapped the man, bristling. 'And my name is Delacroix. I am no man's servant, so do not address me as one.'

'Keep your bruised dignity for later, *Delacroix*,' said Joan acidly, grabbing the hatchet from him and swinging at the walls with all her might.

Splinters flew. Then the massive Eudo arrived with the biggest chopper Bartholomew had ever seen. In three mighty swipes, he had smashed a head-sized hole.

Bartholomew darted forward to peer through it, blinking away tears as fumes wafted out. It was impossible to see anything inside, and it occurred to him that whoever was in there had probably suffocated by now. Then he glimpsed movement. Someone was struggling to stand, and he had a brief impression of a bloodstained kirtle and a bundle shoved at him. He saw golden curls. The bundle was a child.

'Stand back!' he yelled, and indicated that Eudo was to hit the wall again.

More wood shattered. Then Delacroix snatched Joan's axe and began a frenzied assault that had no impact and prevented Eudo from working. Bartholomew tried to stop him, but Delacroix fought him off. Then a fist shot out and Delacroix reeled backwards.

'Put your back into it before it is too late,' roared Joan at Eudo, wringing her bruised knuckles. 'Hurry!'

Eudo obliged, and the hole expanded. Joan struggled to clamber through it, careless of the smoke that belched around her. She was too big to fit, obliging Bartholomew to haul her out again. She emerged smouldering, her wimple alight. Eudo threw her to the ground and rolled her over, whipping off his shirt to smother the flames.

'No, help *her*!' she snarled, pushing him away. Her face was streaked with soot, her habit was rucked up to reveal two powerful white thighs, and her wimple was in a blackened, unsalvageable mess. 'The child!'

Bartholomew thrust his arms through the hole. Immediately, something was pushed into them. He pulled hard. There was an agonising moment when clothes snagged on the jagged edges, but Eudo drew a knife and hacked the material free.

Leaving Eudo and Delacroix to rescue the woman, Bartholomew and Joan carried the child away from the smoke. Her eyes were closed and there was no heartbeat. Bartholomew began to press rhythmically on her chest, pausing every so often to blow into her lungs. Nothing happened, so he did it again. And again, and again.

'No!' snapped Joan, when he stopped. 'Do not give up. Not yet.'

He did as he was told, and was on the verge of admitting defeat when the child's eyes fluttered open. She sat up and began to cough.

'Praise the Lord!' breathed Joan. 'A miracle!'

She fetched Eudo's discarded shirt and wrapped it around the girl, although it was Amphelisa who took the dazed child in her arms and crooned comforting words.

Bartholomew turned his attention back to the shed. Its roof was a sheet of orange flames, and groans and crashes emanated from within as it collapsed in on itself.

'What of the woman?' he asked hoarsely.

'We could not reach her,' rasped Eudo, whose face was ashen. 'It was Mistress Girard, God rest her soul.'

CHAPTER 4

The next morning dawned cool, damp and wet. Bartholomew fancied he could smell burning in the misty drizzle from the still-smouldering Spital shed, although this was impossible as it was too far away. His sleep had teemed with nightmares, so he had risen in the small hours and gone to the hall to read. But even Galen's elegant prose could not distract him from his thoughts, so he had spent most of the time staring at the candle, thinking about the fire.

By the time it was out, the rubble had been far too hot for retrieving bodies, so Tulyet, whose responsibility it was to investigate, had asked him to return the following day to examine the victims. A roll call had revealed five people missing – the rescued girl's parents, uncle, aunt and teenaged brother.

The bell rang to wake the scholars for Mass, so he went to the lavatorium – the lean-to structure behind the hall, built for those interested in personal hygiene. Until recently, only cold water had been available, but Michael liked the occasional wash himself, and had ordered the servants to provide hot as well. It was an almost unimaginable luxury.

Bartholomew stank of burning, so he scrubbed his skin and hair vigorously, then doused himself with some perfume that someone had left behind. He wished he had used it more sparingly when it transpired to be powerful and redolent of the stuff popular with prostitutes. He started to rinse it off, but the bell rang again, this time calling scholars to assemble in the yard, ready to process to the church. He left his soiled clothes in the laundress's basket, and sprinted to his room for fresh ones, wearing nothing but a piece of sacking tied around his waist.

'You had better not do *that* when you are married,' remarked Theophilis, watching disapprovingly. 'Not with a woman about.'

Bartholomew was tempted to point out that Matilde was unlikely to mind, but held his tongue lest Theophilis thought he was being lewd. Back in his room, he donned a fresh white shirt, black leggings and a clean tabard. Then he forced his feet into shoes that were still wet from fire-drenching water, and hurried into the yard.

Michael was already there, hood up to keep the drizzle from his immaculately barbered tonsure. His Benedictine students stood in a small, sombre cluster behind him, while Bartholomew's medics formed a much noisier group near the hall. Aungel was with them and they were laughing. When he caught the words 'chicken' and 'debate', he surmised that they were reviewing William's attempt to debunk Clippesby's thesis the previous day.

Clippesby and Theophilis were by the gate, so he went to join them. The Dominican was kneeling, and Bartholomew thought he was praying until he realised he was talking to the College cat. Theophilis listened carefully as Clippesby translated what the animal had said, then rolled his eyes, mocking the Dominican's eccentricity. Bartholomew bristled, but William strode up before he could take issue with him.

'I have a bone to pick with you, Matthew,' the friar said coolly. 'Your students kept asking questions during my sermon yesterday.'

'Of course they did,' said Bartholomew, aware of Theophilis sniggering. 'They have been trained to challenge statements they deem illogical or erroneous.'

William's scowl deepened. 'My exposition was neither, and the next time I give a lecture, *they* will not be invited.'

Bartholomew was sure they would be delighted to hear it. Then Aungel approached.

'Yesterday was great fun, Father,' he declared enthusiastically. 'I have never laughed so much in all my life. The best part was when you claimed that all robins are nominalists, because they know the names of the worms they eat.'

'I never did! You tricked me into saying things I did not mean.'

'We did it because it was so easy,' said Theophilis in his eerily sibilant voice. 'And our students learned one extremely valuable lesson: to keep their mouths shut when they do not know what they are talking about.'

'But I *do* know what I am talking about!' cried William, aggrieved. 'I am a Franciscan theologian, and my understanding of the realism–nominalism debate is far greater than that of Clippesby's stupid chickens.'

'In that case, Father,' said Theophilis slyly, 'perhaps you should debate with them directly next time. You might find Ma and Gertrude easier to defeat than the students.'

William narrowed his eyes. 'You want me to appear as mad as Clippesby! Besides, all his hens look the same to me. How will I know which are the right ones?'

Theophilis regarded William warily, not sure if he was serious, while Bartholomew laughed at them both.

'Audrey has just mentioned something interesting,' said Clippesby, indicating the cat. Bartholomew was glad he never took umbrage at William's insults, or the College would have been a perpetual battleground. 'She was hunting near the Spital just before dawn, and she saw what appeared to be a ghost – a spectre that undulated along the top of the walls.'

The Dominican often went out at night to commune with his animal friends. When he did, he sat so still that he was all but invisible, which meant he frequently witnessed sights not intended for his eyes. Unfortunately, he invariably reported them in a way that made them difficult to interpret.

'You mean you saw a *person* on the wall,' said Aungel. 'Who was it? A townsman trying to get inside to see the charred bodies? A lunatic trying to escape?'

'It was a white, shimmering shape, which rippled along until it vanished into thin air,' replied Clippesby. 'Audrey has never seen anything like it, and she hopes never to do so again.'

'Are you sure she was not dreaming?' asked Bartholomew, hoping Clippesby would not mention the tale to Cynric, or they would never hear the end of it.

Clippesby nodded. 'She recited prayers to ward off evil, and ran home as fast as her legs would carry her.'

'What was she doing out there in the first place?' asked Theophilis suspiciously. 'It is not safe, given the unsettled mood of the town.'

'She went to make sure that no horses were involved in the fire,' explained Clippesby. 'Burning would be a terrible way to die.'

'It would,' agreed Bartholomew soberly. 'As five hapless people have discovered.'

Eventually, the last student emerged yawning from his room, and Michael led the way to church. This was something else that had changed since he and Bartholomew had returned from Clare. The two of them had spent years walking side by side, talking all the way. Now Michael was obliged to be in front, leaving Bartholomew with William, who was not nearly such good company. Aungel and Theophilis were next, followed by Clippesby and any animal he had managed to snag. The students tagged along last, those in holy orders with their heads bowed in prayer, the remainder a noisy, chatting throng.

They arrived at the church, where it was William's turn to officiate, with Michael assisting. As William prided himself on the speed with which he could rattle through the sacred words, Mass was soon over, and Michael led the way home.

The rain had stopped and the sun was out, bathing the town in warm yellow rays. Everywhere were signs of advancing spring – blossom on the churchyard hedges, wildflowers along the sides of the road, and the sweet smell of fresh growth. Then a waft of something less pleasant wafted towards them, from the ditch that Tyled Hostel used as a sewer.

They reached Michaelhouse, where Agatha, the formidable laundress who ran the domestic side of the College, had breakfast ready. Women were forbidden to enter Colleges, lest they inflamed the passions of the residents, although exceptions were made for ladies who were old and ugly. Agatha was neither, although it would be a brave man who tried to force his attentions on her.

A few students peeled off to change or visit the latrines, but most went directly to the hall, where vats of meat-heavy pottage were waiting. There was also bread and honey for those who disliked rich fare first thing in the morning. Bartholomew opted for the lighter choice – he had already let his belt out once because of Michael's improved victuals, and did not want to waddle down the aisle to marry Matilde.

The meal was soon over, and Michael intoned a final Grace. Usually, Bartholomew went to the conclave to put the finishing touches to his lectures, but that day he went to his room to collect what he would need for examining bodies. Michael joined him there.

'I cannot stop thinking about yesterday,' said the monk, and shuddered. 'Those poor people were inside that burning shed for an age – we did not exactly hurry to the Spital, and even when we did arrive, it was some time before Eudo raised the alarm. Why did no one hear them sooner?'

Bartholomew had wondered that, too. 'Maybe the fire-fighters made too much noise.'

'But they did not, Matt. One of the first things I noticed was that they were labouring in almost complete silence, with none of the yelling and screeching that usually accompanies such incidents. If the victims had shouted, they would have been heard.'

Bartholomew regarded him unhappily – his reflections during the night had led him to much the same conclusion. 'So either their pleas were deliberately ignored or something happened to keep them quiet until it was too late.'

Michael raised his hands in a shrug. 'Yet everyone seemed genuinely shocked by the tragedy – I was watching very closely. Of course, the Spital's patients *are* insane . . .'

'The staff are not. They are all members of Tangmer's family.'

'Could it have been a suicide pact – the victims decided to die together, but one opted to spare the girl at the last minute?'

'Perhaps the bodies will give us answers. But the Spital is a curious place, do you not think? Its patients are like no lunatics that I have ever encountered.'

Michael agreed. 'There is an air of secrecy about it that is definitely suspicious. However, I think I know why. Not one madman spoke the whole time I was listening, and at one point, Prioress Joan shouted orders in French. I assumed no one would understand her, but most of them did.'

Bartholomew regarded him askance. 'You think they are French raiders, poised to attack us as they did in Winchelsea? That does not sound very likely!'

'I think they are French,' said Michael quietly, 'but not raiders. Most are women, children and old men, so I suspect they are folk who have been living peacefully in our country, but who suddenly find they are no longer welcome. The Spital is their refuge.'

Bartholomew considered. The monk's suggestion made sense, as it explained a lot: the peculiar silence, the inmates keeping their distance, the policy of discouraging visitors, and Tulyet, Leger and Norbert being asked to repel spectators.

'Amphelisa is French,' he said. 'Perhaps they are her kin. Moreover, she told me that the child we rescued is called Helene Girard . . . Hélène Girard.' He gave it two different pronunciations – the English one Amphelisa had used, followed by the French. Then he did the same for the other name he had heard: Delacroix.

'Then I am glad I have decided to investigate the matter,' said Michael, 'because if we are right, the chances are that the fire was set deliberately with the Girard family inside. Ergo, five people were murdered. It would have been six if you had not saved Hélène.'

Bartholomew frowned. 'That is a wild leap of logic, Brother! Moreover, the Spital is outside your jurisdiction – you have no authority to meddle.'

'The Senior Proctor will meddle where he likes,' declared Michael haughtily. 'And such a ruthless killer at large most certainly *is* my business, as I have an obligation to keep our scholars safe. Besides, I have not forgotten Paris the Plagiarist, even if you have.'

Bartholomew blinked. 'You think that whoever stabbed him also incinerated an entire family? But what evidence can you possibly—'

'Paris was French, and I am sure we shall shortly confirm that the Girards were French, too. So was Bonet the spicer. It cannot be coincidence, and as Paris was a scholar, it is my duty to find out what is happening. But I cannot sit here bandying words with you. I must visit the castle, and tell our Sheriff what we have reasoned.'

'What *you* have reasoned,' corrected Bartholomew, then

pointed out of the window. 'But you are spared a trek to the castle, because Dick is here to see you.'

The suite allocated to the Master of Michaelhouse was in the newer, less ramshackle south wing, and comprised a bedchamber, an office and a pantry for 'commons' – the edible treats scholars bought for their personal use. Needless to say, Michael kept this very well stocked, so Tulyet was not only furnished with a cup of breakfast ale, but a plate of spiced pastries as well. The Sheriff listened without interruption as Michael outlined his theory, although he gaped his astonishment at the claim that the Spital was a haven for displaced Frenchmen.

'I am right,' insisted Michael. 'The King issued his call to arms because of what the Dauphin did in Winchelsea, so, suddenly, the war is not something that is happening in some distant country, but is affecting people *here*. Even many of our scholars, who should be intelligent enough to know better, are full of anti-French fervour.'

'While the town is convinced that the Dauphin will appear at any moment to slaughter them all,' acknowledged Tulyet ruefully. 'A belief that Sir Leger and Sir Norbert exploit shamelessly to make folk practise at the butts.'

'Leger and Norbert,' said Michael in distaste. 'I have heard them in taverns, ranting that all Frenchmen should be wiped from the face of the Earth. It is a poisonous message to spread among the ignorant, who are incapable of telling the difference between enemy warriors and innocent strangers – as Paris the Plagiarist may have learned to his cost.'

'And Bonet,' sighed Tulyet. 'But Leger and Norbert have been moulded by the army, where they fought French warriors, massacred French peasants and destroyed French crops. I do not offer this as an excuse, but an explanation.'

'So you believe me?' asked Michael. 'About the Spital "lunatics" being French?'

Tulyet nodded slowly. 'On reflection, yes. I heard some of the children whisper in that language yesterday. Moreover, none of the adults seemed mad, which suggests they are there for some other reason.'

'So what will you do about it?' asked Bartholomew uneasily.

'Speak to them – determine whether they are hapless civilians caught in a strife that is none of their making, or spies intent on mischief.'

'They cannot be spies,' objected Bartholomew. 'Half of them are children.'

'It would not be the first time babes in arms were used as "cover" by unscrupulous adults,' said Tulyet soberly. 'However, I can tell you one thing for certain: something or someone prevented the Girards from escaping the fire, which means they were murdered.'

'Do you think they were killed because they were French?' asked Bartholomew.

'Perhaps, but we will find out for certain when you examine the bodies – or when Michael and I poke around the remains of the shed together.'

Michael smiled. 'You do not object to joining forces with the University, a foundation stuffed to the gills with enemy soldiers, if the town is to be believed?'

Tulyet raised his eyebrows. 'Can you blame them? Your scholars strut around whinnying in French, and flaunting the fact that few of them are local. It is deliberately provocative.'

'It is,' conceded Michael. 'And I shall speak to de Wetherset again later, to see if we can devise a way to make them desist.'

'Good,' said Tulyet. 'Because now is not the time to antagonise us – not when so many are being taught how to fight. More than a few itch to put their new skills into practice.'

Michael stood. 'Then we had better make a start. If our killer hates Frenchmen enough to burn women and children alive, we need to catch him fast.'

'I have just come from the Spital,' said Tulyet, not moving. 'The shed is still too hot for retrieving the victims, so I suggest meeting there at noon.'

'Then in the meantime, Matt and I will question the folk who live along the Trumpington road. Perhaps one of them will have noticed someone slinking along intent on murder and arson.' Michael raised a hand to quell Bartholomew's immediate objection. 'I know it will inter- fere with your teaching, but it cannot be helped. We must catch the culprit – or culprits – before any more blood is spilled.'

'I will speak to my informants,' said Tulyet. 'See if they have heard rumours about groups of Frenchmen living in the area. I hope they would have already told me if there were, but there is no harm in being sure.'

'None at all,' agreed Michael.

The three of them left the College, and walked to the high street, where Tulyet turned towards the castle, and Bartholomew and Michael aimed for St Mary the Great. It was Wednesday, the day when the market was dedicated to the buying and selling of livestock, so the town was busier than usual. Herds of cows, sheep and goats were being driven along the main roads, weaving around wagons loaded with crates of poultry. The noise was deaf- ening, as none of the creatures appreciated what was happening and made their displeasure known with a cacophony of lows, bleats, honks, squawks and quacks.

It seemed normal, but Bartholomew knew the town well enough to detect undercurrents. Locals shot chal- lenging glances at the students who trooped in and out of the churches, looks that were, more often than not, returned in full. Then he saw four King's Hall men backed into a corner by a gaggle of angry bakers. The scholars' hands hovered over the hilts of their swords, but it was the bakers who made a hasty departure when Michael bore down on them.

'They accused us of being French,' said one student defensively. His name was Foxlee, and it had been him and his three friends who had tried to pick a fight with Isnard the previous day. 'But I was born not ten miles from here, and I have lived in England all my life.'

'Whereas I hail from Bruges,' put in another, 'and while France may consider Flanders a vassal nation, my countrymen and I will *never* yield to their vile yoke.'

'At least they had heard of Bruges,' said a third. 'When I told them I was from Koln, they asked which part of France it was in. Do none of these peasants have brains, Brother?'

They spoke loudly enough to be heard by passers-by. These included Isnard and one of his more dubious associates – Verious the ditcher, a rogue who supplemented his meagre income with petty crime.

'If you are English, why do you wear them French clothes?' Verious demanded.

'What French clothes?' asked Bruges, startled, although Bartholomew could understand why Verious had put the question, as all four scholars wore elegant gipons, tied around the waist with belts made from gold thread. The skirts fell elegantly to their knees, and their feet were encased in calfskin boots. Around their heads were liripipes – scarves that could double as hoods. All were blue, which was King's Hall livery, although there was no sign of the academic tabards that should have covered their finery. But it was the dash of the exotic that rendered the ensemble distinctly un-English – mother-of-pearl buttons, lace cuffs and feathers.

'He cannot tell the difference between French fashions and those favoured by the Court,' scoffed Foxlee. 'If the

King were to ride past now, this oaf would probably accuse *him* of being French as well.'

'You seem to have forgotten your tabards,' said Michael coolly, preventing Verious from snarling a response by raising an imperious hand. 'Doubtless you will want to rectify the matter before the Senior Proctor fines you.'

'And any townsman who jeers at them will be reported to the Sheriff for breaking the King's peace,' put in Bartholomew hastily, as Verious and Isnard drew breath to cackle their amusement at the speed with which the King's Hall lads departed.

'We will be in flames within a week unless Dick and I impose some serious peacekeeping measures,' muttered Michael as he and Bartholomew went on their way. 'The only problem is that the triumvirate veto anything I suggest.'

Bartholomew frowned his mystification. 'Do they want the University to burn then?'

Michael scowled. 'This is what happens when our colleagues elect a man who thinks he knows better than me. When de Wetherset was last in charge, the town was a very different place. He does not understand that things have changed.'

'Then you had better educate him before he does any irreparable harm.'

They began their enquiries at the Hall of Valence Marie and then Peterhouse, although no one at either College could tell them anything useful. Opposite Peterhouse was a row of houses, some of which were rented to the University for use as hostels. Unfortunately, the residents had either been out or had noticed nothing unusual until they had seen the smoke, at which point the culprit would likely have been well away. The fourth house they visited was larger than the others, and had recently been renovated to a very high standard.

'It is a dormitory for Tyled Hostel,' explained Michael as they knocked on its beautiful new door. 'That place has more money than is decent.'

A student came to escort them to a pleasant refectory at the back of the house, where he and his friends were entertaining – the triumvirate were ensconced there, enjoying cake and honeyed wine. De Wetherset and Aynton were members of Tyled, but it was strange to see Heltisle – the Master of Bene't – in a hostel, as he usually deemed such places beneath him, even wealthy ones like Tyled, and was brazen in his belief that Colleges were far superior foundations. Then Bartholomew saw several metal pens displayed on the table, and realised that Heltisle was there in the hope of making a sale.

The triumvirate looked sleek and prosperous that day, and had donned clothes that were bound to aggravate the locals. De Wetherset's gold pilgrim badge glittered on a gorgeous velvet hat; Heltisle seemed to have done his utmost to emulate the Dauphin; and even the usually sober Aynton wore French silk hose. It was needlessly provocative, and Bartholomew was disgusted that they did not set a better example.

'We have already asked these lads if they saw anything suspicious yesterday,' said Aynton with one of his benign grins. 'None did, because they were all at a lecture.'

'But Theophilis told us that the dead lunatics were from a family called *Girard*,' said Heltisle, pronouncing the name in the English way. 'Is it true?'

'Yes,' replied Michael cautiously. 'Why? Did you know them?'

'They are the ones that de Wetherset and I hired as proxies in the call to arms,' replied Heltisle. 'At considerable expense.'

'What a pity,' said Bartholomew with uncharacteristic acerbity. 'Now you will have to go to the butts yourselves.'

'We are too important to waste our time there,' declared

Heltisle. 'Besides, *I* do not need to practise. I am already an excellent shot and very handy with a sword.'

'Not that we will ever have to put such talents to work, of course,' put in de Wetherset. 'If we are obliged to march to war, we shall be employed as clerks or scribes.'

'No – *generals*,' countered Heltisle. 'Directing battles from a safe distance.'

Bartholomew laughed, although he knew the Vice-Chancellor had not been joking.

'*I* did not hire a Girard,' put in Aynton. 'My proxy was Bruges the Fleming from King's Hall. But after you said such an arrangement smacked of cowardice, Brother, I released him from my service. I do not want to earn the contempt of townsfolk or of fellow scholars.'

'His name is Bruges, you say?' asked de Wetherset keenly.

'Yes, but you are too late to snag him for yourself,' said Aynton apologetically. 'Theophilis overheard me talking to him, and hired him on the spot. He told me the University would need to keep some of its officials back, if the Chancellor, the Vice-Chancellor, the Commissary *and* the Senior Proctor are obliged to go and fight the French.'

'You see, Brother?' murmured Bartholomew. 'You are reckless to trust Theophilis – he has ambitions to rule the University all on his own.'

Michael ignored him. 'How well did you know these Girard men?'

'We met them twice,' replied Heltisle. 'Once to discuss the matter, and once to hand over the money we agreed to pay.'

He named the sum, and Bartholomew felt his jaw drop. It was a fortune.

'We understand one of the children survived,' said de Wetherset. 'Perhaps you would see that the money stays with her, Brother. We had a contract with her kin, and it is hardly her fault that they are no longer in a position to honour it.'

'That is generous,' said Michael suspiciously.

'It is,' agreed Heltisle, and smiled craftily. 'Perhaps word of our largesse will spread, and another lunatic will offer us his sword.'

'No,' said de Wetherset sharply. 'It is *not* self-interest that guides us. The truth is that I feel sorry for the girl – parents, aunt, uncle and brother, all dead. It is a heavy burden to bear.'

Heltisle retorted that he was a sentimental fool, and an ill-tempered spat followed, with Aynton struggling to mediate. While they bickered, Bartholomew pulled Michael to one side and spoke in an undertone.

'Do you think someone heard what the Girards were paid and decided to steal it? There are plenty who would kill for a fraction of that amount.'

'We shall bear it in mind,' Michael whispered back. 'But why would the Girards offer to bear arms against their countrymen? Or did they take the money with no intention of honouring the arrangement? After all, it cannot be cheap to stay in hiding, so any means of gaining a quick fortune . . .'

'Perhaps we should include de Wetherset and Heltisle on our list of murder suspects – they realised the Girards aimed to cheat them and took revenge.'

'If they are capable of incinerating an entire family, they would not be hiring proxies to go to war on their behalf – they would be itching to join the slaughter in person.'

Bartholomew supposed that was true, although he decided to watch both scholars carefully until their innocence was proven. He was about to say so, when there was a knock on the door and two men were shown in bearing missives for the Chancellor's attention. Michael's jaw dropped when he saw the couriers' clothes.

'Those are *beadles'* uniforms!' he breathed, shocked. 'How dare you wear—'

'These are a couple of the new recruits Heltisle has hired,' explained de Wetherset. 'To protect us against the growing aggression of the town.'

Michael gaped at him. It was the Senior Proctor's prerogative to choose beadles, and he took the duty seriously. They were no longer a ragtag band of louts who could gain employment nowhere else, noted for drunkenness and a love of bribes, but professionals, who were paid a decent wage and were treated with respect. They were picked for their ability to use reason rather than force, although they were reliable fighters in a crisis. Heltisle's men were surly giants, who looked as though they would rather start a fight than stop one.

'If you thought we needed more men, you should have told me,' said Michael between gritted teeth. 'I would have been more than happy to—'

'I assumed you would not mind,' said Heltisle slyly. 'After all, you regularly relieve de Wetherset of the duties that go with *his* office, so I thought you would not object to me doing the same to you.'

'I hardly think—' began Michael indignantly.

'I took on a dozen,' interrupted Heltisle, enjoying the monk's growing outrage. 'All good fellows who will make townsmen think twice about crossing us.'

'And how will you pay for them?' demanded Michael curtly. 'Because it will not be out of the Senior Proctor's budget.'

'We shall use the Destitute Scholars' Fund,' replied Heltisle, and shrugged when Michael regarded him in disbelief. 'It is only penniless low-borns who need it, and I do not want them here anyway.'

'These "penniless low-borns" are often our best thinkers,' said Bartholomew quietly. 'Our University will be a poorer place without them.'

'Rubbish,' stated Heltisle contemptuously, and turned back to Michael, indicating the new beadles as he did so. 'My recruits are a cut above the weaklings you favour, and will be a credit to the University.'

'I hope you are right,' said Michael tightly. 'Because any inadequacies on their part will fall at your door, not mine.'

'No, all beadles are *your* responsibility,' said Heltisle sweetly. 'And there is another thing: a letter arrived from the Bishop this morning. It was addressed to you, but I assumed it was really meant for the Chancellor, so I opened it.'

Michael struggled not to give him the satisfaction of losing his temper. 'How very uncouth. I would *never* stoop to such uncivilised antics.'

This was a downright lie, as he stole missives addressed to the triumvirate on a daily basis. Grinning, Heltisle produced the document in question. It was thick with filth, so he had wrapped it in a rag to protect his hands.

'It fell in a cowpat,' he explained gloatingly. 'Are you not going to take it and see what it says?'

'I will tell you, Brother,' said Aynton, shooting the Vice-Chancellor an admonishing look for his childishness. 'It is about a field in Girton. The Bishop owns it, but he wants to transfer the title to St Andrew's Church.'

It was Michael's turn to grin. 'You are right, Heltisle – the Bishop *would* rather the Chancellor sorted it out. Unfortunately, the deeds pertaining to that piece of land are so complex that they will take weeks to unravel. I recommend he delegates the matter to a deputy. You, for example.'

He bowed and sailed out. As Bartholomew turned to follow, he heard de Wetherset remark that perhaps he *had* better do as the Senior Proctor suggested, as a Chancellor could not afford to waste time on trivialities. He did not catch Heltisle's reply, but he did hear Aynton rebuke him for foul language.

* * *

Out on the street, Michael's temper broke, and he railed furiously about Heltisle's effrontery. Bartholomew let him rant, knowing he would feel better for it. The tirade might have gone on longer, but they bumped into Theophilis, who had been in the Gilbertine Priory, giving a lecture on his *Calendarium*. Michael was far too enraged for normal conversation, so Bartholomew took the opportunity to ask the Junior Proctor about the proxy he had snapped up when Aynton had decided against using one.

'Bruges the Fleming.' Theophilis spoke so silkily that Bartholomew's skin crawled. 'I hired him for you, Brother. The University will need strong leaders if lots of us are called to fight, and you are the only man I trust to watch our interests while I am away.'

'You are kind, Theophilis,' said Michael. 'But as a monk in major holy orders, I am exempt from the call to arms. I do not need a proxy.'

'I know that,' said Theophilis impatiently. 'But you will need a good man at your side, so Bruges will stand in for whoever you select to help you. Perhaps you will pick me, but perhaps you will decide on another – the choice will be yours to make.'

'You see, Matt?' said Michael, when the Junior Proctor had gone. 'His intentions *are* honourable. He was thinking of the University, not himself.'

Bartholomew did not believe it for an instant, but knew there was no point in arguing. He and Michael went to the house next to Tyled's dormitory, where they learned that the owners – a tailor and his wife – were 'far too busy to gaze out of windows all day like lazy scholars'.

When they emerged, Tulyet was waiting to report that none of his spies had heard the slightest whisper of groups of Frenchmen in the area – and they had all been alert for such rumours, given what had happened to Winchelsea.

'Perhaps the Gilbertines will have noticed something

useful,' said Michael, although his shoulders slumped; their lack of success was beginning to dishearten him.

They had not taken many steps towards the priory before they met Sir Leger and Sir Norbert, marching along with an enormous train of townsfolk at their heels, most from the nearby King's Head tavern. The two knights wore military surcoats, and their hands rested on the hilts of their broadswords. All their followers carried some kind of weapon – cudgels, pikes or knives.

'What are you doing?' demanded Tulyet, aghast. 'You cannot allow such a great horde to stamp about armed to the teeth! It is needlessly provocative.'

'Needlessly provocative?' echoed Leger with calculated insolence. 'We are preparing to repel a French invasion, as per the King's orders.'

'All true and loyal Englishmen will applaud our efforts,' put in the swarthy, hulking Norbert, 'which means that anyone who does not is a traitor. Besides, if there is any trouble, it will not be us who started it, but that University you love so much.'

'Quite,' said Leger smugly. 'Because all we and our recruits are doing is walking along a public highway, minding our own business.'

'Do not test me,' said Tulyet tightly. 'I know what you are trying to do and I will not have it. Either you behave in a manner commensurate with your rank, or I shall send you back to the King in disgrace. Do I make myself clear?'

Norbert looked as though he would argue, but the more intelligent Leger knew they had overstepped the mark. He nodded sullenly, jabbing his friend in the back to prevent him from saying something that would allow Tulyet to carry out his threat.

'Where were you going?' Bartholomew asked in the tense silence that followed.

'The butts,' replied Leger stiffly. 'For archery practice.'

'The butts are ours on Wednesdays,' said Michael. 'You cannot have them today.'

When the King had first issued his call to arms, a field near the Barnwell Gate had been hastily converted into a shooting range – 'the butts'. As it was the only suitable land available, both the town and the University had wanted it, so Tulyet and Michael had agreed on a time-table: the town had it on Tuesdays, Thursdays, Saturdays and Sundays, while scholars had it on Mondays, Wednesdays and Fridays. There had been no infringe-ments so far, but everyone knew it was only a question of time before one side defaulted, at which point there would be a fracas.

'Take them to the castle instead,' ordered Tulyet. 'It is time they learned something of hand-to-hand combat. I shall join you there later, to assess the progress you have made. I hope I will not be disappointed.'

There was a murmur of dismay in the ranks, as infantry training was far less popular than archery. Norbert opened his mouth to refuse, but Leger inclined his head.

'Good idea,' he said. 'We shall teach everyone how to use a blade. I have always found throat-slitting and stab-bing to be very useful skills. Men! Forward *march*!'

'There will be a battle before the week is out,' predicted Tulyet, watching them tramp away. 'They itch to spill your blood, and the University itches to spill ours. But I had better go and make sure they do as they are told. While I do, ask the Gilbertines if they saw our murderous arsonist slinking past, and we shall go to the Spital as soon as I get back.'

The Gilbertine Priory was a beautiful place, and Bartholomew knew it well, as he was often summoned to tend poorly canons. They had a more liberal attitude towards women than the other Orders, and had not minded at all when Michael had asked them to house a few nuns during the *conloquium*. They had offered them the use of their guesthouse, a building that stood apart from the main precinct, although still within its protective walls.

Its Prior was a quiet, decent man named John, who had one of the widest mouths Bartholomew had ever seen on a person. He appeared to have at least twice as many teeth as anyone else, and when he smiled, Bartholomew was always put in mind of a crocodile.

'We were having a meeting in our chapel, so the first we knew about the blaze was when our porter came to tell us that you were racing out to the Spital,' John said apologetically. 'But perhaps your nuns saw something – our guesthouse overlooks the road.'

He left them to make their own way there. As they went, Michael told Bartholomew that he had housed ten nuns there – nine from Swaffham Bulbeck and one from Ickleton Priory.

'Both foundations are wealthy,' he explained, 'and I thought they might become Michaelhouse benefactors if I put them somewhere nice. It was a serious mistake.'

'Why?'

'Because last year, Abbess Isabel of Swaffham Bulbeck visited Ickleton on behalf of the Bishop. She was so shocked by what she found that its Prioress – Alice – was deposed. And which nun should be sent to represent Ickleton at our *conloquium*? Alice!'

'That must be uncomfortable for both parties,' mused Bartholomew.

'It is more than uncomfortable,' averred Michael. 'It has resulted in open warfare! I offered to find one faction alternative accommodation, but neither will move, on the grounds that it will then appear as if the other is the victor.'

Bartholomew was intrigued. 'What did Abbess Isabel find at Ickleton, exactly?'

'Just the usual – corruption, indolence, licentiousness.'

'Those are usual in your Order, are they?'

Michael scowled. 'I meant those are the most common offences committed by the rare head of house who strays from the straight and narrow. Alice allowed her friends to live in the priory free of charge, and gave them alms that should have gone to the poor. She also let her nuns miss their holy offices, and too many men were regular visitors.'

'Then it is no surprise that the Bishop deposed her. But are you sure that Abbess Isabel did not exaggerate? I have met her, and she is very easily shocked.'

'She is,' acknowledged Michael. 'Probably because she is generally considered to be a saint in the making.'

Bartholomew was surprised to hear it. 'Is she?'

'She was to have married an earl, but when she expressed a desire to serve God instead, he chopped off her hands. That night, he was struck dead and her hands regrew.'

Bartholomew regarded him askance. 'Surely, you do not believe that?'

'The Pope did, and granted her special dispensation to wear a white habit instead of a black one, as an expression of her purity. But how did you meet her?'

'She is the one who found Paris the Plagiarist's body. She was so upset that she fainted, so I carried her into a tavern to recover – where she saw the landlady's low-cut bodice and swooned all over again. I wondered at the time why her habit was a different colour. I wanted to ask, but she did not seem like a lady for casual conversation.'

'No,' agreed Michael. 'Saints are not, generally speaking.'

Abbess Isabel was a slender, sallow woman whose bright white habit made her appear ghostly. She emerged from the Gilbertines' stable on a donkey, and Michael whispered that she was scheduled to speak on humility at the *conloquium* that day.

'Hence her arrival on a simple beast of burden,' he explained. 'A practical demonstration of self-effacement. Of course, the fact that she feels compelled to show us how humble she is does smack of pride . . .'

Suddenly, the Abbess raised her pale eyes heavenwards in a rapt expression. Her black-robed retinue immediately grabbed the donkey's bridle and formed a protective ring around her, to ensure that her communication with God was not interrupted.

'We could be here a while,' murmured Michael. 'She goes into trances.'

'Or perhaps it is a ruse to avoid *her*,' said Bartholomew, nodding to where another nun was coming from the opposite direction. 'The deposed Alice, I presume?'

Alice was short and thin, and her beady black eyes held an expression of such fierce hatred that Bartholomew was sure she should never have been allowed to take holy orders. The malevolent glower intensified when she saw Isabel being pious. Then she began to scratch so frantically at her scalp that he suspected some bothersome skin complaint – perhaps one that rendered the sufferer unusually bad-tempered.

'I was astonished when I learned that *she* was Ickleton's sole delegate,' whispered Michael. 'I assumed she was still in disgrace.'

'Perhaps her replacement wanted rid of her for a while,' suggested Bartholomew. 'Having a former superior under your command cannot be easy.'

'Especially one like Alice, who is bitter and quarrelsome. Of course, Swaffham Bulbeck is not the only convent Alice has taken against. She has also declared war on Lyminster, because the Bishop's sister lives there. Putting them in the Spital was another mistake on my part, as they invariably meet when they ride to St Radegund's each morning. There have been scenes.'

Alice marched towards Michael, bristling with anger. 'I have a complaint to make, Brother. That worldly Magistra Katherine spoke at the *conloquium* today, and she was so boring that I had to leave.'

'You call Katherine worldly?' blurted Michael. 'After you were dismissed for—'

'I made one or two small errors of judgement,' interrupted Alice sharply. 'And was then condemned by people who are far worse sinners than I could ever hope to be.'

'*Hope* to be?' echoed Bartholomew, amused.

Alice ignored him. 'Katherine is like her brother – a hypocrite. How dare he dismiss me when *he* fled the country to escape charges of murder, theft, kidnapping and extortion!'

She had a point: the Bishop had indeed been accused of those crimes, and rather than stay and face the consequences, he had run to Avignon, to claim sanctuary with the Pope. Everyone knew he was guilty, so Bartholomew understood why Alice objected to being judged by him. Michael opened his mouth to defend the man whose shoes he hoped to fill one day, but Alice was already turning her vitriol on someone else she did not like.

'And that Abbess Isabel is no saint,' she hissed. 'She is selfish and deceitful.'

Isabel was not about to hang around being holy while Alice denigrated her to the Bishop's favourite monk. She barked an order that saw her nuns drop the donkey's bridle and step aside. Then she rode forward to have her say.

'You are a disgrace, Alice,' she declared, her pale eyes cold and hard. 'It is wrong to make light of your own crimes by pointing out the errors of others. There is no excuse for what you did.'

'And you never make mistakes, of course,' jeered Alice.

'You are perfect in every way. How wonderful it must be to be you.'

'She *is* perfect,' declared one of Isabel's nuns angrily. 'Just ask the Pope. We are honoured to serve her, so keep your nasty remarks to yourself.'

'Yesterday's fire,' interposed Michael quickly. 'The arsonist almost certainly used the road outside to reach the Spital. Did any of you notice anything suspicious?'

'No,' replied Isabel shortly. 'If we had, we would have told you already.'

'I was not here,' said Alice haughtily. 'I was at the *conloquium.*'

'But I prayed for the Girard family all night,' Isabel went on, as if her enemy had not spoken, 'which was not easy with Alice lurking behind me – I could feel her eyes burning into the back of my head. She will be bound for Hell unless she learns to replace malice with love.'

Alice bristled. '*I* was praying for the Girards, but you were praying for yourself – that your so-called piety will win you a place among the saints.'

'While you are here, Brother,' said another of the nuns frostily, 'perhaps you will tell *Sister* Alice to keep her maggot-infested marchpanes to herself. She will deny sending them to the Abbess, but we all know the truth.'

'Liar!' snarled Alice. 'I have better things to do than buy you lot presents.'

'What time did you arrive at the *conloquium*, Alice?' asked Michael, speaking quickly a second time to nip the burgeoning spat in the bud.

'Not until the afternoon,' admitted Alice. 'Before that, I was in a town church, practising my own presentation, which is later this week.'

'So you cannot prove where you were at the salient time?' asked Isabel, raising her white eyebrows pointedly.

Alice bristled. 'I sincerely hope you are not accusing *me* of setting this fire. Why would I do such a thing?'

'To harm the ladies from Lyminster,' replied another of Isabel's retinue promptly. 'You hate them almost as much as you hate us, and your enmity knows no bounds.'

'And you, Isabel?' asked Michael before Alice could defend herself. 'Where were you?'

'Praying,' replied the Abbess serenely. 'In St Botolph's Church. All my sisters were with me, so none of us can help you identify your arsonist. Now I have a question for *you*, Brother: have you caught Paris the Plagiarist's killer yet? I cannot forget the sight of his dead white face, and it disturbs me to think that his murderer might pass us in the street.'

'He might,' acknowledged Michael. 'And our best – perhaps our only – chance of catching him now is if *you* remember anything new.'

'Then I shall tell God to jog my memory,' said Isabel, and smiled. 'So you will soon have the culprit under lock and key, because He always accedes to my demands.'

'That shows you are no saint,' spat Alice at once. 'No one makes *demands* of God.'

Isabel's entourage took exception to this remark. A furious quarrel ensued, and this time, not even Michael could quell it.

Bartholomew backed away, pulling the monk with him. 'You are brave to have anything to do with this *conloquium*, Brother,' he murmured, 'if these delegates are anything to go by.'

'Fortunately, they are not,' said Michael with a heartfelt sigh. 'Shall we see if Dick is ready for the Spital?'

Tulyet had trailed his knights and their followers to the castle, and was confident that they were all condemned to an unpleasant afternoon wrestling each other in the dusty bailey. He hurried back to the Trumpington road, where he found Bartholomew and Michael still busy with the nuns. While he waited for them to finish, he discussed the town's unsettled atmosphere with Prior John, who was worried that it might spread to infect his peaceful convent.

'It would not normally worry me,' confided John, 'but Michael's nuns are a querulous horde, who never stop squabbling. I would never have agreed to take them had I known what they were like. All I can say is thank God I am a Gilbertine, not a Benedictine!'

Tulyet laughed. Then Michael and Bartholomew appeared, so he bade John farewell and set off towards the Spital with them. They had covered about half the distance when they met big Prioress Joan riding a spirited stallion. He and Michael admired her skill as she directed it over the treacherous, rock-hard ruts, although Bartholomew's attention was fixed on the horse – it had an evil look in its eye and he did not want to end up on the wrong end of its teeth.

'Here is a handsome beast,' said Michael, approvingly. 'The horse, I mean, not you, Abbess. Does he belong to your convent?'

'Do you ask as the Bishop's spy or as a man who appreciates decent horseflesh?' said Joan, a twinkle in her eye. 'Because if it is the former, then of course Dusty belongs to the convent. You know as well as I do that Benedictines are forbidden expensive possessions.'

'Horses do not count,' averred Michael, although Bartholomew was sure St Benedict would have begged to differ. 'You call him Dusty? An unworthy name for such a fine creature.'

'A grand one would raise alarms when we submit our accounts,' explained Joan with a conspiratorial grin. 'But no one questions hay for a nag called Dusty. Would you like to take him for a canter later? I do not usually lend him out, but I sense you could manage him.'

'Are you sure he could bear the weight?' asked

Bartholomew, looking from the monk's substantial girth to the horse's slender legs.

'Ignore him, Brother,' said Joan, giving Bartholomew a haughty glare. 'People accuse me of being too large for a woman, but they do not know what they are talking about. The truth is that I am normal, while everyone else is excessively petite.'

'And I have unusually heavy bones, although few are intelligent enough to see it,' said Michael, pleased to meet someone who thought like him. He eyed Bartholomew coolly. 'Even my closest friend calls me plump, and has the effrontery to criticise my diet.'

'Then that is just plain rude,' said Joan, offended on his behalf. 'A man's victuals are his own affair, just as a woman's size is hers.'

'Quite right,' agreed Michael. 'Shall we ride out together and discuss this vexing matter in more detail? I shall borrow something from King's Hall – they have the best stables.'

Joan revealed her long teeth in a delighted smile. 'After the *conloquium*, when I am not obliged to listen to my sisters whine about the difficulties involved in running a convent. In my opinion, if you have a problem, you solve it. You do not sit about and grumble like men.'

'Problems like your priory's chapel,' mused Michael. 'Part of it collapsed, so you rebuilt it with your own hands. Magistra Katherine told me.'

Joan blushed modestly. 'She exaggerates – I had lots of help. Besides, I would much rather tile a roof than do the accounts. I thank God daily for His wisdom in sending Katherine to me, as she is an excellent administrator. I could not have asked for a better deputy.'

'We are on our way to the Spital, to find out what happened to the Girard family,' said Tulyet. 'You were there when the fire started, so what can you tell us about it?'

'Nothing, I am afraid. I was in the stables grooming Dusty at the time. Katherine was due to give a lecture in St Radegund's, but when I saw the shed alight, I sent a message asking for it to be postponed, as it seemed inappropriate to jaunt off while our hosts struggled to avert a crisis. I spent most of the time calming the horses.'

'Did you notice any visitors to the Spital yesterday?' Tulyet asked. 'I know Tangmer discourages them, but it is possible that someone sneaked in *un*invited.'

'Just Sister Alice, who will insist on paying court to us, even though we find her company tiresome. Moreover, I always want to scratch when she is around, because she claws constantly at herself. When she is with us, my nuns and I must look like dogs with fleas.'

'So you saw nothing to help?' Michael was beginning to be frustrated by the lack of reliable witnesses.

Joan grimaced. 'I am sorry, Brother. All my attention was on the horses. Try asking my nuns – I have left them in the Spital to pray for the dead. I am the only Lyminster delegate who will attend the *conloquium* today, but only because I am scheduled to talk about plumbing. If it were any other day, I would join my sisters on their knees.'

They were nearly at the Spital when they were hailed by Cynric. The book-bearer carried a sword, and had one long Welsh hunting knife in his belt and another strapped to his thigh. He had also donned a boiled leather jerkin and a metal helmet.

'These are what I wore at Poitiers,' he reminded Bartholomew, who was eyeing them disapprovingly. 'When you and me won that great victory.'

Four years before, he and Bartholomew had been in France, when bad timing had put them at the place where the Prince of Wales was about to challenge a much larger army. They had acquitted themselves adequately, but Cynric's account had grown with each telling, and had reached the point where he and the physician had defeated the enemy with no help from anyone else. Bartholomew still had nightmares about the carnage, although Cynric professed to have enjoyed every moment and claimed he was proud to have been there.

'Please take them off,' begged Bartholomew. 'They make you look as though you are spoiling for a fight.'

'I *have* to wear them – Master Heltisle put me in charge of training scholars at the butts,' argued Cynric. 'And if I do not look the part, no one will do what I say. But never mind that – me and Margery have something to tell you.'

They had not noticed the woman at the side of the road. Margery Starre was a lady of indeterminate years, who made no bones about the fact that she was a witch. Normally, this would have seen her burned at the stake, but she offered a valuable service with her cures and charms, many of which worked, so the authorities turned a blind eye. Bartholomew was wary of her, as she believed that the Devil – with whom she claimed to be on friendly terms – had helped him to become a successful physician. He dreaded to imagine what would happen if she shared this conviction with his colleagues. Heltisle, for one, would certainly use it to harm him.

'One of those Black Nuns came to me with a peculiar request,' she began without preamble. 'And I thought you should know about it.'

'Not that,' said Cynric impatiently. 'Tell them about the Spital ghost – about it being the spirit of some hapless soul sacrificed by pagans.'

'I saw it with my own eyes,' said Margery obligingly. 'A white spectre, which wobbled along the top of the wall, then disappeared into thin air.'

'Clippesby saw it, too,' put in Cynric. 'I overheard him telling the hens about it this morning.'

'It did not speak,' Margery went on, 'but I could tell it was a soul in torment.'

'Could you?' said Bartholomew curiously, although he knew he should not encourage her. 'How?'

'By its demeanour. And because it left trails of water on the wall – tears. The Spital should never have been built there, as it is the site of an ancient temple.'

'How can you tell?' demanded Bartholomew, sure she could not. The land on which the Spital was built was no different from its surroundings, and there was nothing to suggest it was special – no ditches, mounds, springs or unaccountable stones.

'Because Satan told me,' replied Margery grandly. 'He dropped in yesterday morning, and said he plans to take up residence there. I imagine it was him who started that fire – not deliberately, of course, but because his fiery hoofs touched dry wood.'

'You are right,' said Bartholomew sombrely. 'The Devil *was* involved in starting the blaze, because only a very evil being could want people roasted alive.'

Margery sniffed. 'Satan is not evil – just misunderstood. He—'

'You mentioned a nun,' interrupted Michael, unwilling to listen to such liberal views about the Prince of Darkness. He was a monk, after all. 'She came to you with "a peculiar request".'

'It was Alice, the short, spiteful one who was deposed from Ickleton,' replied Margery. 'She asked me to make her some candles that reek of manure.'

Michael frowned his bemusement. 'Why would she want something like that?'

'To send to folk she does not like. The recipients will light them in all innocence, then spend days trying to dislodge the stink from their clothes.'

'I see,' said Michael. 'And Alice told you all this willingly?'

Margery nodded. 'She was reluctant at first, but hate burns hot inside her, and once she started, she could not stop. One of her targets is that elegant, arrogant nun, who thinks she is better than everyone else because her brother is the Bishop . . .'

'Magistra Katherine,' supplied Bartholomew.

'Yes, so if *she* dies in suspicious circumstances, you will know who to question first. Another enemy is Prioress Joan, who called her a spiteful little harpy. And a third is Abbess Isabel, whose report to the Bishop saw her disgraced.'

'Did Alice buy spells that would kill or hurt them?' asked Bartholomew uneasily. He did not believe in the efficacy of such things, but if Alice was attempting to purchase some, then her intended victims should be warned to be on their guard.

'I do not deal in those,' replied Margery loftily, although his relief evaporated when she added, 'other than for very special customers.'

'I assume you refused to make these smelly candles, too,' said Bartholomew.

'Of course not! She paid me a fortune to invent them, and I like a challenge. If I succeed, I can sell them to others who want to annoy their foes. You may have one – free of charge – for that nasty old Heltisle if you like.'

Bartholomew laughed. 'It is tempting, but I do not think Matilde would approve.'

'She would! She cannot abide him either. Mind you, that villain Theophilis is worse. He sniffs around poor Master Clippesby like a dog on heat, and I do not like it.'

'We should go,' said Tulyet, tired of listening to her. 'Time is passing.'

He set a cracking pace, and no one spoke again until they reached the Spital. When they arrived, he glanced up at the towering walls.

'God's blood!' he blurted. 'What is *that*?'

Bartholomew and Michael looked to where he pointed,

and saw something pale rise from the ground and ascend the wall. There was an approximate head and body, with two trailing wisps that might have been legs. It floated upwards, then disappeared over the top.

'It is someone playing a trick,' determined Michael. 'Go and look in the undergrowth, Matt. You are better at these things than me.'

Bartholomew took a stick and thrashed around in the weeds at the foot of the wall, but there was nothing to see – no tell-tale footsteps or hidden pieces of twine.

'If it is a prank, then it is a very clever one,' he told Michael eventually. 'I have no idea how it was managed. Perhaps it really was a ghost.'

'Do not be ridiculous,' said Michael firmly. 'There is no such thing as ghosts. Well, other than the Holy Ghost, of course, but that is different.'

CHAPTER 5

There was a bell rope outside the Spital's main entrance so that visitors could announce their arrival. Michael gave it a tug, and when nothing happened, pulled harder. Then he exchanged a look of astonishment with Bartholomew and Tulyet when, instead of the usual cheery jangle that characterised such arrangements, a bell of considerable size boomed out. It echoed mournfully around them, stilling the merry chatter of sparrows in the nearby bushes.

'Goodness!' murmured Bartholomew, when the deep hum had died away. 'How very sinister! It feels as though we are about to ask for admittance to the Devil's lair.'

'Do not jest about such matters,' admonished Tulyet uneasily. 'There is something distinctly odd about this place. Perhaps Margery is right about Satan making it his own – and the thing we just watched shimmer over the wall was one of his familiars.'

'It was a trick,' said Michael firmly, 'even if we did find no evidence to prove it. However, we shall use it to our advantage, because if folk believe this place is infested by evil sprites, they will keep their distance. Then if the lunatics do transpire to be French, they are less likely to be discovered.'

'Alternatively,' cautioned Bartholomew, 'local folk may object to such a place on their doorstep, and will raze it to the ground. Then we shall have dozens of victims, not five.'

They were still debating when the massive Eudo opened the gate. He peered out warily, standing so that his bulk prevented them from seeing inside.

'You cannot come in,' he stated in a tone designed to brook no argument.

'Oh, yes, we can,' countered Tulyet. 'People died here yesterday, and it is our duty to investigate. So either let us in now or we shall return with soldiers.'

His stern face convinced Eudo to do as he was told. The moment they were inside, the big man closed the gate and secured it with a thick bar.

'People do not like lunatics,' he explained. 'Ergo, we have to protect ours.'

'So I see,' remarked Tulyet, looking to where several men were stationed on the walls, clearly standing guard. They were not armed, but sack-covered mounds revealed where weapons were stashed.

The Spital was a very different place than it had been the previous day. The inmates no longer stood in a frightened cluster, but joined the staff in a variety of humdrum activities – sweeping, gardening, laundry. There was not a child in sight. Two inmates moved as though they were not in complete control of their limbs, while three others jabbered self-consciously.

'Not even madmen do dirty household chores without aprons to protect their clothes,' Michael murmured as they followed Eudo to the hall. 'That bell is not to announce visitors, but to warn the inmates to take up pre-agreed roles and positions. All this quiet industry is an act, although not a very convincing one.'

'I agree,' whispered Tulyet. 'But let us go along with the charade, and see what we can learn before we reveal that we know they are Frenchmen in disguise – wealthy Frenchmen, as hiring an entire hospital cannot be cheap.'

'I suspect they are middling folk – craftsmen and traders,' said Bartholomew. 'The one beating rugs has burns like a blacksmith, while the woman weaving baskets is so dexterous that it must be her profession.'

They turned at a shout, and saw the portly Warden Tangmer waddling towards them, red-faced and breathless in his haste. Eudo's tiny wife Goda was with him, wearing an elaborately embroidered kirtle that made her look like an exotic doll. Bartholomew wondered if her everyday one had been spoiled fighting the fire.

Tulyet opened his mouth to explain why they were there, but the Warden spoke first.

'We shall bury our dead behind the chapel,' he announced. 'We are digging their graves now, so please leave us to do it in peace.'

'Not until we have ascertained why a whole family was trapped inside a burning shed,' said Tulyet sharply.

Tangmer winced. 'It was an accident. We are bursting at the seams with lunatics, so every building is needed to accommodate them all, even ramshackle ones that go up in flames when candles are knocked over.'

Eudo glared at Michael. 'Which is your fault for foisting those nuns on us.'

Michael raised his eyebrows. 'I did it because *you* told me that all your patients are held in secure accommodation inside the hall, and that the guesthouse was never used for that purpose. If you had been honest with me, I would have billeted my sisters elsewhere.'

'I did not know you were fishing for beds at the time,' retorted Eudo sullenly. 'I thought you wanted assurances that your precious University is in no danger from escaped madmen.'

'So the nuns' arrival meant that some patients were moved to the shed?' asked Tulyet. He waited until Eudo and Tangmer nodded before continuing. 'You are lying again – yesterday, you told me that it was full of tools and building supplies.'

Tangmer gave a pained smile. 'It is. However, the Girards elected to use it anyway – like a family house.'

'There were no windows,' added Eudo, 'so you had to

use candles or a lamp inside. It was also full of dry timber, so if one of the youngsters knocked one over . . .'

'The door was open when the alarm was first raised,' said Tangmer, his heckling defiance replaced by anguish. 'I ordered it closed, thinking it was the best way to contain the blaze. There had been plenty of time for anyone inside to get out, so I do not understand how this terrible thing could have happened. Goda said the shed was empty.'

'I was sure it *was* empty,' put in Goda, shaking her head unhappily. 'I could not believe it when voices . . .'

'Did you search it?' asked Tulyet. 'Properly?'

Goda grimaced. 'I went in as far as I dared, but no one was there. All I can think is that they were hiding behind the logs at the very back.'

Tulyet frowned. 'Why would they hide?'

'Because we had a visitor, and they were terrified of those,' explained Goda. 'I see now that I should have looked harder, but it never occurred to me that they would be more frightened of strangers than a fire.'

'What visitor?'

'Sister Alice, who came to see the nuns. I do not know why, as they loathe each other.'

'Alice did not mention that to us just now,' muttered Bartholomew. 'Curious.'

'She came today as well,' Goda went on, 'even though it was early and we were not really ready for . . .'

She trailed off, chagrined, when she realised she had almost let slip something that was meant to be kept quiet. Eudo blundered to her rescue.

'Ready for the day's chores,' he blustered. 'Some patients were not even dressed, and we were afraid that Alice would go away thinking we are all as lazy as . . . as *Frenchmen*. That race is worthless, and we hate them.'

'We do,' agreed Tangmer with a sickly smile. 'After what happened at Winchelsea, I shall kill any Frenchman on sight. We all would – every last soul among us.'

'Does that include your wife?' asked Bartholomew archly. 'Or is she exempt?'

'Amphelisa?' gulped Tangmer, eyes wide in his panicky face. 'She is not French!'

Tulyet indicated Bartholomew. 'I have brought the University's Corpse Examiner to look at the bodies, because I find it very strange that an entire family would rather roast alive than meet a nun.'

'Do you?' Tangmer exchanged an agitated glance with Eudo. 'Well, I suppose there is no harm in it, but I have a condition – that none of you speak to our patients. They are in a very fragile state after yesterday, and we cannot have them distressed further.'

'Where are the bodies?' asked Tulyet briskly. 'Still in the shed?'

'We retrieved them and put them in the chapel,' replied Tangmer. 'Poor souls.'

The Spital's chapel was a pretty place adjoining the central hall. There were two ways in – a small priests' door in the north side and a larger entrance from the hall itself. Tangmer opted to use the former, clearly to prevent his visitors from seeing more of his domain than absolutely necessary. As soon as they were inside, he dismissed Eudo and Goda, obviously afraid one would inadvertently say something else to arouse suspicion.

Inside, the first thing that struck Bartholomew was the smell – not the scent of damp plaster, incense and dead flowers that characterised most places of worship, and not the stench of charred corpses either. Instead, there was a powerful aroma of herbs, so strong that he wondered if it was safe.

'Amphelisa distils plant oils in here,' explained Tangmer, seeing his reaction. 'Under the balcony at the back. Well, why not? It uses space that would be redundant otherwise. Come. Allow me to show you.'

The chapel comprised a nave and a chancel. The balcony was suspended over the back half of the nave, reached by a flight of steps with a lockable door at the top. A knee-high wall ran across the front of the balcony, topped by a wooden trellis screen that reached the roof.

'We installed that so lepers can watch the holy offices without infecting the priest,' explained Tangmer, as Bartholomew, Michael and Tulyet stopped to stare up at it.

'But lepers are rare these days,' Bartholomew pointed out. 'So why bother with something that is never likely to be used?'

Tangmer looked pained. 'We had no idea they *were* scarce here until after we opened our doors, because there are plenty of them in Fra—' He stopped abruptly, alarm in his eyes.

'In France?' finished Bartholomew. 'You may be right.'

'In *Framlingham*, where Amphelisa comes from,' blurted Tangmer unconvincingly, and hastened on before anyone could press him on the matter. 'So it was a shock to find our charitable efforts might be wasted. Then Amphelisa suggested taking lunatics instead, on the grounds that they are also shunned by society through no fault of their own.'

The area below the balcony was low and dark. The left side was stacked with unseasoned firewood, while the remainder served as Amphelisa's workshop – two long benches loaded with equipment, and shelves for her raw ingredients. She was there when they arrived, bent over a cauldron, wearing another burgundy-coloured robe. Bartholomew recalled the reek of powerful herbs around her the previous day, strong enough to mask the reek of burning shed.

'As we have no lepers, we use the balcony to store her finished oils,' gabbled Tangmer, obviously aiming to distract his visitors in the hope of preventing them from asking more awkward questions. 'It locks, which is helpful, as most are expensive to produce. And some are toxic. Would you like to see them?'

He indicated that Amphelisa was to lead the way before they could decline. She nodded briskly and hurried up the steps to unlock the door with a key she kept around her neck, calling for them to follow. Bartholomew was willing, although Michael and Tulyet were less enthusiastic, neither liking the aroma of the highly concentrated oils.

The balcony was a large, plain room, lit only by the light that filtered through the screen at the front. Peering through the trellis afforded a fine view down the nave and into the chancel beyond. Opposite the screen was a stack of crates. Amphelisa opened the nearest to reveal a mass of tiny pots, each one carefully labelled – Bartholomew read lavender, rosewood, pine and yarrow before she closed it again.

'We send them to London,' she said. 'And as we spent nearly all our money on building this Spital, every extra penny is welcome. Would you like a free pot of cedarwood oil, Doctor? There is nothing quite like it for killing fleas and other pestilential creatures.'

'I might try some on my students then,' drawled Michael, while Bartholomew wished she had offered him some pine oil instead, as it was useful for skin diseases.

'This is not the best place for a distillery,' he said, pocketing the phial before following her back down the stairs. 'It is poorly ventilated and the fumes may be toxic. Moreover, you work with naked flames and there is firewood nearby. It is asking for trouble.'

Amphelisa waved a hand in a gesture that was unmistakably Gallic. 'The wood is still damp – it will smoke, but will take an age to ignite. But you are not here to discuss oil with me – you want to see the dead. They are in the chancel. Follow me.'

'And then you can leave,' said Tangmer, although with more hope than conviction.

The bodies had been placed in front of the altar. Two men knelt beside them. One was the dark-featured 'lunatic' who had said his name was Delacroix. The other was an elderly man with a shock of white hair, who was praying aloud in Latin – Latin that had the distinctive inflection of northern France. Both men leapt up when they realised they were not alone.

'Go, go!' cried Tangmer in English, flapping his hands at them. 'This is no place for madmen. Amphelisa – take them out. They cannot be in here unsupervised.'

'No, wait,' countered Michael in French. The two men stopped dead in their tracks, causing Tangmer and Amphelisa to exchange an agitated glance. 'Are you priests?'

Tangmer frantically shook his head, warning them against engaging in conversation. The pair edged towards the door, clearly aiming to bolt, but Tulyet barred their way. The two inmates regarded each other uncertainly.

'I am Father Julien,' replied the old one eventually. He had a sallow, lined face, although wary grey eyes suggested that his mind was sharp. 'I am ill. I came here to recover.'

'We aim to find out what happened to your friends,' said Michael, aware that the clipped English sentences were designed to give nothing of the speaker's origins away. 'So Matt will look at their bodies, to see how they died.'

'Why bother?' snarled Delacroix in French. He was in shirtsleeves that day, which revealed his neck; a scar around it that suggested someone had once tried to hang him. 'No one wants us here, and now you have five less to worry about. But we are not—'

'Hush, Delacroix!' barked Tangmer, while Amphelisa

104

and Julien paled in horror. 'Do not use that heathen language in this holy place. You know what we agreed.'

'Enough of this charade,' said Tulyet, tiring of the game they were playing. 'We are not fools. We know there are no lunatics here – just Frenchmen in hiding.'

There was a brief, appalled silence. Then Amphelisa opened her mouth to deny it, but Tangmer forestalled her by slumping on a bench with a groan of defeat.

'How did you guess?' he asked in a strangled whisper.

Amphelisa stood next to him, one hand on his shoulder and her face as white as snow. Julien's expression was resigned, but Delacroix scowled in a way that suggested he was more angry than dismayed at being found out.

'Tell us your story,' ordered Tulyet. 'If your presence here is innocent, you will come to no harm.'

'No harm?' sneered Delacroix. 'I walked through your town yesterday, and I heard what was being said about France on the streets. You hate us all, regardless of whether or not we support the Dauphin and his army.'

'Yes,' acknowledged Michael, 'there *is* much anti-French sentiment, and had you been caught there, you might well have been lynched. But we are not all ignorant bigots. We will hear what you have to say before passing judgement.'

'I *had* to do it,' whispered Tangmer, head in his hands. 'They came to me – a host of bewildered, frightened people, including children. How could I turn them away?'

'We paid you,' spat Delacroix. 'That is what convinced you to hide us, not compassion.'

'The money was a consideration,' conceded Tangmer stiffly, 'but our chief motive was pity. These people are not soldiers, but families driven from their homes by war. We call them our *peregrini*, which is Latin for strangers.'

'Why choose here?' asked Tulyet, before Michael could say that he did not need Tangmer to teach him a language he used on a daily basis. 'Cambridge is hardly on the beaten track.'

'Because Julien is my uncle,' explained Amphelisa. Her French was perfect, and was the language used for the rest of the conversation.

'So he is your uncle and every member of the Spital's staff is a Tangmer,' said Tulyet drily. 'You are fortunate to boast such a large family.'

'My husband has a large family,' said Amphelisa with quiet dignity. 'I only have Julien, as all the rest were killed in France two years ago. After their deaths, Julien brought the surviving villagers to England, where they lived peacefully until the raid on Winchelsea . . .'

'Winchelsea was where we settled, you see,' explained Julien. 'But it was attacked twice, and each time, the Mayor accused us of instigating the carnage – that we told the Dauphin when best to come.'

'Why would the Mayor do that?' asked Tulyet sceptically.

'Because he should have defended his town,' replied Julien, 'but instead, he hid until it was safe to come out. He needed a way to deflect attention from his cowardice, so he found some scapegoats – us.'

'*We* fought for Winchelsea,' said Delacroix bitterly. 'My brothers and I tried to repel the raiders at the pier, and both of them died doing it. The town should have been grateful, but instead, they turned on us.'

'We had to abandon the lives we had built among folk we believed to be friends,' said Julien. 'Our situation looked hopeless, but then I remembered Amphelisa's new Spital . . .'

'But why stay in England?' pressed Tulyet. 'Why not go home?'

Bartholomew knew the answer to that, because the marks on Delacroix's neck were indicative of a failed lynching, plus there was the fact that these *peregrini* had fled France *two years ago* . . .

'You are Jacques,' he surmised. 'Men who rebelled against their aristocratic overlords, and who were outlawed when that rebellion failed.'

This particular revolt, known as the Jacquerie, had been watched with alarm in England, as there had been fears that it might spread – French peasants were not the only ones tired of being oppressed by a wealthy elite. The Jacques had voiced a number of grievances, but first and foremost was the fact that they were taxed so that nobles could repair their war-damaged castles, on the understanding that the nobles would then protect the peasants from marauding Englishmen. The nobles did not keep their end of the bargain, and village after village was looted and burned. Crops were destroyed, too, and the people starved.

The Jacquerie foundered when its leader was executed, after which the nobles retaliated with sickening brutality. Thousands of peasants were slaughtered, many of whom had had nothing to do with the uprising. Those who could run away had done so, although most of them had nowhere else to go.

'Only six men from our village dabbled in rebellion,' said Julien quietly. 'The remaining two hundred souls did not, but they were murdered anyway. Thirty of us escaped, mostly old men, women and children. I led them, along with the six Jacques, to Winchelsea, thinking it would be safe.'

'Were the Girards among the six?' asked Bartholomew.

'Only the two men,' replied Julien, then nodded at Delacroix. 'He is another, along with three of his friends.'

Delacroix went pale with fury. 'You damned fool! Now we will *have* to leave. We cannot stay here if the truth is out.'

'Where will you go?' asked Tulyet, obviously hoping it would be soon.

Bartholomew understood why the Sheriff wanted them

gone. First, he had his hands full keeping the peace between University and town, and did not have the time or the resources to protect strangers as well. But second and more importantly, there was a radical minority – Cynric among them – who thought the Jacquerie had been a very good idea, and who would love to hear what Delacroix had to say about social justice and insurrection.

'Delacroix is right,' said Michael gently, when there was no reply to Tulyet's question. 'You cannot stay here – it is too dangerous.'

'You have been dissuading folk from visiting this place with rumours of hauntings and pagan sacrifices,' put in Bartholomew, 'and the "ghostly manifestation" you staged for us was clever, too. But it will not work for much longer. Curiosity will win out over fear, and people will come to see these things for themselves.'

'Especially if Margery Starre sells them protective charms,' added Michael. 'And they feel themselves to be invulnerable.'

Meanwhile, Tulyet was regarding Delacroix appraisingly. 'The Girard men sold themselves as proxies when our King issued his call to arms. Why? It was a needless risk.'

Delacroix shrugged. 'We needed the money – we are running out, and we cannot expect Tangmer to feed us all for nothing.'

'No,' agreed Tangmer fervently; Amphelisa shot him a reproachful glance.

'But they would never have gone to the butts,' continued Delacroix. 'It would have been suicide. They were going to get Tangmer to declare them too mad to venture out.'

Michael drew Bartholomew aside while Tulyet continued to question the two *peregrini*. 'Perhaps you were right – de Wetherset and Heltisle *did* guess that the Girards aimed to cheat them, and killed them for revenge.'

But Bartholomew was no longer sure. 'I do not see the

Chancellor and his deputy scrambling over walls with a tinderbox. Also, de Wetherset told us to give the money to Hélène. If he had been angry enough to kill her kin, he would have demanded it back.'

'Maybe he was salving his guilty conscience,' shrugged Michael. 'He is not entirely without scruples, although I cannot say the same about Heltisle. I say we put them both on our list. Of course, Delacroix is an angry man, so perhaps these murders can be laid at his feet. Look at the bodies now, Matt, and see what they can tell you.'

Unwilling to perform in front of an audience, Bartholomew ordered everyone out. They went reluctantly and stood by the side door, where Tulyet demanded to know what had prompted Delacroix to join the Jacquerie, and Delacroix snarled answers that did nothing to secure his removal from a list of murder suspects.

Bartholomew took a deep breath and began. Four victims were burned beyond recognition, although one was relatively undamaged. He began with him, and immediately made a startling discovery. He considered calling Tulyet and Michael at once, but decided to spare them the sight of what needed to be done next. He worked quickly, and when he had finished, put everything back as he had found it.

He went outside to wash his hands. Even after a vigorous scrub, they still stank of charred flesh, so he splashed them with some of Amphelisa's cedarwood oil. Then he went to where Michael and Tulyet were waiting for him.

'The fire did not kill them,' he began. 'Or rather, it did not kill the adults – the lad died from inhaling smoke. The other four were stabbed.'

'Stabbed?' echoed Michael, startled.

'Death was caused by one or more wounds from a double-edged blade, inflicted from behind,' Bartholomew went on. 'A dagger. If you find the weapon, I may be able to match it to the wounds.'

'But the boy died from the smoke?' asked Tulyet. 'How do you know?' His expression was one of dismay and disgust. 'Please do not tell me that you looked inside him!'

'It was the only way to be sure,' said Bartholomew defensively.

He had long believed that dissection would be a godsend in cases such as this, where answers would otherwise remain elusive, and for years he had itched to put his skills to the test. But now he had formal permission from the University to do it, he found it made him acutely uncomfortable. He was nearly always assailed by the notion that the dead knew what he was doing in the name of justice and did not like it.

'So you found smoke in his innards,' surmised Michael, speaking quickly before Tulyet could further express his disquiet. He was not keen on the dark art of anatomy either, but he certainly appreciated the answers it provided.

Bartholomew nodded. 'There are no other marks on him, so I suspect he was dosed with a soporific – that he went to sleep and never woke up. The same must have happened to Hélène, who is also wound-free. There was smoke in the lungs of one of the women, too – almost certainly the one who passed Hélène to safety.'

'So her injury was superficial?' asked Tulyet.

'No, it was fatal – it punctured her lung. It just did not kill her instantly.'

'Probably Hélène's mother,' mused Tulyet, 'using her dying strength to save her child. It is a pity you failed to rescue her – she could have told us who did this terrible thing before she breathed her last.'

'Does Hélène know?' asked Bartholomew. 'Has anyone spoken to her?'

'I did, and so did Amphelisa, but with no success. I

have asked Amphelisa to persist, but do not expect answers – if you are right about the soporific, Hélène may have slept through the entire thing.'

'Matt's findings explain a good deal,' said Michael. 'Such as why the family did not leave when the shed began to burn. They were either dead, wounded or asleep. The killer must have left the bodies where they would not be spotted by the casual observer.'

At that point, the Spital folk began to edge towards them, keen to learn what had been discovered. Amphelisa was holding Hélène, who drowsed against her shoulder, making Bartholomew suspect that whatever she had been fed the previous day was still working. It meant the dose had been very powerful.

Delacroix's face darkened in anger when Tulyet told them what Bartholomew had found, while Father Julien's hands flew to his mouth in horror. Amphelisa held Hélène a little more tightly, and Tangmer closed his eyes, swaying, so that Eudo and Goda hastened to take his arms lest he swooned.

'Hélène refused to drink her milk today,' whispered Amphelisa, stroking the child's hair, 'because she said yesterday's was sour. So she was right – someone put something in it that changed the taste.'

'Did she say anything else?' asked Tulyet keenly.

'That she did not finish it, so her brother had it instead.' Amphelisa looked away. 'All I hope is that it rendered him unconscious before . . .'

'Does she remember who gave it to her?'

'She collected it from the kitchen, which is never locked, so anyone could have sneaked in to . . .' Tangmer was ashen-faced. 'How could anyone . . . to poison a child's milk!'

'Hélène had a daily routine,' said Julien wretchedly. 'After church, she fetched the milk from the kitchen for herself and her brother, which she took to the shed to

111

drink. Her family liked that shed. They called it their house and treated it as such.'

'Who else knew all this?' asked Michael.

Amphelisa raised her hands in a Gallic shrug. 'Everyone here. However, none of us is responsible for this terrible deed. The staff are all Henry's kin, while the *peregrini* would never hurt each other.'

'There were visitors yesterday,' said Delacroix in a strained voice. His fists were clenched at his sides and he looked dangerous. 'Tell them, Tangmer.'

Tangmer took a deep breath to pull himself together. 'First, Verious the ditcher came to clear a blocked drain, after which the miller delivered flour. Then there were your two new knights, Sheriff, who arrived with tax invoices for me to sign.'

'Do not forget the nuns,' said Delacroix tightly. 'Twenty from Lyminster, plus the one who was deposed for whoring – Sister Alice.'

'I hardly think nuns poison children and burn the bodies,' said Michael coolly. 'Especially ones from my Order.'

Delacroix regarded him with open hatred. 'You would not say that if you had been in France two years ago. The Benedictines were as rabid as anyone in their desire for vengeance against those who baulked at paying crippling taxes to greedy landowners.'

'Do the nuns know your "lunatics" are Jacques, Tangmer?' asked Tulyet before Michael could respond.

'No, because we have taken care to keep them in the dark,' replied Amphelisa. 'Although it has not been easy. Fortunately, they spend most of their day at the *conloquium*, and only come here to sleep.'

'The soporific fed to Hélène must have been uncommonly strong,' mused Bartholomew, examining the child. 'She did not finish her milk, but she is still drowsy. Do you keep such compounds here?'

Amphelisa regarded him warily, knowing what was coming next. 'This is a hospital for people with serious diseases. Of course we have powerful medicines to hand.'

'How easy is it to steal them?'

'They are stored in the balcony, which you have already seen is secure. I keep the only key on a string around my neck.'

'Then can you tell if anything is missing?' asked Michael.

'I could try, although it would entail examining every pot in every crate, and there are dozens of them. It would take a long time.'

'Do not bother,' said Bartholomew. 'The culprit may not have taken a whole jar, just helped himself to what he needed, then disguised the fact by topping it up with water. I doubt you will find answers that way.'

He glanced at Michael and Tulyet, glad it was not *his* responsibility to solve the crime. He did not envy them their task one bit.

It was a grim procession that trudged from the chapel to the remains of the shed. Tangmer was sobbing brokenly, although it was impossible to know whether his distress was for the victims or because their deaths reflected badly on the place he had founded. Amphelisa walked at his side with the sleeping Hélène, her face like stone. Tiny Goda and massive Eudo followed, hand in hand, with the *peregrini* in a tight cluster behind them. Bartholomew, Michael and Tulyet brought up the rear, but hung well back, so they could talk without being overheard.

'I think the Girards were killed by a fellow *peregrinus*,' whispered Tulyet. 'None are strangers to bloodshed and some are Jacques – violent revolutionaries.'

But Bartholomew was uncertain. 'They are alone in the middle of a hostile country. I should think they know better than to fight among themselves.'

'There were thirty of them – now twenty-five – which makes for a sizeable party,' argued Tulyet. 'Differences of opinion will be inevitable. Moreover, living in constant fear of exposure will test even the mildest of tempers, as all will know that the wrong decision may cost the lives of their loved ones. *I* would certainly kill to protect my wife and son.'

'Would you?' asked Bartholomew, rather startled by the confidence.

Tulyet reflected. 'Well, to protect my wife. Dickon can look after himself these days.' He smiled fondly. 'He is in Huntingdon at the moment, delivering dispatches for me. Did I tell you that he is going to France soon? Lady Hereford wrote to say that her knights "can teach him no more". Those were her exact words.'

He swelled with pride, although Bartholomew struggled not to smirk. Lady Hereford had offered to help Dickon make something of himself, but the little hellion had defeated even that redoubtable personage, because Bartholomew was sure her carefully chosen phrase did not mean that Dickon had learned all there was to know. The lad was a lost cause, and Bartholomew was always astonished that Tulyet, usually so shrewd, was blind when it came to his horrible son.

'The strain on these people must be intolerable,' said Michael, prudently changing the subject. 'Delacroix is on a knife-edge, and it would take very little for him to snap.'

'Yet this does not feel like a crime where someone has snapped,' mused Bartholomew. 'It was carefully planned, almost certainly by someone who knew the Girards' liking for a flammable building.'

'I agree,' said Tulyet. 'We should also remember that four people were stabbed and none fought back, which suggests the culprit knew how to disable multiple victims at once. Delacroix and his cronies were active in the violence that was the Jacquerie . . .'

'They certainly top my list of suspects,' said Michael. 'But here we are at the shed, so we shall discuss it later. We do not want them to know what we are thinking quite yet.'

The shed was barely recognisable. It had collapsed in on itself, and comprised nothing but a heap of blackened timber and charred thatch. Amphelisa pointed out the spot where the bodies had been found.

'There were stacks of wood between them and the door,' she explained. 'So the only way Goda could have seen them was if she had gone to the very back of the building and peered behind the pile. That is beyond what could reasonably be expected of her.'

'The place was thick with smoke,' added Goda. 'It was hard to see anything at all.'

Tulyet, Michael and Bartholomew were meticulous, but there was nothing to explain why anyone should have stabbed four people and left them with their sleeping children to burn. Tulyet was thoughtful.

'This reminds me of the first Winchelsea raid,' he said, 'where other families were shut inside a burning building and left to die. It was in a church, and became known as the St Giles' Massacre.'

'But those victims were not stabbed and poisoned first,' Michael pointed out. 'At least here, no one was burned alive.'

'Hélène's mother was,' countered Bartholomew soberly.

Feeling they had done all they could at the Spital, they turned to leave, but as Bartholomew picked his way off the rubble, a charred timber cracked under his foot. He stumbled to one knee, and it was then that he saw something they had missed.

'Here is the weapon that killed the Girards,' he said. 'The blade is distinctive, because it is abnormally wide and thick. Shall we test it against the wounds, to be certain?'

'We believe you,' said Michael hastily, keen to be spared the ordeal.

Bartholomew hesitated. 'There is something else, although I cannot be sure . . .'

'Just tell us,' ordered Tulyet impatiently.

'Bonet the spicer,' said Bartholomew. 'His wounds were unusually wide, too.'

'You think *this* weapon killed him as well?' asked Tulyet sceptically.

'The only way to be sure is to measure his injury against the blade,' replied Bartholomew. 'I can do that, if you like.'

'Bonet was buried today, and we are *not* digging him up,' said Tulyet firmly. 'But what about the scholar who was stabbed – Paris? Could this blade have killed him as well?'

'No,' replied Michael, before Bartholomew could speak, 'because I have that in St Mary the Great. I shall show it to you tomorrow.'

Tulyet turned the dagger over in his hands. 'This is an unusual piece – I have never seen anything quite like it. However, I can tell you that it would have been costly to buy. The hilt is studded with semi-precious stones and the blade is tempered steel.'

He took it to where the Spital's people – staff and *peregrini* – were milling around restlessly. They all craned forward to look, then shook their heads to say none of them had seen it before.

'Ask in the town,' suggested Delacroix tightly. 'Or at the castle – your two new knights are rich enough to afford quality weapons, and they hate the French, too.'

'They do,' acknowledged Tulyet. 'But they are also blissfully ignorant about who is hiding here.'

'Are you sure?' asked Bartholomew in a low voice. 'Tangmer mentioned them coming to deliver tax documents. Perhaps they saw something to raise their suspicions then.'

'They will be questioned,' said Tulyet firmly. 'Along with the miller, Verious and the nuns. It seems our killer has claimed seven French victims, so we must do all in our power to stop him taking an eighth.'

CHAPTER 6

Bartholomew did not want to investigate seven murders, especially as it was his last term as a scholar, so every day was precious. He tried to slip away, but Michael blocked his path and demanded to know where he thought he was going.

'You cannot need me when you have Dick,' objected Bartholomew. 'Besides, I have no jurisdiction here. It is not University property and no scholar has died.'

'Paris the Plagiarist was a scholar,' said Michael soberly. 'And as I am sure all seven deaths are connected, you *do* have jurisdiction here. Moreover, the Girards were hired as proxies by our Chancellor and his deputy, which is worrisome. You *must* help me find out what is going on.'

Tulyet agreed. 'I should tell you now that de Wetherset and Heltisle are on my list of suspects. It is possible that they found out the Girards had no intention of honouring the arrangement and killed them for it.'

'Much as I dislike Heltisle, I do not see him dispatching children,' said Bartholomew. 'And if de Wetherset cared about the money, he would not have given it all to Hélène.'

'We should not lump the two of them together in this,' said Michael. 'De Wetherset is unlikely to soil his hands with murder – he is an intelligent man, and would devise other ways to punish a deceitful proxy. Heltisle, however, is cold, hard and ambitious. I would not put any low deed past him.'

'I can see why he dispatched the plagiarist – a man who brought our University into disrepute – but why kill the spicer?' asked Bartholomew uncertainly.

'Bonet supplied the University with goods,' shrugged Michael. 'Perhaps there was a disagreement over prices. I know for a fact that Heltisle wants to renegotiate some of our trade deals when the current ones expire.'

'I shall leave de Wetherset and Heltisle to you,' said Tulyet. 'But first, we should speak to the people here – staff, Frenchmen *and* nuns.'

He marched away to organise it, while Bartholomew grumbled about losing valuable teaching time. The monk was unsympathetic.

'You may have no University to resign from unless we find our culprit. It is possible that these murders are a sly blow against us – Paris was a scholar; Bonet sold us spices; and now we have our Chancellor and his deputy's proxies murdered.'

Bartholomew was not sure what to think, but there was no time to argue, as Tulyet was waving for them to join him in the hall. Once inside, all three gazed around in admiration. It was a high-ceilinged room with enormous windows that allowed the sunlight to flood in. The tables and benches were crafted from pale wood, while the floor comprised creamy white flagstones, a combination that rendered it bright, airy and cheerful.

'This is wasted on lepers and lunatics,' muttered Michael. 'Indeed, I could live here myself. It is much nicer than Michaelhouse.'

Tulyet wanted to question the *peregrini* first. They shuffled forward uneasily. All hailed from the wealthier end of village life – craftsmen and merchants who earned comfortable livings, and who had been respected members of the community before war and rebellion had shattered their lives. There were nine children including Hélène, seven women of various ages, five very old men and the four Jacques.

Most questions were answered by Father Julien, with occasional help from a stout woman named Madame

Vipond – the weaver Bartholomew had seen outside. While the two of them spoke, Delacroix and his companions snarled and scowled, so it soon became apparent that the Jacques resented the priest's authority and itched to wrest it from him.

'We had no choice but to leave France,' Julien told Tulyet. 'The barons burned every house in our village, and as I have already said, they murdered all but thirty of our people. None of the dead were Jacques.'

'Because we were away when the barons came,' objected Delacroix, detecting censure. 'How could we defend our village when we were not there?'

'My point exactly,' murmured Julien acidly.

'We chose to resettle in Winchelsea because my husband and I had sold baskets there for years,' said Madame Vipond after a short, uncomfortable silence. 'I knew it well and thought we could rebuild our lives among good and kindly people. We gave money to charitable causes and adopted their ways. We tried to become part of the town.'

'And when the Dauphin's raiders came, my brothers died trying to defend it,' spat Delacroix. 'Then what did those *good and kindly people* do? Accuse us of being spies! So we ran a second time, abandoning all we had built there. We have virtually no money, so it will be difficult to leave here and settle somewhere else. Perhaps you will give us funds, Sheriff.'

'Why would I do that?' asked Tulyet, startled. 'I have my own poor to look after.'

'Because we could stir up trouble if you refuse,' flashed Delacroix. 'You want to stay on our good side, believe me. We—'

'Delacroix, stop!' cried Julien. 'We are not beggars, and we do not make threats.'

'Well, I suppose we have this,' said Delacroix, brandishing a fat purse. 'The money earned by the Girards for being proxies. It will keep the wolf from the door for a while.'

'How does it come to be in *your* possession?' demanded Michael immediately.

Delacroix regarded him evenly. 'I took it from their bodies when we removed them from the shed – for safe-keeping.'

'Give it to Michael,' ordered Julien. 'He will return it to its rightful owners.'

'It is Hélène's now,' said Michael, before Delacroix could refuse and there was more sparring for power. 'Chancellor de Wetherset wants her to have it.'

Unexpectedly, Delacroix's eyes filled with tears at the kindness, while a murmur of appreciation rippled through the others.

'Are you sure?' asked Julien warily. 'He will receive nothing in return except our gratitude.'

'He knows,' said Michael. 'However, the offer was made when he thought Hélène was the child of lunatics. He may reconsider if he learns the truth, so I recommend you stay well away from the town.' He looked hard at the Jacques. 'Especially you.'

'He is right,' agreed Tulyet. 'Tensions are running unusually high at the moment, so you must leave as soon as possible. How soon can it be arranged?'

'We will go today,' sniffed Delacroix. 'We know where we are not wanted.'

'It takes time to prepare twenty-five people for travel when most are either very old or very young,' countered Julien. 'We shall aim for Friday – the day after tomorrow.'

'Very well,' said Tulyet. 'Now tell us about the Girard family. Did you like them?'

'We did,' replied Madame Vipond, although she did not look at the Jacques. 'They were strong and wise, and our lives here will be harder without them.'

'Did you see anything that might help us catch their

killer?' asked Tulyet. 'Or did any of you visit them in the shed yesterday?'

'It was their private place,' explained Julien, 'where they went for time together as a family. They disliked being disturbed.'

'So what happened when the fire began? Who first noticed it?'

'Delacroix saw smoke when he went to the kitchen for bread,' replied Julien. 'He sent Goda to raise the alarm, while he went to see about putting it out. The rest of us stayed well back, so we would not get in the way.'

'Did it cross your minds that the Girards might still be inside?'

'Of course not!' snarled Delacroix. 'The door was open, so we naturally assumed they had left.'

'And Goda seemed certain that it was empty,' elaborated Julien. 'Then Tangmer ordered it shut to contain the blaze – at that point, he still thought we could put it out.'

'Goda,' mused Michael. 'Are you on good terms with her?'

'You think *she* is the killer?' Delacroix laughed derisively. 'The Girards knew how to look after themselves – they would never have been bested by a tiny little woman.'

'Besides, Goda has no reason to harm us,' added Julien, shooting him a glance that warned him to guard his tongue. 'No one here does.'

'What about the dagger?' asked Tulyet, laying it on the table. 'I have scrubbed the soot off it, so examine it again now it is clean. Do you recognise it?'

There was a moment when Bartholomew thought he was playing tricks – that Tulyet had substituted the murder weapon for another in the hope of catching the culprit out – but then he saw the wide blade and the jewelled hilt, both of which gleamed expensively. It was a world apart from the greasy black item he had plucked from the rubble.

'No,' said Julien, peering at it. 'But it is ugly – a thing specifically designed for the taking of life. You should throw it in a midden, Sheriff, where it belongs.'

'I think it is handsome,' stated Delacroix, a predictable response from a warlike man. 'But I have never seen its like before.'

One by one, the other *peregrini* approached to look, but all shook their heads.

'So none of you noticed anything unusual about the shed before the fire?' pressed Michael when they had finished. 'No strangers loitering? No visitors you did not know?'

'Just the ones we have already mentioned,' replied Julien. 'The miller, the ditcher and the two knights from the castle.'

'Plus all those Benedictine nuns,' put in Delacroix, glaring at Michael.

They interviewed the Spital staff next, beginning with Tangmer and Amphelisa, although Bartholomew quickly became distracted when Amphelisa described how she had mended a persistently festering cut on Delacroix's leg. He asked how she had come by such skills.

'From being near Rouen when the Jacquerie struck,' she replied. 'The slaughter was sickening. Delacroix will tell you that the barons were worse, but the truth is that both sides were as bad as each other.'

'Yet you agreed to house him here,' Bartholomew pointed out. 'Him and his five renegade friends.'

'Because Julien begged me to. Besides, the Girards said they wished they had never become involved with the Jacquerie, and I suspect Delacroix and his friends will feel the same way when they are older and wiser.'

Bartholomew was not so sure about that, but she changed the subject then, telling him her views on treating ailments of the mind with pungent herbs. He listened keenly, aware all the while of the scent of oils in her clothes. They made him wonder if he should distil some in Michaelhouse, as there were times when the presence of a lot of active young men, few of whom bothered to wash, drove him outdoors for fresh air. Then he remembered that it would not matter after July, because he would be living with Matilde.

Meanwhile, Michael and Tulyet questioned Tangmer, who seemed smaller and humbler than he had been before he had been caught harbouring Frenchmen.

'I founded this place to atone for my niece's crimes,' he said miserably, 'and to redeem the Tangmer name. But now foul murder is committed here. Will we never be free from sin?'

'Not as long as you shelter dangerous radicals and pass them off as lunatics,' said Tulyet baldly. 'So, what more can you tell us about yesterday?'

'Nothing I have not mentioned already. I *knew* I should have refused these people sanctuary, but Amphelisa . . . well, she is a compassionate woman. Of course, having those nuns here at the same time has been a nightmare. I live in constant fear that one will guess what we are doing and report us.'

He had no more to add, so Tulyet beckoned Eudo forward. The big man approached reluctantly, twisting his hat anxiously in his ham-like hands.

'Where were you when the fire started?' asked Tulyet, watching him fidget and twitch.

'Out,' replied Eudo, furtively enough to make the Sheriff's eyes narrow. 'I arrived home just as the alarm was being raised. I opened the gates then, so we could get water from the stream. We used buckets, you know. They were—'

'"Out" where exactly?' demanded Tulyet, overriding Eudo's clumsy attempt to divert the discussion to safer ground.

124

Eudo would not look at him. 'On private Spital business. I cannot say more.'

'Did you go alone?'

Eudo glanced at Tangmer, who nodded almost imperceptibly. 'Yes, but I cannot—'

'Who did you see on this mysterious excursion?' snapped Tulyet. 'And bear in mind that I am asking for your alibi. If you cannot provide one, I shall draw my own conclusions from all these brazen lies.'

'He is doing it for me,' interposed Tangmer, much to Eudo's obvious relief. 'I sent him to the town to buy some decent ale. You see, Amphelisa makes ours, but . . . well, she has a lot to learn about brewing. I am loath to hurt her feelings, so Eudo gets it for me on the sly.'

'I do,' nodded Eudo. 'But I cannot prove it, because I am careful never to be recognised there. Obviously, we cannot have word getting back to Amphelisa.'

It sounded a peculiar tale to Michael and Tulyet, who pressed Eudo relentlessly in an effort to catch him out. They failed.

'He has just put himself at the top of my list of suspects,' muttered Michael, when they had given up, leaving the big man to escape with relief. 'He is not even very good at prevarication – I have rarely heard such embarrassingly transparent falsehoods.'

'He is third on mine,' said Tulyet. 'After de Wetherset and Heltisle.'

Goda was next. She flounced towards them, resplendent in her handsome kirtle. Her shoes were new, too, and over her hair she wore a delicate net that was studded with beads. She was so tiny that when she sat on the bench, her feet did not touch the floor, so she swung them back and forth like a restless child.

'I was in the kitchen all morning, making bread,' she began. 'Delacroix came to beg some, then left. He was back moments later, jabbering about a fire. I ran outside, and saw smoke seeping through the shed roof.'

'Then what?' asked Michael.

'I yelled the alarm. All the staff dropped what they were doing and raced to put it out. However, I can tell you for a fact that none of them were near the shed when it started – I would have noticed.'

'Obviously, the fire was lit some time before the smoke became thick enough to attract your attention,' said Michael. 'Ergo, how do you know that a member of staff did not set the blaze and then slink away, ready to come running when the alarm was raised?'

'Because I was kneading dough, which is boring, so I spent the whole time gazing through the open door,' she replied promptly. 'I would have seen anyone go to the shed.'

'Yet someone did,' Michael pointed out. 'And we have five dead to prove it.'

'Oh, I saw the *Girards* popping in and out,' said Goda impatiently. 'But no one else. Perhaps they were weary of being persecuted, and decided to kill themselves.'

Michael felt he could come to dislike this arrogantly flippant woman. 'You think they stabbed themselves in the back? I am not even sure that is possible. And even if it is, why not choose an easier way to die?'

Goda shrugged. 'Unless you can find a way to quiz the dead, you may never know. However, I can assure you that no staff member had anything to do with it.'

'What about the *peregrini*?' asked Tulyet. 'There are tensions among them. Were any of them near the shed?'

'Not that I saw. And before you ask, the nuns were in the guesthouse, although they emerged to gawp when the shed began to burn in earnest.'

'Are you sure it was the Girards "popping in and out" of the shed?' asked Tulyet. 'Because someone committed a terrible crime there, and as you claim no one else was

126

in the vicinity and we know the victims did not kill themselves . . .'

'Oh, I see,' she said, nodding. 'One time, it could have been the killer impersonating them. It is possible – the shed is some distance from the kitchen, and I was not watching particularly closely.'

'So, with hindsight, is there anything that struck you as odd?'

Goda shook her head. 'Obviously, this person took care *not* to be suspicious. What would be the point of donning a disguise, if you then go out and give yourself away with attention-catching behaviour?'

Michael fought down his growing antipathy towards her. 'The Spital had several visitors before the fire began. What can you tell us about those?'

'I only saw Sister Alice. She is always pestering our nuns, even though Magistra Katherine has told her that she is not welcome here. Prioress Joan is kinder, but even her patience is wearing thin. Magistra Katherine has the right of it, though: Alice is a thief, so the other nuns should have nothing to do with her.'

'A thief?' echoed Michael warily. 'How do you know?'

'Well, once, when all our nuns were at the *conloquium*, Alice visited the guesthouse while I happened to be cleaning under the bed. Rashly assuming she was alone, she began riffling through their things. I saw her slip a comb up her sleeve and walk off with it.'

Michael was not sure whether to believe her. 'Was it valuable?' he asked warily.

For the first time, Goda considered her answer with care, and he saw that the cost of things mattered to her.

'I would not have paid more than sixpence for it,' she replied eventually. 'I told our nuns when they got back, and it transpired that the comb belonged to Prioress Joan. I thought she would not care, given that she is not a vain woman, but she was very upset.'

'Could Alice have set the fire?' asked Tulyet, while Michael held his breath; he did not want a Benedictine to be the culprit.

'Possibly,' said Goda. 'But we have let no nun get anywhere near the *peregrini*, which would mean she killed five people she never met. That seems unlikely.'

'Look again at the murder weapon,' ordered Tulyet, laying it on the table in front of her. 'Have you seen it before?'

Goda spent far more time than necessary turning it over in her hands. When it became clear that she was more interested in assessing its worth than identifying its owner, Tulyet tried to take it back. There was a tussle when she declined to part with it.

'It is a nice piece,' she said watching covetously as Tulyet returned it to his scrip. 'What will you do with it once your enquiries are over? I doubt you will want to keep it, but I will give you a fair price.'

'I shall bear it in mind,' said Tulyet, taken aback and struggling not to let it show.

'That is a fine new kirtle,' said Michael, wondering if Alice was not the only one with sticky fingers. 'How did you pay for it?'

Goda regarded him coolly. 'By saving my wages. Unlike most people, I do not fritter them away on nothing. Not that my clothes are any of your affair. Now, is that all, or do you have more impertinent questions to put to me?'

'You may go,' said Tulyet coldly. 'For now.'

As time was passing, Tulyet suggested that he finished speaking to the staff on his own, while Bartholomew and Michael tackled the nuns.

'Prioress Joan has just returned from the *conloquium*,' he said, watching her dismount her handsome stallion while her ladies flowed from the guesthouse to welcome her back. Bartholomew recalled that she had left them to pray while she went to give a lecture on plumbing.

'And let us hope one of us has some luck,' sighed Michael, 'because I cannot believe that someone could stab four people, drug two children, set a building alight, and saunter away without being seen.'

The guesthouse was a charming building. Its walls were of honey-coloured stone, it had a red-tiled roof, and someone had planted roses around the door. Most of the windows were open, allowing sunlight to stream in, and the furniture was simple but new and spotlessly clean. All the nuns were there, except one.

'Our Prioress went to settle Dusty in the stables,' explained Magistra Katherine de Lisle. 'She spends more time with him than she does at her devotions.'

Bartholomew studied Katherine with interest. Like her prelate brother, she was tall, haughty, and had a beaky nose and hooded eyes. She was perhaps in her sixth decade, but her skin was smooth and unlined. A smirk played at the corners of her mouth, and he was under the impression that she considered herself superior to everyone else, and thought other people existed only for her to mock. He wondered if arrogance ran in the family, because her brother was also of the opinion that he was the most important thing in the universe.

'Caring for God's creatures is a form of worship,' said Michael, who was known to linger in stables at the expense of his divine offices himself. 'I will fetch her while the rest of you tell Matt about yesterday's tragedy.'

Bartholomew was happy with that, as he had no wish to visit a place where he would meet an animal that would almost certainly dislike him on sight – horses instinctively knew he was wary of them, and even the most docile of nags turned mean-spirited in his presence.

'There are a lot of you,' he remarked when the monk had gone.

'Twenty,' replied Katherine, a faint smile playing about her lips. 'We brought more delegates than any other convent.'

'Why?'

'Because Prioress Joan offered to bring any nun who wanted to travel. Some came for the adventure, others to meet fellow Benedictines, the rest to learn something useful. But *I* was invited personally by the organisers because I am a talented speaker who can preach on a variety of interesting subjects. I am not styled *Magistra* Katherine for nothing, you know.'

She began to list her areas of expertise, although as most pertained to theology, Bartholomew thought she was sadly mistaken to describe them as 'interesting'. Sensing she was losing his attention, she finished by saying that Joan's relaxed rule made for a contented little community of nuns at Lyminster.

While she spoke, the other sisters occupied themselves with strips of leather and pots of oil, filling the room with the sweet scent of linseed. Eschewing such menial work, Katherine picked up a book, clearly aiming to read it the moment Bartholomew left.

'To thank her for bringing us here, we are making new reins for Prioress Joan,' explained one nun, smiling. 'Or rather, for Dusty. He is strong, and is always snapping them.'

'They know the surest way to her heart,' said Katherine, then indicated the tome in her lap. 'Whereas I prefer to study Master Clippesby's treatise. He must be a remarkable man, because I have never encountered such elegant logic.'

'He is a remarkable man,' agreed Bartholomew, hoping they would never meet. The mad Dominican would not be what Katherine expected, and they would almost certainly disappoint each other. 'He has a unique way with animals.'

'Joan would like him then,' said Katherine with a smirk. 'Especially if he is good with horses. But his theories are astonishing. And what an imagination, to use chickens to speak his views.'

Clippesby would argue that the views were the birds' own, but Bartholomew decided not to tell her that. He changed the subject to Alice.

'Yes, the wretched woman did visit shortly before the fire started,' said Katherine. 'She will not leave us alone, despite our efforts to discourage her. You know why, of course.'

'Do I?'

'Because my brother was so shocked by the way she ran Ickleton Priory that he deposed her. Now she aims to avenge herself on him through me. But she will not succeed, because she is not clever enough.'

Unwilling to be dragged into that dispute, Bartholomew returned to the subject of the fire. 'Did you see Alice near the shed? Or talking to the . . . patients, particularly those who died?'

'Not yesterday or any other day,' replied Katherine. 'However, that is not to say she did not do it – just that we never saw her.'

All the nuns denied recognising the murder weapon, too, although Bartholomew had to be content with sketching it on a piece of parchment, as Tulyet had the original.

'We are unlikely to know anything to help you,' said Katherine, clearly impatient to get to her reading, 'because a condition of us staying here is that we keep away from the lunatics. We have obliged, because none of us want to exchange these nice, spacious quarters for a cramped corner in St Radegund's.'

'But you must look out of the windows,' pressed Bartholomew, loath to give up. 'And one faces the shed.'

'It does,' acknowledged Katherine. 'But it is nailed shut, and the glass is too thick to see through. The only ones that open overlook the road.'

Bartholomew saw she was right, and wondered if it was why Alice had rummaged through the nuns' belongings when they were out – no one from inside the Spital could have looked in and seen her, and she would have got away with it, if Goda had not been cleaning under the beds. Assuming Goda was telling the truth, of course.

'Is Joan missing a comb?' he asked.

'Yes,' replied Katherine. 'An ivory one. She was upset about it, as it was the one she used on Dusty's mane. Goda says Alice took it, which Alice denies, of course. If it is true, it will be part of some malicious plot against me or my brother. Her vindictiveness knows no bounds, so if you do arrest her for roasting lunatics, I should be very grateful.'

'Where were you when the blaze began?' asked Bartholomew, and when her eyebrows flew upwards in instant indignation, added quickly, 'Just for elimination purposes.'

Katherine indicated her sisters. 'We were all in here, except for the hour before the fire. At that point, I was in the garden behind the chapel and Joan was in the stables. We predicted that Alice would come, you see, and we aimed to avoid her.'

'Alice *did* come,' put in another nun. 'But she left when we told her that Magistra Katherine and Prioress Joan were unavailable. The rest of us were here until the alarm was raised, at which point Prioress Joan came to take us outside lest a stray spark set this building alight, too.'

Bartholomew regarded Katherine thoughtfully. 'You cannot see the shed from in here, but you can from behind the chapel . . .'

There was a flash of irritation in the hooded eyes. 'Very possibly, but I was engrossed in Clippesby's book and paid no attention to anything else.'

'But you heard the alarm raised,' pressed Bartholomew.

Katherine regarded him steadily. 'I was absorbed, not on another planet. Of course I stopped reading when everyone started shouting and I saw the smoke.'

'So you have no alibi,' said Bartholomew, hoping she would not transpire to be the killer, as the Bishop would be livid.

Katherine gave another of her enigmatic smiles. 'I am afraid not, other than my fervent assurance that high-ranking Benedictine nuns have better things to do than light fires in derelict outbuildings.'

Unfortunately, her fervent assurance was not enough, thought Bartholomew, watching her open the book to tell him that the interview was over.

He was about to leave when Michael walked in with Joan, deep in a conversation about hocks and withers. She was taller than Michael, who was not a small man, and her hands were the size of dinner plates.

'Have you answered all his questions?' she asked of her nuns, jerking a huge thumb in Bartholomew's direction. 'Nice and polite, like I taught you?'

'We have,' replied Katherine, resignedly closing her book again. 'Although he is disturbed by my inability to prove that I did not incinerate an entire family.'

'Katherine often disappears to read on her own,' said Joan. 'Of course, you will probably say that *I* cannot prove my whereabouts either, given that I was with Dusty. Or will you? I understand your Clippesby talks to animals – perhaps he will take Dusty's statement.'

'It is no laughing matter,' said Michael sternly. 'People died in that fire.'

'Yes,' acknowledged Joan, contrite. 'And we shall continue to pray for their souls. However, as it happens, I can do better than Dusty for an alibi. One of the servants – that ridiculously tiny lass – was in the kitchen the whole time. And if I could see her, she must have been able to see me.'

'Goda?' asked Michael. 'So you can vouch for her?'

'I suppose I can,' said Joan. 'I would not normally have

noticed her, but she was wearing yellow, a colour Dusty does not like, and he kept snickering in her direction. She was certainly in the kitchen when the blaze would have started.'

'So, Brother,' drawled Katherine, amused, 'I am your only Lyminster suspect. My brother will be horrified when he learns that you have me in your sights.'

'Then let us hope we find the real culprit before it becomes necessary to tell him,' said Michael, smiling back at her.

'That poor family,' said Joan, sitting heavily on a bed. 'What will happen to their friends now? There cannot be many places willing to hide Frenchmen.'

'You know?' breathed Michael, shocked, while Bartholomew gaped at her. 'But how?'

'We are not fools,' replied Joan softly. 'Tangmer nailed the window shut to prevent us from seeing them, but we have ears – we often hear the children chattering in French.'

'Joan took a few of us to Winchelsea when we heard about the raid,' said Katherine. 'We wanted to help, and the town is only sixty miles from our convent. We arrived five days later, and although we were spared the worst sights, what remained was terrible enough. We heard the rumours about the "spies" who told the Dauphin when best to come. It did not take a genius to put it all together. We know exactly who these folk are.'

'Have you told anyone else?' asked Michael uneasily.

She shot him a withering glare. 'Of course not! These people have a right to sanctuary, just like any Christian soul. I shall not even tell my brother.'

'I hope the murders do not panic them into flight again,' said Joan. 'It will be more dangerous still on the open road, as I imagine the sentiments spoken on Cambridge's streets will be just the same in other towns and villages.'

'We shall include them in our prayers, along with the victims of Winchelsea.' Katherine nodded to her Prioress. 'Joan has already started work on a chantry chapel for those who lost their lives there.'

Joan blushed self-effacingly. 'It is the least we can do,' she mumbled.

'God only knows what led the Dauphin's men to do such dreadful things,' Katherine went on. 'All I can think is that they were possessed by the Devil.'

'I rather think they decided to murder, loot and burn without any prompting from him,' said Joan grimly. 'I trust they will make their peace with God, because *I* cannot find it in my heart to forgive them.'

Katherine touched her arm in a brief gesture of sympathy, and the Prioress turned away quickly to hide her tears, embarrassed to show weakness in front of strangers. Two or three of the younger nuns began to sob.

'Yesterday brought it all back to us,' said Katherine, and for once, there was no smug amusement in her eyes. 'Burned bodies and wounds inflicted in anger . . .'

Joan took a deep breath and dabbed impatiently at her eyes. 'I am more sorry than I can say that we failed to save the family here.'

'You will move to St Radegund's today,' decided Michael. 'The killer may strike again, and the Bishop would never forgive me if anything happened to his sister. Or any nun.'

'I would rather stay here,' said Katherine at once. 'St Radegund's is too noisy.'

'Worse, there will be no decent stabling for Dusty,' put in Joan, clearly of the opinion that his comfort was far more important than that of her nuns.

'I will arrange something for him,' promised Michael. 'He will not suffer, I promise.'

'I cannot see that *we* are in danger,' argued Katherine stubbornly. 'We are not French.'

'We do not know for certain why the Girards were targeted,' said Michael. 'It may have nothing to do with their nationality.'

'Oh, come, Brother,' said Katherine irritably. 'Of course it does! Why else would their children have been dispatched, too? But please do not uproot us now. The *conloquium* will finish in a few days, after which we will be gone.'

'*Five* days,' said Michael promptly. 'Too many to justify the risk. Please do as I ask.'

'Then we shall stay in the Gilbertine Priory instead,' determined Katherine. 'It will put us in Alice's objectionable presence, but that is a small price to pay for a quiet place to read.'

'Alice and Abbess Isabel's flock will be moving to St Radegund's as well,' said Michael. 'So pack your belongings, and I shall arrange for an escort as soon as possible.'

Katherine rolled her eyes, although Joan nodded briskly and ordered her nuns to begin preparations. They did as they were told reluctantly, and it was clear that Katherine was not the only one who resented the loss of their comfort.

'Speaking of Alice,' said Michael, 'did Matt ask you about the comb she took?'

Joan scowled. 'It was Dusty's favourite, and I was vexed when I found it gone. Alice denies it, of course, although Goda has no reason to lie. Doubtless she aims to use it for mischief, so if it does appear in suspicious circumstances, please remember the malice she bears us.'

'The malice she bears *me*,' corrected Katherine. 'It was my brother who deposed her.'

'My head is spinning,' confessed Tulyet, as he, Bartholomew and Michael walked back to the town at the end of the day. 'I need to sit quietly and reflect on all we have been told – although I can confirm that Goda *did* see Joan in the stables, so they have alibis in each other. We can cross them off our list of suspects.'

'Then who remains on it?' asked Michael. 'I would say—'

'Not tonight,' interrupted Tulyet wearily. 'I cannot think straight. We shall discuss it in the morning, by which time I will have questioned the ditcher, the miller and my two knights. Who knows? Perhaps one will confess, and we shall be spared the chore of pawing through all these facts, lies, claims and suppositions.'

'Then meet us in the Brazen George,' said Michael, naming his favourite tavern, a place where he was so regular a visitor that the landlord had set aside a chamber for his exclusive use. 'You are right: our minds will be fresher tomorrow.'

'I am not sure what to do about the *peregrini*,' sighed Tulyet. 'Instinct tells me to set guards, to prevent the surviving Jacques from spreading their poisonous message. But if I do, I may as well yell from the rooftops that the Spital holds a secret.'

Michael agreed. 'We should let Tangmer continue what he has been doing. It will only be for two more days, and then they will be gone. Do not worry about the rebels – Julien has promised to keep them under control.'

'I hope he can be trusted,' said Tulyet worriedly. 'We do not need a popular uprising to add to our troubles. What will you do now, Brother?'

'Matt and I will visit Sister Alice and demand to know why she neglected to mention visiting the Spital before the fire broke out. Then I must arrange for the nuns to move to St Radegund's. After that, there is a rehearsal of the Marian Singers.'

'I do not know them,' said Tulyet politely. 'Are they new?'

'You *do* know them,' countered Bartholomew wryly. 'They were formerly known as the Michaelhouse Choir.

However, as even speaking that name causes grown men to weep, Michael has decided to revamp their image.'

The monk's eyes narrowed. He was fiercely defensive of his talentless choristers, and hated any hint that they were less than perfect.

Tulyet laughed. 'You think naming them after the Blessed Virgin will make folk reconsider their opinions?'

'I named them after the church where we practise,' said the monk stiffly. 'St Mary the Great is the only place large enough to hold us all these days.'

Tulyet changed the subject, seeing it would be too easy to tread on sensitive toes. 'Then *you* can speak to the ditcher and the miller. They sing bass, do they not?'

Michael inclined his head. 'But here we are at the Gilbertine Priory, where Sister Alice is staying. She has filched combs, commissioned stinking candles, and foisted her company on people who do not want it, so perhaps the Spital murders are just a case of unbridled spite, and we shall have our killer under lock and key tonight.'

'I do not envy you the task of challenging her, Brother,' said Tulyet. 'I have met her twice: once when she informed me that Abbess Isabel aims to assassinate the King, and once when she claimed that Lyminster Priory cheats on its taxes. When I declined to act on either charge, she called me names I never expected to hear on the lips of a nun.'

The Gilbertine Priory looked pretty in the early evening sunlight, and Bartholomew and Michael arrived to find the hospitable canons fussing over their guests with cordials and plates of little cakes. Alice was not there, but the nuns from Ickleton were, including their saintly Abbess, whose habit was so white it glowed. Needless to say, none were pleased to learn they were to be moved to a place that was already bursting at the seams.

'But why should we go?' demanded Isabel, her voice rather petulant for someone with aspirations of sainthood. 'None of us are French and I like it here.'

'I cannot risk it,' said Michael firmly. 'Please do as I ask.'

'Very well,' sighed Isabel with very ill grace. 'Although it is foolish and unreasonable. However, you must find us a spot well away from Alice. We find her company irksome.'

'Did she mention the Spital fire to you?' asked Michael hopefully. 'I know she went there the morning it happened.'

'In the last forty-eight hours, she has uttered less than a dozen words to me,' replied Isabel tartly, 'none of which should have come from the mouth of a lady. She is so eaten up with bitterness that she is barely sane.'

Bartholomew and Michael went to Alice's room, and found her sitting at a table. She scrabbled to hide what she was doing when she saw them at the door, but Michael swooped forward and discovered that she had made a reasonable imitation of the Bishop's seal and was busily forging letters from him. She was more angry than chagrined at being caught, and began to scratch her shoulder.

'So tell the Bishop about it,' she challenged. 'He has already stripped me of my post and treated me with callous contempt. What more can he do?'

Michael read one of the counterfeit messages and started to laugh. 'Abbess Isabel is unlikely to believe that he wants her to walk naked from the castle to St Mary the Great. Or that she is then to stand in the market square and pray for the French.'

Alice scowled. 'It is not—'

'Just as the Sheriff did not believe that she wants to kill the King,' Michael went on. 'You make a fool of yourself with these ridiculous plots. It is time to stop.'

Alice regarded him sullenly. 'Why should I? I am the victim here and—'

'Speaking of victims, we have witnesses who say you were in the Spital when five people died. What do you have to say about that?'

'That I had nothing to do with it. I tried to pay my respects to Magistra Katherine and Prioress Joan, but they were too busy to receive me, so I left – *before* the blaze began. Next, I went to practise my lecture in an empty church, and I arrived at the *conloquium* later that afternoon. I told you all this yesterday.'

'No, you did not,' countered Michael. 'You failed to mention the Spital at all.'

Alice regarded him with dislike. 'It slipped my mind. So what?'

'Can you prove you left before the fire started?' asked Michael, keeping his temper with difficulty. 'Because you were seen arriving at the Spital, but no one mentioned you leaving.'

'Is it my fault that your so-called witnesses are unobservant asses? However, if you want a culprit, look to Magistra Katherine. I imagine she claims she was reading, and thus has no alibi. Am I right?'

'Yes,' acknowledged Michael. 'But—'

'I saw her sneaking around in a very furtive manner,' interrupted Alice. 'So was that hulking Joan, who is too stupid to be a prioress. She is more interested in horses than her convent, and delegates nearly all her own duties to her nuns.'

Bartholomew went to the window, well away from her, partly because her scratching was making him itch, but mostly because he was repelled by her malevolence. Moreover, one of Vice-Chancellor Heltisle's patented metal pens lay on the table, and it was very sharp – he felt Alice was deranged enough to snatch it up and stab him with it.

140

'Explain why you stole her comb.' Michael raised a hand when Alice started to deny it. 'You were seen.'

Alice struggled to look nonchalant. 'Perhaps I did pick it up, but only to look at – I never took it away. Joan is careless with her things, and probably mislaid it since.'

'Even if that is true, there is no excuse for poking about among other nuns' belongings.'

'I was looking for a nose-cloth, if you must know. Joan always keeps a good supply in her bag.' Alice smiled slyly. 'If you do not believe me about the comb, then search this room right now. You will not find it.'

The offer told them that she had hidden it somewhere they were unlikely to look, so they did not waste their time. Michael continued to bombard her with questions, but she stuck to her story: that she had visited the Spital the previous morning, but left when the nuns declined to receive her. She had seen or heard nothing suspicious near the shed, and was well away before the fire started.

'Your culprit will be Magistra Katherine, Prioress Joan, one of their sanctimonious nuns, or a lunatic,' she finished firmly. 'Not one of them can be trusted. I, however, am entirely innocent.'

They reached the Trumpington Gate, where Cynric was waiting to say that Bartholomew had a long list of patients waiting to see him. Bartholomew was pleased, as most lived some distance from the high street, so he would not be forced to listen to the Marian Singers massacre Michael's beautiful compositions. He visited a potter near the Small Bridges, and was amazed when he could still hear the racket emanating from St Mary the Great.

He took the long way around to his next patients – two elderly Breton scholars from Tyled Hostel, who were more interested in informing him that they had not voted for de Wetherset as Chancellor than explaining why they needed his services. Eventually, it transpired that they were suffering from a plethora of nervous complaints, all resulting from fear that they might be attacked for being French.

His next call took him past the butts. This was bordered by the Franciscan Priory to the north, the Barnwell Gate in the south, the main road to the west and the filthy King's Ditch to the east. It comprised a long, flat field with a mound, like an inverted ditch, at the far end. The mound was the height of a man and was topped with targets – circular boards with coloured rings. A line in the grass marked where the archers stood to shoot.

It was Wednesday, so it was the University's turn to use the ground, and as darkness had fallen, it was lit with torches. Night was not the best time for such an activity, but the daylight hours were too precious – to working men and University teachers – to lose to warfare, so practices had to be held each evening.

The University's sessions were meant to be supervised by the Junior Proctor, but Theophilis had left Beadle Meadowman to write the attendees' names in a ledger and ensure an orderly queue, while he joined the Michaelhouse men at the line. The students were trying to listen to Cynric, but Theophilis kept interrupting, and when they stepped up to the mark, most of their arrows flew wide. Cynric turned and stamped away in disgust.

'That stupid Theophilis!' he hissed as he passed Bartholomew. 'He keeps interfering, and now our boys are worse than when we started. He has undone all my good work.'

'Come and shoot, Matthew,' Theophilis called, his hissing voice distinctly unsettling in the gloom. 'Or you will be marked as absent.'

'I have patients,' Bartholomew called back, pleased to have an excuse.

'And I have documents to read, teaching to prepare, and lecture schedules to organise,' retorted Theophilis.

'But the King issued an edict, and *I* am not so arrogant as to ignore it.'

Inwardly fuming – both at the wasted time and the public rebuke – Bartholomew marched up to the line, grabbed a bow and sent ten arrows flying towards the targets. As he did not aim properly, most went wide, although four hit the mark, showing that he had not forgotten everything he had learned at Poitiers. He handed the weapon back without a word and went on his way, pausing only to ensure that his name was in the register.

He visited two customers near the castle, and was just crossing the Great Bridge on his way home when he met Tulyet hurrying in the opposite direction.

'I have been looking everywhere for you, Matt! Poor old Wyse is dead. Will you look at him? It seems he fell in a ditch and drowned. As it is a Wednesday, he was probably drunk.'

Will Wyse was a familiar figure in Cambridge. He eked a meagre living from selling firewood, and would have starved but for the generosity of the Franciscans, who gave him alms every Wednesday. He always celebrated his weekly windfall by spending exactly one quarter of it on ale in the Griffin tavern.

Tulyet led Bartholomew across the river, then a short way along the Chesterton road, to where the unfortunately named Pierre Sauvage stood guard over Wyse's body. Sauvage handed Bartholomew a lamp, and the physician saw that Wyse had apparently stumbled, so that his head had ended up in the ditch at the side of the road. The rest of the body was dry. Bartholomew knelt to examine it more closely.

'An accident?' asked Tulyet, watching him. 'A fall while he was in his cups?'

'He was murdered,' replied Bartholomew. 'You see that blood on the back of his head? It is where someone hit him from behind. The blow only stunned him, but his assailant dragged him here, dropped him so his face was in the water, and left him to drown.'

Tulyet gaped at him. 'Murdered? But who would want to kill Wyse?'

'Someone who wanted his money,' predicted Sauvage. 'Everyone knows he had some on a Wednesday, and that he always staggered home along this road after the Griffin.'

'But his purse is still on his belt,' countered Tulyet.

'Perhaps the culprit was also drunk,' shrugged Sauvage, 'but sobered up fast and ran away when he realised what he had done.'

Tulyet shook his head in disgust. 'Carry the body to St Giles's, then go to the Griffin and see what his friends can tell you. Perhaps there was a drunken spat. Take Sergeant Orwel – he is good at prising answers from reluctant witnesses.'

'He is at choir practice,' said Sauvage. 'But he should be finished by the time I have taken Wyse to the church. Of course, no townsman did this. We would never risk the wrath of the Franciscans – they were fond of Wyse and will be furious when they find out what has happened to him. It will be the work of a University man.'

Bartholomew blinked. 'What evidence do you have to say such a thing?'

'First, Wyse was old and frail, so posed no threat to a puny book-man,' began Sauvage, suggesting he had given the matter some serious thought while he had been guarding the body. 'Second, the culprit was clever, like all you lot, so he killed his victim in a place where no one would see. And third, scholars hate the sight of blood, which is why Wyse was drowned rather than stabbed.'

'That is not evidence,' said Bartholomew impatiently. 'It is conjecture. There is nothing to suggest that a scholar did this. Indeed, I would say the Sheriff has the right of it, and Wyse died as a result of a disagreement with his friends.'

'Well, you are wrong,' stated Sauvage resolutely. 'You wait and see.'

While Bartholomew visited patients, Michael organised an escort for the nuns, then went to St Mary the Great, his mind full of the music he would teach that evening. There was a *Jubilate* by Tunstede, followed by a *Gloria* he had composed himself, and finally some motets for the next matriculation ceremony. De Wetherset had vetoed the Marian Singers taking part in such an auspicious occasion, but Michael was not about to let a mere Chancellor interfere with his plans, and continued to rehearse so as to be ready for it.

He entered the nave and looked around in astonishment, sure half the town had turned out to sing. He experienced a stab of alarm that there would not be enough post-practice food. As it was, they were obliged to share cups – one between three.

Of course, it was his own fault that the choir had grown so huge. He had always known that some of its members were women, and had never been deceived by the horsehair beards and charcoal moustaches. However, he had recently been rash enough to say there was no reason why a choir should consist solely of men, at which point the disguises were abandoned and women arrived in droves. Feeding everyone was an ever-increasing challenge.

He looked fondly at the many familiar faces. There were a host of beadles, Isnard the bargeman and Verious the ditcher, although Michael was less pleased to see Sergeant Orwel among the throng. Orwel was a hard-bitten, vicious, bad-tempered veteran of Poitiers, who had been the cause of several spats between scholars and townsfolk. Michael had never understood why Tulyet continued to employ him, unless it was for his ability to intimidate.

However, the moment Orwel began to sing, Michael forgot his antipathy: the sergeant transpired to be an unexpectedly pure, clear alto. Outside, passers-by were astounded to hear a haunting quartet, sung by Michael, Orwel, Isnard and Verious.

Afterwards, over the free bread and ale, Michael cornered the witnesses he hoped would have insights into the fire. Unfortunately, the miller had been hurrying to unload his wares lest close proximity to lunatics turned him insane himself, so had noticed nothing useful. Disappointed, Michael went in search of Verious, who he found sitting with Isnard and Orwel.

'Terrible business about the Spital,' said Isnard conversationally. 'We heard forty lunatics were roasted alive.'

Michael marvelled at the power of rumour. 'There were not—'

'It was that dolphin and his rabble,' growled Verious. '*They* did it.'

'What do you mean?' asked Michael worriedly. Had the ditcher guessed the truth when he had been at the Spital and shared the secret with his dubious friends? If so, the *peregrini* would have to leave at once, before hotheads from the town *and* the University organised an assault.

'The dolphin came up the river from the coast,' explained the ditcher darkly. 'Looting and burning as he went. Our soldiers guard the gates, so he dared not invade the town, but the Spital is isolated. The Frenchies saw it and seized their chance. Poor lunatics!'

'I think the Sheriff would have noticed an enemy army rampaging about the countryside,' said Michael drily. 'However, someone burned a shed with six people inside it, and I intend to find the culprit. You were in the Spital yesterday, Verious – did *you* notice anything unusual?'

The ditcher swelled with importance as everyone

looked expectantly at him. 'I saw the lunatics doing what lunatics do – swaying and gibbering.'

'But did you see anyone near the shed?' pressed Michael. 'Or go near it yourself?'

Verious grimaced. 'No, because them Tangmer cousins would not leave me alone. Every time I tried to slip away to have a nose around, one would stop me. It meant I saw nothing very interesting.'

'I spotted two of Tangmer's madmen in the town the day before the fire,' put in Isnard helpfully. 'They were chatting to Sir Leger and Sir Norbert, who addressed one as Master Girard. Was he among the dead?'

Michael nodded, although he hated providing Isnard with information that would almost certainly be repeated in garbled form. There was no point in begging discretion, as this would only lead to even wilder flights of imagination.

'What were they saying?' he asked.

'I could not hear,' came the disappointing reply.

'I could,' growled Orwel. 'Because *I* saw them talking together, too. But I could not tell what lies the lunatics were spinning to our two good knights, because they were speaking French, and I have never befouled my brain by learning that vile tongue.'

'French?' asked Michael, alarmed.

It would be the knights' first language, given that they were part of the ruling elite, but he was appalled that the Girards should have used it with strangers. Had Leger and Norbert guessed the truth and acted on it? If so, it would put Tulyet in an invidious position – he could hardly hang the King's favourites, yet nor could he over-look their crime.

'Here comes Cynric,' said Isnard, glancing up. 'Driven away from the butts again by your interfering Junior Proctor, no doubt. That Theophilis cannot keep his opin-ions to himself, even though he knows less about archery than a snail.'

'I have something to tell you about the Spital, Brother,' announced Cynric grandly. 'We need not worry about the French attacking it again.'

'No?' asked Michael warily. 'Why not?'

'Because I have just been to see Margery Starre, and she says it is now Satan's domain,' explained Cynric. 'And he has put it under his *personal* protection. Anyone assaulting it can expect to be sucked straight down to Hell.'

'Well, then,' said Michael, hoping that would be enough to protect the *peregrini* until they could slip away. 'We had all better keep our distance.'

CHAPTER 7

By the following morning, everyone knew that Satan had moved into the Spital, and would not welcome uninvited guests. However, while the news encouraged superstitious townsfolk to stay away, it had the opposite effect on those in holy orders.

'The Devil will not tell *me* what I can and cannot do in my own town,' declared Father William indignantly, as he and the other Fellows sat in the conclave after breakfast. 'Who does he think he is?'

'That tale is a lot of nonsense started by Cynric,' said Theophilis in the sinister whisper that Bartholomew was coming to detest. 'I shall be glad when you leave the University and take that heretic with you, Bartholomew. I dislike the fact that he – and you, for that matter – has befriended a witch.'

'Cynric is not a heretic,' objected Bartholomew, although he was aware that the book-bearer was not exactly a true son of the Church either. 'And I am no friend of Margery Starre.'

'Really?' asked Aungel guilelessly. 'Because she always speaks very highly of you. When I collect the cure she makes for my spots, she always says—'

He stopped abruptly, aware that he had not only dropped his former teacher in the mire, but had done himself no favours either. Theophilis was quick to pounce.

'You will not buy her wares again, Aungel,' he ordered sharply. 'And I shall put Bartholomew's association with that woman in my weekly report to the Chancellor.'

'Come to the Spital with me, Theophilis,' said William,

eyes blazing fanatically. 'You and I will send Lucifer packing together.'

'Good idea,' said Theophilis, and turned to Michael. 'And while we are there, I shall investigate the murdered lunatics. *I* am your Junior Proctor, so if anyone helps you solve the mystery, it should be *me*.' He glared pointedly at Bartholomew.

'It is kind of you to offer,' said Michael. 'But I need you to monitor the triumvirate. I say this not for my benefit, but for your own – you will never rise in the University hierarchy if the Chancellor regains too much power, as he will prevent me from promoting you.'

'Of course,' said Theophilis, paling at the awful prospect of political stagnation. 'I shall go to St Mary the Great at once. Meadowman told me that a letter arrived for de Wetherset at dawn, so I should find out who sent it.'

'You should,' agreed Michael. 'It is the time of year when nominations for lucrative sinecures arrive, and it would be a shame if you lose out to someone less deserving.'

Theophilis made for the door at such a lick that he startled the hens that Clippesby was feeding under the table. They scattered in alarm.

'Keep those things away from me,' he snarled, flapping his hands at them. 'They should not be in here anyway – unless they are roasted in butter.'

'You would eat Gertrude?' breathed Clippesby, shocked. 'The nominalist?'

Theophilis forced a smile. 'Of course I would not eat her, Clippesby. I am too fervent an admirer of her philosophy. Forgive me, Gertrude. I spoke out of turn.'

He bowed to the bird and left, leaving Clippesby to smooth ruffled feathers. William watched him go, then went to recruit Aungel for a holy assault on the Spital.

'I do not understand why you trust Theophilis,' said

Bartholomew, once he and Michael were alone. 'He is only interested in furthering his own career, and cares nothing for yours.'

'Almost certainly. However, he also knows that the only way he will succeed is with my support, so he will do anything to keep my approval.' Michael stood and stretched. 'We should go to meet Dick. We have a lot to do today.'

'Have we?' asked Bartholomew without enthusiasm.

Michael nodded. 'Once we have discussed our findings with him, we must speak to Leger and Norbert about their conversation with the Girards. I want to know why they kept an encounter with two murder victims to themselves.'

'It might be wiser to let Dick do that,' said Bartholomew, thinking that while the ruffianly pair might not assault a monk, the same could not be said about a physician. He was no coward, but there was no point in deliberately courting danger.

'You may be right. Next, we shall go to St Mary the Great, where I will show you the blade that killed Paris the Plagiarist. You never saw it, because it got kicked under a stone and Theophilis did not find it until the following day.'

'*Theophilis* found it? And it was missed during the initial search?'

'Yes, but when he showed me where it had fallen, I was not surprised that no one had spotted it sooner. I want you to compare it to the weapon that killed the Girards.'

'The wounds on them and Paris were not the same size,' said Bartholomew. 'I told you that yesterday. Theirs were more akin to Bonet's, but he is buried, so we will never know if he was killed with the weapon we found at the Spital. Incidentally, have you asked where Theophilis was when the fire started?'

Michael's eyes were round with disbelief. 'Lord, Matt!

What is it about my poor Junior Proctor that you so dislike? He never says anything nasty about you.'

'Spying is distasteful, but he happily rushed to do it, which says nothing good about him. He spends a lot of time with de Wetherset and Heltisle, and he is ambitious. If they offer him a better deal, he will take it – then it will be *you* who is the subject of his snooping.'

'I shall bear it in mind, although I am sure you are wrong.'

'So *did* you ask where he was when the fire started?'

Michael was growing exasperated. 'Why would Theophilis, a Fellow of Michaelhouse, renowned canon lawyer and possible future Chancellor, stab a few frightened Frenchmen? I have discussed the war with him in the past, and he is of the same opinion as you and me – that the leaders of both sides should bring about a truce before any more blood is spilled.'

'So you have not asked him,' surmised Bartholomew in disgust.

'You *know* where he was – here, in the hall, keeping the peace while William revealed his ignorance of the nominalism–realism dispute.'

Bartholomew raised a triumphant finger. 'No, he was not! Aungel said he left shortly after it started, and did not return for some time – which is why my students were able to savage William so ruthlessly. Theophilis was not here to keep them in line.'

'I forgot – he *did* mention going out,' said Michael. 'Heltisle had a meeting, and refused to reveal who with, so Theophilis followed him. Unfortunately, he lost him by King's Hall, so he returned to his duties here.'

'It is not a very convincing alibi, is it?' said Bartholomew, unimpressed. 'No one can really verify what he was doing.'

'I suspect that is true for half the town, which is why this case will not be easy to solve. But solve it we must, because we cannot rest until this killer is caught. So if you are ready . . .'

Bartholomew nodded to where William was still badgering Aungel to join him in a righteous assault on Satan. 'What about him? We cannot let *him* go anywhere near the Spital, because if he learns who is inside . . .'

'I shall ask him to visit his fellow Franciscans and find out what they know about Wyse. He will enjoy that, as he is always clamouring to be a proctor. By the time he has finished, he will have forgotten all about his holy mission against the Devil.'

Bartholomew hoped Michael was right.

Taverns were off limits to scholars, on the grounds that they tended to be full of ale-sodden townsfolk. In times of peace, Michael turned a blind eye to the occasional infraction, but Paris's murder meant the stricture had to be enforced much more rigidly. Unfortunately, several hostels had flouted the rule the previous night, and there had been drunken fights.

'We have seen trouble in the past,' muttered Michael as he and Bartholomew hurried to their meeting with Tulyet, 'but it is worse this time because everyone is armed.'

He and Bartholomew entered the Brazen George via the back door, where they were less likely to be spotted. The room the landlord always kept ready for him was a pleasant chamber overlooking a yard where hens scratched happily. They reminded Bartholomew of Clippesby's treatise.

'How many copies has Heltisle sold?' he asked. 'Do you know?'

'Enough to build the dogs a veritable palace *and* pay for the conclave windows to be glazed.' Michael shook his head admiringly. 'Clippesby has been stunningly clever – he also added a clause that obliges Heltisle to bear the cost of all these new copies himself. Unless he builds a kennel in the next few days, our Vice-Chancellor will be seriously out of pocket.'

'Then let us hope no one warns him,' said Bartholomew pointedly.

'Theophilis would never betray us. Stop worrying about him, Matt.'

There was no point in arguing. Landlord Lister arrived, so Bartholomew sat at the table and listened as Michael began to order himself some food.

'Bring lots of meat with bread. But no chicken. I am disinclined to eat those these days, lest one transpires to be a nominalist and thus a friend to my Order.'

'You cannot be hungry, Brother,' said Bartholomew disapprovingly. 'You have just devoured a huge meal at College—'

'Unfortunately, I did not,' interrupted Michael stiffly. 'You stuck that dish of peas next to me, which meant I could not reach anything decent. Besides, I was up half the night, and I need sustenance. After choir practice, there were the brawls to quell *and* I had to make sure the nuns from the Spital and the Gilbertine Priory were safely rehoused in St Radegund's.'

'Was there room for them all?'

'Not really, and the *conloquium* is a nuisance, getting in the way of preventing civil unrest, solving Paris's murder and controlling de Wetherset. Or rather, controlling Heltisle and Aynton, as they are where the real problem lies. They have never liked me, and de Wetherset is far too willing to listen to their advice.'

'Heltisle is a menace, but Aynton—'

'Did I tell you that most spats last night were about Wyse?' interrupted Michael, unwilling to hear yet again that the Commissary was harmless. 'You said he was murdered.'

'He *was* murdered. I hope Dick catches the culprit

soon, because he was an inoffensive old sot who would have put up no kind of defence. It was a cowardly attack.'

'The town cries that a scholar killed him, and the University responds with angry denials. Wyse's death may not come under my jurisdiction, but we shall have no peace until the suspect is caught, so I will have to look into the matter. And you will help. Do not look irked, Matt – your town and your University needs you.'

Tulyet arrived a few moments later, looking tired – keeping the King's peace in the rebellious little Fen-edge town was grinding him down, too. He immediately began to complain about de Wetherset, who was in the habit of obsessing over minute details in any agreements the town tried to make with him. Thus negotiations took far longer than when the Senior Proctor had been in charge.

'He never used to be this unreasonable,' he grumbled. 'What is wrong with the man?'

'He just needs a few weeks to assert himself, after which he will be much more amenable,' said Michael soothingly. 'The situation will ease even further once I persuade him to dismiss Heltisle and Aynton.'

Tulyet brightened. 'Will you? Good! I am sure Heltisle encourages de Wetherset to be awkward, although Aynton is a bumbling nonentity whom you should ignore. But you are sensible and accommodating, and I have grown complacent. This new regime is an unpleasant reminder that your University contains some very difficult men.'

'Here is Lister,' said Michael, more interested in what was on the landlord's tray. 'You two may discuss the murders while I eat.'

'I believe we have one killer and seven French victims,' began Bartholomew. 'We may know for certain once we have compared the dagger that killed Paris to the one used on the Girard family. It is a pity Bonet's was stolen, and that he is already buried.'

Tulyet helped himself to a piece of Michael's bread. 'So we have a French-hating killer *and* a rogue who drowns helpless old drunks. Two culprits, not one.'

'Did Sauvage learn anything useful in the Griffin last night?' asked Bartholomew.

'Yes, but only after Sergeant Orwel arrived to help him,' said Tulyet. 'Orwel knows how to get the truth from recalcitrant witnesses. Sauvage does not.'

'And?' asked Michael, his mouth full of cold beef.

'The other patrons *did* see someone watching Wyse with suspicious interest – someone who then followed him outside. Unfortunately, the bastard kept his face hidden. However, his cloak was of good quality, and his boots were better still.'

'Really?' asked Michael. 'The Griffin does not usually attract well-dressed patrons.'

'These witnesses also saw this man take a book out of his scrip, and they noticed his inky fingers,' Tulyet went on. 'Two things that "prove" the culprit is a scholar. It is what ignited the trouble between us and your students last night.'

'*Did* he read and have inky fingers?' asked Bartholomew. 'Or did these so-called witnesses make it up?'

'I suspect he did, as too many of them gave identical testimony for it to be fiction. Of course, some townsmen can read . . .'

'And are clever enough to know who will be blamed if books and inky hands are flashed around,' finished Michael. 'It could be a ruse to lead us astray. Now, what about the Spital deaths? Summarise what we know about those while I nibble at this pork.'

'The Girard family considered the shed to be theirs,' began Tulyet, 'which I suspect created friction, as petty things matter to folk under strain.'

'We saw for ourselves that there are two distinct factions among the *peregrini*,' added Bartholomew. 'The majority side with Father Julien, but the Jacques follow Delacroix.'

'The Jacques,' muttered Tulyet. 'Members of a violent uprising that destabilised an entire country. I am not happy with such men near my town.'

'No,' agreed Michael, dabbing his greasy lips with a piece of linen. 'But take comfort from the fact that there are only four of them – hopefully too few to be a problem.'

Tulyet looked as if he disagreed, but did not argue, and only returned to analysing the murders. 'Hélène collected milk from the kitchen, then joined her family in the shed. There, she found the milk had a peculiar taste and refused to drink most of it, which saved her life. Shortly afterwards, the adults had been stabbed and the fire started.'

'Has Hélène recalled anything new?' asked Bartholomew.

'Unfortunately not,' replied Tulyet. 'She just remembers feeling sleepy.'

Bartholomew thought about the milk. 'The soporific must have been added in the kitchen. Does that mean the culprit is a member of staff? No one else can get in there.'

Tulyet grimaced. 'If only that were true! Last night, I broke in with ease. Then I entered the kitchen, refectory and dormitory without being challenged once. I was obliged to teach the Tangmers how to implement some basic security measures.'

'But the Girards were killed in broad daylight,' argued Bartholomew. 'It is one thing to sneak in under cover of darkness, but another altogether to do it during the day.'

'Unfortunately, the layout of the Spital offers plenty of cover for a competent invader,' countered Tulyet. 'Ergo, the culprit might well hail from outside.'

'Suspects,' said Michael briskly. 'First, the *peregrini*.'

'They are high on my list, too,' said Tulyet. 'Especially as I have learned that they arrived in the area two days before Paris was stabbed. Now, the Girards were no angels – they were territorial over the shed, they took money with no intention of honouring agreements, and two were Jacques. Meanwhile, Delacroix is angry, bitter and violent – perhaps the Girards quarrelled with him.'

'Or Father Julien did,' said Michael. 'I like the man, but perhaps he decided that dispatching one awkward, divisive family was the best way to save the rest.'

'What about the Spital staff?' asked Bartholomew. 'Little Goda is in the clear, because Prioress Joan saw her in the kitchen when the fire was set. The two of them can have no more than a passing acquaintance, so there is no reason to think they are lying for each other.'

'My clerks cross-checked my notes about who was with whom when,' said Tulyet. 'And it transpires that every member of staff has at least two others to vouch for him except Tangmer, his wife and Eudo. Eudo and Tangmer *say* they were together, but their accounts are contradictory.'

'So they lied,' mused Michael. 'Interesting.'

'Very. Amphelisa was alone in her workshop, and I am inclined to believe her because of the way she cares for Hélène – you do not try to kill a child, then adopt her as your own. Moreover, she is the one who agreed to house the *peregrini* in the first place, very much against her husband's better judgement.'

'Then there is Magistra Katherine,' Bartholomew went on. 'She was reading behind the chapel, so she has no alibi either.'

'I cannot see the Bishop's sister dispatching a family of strangers,' said Michael.

'Why not?' asked Bartholomew. 'Her brother sanctions murder.'

'I hardly think it is something that runs in a family,' retorted Michael stiffly. 'A more likely suspect is that spiteful Sister Alice, who went a-visiting at the salient time.'

158

'Then we have an entire town that hates the French,' added Tulyet. 'I know no one is supposed to know that the Spital is full of them, but these secrets have a way of leaking out. What did the ditcher and the miller tell you, Brother? Could either of them be the killer?'

'No,' said Michael with conviction. 'Neither is clever enough to have devised such an audacious plan, and nor would they kill children with poisoned milk. Furthermore, they are not observant, and would never have identified the "lunatics" as French.'

'Sir Leger and Sir Norbert might have done, though,' mused Bartholomew. 'And Isnard and Sergeant Orwel did see them talking to the Girards.'

Tulyet grimaced. 'My new knights hate the French, and if the Girards gave themselves away . . . But let us not forget that de Wetherset and Heltisle hired the Girards as proxies.'

'I wonder if Theophilis was there when that happened,' said Bartholomew reflectively, 'perhaps spying on them for you, Brother.'

'If Theophilis had the slightest inkling that Frenchmen were posing as lunatics, he would have told me,' said Michael firmly. 'However, Aynton would not – *he* cannot be trusted at all.' He scowled when Bartholomew began to object. 'If you insist on including Theophilis, then I insist on including Aynton.'

Bartholomew raised his hands in surrender. 'Although neither of us really thinks de Wetherset and Heltisle are the kind of men to poison children.'

'*I* would not put it past them,' countered Tulyet. 'It would not be the first time seemingly respectable scholars resorted to abhorrent tactics to get their own way.'

'So where does that leave our list?' asked Michael. 'Summarise it for me.'

'The *peregrini*, specifically Julien and the Jacques,' began Tulyet. 'Amphelisa, Tangmer and Eudo from the Spital;

Magistra Katherine and Sister Alice from the Benedictine Order; Leger and Norbert from the castle; and de Wetherset, Heltisle, Aynton and Theophilis from the University.'

'And a lot of dim-witted townsfolk and students who think we are about to be invaded by the Dauphin,' added Michael. 'Although we all have reservations about Amphelisa being the culprit, while I sincerely doubt de Wetherset and Theophilis are involved, and Matt thinks Aynton is as pure as driven snow.'

'So how do we set about finding the culprit?' asked Bartholomew.

'You tackle the scholars and the nuns,' replied Tulyet, 'while I concentrate on the townsfolk. We shall share the suspects at the Spital.'

'And your knights?' asked Michael. 'Will you take them, too?'

'No – we shall do that together.' Tulyet winced. 'Their military service has turned them into French-hating fanatics. They also know how to break into buildings and set fires. It is entirely possible that one of them – Leger, most likely – guessed what the Spital is hiding.'

Michael stood abruptly. 'Come with us to look at the knife that killed Paris, Dick. You know weapons better than we do.'

On their way out of the Brazen George, a message arrived for Michael. It was from Heltisle, and ordered him to report to St Mary the Great immediately. The monk read it once, then again to be sure. When he had finished, he screwed it into a ball and flung it on the ground.

'How dare he summon me!' he fumed. 'I have enough to do, without being sent hither and thither at the whim of a man whose appointment I did not sanction.'

'You are on your way there anyway,' said Tulyet pragmatically. 'And he might have something important to tell you. If not, it can be your pretext for ignoring him next time.'

'There will not be a next time! And I am glad you two will be with me – it means that if I feel compelled to punch him, one can drag me off while the other sets his broken nose.'

Tulyet backed away. 'I rather think this is a confrontation that an outsider should not witness. Go and do your punching and meet me by the Great Bridge in an hour. Bring the knife that killed Paris. In the interim, I will start questioning townsfolk about the fire.'

He hurried away, and Bartholomew and Michael stepped on to the high street just as Aynton was passing. The Vice-Chancellor beamed amiably and fell into step beside them, so Michael used the opportunity for an impromptu interrogation.

'Where were you when the Spital fire started?' he asked, cutting into the Commissary's rambling account of a brawl he had witnessed the previous night.

Aynton blinked his surprise. 'Me? Why?'

'Because I should like to know,' replied Michael coolly.

Aynton gave a little laugh. 'I am afraid I cannot tell you *precisely*, because I do not know *precisely* when the fire began. However, I was probably in St Mary the Great with de Wetherset and Heltisle. Oh, and Theophilis, who was spying on us, as is his wont. Can you not find him anything more respectable to do, Brother?'

'You were there all morning?' asked Michael, irked to learn that his Junior Proctor was compromised, although Bartholomew wondered if Theophilis had done it on purpose, to let the triumvirate know whose side he was really on.

Aynton continued to grin amiably. 'Yes, other than the time I went out. I shall pontificate on the Chicken Debate later this month, so I take every opportunity to practise.

I go to the Barnwell Fields, where I can speak as loudly as I like without disturbing anyone.'

Michael stifled a sigh of exasperation. 'So you were alone for part of the time?'

Aynton raised his eyebrows. 'I was, although I hope you do not suspect *me* of the crime.' He chortled at the notion. 'Perhaps Clippesby will ask the sheep to give me an alibi. Would that suffice?'

'Not really,' said Michael coldly. 'Because it transpires that you knew two of the victims – they were the proxies hired by de Wetherset and Heltisle.'

'I did not *know* them,' argued Aynton pedantically. 'I met them twice. All I can tell you is that they had shifty eyes and looked around constantly, as if they feared an attack. So, now I have proved that my acquaintance with them was superficial, you can cross my name off your list of suspects. Eh?'

He gave a cheery wave and sailed away. Michael watched him go with narrowed eyes.

'If that was not the response of a guilty man, I do not know what is. How dare he claim he was in a field talking to sheep and expect me to believe it!'

'Perhaps it was the truth,' said Bartholomew. 'He has always been eccentric.'

They entered St Mary the Great, and headed for Michael's sumptuous office. Theophilis was in it, riffling through the documents on the desk.

'What are you doing?' demanded Bartholomew, indignant on Michael's behalf.

Theophilis regarded him with an expression that was difficult to read. 'Looking for next week's theology lecture schedule,' he replied smoothly. 'Father William assures me that he is on it. I hope he is not, because I refuse to listen to him again.'

Michael sighed. 'He has used this tactic to win a slot before, and it occasionally works. Tell him the programme

162

is full. Or better yet, suggest he delivers his tirade to his fellow Franciscans. They are less likely to lynch him, and it will still satisfy his desire to be heard.'

Theophilis inclined his head and slithered away to do the monk's bidding.

Bartholomew picked up the document on the top of the pile. 'Here is the schedule. I wonder why he felt the need to rummage when what he wanted was in plain sight.'

'He could not see the wood for the trees, I suppose,' shrugged Michael. 'But do not worry about him prying. I keep nothing sensitive here – not as long as the likes of Aynton and Heltisle are at large. Now where did I put that dagger? Hah! Here it is.'

The weapon was a handsome thing, one its owner would surely be sorry to lose. It was also distinctive, with a jewelled handle of an unusual shape and a blade of tempered steel.

'It is not the same as the one that killed the Girards,' said Bartholomew, turning it over in his hands. 'The blade is longer and thinner. However, the design is almost identical, and it would not surprise me to learn that they came from the same place.'

'You mean the same forge?'

'No, I mean the same geographical region. Have you seen Cynric's knives? They look alike, because they were all made in Wales. But I am no expert – Dick will tell you more.'

Michael put the weapon in his scrip. 'We shall do it as soon as I find out why Heltisle feels the need to flex muscles he does not have. And while we are there, we shall ask him where *he* was when his proxy was stabbed and incinerated.'

De Wetherset was in his poky office, assessing applications from prospective students. Bartholomew was impressed to note that each was given meticulous attention before a decision was made – Suttone had delegated the entire process to his clerks, while the Chancellor before that had only read the first line. His iron-grey hair was perfectly groomed, and he exuded authority and efficiency.

Heltisle was behind him, leaning over his shoulder to whisper. His clothes would not have looked out of place at Court – he had abandoned his College livery in favour of a purple mantle that any baron would have envied, while his hat was trimmed with fur. He oozed a sense of wealth and entitlement – just the attitude that townsfolk found so aggravating.

His shifty blush when Michael and Bartholomew walked in made it clear that he had been talking about them. As he straightened, a strand of his hair snagged on the pilgrim badge in de Wetherset's hat. De Wetherset sighed and fidgeted impatiently while Heltisle struggled to free himself, and the process was complicated further still when the Chancellor jerked away suddenly and caught his hand on one of his deputy's metal pens. The resulting cut was insignificant, but de Wetherset made a terrible fuss, obliging Bartholomew to provide a salve.

'Why did you want me, Vice-Chancellor?' asked Michael, when the kerfuffle was finally over. 'Please state your case quickly. I am a busy man.'

Heltisle eyed him coldly. 'Why are you still involved in the Spital affair?'

'The Spital *murders*. And of course I am still involved. Why would I not be?'

'Because it is not University property and the victims were not scholars,' replied Heltisle. 'Ergo, it is not our concern. Moreover, the place is said to be under Lucifer's personal control, and we cannot be associated with that sort of thing.'

'Superstitious nonsense,' declared Michael. 'And the

murders *are* my concern, because they were almost certainly committed by the same rogue who killed Paris, who *was* a scholar. Moreover, you hired two of the victims to train at the butts on your behalf. Surely you want to know who deprived you of your proxies?'

'Not really,' sighed de Wetherset. 'It will not bring them back, poor souls. Did you arrange for our money to be given to the orphaned child, by the way? You must let us know if we can do anything else to help her.'

'There is, as a matter of fact,' said Michael. 'You can answer a question: where were you both on Wednesday morning?'

De Wetherset's eyes widened with shock. 'Surely you cannot think we had anything to do with these deaths?'

'He does,' growled Heltisle, tight-lipped with anger. 'And it is a gross slur on our character. You should dismiss him at once for his—'

'No, Heltisle,' interrupted de Wetherset, raising a hand to stop him. 'Michael is right – we had a connection to the victims, so of course we must account for our whereabouts.' He turned back to Michael. 'We were in here, working.'

'Just the two of you?' asked Bartholomew, enjoying the way that Heltisle bristled at the indignity of being interrogated like a criminal.

'Aynton was here for a while,' said de Wetherset. 'But then he went out, probably to practise a lecture he intends to give.'

'Can anyone confirm it?'

'No,' replied Heltisle, barely able to speak through his clenched teeth. 'The door was closed, because we were engaged in *confidential* University business, and it was necessary to thwart eavesdroppers.'

The look he gave Michael suggested that Theophilis's usefulness as a spy was well and truly over.

'But it does not matter, because Heltisle and I have

alibis in each other,' said de Wetherset. 'That is what alibis are, is it not – one person proving that another is entirely innocent?'

Michael nodded. 'Although we prefer independent witnesses, rather than friends who owe each other their loyalty. But if that is all you have, we shall have to make the best of it.'

'You were ensconced in here together all morning?' pressed Bartholomew, suspicious of Heltisle's aggressively defensive answers.

'Yes,' said Heltisle shortly.

'No,' said de Wetherset at the same time. He gave his Vice-Chancellor an exasperated glance. 'You know we were not – you went out to buy parchment and you were gone for quite a while.'

'Because there was a long queue in the shop,' said Heltisle, struggling to mask his annoyance at the revelation. 'Then I had an errand to run for my College.'

'But I stayed here, and I am sure some clerk or other will confirm it,' said de Wetherset rather carelessly. 'Just ask around.'

'Your theory is wrong anyway, Brother,' said Heltisle, launching an attack to mask his discomfiture. 'Paris and the others were *not* dispatched by the same hand. How could they be when there is no connection between them? No wonder you have failed to catch the killer – you cannot see the obvious.'

'I am afraid I agree, Brother,' said de Wetherset apologetically. 'Your premise is indeed flawed.' Then he grimaced. 'We were too lenient with Paris. Plagiarism is a terrible crime, and we should have made an example of him, to prevent others from following suit.'

'Quite right,' nodded Heltisle. 'The next culprit should be hanged.'

'Unfortunately, plagiarism is not a capital offence,' said de Wetherset ruefully. 'Much as we might wish it were otherwise. There is nothing more vile than stealing an idea and passing it off as one's own.'

'But as it happens, you no longer need concern yourself with Paris,' Heltisle went on, smugness restored. 'As you have failed to catch his killer, Aynton will investigate instead.'

'Impossible!' snapped Michael. 'Only proctors have the authority to—'

'We have amended the statues to say that he can,' interrupted Heltisle, positively overflowing with spiteful glee. 'Aynton will succeed where you have let us down.'

'I am sorry, Brother,' said de Wetherset; he sounded sincere. 'But I feel the case requires fresh eyes. The unsolved murder of a scholar is causing friction with the town, and we need answers before it becomes even more problematic. I hope you understand.'

'Aynton mentioned nothing of this when we met him just now,' said Michael stiffly.

'Perhaps it slipped his mind,' said de Wetherset charitably, although Bartholomew suspected that the Commissary's courage had failed him and he had opted to let someone else break the news. 'But look on the bright side: it will leave you more time for your peace-keeping duties.'

'I have ideas about how to improve your performance there, too,' said Heltisle, before Michael could respond. 'For a start, you can order Tulyet to impose a curfew on all townsfolk. If they are indoors, our scholars can wander about where they please without fear of assault, and the town will be a much nicer place.'

'I hardly think—' began Bartholomew, shocked.

Heltisle cut across him. 'However, this curfew is the *only* matter on which you may converse with him. For all other business, you must refer him to us. The University has made far too many concessions over the last decade, and it is time to seize back the rights that you have allowed him to leech away.'

'Then thank you very much,' said Michael with a sudden, radiant smile. 'It will be a great relief to lose that particular burden. You are most kind.'

'Am I?' said Heltisle, smugness slipping. 'I thought you would object.'

'Oh, no,' replied Michael airily. 'I am delighted. After all, why should *I* be blamed when the town takes umbrage at all these harsh new policies, and takes revenge by placing the instigators' severed heads on a pike?'

Heltisle paled. 'Severed heads?'

'I have been walking a tightrope with the town for years,' said Michael, continuing to beam. 'So I am most grateful to pass the responsibility to someone else.'

Heltisle was so angry that Bartholomew edged towards the door, afraid the Vice-Chancellor might fly at them with one of his sharp metal pens. De Wetherset swallowed hard, and glared accusingly at his Vice-Chancellor.

'Perhaps this is not the best time to—'

Michael went on happily. 'But now the onus of dealing with the town lies with you, it should be *you* who informs the Sheriff about the curfew you want. Good luck with that! However, you might want to exempt bakers, or our scholars will have no bread to break their fast. And brewers who need to tend our ale. And dairymaids who—'

'We do not need you to tell us what to do,' snapped Heltisle, struggling to hide his dismay when he realised his solution would be impossible to implement.

'Yet the town *must* learn that we are not to be trifled with,' said de Wetherset thoughtfully. 'So we shall put on a good show at the butts tonight. Then they will see we are a force to be reckoned with, militarily speaking.'

'Not tonight, Chancellor,' Michael reminded him. 'It is the town's turn to practise.'

'I know that,' said de Wetherset. 'It is the point – they cannot witness our superior skills unless they see us in action, and the only way to do that is by joining them.'

'That would be a serious mistake,' warned Bartholomew. 'We cannot have armed scholars and armed townsfolk in the same place. It would be begging for trouble!'

'How dare you argue with the Chancellor!' snapped Heltisle, then glowered at Michael. 'Moreover, this would not be an issue if *you* had secured the University a good bargain at the butts. I shall summon Tulyet here later, with a view to renegotiating.'

'You can try,' said Michael, 'although I doubt he will respond to messages ordering him to report to you. Besides, the butts are town property, and he lets us use them out of the goodness of his heart. Be wary of unreasonable demands.'

'I know what I am doing,' retorted Heltisle tightly, not about to lose another battle to Michael's greater understanding of the situation. 'And I will prevail.'

'Incidentally, Heltisle has hired another half-dozen beadles for you, Brother,' said de Wetherset with a conciliatory smile. 'Do not worry about the cost, as we shall pay for them with the funds set aside for sick scholars.'

Bartholomew was shocked and angry in equal measure. 'And what happens to students who fall ill or suffer some debilitating accident? How will they survive until they are back on their feet again?'

'Their friends will have to bear the burden,' replied de Wetherset, and turned back to Michael before Bartholomew could remonstrate further. 'Increasing our little army will show the town that we are not to be bullied. You can teach them their trade, and Bartholomew can help you.'

'Me?' blurted Bartholomew. 'But I have classes to take.'

'If that were true, you would be lecturing now,' sneered Heltisle. 'But you are here, so they cannot be that important. Besides, you only teach medicine, which is a poor second to theology and law.'

'I am training physicians,' said Bartholomew indignantly.

'Who will be a lot more useful than theologians or lawyers when the plague returns.'

'They were not very useful last time,' retorted Heltisle. 'At least lawyers could make wills, while theologians knew how to pray. Besides, I do not believe the Death will return.'

'I do,' said de Wetherset, and crossed himself. 'So did Suttone, which is why he left us.'

'Is it?' asked Heltisle slyly. 'Or was there another reason?'

Bartholomew's eyes narrowed. 'What are you saying?'

Heltisle smirked. 'My lips are sealed. You must find another source of gossip.'

'Ignore him, Matt,' said Michael, once they were outside. 'It is not the first time Heltisle has hinted that Suttone resigned for unsavoury reasons of his own. But it is a lie – a shameful attempt to hurt someone who is not here to defend himself. He aims to besmirch Michaelhouse and unsettle us at the same time.'

'I wish de Wetherset had not appointed him,' said Bartholomew unhappily. 'The power seems to have driven him mad, and all he cares about is besting you. And to be frank, I am not sure de Wetherset is much better. How dare he raid the funds reserved for the sick and poor! It is an outrage! Moreover, it is sheer lunacy to alienate Dick.'

'It is, and de Wetherset knows it. However, he was elected on a promise to stand up to the town, so that is what he is doing. He will posture and strut to show the University gaining the upper hand, but once he has won a few battles, he will settle down.'

Bartholomew hoped he was right, and that irreparable harm was not done in the process. 'What will you do now?' he asked. 'Leave the murders to Aynton and concentrate on training these new beadles?'

Michael regarded him askance. 'Of course not! I shall

continue to do my duty as I see fit, and Meadowman can lick Heltisle's men into shape. We shall speak to Leger and Norbert with Dick, as planned, then make enquiries about the triumvirate, and find out what they were really doing on Wednesday.'

'You do not believe what they told you?'

'I do not believe anything without proof, and I am suspicious of their need to shut themselves up together. I suspect they were just plotting against me, but we should find out for certain.'

They reached the Great Bridge, where Tulyet was waiting, angry because Sergeant Orwel had reported that Leger and Norbert had taken themselves off hunting and were not expected back until the following day.

'It is our turn at the butts tonight, and they are supposed to supervise,' he said between gritted teeth. 'I suppose this is their revenge for me refusing to let them do it yesterday.'

'You think you have troubles,' sighed Michael, and told him about his confrontation with the Chancellor and his deputy.

Tulyet grimaced. 'Their antics are absurd, but I will not allow them to destroy all we have built. I shall find an excuse to avoid them until they no longer feel compelled to challenge me at every turn. Now, what about the knife that killed Paris? Do you have it?'

Michael handed it to him. 'Matt says there are similarities to the one that claimed the Girards' lives. What do you think?'

Tulyet examined it carefully. 'He is right. I would bet my life on the hilts being made in the same area, while the blades are crafted from steel of matching quality. However, I have never seen their like manufactured in this country.'

Bartholomew stared at him. 'Could they be French?'

Tulyet shrugged. 'It would be my guess, but I cannot

be certain. Perhaps Leger and Norbert will know. They were a-slaughtering there until recently.'

'Leger is not stupid enough to admit to anything incriminating,' predicted Bartholomew. 'Norbert, on the other hand . . .'

'Of course, my two knights are not the only ones with French connections,' said Tulyet. 'Do not forget that the *peregrini* hail from there.'

They agreed what each would do for the rest of the day: Tulyet to see what more could be learned about Wyse's killer, and Michael and Bartholomew to re-question everyone on their list of suspects. Tulyet would show the blade that had killed the Girards around, and Michael would do the same with the one found at the scene of Paris's murder.

'Good hunting,' said Tulyet, as he strode away.

The first thing Bartholomew and Michael did was return to St Mary the Great to ask if any clerks or secretaries could confirm the triumvirate's alibis. None could, but someone suggested they ask a Dominican friar who had been near de Wetherset's office at the time in question, repairing a wall painting. Bartholomew and Michael hurried to his priory at once, only to learn that the artist had been absorbed in his work and had not noticed the triumvirate's comings and goings at all.

As they passed back through the Barnwell Gate, they met a group of thirty or so nuns who had played truant from the *conloquium*, brazenly flouting Michael's order for them to stay at St Radegund's. The working sessions that day were aimed at sisters who struggled to balance the books, which was dull for those for whom arithmetic was not a problem. Ergo, a few of the more numerate delegates had organised a jaunt to the town – a foray to the market to shop for bargains, followed by a guided tour of the Round Church.

Leading the little cavalcade was Joan, wheeling Dusty around in a series of intricate manoeuvres that drew admiring glances from those who appreciated fine horsemanship. She looked more like a warrior than a nun, with her powerful legs clad in thick leather riding boots, and her monastic wimple covered by a functional hooded cloak. Her delight in the exercise was obvious from the glee on her long, horsey face.

Behind her was Magistra Katherine, clinging to the pommel of her saddle for dear life, although her mount was a steady beast with a dainty gait. Like its rider, it seemed to regard those around it as very inferior specimens, and it carried itself with a haughty dignity.

Abbess Isabel was astride her donkey, and Bartholomew nearly laughed when he saw that someone had dusted it with chalk to make it match its owner's snowy habit. She rode with her hands clasped in prayer, eyes lifted to the skies, and looked so saintly that people ran up to beg her blessing. Katherine smirked sardonically at the spectacle.

At the end of the procession was Sister Alice, although as her dubious accounting skills were what had led the Bishop to investigate her priory in the first place, she was someone who might have benefited from lessons in fiscal management. She was scowling at the other nuns, her expression so venomous that those who were asking for Abbess Isabel's prayers crossed themselves uneasily.

The ladies had evidently found much to please them at the market, as they had hired a cart to tote their purchases back to St Radegund's. It was driven by Isnard, while Orwel walked behind it to make sure nothing fell off. The boxes were perfectly stable, but the sergeant steadied them constantly, at the same time contriving to slip a hand inside them to assess whether they held anything worth stealing.

'The offer still stands, Brother,' called Joan. 'You may borrow Dusty here whenever you please. The roads make for excellent riding at the moment, as they are hard and dry.'

'It is tempting to gallop away, and let de Wetherset and Heltisle run the University for a week,' sighed Michael, 'by which time everyone will be frantic for me to return. But I know where my duty lies.'

'Are you still exploring the Spital murders?' asked Katherine, struggling to keep her seat as her proud horse decided it could do better than Dusty and began to prance.

'The Chancellor has asked Commissary Aynton to do it instead,' replied Michael, artfully avoiding the question.

'Then perhaps you will do us the honour of joining the *conloquium*,' said Katherine. 'Not today – you will learn nothing from watching Eve Wastenys struggle to teach the arithmetically challenged – but tomorrow, when we discuss the Chicken Debate. You will discover that female theologians have some very intelligent points to make.'

'Some of them do,' muttered Joan, and glared at Alice, who had baulked at exchanging pleasantries with the Senior Proctor and had ridden on ahead. 'But other nuns' tongues are so thick with poison that it is best not to listen to anything they say.'

Katherine hastened to elaborate. 'Last night, Sister Alice announced to the entire gathering that Lyminster reeks of horse manure and should be suppressed.'

'Her venom towards us springs purely from the fact that Magistra Katherine is the Bishop's sister,' said Joan in disgust. 'Even though Katherine had nothing to do with the decision to depose her. This malevolence is grossly and unjustly misplaced.'

'I will speak to her,' promised Michael. 'You are right to be vexed: her behaviour is hardly commensurate with a Benedictine. Incidentally, Goda has confirmed your alibi for the fire – she says she saw you in the stables.'

Joan smiled toothily, natural good humour bubbling

to the fore again. 'I am relieved to hear it! I should not like to be on anyone's list of suspects.'

Katherine grimaced. 'What about me? Or is it just God and His angels who can verify my whereabouts? Are you on speaking terms with them, Brother? If so, they will assure you that I was engrossed in Clippesby's treatise.'

'I tried to read that,' said Joan, 'but I only managed the first page. He should have had *horses* discussing these philosophies, as I could not imagine chickens doing it. Perhaps you will recommend that he uses something more sensible next time, Brother.'

'But he chose chickens for a reason,' explained Katherine earnestly, while Bartholomew smothered a smile that Joan could not envisage talking hens, but had no issue with talking nags. 'Namely to demonstrate that two small, simple creatures can grasp the essence of—'

'I have never been much of a philosopher,' interrupted Joan, making it sound more like a virtue than a failing. 'My steeds do not care about such matters, and if my nuns do . . . well, I can refer them to you.'

And with that, she began to show off Dusty's side-stepping skills, while Katherine fought to prevent her own mount from doing likewise. Between them, they hogged the whole road, although as they were nuns, no one swore or cursed at them. While they were occupied, Abbess Isabel abandoned her circle of admirers and came to talk.

'Have you caught the plagiarist's killer yet, Brother?' she asked, crossing herself with a thin, unnaturally white hand. 'I cannot get his dead face out of my mind, and I know his soul cries out for vengeance.'

'You will have to rely on Commissary Aynton to supply that,' said Michael, but then produced the dagger from his scrip. 'Here is the blade used to stab him. Is it familiar?'

The Abbess stared at it for a long time, but eventually shook her head. 'Will you be able to identify the killer from it?'

'Perhaps. It is distinctive, so someone may recognise the thing.'

'Then I shall pray for your success,' said Isabel. 'Right now, in fact. Goodbye.'

She jabbed her donkey into a trot, and was off without another word. A train of folk ran after her, still begging for her prayers, but she barely glanced at them, and seemed keen to put as much space between her and Michael as possible.

'That was peculiar,' remarked Bartholomew, watching her disappear. 'I wanted her to repeat exactly what she saw when she stumbled across Paris's body, but she was gone before I could ask.'

'She did leave rather abruptly,' acknowledged Michael, 'almost as if she had something to hide. Yet I do not see her stabbing anyone. You can see just by looking that she is holier than the rest of us.'

'And if you do not believe it, ask her,' said Bartholomew drily. 'However, I *can* see her killing Paris. She is a fanatic, and they tend to consider themselves bound by different rules than the rest of us.'

Michael scoffed at the notion of the pious nun being a murderer, but they were prevented from discussing it further by Joan, who had finished showing off with Dusty, and came to find out what they had said to disconcert Isabel. Michael showed her – and Katherine – the dagger. Joan leaned down to pluck it from the monk's hand, although Katherine fastidiously refused to touch it.

'It is an ugly thing,' Katherine declared with a shudder. 'No wonder Isabel fled! I do not like the look of it myself, and I am used to such things, as my brother collects them.'

'The Bishop collects murder weapons?' asked Bartholomew warily.

'When he can get them,' replied Katherine. 'And they—'

'Actually, this *is* familiar,' interrupted Joan, frowning. 'I am sure I have seen it before.'

'Seen it where?' demanded Michael urgently. 'Or, more importantly, carried by whom?'

Joan closed her eyes to struggle with her memory, but eventually opened them and shook her head apologetically. 'It will not come, Brother. And even if it did, you would have to treat it with caution, as one weapon looks much like another to me. However, I shall keep mulling it over. Perhaps something will pop into my head.'

'I doubt it will,' predicted Katherine. 'And you would do better to reflect on spiritual matters. Or, better yet, praying that the *conloquium* will be a success, even when women like Sister Alice stain it with spite.'

'Oh, I pray for that all the time,' said Joan, 'although it does not seem to be working.'

CHAPTER 8

Although Bartholomew and Michael spent the rest of the day quizzing and re-questioning witnesses, they learned nothing new. As evening approached, Michael went to watch Heltisle's new beadles embark on their first patrol, while Bartholomew dismayed his students by informing them that they were going to study – it was rare that classes continued after the six o'clock meal, and they had been looking forward to relaxing.

They grumbled even more when it became clear that they were going to work in the orchard, as it was chilly there once the sun had set. But Bartholomew's room was too small to hold everyone, and Theophilis had bagged the hall for Clippesby, who had agreed to present a preview of his next treatise. This would feature the philosophising hens again, and was a more in-depth look at some of the issues raised in his first exposition.

The Dominican's lecture sparked a vigorous debate, and Theophilis in particular asked a great many questions. It ended late, although not as late as Bartholomew, who lost track of time entirely and only stopped when his lamp ran out of oil, plunging the orchard into darkness. As a result, there were yawns and heavy eyes aplenty when the bell rang for church the following morning.

After their devotions, Michael led everyone back to the College for breakfast. With the resilience of youth, the students quickly rallied, and the hall soon rang with lively conversation, most of it about Clippesby's latest hypotheses. Michael summarised them for Bartholomew and his medics, then made some astute observations of his own. Theophilis jotted everything down on a scrap of parchment.

'For Clippesby to incorporate in his final draft,' he explained as he scribbled. 'What was that last point again, Brother?'

'There is no need to make notes for me, Theophilis,' said Clippesby politely. 'I can remember all these suggestions without them.'

'What, *all* of them?' asked William, astonished and disbelieving in equal measure.

'I have help.' Clippesby indicated the two hens that he had brought with him, which hunted among the rushes for scraps of dropped food. 'Ma and Gertrude act as amanuenses.'

'Can they write, then?' asked Theophilis with a smirk to let everyone know he was having fun at the Dominican's expense.

'Of course not!' said Clippesby, regarding him askance. 'They are chickens.'

The students laughed harder and longer than the rejoinder really warranted, which told Bartholomew that he was not the only one who disliked the Junior Proctor. Or perhaps it was just that they were protective of Clippesby, who had always been a great favourite of theirs. Thus snubbed, Theophilis fell silent, although he continued to record all that was said about Ma's new and intriguing definition of hermeneutic nominalism.

Bored with theology, Aungel began to whisper to Bartholomew. 'I hope Brother Michael will not win a bishopric or an abbacy very soon, because if he leaves the University, Theophilis will become Senior Proctor, and he will not be very good at it. He is too deceitful. For a start, we do not even know his real name.'

Bartholomew frowned. 'What do you mean?'

Aungel shrugged. 'No one calls their child *Theophilis*, so he must have chosen it for himself. "Loved by God" indeed! He should let us be the judge of that. Incidentally, Chancellor de Wetherset has been going around saying that Michael is no longer allowed to investigate murders. I hope he is wrong, or Paris will never have justice.'

'Have you heard any rumours about who might have killed Paris?'

'Oh, plenty,' replied Aungel, 'including one that claims de Wetherset, Heltisle and Aynton did it, because his plagiarism brought disgrace to the University. Which it did, of course. They do not do that sort of thing at Oxford.'

'We do not do that sort of thing here,' averred Bartholomew. 'Paris was an aberration.'

'A dead aberration,' said Aungel, 'although even he deserves vengeance.'

A short while later, Bartholomew and Michael discussed their plans for the day, which did not include training Heltisle's new beadles, as Michael's time with them the previous evening led him to declare them a lost cause.

'They are useless,' he spat. 'Not worthy to be called beadles, so I shall refer to them as "Heltisle's Horde" from now on. Worse, monitoring them took my attention away from my real duties, and there was nearly a skirmish because of it.'

'What happened?'

'It was the town's turn to practise at the butts, but some of our scholars tried to join in. Dick managed to keep the peace, but only just. But to business. We shall go to the castle first, as he sent word that Leger and Norbert are home and available for questioning. Perhaps they will recognise the daggers.'

'I wish someone would,' said Bartholomew. 'I thought Joan might, and I was disappointed when her memory failed her.'

'Perhaps she will remember today. I hope so, as there will be serious trouble unless we can present some answers soon. Last night, the town again accused the University of killing Wyse. I managed to avert trouble, but it was not easy.'

'How are the *peregrini*?' asked Bartholomew. 'Still safe?'

'For now, although they must leave tomorrow, because there will be a bloodbath if they are caught here. Of course, if it transpires that the Jacques murdered Paris, Bonet and the Girards, we shall have to hunt them down and bring them back.'

'But only the Jacques,' said Bartholomew. 'Not the old men, women and children.'

'So perhaps we had better speak to them again before they go,' Michael went on. 'And tonight, we shall both have to make an appearance at the butts.'

'Not you – as a monk, you are exempt from wasting your time there.'

'Exempt from training, but not from supporting the efforts of my colleagues,' sighed Michael. 'If I stay away, the triumvirate will accuse me of being unpatriotic.'

'Not the triumvirate,' growled Bartholomew. 'Heltisle. He is the poisonous one, aided and abetted by the insidious Theophilis.'

'Aided and abetted by Aynton,' countered Michael. 'De Wetherset must be sorry he appointed them, because they are losing him support hand over fist.'

'They are losing you support, too,' warned Bartholomew. 'Their antics reflect badly on all the University's officers, not just the Chancellor.'

'Yes,' acknowledged Michael. 'But to win a war, you must make some sacrifices, so I shall let them continue for now. Do not look so worried! I know what I am doing.'

Bartholomew hoped he was right, and that overconfidence would not see the downfall of a man who really did have the University's best interests at heart.

The castle lay to the north of the town. It had started life as a simple motte and bailey, but had since grown into a formidable fortress. It stood atop Cambridge's only hill, and was enclosed by towering curtain walls. Its function was usually more administrative than military, but the King's call to arms had resulted in a flurry of repairs and improvements. The chains on the portcullis had been replaced, unstable battlements had been mended, and the dry moat was filled with sharpened spikes.

'Do you really think the French will raid this far inland, Dick?' asked Bartholomew.

Tulyet shrugged. 'We are not difficult to reach from the sea, and it is better to be safe than sorry. However, an invasion worries me a lot less than the presence of Jacques in the Spital. True, our local hotheads are more likely to kill them than listen to their seditious ideas, but they make me uneasy, even so.'

Michael was more concerned with his own troubles. 'I have been ordered to leave the Spital murders to Aynton.'

Tulyet eyed him keenly. 'Because he will never find answers, thus leaving the killer to go free? If de Wetherset and Heltisle are the guilty parties, that would suit them very nicely.'

Michael's expression was wry. 'I did wonder if one of them had his own reasons for wanting an unskilled investigator on the case.'

'I sincerely hope this is an order you intend to flout,' said Tulyet.

Michael smiled. 'Naturally, although I shall need some help from you. I do not want Aynton knowing about our findings, lest he impedes the course of justice, either by design or accident. When he comes to you for information, would you mind misdirecting him?'

'With pleasure. Now, did anyone recognise the dagger you showed around yesterday?'

'Prioress Joan thought it was familiar,' replied Michael. 'She could not recall why, but I suspect she has seen it – or one similar – on someone's belt.'

'And where has she been staying?' pounced Tulyet. 'In the Spital, with the Jacques!'

'She has promised to reflect on the matter,' said Michael, 'so perhaps she will surprise us and produce a name.'

'Leave Paris's blade with me when you go,' instructed Tulyet. 'I will show it and the one from the Girards to the garrison. However, my money is on the culprit being at the Spital. I went there again at dawn, just to keep the Tangmers and their guests on their toes.'

'Did you learn anything new?' asked Michael.

Tulyet nodded. 'The Jacques intended to slip away this morning, leaving the rest of the *peregrini* to fend for themselves, but Delacroix fell ill during the night. He accuses Father Julien of poisoning him, which is possible, as the priest will not want his flock to be without men who can protect them.'

'And is Delacroix poisoned?' asked Bartholomew. 'Or just unwell?'

'He cannot stray more than two steps from the latrines, so who knows? Are you ready for Leger and Norbert? We should tackle them before they decide to go hunting again.'

The two knights were in the hall, the vast room that served as a refectory for Tulyet's officers, staff and troops. They had taken seats near the hearth, where a fire blazed, even though the day was warm. They lounged comfortably, boots off, armour loosened, and weapons arranged on the bench next to them. Neither acknowledged Tulyet as he approached, which was a deliberate affront to his authority.

'I have questions for you,' said Tulyet, sweeping the arsenal on to the floor with one swipe of his hand before sitting down and indicating that Bartholomew and Michael were to perch next to him.

The faces of both knights darkened in anger as their precious swords and daggers clattered on the flagstones. Bartholomew hoped Tulyet knew what he was doing, feeling it was rash to antagonise such brutes. It was the first time he had studied them closely, and he could not help but notice the array of scars, thickened ears and callused hands, especially on Norbert. All were signs of lives spent fighting.

'What questions?' snarled Leger, retrieving his sword and inspecting it for damage.

'We can begin with what you discussed with the Girard men the morning they were murdered,' said Michael. 'Then you can tell us why you did not bother to mention it to us.'

The pair exchanged glances. Leger's expression was calculating, but there was a flash of panic in Norbert's eyes.

'Who told you—' the bigger knight began belligerently.

'That does not matter,' interrupted Tulyet. 'The point is that you were seen, and I demand an explanation.'

'You *demand*?' echoed Leger incredulously. 'We are representatives of His Majesty, personally appointed by him to oversee Cambridge's preparations for war.'

'And I am his Sheriff,' retorted Tulyet. 'So I outrank you. Now, answer our questions or I shall send you back to the King in disgrace.'

Norbert bristled, but Leger was intelligent enough to know that Tulyet meant it, and began to answer the question, albeit sullenly. 'We did not know they were Spital lunatics at the time. We just saw them walking along, and we could tell, just by looking, that they were warriors, so we asked why they had not been to the butts.'

'How did they respond?'

'We could barely understand them,' shrugged Leger. 'One was mute, while the other had a toothache that mangled his words. Our English was not equal to the conversation, so we forced them to use French, which was better, but only marginally.'

It was impossible to tell if the two knights had fallen for the Jacques' ruse, although Bartholomew wondered why the Girards had gone out in the first place, as it was a reckless thing to have done.

'Did they tell you they were from the Spital?' he asked.

'No, they said they were fletchers, and thus exempt from the call to arms,' growled Norbert. 'It is only now that we learn they were lunatics – and lying lunatics into the bargain.'

'We are going to the Spital this afternoon, to assess the rest of them,' added Leger. 'If they seem as rational as the pair we met, I want them all at the butts.'

'I would not recommend putting weapons in the hands of madmen,' said Bartholomew hastily. 'They might run amok and turn on you. And that is my professional medical opinion.'

It was pure bluster, but the knights agreed to leave the Spital men in peace anyway.

'Now, let us discuss the fire,' said Tulyet. 'Where were you when it began?'

Norbert regarded him coolly. 'I hope you are not accusing us of setting it.'

'Just answer the question,' barked Tulyet.

Norbert came to his feet fast. Tulyet did not flinch, even though the other man towered over him. Prudently, Leger gestured that his friend was to sit back down.

'We cannot recall, Sheriff,' he said with a false smile. 'Our remit is to train troops, so we spend a lot of time trawling taverns for likely recruits. We were in the King's Head at one point on Wednesday morning, but I cannot tell you precisely when.'

'The King's Head is near the Spital,' remarked Bartholomew.

Leger ignored him and continued to address Tulyet.

185

'So you will just have to take our word that we were else-where at the salient time. That should not present too great a difficulty, given that we are fellow knights.'

'Why should he believe you?' asked Michael acidly. 'You failed to report meeting two of the victims not long before their murders, which hardly presents you in an honest light.'

'It slipped our minds,' shrugged Leger. 'It was a discussion about nothing, so why should we remember? Or do you think we should tell the Sheriff every time we exchange words with men of fighting age? If we did, none of us would get any work done.'

He regarded the monk with sly defiance, and it was clear that pressing the matter further would be a waste of time, so Tulyet showed them the weapons that had killed Paris and the Girards. Leger gave them no more than a passing glance, but Norbert took them and studied them carefully.

'Such fine craftsmanship,' he breathed appreciatively. 'Where did you find them?'

'One was planted in the back of an elderly priest,' replied Michael pointedly. 'The other was used to murder defenceless lunatics.'

Norbert handed them back to Tulyet. 'Then the killer is a fool for leaving them behind. And if he is a fool, even you should be able to catch him.'

There was no more to be said, so Bartholomew, Michael and Tulyet took their leave.

'Do you believe they "forgot" their encounter with the Girards?' asked the physician when they were out in the bailey again. 'Because I do not. Moreover, they cannot prove where they were, and I can certainly see them dispatching a family with ruthless efficiency.'

'So can I,' replied Michael. 'Leger's answers were too glib, and I sense there was more to the encounter than they were willing to confess.'

'I agree,' said Tulyet, 'although I am not sure it involves murder. They are not poisoners – they would have stabbed everyone, including the children.'

'So are they on your list of suspects or not?'

'They are,' said Tulyet. 'Just not right at the top. But I shall show both weapons to the garrison, and if Leger and Norbert ever owned them, I will find out – soldiers notice such things. And if that yields no answers, I shall flash them around the town. Someone will recognise them, I am sure of it.'

But Bartholomew had a bad feeling the Sheriff's confidence was misplaced.

Bartholomew and Michael headed for St Radegund's. To reach the convent, they had to pass through the Barnwell Gate, which was manned that day by some new and vigilant sentries, who had been given the choice of a week's military service or the equivalent time spent in gaol as punishment for brawling with scholars. Among them was Verious the ditcher. All were under the command of the sullen Sergeant Orwel and his helpmeet Pierre Sauvage. Orwel sported a new hat that was black and rather feminine, leading Bartholomew to suppose he had stolen it from the nuns the previous day.

'Stop,' Orwel ordered roughly, whisking the headpiece out of sight when he saw the physician staring at it. 'The Barnwell Gate is closed today.'

'Is it?' asked Michael coolly. 'Then why has that cart just driven through?'

'You cannot pass, Brother,' said Verious apologetically. 'Sir Leger thinks there are French spies in the area, and we are under orders to keep them out.'

'We are not French spies,' said Michael. 'Moreover, we want to leave, not come in.'

Verious became flustered, unwilling to annoy the man who provided his choir with free victuals *or* the physician who never charged him for medicine when he was ill. He turned to the others for help. 'Brother Michael makes a good point. He is—'

'*I* am in charge here,' snapped Orwel. 'And I say the gate is closed. Sir Leger told me that *anyone* might be a French spy, even folk we know.'

'For heaven's sake!' snapped Michael irritably. 'I am the University's Senior Proctor!'

'I do not care what you call yourself,' growled Orwel. 'Now bugger off.'

There was a murmur of consternation, as the others saw membership of the choir and complimentary medical care flash before their eyes. They backed away, aiming to put some distance between themselves and the gruff sergeant, but Orwel barked at them to stand fast.

'But Brother Michael and Doctor Bartholomew cannot be spies,' protested Verious, distraught. 'If they were, they would be slinking about on tiptoe.'

Bartholomew struggled not to laugh at this piece of logic.

'Sir Leger said to stop all scholars from leaving town,' Orwel persisted, although only after he had given Verious's remark serious consideration. 'Or have you forgotten that one of them murdered poor Wyse?'

'Of course not,' snapped Verious. 'But these two did not do it. The culprit will be some foreigner – a man from King's Hall or Bene't College, which are full of aliens.'

'Sir Leger gave us our orders,' stated Orwel stubbornly. 'So we must follow them.'

'Sir Leger this, Sir Leger that,' mocked Michael. 'Can no one here think for himself?'

'Sir Leger recommended that we stay away from doing that, so he can do it for us,' replied Verious, quite seriously. 'We are all relieved, as thinking for ourselves has led to a lot of trouble in the past.'

This time, Bartholomew did laugh, although Michael failed to see the funny side.

'Stand aside before you make me angry,' he snapped. 'Matt and I need to visit the nuns. And do not smirk like that, Verious. Our intentions are perfectly honourable.'

'Of course they are,' said Verious, and winked.

'When the King calls us to arms, I shall be first over the Channel,' confided Sauvage, somewhat out of the blue. 'Then I shall avenge Winchelsea by slaughtering entire villages.'

'"Entire villages" were not responsible for Winchelsea,' argued Michael impatiently. 'That was a small faction of the Dauphin's—'

'Every Frenchman applauds what was done,' interrupted Orwel fiercely. 'So they all deserve to die. Now are you two going to piss off, or must we arrest you?'

'Arrest Brother Michael and Doctor Bartholomew?' cried Sauvage, horrified. 'You cannot do that! They will tell the Sheriff and he will be furious with us – they are his friends.'

'Besides, you will die if you try to take Doctor Bartholomew somewhere he does not want to go,' added Verious. 'He fought at Poitiers, where Cynric said he dispatched more of the enemy than you can shake a stick at. And look at my nose. You see where it is broken? Well, he did that. I tell you, he is *lethal*!'

Verious and Bartholomew had once come to blows, although it had been more luck than skill that had seen the physician emerge the victor. He was about to say so, disliking the notion that he should own such a deadly reputation, when Orwel stepped aside.

'I did not realise you were a veteran of Poitiers,' he said obsequiously. 'You may pass.'

'Will I be allowed back in again?' asked Bartholomew warily.

Orwel nodded. 'And if this lot give you any trouble,

send for me. I was at Poitiers, too, so we are comrades-in-arms. Those always stick together, as you know.'

'He does know,' said Michael, sailing past. 'But he does not countenance insolence or stupidity, so you might want to watch yourself in future.'

St Radegund's Priory was a sizeable foundation, far larger than was necessary for the dozen or so nuns who lived there. However, even the spacious refectory, massive dormitory and substantial guest quarters were not large enough to accommodate all the *conloquium* delegates, especially now that the twenty from the Spital and the ten from the Gilbertine Priory had joined them. Most bore the discomfort with stoic good humour, although a few complained. Needless to say, Sister Alice was among the latter.

'I had to reprimand her,' said Prioress Joan, who was basking in the adulation of her colleagues for a thought-provoking presentation entitled *Latrine Waste and Management*. 'Her moaning was beginning to cause friction.'

She looked larger and more horse-like than ever that day, towering over her sisters like a giant, but there was a rosy glow about her, and she radiated vitality and robust good health.

'Joan was the only one brave enough to do it,' put in Magistra Katherine, the inevitable smirk playing around her lips. 'Everyone else is afraid of annoying Alice, lest the woman turns her malevolent attentions on them.'

'No one wants to suffer what I have endured at her hands since we arrived,' elaborated Abbess Isabel, whose white habit positively glowed among all the black ones. 'But Prioress Joan took the bull by the horns, and Alice has been quiet ever since.'

'Well, something had to be done,' shrugged Joan, clearly pleased by the praise. 'I told her to bathe, too, because if I have to watch her claw at herself like a horse with fleas for one more day . . .'

Even the thought of it made some nuns begin scratching, and Bartholomew watched in amusement as Michael did likewise. Others joined in, until there were upwards of twenty Benedictines busily plying their nails. Then the monk asked if there was anything he could do to make their stay more pleasant, and the scratching stopped as minds turned to less itchy matters.

'I will survive a few cramped nights, but poor Dusty may not,' declared Joan, fixing Michael with a reproachful eye. 'You said he could have the old bakery, but the moment I finished cleaning it out, the nuns from Cheshunt dashed in, claiming they would rather share with him than with Alice. But he prefers to sleep alone, so shall I oust them or will you?'

'Neither,' said the monk, thinking fast. 'I will take him to Michaelhouse. Cynric knows horses, so he will be well looked after there.'

Joan beamed and clapped him on the shoulder. 'I was right about you, Brother! You are a *good* man. May I visit him whenever I please?'

Michael hesitated, uneasy with women wandering unsupervised in his domain. Then he glanced at Joan, and decided that it would be a deranged scholar indeed who considered her to be the lady of his dreams. He nodded, then changed the subject by asking about the dagger that had killed Paris, which she had half-recognised earlier.

'I *know* it is familiar,' she said with a grimace. 'But the answer continues to elude me, even though I have been wracking my brain ever since. But I shall not give up. It will come to me eventually.'

'Then let us hope it is sooner rather than later,' said Michael, disappointed, and moved to another matter. 'How is the *conloquium* going?'

'Not well,' sighed Abbess Isabel, although Bartholomew

was sure that every other nun had been about to say the opposite. 'We have made no meaningful policy decisions, despite the fact that I have been praying for some ever since I arrived. This is unusual, as God usually does exactly what I want.'

'Oh, come, Isabel,' chided Joan. 'We have decided a great deal. For example, none of us will ever store onions in a damp place again, having heard Abbess Sibyl of Romsey wax lyrical on the subject.'

'So there you are,' drawled Katherine. 'A decision that will impact every nun in our Order, made by us, here at St Radegund's.'

Joan was oblivious to sarcasm. 'And it is an important one! I use an onion poultice on Dusty's hoofs, so it is imperative to ensure a year-round supply.' She beamed. 'And the *conloquium* has certainly made *me* count my blessings. I have listened to other prioresses list the problems they suffer with their flock, and mine are angels by comparison.'

Isabel sniffed. 'Anyone would be an angel compared to Alice. She was on the verge of turning Ickleton into a brothel before I came along. Your brother should have done more than depose her, Magistra Katherine – he should have ordered her defrocked.'

'Perhaps he did not want to be denounced as a hypocrite,' suggested Joan with a shrug of her mighty shoulders. 'We all know *he* enjoys a romp with—'

'He believes in second chances,' interrupted Katherine swiftly, and changed the subject. 'The *conloquium* has been worthwhile for me, because it brought Clippesby's thesis to my attention. Unfortunately, I still have not had the pleasure of meeting him.'

'No,' said Michael ambiguously. 'You have not.'

'I suppose the conference has been worthwhile,' conceded Isabel grudgingly. 'Magistra Katherine explained the nominalism–realism debate in a way we all understood. Then

Sister Florence of York showed us how to get an additional habit out of an ell of cloth, while Alice taught us something called "creative accounting".'

'I would not recommend you follow *that* advice,' said Katherine drily. 'Her intention was to land you all in deep water with your bishops.'

Isabel shrugged off her bemusement and turned to Michael. 'What of the murders? I have been praying for the victims' souls, even though the ones at the Spital were insane and thus outside God's grace.'

'The insane are not outside God's grace,' objected Bartholomew, startled. 'If anything, they are further *inside* it, as they cannot be held responsible for their sins. Unlike the rest of us.'

'I would not know,' retorted Isabel loftily. 'I do not have any sins.'

'Right,' said Michael, after a short, startled silence. 'We need to speak to Alice. Will someone fetch her? While we wait, I shall ensure your victuals are up to scratch. I am obliged to monitor *all* aspects of this *conloquium*, including the quality of the food.'

It was some time before Michael declared himself satisfied that the delegates were being properly fed. Then he and Bartholomew went to the church, where Alice had been ordered to sit until he was ready to see her.

The church was the convent's crowning glory, a large, peaceful place with a stout tower. Parts of it had suffered from the lack of funds that affected many monastic foundations, so there were patches of damp on the walls, while some of the stained glass had dropped out of its frames. It smelled of mould, old wood and the wildflowers that someone had placed on every available surface.

Most nuns waiting in a holy place would have used the time for quiet prayer, but such a rash thought had not crossed Alice's mind. She paced angrily, muttering under

193

her breath about the indignities she was forced to endure. Abbess Isabel and Magistra Katherine were the names most frequently spat out, although some venom was reserved for the nuns who had opted to share their sleeping quarters with a horse rather than her. She scratched so vigorously as she cursed that Bartholomew asked if she needed the services of a physician.

'All I need is to know why I was dragged here,' she snarled. 'I was in a session on medicine, learning lots of useful things. You hauled me out, so I missed most of it.'

'Medicine?' asked Bartholomew with interest.

'Strong ones, used to cure serious ailments. I was enjoying myself.'

'Perhaps you were,' said Michael. 'But only qualified *medici* should administer such potions, and we do not want any more suspicious deaths to explore.'

'*I* am not a killer,' declared Alice indignantly. 'And if you are here to accuse me of stealing Joan's comb again, I shall complain to the Bishop about being hounded for an incident that I have already explained away.'

'We came to ask if you have remembered anything new since we last spoke,' said Michael. 'You will appreciate that we are eager to catch the rogue who murdered five Spital people, particularly as I suspect that he also stabbed a spicer and an elderly priest.'

'You mean an elderly *plagiarist*,' mused Alice. 'Perhaps you should look to your University for a suspect, Brother, rather than accusing innocent nuns.'

'I accuse no one,' said Michael. 'All I want from you is information. You were in the Spital when the killer struck, and I thought you might have noticed something to help us.'

Alice's face was full of spite. 'I can only repeat what I told you before – that I saw Katherine scurry off alone. She doubtless told you she was reading, but you cannot believe her. She is kin to the most evil, corrupt, dishonest man who ever lived – the Bishop of Ely!'

'Of course,' said Michael flatly. 'Anything else?'

Alice gave the matter serious consideration, and for a while no one spoke. A bell rang to announce the end of one set of lectures, followed by a genteel rumble of voices as the nuns discussed which talk they wanted to attend next. Then the bell chimed to mark the beginning of the next session, after which there was silence. A dog barked in the distance, and an irritable whinny suggested Dusty was eager for attention.

'I can tell you that it was easy to enter the Spital,' said Alice eventually. 'The Tangmers will claim they guard the gate assiduously, but I walked in unchallenged several times. Of course, I imagine they are more careful now.'

'I hope so,' muttered Bartholomew.

'So the killer may have come from outside?' asked Michael.

'Well, the staff *were* more interested in monitoring the billeted nuns than guarding their madmen, so it is possible. The Tangmers are an odd horde, and their chapel is an accident waiting to happen, as it is stupid to store firewood in a place where oils are heated with naked flames. Perhaps that is what happened to the shed: Amphelisa was experimenting in it.'

'Why would she do that when she has a well-equipped workshop?'

'Because the workshop is in the chapel,' explained Alice. 'And thus out of bounds during services. Perhaps she could not wait until Mass was finished, so found somewhere else to work in the interim – in which case, she did the killer a favour by incinerating his victims.'

Bartholomew pondered the suggestion. Perhaps Amphelisa did find it frustrating to be ousted every time the chapel was needed, especially if Julien was the kind

195

of priest who kept all his sacred offices. It was entirely possible that she had opted to use the shed, which everyone said was tinder-dry and filled with wood. No one had seen her near it, but the staff were her kin by marriage, so unlikely to betray her.

Michael continued to press Alice for more information, but when it became clear that she had said as much as she was going to, they took their leave.

'I do not know what to think about this comb Alice is supposed to have stolen,' said Michael, when he and Bartholomew were heading back to the town. He was astride Dusty and the physician walked at his side, careful to stay well away from an animal that he sensed was keen to bite, kick or butt him. 'Is she guilty? Or is she falsely accused, as she claims?'

'Does it matter?' asked Bartholomew. 'It hardly compares to murder, and I do not know why we are even talking about it.'

'Because it is the key to the characters of some of our suspects and witnesses,' replied Michael. 'Whether they are thieves, liars or vindictive manipulators.'

'Alice stole it,' said Bartholomew impatiently. 'Unless you believe she really was riffling through someone else's bags in search of nose-cloths. There is something so distasteful about her that she is currently at the top of my list of suspects.'

'Above Theophilis?' asked Michael. 'The Devil incarnate, according to you?'

'Perhaps not above him,' acknowledged Bartholomew. 'He is deceitful, as illustrated by the fact that he spied on the triumvirate for you – betraying men who trust him.'

'But he did not betray them,' Michael pointed out. 'Not when they seem to know exactly what he was doing. And the last time we discussed this, you said he had failed me deliberately, because he was actually on their side. You cannot have it both ways.'

'Then what about the way he behaves towards Clippesby? Pretending to befriend him, but then mocking him behind his back?'

'That is distasteful, but hardly evidence of a criminal mind. But here is where you and I part company. I shall spend the rest of the day at the Spital and St Mary the Great, trying to tease more information from everyone we have already interviewed.'

'You do not want me with you?' asked Bartholomew, brightening.

'I do, but a message arrived when we were with the nuns. You are needed by patients, one of whom is Commissary Aynton. Go to him, and while you ply your healing hands, see if you can find out exactly what *he* was doing on the morning of the fire.'

'He has already told us – he was either with de Wetherset and Heltisle in St Mary the Great, or practising his lecture on the sheep.'

'Then press him to elaborate, and see if you can catch him in an inconsistency.'

CHAPTER 9

Cynric was waiting for Bartholomew by the Barnwell Gate, because the town was growing increasingly restive and he was protective of the physician. Together they walked past the butts, where one or two archers were already honing their skills, taking advantage of the fact that most folk would arrive later, once the day's work was done.

'There will be trouble tonight, boy,' predicted Cynric. 'It is the town's turn to practise, but de Wetherset plans to turn up as well. He wants everyone to think he is brave for not buying another proxy, although the truth is that there is no one left for him to hire.'

'Warn Michael and Theophilis,' instructed Bartholomew. 'One of them *must* convince him to wait until tomorrow before flaunting his courage.'

'I am not speaking to Theophilis,' said Cynric, pursing his lips. 'I cannot abide him. He spent all morning humouring Clippesby by the henhouse, then told Father William that Clippesby is a lunatic who should be locked away.'

'What do you mean by "humouring" him?'

'Making a show of asking the chickens their opinions, then pretending to appreciate their replies. I tried to draw Clippesby away, but Theophilis sent me to de Wetherset with a letter, which he said was urgent. But it was not.'

'How do you know?'

'Because I read it,' replied Cynric unrepentantly. 'All it said was that Brother Michael had gone to St Radegund's to talk to the nuns. It was a ruse to get me out of the way.'

Bartholomew had taught Cynric to read, although he

had since wondered if it had been a wise thing to do. He pondered the question afresh on hearing that the book-bearer had invaded the Chancellor's private correspondence, and yet it was interesting to learn that Theophilis reported Michael's movements to de Wetherset. It confirmed his suspicion that the Junior Proctor was not to be trusted.

'You can tell Michael that as well,' he said. 'Although you should make sure Theophilis never finds out what you did.'

Cynric turned to what he considered a much more interesting subject. 'Margery says the Devil is already very comfortably settled in the Spital.'

'Stay away from that place,' warned Bartholomew, afraid Cynric would go to see the sight for himself – he did not want his militant book-bearer to encounter like-minded Jacques.

'I shall,' promised Cynric fervently. 'I have no desire to meet the Lord of Darkness, although Margery tells me that he is not as bad as everyone thinks. But even before Satan moved in, the Spital had a sinister aura. I want nothing to do with it.'

'Good,' said Bartholomew. 'But advise Margery to keep her heretical opinions to herself. The University's priests will not turn a blind eye to those sorts of remarks for ever, and we shall have a riot for certain if they execute a popular witch.'

Bartholomew found Aynton at his home in Tyled Hostel. The Commissary was in bed, one arm resting on a pile of cushions. His face was white with pain.

'It happened at the Spital this morning,' he explained tearfully, 'and if I had a suspicious mind, I might say it was deliberate.'

'What was deliberate?' asked Bartholomew, sitting next to him and beginning to examine the afflicted limb.

'I assume you know that de Wetherset wants me to solve the Spital murders,' whispered Aynton. 'Well, I was interrogating Warden Tangmer, when his cousin – that great brute Eudo – pushed me head over heels. My wrist hurts abominably, but worse, look at my boots! He has ruined them completely!'

Bartholomew glanced at them. They were calf-height, flimsy and so garishly ugly that he thought the scuffs caused by the fall had improved rather than disfigured them.

'Pity,' he said, aware that the Commissary was expecting sympathy. 'But I am sure a good cobbler can fix them.'

'He says the marks are too deep,' sniffed Aynton. 'I shall continue to wear them, as they cost a fortune, but they will never be right again. And my arm is broken into the bargain!'

'Sprained,' corrected Bartholomew, applying a poultice to reduce the swelling. 'Eudo must have given you quite a shove to make you fall over.'

'The man does not know his own strength. I suspect he did it because I was berating Tangmer for allowing his lunatics to play with swords. Some were engaged in a mock fight when I arrived, you see, which is hardly an activity to soothe tormented minds.'

'No,' agreed Bartholomew, supposing the Jacques had been practising the skills they might need to defend themselves, and that their imminent departure meant they were less concerned about being seen by visitors.

'Between you and me, there is something odd about that Spital,' Aynton went on. 'I think it harbours nasty secrets.'

Bartholomew kept his eyes on the poultice lest Aynton should read the truth in them. 'Well, its patients *are* insane, so what do you expect? I wish I could help them, but ailments of the mind have always been a mystery to me.'

The last part was true, at least.

'I would have thought you had enormous experience

with lunatics,' said Aynton caustically. 'Given that most of our colleagues are around the bend.'

Bartholomew laughed. 'A few, perhaps.'

'It is more than a few,' averred Aynton. 'It would take until midnight to recite a list of all those who are as mad as bats. Shall I start with Michaelhouse? Clippesby, Father William, Theophilis and Michael. And you, given your peculiar theories about hand-washing. Then, in King's Hall, there is—'

'Michael is not mad,' objected Bartholomew. 'Nor is Theophilis.'

He did not bother defending Clippesby for obvious reasons, while anyone who had met William would know that he was barely rational. And as for himself, he did not care what people thought about his devotion to hygiene, because the results spoke for themselves – he lost far fewer patients than other *medici*, and if the price was being considered insane, then so be it.

'Theophilis spends far too much time with Clippesby,' said Aynton disapprovingly. 'They are always together, talking and whispering. He should be careful – lunacy is contagious, you know.'

Bartholomew declined to take issue with such a ridiculous assertion. 'And Michael? What has he done to win a place on your list?'

Aynton lowered his voice. 'He does not like me. I cannot imagine why, as I have given him no cause for animosity. Indeed, I have done my utmost to be nice to him, but he rejects my overtures of friendship.'

'So anyone who does not like you is mad?'

'It demonstrates a warped mind, which means he should not hold a position of such power in the University. De Wetherset is right to clip Michael's wings.'

Bartholomew regarded him in surprise, aware that Aynton's eyes had lost their customary dreaminess, and were hard and cold. 'I hardly think—'

'Michael's influence is waning, and unless he wants to be ousted completely, he must learn to accept it. Yes, he has made the University strong, but it is inappropriate for the Senior Proctor to wield more power than the Chancellor, and it is time to put an end to it.'

Bartholomew felt treacherous even listening to such sentiments, and turned his attention back to medicine, eager to end the discussion.

'Does this hurt when I bend it?'

'*Ow!* Be gentle, Matthew! I am not one of your dumb beggars, impervious to pain.'

Bartholomew opened his mouth to retort that his paupers most certainly did feel pain, but decided it was another topic on which he and Aynton were unlikely to agree. He remembered what Michael had asked him to do.

'You say you were practising a lecture on the morning of the Spital fire,' he began.

'I was,' replied Aynton curtly. 'But I have said all I am going to on the subject, so do not press me again. If you do, I shall lodge a complaint for harassment.'

Bartholomew took his leave, disturbed to have witnessed a side of the amiable academic that he had not known existed. Perhaps Michael was right to be wary of him.

But once outside, breathing air that was full of the clean scents of spring – new grass, wild flowers and sun-warmed earth – he wondered if he had overreacted. After all, what Aynton said was true: Michael did wield a disproportionate amount of power. Moreover, lots of patients were snappish when they were in pain, so why should Aynton be any different? Bartholomew pushed the matter from his mind and went to his next customer.

He was just passing King's Hall when he spotted two figures, one abnormally large, the other abnormally small. Eudo had tried to disguise himself by pulling a hood over

202

his head, although his great size made him distinctive and several people hailed him by name. By contrast, his minuscule wife was clearly delighted with the way she looked and made no effort at all to conceal her identity. She wore a light summer cloak pinned with a jewelled brooch, and the gold hints in her hair were accentuated by a pretty fillet.

'We wanted to stay at home and protect the . . . patients,' blurted Eudo when Bartholomew stopped to exchange pleasantries. 'But Hélène is having nightmares, so Amphelisa sent us to buy ingredients for a sleeping potion.'

He indicated the basket he carried. Bartholomew glanced in it once, then looked again.

'Mandrake, poppy juice, henbane,' he breathed, alarmed. 'These are powerful herbs – too powerful for a child. It is not—'

'Amphelisa knows what she is doing,' interrupted Goda shortly. 'And if we want your opinion, we will ask for it.'

'Has she made sleeping potions for Hélène before?' asked Bartholomew. 'One strong enough to make her drowse through a fire, perhaps?'

Rage ignited in Eudo's eyes. He moved fast, grabbing Bartholomew by the front of his tabard and shoving him against a wall. Bartholomew tried to struggle free, but it was hopeless – Eudo's fingers were like bands of iron.

'Eudo, stop!' hissed Goda, glancing around to make sure no one was watching. 'You will make him think Amphelisa *did* poison the children. But she did not, so she does not need you to defend her. Let him go.'

Bartholomew was surprised when Eudo did as he was told.

'Is this what happened to Commissary Aynton?' he asked curtly, brushing himself down. 'He put questions that frightened you, so you pushed him? I know it was no accident.'

203

'Oh, yes, it was,' countered Goda fiercely. 'Aynton *claimed* that some of our patients were playing with swords. We told him he was mistaken, so he began prancing around to demonstrate what he thought he had seen. He bounced into Eudo and lost his balance.'

'Which would never have happened if he had not been jigging about like an ape,' growled Eudo. 'It was his own fault.'

Bartholomew suspected the truth lay somewhere in between – that Eudo had shoved Aynton in an effort to shut him up, but that Aynton had been off balance, so had taken an unintended tumble. Even so, it was unacceptable behaviour on Eudo's part, and Bartholomew dreaded to imagine what he might do without Goda to keep him in line.

'Does Amphelisa distil oils anywhere other than the chapel?' he asked, switching to another line of enquiry.

'That is none of your—' began Eudo in a snarl, although he stopped when Goda raised a tiny hand. There were two silver rings on her fingers that Bartholomew was sure had not been there the last time he had seen her.

'We could tell you,' she said sweetly. 'But our tongues will loosen far more readily if you have a coin to spare.'

Bartholomew raised his eyebrows. 'You want to be paid for helping me catch the person who murdered five people in your home?'

Goda shrugged. 'Why not? You earn three pennies for every corpse you assess, so why should you be the only one to turn a profit from death?'

Bartholomew had never considered himself as one who 'turned a profit from death' before, and the notion made him feel faintly grubby. He floundered around for a response, but Eudo spoke first.

'Your question is stupid! Of course Amphelisa does not work anywhere else. How can she, when all her distilling equipment is in the chapel? It cannot be toted back and forth on a whim, you know. Or do you imagine she produces oils out of thin air?'

Goda glared at him for providing information that could have been sold, but then her attention was caught by someone who was approaching from the left.

'Smile, husband,' she said between clenched teeth. 'Here comes Isnard the bargeman, and if he thinks we are squabbling with his favourite *medicus* . . .'

Eudo's smile was more of a grimace, but it satisfied Isnard, who proceeded to regale them with the latest gossip.

'You need not worry about your Spital being haunted any longer,' he began importantly. 'Because Margery Starre just told me she was mistaken about it standing on the site of an ancient pagan temple.'

Eudo was alarmed. 'But I have seen ghosts with my own—'

'Tricks,' interrupted Isnard with authority. 'Margery went to visit Satan last night, as she and him are on friendly terms, but he was nowhere to be found. What she *did* find, however, was a piece of fine gauze on twine, which could be jerked to make an illusion.'

'Oh,' said Eudo uncomfortably. 'But—'

'Moreover, Margery was *paid* to tell us that the Devil was taking up residence there,' Isnard went on, 'which she did, because she thought it was Satan himself begging the favour.'

Bartholomew frowned. 'Why would she think that?'

'Because she was visited by someone huge in a black cloak with horns poking from under his hood. Naturally, she made assumptions. But when she went to see him at the Spital and found evidence of trickery . . . well, she realised the whole thing was a hoax.'

Bartholomew was secretly gratified to learn that the self-important witch had been so easily duped. Perhaps it would shake her followers' faith in her, which would be no bad thing, especially where Cynric was concerned.

'You say she was tricked by someone huge?' he asked, looking hard at Eudo.

'Yes – someone *pretending* to be Satan,' said Isnard, lest his listeners had not deduced this for themselves. 'Well, two someones actually, as the deceiver had a minion with him, who did all the talking.'

'Is that so?' said Bartholomew, aware that neither Goda nor Eudo would meet his eyes.

'Margery is none too pleased about it,' said Isnard, 'so you Spital folk might want to stay out of her way for a while. She says it is heresy to take the Devil's name in vain.'

The warning delivered, Isnard went on his way, swinging along on his crutches as he looked for someone else to gossip with. Bartholomew watched him go, aware of a rising sense of unease as it occurred to him that there would now be repercussions.

'Go home and inform Tangmer that his ruse has failed,' he told Goda and Eudo. 'And that some folk may resent being deceived and might want revenge.'

'Let them try,' snarled Eudo. 'We will teach them to mind their own business.'

'The Lyminster nuns saw through the *peregrini*'s disguises,' Bartholomew went on, 'which means that others will, too. They must leave at once.'

Goda softened. 'They plan to go at dusk.'

'I hope they find somewhere safe,' said Bartholomew sincerely. 'But when did you pretend to be Satan, exactly, Eudo? I was under the impression from Margery that it was on Wednesday morning, more or less at the time when the fire started.'

Eudo opened his mouth to deny it, but then shrugged. 'It was. So what?'

'It means you have an alibi,' explained Bartholomew.

'Who was the minion? It was not Goda – she was baking all morning, in full view of Prioress Joan. Was it Tangmer?'

Eudo sagged in defeat. 'He is better at that sort of thing than me, so we decided to do it together. But we could hardly tell you, the Sheriff and Brother Michael that we were off bribing witches when the Girards were murdered, could we? So he invented the tale about Amphelisa not being very good at brewing . . .'

Which explained why Tangmer and Eudo had been so furtive when asked to give an account of their where-abouts, thought Bartholomew. But they were definitely in the clear for the murders, as it would have taken time to dress appropriately and then convince Margery to do what 'Satan' wanted. The list of suspects was now two people shorter.

Bartholomew returned to College, where he dashed off messages telling Michael and Tulyet what he had learned. He sent Cynric to deliver them, then went to the hall and interrogated his students on the work he had set them to do. Unimpressed with their progress, he lectured them on what would be expected of the medical profession if the plague returned, aiming to frighten them into working harder. Islaye, the gentle one, looked as though he might be sick; the callous, self-interested Mallett was dismissive.

'It will not return, sir,' he declared confidently. 'God has made His point, and He has no reason to punish us a second time.'

'Actually, He does,' said Theophilis, who had been listening. His soft voice sent an involuntary shiver down Bartholomew's spine. 'It has only been ten years, but we are already slipping back into evil ways. For example, there is a rumour that someone has been dressing up as Satan. That is heresy, and if I catch the culprit, I will burn him in the market square.'

Unwilling to discuss that, Bartholomew returned to his

original theme. 'There are reports of plague around the Mediterranean, and local physicians predict that it will spread north within a year. Ergo, you must work hard now, to be ready for it.'

'Just like physicians were ready last time,' scoffed Theophilis. 'No wonder poor Suttone upped and left in the middle of term – he did not trust you lot to save him.'

At that point, Theophilis's students, deprived of supervision, grew rowdy enough to disturb Father William. Irritably, the Franciscan ordered him back to work, and there was an unseemly spat as one took exception to being bossed around by the other.

'Master Suttone *was* terrified of the plague,' said Mallett to Bartholomew, while everyone else watched the spectacle of two Fellows bickering. 'But that is not why he left.'

Heltisle had claimed much the same, and Bartholomew hoped the malicious Vice-Chancellor had not been spreading nasty untruths.

'Then what was?' he asked coolly, a warning in his voice.

Mallett was uncharacteristically tentative. 'I happened to be passing St Mary the Great one night, when I overheard a conversation between Suttone and Heltisle . . .'

'And?' demanded Bartholomew, when the student trailed off uncomfortably.

'And I did not catch the whole thing, but I did hear Heltisle tell Suttone that there would be repercussions unless he did as he was told. The next day, Suttone resigned. You will not repeat this to Heltisle, will you, sir? I do not want to make an enemy of him – he has connections at Court, and I want a post with a noble family when I graduate.'

Bartholomew frowned. 'Are you saying that Suttone was *coerced* into leaving? How? Did he have some dark secret that he wanted kept quiet?'

'I got the impression that he did,' replied Mallett. 'But I have no idea what it was.'

Bartholomew was exasperated. 'Why have you waited so long before mentioning it? If your tale is true, then it means Heltisle may have the means to hurt Michaelhouse. You must know how much he hates us.'

Mallett shrugged. 'I do, but I have to think of myself first. I was going to tell you at the end of term, once my future is settled, but . . . well, I suppose I owe this place some loyalty.'

'You do,' said Bartholomew angrily, and indicated the other students, whose attention had snapped away from William and Theophilis at the sound of their teacher's sharp voice. 'And to your friends, who will still be here after you leave.'

'Yes,' acknowledged Mallett sheepishly. 'But there is another reason why I was reluctant to speak out. You see, I overheard this discussion very late at night . . .'

'After the curfew bell had sounded and you should have been at home,' surmised Bartholomew, unimpressed.

'What were you doing?' asked Islaye coolly. 'Visiting that sister you have been seeing – the one who was billeted at the Spital, and who you insist on meeting at the witching hour?'

Mallett shook his head. 'She only arrived a couple of weeks ago. The confrontation between Heltisle and Suttone was back in March, when Suttone was still here.'

'Just tell me what was said,' ordered Bartholomew tersely. 'I do not want to know about your dalliances with nuns.'

Mallett gaped at him. 'Dalliances? No, you misunderstand! I went to the Spital to meet my *sister*. She is one of the Benedictines who lodged there before Brother Michael moved them to St Radegund's. I had to visit her on the sly, because Tangmer refused to let me in. He said I might upset his lunatics.'

'Well, you might,' muttered Islaye sourly. 'You are not very nice.'

'I even offered to cure his madmen free of charge,' Mallett went on, ignoring him, 'but Tangmer remained adamant. He is an ass – my sister says that founding the Spital broke him and he has no money left. Ergo, he should have accepted my generous offer.'

'How does she know about his finances?' asked Bartholomew, although he was aware that they were ranging away from what Heltisle had said to Suttone.

'She overheard him telling his cousins. Everyone thinks he is rich, but his fortune is gone, and he will only win it back when he has some rich lunatics to look after. She says the current batch – who are not as mad as you think – only pay a fraction of what they should. Amphelisa does not mind, but Tangmer does.'

'I see,' said Bartholomew, wondering if he had been precipitous to declare Tangmer and Eudo innocent of murder. Perhaps killing the Girards had been a way to oust guests who prevented them from recouping their losses. 'But never mind the Spital. Tell me about the quarrel between Heltisle and Suttone.'

'There is no more to tell,' said Mallett apologetically. 'Other than that Suttone was on the verge of tears, while Heltisle was gloatingly triumphant. It should not surprise you: Heltisle has been dabbling in University politics for years, and is as crafty as they come, whereas Suttone was an innocent in that respect.'

'He was,' agreed Islaye. 'However, if Heltisle did harm him, he will answer to Brother Michael. *He* will not let that slippery rogue get away with anything untoward.'

Bartholomew was sure Islaye was right.

Mallett's story had infuriated Bartholomew, because he was sure that Heltisle *had* done something unkind to Suttone, especially since it had happened when Michael was away and thus not in a position to intervene. As a consequence, he did not want to spend his evening at the butts, where he was likely to run into the Vice-Chancellor, afraid his antipathy towards the man would lead to an unseemly confrontation.

Unfortunately, he knew his absence would be noted, and he was loath to provide Heltisle with an opportunity to fine him. Faced with two unattractive choices, he asked Aungel to go with him, hoping the younger Fellow's company would take his mind off Heltisle's unsavoury antics. They chanced upon Theophilis in the yard, and the three of them began to walk there together. Theophilis held forth conversationally as they went.

'There was nearly a fight at the butts last night. De Wetherset and Heltisle took their students there, but it was the town's turn, and insults were exchanged.'

Bartholomew was disgusted. 'They went anyway, even after Michael told them not to? What were they thinking?'

'Apparently, Heltisle had informed de Wetherset that the Sheriff had invited them to share the targets. It was only when they were at the butts that Heltisle admitted to lying.'

'So what happened?' asked Aungel, agog.

'Tulyet threatened to hang the first person who drew a weapon in anger,' replied Theophilis. 'You could see he meant it, so our lot went home.'

Bartholomew shook his head in disbelief. Did Heltisle *want* the University to be held responsible for igniting a riot? Then he stopped walking suddenly, and peered into the shadows surrounding All Saints' churchyard.

Sister Alice was slinking along in a way that was distinctly furtive, pausing every so often to check she was not being watched. Curious, Bartholomew began to follow her, and as Theophilis and Aungel were also intrigued by her peculiar antics, they fell in at his heels. None of them

211

were very good at stealth, so it was a miracle she did not spot them.

Eventually, they reached Shoemaker Row, where Alice peered around yet again. The three scholars hastily crammed themselves into a doorway, where Bartholomew struggled to stifle his laughter, aware of what a ridiculous sight they must make. Irked, Theophilus elbowed him sharply in the ribs.

Alice stood for a moment, listening to the sounds of the night – a dog barking in the distance, the rumble of conversation from a nearby tavern, the mewl of a baby. Then she scuttled towards a smart cottage in the middle of the lane and knocked on the door.

'That is where Margery Starre lives,' whispered Aungel, as the door opened and Alice slithered inside. 'Visiting witches is hardly something a nun should be doing. No wonder she did not want to be seen!'

Bartholomew crept towards the window. The shutter was closed, but by putting his ear to the wood he could hear Margery's voice.

'Of course I can cast cursing spells,' she was informing her guest. 'But are you sure that is what you want? Once you start down such a path, there is no turning back.'

'I started down it ages ago,' Alice retorted harshly, 'after I was ousted from my post for no good reason. They started this war, but I shall finish it.'

The voices faded, leading Bartholomew to suppose they had gone to a different room. He was disinclined to hunt out another window, because he was suddenly assailed by the conviction that Margery knew he was out there – she had other uncanny abilities, so why not seeing through wood? He slipped away, and told the others that he had been unable to hear. He would happily have confided in Aungel, but he could not bring himself to trust Theophilis.

'I thought Alice was trouble the first time I set eyes on her,' the Junior Proctor declared as they resumed their journey to the butts. 'I have an instinct for these things, which is why Brother Michael appointed me as his deputy, of course.'

'You mean his inferior,' corrected Aungel. 'He does not have a deputy.'

Theophilis shot him a venomous look. 'I shall be Chancellor in the not-too-distant future, so watch who you insult, Aungel. You will not rise far in the University without influential friends.'

'Is that why you are always pestering Clippesby?' asked Aungel, regarding him with dislike. 'Because he is a great theologian, and you aim to bask in his reflected glory? His next thesis is almost ready and—'

'On the contrary,' interrupted Theophilis haughtily. 'All the time I have spent with him has been for one end: to assess whether he should be locked in a place where he can do no harm.'

Aungel bristled. 'Clippesby would never hurt anyone – he is the gentlest man alive. Besides, it was *you* who insisted on sitting in the henhouse all afternoon, not him. He wanted to read in the hall.'

'The way I choose to evaluate another scholar's mental competence is none of your business,' snapped Theophilis, nettled. 'So keep your nose out of it.'

'It *is* his business,' countered Bartholomew. 'And mine, too. We look out for each other at Michaelhouse.'

'I *am* looking out for Clippesby,' said Theophilis crossly. 'I am trying to determine whether he should be allowed to wander about unsupervised in his fragile state. He may come to grief at the hands of those who do not understand him. I have his welfare at heart.'

Bartholomew was far from sure he did, but the Junior Proctor's claims flew from his mind when they arrived at the butts. The town had not forgiven the University for disrupting its turn the previous evening, and had turned out in force to retaliate in kind.

As ordering one side home would have caused a riot for certain, Michael and Tulyet had divided the targets in half, so that the University had the four on the left part of the mound, and the town had the four on the right. Neither faction was happy with the arrangement, and Michael's beadles and Tulyet's soldiers were struggling to keep the peace.

'Lord!' breathed Aungel, looking around with wide eyes. '*Everyone* is here – the whole University and every man in the town. We will never get a chance to shoot.'

'No,' agreed Bartholomew, 'so round up everyone from Michaelhouse and take them home. There is no point in risking them here needlessly. No, not you, Theophilis. You must stay and help Michael.'

'But it might be dangerous,' objected Theophilis. 'Or do you mean to place me in harm's way because I believe Clippesby is mad?'

'I place you there because you are the Junior Proctor,' retorted Bartholomew tartly. 'It is your job.'

Aungel was wrong to say that the whole University and every man in the town was at the butts, because more were arriving with every passing moment, adding to what was becoming a substantial crush. The beadles and soldiers had joined forces to keep the two apart, but Bartholomew could tell it was only a matter of time before their thin barrier was breached.

He looked around in despair. There were far more townsmen than scholars, but many students were trained warriors who could kill stick-wielding peasants with ease. If the evening did end in a fight, he would not like to bet on which side would win.

'Why not send them *all* home?' he asked Tulyet.

The Sheriff was watching Leger and Norbert try to instruct a gaggle of men from the Griffin, all of whom were much more interested in exchanging insults with the Carmelite novices than anything the knights could tell them about improving their stance and grip.

'Because as long as they are here, we can monitor them,' explained Tulyet tersely. 'If we let them go, they will sneak around in packs and any control we have will be lost.'

'How long do you think you can keep them from each other's throats?' asked Bartholomew uneasily.

'Hopefully, for as long as is necessary. Unfortunately, your new beadles are useless. Half are cowering behind the Franciscan Friary, while the rest itch to start a fight.'

He darted away when a Carmelite novice 'accidentally' hit Leger with a bow. Then Bartholomew heard Sauvage calling to him, urging him to abandon 'them French-loving University traitors' and stand with loyal Englishmen instead. Bartholomew pretended he had not heard, and retreated behind a cart, where he watched the unfolding crisis with growing consternation.

Most of King's Hall had turned out. They included the four friends who had nearly come to blows with Isnard on the way to the Spital fire. They strutted around like peacocks, and other foundations were quick to follow their example, causing townsmen to bristle with indignation. The name Wyse could be heard, as townsfolk reminded each other that one such arrogant scholar had slaughtered a defenceless old man.

The King's Hall men considered themselves far too important to wait for their turn to shoot, so they strode to the front of the queue and stepped in front of the Carmelites. Bartholomew held his breath, hoping the University would not start fighting among itself. If it did, the town would pitch in and that would be that. But Michael saved the day by promising the friars a barrel of ale if they allowed King's Hall to go ahead of them.

First at the line was the scholar who had declared himself to be a Fleming – Bruges. He took a bow from

Cynric without a word of thanks, and to prove that he was an accomplished warrior, he carried on a desultory conversation with his friends while he sent ten missiles thudding into the target. There was silence as everyone watched in begrudging admiration.

'King's Hall will never allow the French to invade,' he bragged, thrusting the bow so carelessly at Cynric that the book-bearer dropped it. 'It does not matter if these ignorant peasants can shoot, because Cambridge has *us* to defend it.'

'We are not ignorant, you pompous arse,' bellowed Sauvage, a 'witticism' that won a roar of approval from the town. 'And *we* will defend the town, not you.'

'You?' drawled Bruges with a provocative sneer. 'I hit the target ten times. What was your score, peasant?'

'It was only four,' scoffed the student from Koln. 'And not one hit the middle.'

'You two are *foreign*,' yelled Sauvage, red with mortification as Koln's cronies hooted with derisive laughter. 'You are here to spy and report to your masters in Paris.'

'And we cannot allow that,' shouted Isnard, although what a man with one leg was doing at the butts, Bartholomew could not imagine. Archery required two hands, and the bargeman needed at least one for his crutches. 'We should trounce them.'

'Come and try, cripple!' goaded Bruges. 'We will show you what we do to cowardly rogues who stab elderly plagiarists.'

'We did not kill Paris!' declared Isnard, outraged. '*You* did. He—'

'Enough!' came Michael's irate voice, as he and Tulyet hurried forward to intervene. 'Koln, if you are going to shoot, get on with it. If not, stand back and let someone else have a turn.'

'And do not even think of jeering at him, Sauvage,' warned Tulyet, 'unless you fancy a night in gaol. Now, take your bow again, and this time mark your target *before* you draw. Isnard, if you must be here, do something useful and sort these arrows into bundles of ten.'

'Can he count that high?' called Bruges, although he blanched and looked away when Michael swung towards him with fury in his eyes.

Tulyet began to instruct Sauvage, who was delighted to be singled out by so august a warrior, and called his friends to watch, drawing their attention away from the scholars. Unsettled by the Senior Proctor's looming presence, there was no more trouble from King's Hall either. Bartholomew heaved a sigh of relief. Trouble had been averted – for now, at least.

For an hour or more, the two sides concentrated on the business at hand, each studiously ignoring the efforts of the other. Bartholomew began to hope that the evening would pass off without further incident after all, but then it was Bene't College's turn to shoot. Heltisle and his students shoved their way forward, full of haughty pride.

'Allow me to demonstrate,' Heltisle began in a self-important bray and, to everyone's astonishment, proceeded to send an arrow straight into the centre of the target.

It was the best shot of the evening, and raised a cheer from the University, although the townsfolk remained silent. His second missile split the first, and he placed the remaining eight in a neat circle around them. Then he shoved Cynric aside, and began to instruct his students himself. He took so long that a number of hostel men grew impatient with waiting.

'Take your lads home,' ordered Michael, easing the Vice-Chancellor away from the line so that Ely Hall could step up. 'There is no need to keep them here.'

'I would rather they stayed, Brother,' came a familiar voice. 'There is much to be learned from watching the efforts of others.'

It was de Wetherset. Bartholomew had not recognised him, because it was now completely dark, and while torches illuminated the targets and the line, it was difficult to make out anything else. Moreover, the Chancellor had dressed for battle – a boiled leather jerkin, a metal helmet, and a short fighting cloak on which was pinned his pilgrim badge. Unfortunately, rather than lending him a warlike mien, they made him look ridiculous, and a number of townsfolk were laughing. So far, he had not noticed.

'There will be a scuffle if too many men crowd the line,' argued Michael tightly, 'so, I repeat – Heltisle, go home.'

'If he does, it will leave us in a vulnerable minority,' countered de Wetherset. 'Besides, this is *our* night – if we concede the butts today, what is to stop the town from taking advantage of us in other ways tomorrow?'

'And you are here, Brother,' said Heltisle silkily. 'Or are you unequal to keeping us safe from revolting townsmen?'

'Oh, we need have no fears on that score, Heltisle,' said de Wetherset pleasantly. 'I trust Michael to protect us. If I did not, I would have stayed at home.'

'Then do what I tell you,' hissed Michael, exasperated. 'I cannot keep the peace if you overrule my decisions.'

'Very well,' conceded de Wetherset with an irritable sigh. 'We shall leave the moment we have seen what Ely Hall can do.'

'Did Suttone ever see you shoot, Heltisle?' asked Bartholomew casually, although he knew it was hardly the time to quiz the Vice-Chancellor about what Mallett claimed to have overheard. 'He often mentions you in his letters.'

'Does he?' asked Heltisle, instantly uneasy. 'What does he say?'

'That he wishes he had not resigned,' bluffed Bartholomew, glad it was dark, so Heltisle could not see

218

the lie in his face. 'He is thinking of coming back and standing for re-election.'

'He cannot,' declared Heltisle in alarm. 'No one would vote for him – not now our scholars have had a taste of de Wetherset.'

'You are too kind, Heltisle,' said the Chancellor smoothly, and turned to smile at Bartholomew. 'I am glad to see *you* here – a veteran of Poitiers is just the example our students need. Perhaps you would give us a demonstration of your superior skills.'

'My skills lie not in shooting arrows, but in sewing up the wounds they make,' retorted Bartholomew. 'I can demonstrate *that*, if you like.'

De Wetherset laughed, although Bartholomew had not meant to be amusing. 'Regardless, I hope you are stockpiling bandages and salves. We shall need them when the Dauphin's army attacks our town.'

Bartholomew raised his eyebrows. 'I doubt he will bother with us – not when there are easier targets on the coast.'

But de Wetherset shook his head. 'He will know about our rich Colleges, wealthy merchants, and opulent parish churches. Of course he will come here, and anyone who thinks otherwise is a fool.'

Again, there was relative peace, as all attention was on the archers and their targets, although Heltisle did not take his scholars home and his example encouraged other Colleges and hostels to linger as well. For a while, the only sounds were the orders yelled by Cynric and Tulyet.

'Ready your bows!'

'Nock!'

'Mark!'

'Draw!'

'Loose!'

Then the twang and hiss as the missiles sped towards their targets, followed by a volley of thuds as they hit or jeers from onlookers if they went wide. Even as the arrows flew, Cynric and Tulyet were repeating the commands – the power of the English army lay in the ability of its archers to shoot an entire quiver in less than a minute, and it was not unknown for a good bowman to have two or more arrows in the air at the same time.

'Heltisle is the best shot so far,' said Cynric, when it was the physician's turn to step up to the mark. There was a short delay while White Hostel, which had just finished, went to retrieve the arrows so they could be reused. 'Although Valence Marie was almost as good. Gonville is rubbish, though.'

Bartholomew peered into the gloom. 'The Carmelite novices were here earlier – no surprise, as they have always been a bellicose horde – but do I see the Franciscans, too?'

'Yes – friars and monks are exempt, but not novices, so youngsters from all the Orders are here. Normally, our overseas students would stand in for them, but most of those are lying low, lest they are accused of being French.'

'*I* would not want to be an overseas scholar at the moment,' came a voice from the shadows. It was Aynton, the bandage gleaming white around his wrist. He walked carefully, so as not to soil his ugly boots. 'I hope we can protect them, should it become necessary.'

So did Bartholomew. 'How is your arm? You should be resting it at home.'

'Heltisle said there might be trouble tonight, so I felt obliged to put in an appearance,' explained Aynton. 'Hah! It is your go. Show us what a hero of Poitiers can do, eh?'

Bartholomew was horrified when scholars and towns-folk alike stopped what they were doing to watch him, and heartily wished Cynric had kept his tall tales to himself. Feeling he should at least try to put on a good show, he was more careful than he had been the last time, and listened to the advice Cynric murmured in his ear. His first shot went wide, but the next nine hit the target. None struck the centre, but he was satisfied with his performance even so.

'I thought you would be a lot better than that,' said Sergeant Orwel, disappointed.

'If you really were at Poitiers, you should know that accuracy was not an issue there,' said Cynric loftily. 'The enemy was so closely packed that it was impossible *not* to hit them, no matter where you pointed your bow.'

'Bartholomew never fought at Poitiers,' sneered Bruges. 'What rubbish you believe! Next you will claim that *Sauvage* is English, when it is obvious that he is a filthy French—'

'*You* dare question the origin of another man's name?' demanded Norbert, his face hot with indignation. 'You, who has one that the King of France would be proud to bear?'

'I am Flemish,' declared Bruges, offended. 'Only imbeciles cannot tell the difference.'

'How about a wager, Frenchie?' called Orwel. 'A groat says that four of us can beat any four of you.'

'A whole groat,' drawled Bruges caustically, while on the University side, a frantic search was made for Heltisle. 'I am dizzy with the excitement of winning such a heady sum. How shall we give our best when the stakes are so staggeringly high?'

'So you can pay then?' called Orwel, not a man to appreciate sarcasm. 'Good.'

Unfortunately for the scholars, Heltisle was nowhere to be found, so four King's Hall men – Bruges, Koln and two local students named Foxlee and Smith – stepped up to the line. They ignored the anxious clamour from the other scholars, who pointed out that while Bruges was a decent shot, the other three were only average, so room should be made for a trio from Valence Marie. Meanwhile, four townsmen were chosen and stood waiting.

'Ready your bows,' shouted Cynric quickly, when King's Hall refused to yield and tempers on the University side looked set to fray. 'Nock! Mark!'

There was a flurry of activity as all eight participants scrambled to obey.

'Draw! *Loose!*'

Thuds followed hisses, and everyone peered down the field. All the targets bristled with arrows, and it was clear that the result would be very close. The eight archers trotted off to inspect them more closely. Meanwhile, someone yelled that one round was not enough, so two more teams were assembling, ready to shoot the moment the targets were clear.

'Which of you will pay the groat?' demanded Leger triumphantly. 'Because *we* won.'

'You cannot know that!' objected Cynric. 'Not yet.'

'I can see all our arrows clustered together,' argued Leger. 'Whereas your bowmen are hunting in the grass for theirs. We *did* win!'

'Lying scum!' yelled someone from White Hostel. '*We* won and I will punch anyone who claims otherwise.'

'Come here and say that,' roared Leger. 'Now give us the groat or—'

'Ready your bows!'

Bartholomew was not sure who had called the next archers to order, because the speaker was deep in the shadows. However, it came from the town side, and mischief was in the air, as the first teams were still down at the targets.

'Wait!' he shouted urgently. 'Not yet.'

'Nock! Mark! Draw! *Loose!*'

The commands came in a rapid rattle, so authoritatively that eight arrows immediately flew from eight bows. A

222

good part of butts training was conditioning men to follow orders immediately and unquestioningly, so it was no surprise that the second teams had reacted without hesitation. There was a collective hiss, followed by several thuds and a scream.

'Down bows! Down bows!' howled Cynric frantically, snatching the weapons away before anyone could reload. 'No one shoot! *Down* bows!'

Bartholomew did not wait to hear if it was safe to go. He set off towards the mound at a run, aware of others sprinting at his heels. He aimed for the shrieks.

He arrived to see that Foxlee had been shot in the leg, while Koln – mercifully unhurt – lay on the ground with his hands over his head, crying for a ceasefire. Others had not been so fortunate. Bruges and Smith from King's Hall were dead, as was one townsman.

De Wetherset was among those who had hurried after Bartholomew. He scrambled up the mound, breathing hard, his face a mask of horror. Then Tulyet arrived.

'Christ God!' the Sheriff swore when he saw the bodies. 'Who gave the order to shoot?'

'A townsman,' replied de Wetherset shakily. 'But I cannot believe he intended anyone to die, as his own side was down here, too. Clearly, it is a prank gone badly wrong.'

Bartholomew was not so sure. Nor was Koln, now on his feet and shaking with fury.

'Of course the culprit meant there to be bloodshed!' he yelled. 'It was brazen murder! Someone will pay for this!'

'Just stop and think,' snapped de Wetherset. 'The town would never hurt one of—'

'I want revenge,' howled Koln. 'Well, lads? What are you waiting for? Will you allow town scum to dispatch our friends?'

There was a short silence, then all hell broke loose.

* * *

There were moments during the ensuing mêlée when Bartholomew wondered if he was dreaming about Poitiers. He still had nightmares about the battle, and the screams and clash of arms that resounded across the butts were much the same. He yelled himself hoarse calling for a ceasefire, but few heard, and those who did were disinclined to listen.

'Stay with me, boy,' gasped Cynric, whose face was spattered with someone else's blood. 'Back to back, defending each other. You were wise to take the high ground – it will be easier to fight them off from here.'

Bartholomew knew there was no point in explaining he had not chosen the mound for strategic reasons but because it was where the first victims lay.

'No killing, Cynric,' he begged. 'Try to disarm them instead.'

'Right,' grunted Cynric, as he swung his cutlass at a stave-wielding townsman with all his might. 'After all, they mean us no harm.'

'Norbert!' gulped Bartholomew, watching in shock as a lucky thrust by a baying Bene't student passed clean through the knight's lower body. 'I must help—'

Cynric grabbed his arm before he could start towards the stricken man. 'You will stick with me if you value your life. And the lives of others – your skills will be needed later.'

'Goodness!' cried Aynton, stumbling up to them. He carried a bow in his uninjured hand, which he was waving wildly enough to deter anyone from coming too close. His face was white with terror. 'What do we do? How can we stop it?'

'You cannot,' gasped Cynric. 'Now stay behind us. You will be safe there.'

Bartholomew watched in despair as a phalanx of flailing swords from King's Hall, led by the enraged Koln, cut a bloody swathe through a contingent of apprentices.

Then his attention was caught by a seething mass of townsfolk, all of whom were howling for French blood, and seemed to think it could be found on the mound. None of them believed Aynton's frightened bleat that he had none to offer, and they surged upwards with murder in their eyes.

Just when Bartholomew thought his life was over, there came a thunder of hoofs. It was Tulyet on a massive warhorse, next to Michael on Dusty and several mounted knights from the castle. None slowed when they reached the skirmishers, so that anyone who did not want to be trampled was forced to scramble away fast. The riders wheeled their destriers around and drove them through the teeming mass a second time, after which most combatants broke off the fight to concentrate on which way they would have to leap to avoid the deadly hoofs. Tulyet reined in and stood in his stirrups, towering over those around him.

'How dare you break the peace!' he thundered, his voice surprisingly loud for so slight a man. 'Is this how you serve your country? By fighting each other? Disarm at once!'

'But we were fighting *French* scholars,' shouted a potter, too full of bloodlust to know he should hold his tongue. 'They are the enemy. We were—'

'Arrest that man,' bellowed Tulyet, pointing furiously at him.

Two of his soldiers hurried forward to oblige, much to the potter's dismay.

'*We* did not start this,' shouted Koln, whose face was white with rage in the flickering torchlight. '*They* did – the town scum.'

'You are under arrest, too,' snarled Michael. 'See to it, Meadowman.'

The beadle bundled the startled King's Hall man away before he could draw breath to object. Then de Wetherset spoke, begging his scholars to disperse. Most did, although the livid faces of Michael and Tulyet did more to shift them than any of the Chancellor's nervous entreaties. Soon, all that were left were the dead and wounded.

'Casualties?' demanded Tulyet in a tight, clipped voice.

'Eight dead,' replied Bartholomew, not looking up from the miller he was struggling to save. 'Three scholars and five townsmen. There will be others before morning.'

'Eight,' breathed Michael, shaking his head in disgust. 'All lost for nothing.'

'Take the wounded to the Franciscan Friary,' ordered Tulyet. 'And spread word that if anyone, other than soldiers or beadles, is out on the streets tonight, he will hang at dawn.'

'Not scholars,' said de Wetherset hoarsely. 'You do not have the authority to impose that sort of sanction on us. Tell him, Brother.'

'Then *I* will impose it,' said Michael shortly. 'Because he is right – *anyone* out tonight will be presumed guilty of affray and punished accordingly.'

Tulyet nodded curt thanks, then hurried away to organise stretchers and bearers, while Michael went to give what comfort he could to the dying – he was not a priest, but had been granted dispensation to give last rites during the plague and had continued the practice since. Bartholomew turned to Cynric, knowing he needed the help of other *medici*.

'Fetch Rougham and Meryfeld. Then go to Michaelhouse and tell my students to bring bandages, salves, needles and thread.'

Fleetingly, it occurred to him that when de Wetherset recommended that he stockpile medical supplies, he had not imagined that he would be needing them that very night.

Cynric nodded briskly. 'Anything else?'

'Yes – go to the Spital and ask Amphelisa for a supply

of the strong herbs that she uses for pain. I do not have nearly enough to do what will be necessary this evening.'

'Then thank God Margery found out that the Devil does not live there,' muttered the book-bearer, crossing himself before kissing a grubby amulet. 'I would not have been able to go otherwise, as I have no wish to encounter Satan.'

'You already have,' said Bartholomew soberly. 'I am sure he was here tonight.'

CHAPTER 10

The bells were chiming for the night office by the time Bartholomew and his helpers had carried all the wounded to the Franciscan Priory. Despite their best efforts, another three men died, bringing the death toll to eleven – four scholars and seven townsfolk. Their bodies were taken to the chapel, where the friars recited prayers for their souls.

Rougham and Meryfeld, physicians who only ever tended paying customers, quickly bagged the wealthy victims, leaving Bartholomew with the rest. This did not bother him, as he had always been more interested in saving lives than making money. However, he was pleasantly surprised to learn that Amphelisa felt the same way – she not only donated her pain-dulling herbs for free, but stayed to help him saw and stitch. She was a constant presence at his side, always ready with what was required and enveloping him in the sweet scent of the distilled oils that had soaked into her burgundy work-robe.

'It is a good thing I sent Eudo and Goda to replenish my stocks today,' she murmured, helping Foxlee to sip a poppy juice cordial. 'Or we would have run out by now.'

'For Hélène.' Bartholomew spoke absently, because he was removing the arrowhead from Foxlee's leg, and it was perilously close to an artery. 'To help her sleep.'

Amphelisa shot him a startled look. 'Hélène will have camomile and honey. I am not in the habit of dosing small children with henbane and mandrake.'

Bartholomew glanced up at her. 'Then why did Eudo and Goda tell me—'

'I cannot control what they say when I am not there to correct them,' she interrupted shortly. 'Goda is a fey soul who probably misheard, while Eudo is slow in the wits.'

'He is not too stupid to convince the town's favourite witch that he was Satan.'

Amphelisa scowled. 'That was *your* fault! Until then, we had kept the curious away by jigging bits of gauze around on twine. But did you run away screaming? Oh, no! You had to poke about in the bushes for evidence of trickery. We had to devise another ruse, and claiming that Satan had moved in was the best we could manage in a hurry.'

'What will you do now that Margery is telling everyone the truth? Ask for your money back? I understand that "Satan" paid a handsome fee to ensure her cooperation.'

'It no longer matters, because the *peregrini* have gone,' said Amphelisa. 'Someone started a rumour about French spies, so they decided to leave at once.'

'All of them? Delacroix was ill the last I heard.'

'I gave him nettle root to stop his bowels, and he was first through the gate.' She gave a wan smile. 'Then I started a tale of my own – that our patients went to London for specialist treatment. London is south, but the *peregrini* went north, so if anyone gives chase . . .'

'So the Spital no longer has "inmates"?'

'None, and anyone may come to check our hall. Indeed, I hope they do. Then they will see it is a good place, and will give us some real lunatics to look after.'

'And you need fee-paying patients,' said Bartholomew, dropping the arrowhead into a basin, and pressing a clean cloth to the wound.

'How do you . . .' She trailed off, then shook her head in disgust. 'Mallett! I thought I saw him sneaking about with one of the nuns, and he is your pupil. *He* told you!'

Bartholomew glanced to where Mallett was arguing with two tailors over payment for services rendered. He had no doubt that the student would win. He turned back to his own patient. Foxlee barely flinched as he began to sew, which was testament to Amphelisa's skill – she had administered enough medicine to blunt the pain, but not enough to send their patient into too deep a sleep.

'If Eudo and your husband were pretending to be denizens of Hell when the Girards were murdered, we can cross them off our list of suspects,' said Bartholomew, his eyes on his stitching. 'While the rest of the staff have alibis in each other . . .'

'But I was alone,' finished Amphelisa, guessing exactly where he was heading. 'I am not your culprit, though. I was the one who offered them sanctuary.'

Tulyet had said the same, Bartholomew recalled, and had claimed that she would not have taken such loving care of Hélène if she had murdered the girl's family. He said nothing, and Amphelisa grabbed his arm, forcing him to look at her.

'Henry and I founded the Spital – a place of comfort and healing – because we wanted to do some good, as well as to make amends for the wrongs of the past. Do you really think we would undo all that by committing murder?'

It was a good point, but hardly the time to discuss it. Bartholomew left her to bandage Foxlee's leg and moved to his next patient, who had suffered a serious gash across the chest. After that there were more wounds to clean and sew shut, so many that he began to wonder if anyone had escaped the mêlée unscathed. He finished eventually and slumped on a bench, flexing shoulders that were cramped from bending. By then, all his helpmeets had gone except two of his senior students.

'Go home now,' he told them tiredly. 'You did well tonight.'

'No, *you* go home sir,' said Mallett, whose purse looked a lot fuller than it had been before the skirmish. 'It will be light in a couple of hours, at which point you will have to examine this lot again. So snatch a bit of sleep, while Islaye and I mind things here.'

'Everyone is resting peacefully now anyway,' put in Islaye, who had wept every time a patient had died, and had been unable to look at some of the wounds Bartholomew had been obliged to repair. 'Except Norbert, who is in too much pain.'

'Serves him right,' muttered Mallett, who had not uttered a word of comfort to anyone. 'He called me a Frenchman yesterday.'

Bartholomew was too exhausted to point out that such an 'insult' hardly warranted being fatally stabbed through the bowels. He went to tend Norbert himself, thinking that neither student was suitable company for a man on the verge of death. The knight opened pain-filled eyes as Bartholomew knelt next to his pallet.

'Give me medicine to ease the agony,' he whispered. 'And stay with me awhile.'

Bartholomew set about preparing a potion so strong that Norbert would be unlikely to wake once he had swallowed it. It would not kill him – the wound would – but Norbert would sleep until he breathed his last. He cradled the dark, greasy head in his arm, and helped him drink until every drop was gone. Norbert lay back, his face sheened in sweat.

'And now I shall confess my crimes.'

'Not to me,' said Bartholomew, beginning to rise. 'You need a priest.'

Norbert gripped his arm. 'I said *crimes*, not sins. The Franciscans have already given me absolution, so I do not fear for my soul. But I want to tell you what happened tonight, because it was me who called the order to ready bows. However, I did *not* call the order to shoot.'

Bartholomew reflected on what he could remember of the sequence of events. 'Yes – the voice of whoever shouted the first order *was* different from whoever bellowed the second. But both came from the town's side of the butts.'

'It was someone behind me. I looked around, but it was too dark to see, and there were so many people . . . It was some fool mouthing off without considering the consequences.'

'Even fools know that if you shoot at people you might hit them.'

Norbert winced. 'I wanted to give those arrogant King's Hall bastards a fright by making them *think* they were about to be shot. I never meant for it to actually happen.'

'Close your eyes,' said Bartholomew, not sure what to think. 'Sleep is not far off now.'

'I have not finished. You should also be aware that the Spital's secret is out. By morning, everyone will know the place is full of Frenchmen. A nun told me last Monday.'

Bartholomew frowned. 'Which nun?'

'She spoke through a half-closed door, so I never saw her face. She said it was an abomination that French scum were hiding in our town, and she wanted me to kill them.'

Bartholomew struggled to understand the implications of what he was being told. 'If this nun spoke to you on Monday, it means that you knew there were Frenchmen in the Spital when the fire broke out on Wednesday.'

'Yes, I did. Leger and I were pleased that some were roasted, but *we* did not do it. I swear on my immortal soul that neither of us went anywhere near the Spital that morning.'

'Why did you not tell Dick all this?'

'Because Leger wants to be Sheriff, so it is in our interests to see Tulyet's investigation fail. But now my end is near . . . well, his ambitions are less important than my conscience.'

Bartholomew was still grappling to understand what Norbert had done. 'But some of the Spital's fugitives were

Jacques – rebels. You should not have kept that to your-selves.'

'We didn't – we have been spreading the word slowly and carefully through the town. Leger says that instant rumours can be dismissed as falsehoods, but measured hints and whispers are far less easy to ignore. We watched the tale take hold more strongly tonight, and by morning, everyone will know who is in the Spital.'

Bartholomew was glad the *peregrini* had gone, although he hoped the generous souls who had taken pity on them would not suffer in their stead. 'Where did you meet this nun?'

'At St Radegund's, when I was delivering messages from the King to various abbesses.'

'What else can you tell me about her?'

'Just that I could hear her scratching as she spoke. It is not a nice habit in a woman.'

Alice, thought Bartholomew. The Lyminster nuns had guessed the truth about the Spital's lunatics, so it was no surprise that Alice had done so, too. Yet confiding in Norbert was akin to arranging a massacre. Was she so twisted by hatred that she would bring about the deaths of harmless women and children?

Norbert seemed to sense his thoughts. 'Yes,' he whis-pered. 'She *is* evil. I could hear the malevolence in her voice as she spoke to me.'

Bartholomew hurried straight home to tell Michael what Norbert had confessed, only to find the Master's quarters empty. He scribbled a note detailing his findings, and left it on the desk. Then he returned to his own room and fell into an exhausted sleep. Not long after, the bell rang to call everyone to morning prayer. He rose and shuffled wearily into the yard, where Cynric was waiting to talk to him – the book-bearer had visited the Franciscans' chapel during the night, and had made an alarming discovery among the dead. Bartholomew listened to his tale in horror.

Michael did not appear for the service, so Bartholomew fretted all through it, unsettled by Cynric's news. The monk was missing for breakfast, too, and Bartholomew only picked at the meaty pottage that was served. William took Michael's place at the high table, booming the pre- and post-prandial Graces with great relish and many grammatical mistakes.

When the meal was over, Bartholomew told Aungel which texts to teach that day, oblivious to the young Fellow's dismay at what he considered to be unrealistic goals, then hurried to his room, where he gathered fresh supplies for the wounded at the friary. Michael arrived just as the physician was about to leave, his face grey with fatigue and his habit bearing signs of the previous night's skirmish.

'We declared a total curfew in the end,' he said. 'But that did not stop some feisty souls from sneaking out. Dick, Theophilis and I raced about like hares all night, quelling one spat only for another to break out. Dick hanged three of the worst offenders this morning.'

'They were executed for affray?' asked Bartholomew uneasily.

'For murder – they were caught red-handed and there is no doubting their guilt. However, he is keen for everyone to think it was for rioting – he made the threat, and must be seen to carry it out, or no one will believe him the next time he is compelled to do it.'

'What is happening on the streets now?'

'Nothing – the mischief-makers have gone home at last.' Michael grimaced. 'We should be hunting the rogue who stabbed Paris, Bonet and the Girards – and whoever dispatched poor old Wyse – but instead all we do is struggle to keep a lid on this brewing war.'

'What did the triumvirate do to help last night?'

'They disappeared into St Mary the Great, where they stayed until dawn. No doubt they were plotting against me while I risked life and limb outside. What was the final death toll?'

'It will be fourteen by now, although only four were scholars.'

'Eighteen, then,' said Michael softly, 'if we include the three who were hanged and their victim. Eighteen dead for nothing!'

'Do you want official causes of death?' asked Bartholomew, and gave his report without waiting for an answer. 'Nine townsmen died of knife wounds, while the tenth was shot. Of the scholars, two were bludgeoned, one was shot, and Bruges was stabbed.'

'Stabbed?' asked Michael. 'You mean shot – he and the other King's Hall lad were caught by the first volley of arrows. You said he was dead when you reached the mound.'

'He *was* dead, which is why I did not examine him very carefully – I was more concerned with the living at that point. But Cynric went to the Franciscans' chapel and saw the dagger still in Bruges's back. He pulled it out and brought it home. It is on the table.'

Michael went to look at it, then gaped his shock. 'But it is almost identical to the ones that were used on Paris and the Girard family! Are you telling me that the killer struck again – *while we were watching?*'

Bartholomew raised his hands in a shrug. 'He must have done, because Bruges was dead when I arrived at the targets. Cynric asked the surviving archers if they saw anyone else lurking around, but none of them did. The fact that it was dark did not help – the targets were illuminated, but the area around them was not.'

'Lord!' breathed Michael. 'Do you think one of them did it – that there were sour words between the opposing teams while they were deciding who won the contest?'

'Cynric said they watched each other very carefully, as everyone knew their rivals would try to cheat. Bruges was alive when the arrows were loosed, which means the killer struck *after* they landed, but *before* we all reached the targets to see who had been hit.'

'There goes our theory that Paris, Bonet and the Girards were killed for being French,' sighed Michael. 'Bruges is from Flanders.'

'I am not sure everyone appreciates the difference,' said Bartholomew soberly. 'I wager anything you please that the killer is sitting in his lair at this very moment, congratulating himself on ridding the town of another enemy.'

'Do you think *he* gave the order to shoot? The killer?'

Bartholomew rubbed his eyes tiredly. 'I explained all this in the message I left in your room. Did you not read it?'

'What message? My desk was empty.'

Bartholomew outlined what he had written, at the same time wondering who had taken the note. The obvious suspect was Theophilis, who had then carried it to his real masters in St Mary the Great. Or perhaps he was the killer, and was even now working out how to avoid being caught while simultaneously continuing his evil work.

'So Norbert yelled the order for the archers to prepare, to give King's Hall a fright, but someone else hollered the command to shoot,' summarised Michael when Bartholomew had finished. 'And all the while, our killer loitered boldly, awaiting his next victim.'

Bartholomew nodded. 'Norbert thought the second command came from a townsman who acted without considering the consequences. The killer just took advantage of it.'

'So we can discount Norbert and Leger for the Spital murders, because you believe what Norbert told you regarding their whereabouts?'

'Yes, and we can discount Tangmer and Eudo, too, which means we are left with the *peregrini*, Amphelisa, Sister Alice, Magistra Katherine, the triumvirate, Theophilis—'

'Not Theophilis or de Wetherset,' interrupted Michael. 'And not Heltisle either, much as it pains me to admit it. They are more likely to wound with plots than daggers.'

'But you see Aynton as a stabber?'

'I do. I told you: there is something about him that I do not trust at all.' Michael returned to the list. 'I cannot see nuns committing murder either.'

'Not even Sister Alice, who betrayed the *peregrini* to Norbert, along with the injunction to kill them all? Moreover, far from narrowing our list of suspects down, her gossip means that we now have to expand it to anyone who might have heard the rumour about Tangmer sheltering French spies.'

'Are you sure Norbert was telling the truth? I would not put it past him to lie on his deathbed, just to confound us.'

'He seemed sincere. Will you confront Alice today?'

'Of course, although you should not forget that Norbert did not see her face, and it is not difficult to don a habit, stand in the shadows and impersonate a nun. But first, I must sleep. There is no point in challenging anyone when my wits are muddy from fatigue. Will you come with me to St Radegund's later?'

'If I must,' replied Bartholomew without enthusiasm.

The Franciscans occupied a large swathe of land in the east of the town. It was bordered by the main road at the front and the King's Ditch at the back. Inside, it was pretty, dominated by its church, refectory and dormitory. It also had a substantial guesthouse, which had been converted into a makeshift hospital. Bartholomew walked in and satisfied himself that the surviving wounded were doing as well as could be expected.

'Norbert died,' reported Mallett. 'In his sleep, which was a pity, as I could have charged him for another dose of poppy juice if he had woken.'

'You will go far,' muttered Bartholomew in distaste. 'You already think like most successful *medici*.'

'Thank you, sir,' said Mallett, flattered. 'But Islaye and I can manage here for a bit longer, if you have other things to do. It will be no trouble.'

Bartholomew was sure it would not, especially if fees were pocketed in the process. He replaced them with two of their classmates, and went in search of Prior Pechem, a dour, humourless man who had just completed his morning devotions and was on his way to the refectory to break his fast.

'Your tyranny in the classroom has paid off,' Pechem remarked. 'Your lads are much better than Rougham and Meryfeld, who have fifty years' medical experience between them.'

As Bartholomew had scant regard for his colleagues' abilities, this compliment fell on stony ground. 'I saw you and some of your novices at the butts last night,' he began.

Pechem nodded. 'The ones who are not exempt from this wretched call to arms. I accompanied them, lest there was trouble.'

'Were you there when the fight erupted?'

'Yes, but I whisked them all home the moment the knives came out. I know they were there to learn how to kill, but I am unwilling to let them put theory into practice just yet.'

'So what did you see?'

'Not much, because it was dark. I heard a yell to ready bows, followed by another – a different voice, from further away – to shoot. Then all was chaos, blood and confusion.'

'Did you recognise either of the voices?'

'Unfortunately not. However, both came from the townsfolk's side – the first from near the front, and the second from the back. Indeed, it was so far to the rear that the culprit may not have been part of the town faction at all.'

'What are you saying? That he may have been one of us?'

Pechem shrugged. 'I would hope not, but who knows? You do not need me to tell you that some of our students are eager to test their newly acquired skills on living flesh.'

'I hope you are wrong,' said Bartholomew unhappily.

'So do I, but I fear I am not. The first order was from some ass who aimed to give everyone a scare, but the second was from someone who wanted to see blood. He knew exactly what he was doing, suggesting a cold and calculating mind. I doubt he will be caught.'

'Do not underestimate Michael. He has snared cunning criminals before.'

'Yes, but that was when he had power. Now he must dance to de Wetherset's tune, and de Wetherset listens too much to Heltisle and Aynton.'

'You do not like them?'

'Let us just say that I have reservations. Of course, if there are any more incidents like last night, some of us will demand their resignation.'

'Please do not,' begged Bartholomew. 'They will shift the blame to Michael, because keeping the peace is the Senior Proctor's responsibility.'

'They can try, but we are not stupid – we know who is better for the University, and it is not de Wetherset and his power-hungry cronies.' Then Pechem gave one of his rare smiles and changed the subject. 'How is Clippesby? That man is a treasure.'

Bartholomew regarded him in surprise. 'We think so, but have you forgotten that he is a Dominican? A member of a rival Order?'

'His treatise means we are more kindly disposed towards those now. Before, we deplored their reckless adherence

239

to nominalism, but Clippesby's hens demonstrated how we can accept their arguments while still remaining true to our own. He is a genius.'

'Yes,' agreed Bartholomew. 'We have known it for years.'

The wounded kept Bartholomew in the Franciscan Priory until mid-morning, after which he left Dr Rougham in charge and walked home. When he arrived, Michael's window shutters were open and voices emanated from his quarters. He climbed the stairs, and found the Master and his Fellows discussing the previous night's skirmish.

Michael reclined in his favourite chair, the colour back in his cheeks after a nap and a snack from his private pantry. Theophilis was on a bench next to him, while William sat on the windowsill. Aungel perched on a stool, straight-backed and formal, not yet ready to relax in the presence of men who had so recently been his teachers. Clippesby lay on the floor with two hedgehogs.

'You made friends of the Franciscans with your treatise,' Bartholomew told the eccentric Dominican.

'Not *all* Franciscans,' growled William, eyeing Clippesby with a combination of resentment and envy. 'Some of us still think your arguments are seriously flawed.'

'Are they?' asked Clippesby with a sweet smile. 'Please tell me how, so I can amend them. My next thesis is almost finished, and I should not like to repeat any mistakes.'

'I am not telling you,' blustered William. 'You must work them out for yourself.'

The others exchanged amused glances. William noticed and went on the offensive, aiming for Clippesby, because he knew the Dominican would not fight back.

'I suppose *they* are philosophers, too,' he scoffed, jabbing a filthy finger at the hedgehogs. 'And will tell you what to pen in your next "seminal" work.'

'Oh, no,' said Clippesby, all wide-eyed innocence. 'Hedgehogs have no time for logical reasoning – they prefer to spend their time exploring the town. It is *hens* who are the theologians, as you would know if you had read their discourse.'

'Exploring?' queried Theophilis, and when Clippesby's attention returned to the animals, he grinned at the others. 'Exploring what? Libraries, in search of tomes that will lead them to a greater understanding of theology?'

'Exploring the *town*,' repeated Clippesby patiently. 'For example, Olive and Henrietta here went to the Chesterton road on Thursday, where the scholar killed that old man.'

'So they did not analyse the naturalism of—' began Theophilis.

'Wait a moment,' interrupted Michael sharply. 'You witnessed Wyse's murder?'

'*I* did not,' replied Clippesby. 'Nor did Olive and Henrietta. However, they saw the culprit running away. They did not know he was a killer at the time, of course – they only realised it later, after the body was discovered.'

'And you only mention this now?' cried Michael. 'After Dick and I have been running ourselves ragged in a hunt for clues?'

'I have been busy,' shrugged Clippesby. 'Heltisle keeps lying about how many copies of my treatise have been sold, while Theophilis insists on entangling me in theological dis—'

'The killer,' snapped Michael in exasperation. 'His name, please.'

'Olive and Henrietta did not see his face,' said Clippesby. 'But his cloak fell open as he passed, revealing his scholar's tabard. There was also an academic hat tucked in his belt.'

'Did you recognise the livery?' pressed Michael.

'No, because it was too dark.'

'So how do you know it was the killer you saw?' interrupted Bartholomew.

'Because he held a bloodied rock, which he tossed into

241

the copse where Olive and Henrietta were sleeping. It is what caught their attention, you see, otherwise they might have dozed through the entire incident.'

'*Were* they asleep?' asked Theophilis with a sly smile. 'Or philosophising?'

Even Clippesby was beginning to tire of Theophilis's persistence. 'I just told you – hedgehogs do not engage in academic pursuits. Olive and Henrietta wanted a rest, away from the fuss generated by the chickens' theories.'

'In other words, stop asking stupid questions,' translated William. 'The hens have already written all they know about nominalism and realism, so if you want to delve any deeper into the matter, you will have to consult with me.'

Theophilis laughed and the others joined in. Their mirth was short-lived, though, as William glanced out of the window to see Commissary Aynton walking across the yard. As he could think of no clever riposte to put his colleagues in their place, he vented his spleen on the visitor instead.

'Here comes one of the Chancellor's dogs,' he sneered. 'Do you want me to send him packing, Brother? I will do it if your Junior Proctor is unequal to the task.'

Michael made a warning sound in the back of his throat as Theophilis started to reply. No foundation liked outsiders to know its members quarrelled, so by the time Aynton was shown in, he might have been forgiven for thinking that all Michaelhouse Fellows loved each other like brothers.

'Good morning, Commissary,' said Michael pleasantly. 'How may we help you?'

'I am here to help *you*, Brother,' said Aynton, beaming. 'With a report. De Wetherset, Heltisle and I questioned witnesses while you lay around in bed this morning. Not that there is anything wrong with sleeping, of course. I am sure you needed the rest.'

'I did,' said Michael stiffly. 'I was up all night.'

'So were we,' said Aynton. 'Working for the University's greater good. We discussed the riot *ad nauseum*, although we reached no firm conclusions.'

'I imagine not,' said Michael haughtily. 'There are none to reach with the information currently available. If there were, I would have drawn them myself and acted on them.'

'Of course you would,' said Aynton, so condescendingly that Bartholomew glanced uneasily at Michael, knowing that umbrage would be taken. 'I would never suggest otherwise.'

'Good,' said Michael, controlling himself with difficulty. 'So make your report. What did these witnesses tell you?'

'Well, we started by asking all those scholars who attended the butts if they knew who gave the order to shoot. They did – it was a townsman.'

'Any particular one?'

'They did not see, as he skulked behind his cronies. However, we know his motive – to avenge that old rogue Wyse by taking the lives of innocent scholars. Every University man we interviewed said the same thing, so it must be true.'

Michael gave a tight smile. 'But every townsman who was there claims the culprit is a scholar. So who should we believe, when everyone is convinced of his own rectitude?'

'Why, scholars, of course,' replied Aynton, astonished he should ask. 'Townsmen are given to lying. Besides, the command came from *their* side of the butts. I heard it myself.'

'So did I,' put in Theophilis. 'I agree with Aynton – a townsman *is* responsible. But we will catch him, Brother. You and me together.'

'Let us hope so,' said Michael. 'Is there anything else, Commissary, or are you ready to resume your enquiries into the murders of Paris and the others? Unless you have solved the mystery already, of course?'

Aynton chuckled. 'Not yet, Brother, not yet. But before I set off, I must pass you a message from the Chancellor: he would like to see you in his office at your earliest convenience. He asks if Bartholomew would attend, too, as he has more griping in the guts.'

'Probably from listening to you and Heltisle spout nonsense all night,' muttered William, and for once, Bartholomew thought the friar might be right.

Michael did not go to St Mary the Great immediately, aiming to make the point that the Senior Proctor could not be summoned like a minion. And as de Wetherset's medical complaint was not urgent, Bartholomew went to replenish his medical bag first.

Eventually, both were ready and they walked across the yard towards the gate. Before they could open it, Tulyet arrived with Sir Leger and Sergeant Orwel. Orwel was a bristling bundle of hostility, and looked around the College with calculated disdain. Leger was pale, and seethed with anger and grief for Norbert.

'I did all I could for him,' Bartholomew said gently, 'but his wound was too severe.'

'I know,' replied Leger, softening a little. 'The Spital woman – Amphelisa – told me.'

'He confessed things before he slipped into his final sleep,' said Bartholomew. 'About being cornered in St Radegund's on Monday, probably by Sister Alice, who urged him to kill the French spies hiding in the Spital.'

There was a moment when he thought Leger would deny it, but then the knight inclined his head. 'It surprised us – we are not used to nuns encouraging slaughter.'

'I hope it was not you two who started the rumour about the Spital,' said Tulyet coolly. 'The one that is all over the town this morning.'

Leger regarded him levelly. 'The nun confided in Norbert on Monday, but, as you have just remarked, the tale was not "all over the town" until today. If we were responsible, it would have been common knowledge on Tuesday or Wednesday, would it not?'

Bartholomew felt like reporting what Norbert had told him about the delay, but then decided against challenging a knight who was loaded with weapons. Besides, the spreaders of the tale were far less important than its originator.

'Why did you not mention this at once?' demanded Tulyet crossly. 'Surely, you must see it has a bearing on the murders we have been struggling to solve?'

Leger shrugged. 'We did not believe it could be true, so we dismissed it as malicious nonsense. Moreover, Norbert did not see this nun's face, and she certainly did not tell him her name. If it was Sister Alice, this is the first I know about it.'

'I will go to St Radegund's this morning,' determined Michael. 'If she hates the French enough to want them lynched by an ignorant mob, then she might well have stabbed Paris, Bonet, the Girards and now Bruges. After all, she did visit the Spital on the day of the fire.'

Bartholomew was suddenly aware that Orwel was listening rather gleefully, as if he was pleased by the route their suspicions had taken.

'Where were you when the order was given to shoot last night?' Bartholomew asked him sharply.

Leger spoke before the sergeant could reply for himself. 'He was with me – at the *front* of the crowd, and in the plain sight and hearing of many witnesses. But I am sure you were not about to accuse him of being the culprit, just as I am sure you would not accuse me. Why would you? You have no evidence to suggest that either of us was responsible.'

Bartholomew was not sure what to think about Orwel,

although he knew Leger was innocent, as he himself had seen the knight arguing with scholars at the salient time. He let the matter drop.

'Unfortunately, the rumour is not just that the Spital sheltered French spies,' said Tulyet to Michael. 'It is also that the University knew about it but chose to look the other way.'

'I *did* look the other way,' said Michael. 'Out of compassion and decency. So did you.'

'Yes, but our Sheriff is not a traitor,' said Orwel smugly, as if the same could not be said of the Senior Proctor. 'How can he be? He is kin to the King.'

'I am?' asked Tulyet, startled to hear it.

Orwel nodded. 'Your son Dickon told me before you sent him to Huntingdon. Ergo, *you* never ignored the fact that a nest of spies was on our doorstep. However, most scholars are French and proud of it. Take King's Hall, for example – it has members named Bruges, Koln, Largo, Perugia, San Severino—'

'None of those are French,' interrupted Bartholomew. 'And Bruges was from Flanders.'

'They are foreign and thus suspect,' said Orwel with finality, and glared at the physician. 'We probably fought some of them at Poitiers, so I do not understand how you can bear to be in their company.'

'Take a dozen soldiers and go to the Spital,' ordered Tulyet, before Bartholomew could reply. 'I am making you personally responsible for its safety, which means that if it suffers so much as a scratch, I shall blame you. And you do not want that, Orwel, believe me.'

Orwel opened his mouth to refuse the assignment, but a glance at Tulyet's angry face made him think better of it. He nodded curtly and stamped away.

'No one will bother with the Spital now,' said Leger when Orwel had gone. 'Amphelisa told me last night that the spies – or lunatics, if you prefer – have fled.'

'That is irrelevant,' said Tulyet wearily. 'The Spital took them in, and there are many hotheads who will see that alone as an excuse to attack it.'

'There is more likely to be an assault on King's Hall than the Spital,' argued Leger. 'Orwel may not have put his case very eloquently, but he is right – it *does* possess the lion's share of the University's foreign scholars, so it is where any trouble will start.'

'You had better hope not,' said Michael coolly. 'It is full of influential nobles and favourites of the King, and if any more of them are killed by townsmen—'

'*Norbert* was a favourite of the King,' interrupted Leger tightly, 'and *he* was murdered by a scholar. The University must pay for his death.'

'He died because he was fighting when he should have been keeping the peace,' countered Tulyet shortly. 'He would still be alive if he had done his duty.'

'You take their side in this?' breathed Leger, shocked. 'When they killed innocent townsfolk last night and Wyse before that?'

'No one who died last night was innocent,' said Tulyet shortly. 'They chose to take up arms and they paid the price. However, I will not tolerate lawlessness in my town, so I *will* find who yelled the order to shoot and I *will* catch whoever killed Wyse, Paris and the others. The culprits will be brought to justice, no matter who they transpire to be.'

'Good,' said Leger. 'I will help. It will be a scholar and I shall see him swing.'

'Will you arrange for Norbert to be buried?' asked Tulyet, tired of arguing with him. 'I am sure he would rather you did it than anyone else.'

'So now we have another mystery to solve,' sighed Michael when Leger had gone. 'Because you are right: we should hunt down the rogue who gave the order to shoot. It is ultimately *his* fault that we have eighteen dead.'

'Yes,' agreed Tulyet tautly. 'And I meant what I told Leger: the culprit will suffer the full extent of the law regardless of who he is – townsman or scholar. I hope you will support me in this.'

'Of course,' Michael assured him. 'He will answer for his actions, and so will three other criminals: the killer with the fancy blades; the coward who dispatched poor old Wyse; and the poisonous nun who spread the rumour about the *peregrini*.'

'Perhaps Alice will confess to everything,' said Tulyet. 'Then there will be no reason for the town and the University to fight. It will reflect badly on your Order, though . . .'

'Alice did not give the order to shoot,' said Bartholomew. 'It was a man's voice.'

'Interrogate her,' instructed Tulyet. 'I will try to keep the peace here. And when you come back, would you mind telling Heltisle that the Mayor did *not* order the archers to massacre scholars last night – he was nowhere near the butts and has a dozen witnesses to prove it.'

'I had better do that first,' said Michael wearily. 'It will take very little to spark another riot, and that sort of accusation might well be enough.'

'Perhaps that is what Heltisle hopes,' said Tulyet soberly. 'So that you and de Wetherset will be held responsible, leaving the way open for him to step into your shoes.'

'With Theophilis as his loyal deputy,' added Bartholomew.

CHAPTER 11

Bartholomew and Michael hurried towards St Mary the Great, both aware that the atmosphere on the streets had deteriorated badly since they had last been out. Townsmen blamed the University for the riot, while scholars accused the town. The situation was exacerbated by wild and unfounded rumours – that King's Hall had installed French spies in the Spital, that the Dauphin was poised to march on Cambridge at any day, and that the Mayor intended to poison the University's water supply.

'I know hindsight is a wonderful thing,' said Bartholomew, 'but you should never have let the triumvirate take so much power. The next time someone tells me that the Senior Proctor has too much authority, I shall say that I wish you had more of it.'

'Quite right, too,' said Michael. 'I admit I hoped that Heltisle and Aynton would make a mess of things so de Wetherset would have to dismiss them, but I did not anticipate that they would create this much havoc in so short a space of time.'

They arrived at the church, where scholars had gathered to mutter and plot against the town. Most were armed, even the priests. Bartholomew paused to gaze around in alarm, but Michael pulled him on, whispering that time was too short for gawping.

They reached de Wetherset's poky office, although it was Heltisle, not the Chancellor, who sat behind its desk. The floor was covered with Michael's personal possessions, which had been unceremoniously dumped there. The monk's eyes narrowed.

'What is going on?' he demanded dangerously. 'And why are you reading my private correspondence with the Bishop? Those letters were locked in a chest.'

Heltisle was unable to prevent a triumphant grin. 'I know – we had to smash it to get inside. De Wetherset did not want your rubbish cluttering up his new quarters, and as we had no key, we had to resort to other means of clearing the decks. Where have you been?'

'Tending to urgent University business,' replied Michael tightly. 'Such as the scholars who died in last night's brawl, along with Paris the—'

'Paris!' spat Heltisle. 'The town did us a favour when they dispatched him. He should have been hanged the moment his crime was discovered.'

Michael eyed him coolly. 'Should he, indeed? Perhaps I have been looking in the wrong place for his killer. I doubt townsmen feel strongly about plagiarism, whereas scholars . . .'

Heltisle sneered. 'Do not accuse me of fouling my hands with his filthy blood. And before you ask, I did not kill the spicer or that drunken nobody on the Chesterton road either.'

'Wyse was not a nobody,' said Bartholomew, amazed to discover that he was capable of disliking the arrogant Master of Bene't even more than he did already. 'The Franciscans were fond of him, he was one of my patients, and he was a member of the Michaelhouse Choir.'

'The Marian Singers,' corrected Michael.

'Clippesby's treatise is selling very well, by the way,' said Heltisle, moving to another matter in which he felt victorious. 'What a pity your College will not reap the profits.'

Michael thought it best to stay off that subject, lest he or Bartholomew inadvertently said something to make Heltisle smell a rat. 'You have not answered my first question. Why are you so busily nosing through my private correspondence?'

'And what is it doing in here anyway?' put in Bartholomew.

Heltisle leaned back in the chair, his expression so gloating that Bartholomew did not know how Michael refrained from punching him.

'Forgive me, Brother,' he drawled. 'I was just passing the time until you deigned to appear. This is now your office. It was inappropriate for the Senior Proctor to have a grander realm than the Chancellor, so I told de Wetherset to put matters right.'

'So that is why lights burned in the church all night,' mused Michael. 'While I was busy preventing our University from going up in flames, you two were playing power games.'

Heltisle's smirk slipped. 'We were setting all to rights after your farce of a reign.'

'If the room was so important, why did you not just ask for it?' Michael was all bemused innocence. 'I would have moved. There was no need for you to demean yourselves with this sort of pettiness.'

'You would have refused,' said Heltisle, wrong-footed by the monk's response.

'I assure you, Heltisle, I have far more important matters to occupy my mind than offices. But you *still* have not explained why you see fit to paw through my correspondence.'

Heltisle glared at him. 'It is not *your* correspondence – it is the University's. And of course the Chancellor's deputy should know what it contains.'

Michael stepped forward and swept all the documents into a box. 'Then take it. I am glad to be rid of it, to be frank. It represents a lot of very tedious work, which I now willingly hand to you, Vice-Chancellor.'

'Now wait a moment,' objected Heltisle. 'I cannot waste my time with—'

'No, no,' said Michael, pulling him to his feet, shoving

251

the box into his hands and propelling him towards the door. 'You wanted it, so it is yours. I shall tell the Bishop to correspond with you about these matters in future. However, a word of warning – he does not tolerate incompetence, so learn fast. It would be a pity to see a promising career in ruins.'

'But none of these missives make sense to me,' snapped Heltisle, peering angrily over the top of the teetering pile. 'You will need to explain the background behind—'

'I am sure you can work it out.' Michael smiled serenely. 'A clever man like you.'

'No! I am too busy for this sort of nonsense. I am—'

'I suggest you make a start immediately. Some of it is urgent, and you do not want the Bishop vexed with you for tardiness. Perhaps you can do it instead of spreading silly lies about the Mayor. Oh, yes, I know where those tales originated, and I am shocked that you should stoop so low.'

Heltisle's face was a combination of dismay, anger and chagrin. 'You cannot berate *me* like an errant schoolboy. I am—'

'Go, go,' said Michael, pushing him through the door. 'I am needed to save the University from the crisis your puerile capers has triggered. I cannot stand here bandying words with you all day.'

'You might dismiss me, but you had better make time for de Wetherset,' said Heltisle in a final attempt to save face. 'He wants to see you at once.'

'Of course,' said Michael. 'I would have been there already, but I trod in something nasty on my way. I shall attend him as soon as I have scraped the ordure from my boot.'

When Heltisle had gone, Michael looked thoughtfully around the tiny space that was now his, while Bartholomew waited in silence, waiting for the explosion. It did not come.

Michael saw what he was thinking and laughed. 'Do not look dismayed on my account, Matt. I shall be back in my own quarters within a week.'

'Then what about the documents? Do you really not mind him nosing through them?'

Michael laughed again. 'I would have been vexed if he had not, given all the time I spent picking out the ones that would cause him the greatest problems.'

Bartholomew blinked. 'So you predicted this would happen and prepared for it?'

Michael raised his eyebrows in mock astonishment. 'Whatever gave you that idea?'

De Wetherset looked supremely uncomfortable in Michael's chair, behind Michael's desk and with Michael's rugs under his plump feet. Aynton was behind him, beaming as usual. The Commissary was immaculately dressed, right down to a fresh white bandage on his wrist – not one of Bartholomew's, which meant he had gone to a different physician for his follow-up appointment. His boots gleamed, although not even the herculean efforts of his servant could disguise their ugliness or the marks caused by his fall at the Spital.

'I knew you would understand,' said de Wetherset in relief, when the monk wished him well in his new domain, although Heltisle, who had followed, glowered furiously. 'A Chancellor cannot expect to be taken seriously if he operates from a cupboard at the back of the church while his Senior Proctor sits in splendour at the front.'

Michael grinned wolfishly. 'It does not matter to me who works where. Now, why did you want to see me, Chancellor? Or would you rather have your consultation with Matt first?'

'My stomach, Bartholomew,' said de Wetherset piteously. 'It roils again, and I need more of the remedy you gave me last time.'

'Nerves,' Bartholomew said, pulling some from his bag and handing it over. 'Arising from fear of how the Senior Proctor might react at being displaced.'

'Almost certainly,' agreed de Wetherset with a wry smile. 'But to business. How are the wounded in the friary? Should we expect more deaths?'

Bartholomew kept his reply brief when he saw that neither the Chancellor nor his deputy were very interested. Only Aynton was concerned, and announced his intention to visit the injured in their sickbeds, where he would caution them against future bad behaviour.

'Of course, none of it would have happened if the town had stayed away from the butts,' said de Wetherset, when the Commissary had finished babbling. 'It was our turn to use them, and they should have respected that.'

'They did it because you invaded their practice the night before,' said Bartholomew tartly.

'I hope you do not suggest that the skirmish was *our* fault,' said Heltisle indignantly. 'We are innocent victims in this unseemly affair.'

'We are,' agreed de Wetherset. 'However, I am sure Michael and I can work together to ensure it does not happen again. We want no more trouble with the town.'

'The best way to achieve that is to present culprits for some of the crimes that have been committed against us,' said Heltisle curtly. 'Unfortunately, the Senior Proctor is incapable of catching them.'

'Because I was ordered to leave it to Aynton,' Michael reminded him. 'Ergo, the failure cannot be laid at my feet. However, I have continued to mull the matter over in my mind, and I was on my way to confront one culprit when you dragged me here.'

'Really?' asked Aynton keenly. 'Who is it?'

'You will be the first to know when an arrest is made,' lied Michael. 'However, as I am here, perhaps you will tell me what *you* saw and heard at the butts last night.'

De Wetherset raised his hands apologetically. 'It was dark, and I was more concerned with staying away from jostling townies. I knew the contestants had gone to assess the targets, but I assumed they were all back when the order came to send off the next volley. I did not see who called it.'

'Nor did I,' said Heltisle. 'But I heard it, and I can tell you with confidence that it was a townsman. For a start, it was in English, and what scholar demeans himself by using the common tongue?'

'You were there?' asked Bartholomew suspiciously. 'You are our best archer, but neither you nor your students could be found when the town issued the challenge. Ergo, you were not at the butts at that point.'

Heltisle regarded him with dislike. 'We were on our way home, but raced back when we heard about the contest. So I *am* able to say with total conviction that the order to shoot came from the town.'

'I am not so sure,' demurred Aynton. 'The yell *was* in the vernacular, but I thought it had a French inflection.'

'I hope you are mistaken, Commissary,' gulped de Wetherset. 'Because if not, your testimony might lead some folk to think that the culprit is a scholar.'

'We are not the only ones who speak French,' said Aynton. 'Have you not heard about the spies in the Spital? It seems you two did not hire lunatics to act as your proxies in the call to arms, but members of the Dauphin's army!'

Heltisle gaped his horror. 'If that is true, I want my money back! I do not mind giving charity to a lunatic's orphan, but I will not have it used to coddle some French brat.'

De Wetherset was equally appalled, but not about the money. 'Are you saying that one of these French spies came to the butts with the express purpose of making us and the town turn on each other?' he asked in a hoarse, shocked voice. 'And we obliged him with a riot?'

Aynton nodded. 'Perhaps in revenge for his five coun-trymen being stabbed and burned.'

Bartholomew and Michael took their leave as the trium-virate began to debate the matter among themselves.

'Personally, I think Aynton yelled the order to shoot,' said Michael, once he and Bartholomew were out of earshot, 'and he accuses the *peregrini* to throw us off his scent. But his claim is outrageous, because not even Delacroix would take such a risk.'

'Are you sure?' asked Bartholomew soberly. 'It was dark and crowded, so none of us would have recognised him. Moreover, Aynton was right about one thing – setting us at each other's throats would be an excellent way to avenge his murdered friends.'

'I suppose it would,' conceded Michael unhappily.

Outside in the street, they met Warden Shropham from King's Hall, who had come to discuss funeral arrange-ments for his two dead scholars. He was a shy, diffident man, who was not really capable of controlling the arrogant young men under his command, which ex-plained why his College was nearly always involved when trouble erupted. Feeling he should be there when the Warden spoke to de Wetherset, Michael accompa-nied him back inside the church. Bartholomew went, too.

'De Wetherset is in *there*?' whispered Shropham when Michael indicated which door he should open. 'But that is your office, Brother!'

'Heltisle decided to make some changes,' said Michael, speaking without inflection.

Shropham made an exasperated sound. 'It was a bad day for the University when he was appointed. Do not let him best you, Brother – we shall all be the losers if you do.'

He opened the office door and walked inside, leaving

256

Michael smugly gratified at the expression of support from the head of a powerful College.

'We have been discussing your deceased students, Shropham,' de Wetherset told the Warden kindly. 'And we have agreed that the University will pay for their tombs – two very grand ones.'

Shropham looked pained. 'I would rather not draw attention to the fact that they died fighting, if you do not mind – their families would be mortified.' His grimace deepened. 'I still cannot believe that you kept everyone at the butts once the townsfolk began to show up. If you had sent us home, Bruges and Smith would still be alive.'

'You blame *us* for last night?' demanded Heltisle indignantly. 'How dare you!'

De Wetherset sighed. 'But he is right, Heltisle – it *was* a poor decision. I assumed the beadles would keep the peace, but I was wrong to place my trust in a body of men who are townsmen at heart.'

Michael's jaw dropped. 'My beadles did their best – and they are loyal to a man.'

'Although the same cannot be said of the ones Heltisle hired,' put in Bartholomew, who had tended enough injured beadles to know who had done his duty and who had not. 'Most fled at the first sign of violence, and the ones who stayed were more interested in exacerbating the problem than ending it.'

'I am glad you are leaving at the end of term,' said Heltisle coldly. 'It will spare me the inconvenience of asking you to resign. I will not tolerate insolence from inferiors.'

'Even though he speaks the truth?' asked Shropham. 'Because I saw these men myself – they *were* useless.'

Heltisle indicated Michael. 'Then *he* should have trained them properly.'

Michael shot him a contemptuous look before turning back to Shropham. 'Do you know who called for the archers to shoot? Could you see him from where you stood?'

Shropham shook his head. 'I wish I had, because I should like to see him face justice. It is ultimately his fault that Bruges and Smith died.'

'Bruges was stabbed with this,' said Michael, producing the dagger. 'Is it familiar?'

'We scholars do not demean ourselves with weapons,' declared Heltisle before Shropham could reply. 'Of course, if it were a pen—' He picked up a metal one from the table, and turned it over lovingly in his fingers. 'Well, we can identify those at once.'

Bartholomew was not about to let him get away with so brazen a lie. 'You had the only perfect score at the butts last night *and* you once told us that you are handy with a sword. Ergo, you *do* demean yourself with weapons.'

Heltisle regarded him with dislike. 'Skills I acquired *before* I devoted my life to scholarship, not that it is any of your business.'

Meanwhile, Shropham had taken the dagger from Michael and was studying it carefully. He had been a soldier before turning to academia, although Bartholomew found it difficult to believe that such a meek, sensitive man had once been a warrior of some repute.

'It is French,' he said, handing it back. 'From around Rouen, to be precise. I had one myself once, but most are sold to local men. You should find out who hails from that region and ask them about it.'

'So there you are, Brother,' said Heltisle. 'Run along and do as you are told, while the rest of us decide how best to honour King's Hall's martyred scholars.'

Michael bowed and took his leave, while Bartholomew marvelled at his self-control – *he* would not have allowed himself to be dismissed so insultingly by the likes of Heltisle.

'The *peregrini* hail from near Rouen,' the physician said, once they were outside. 'And the Jacquerie was strong in that region . . .'

'So the daggers may belong to them,' surmised Michael. 'Aynton was right to suggest they might have ignited last night's trouble with an order to shoot. And we were right to consider the possibility of a falling-out among them that saw the Girards murdered.'

'If so, we can never interrogate them about it, because they have gone. Will you still speak to Alice? I doubt she has connections to Rouen.'

'Even if she is not the killer, we cannot have nuns from my Order waylaying knights and urging them to kill people. We shall speak to her first, then see what Amphelisa can tell us about daggers made near Rouen.'

'We have already shown her the one that killed the Girards. She did not recognise it.'

Michael's expression was sober. 'That was before Shropham told us where it was made. Perhaps she will recognise it when confronted with the truth. After all, it would not be the first time she has lied to us.'

In the event, Bartholomew and Michael were spared a trek to St Radegund's, because Sister Alice was walking along the high street. She was with Prioress Joan and Magistra Katherine, talking animatedly, although neither was listening to what she was saying. Katherine's distant expression suggested her thoughts were on some lofty theological matter, while Joan was more interested in the fine horse that Shropham had left tethered outside the church.

'Good,' said Michael, homing in on them. 'I want a word with you.'

'Me?' asked Joan, alarm suffusing her homely features. 'Why? Not because of Dusty? What has happened to him? Tell me, Brother!'

'He is quite well,' Michael assured her, raising his hands to quell her rising agitation, while Katherine smirked, amused that her Prioress's first concern should be for an animal. 'And perfectly content with Cynric.'

Joan sagged in relief. 'Is it about that dagger then? I have been mulling the matter over, and it occurs to me that I did not see it here, but at home. Obviously, we do not have that sort of thing in the convent, so now I wonder whether I spotted it in Winchelsea . . .'

'We went there after it was attacked, if you recall,' said Katherine. 'To offer comfort to the survivors and to help them bury their dead.'

'But I cannot be *certain*,' finished Joan unhappily. 'I am sorry to be such a worthless lump, but my brain refuses to yield its secrets.'

'Keep trying, if you please,' said Michael, disappointed. 'It is important. However, it was not you we wanted to corner – it is Alice.'

'Me?' asked Alice, scratching her elbow. 'Why? I have nothing to say to you. Besides, we are busy. The Carmelite Prior was so impressed by Magistra Katherine's grasp of nominalism that he offered to show us his collection of books on the subject.'

'To show *me* his books,' corrected Katherine crisply, 'while Joan is to be given a tour of his stables. You are invited to neither.'

Alice sniffed huffily. 'I do not want to see smelly old books and horses anyway.'

'No?' asked Katherine archly. 'Then why have you foisted yourself on us?'

'Because the streets are uneasy after last night's chaos,' retorted Alice, 'and there is safety in numbers. If anyone else had been available, I would have chosen them instead.'

'Of course you would,' said Katherine, before glancing around with a shudder. 'My brother always said this town

260

is like a pustule, waiting to burst. He is right! I heard there are more than a dozen dead and countless injured.'

'But no horses harmed, thank God,' said Joan, crossing herself before glaring at Michael. 'Although I understand Dusty was ridden into the thick of it.'

'He behaved impeccably,' Michael informed her, unabashed. 'You would have been proud. Indeed, it is largely due to him that the death toll was not higher.'

Joan was unappeased. 'If there is so much as a scratch on him . . .'

'There is not, and he enjoyed every moment – he is far more destrier than palfrey. Did I tell you that Bruges the Fleming declared him the finest warhorse that ever lived? Coming from King's Hall, that was a compliment indeed.'

'Bruges is from Flanders?' asked Joan, surprised. 'I assumed he was French. He spoke to me in that tongue – loudly and arrogantly – the other day, when he told me that he wanted to buy Dusty. It made passers-by glare at us, which was an uncomfortable experience.'

'He will not do it again,' said Bartholomew soberly. 'He was among last night's dead.'

Joan gaped at him, but then recovered herself and murmured a prayer for his soul. 'Yet I am astonished to learn he was rioting. I assumed he was more genteel, given that he had such good taste in horses.'

'I do not know what you see in that ugly nag, Prioress,' put in Alice unpleasantly. 'Sometimes, I think you love him more than us, your Benedictine sisters.'

'I do,' said Joan baldly. 'Especially after this *conloquium*, where I have learned that most are either blithering idiots, greedy opportunists or unrepentant whores.' She regarded Alice in distaste. 'And *some* are all three.'

'I am none of those things,' declared Alice angrily. 'I am the victim of a witch-hunt by Abbess Isabel and the Bishop. I did nothing wrong.'

'You made bad choices and you were caught,' said Joan sternly. 'Now you must either accept your fate with good grace or renounce your vows and follow some other vocation.'

'As a warlock, perhaps,' suggested Katherine. 'Given that you know rather too much about maggoty marchpanes, stinking candles and cursing spells.'

'You malign me with these vile accusations,' scowled Alice, although the truth was in her eyes. 'I am innocent of—'

'Speaking of vile accusations,' interrupted Michael, 'perhaps you will explain why you have been gossiping about spies in the Spital. And do not deny it, because Sir Norbert identified you by your constant scratching.'

Alice had been about to claw her arm again; Michael's words made her drop her hand hastily. 'But everyone is talking about the spies in the Spital. Why single me out for censure?'

'Because you are the originator of the tale,' said Michael harshly. 'You discovered the "lunatics" were French – oldsters, women and children fleeing persecution from those they considered to be friends – and you urged Norbert to kill them.'

'Did you?' asked Katherine, regarding her in distaste. 'And what would have happened to us during this slaughter? Or would our deaths have been an added bonus?'

'I had no idea you were living with French spies until I heard it from Margery Starre last night,' declared Alice. 'Those rumours did *not* start with me.'

'Look at this dagger,' ordered Michael, holding it out to her. 'It was used to kill Bruges. Others like it were employed on Paris, Bonet and the Girard family.'

'But not by me,' said Alice, barely glancing at it. 'Do you really think that I, a weak woman, could plunge blades into the backs of strong and healthy men?'

262

'How do you know they were stabbed in the back?' pounced Bartholomew.

Alice's eyes glittered. 'Because someone told me. I forget who.'

'Margery, probably,' muttered Katherine. 'A witch, who is hardly suitable company for nuns. And it takes no great strength to drive a blade into someone from behind anyway, which I know, because the survivors at Winchelsea told me.'

Alice sighed to show she was bored of the conversation. 'Shall we talk about something more interesting, such as getting me reinstalled as Prioress at Ickleton?'

Suddenly, Michael had had enough of her. 'You are under arrest for the murders of Paris, Bonet, the Girards and Bruges,' he said briskly. 'And for spreading malicious rumours.'

'Oh, yes,' sneered Alice. 'Pick on the innocent nun *again*. Well, I have killed no one, although that might change if you persist with these ridiculous charges.'

'Stop your whining – it is tedious beyond belief,' snapped Joan, then turned to Michael, tapping the dagger with a thick forefinger. 'This is similar to the other one you showed me, and the more I think about it, the more I suspect I *did* see its like in Winchelsea—'

'Which proves I am innocent, as I have never been there,' put in Alice triumphantly.

'Oh, yes, you have,' countered Katherine. 'You visited us in Lyminster a few months ago, delivering letters from your own convent.'

'Lyminster is not Winchelsea,' argued Alice. 'They are more than sixty miles apart. I went to one, but not the other, and you cannot prove otherwise.'

'Actually, I can.' Katherine gestured to Alice's clothes. 'There is Winchelsea-made lace at your wrists and Winchelsea-made buttons on your habit. Moreover, your Prioress told me that you took far longer to complete the return journey than you should have done, which is indicative that you treated yourself to a major diversion.'

Alice glared malevolently at her. 'There were floods and other perils, so I had to make my way along the coast instead of plunging straight back inland. It means nothing.'

Katherine regarded her with contempt. 'I knew you were a liar, a cheat and a whore, but I am shocked to learn you are a killer as well.'

'I am *not*!' cried Alice furiously. 'So what if I stopped briefly at the port where Joan saw those particular weapons? It does not mean—'

'Where will you keep her, Brother?' interrupted Joan. 'Not near Dusty, I hope.'

Michael hesitated. The proctors' cells were full of angry young men from the riot, and he could hardly put a nun among those, not even one as unlikeable as Alice.

'Leave her to us,' said Katherine, guessing his dilemma. 'St Radegund's has cellars.'

Bartholomew was relieved when Alice was marched away, although Michael fretted over what a public announcement of her crimes might do to his Order.

'*Is* she the killer?' the monk asked worriedly. 'She is vicious and deranged, but only against those she thinks have wronged her. What could she possibly have had against Bruges? Or any of the victims, for that matter?'

'Question her again later,' suggested Bartholomew. 'Once she is confined, she may be more willing to cooperate. And even if she is innocent of the murders, she still has the rumours to answer for – rumours that may yet spark more trouble.'

'True,' acknowledged Michael. 'But before we do anything else, we should see what Amphelisa has to say about these weapons being made near Rouen.'

They set off towards the Spital, both acutely aware of

the atmosphere of rage and resentment that continued to simmer after the previous night's skirmish. Townsmen knew they had suffered more casualties than the University, and were keen to redress the balance, while scholars itched to avenge the deaths of four students with promising futures.

The Trumpington road was busy, and Bartholomew noted with alarm that most people were going to or from the Spital – Tulyet was right to predict that it might suffer from the decision to shelter the *peregrini*. They arrived to find the gates closed and Tangmer's family standing an uneasy guard atop the walls. Outside was a knot of protestors, who were vocal but not yet physically violent. They were being monitored by Orwel and a gaggle of soldiers from the castle, all of whom bitterly resented being there.

Michael knocked on the gate, which was opened with obvious reluctance by the huge Eudo. He and Bartholomew were pulled inside quickly before it was slammed shut again. This provoked a chorus of accusations from those outside, who jeered that the Senior Proctor and his Corpse Examiner had gone to confer with fellow French-lovers. Inside, any staff not guarding the walls had clustered at the gate, ready to repel anyone who tried to enter by force.

'My wife is not here,' said Tangmer, who was pale with worry. 'She went to tend the wounded in the Franciscan Friary again. I hoped her compassion to the injured would make everyone think more kindly of us, but you all still howl for our blood.'

'The claim is that we sheltered spies,' put in Eudo, clenching his ham-sized fists in impotent anger. 'But all we did was take pity on frightened women and children.'

'And eleven men,' his little wife Goda reminded them. She was wearing a new fret in her hair, which had been sewn with silver thread and looked expensive. 'Six of whom were Jacques. We should not have done it, as it made us enemies in the University *and* the town.'

'Look at this dagger,' said Michael, presenting it. 'It and the ones that killed Paris, Bonet and the Girard family were made in or near Rouen.'

'Amphelisa hails from there,' said Goda at once. 'So do the *peregrini*.'

'Yes,' said Michael, watching Tangmer shoot her an agonised glance, while Eudo delivered a warning jab to the ribs that almost knocked her over. 'I know.'

'It is not Amphelisa's,' said Tangmer quickly. 'She does not own weapons. She is a gentle soul, dedicated to helping those in need, regardless of their colour or creed.'

'Then what about you?' asked Michael. 'Is this a gift from those grateful "lunatics"? We have reason to believe that daggers like these were seen in Winchelsea, which is where your *peregrini* settled after fleeing France.'

'They gave us a little money,' said Tangmer. 'They had to – we could not have fed them otherwise. But they never offered us gifts.'

'Delacroix and his friends carried plenty of knives,' said Eudo, 'but I paid them no heed. If you want to know if this blade is theirs, you will have to ask them. Unfortunately, they left us last night, as I am sure you have heard.'

'Without leaving the money for the food they ate last week,' put in Goda sourly. 'So if you go after them, perhaps you will collect it for us.'

Bartholomew and Michael stayed a while longer, quizzing every member of staff about the dagger, but no one admitted to recognising it. Eventually, they took their leave.

'Well?' asked Bartholomew, once they had run the gauntlet of the taunting, jeering throng outside and were heading back towards the town. 'What do you think? I have no idea whether any of them were telling the truth.'

'Nor do I,' admitted Michael. 'I doubt we will have it from Amphelisa either, but you had better go to the friary and try. Take the dagger with you. I will find Dick, and tell him we have arrested Alice. I imagine he will want to be there when I question her again.'

Bartholomew was glad to reach the Franciscans' domain, which was an oasis of peace after the uneasy streets. Yet not even it was immune to the festering atmosphere outside, and Prior Pechem had made arrangements similar to those at the Spital – guards on the gate and archers on the walls.

Bartholomew arrived at the guesthouse to find all his students there, ranging from the boys who had only recently started their studies, to Islaye and Mallett who would graduate at the end of term. There were so many that the wounded had been allocated two apiece. The reason soon became clear: tending the sick was a lot easier than the punishing schedule he expected them to follow at Michaelhouse, and they were eager for a respite. He was tempted to send them all home, but then decided that there was nothing wrong with some practical experience. Moreover, it would keep them too busy to join in any brawls.

Amphelisa was there, too, moving between the beds and talking softly to patients and students alike. She wore a very old burgundy cloak that day, because changing soiled dressings was messy work. It was one she used while distilling oils, so the scent of lavender and pine pervaded the room. Bartholomew waited until she was free, then cornered her by a sink, where he was pleased to see her washing her hands before tending the next customer.

'I would not know if Rouen produced beautiful weapons or not,' she informed him when he showed her the one that had killed Bruges. 'I have no interest in things that harm – only in things that heal. I have told you this before.'

'Then perhaps you noticed if Delacroix or one of his friends had one,' he pressed.

'I did not – I was more concerned about their well-being than their belongings.'

Bartholomew opened his mouth to ask more, but there was a minor crisis with a patient, and by the time it was over, Amphelisa was nowhere to be seen. He was instantly suspicious, but Mallett informed him that she had been helping out for hours, and had expressed a perfectly understandable wish to go home and change her clothes.

'Although I like the smell of the cloak she was wearing,' he confided. 'So do our clients – it calms them. It must be the soporific oils that have soaked into it.'

Bartholomew remained in the friary for the rest of the day, taking the opportunity to do some impromptu teaching. He did not notice his students' exasperated glances when they saw their plan to escape him had misfired – he was working them harder than ever. He might have gone on all evening, but at dusk he was summoned by Isnard, who was complaining of a sore throat. The relief when he left was palpable.

He arrived at the bargeman's cosy riverside cottage to find him in despair. It was difficult to fight on crutches, so his contribution to the brawl had been to howl abuse at the enemy. He had done it with such gusto that he was now hoarse.

'And tomorrow is Sunday,' he croaked, 'when the Marian Singers will perform at High Mass. It would break my heart to miss it.'

Bartholomew prescribed a cordial of honey and black-currant, and told him to rest his voice. Unfortunately, Isnard had things to say, so there followed an exasperating interlude in which the bargeman mouthed the words and Bartholomew struggled to understand them.

'You arrested a nun,' Isnard began. 'But she did not kill Wyse. That was a scholar. We all saw him sitting in the Griffin, watching us with crafty eyes.'

'*You* saw him?' demanded Bartholomew. 'What did he look like?'

'We never saw his face, as he was careful to keep in the shadow. But I can tell you that he was fat.'

As a great many scholars were portly, this description was not very helpful. Bartholomew ordered Isnard to stay indoors and keep warm – it would make no difference to his voice, but would stop him from fighting scholars – and trudged back to Michaelhouse. As he was passing St Mary the Great, a door opened and Orwel slipped out. The sergeant looked around furtively before slinking away. Bartholomew frowned. Why was he in the church when he was supposed to be guarding the Spital?

He started to follow, aiming to ask, but lost him in the shadows of the graveyard.

Back in Michaelhouse, Bartholomew had done no more than drop his bag and look to see if his students had left any food lying around when Michael appeared. The monk turned his nose up at the slice of stale cake that Bartholomew offered to share, and invited him to the Master's suite for something better instead.

'Did you interview Alice?' asked Bartholomew, aware that his slice of beef pie was considerably smaller than the lump the monk had cut for himself.

'Dick and I decided to leave it until tomorrow, to give her time to reflect on the situation and hopefully come to her senses. Did you speak to Amphelisa?'

'Yes, but she had nothing to say. I did see Orwel sneaking out of St Mary the Great just now, though. I thought he was supposed to be guarding the Spital.'

'Perhaps Dick relieved him,' shrugged Michael. 'However, he may have been looking for me. He claims to have information about Wyse's murder, so I agreed to meet him behind the Brazen George at midnight. It is possible that he wanted to make sure I would be there – along with the money I agreed to pay.'

'Midnight?' asked Bartholomew uneasily. 'That is an odd time. Will it be safe? His intention may be to coax you to a dark place where you can be dispatched.'

'It might, which is why Dick will be there, too. However, I am fairly sure Orwel's motives are purely pecuniary.'

'What else did you do after we parted company?'

'I went to King's Hall and ordered them to stay indoors tonight. Unfortunately, Warden Shropham had already told them that the weapon used to dispatch Bruges was French, so now they think the town is sheltering a lot of enemy soldiers.'

'I have been thinking about these daggers,' said Bartholomew, handing back the one he had shown Amphelisa. 'They are well-made and expensive, yet the killer is happy to leave them in or near his victims. One of the reasons Alice was deposed was greed – she lined her own pockets at her priory's expense . . .'

'So you believe she is unlikely to be the culprit, because she is too mean to abandon a costly item,' surmised Michael. 'She would have taken it with her.'

Bartholomew nodded. 'The same is true of most towns-folk and scholars. Ergo, the culprit is wealthy – someone who can afford to lose them.'

'A rich scholar or a rich townsman,' mused Michael.

'Or a Jacques – a man who looted the houses of aris-tocrats in France and who may think he can do the same here when he runs low on funds. Of course, we must not forget de Wetherset, Heltisle and Theophilis – none of them are poor.'

'Nor is Aynton,' added Michael, and grimaced. 'The culprit is using these daggers to taunt us – daring us to link them to him.'

Bartholomew agreed, and wished he knew how to prompt Joan's memory, as he was sure the mystery would be solved once she remembered where – and with whom – she had seen the weapon before. 'Regardless, I do not think Alice stabbed anyone.'

'I am inclined to agree, although we shall keep her under lock and key anyway. She still started vicious rumours, and she is a divisive force at the *conloquium*. It is best she stays where she can do no more harm.'

'Is there any news about who gave the order to shoot last night?' asked Bartholomew hopefully. 'Or about Wyse's murder?'

Michael shook his head. 'Although every townsman blames us, and every scholar accuses the town. Dick and I have imposed another curfew until dawn, although a lot of hotheads have elected to ignore it. I fear for our foreign scholars, Matt – all of them, not just the French ones. I hope they have the sense to stay indoors.'

'So we know nothing new,' surmised Bartholomew despondently.

'Dick heard a rumour that the *peregrini* have taken up residence near the Austin Priory,' said Michael, referring to the foundation located a mile or so outside the town. 'So we rode out there to investigate.'

'I assume you did not find them.'

'Of course not. I decided to take Dusty, and as Prioress Joan was visiting him when I went to saddle up, she came, too, for the sheer joy of a canter along an empty road. She let me have Dusty, while she rode Theophilis's mean old brute. You should have seen how she handled him – he was a different horse.'

'Was he?' asked Bartholomew without much interest.

'The excursion allowed me to quiz her in depth about Alice. Apparently, Alice visited the Spital seven or eight times before the murders, so she probably did guess the "lunatics" were nothing of the kind. Ergo, I am sure it *was* her who told Norbert, no matter how vigorously she denies it.'

'Probably.'

'She also sent Magistra Katherine some very dangerous gifts – candles that leaked poisonous fumes, a lamp that burst into flames, a book impregnated with a potion to burn the reader's fingers, blankets infested with fleas . . .'

'Fleas?'

Michael grinned. 'And in a twist of irony, she is the one who crawls with them. We should not forget the comb she stole from Joan either. That is still missing, and I am sure she intends it to be a part of some mischief yet to unfold. Shall we go to meet Orwel now?'

'Now?' asked Bartholomew, startled by the abrupt change of subject. 'It is too early.'

'I know, but Lister makes a lovely roasted pork on a Saturday night and I am ravenous.'

'You cannot be! You have just devoured most of a pie.'

'To line my stomach, Matt – to prepare it for the proper meal to come.'

It was not only Michael who liked Lister's roasted pork, and the tavern was full of muttering townsmen when they arrived. Bartholomew was glad of the private room at the back. Tulyet appeared much later, footsore and weary from asking questions of witnesses.

'The town is now certain that scholars killed Wyse, hid French spies in the Spital *and* engineered last night's riot,' he reported. 'A riot in which four of you died, but ten of us. I have done my best to quell the gossip, but folk believe what they want to believe.'

'Then let us hope Orwel knows who killed Wyse,' said Michael. 'They may be appeased if that culprit is brought to justice. I imagine he will name Aynton – the gently smiling spider in the web.'

'Or Theophilis,' countered Bartholomew.

'Theophilis would never betray me,' said Michael. 'Why would he, when I gave him his Fellowship, his post as Junior Proctor, a lucrative benefice—'

'No man likes to be beholden to another,' interrupted Tulyet. 'However, Theophilis does not have the courage for murder, so my money is on de Wetherset or Heltisle. It was a bad day for the University *and* the town when they took power.'

Bartholomew told him that he and Michael now thought the dagger belonged to someone wealthy. Tulyet scrubbed his face with his hands.

'Then I will interview burgesses tomorrow. You can do the same with rich scholars. However, the culprit cannot be a Jacques – they fled *before* Bruges was killed.'

'*If* they left,' said Bartholomew. 'Perhaps one lingered long enough to avenge himself on the place that killed his friends and forced him out of his cosy refuge.'

'Twenty-six dead,' sighed Michael. 'Paris, Bonet, five members of the Girard family, Wyse, the fourteen from the riot, plus the three who were hanged for murder and their victim. And more will follow unless we stop the contagion.'

Lister arrived at that point to collect the empty platters, and Bartholomew noticed that the landlord was careful to keep the door closed – he did not want his other customers to know that he welcomed scholars in his fine establishment.

'Did I tell you that the Chancellor came here earlier, Brother?' Lister asked. 'He and his henchman Heltisle. They wanted to hire this room for *their* sole use, so that you would have to find somewhere else.'

Michael gaped at him in disbelief. 'They did *what?*'

'I had to lie – tell them that it is out of commission due to a smoking chimney. Yet it is rash for me to make enemies of such powerful men – they could break me by deciding to drink here, as my other regulars would leave.'

'Do not worry, Lister,' said Michael between gritted teeth. 'They will never harm you or your business. I promise.'

Lister smiled wanly. 'Thank you, Brother. Of course, it will be irrelevant if the town erupts into violence again. The streets felt more dangerous today than they have ever done.'

The moment Lister had gone, Michael embarked on a furious tirade. 'How *dare* they! This is *my* refuge. I do not care about my office in St Mary the Great, but to invade a man's tavern ... I will *not* share it with de Wetherset and Heltisle!'

'They do not want to share it,' Bartholomew pointed out. 'They want it all for themselves. It is another attempt to weaken you.'

'Well, they will never interfere with the important business of victuals,' vowed Michael. 'I will not permit it. But there is the linkman calling the hour. It is time to meet Orwel.'

They trooped outside. Tulyet took up station near the back gate, which he said was the one Orwel would use, while Bartholomew was allocated the door at the side. Michael went to stand in the middle of the yard. It was very dark, and Bartholomew was just wondering how he would be able to help should there be trouble, when Michael gave a sharp cry.

'What the— Help! There is a body!'

Bartholomew darted forward, but collided heavily with someone coming the other way. At first he thought it was Tulyet, but something caught him a glancing blow – aimed at his head but hitting his shoulder. He lunged blindly and grabbed a wrist, yelling for Tulyet. The arm was ripped free and he heard the side door open and slam shut again. Tulyet blundered past, fumbling for the latch in the dark. Then he was gone, too.

The commotion alerted Lister, who arrived with a lamp.

It illuminated Michael crouching next to someone on the ground. Bartholomew hurried towards them.

'It is Orwel,' said Michael, rolling the body over to look at its face. 'Is he dead?'

Bartholomew nodded. 'Struck on the head – just like Wyse. Only this time the blow was powerful enough to kill him outright.'

They looked up as Tulyet arrived empty-handed, his face a mask of anger and frustration.

'Who was it?' he demanded. 'Did you see?'

'It was too dark,' replied Bartholomew, and grimaced. 'But I think we have just let Wyse's killer slip through our fingers.'

'I would keep that quiet, if I were you,' advised Lister. 'Or the town will lynch you.'

CHAPTER 12

The next day was Sunday, when bells all over the town rang to advertise their morning services. Scholars in academic or priestly robes hurried to and from their Colleges and hostels, while townsfolk donned their best clothes – if they had any – and stood in naves to listen to the sacred words that were sang, mumbled or bellowed, depending on the preference of the presiding priest.

Bartholomew had been summoned before dawn to tend one of the wounded at the Franciscan Priory. When he had finished, he went to St Edward's, where Orwel's body had been taken. This church celebrated Mass later than everyone else, so was empty, other than its ancient vicar, who was fast asleep on a tomb.

Bartholomew examined Orwel carefully, this time without the distraction of Michael and Tulyet clamouring questions at him. But there was no more to be learned in the cold light of day than there had been the previous night: Orwel had been struck, very hard, with a stone. Assailed by the uncomfortable sense that he was being watched – something he often experienced when he examined corpses on his own – Bartholomew put all back as he had found it, and hurried out into the warm spring sunshine with relief.

As he walked along the high street, he saw the Marian Singers assembling outside St Mary the Great, ready to bawl the *Jubilate* they had been practising. As Michael was late, Isnard assumed command, assisted by Sauvage. At first, the still-hoarse bargeman tried to impose order by whispering, and when that did not work, told Sauvage to relay his orders in a bellow. When he was satisfied with the way they looked, Isnard began to lead the choir inside – only to find his way barred by Aynton and some of Heltisle's Horde.

'Not today, Isnard,' said Aynton apologetically. 'Vice-Chancellor Heltisle is conducting the service, and he has opted for a spoken Mass – one without musical interludes.'

'There is no music involved with the Michaelhouse Choir,' quipped one of the Horde, a rough, gap-toothed individual whose name was Perkyn. 'Just a lot of tuneless hollering. Master Heltisle plans to disband them soon, on the grounds that they bring the University into disrepute.'

'The Michaelhouse Choir no longer exists,' croaked Isnard loftily. 'We are the *Marian Singers*. Moreover, we have nothing to do with the University, for which we thank God, because we would not want to belong to an organisation that is full of Frenchmen.'

'And none of *us* is foreign,' declared Pierre Sauvage. 'Unlike you lot – we know you turned a blind eye when all them French spies escaped from the Spital.'

'What are you saying, *Sauvage*?' sneered Perkyn, giving the name a distinctly foreign inflection. 'That we should have made war on women and children?'

'The French do,' stated Isnard. 'They slaughtered them by the hundred in Winchelsea. Besides, unless you hate the whole race, it means you love them all, and you are therefore a traitor. Chancellor Suttone said so in a sermon.'

Bartholomew was sure Suttone had said nothing of the kind – the ex-Chancellor had had his flaws, but making that sort of remark was certainly not among them.

'Suttone!' spat Perkyn. 'A rogue from Michaelhouse, who left Cambridge not because he was afraid of the plague, but because he wanted to get married.'

There was a startled silence.

'You are mistaken, Perkyn,' said Aynton, the first to find his voice. 'Suttone is a Carmelite, a priest who has sworn vows of celibacy.'

'He ran off with a woman,' repeated Perkyn firmly. 'I was there when de Wetherset and Heltisle discussed it.'

'They would never have held such a conversation in front of you,' said Aynton sternly. 'Not that Suttone is guilty of such a charge, of course.'

Perkyn glared at him. 'I was listening from behind a pillar, if you must know. They tried to keep their voices low, but I have good ears. And I am happy to spread the tale around, because I hate Michaelhouse – it is full of lunatics, lechers and fanatics.'

'Not lechers,' objected Isnard, which Bartholomew supposed was loyalty of sorts.

'You cannot keep us out, Perkyn,' said Sauvage, aware that he might not get his free victuals if the choir failed to fulfil its obligations. 'St Mary the Great belongs to everyone.'

'It is the *University* Church,' argued Perkyn. 'Not yours. Now piss off.'

'It will not be the University's for much longer,' rasped Isnard. 'It was ours before you lot came along and stole it, and the only reason we have not kicked you out before is because Brother Michael works here. However, now de Wetherset has ousted him, we are free to eject your scrawny arses any time we please.'

'De Wetherset did not *oust* Michael,' squawked Aynton, cowering as the choir surged forward threateningly. 'They agreed to exchange rooms.'

Bartholomew could bear it no longer, so went to intervene. He was too late. Isnard shoved past the Commissary, and entered the church with the rest of the Marian Singers streaming at his heels. Aynton followed like a demented sheepdog, frantically struggling to herd them in the opposite direction.

Inside, Heltisle had already started the office, confidently assuming that Aynton was equal to excluding those he had decided to bar. He faltered when he heard the patter of many feet on the stone floor.

Moments later, a terrific noise filled the building – the Marian Singers had decided to perform anyway, regardless of the fact that they had no conductor. They plunged into the *Jubilate*, gaining confidence and volume with every note. Bartholomew put his hands over his ears, and imagined Heltisle was doing the same. Certainly, the Mass could not continue, because the president would be unable to make himself heard.

The music reached a crescendo, after which there was a sudden, blessed silence. Delighted by their achievement, Isnard indicated that the singers were to go for an encore. After three more turns, he declared that they had done their duty, and led the way outside. When they had gone, Michael stepped out of the shadows by the door.

'Do not tell me you were there all along,' said Bartholomew.

Michael grinned. 'Just long enough to know that my choristers did themselves proud today, and annoyed Heltisle into the bargain.'

As it was Sunday, teaching was forbidden, but few masters were so reckless as to leave a lot of lively young men with nothing to do, so it was a Michaelhouse tradition that the Fellows took it in turns to organise some entertainment. Bartholomew usually opted for a light-hearted disputation, followed by games in the orchard or riddle-solving in the hall. Clippesby invariably contrived an activity that would benefit his animal friends – painting the henhouse or playing with dogs – while William always chose something of a religious nature.

That week, it was Theophilis's turn, and his idea of fun was a debate on the nominalism–realism controversy, followed by him intoning excerpts from his *Calendarium* – the list of texts that were to be read out at specific times over the Church year.

'Goodness!' breathed Michael, unimpressed. 'He will set them at each other's throats in the first half, and send them to sleep in the second.'

'Perhaps he *wants* them to quarrel, so he can tell everyone that we have a Master who cannot keep order in his own house,' suggested Bartholomew.

Michael made a moue of irritation. 'Hardly! He is in charge today, so if there are any unseemly incidents, the blame will be laid at his door, not mine.'

But Bartholomew looked at the Junior Proctor's artful, self-satisfied face, and knew he had chosen to air a contentious subject for devious reasons of his own. He realised he would have to stay vigilant if he wanted to nip any trouble in the bud. Unfortunately, Michael had other ideas.

'I need you with me today, Matt. I feel responsible for Orwel's death, given that he was trying to talk to me when he was murdered. It seems likely that a scholar killed Wyse, and as Wyse and Orwel were both brained with a stone . . . well, we must catch the culprit as quickly as possible to appease the town. Then there is the killer of Paris and the others . . .'

'Who is almost certainly not Alice, although she is arrested for it.'

'If we can identify the real killer, it may ease the brewing trouble,' Michael went on. 'Although I fear it is already too late, and we shall only have peace once we have torn each other asunder. And to top it all, I am obliged to waste my time fending off petty assaults on my authority from the triumvirate.'

Bartholomew was unhappy about leaving his College in hands he did not trust. He warned Aungel and William to be on their guard, but Aungel was too inexperienced to read the warning signs, while the Franciscan would be too easily distracted by the theology.

'Our lads may misbehave because they are angry,' said Aungel worriedly. 'Offended by the town braying that we harbour French soldiers, who will slaughter them all.'

'Whereas they are the ones whose patriotism should be questioned,' added William venomously. '*They* looked the other way while Frenchmen lurked in the Spital. I wish I had known they were there – I would have driven them out.'

'You would have ejected frightened women, old men and small children, whose only "crime" was to flee persecution?' asked Bartholomew in distaste.

'Why not?' shrugged William. 'We did it when I was with the Inquisition. And evil takes many different forms, Matthew, so do not be too readily fooled by "harmless" oldsters or "innocent" brats.'

'I am offended by this nasty gossip about Master Suttone,' said Aungel, before Bartholomew could inform William that he was not with the Inquisition now, and such vile opinions were hardly commensurate with a man in holy orders. 'I know he enjoyed ladies on occasion, but he would never have run off to marry one.'

At that moment, the gate opened and Cynric cantered in on Dusty, having just given the horse a morning gallop along the Trumpington road.

'Come quick,' he gasped. 'There is trouble at the Spital. When Orwel was killed, Sauvage was given the job of keeping it safe, but he abandoned it to sing in St Mary the Great. Now the Spital is surrounded by hostile scholars and townsfolk.'

'They have united against a common enemy?' asked William.

'Not united, no,' replied Cynric. 'They each have their own ideas about what should be done, and spats are set to break out. The Sheriff has the town element under control, but he begs you to come and deal with the scholars. He said to hurry.'

The monk was not about to run to the Spital – it was too far, and he did not want to arrive winded and sweaty. He rode Dusty, shouting for Bartholomew to follow. It was not difficult for the physician to keep up with him at first, as no one could ride very fast along Cambridge's narrow, crowded streets, but it was a different matter once they were through the town gate. Then all Bartholomew could see was dust as Michael thundered ahead.

By the time Bartholomew arrived, the crisis had been averted, largely due to the fact that the troublemakers remembered Dusty from the riot – some were still nursing crushed toes and bruised ribs from when the horse had bulled through their ranks, and they were unwilling to risk it again. Many scholars began to slink home, and townsmen followed suit when Leger galloped up in full battle gear. Eventually, only two clots of people remained: a motley collection of students who always preferred brawling to studying; and some patrons from the King's Head, who were never happy unless they had something to protest about.

'I can manage now, Sheriff,' said Sauvage. He was pale – the near loss of control had given him a serious fright. 'These few will be no problem, especially if Brother Michael leaves me some beadles to keep the scholars in line.'

Unfortunately, the only beadles available were Heltisle's Horde, who had no more idea about controlling crowds than Sauvage. Michael gave them instructions, but was far from certain they could be trusted to carry them out. Tulyet finished briefing Sauvage and came to stand with Michael and Bartholomew. So did Sir Leger, whose sour expression showed he was disappointed that a skirmish had been averted.

'The situation will not stay calm for long,' he predicted with more hope than was appropriate for a man who was supposed to be dedicated to keeping the King's peace. 'Tangmer was stupid to take the enemy under his roof. He brought this on himself.'

'The *peregrini* were not "the enemy",' said Bartholomew sharply. 'They were civilians, who left France to avoid being slaughtered.'

'They were Jacques,' growled Leger. 'And spies, who told the Dauphin when to attack Winchelsea. It was a pity they escaped that town before its Mayor could hang them.'

'The Mayor lied,' argued Bartholomew, more inclined to believe Julien's version of events than the one given by a politician who was alleged to be a coward.

'He did not,' countered Leger. 'But we will have our revenge, because the truth is that they have not vanished, but are still in the area. Sauvage spotted Delacroix behind Peterhouse last night, while I saw that priest near St Bene't's Church.'

'Are you sure it was Julien?' asked Bartholomew, wondering what reason the group could possibly have for lingering somewhere so dangerous.

'No,' admitted Leger. 'I gave chase, but lost him in the undergrowth – my armour is too bulky for slithering through bushes like a snake. However, I *am* sure that he and his friends mean us harm.' He gestured to the Spital. 'It would not surprise me if they were still in there.'

'Then let us go and see,' said Tulyet. 'If they are, we shall take them to the castle – for their own protection as much as ours. If they are not, we will make sure that everyone knows the Spital is empty. Agreed?'

The moment Bartholomew, Michael, Tulyet and Leger stepped into the Spital, it was clear that something was wrong. As before, the staff guarded the gates and patrolled the walls, but there was no sign of Tangmer, Eudo or their wives. Moreover, there was a sense of distress among them that seemed to have nothing to do with the situation outside.

The cousin who had opened the gate led the visitors to the chapel without a word, where all four recoiled at the stench emanating from Amphelisa's workshop. It was far more pungent than the last time they had been, and they saw that one workbench had been knocked over, spilling oils all across the floor. Amphelisa was mopping up the mess with a cloth, and her old burgundy cloak was soaked in it.

'The fumes may be toxic in so confined an area,' warned Bartholomew, covering his nose with his sleeve. 'Open the windows and both doors.'

'Come upstairs first,' rasped Amphelisa; her eyes were bloodshot. 'The balcony.'

She led the way to the room above, with its curious wooden screen. Tangmer was there with Eudo, who was sobbing uncontrollably. Goda lay on the floor like a discarded doll.

Bartholomew glanced at Amphelisa. 'Is she . . .'

'Dead,' whispered Amphelisa. 'She was supposed to be baking today, and when she failed to appear, Eudo went to look for her. He found her here.'

Bartholomew crouched next to the little woman. She had been stabbed, and the weapon was still in her chest. He could not bring himself to yank it out while her distraught husband was watching, but Leger had no such qualms. He grabbed it and hauled until it came free.

'Not French,' he said. 'Just a kitchen knife. What happened?'

As Eudo was incapable of speech – he retreated to a corner, where he rocked back and forth, weeping all the while – Tangmer replied. The Warden's face was ashen.

'She must have come to the chapel to pray, but encountered the killer instead. There was a struggle – I assume you saw the mess downstairs? At some point, she managed to escape up here, but he got her anyway.'

The floor was covered in oily footprints, which suggested that Goda and her assailant had done a lot of running about before the fatal blow was struck. There were two distinctive sets: the tiny ones made by the victim, and the much larger ones of her attacker.

'I thought you kept this room locked,' said Bartholomew, bending to inspect them. 'Amphelisa told us that she carries the only key around her neck. So how did they get in?'

Amphelisa glanced uncomfortably at her husband.

'Tell them the truth,' said Tangmer wearily. 'Lies will help no one now.'

'I sometimes gave Goda my key when I needed something fetching from here,' replied Amphelisa unhappily. 'Unbeknownst to me, she made herself a copy. It is in her hand.'

The dead woman's fingers were indeed curled around a piece of metal. Bartholomew removed it and knew at once that it had been cut illicitly, as it was suspiciously plain and had no proper head. Then he looked at Goda's fine new kirtle, and answers came thick and fast.

'Was she stealing your oils and selling them on her own account?'

Amphelisa nodded slowly. 'We think so, although she must have negotiated a very canny deal with an apothecary to explain all the handsome clothes she has acquired recently. She has not worn the same outfit twice in days . . .'

'So who killed her?' demanded Tulyet. 'A member of staff? You have already said that these oils represent a vital source of income, so her thievery will impact on everyone here.'

'None of us hurt her,' said Tangmer firmly. 'She was family. Besides, we knew she was light-fingered when she married Eudo, but she made him happy, so we overlooked it.'

'Then have you had any visitors today?' asked Tulyet.

'No – we thought it best to dissuade them,' replied the Warden. 'For obvious reasons.'

'Then how do you explain her murder, if you are innocent and no one else came in?'

'A townsman or a scholar must have climbed over the wall,' said Tangmer helplessly. 'Like they did when the Girard family died. We try to be vigilant, but our Spital is huge, and it is not difficult to sneak in undetected. You know this, Sheriff – you did it yourself, to prove that our defences are less stalwart than we believed.'

'So you had a mysterious invader,' said Tulyet flatly. 'How convenient!'

Before he could ask more, Leger made an urgent sound. He was standing near the screen, and had been peering through it into the nave below.

'Someone is down there,' he whispered tightly. 'Eavesdropping.'

Tulyet was down the stairs in a flash, and Bartholomew ran to the screen just in time to see him lay hold of someone by the scruff of his neck.

'Hah!' exclaimed Leger triumphantly. 'It is that French priest. I said those bastards were still in the area, but I was wrong. The truth is that they never left!'

It did not take long to determine that Leger was right. The old men, women and children – but not the Jacques, who were conspicuous by their absence – were huddled in the guesthouse recently vacated by the nuns. They looked frightened and exhausted, and Bartholomew's heart went out to them. Before any questions could be asked, there was a commotion outside the gate. Tulyet told Leger to make sure the Spital was not about to be invaded.

286

'What if it is?' shrugged Leger insolently. 'Or would you have me defend French scum from loyal Englishmen?'

'I would have you defend a charitable foundation from a mindless mob,' retorted Tulyet sharply. 'This is a hospital, built to shelter people in need, and the King will not want it in flames. Now go and restore the peace – and not a word about what you have seen here, or you will answer to me. Is that clear?'

With ill grace, Leger stamped away. Once he had gone, the *peregrini* relaxed a little, and one or two of the smaller children even began to play. The Sheriff had been wise to dispense with Leger's menacing presence before starting to question them.

'Where are the Jacques?' he began.

'We do not know,' replied Julien tiredly. 'They left during the night. I did my best to find them and persuade them to come back, but to no avail. Sir Leger saw me in a churchyard, and I was lucky to escape from him.'

'Their flight is a bitter blow,' said the weaver – Madame Vipond – worriedly. 'Who will protect us now? Even Delacroix has gone, despite the rhubarb decoction I slipped into his ale to make sure he stayed put.'

Julien gaped at her. 'So he was right to claim he was poisoned?'

'It was not poison,' she sniffed. 'It was a tonic. He just happened to swallow rather a lot of it. Goda got it for me, although it cost me the last of my savings. Do not look at me like that, Father – I did what I thought was best for the rest of us.'

Julien turned back to Tulyet. 'Well, all I hope is that they have the sense to get as far away from here as possible. I am beginning to realise that we should have done the same.'

'So why did you stay?' asked Tulyet, making it clear that he wished they had not.

'Because Michael moved the nuns, and suddenly there

was an empty guesthouse available,' explained Julien. 'It seemed as if God was telling us to hide here for a while longer – to make proper plans, rather than just traipsing off and hoping for the best.'

Bartholomew looked at the children's bewildered faces, and the dull resignation in the eyes of the adults, and was filled with compassion. Could he take them to Michaelhouse? Unfortunately, word was sure to leak out if he did, and then there would be a massacre for certain – of his colleagues as well as the refugees. He wracked his brain for another solution, but nothing came to mind.

'We could not bring ourselves to oust them,' said Amphelisa. 'So we agreed to tell people that they had gone to London instead. After all, who would ever know the truth?'

'Everyone you invited here to search the place,' replied Bartholomew, shocked by the reckless audacity of the plan. 'You said you hoped they would see it is a good place, and would bring their lunatics here.'

'The offer was for folk to look around our hall, not the guesthouse,' argued Amphelisa pedantically. 'No one would have seen the *peregrini*.'

'If you had declared one building off-limits, even the most dull-witted visitor would have smelled a rat,' said Tulyet, disgusted. 'Your decision was irresponsible, especially as Delacroix *and* Julien were seen after they were supposed to have left. I appreciate your motives, Amphelisa, but this was a foolish thing to have done. Now none of you are safe.'

'Dick is right,' said Michael. 'You must leave today. All of you – staff and *peregrini*.'

'And go where?' asked Madame Vipond helplessly. 'The open road, where we will be easy prey for anyone? Another town or village, where we will be persecuted as we were in Winchelsea? At least here we have food and a roof over our heads.'

'Not food,' put in Tangmer. 'I have no money to buy more, and nor do you.'

'You mentioned the castle,' said Bartholomew to Tulyet. 'They would be safe there, under your protection.'

'That was before Goda was murdered,' said Tulyet. 'Once it becomes known that a local lass was stabbed in a place where Frenchmen were staying . . . well, you do not need me to tell you what conclusions will be drawn. None of us can guarantee their safety now, and the only thing these *peregrini* can do is get as far away as possible.'

'Goda,' said Michael, looking around at the fugitives. 'Do *you* know who killed her?'

'She brought us bread at dawn,' replied Julien. 'But since then, we have been huddled in here, trying to keep the children quiet. The windows are either nailed shut or they open on to the road rather than the Spital, which means we have no idea what is happening in the Tangmers' domain.'

'We had better pack,' said Madame Vipond exhaustedly to the others. 'And trust that God will protect us, given that people will not.'

'We cannot send them off to fend for themselves,' protested Bartholomew to Michael and Tulyet. 'It would be inhuman. We must find another way.'

Michael pondered for a moment. 'The *conloquium* will finish the day after tomorrow, and nuns will disperse in all directions to go home. Most are good women, and many hail from very remote convents. Let me see if one will accept some travelling companions.'

'Two days is too long,' argued Tulyet. 'We cannot trust Leger to keep his mouth shut for ever, and these folk will die for certain if they are discovered here.'

'Then we will just have to protect them,' said Bartholomew doggedly. 'Detail more soldiers to stand guard.'

'I cannot spare men to mind the Spital when I am

struggling to prevent my town from going up in flames,' said Tulyet irritably.

'Please, Dick,' said Michael quietly. 'I seriously doubt these people can move quickly enough to escape the bigots mustering outside, so they will be caught and murdered. I do not want that on my conscience and nor do you.'

Tulyet sighed in resignation. 'Very well – you have until dawn the day after tomorrow to organise an escape. But the agreement is conditional on the *peregrini* staying out of sight. If one is so much as glimpsed through a window or a gate, the deal is off. Do you understand?'

'Thank you, Sheriff,' said Julien with quiet dignity. 'We accept your terms. But what about Delacroix and his friends?'

'You had better hope they are well away,' said Tulyet sourly, 'because if they are lurking here, they are dead already.'

'Do you think Goda tried to stop them from leaving?' asked Bartholomew. 'And they stabbed her for it?'

Julien and Madame Vipond exchanged a glance that suggested it would not surprise them. Amphelisa was the only one who protested their innocence, although not for long.

Outside, Leger listened in mounting anger to what had been agreed. His face darkened and his fists clenched at his side.

'You place the comfort of foreigners above the safety of your town,' he snarled. 'How long do you think it will take before the truth seeps out? After that, anyone trying to defend this place will die, and for what? To protect *Frenchmen*?' He spat the last word.

'We four are the only ones outside the Spital who know the secret,' said Tulyet curtly. 'Michael, Matt and I will say nothing, so unless you cannot keep quiet . . .'

'I can,' said Leger sullenly. 'Although this is a stupid decision, and I will tell the King so when he demands to know why good men died for nothing.'

'No one will die, because you will prevent it,' said Tulyet briskly. 'I am assigning *you* the task of ensuring the Spital comes to no harm.'

'I refuse,' said Leger immediately. 'You cannot make me act against my principles.'

'Your principles preclude you from defending a charitable foundation?' asked Tulyet archly. 'Because that is all I require you to do – to keep the *building* safe.'

'A building with Frenchmen inside it,' retorted Leger. 'The enemy.'

'Oh, come, man,' snapped Tulyet. 'We are talking about a gaggle of women, old men and terrified children. Do you really think such folk represent a danger to you? However, if the challenge of defending this place from a ragtag mob is beyond your abilities, I can easily pick someone else to do it.'

'Then do,' flashed Leger. 'Because I am not—'

'Although if the Spital is damaged because you refuse to do your duty, you will answer to the King,' Tulyet went on. 'He has taken a personal interest in this place, and wants it to thrive. I seriously doubt you will keep his favour once he learns that you let it burn down because a few displaced villagers from Rouen were within.'

'Very well,' snarled Leger, throwing up his hands in defeat. 'But I want my objections noted, and I shall be making my own report to His Majesty.'

He stamped away without another word, his expression murderous. Tulyet watched him begin his preparations, then started to walk back to the town with Bartholomew and Michael.

'Are you sure he can be trusted?' asked Bartholomew uneasily. 'Because if not, it will cost the lives of everyone inside – *peregrini* and staff.'

'I am sure,' replied Tulyet. 'A massacre will reflect badly on his military abilities, and he will not want that on his record. Besides, now that Orwel and Norbert are dead, he is the only man with the skills and experience to mount a workable defence – other than my knights, and I cannot spare them. However, it is not Leger who concerns me, but the Jacques.'

'Why?' asked Bartholomew. 'They will be miles away by now. They would have gone after the Girards were killed, but Julien stopped them. They never wanted to linger here.'

'There is a rage in them that I have seen before,' explained Tulyet soberly. 'Their time in the Jacquerie and then in Winchelsea has turned them angry, bitter, violent and unforgiving. They will not overlook the Girard murders, no matter how much they and the victims might have quarrelled. They will want vengeance.'

'Unless they are the ones who killed them,' Bartholomew pointed out. 'They are on our list of suspects.'

'Regardless, I fear they have *not* disappeared into the Fens to escape the tedious business of protecting Julien's flock, but are here, in Cambridge, biding their time until they can avenge themselves on the country that took them in and then turned against them.'

'Perhaps,' said Michael. 'Yet I cannot believe that one of them stabbed Bruges at the butts. It would have been a shocking risk, and none of them are fools.'

'But it would be a good solution to the murders, would it not?' asked Tulyet. 'The culprit being neither a townsman nor a scholar?'

'Yes,' acknowledged Michael. 'But only if it is true.'

As the mood of the town felt more dangerous than ever, Tulyet decided it would be safer for Bartholomew and Michael to remain with him while they hunted killers. Michael objected, on the grounds that no one would dare assault the Senior Proctor, but Bartholomew was glad of Tulyet's protection. They went to the castle first, where Tulyet organised a hunt for the Jacques, promising a shilling to the soldiers who brought them back.

'Alive,' cautioned Bartholomew, visions of corpses galore delivered to the Sheriff's doorstep, the triumphant bearers safe in the knowledge that the dead could not say there had been a terrible mistake.

When the patrols had gone, Tulyet, Bartholomew and Michael went to the Griffin, to question its patrons about Wyse's killer, after which they interviewed rioters about the person who had yelled the order to shoot. They spent an age in King's Hall asking about its murdered scholars, and then went to St Radegund's, where Sister Alice informed them that all the evidence against her was fabricated. Finally, they spoke to the staff at the Brazen George, to see if they had noticed anything untoward around the time when Orwel had died.

But they learned nothing to take them forward. Afternoon faded to evening, and then night approached, dark and full of whispering shadows. Tulyet scrubbed vigorously at his face to wake himself up as the church bells rang to announce the evening services.

'We have done all we can with the murders today,' he said. 'Now I must go and keep the peace on our streets.'

'I have already briefed my beadles,' said Michael, 'although I told Meadowman not to trust Heltisle's Horde. I shall offer them to Leger soon – a gift of two dozen "prime fighting men" for the King's army.'

He and Bartholomew trudged back to Michaelhouse, where they sat on a bench in the yard and ate a quick meal of bread and cheese before Michael went to join his beadles. The yard used to be dark once the sun went down, but he had ordered it lit with lanterns after he had taken an embarrassing tumble. In the hope that logical analysis would present the answers that had eluded them all day, Bartholomew began to list his remaining suspects.

'The Jacques or Theophilis,' he said. 'I would like to include Heltisle, too, as he keeps trying to drag your attention away from the investigations by playing petty power games, but the truth is that I cannot see him stabbing anyone.'

'The Jacques are on my list, too,' said Michael, 'but with Aynton above them, rather than Theophilis. You are right about Heltisle – he is objectionable, but no killer. We can exclude de Wetherset for the same reason.'

'The only other people left are nuns – Sister Alice and Magistra Katherine, who cannot prove their whereabouts when the Girards were murdered.'

'But Katherine is the Bishop's sister, and too busy being intelligent and superior at the *conloquium* to stab people. I do not see Alice braving the butts either, much as I dislike her.' Michael stood and brushed crumbs from his habit. 'That meagre dinner will not see me through the night. I need something else. Come and have a couple of Lombard slices.'

He marched to his quarters and flung open the door. Theophilis was inside, going through the documents on the desk. The Junior Proctor jerked his hand back guiltily, but managed an easy smile.

'There you are, Brother. I am looking for the beadles' work schedules for the coming week. They are not in St Mary the Great, so I assumed they were here.'

'I gave them to Heltisle,' said Michael. 'Why did you want them?'

'Because Perkyn is ill, and must be removed from the rosters until he is well again. He complains of ringing ears after listening to the Marian Singers.'

Michael's expression hardened. 'Then tell him his services are no longer required. I heard the choir, and *my* ears are not ringing.'

Theophilis inclined his head and left, while Bartholomew wondered what lie the Junior Proctor would tell Perkyn to explain why he no longer had a job.

'He did not want the rotas,' he said, looking through the window to watch Theophilis cross the yard. 'The truth is that Heltisle uncovered nothing to hurt you in your office last night, so he sent him here to find something instead.'

'Well, if he did, Theophilis would not be looking for it on my desk, lying out for all to see. He knows anything important will be locked away. You are wrong about him, Matt.'

Bartholomew failed to understand why the monk refused to accept what was so patently obvious. He looked out of the window again while Michael riffled about in his pantry for treats, and saw Clippesby with a drowsing chicken – he was going to the henhouse to put her to roost. Theophilis changed course to intercept him, and asked a question to which the Dominican shook his head. Theophilis persisted, and Clippesby became agitated. So did the bird, which flew at Theophilis with her claws extended.

The Junior Proctor jerked away with a yelp. He looked angry, so Bartholomew hurried down to the yard to intervene – the hen was Gertrude, and it would be unfortunate if Theophilis hurt her, as the nominalists in the University were likely to see it as an act of war. The last thing they needed was another excuse for strife.

'This lunatic knows something about the murders,' spat Theophilis, jabbing his finger accusingly at Clippesby. 'He saw something last night, but declines to tell me what.'

'What did you see, John?' asked Bartholomew, while Clippesby retrieved the hen and stroked her feathers. She relaxed, although her sharp orange eyes remained fixed on Theophilis.

'You will not get a sensible answer,' hissed Theophilis.

'Just some rubbish about a mouse. He ought to be locked away where he can do no harm. All this nonsense about philosophising fowls! He is an embarrassment, and as soon as I have a spare moment, I am taking him to the Spital. They know how to deal with madmen.'

Clippesby regarded him reproachfully. 'But you have been fascinated by the birds' theories for weeks, so why—'

'You are a fool,' interrupted Theophilis, so vehemently that Clippesby flinched and the hen's hackles rose again. 'I thought you were more clever than the rest of us combined, but I was wrong. I should never have befriended you.'

'Not befriended,' said Bartholomew, suddenly under-standing exactly why Theophilis had spent so much time in the Dominican's company. 'Milked for ideas.'

Theophilis regarded him contemptuously. 'You are as addle-witted as he is if you think I am interested in any theory *he* can devise.'

'But you *are* interested,' argued Bartholomew. 'Because Clippesby *is* cleverer than the rest of us combined. The whole University is talking about the Chicken Debate, and his arguments are respected by people on both sides of the schism. He has single-handedly achieved what others have been striving to do for decades.'

He saw that Michael had followed him outside and was listening. William had sidled up, too, although Theophilis was too intent on arguing with Bartholomew to notice either.

'Clippesby is a one-idea man,' the Junior Proctor said contemptuously. 'He has shot his bow and now his quiver is empty.'

'On the contrary, he has been working on his next treatise all term, and it promises to be every bit as brilliant as the first. It is almost ready, so you aim to steal it and pass it off as your own. *That* is why you have quizzed him so relentlessly.'

'Lies!' cried Theophilis outraged. 'I would never—'

'But first, you must get rid of him,' Bartholomew forged on. 'You began calling him a lunatic a few days ago, rolling your eyes and smirking behind his back. Now you aim to have him locked him away, so that no one will hear when he says "your" treatise is really his.'

'But he *is* insane! He *should* be shut in a place where he cannot embarrass us. And I resent your accusations extremely. Why would *I* claim credit for a discussion between hens?'

'Oh, I am sure you can adapt it to a more conventional format. And that is why you were in Michael's room just now – not spying for Heltisle, but looking for something that will allow you to discredit Clippesby.'

'What if I was?' flared Theophilis, capitulating so abruptly that Bartholomew blinked his surprise. 'I will make sure that this new treatise honours Michaelhouse, whereas Clippesby will just draw attention to the fact that we enrol madmen. It is better for the College if I publish the work under my name. Surely, you can see that I am right?'

Bartholomew was so disgusted that he could think of no reply, although the same was not true of William, who stepped forward to give Theophilis an angry shove.

'You are despicable,' he declared, as Theophilis's eyes widened in horror that his admission had been heard by others. 'There is no room in Michaelhouse for plagiarists.'

'There is not,' agreed Michael, regarding his Junior Proctor with hurt disappointment. 'Consider your Fellowship here terminated.'

'Do not expel him on my account,' begged Clippesby, distressed as always by strife. The hen clucked, so he put his ear to her beak. 'Gertrude says that—'

'You see?' snarled Theophilis, all righteous indignation. 'He is stark raving mad!'

'He is,' agreed William. 'Because *I* would not speak in

your defence if you had been trying to poach *my* ideas. It takes a very special lunatic to be that magnanimous.'

'You cannot eject me, because I resign,' said Theophilis defiantly. 'From Michaelhouse *and* the Junior Proctorship. I want nothing more to do with any of you.'

'Good,' said William. 'I will help you pack. Is *now* convenient?'

When Theophilis had been marched away by a vengeful William, Michael invited Bartholomew and Clippesby to his rooms for a restorative cup of wine. Bartholomew supposed he should feel triumphant that his doubts about the Junior Proctor's integrity should be correct, but instead he felt soiled. He glanced at Clippesby, who perched on a stool with the hen drowsing on his lap.

'What will poor Theophilis do now?' asked the Dominican unhappily. 'No other College will take him once they learn what he did. His academic career is over.'

'You are too good for this world,' said Michael. 'If he had tried to steal my ideas, I would have driven him from the country, not just the College.'

Clippesby kissed the chicken's comb. 'There was never any danger of him taking my ideas. Gertrude and Ma warned me weeks ago that his interest in them was not quite honourable, so they have been having a bit of fun with him.'

Michael regarded him warily. 'What kind of fun?'

A rare spark of mischief gleamed in the friar's blue eyes. 'Theophilis *will* publish a thesis soon, but as Gertrude and Ma have been largely responsible for its contents, it will have some serious logical flaws. Then they will help William prepare a counterclaim.'

Bartholomew shook his head wonderingly. 'Which will have the dual purpose of bringing more academic glory to Michaelhouse – William's refutation is sure to be flawless if your hens are involved – and embarrassing Theophilis by having his errors exposed by the least able scholar in the University. My word, John! That is sly.'

Clippesby kissed the bird again. 'Gertrude has a very wicked sense of humour.'

Michael eyed him with a new appreciation. 'It is a scheme worthy of the most slippery of University politicians. Perhaps I should appoint you as my new Junior Proctor.'

'No, thank you,' said Clippesby vehemently, then turned to Bartholomew. 'When you confronted Theophilis, did I hear you accuse him of spying for Heltisle?'

Bartholomew nodded. 'Why? Do you know something to prove it?'

'I know something to *disprove* it. Hulda the church mouse often listens to Heltisle and de Wetherset talking. She says they *did* ask Theophilis to monitor you, but he refused.'

'Did he say why?' asked Michael. 'And more to the point, why did this mouse feel compelled to eavesdrop on high-ranking University officials in the first place?'

'Because she was afraid they would conspire against you – which they did, by trying to buy your Junior Proctor. But Theophilis was loyal. He refused to betray you, even for the promise of your job.'

'Then what a pity he transpired to be an idea-thief,' spat Michael in disgust. 'Faithful deputies do not grow on trees. I do not suppose he was pumping you for ideas when any of these murders was committed, was he? Matt has him at the top of his list of suspects.'

'He was with Gertrude, Ma and me when Paris was stabbed,' replied Clippesby promptly. 'Does that help?'

Bartholomew was not sure whether to be disappointed or relieved. He had wanted Theophilis to be the culprit, especially in the light of what the man had tried to do to Clippesby, but it would be better for Michaelhouse if the killer was someone else. Then he recalled another thing that Theophilis had said.

'He mentioned you knowing something about the murders. Do you?'

'Just another snippet from Hulda the mouse – that she saw a nun running away from the Brazen George last night. It was not long after Orwel was bludgeoned, although Hulda did not know this at the time, of course.'

Michael gaped at him. 'A *nun* killed Orwel? Which one?'

'Hulda did not say this nun killed Orwel,' cautioned Clippesby. 'She said the nun was running away from the Brazen George shortly after Orwel died. She does not know her name, but the lady was thin, pale, and wore a pure white habit.'

Michael blinked. 'Abbess Isabel? She would never leave St Radegund's at that time of night! She knows the town is dangerous, because she is the one who found Paris's body.'

'How was she running?' asked Bartholomew of Clippesby. 'In terror? In triumph?'

The Dominican shrugged. 'She was just running.'

'Abbess Isabel is *not* the killer,' said Michael firmly. 'She would never risk her place among the saints by committing mortal sins.' He turned back to Clippesby. 'Was this mysterious white figure alone?'

Clippesby nodded. 'And not long before, Hulda saw her calling on Margery Starre.'

'Then it cannot have been Isabel,' said Michael at once. 'She would never visit a witch. I imagine someone stole her distinctive habit and used it as a disguise.'

'So ask Margery who it was,' suggested Clippesby. He bent his head when the hen on his lap clucked. 'But not tonight. Gertrude says she is busy casting spells to prevent another riot.'

'Then we shall see her tomorrow,' determined Bartholomew, although he could see that Michael itched to have answers immediately. 'We cannot disrupt Margery's efforts to keep the peace, Brother. If we do, and trouble breaks out again, everyone will say it is our fault for getting in her way.'

'They will,' agreed Clippesby. 'And if more people die fighting, it will be even harder to restore relations between us and the town.'

Reluctantly, Michael conceded that they were right.

CHAPTER 13

The next day saw a change in the weather. Blue skies were replaced by flat grey ones, and a biting north wind scythed in from the Fens. Bartholomew rose while it was still dark, woke Aungel with instructions for the day's teaching, then joined Michael for a hurried breakfast in the kitchen with Agatha the laundress, who had a great many things to say about the fact that the town and the University were teetering on the brink of yet another major confrontation.

'And it is not just each other they hate,' she declared, pursing her lips. 'There are divisions in both that mean the strife will be all but impossible to quell. I would not be in your shoes for a kingdom, Brother. Or the Sheriff's, for that matter.'

'She is right,' muttered Michael, as he and Bartholomew hurried to Margery's home in Shoemaker Row. 'Dick managed to stamp out some trouble last night, but all it did was give the would-be rioters more cause to resent him – and us.'

'Have you arranged an escape for the *peregrini* yet?' asked Bartholomew.

Michael grimaced. 'I need to be careful, because if I confide in the wrong nun . . . well, I do not need to explain to you that the matter is delicate.'

Although it was only just growing light, the streets were busy as folk took advantage of the curfew's end to see what was happening outside. They included both townsmen and scholars, the latter making no effort to pretend they were going to church. On the high street, some of Heltisle's Horde were engaged in a fracas with students from King's Hall, while there was a quarrel in the market square between those who wanted to fight the French spies at the Spital and those who thought it was better to lynch them.

'Vengeance is for God to dispense, not you,' declared Prior Pechem of the Franciscans as he passed – a remark that meant there were then three factions yelling at each other.

An angry bellow from Michael was enough to make them disperse, although Bartholomew sensed it was only a matter of time before they were at it again. He suspected most cared nothing about the issues they supported, and their real objective was just a brawl.

He and Michael reached Shoemaker Row, where Margery's cottage looked pretty in the daylight – painted a cheerful yellow, with an array of potted plants on the doorstep. It was not how most folk would picture the lair of a witch.

'You will have to go in alone,' said Michael, who had been walking ever more slowly towards it. 'I cannot be seen dropping in on her – our students might interpret it as licence to do the same, and enough of them beat a track to her door as it is. Besides, I have my reputation to think of.'

'What about my reputation?' demanded Bartholomew indignantly.

'Already compromised – it is common knowledge that she likes you. Now hurry up! We cannot afford to waste time. If Margery confirms that Abbess Isabel was indeed out and about when Orwel was murdered, we will have to go to St Radegund's and demand an explanation.'

Bartholomew entered Margery's home with the same fear that always assailed him when he stepped across her threshold – that he would find her having a cosy chat with her good friend Lucifer. Or worse, brewing some concoction that contained human body parts. Instead, it was to discover Cynric there, the two of them sitting companionably at the hearth, drinking cups of her dangerously strong ale.

'I am here for Dusty,' explained the book-bearer, not at all sheepish at being caught in such a place. 'He has a sore hoof, and Margery makes an excellent onion poultice for those.'

'She probably got the recipe from Satan,' muttered Bartholomew to himself, 'who uses it on his cloven feet.'

'No, it is my own formula,' said Margery pleasantly, startling him with her unusually acute hearing. 'So what brings you here, Doctor? And openly, too! The last time you came, you skulked outside with your ear to my window shutter.'

Bartholomew felt himself blush. 'I was following Sister Alice. She was walking along so furtively that I thought I should see what she was up to.'

'She wanted a cursing spell,' recalled Margery. 'But I did not give her one. I decided she was unworthy, so I fobbed her off with a pot of coloured water.'

'Oh,' said Bartholomew, wondering how 'unworthy' one had to be not to pass muster with one of the Devil's disciples. 'Did she say what she intended to do with it?'

'Wreak revenge on her enemies, who seem to include everyone she meets. I did not take to her at all, which is why I do not mind disclosing her secrets. I am more discreet with folk I like, such as yourself.'

'How about Abbess Isabel?' asked Bartholomew, speaking quickly to mask his discomfiture. 'Do you like her?'

Margery nodded. 'She is a little over-passionate about Christianity, but that happens when you spend all your life in a convent, and she cannot help it, poor soul. However, my fondness for her means I will not break her confidence.'

'No?' asked Bartholomew, wondering how to convince

her that it was important she did. Fortunately, he did not have to ponder for long.

'Unless you make it worth my while,' Margery went on. 'Do I detect the scent of cedarwood oil about you? Amphelisa's perhaps? That is excellent stuff – always useful.'

Bartholomew fished it from his bag and handed it over, marvelling that her sense of smell should be as sensitive as her hearing. 'She said it kills fleas.'

'I imagine it does, but it is also good for dissolving unwanted flesh.'

Bartholomew regarded her uneasily. 'Unwanted by whom?' But then he decided he did not want to know the answer, so changed the subject. 'Tell me about the Abbess.'

'She came to me on Saturday evening, shortly after you and Brother Michael went to the Brazen George – I saw you slip through its back door while I was walking home.'

'How did she seem to you?'

'You mean did she race out afterwards and brain Orwel?' asked Margery shrewdly. 'If she did, it had nothing to do with her discussion with me – which was all about a nun she aims to defrock. She is too tactful to mention names, but I knew she meant Alice.'

'How?'

'By her description of a discontented lady with a penchant for stinking candles. She wanted a list of all those Alice intends to hurt, so she could warn them to be on their guard. I obliged her, and in return she gave me a lock of her hair, which she says will be worth a lot of money after she is canonised.'

Bartholomew decided not to tell Margery that it took years for such matters to be decided, and that those arrogant enough to believe they were in the running would probably be rejected on principle.

'Is Isabel herself on Alice's list?' he asked.

'Oh, yes, along with the Bishop and a hundred others. I told her to watch herself, because while I am the best wise-woman in Cambridge, I am not the only one, and others are not as scrupulous as me. When Alice realises my coloured water is not having the desired effect, she will take her custom elsewhere.'

'Did Isabel heed the warning?'

'She promised she would. However, she said one thing that bemused me. She said that finding Paris the Plagiarist's body still haunts her dreams. But why would it? He cannot have been her first corpse, and I am told that his stabbing was not particularly bloody.'

'No more than any other,' said Bartholomew. 'And less than some.'

'There is more to her distress about him than she lets on,' finished Margery. 'It puzzles me, and if you aim to solve his murder, it should puzzle you, too.'

To reach St Radegund's, Bartholomew and Michael had to cross the market square, where there was no sign of the people who had been quarrelling there earlier. There were others, though, using the stalls as an excuse to loiter. The traders were becoming irked by all the looking but no buying, and it would not be long before it caused a spat.

Scholars prowled in packs, armed to the teeth. Some clustered around the baker's stall, a business owned by generations of Mortimers. Bartholomew was not sure which Mortimer ran it now, as they all looked alike, but the present incumbent's face was red with fury.

'They have no right,' he bellowed. 'It is illegal and immoral!'

His angry voice attracted an audience. It included Isnard the bargeman and Verious the ditcher, the latter excused sentry duty at the town gates on the grounds that he was not very good at it.

'What is illegal and immoral?' asked Michael.

'Cutting the price of bread,' snarled Mortimer, so enraged that Bartholomew was afraid he would give himself a seizure. 'We had a deal, and the University cannot suddenly decide only to pay half of it. That will barely cover the cost of the ingredients!'

Michael was bemused. 'Our contract fixes the price of bread until next year. Neither of us can change anything until then.'

'So you say, but Heltisle has declared all the agreements you negotiated null and void. He has a new list of prices – ones that favour scholars at *our* expense.'

'Refuse to sell him anything, then,' shrugged Isnard. 'He and his cronies will starve without bread, and he will soon come back with his tail between his legs.'

'No – he will buy it in Ely and I will be ruined,' said Mortimer bitterly. 'The bastard! He has me over a barrel.'

'You should not trade with scholars anyway,' put in Verious. 'Not when they hid French spies in the Spital – spies who then crept out and murdered Sauvage.'

'*Murdered* Sauvage?' echoed Bartholomew uneasily. 'He is dead?'

'Did you not hear?' asked Isnard. 'We found him this morning, not ten paces from here. He was stabbed, and his killer left the dagger sticking out of his back – a challenge for us to identify it and catch him.'

'*What?*' cried Michael, shocked. 'Why did no one tell me?'

'Because it is none of your business,' spat Mortimer. 'Sauvage was a townsman and he was murdered by the French. His death has nothing to do with the University, so you can keep your long noses out of it.'

'Poor Sauvage,' sighed Isnard. 'He should have told them his name – then they might have thought he was one of them and left him alone.'

'He would not have wanted that,' averred Verious. 'He would rather be dead than be thought of as French.'

'Where is his body?' demanded Michael. 'Holy Trinity?'

'Yes,' replied Isnard. 'Although we kept the dagger. Show him, Verious. Brother Michael is good at catching criminals – maybe he will win justice for poor Sauvage.'

'Do not bother, Verious,' sneered Mortimer contemptuously. 'Michael will do nothing about Sauvage, because all townsmen are dirt to the University.'

'We are not dirt to Brother Michael,' declared Isnard stoutly. 'He would not let us join his choir if we were.'

Verious produced the dagger from about his grimy person. There was no need to study it closely: it was of an ilk with the ones used on the other victims. Michael took it and slipped it in his scrip, much to Verious's obvious dismay.

'What makes you think French spies killed Sauvage?' asked Bartholomew of Verious, although it was Isnard who answered.

'First, because that dagger is the same as the ones used on their other victims, and we know those blades were French, because the Sheriff said so when he showed them to us. And second, because it is an expensive thing, but the killer left it behind. Only spies can afford that sort of extravagance.'

'Because they are paid directly by the dolphin,' elaborated Verious confidently, 'who is fabulously rich after plundering Winchelsea.'

Bartholomew opened his mouth to argue, then closed it again. There was no point when Verious and Isnard had already made up their minds. Michael continued to question them, but when it became clear they had no more to tell, he turned back to the enraged baker.

'I will see you receive a fair price for your bread, Mortimer. You have my word.'

Mortimer scowled at him. 'Unfortunately, your word is

worthless. Heltisle told us that the new Chancellor wants to rule for himself, so you are now irrelevant. You have dealt justly with us in the past, but a new order has arrived, and you are not part of it.'

Michael's face went so dark with anger that Bartholomew was alarmed for him.

'Take a deep breath, Brother,' he advised hastily. 'It is not worth—'

'What is de Wetherset *thinking*?' exploded Michael. 'Not just to antagonise tradesmen when we are on the verge of serious civil unrest, but to undermine my authority when I most need it? Does he *want* the University burned to the ground?'

'It was not him – it was Heltisle,' said Isnard, frightened by the sight of the Senior Proctor trembling with fury. 'Perhaps de Wetherset knows nothing about it.'

Michael closed his eyes and took the recommended deep breath, so that when he next spoke, his voice was calmer.

'It will not matter to Heltisle if we are attacked, because his College is surrounded by high walls, but what about the hostels? They have no such means to defend themselves.'

'He does not care about those,' said Bartholomew. 'He has always been an elitist.'

Michael stormed towards St Mary the Great, aiming to have strong words with Heltisle, but before he and Bartholomew could reach it, they saw him walking along the high street with de Wetherset and Aynton. The triumvirate had been to visit the Mayor, and carried documents bearing his seal. Two dozen beadles – the real ones, not the Horde – formed a protective phalanx around them, which was a necessary precaution as they were attracting a lot of hostile attention.

'Why are these men guarding you?' demanded Michael

between gritted teeth. 'They are supposed to be patrolling the streets to prevent brawls.'

Heltisle's eyes narrowed at the disrespectful tone, although de Wetherset had the grace to look sheepish. Meanwhile, Aynton beamed at everyone who glanced in his direction, clearly under the illusion that a friendly smile was all that was needed to heal the rifts that he and his two cronies were opening.

'Would you have us lynched by a mob?' asked Heltisle archly. 'An assault on us is an assault on the University, so it is imperative that we do not allow it to happen.'

'You would not need protection if you had an ounce of sense,' snarled Michael. 'I negotiated fair trade agreements with the town, and you are fools to meddle with them.'

'They were skewed in the town's favour,' argued de Wetherset, although his voice lacked conviction, as if he already doubted the wisdom of what he had done. 'And I *do* have the authority to broker new ones. It says so in the statutes.'

'It does,' put in Aynton timidly. 'But I am not sure that we went about it in the most diplomatic manner, Chancellor. Peace is—'

'To hell with peace,' growled Heltisle. 'The town attacked us at the butts and killed four of our most promising scholars. Such behaviour cannot be tolerated, and harsher trade deals are its reward.'

'The contracts you signed *were* to our detriment, Brother,' said de Wetherset, simultaneously uncomfortable and defensive. 'So we felt obliged to offer the town a choice: sell at more attractive prices, or have us buy supplies in Ely.'

Michael regarded him furiously. 'Yes, I agreed to higher premiums, but it bought us much goodwill, which will save us a fortune in the long run, as you should know from the last time you were Chancellor. But did you have to start all this nonsense now, when relations are so strained?'

'Relations are always strained,' said de Wetherset, not unreasonably. 'Ergo, there will never be a good time to initiate reform.'

'And if you cannot quell the resulting rumpus, you should resign,' finished Heltisle, his face a mask of triumph. 'Theophilis has already offered to take your place.'

'It is tempting,' said Michael icily, 'just for the pleasure of watching *you* destroyed. But I love the University too much to see it harmed, so I shall stay at my post. However, you have created an ugly mood, so I suggest you go home and stay there. Then my beadles can return to their real duties.'

'No, they will continue to guard us,' countered Heltisle challengingly. 'Oh, and Meadowman is under arrest, by the way. He refused to obey my orders, so I had to make an example of him. The others fell into line when they saw which way the wind was blowing.'

Bartholomew glanced at the beadles who guarded the triumvirate. None were happy with the situation in which they found themselves, and he was sure that if Michael asked, they would abandon the triumvirate and follow him in a heartbeat. But the monk had too much affection for his men to put them in such an invidious position.

'I understand you have continued to investigate the murders,' said de Wetherset, turning to another matter, 'even though we told you to leave them to Aynton.' He raised a hand when Michael opened his mouth to reply. 'I do not aim to scold you, Brother, but to ask if you have made any progress.'

'Because I have not,' said Aynton ruefully. 'I tried, but then I gave up, lest I inadvertently made matters worse.'

'You are wise, Commissary,' said Michael tightly. 'If only others had the intelligence to follow your example.' He did not look at Heltisle. 'And to answer your question, Chancellor, we shall have answers after we have been to St Radegund's.'

'St Radegund's?' echoed de Wetherset, puzzled. 'Why there?'

'Abbess Isabel was in the vicinity when Orwel was brained, and can identify the culprit,' replied Michael with rather more confidence than was warranted, especially given that Isabel might be the killer herself.

'Orwel?' asked Heltisle. 'Who is he?'

'A man who had information about Wyse's murder,' said Michael, continuing to address de Wetherset. 'Unfortunately, he was killed before he could share it.'

'I have never liked the Benedictines,' said Heltisle with a moue of distaste. 'Perhaps this abbess dispatched Paris and the others. I would not put such wickedness past a member of that unsavoury Order.'

'Then you have to admire her courage,' mused Aynton. 'The plagiarist was weak and old, but her other victims cannot have been easy meat.'

'Go, then, Brother,' said de Wetherset with an amiable smile. 'But visit the Jewry first, because a spat was brewing there when we walked past, and you should stamp it out before it erupts. Meanwhile, I shall heed your advice and return to St Mary the Great, where I will remain until all the fuss dies down. What about you, Aynton?'

'Oh, I shall be here and there,' replied the Commissary airily, 'healing rifts and urging everyone to be nice to each other. Or would you rather I stayed with you, Chancellor?'

'No, keeping the peace is more important,' replied de Wetherset. 'Heltisle?'

'I shall go home,' said Heltisle grimly. 'If there is to be a battle, I want Bene't ready to defend its rights and privileges.'

'Preparing for a skirmish is hardly the example our

Vice-Chancellor should be setting,' began Michael sharply. 'It is not—'

'Oh, yes, it is!' interrupted Heltisle. 'And if Michaelhouse does not do the same, it will reveal you to be cowards and traitors.'

'Michaelhouse will do what is right,' countered Michael. 'And that does *not* include indulging in unseemly acts of violence against the town.'

Although Bartholomew itched to race to St Radegund's at once, events conspired against him. First, there was the quarrel in the Jewry to defuse, then Michael insisted on freeing Meadowman. Bartholomew fretted at the lost time, feeling the crisis loom closer with every lost moment.

When they arrived at the gaol, Michael was appalled to discover that all the rioters he had arrested had been released without charge. Their places had been taken not just by Meadowman, but by half a dozen other beadles who had also refused to obey Heltisle.

'He wanted us to guard his College rather than patrol the streets,' said Meadowman indignantly as Michael let him out. 'He thinks it will be targeted in the event of trouble, because it houses one of the University's top officials. I pointed out that Bene't has high walls, stout gates and warrior-students, so can look after itself.'

'Whereas the hostels have no protection at all,' growled another man. 'Other than us.'

'He should not have released the prisoners either,' Meadowman went on angrily, 'although half were Bene't lads, so what do you expect? Now they will hare off to foment more unrest, while Heltisle's Horde looks on like the useless rabble they are.'

'You cannot return to normal duties now,' said Michael. 'Heltisle will just rearrest you. So don everyday clothes, monitor what is happening, and report back to me.'

'We can report to you now,' said Meadowman grimly.

'The town believes the University aims to crush it into penury; the University thinks the town intends to destroy it once and for all; and everyone is convinced the Dauphin is poised to do to us what he did to Winchelsea – with the connivance of either the town or the University, depending on which side you are on.'

'Then identify the ringleaders and shut them up,' ordered Michael. 'You may lock them in their cellars, hand them to the Sheriff, or threaten them in any way you please. Perhaps the trouble will fizzle out if they are muzzled.'

The beadles did not look hopeful, but sped away to do his bidding. Their disquiet and Michael's grim expression combined to make Bartholomew's stomach churn more than ever.

'Dusk,' predicted the monk hoarsely. 'That is when the crisis will come. Tempers will fester all day, and as soon as darkness cloaks everyone with anonymity, we will go to war.'

'There must be a way to stop it. We have averted catastrophes before.'

'But that was when *I* was in charge,' Michael pointed out bitterly. 'Now we have the triumvirate, who undermine all my efforts to restore calm. Heltisle accuses me of wielding too much power, but what about him? He seems to have gone mad with it.'

They resumed their journey to St Radegund's, but met Tulyet by the Barnwell Gate. The Sheriff was astride his massive warhorse, and had donned full armour. The men who rode with him were similarly attired.

'I have done my best to quash the rumours about French spies in the Spital,' he said, reining in. 'But it is only a matter of time before the whispers start again and folk march out there to besiege it. I have ordered Leger to spirit the Tangmers and their guests away the moment it is dark.'

'Perhaps he should do it now,' said Bartholomew worriedly.

Tulyet shot him a scornful glance. 'Then there will be a massacre for certain, because they will be seen by the mob already outside. He needs the cover of night to succeed.'

'Can you trust him to do it?' asked Bartholomew. 'He agreed to protect the buildings, not the people inside.'

'He will do it or answer to the King,' replied Tulyet savagely. 'Besides, once the Spital folk are safe, I hope our warring factions *will* converge on the place, as I would sooner that bore the brunt of their destructive fury than the town.'

'You seem to think a clash is inevitable, but we still hope to avert one. Michael and I are going to see Abbess Isabel, who may have killed Orwel and perhaps the others, too. An arrest may appease—'

'It is far too late for that,' interrupted Tulyet harshly. 'Any hope of a peaceful resolution disappeared when the University chose to renege on its trade deals. So, yes, there will be a clash, and *you* brought it about.'

'Not us,' objected Bartholomew. 'The triumvirate.'

Tulyet shook his head in disgust. 'I thought we had cast aside our differences and were moving towards a lasting peace, but it was all based on the sense and good-will of one man. Now others are in charge . . .'

One of his knights – a rough, hard-bitten warrior who had never approved of Tulyet's efforts to befriend the University – spat. 'We will never have peace with scholars, and unless we take a firm stand against them today, they will crush us for ever.'

'He is right,' said Tulyet sourly, watching him wheel away to bear down on a group of tanners who were preparing to lob stones at someone's windows. 'I *have* signed away rights in exchange for amity, and so have you, Brother. Perhaps we should not have done.'

'Of course you should,' said Bartholomew. 'Neither of us is going anywhere, so we have no choice but to work together, and if that means making compromises, then so be it.'

'What about the Jacques?' asked Michael. 'Have they been found yet?'

Tulyet shook his head. 'But if they are here, whispering poisonous messages in susceptible ears, I will hang them. Now, go to St Radegund's if you must, but do not be long. You will be more useful here than chasing killers who no longer matter.'

Bartholomew glanced up at the sky as they hurried on, wishing it would rain. No one liked getting wet, and inclement weather would drive most would-be rioters indoors. Unfortunately, the clouds were breaking up and it promised to be another fine day.

'It is about noon,' said Michael, wrongly thinking he was estimating the time. 'Which means we have just a few hours before the trouble begins in earnest. We must hurry.'

They passed through the Barnwell Gate unchallenged, as the sentries were patrolling the streets instead. This allowed folk to pour in from the outlying villages. Few carried goods to sell, and Bartholomew realised that word had spread about the brewing unrest, so they were coming to stand with the townsfolk. Tulyet was right: a clash was now inevitable.

They arrived at the convent to find the nuns just finishing a session on the burning issue of whether peas were better served with fish or meat.

'We spent four times longer on that than on apostolic poverty – a debate that has tied the Church in knots for years,' smirked Magistra Katherine. 'We resolved *that* inconsequential problem in less than an hour!'

'Fortunately, the *conloquium* is over tomorrow,' said

Prioress Joan. 'And we shall waste no more time indoors when we should be riding out in God's good clean air. How is Dusty?'

'Quite content,' replied Michael shortly. 'Now where is—'

'Is it true that your town is on the verge of a major battle?' interrupted Katherine. 'And if so, should we make arrangements to leave early?'

'Please do,' begged Michael. 'I cannot see the disorder spreading out here, but there is no point in courting trouble. Tell your sisters to start their journeys as soon as possible.'

Katherine inclined her head. 'Is it because of the *peregrini*? The town and the University are accusing each other of harbouring French spies?'

'Yes,' said Michael. 'But we need to speak to—'

'I hope no one remembers that *we* lodged in the Spital,' said Joan anxiously. 'They might accuse us of being French-lovers, and I do not want my nuns subjected to any unpleasantness.'

'Where is Abbess Isabel?' Michael managed to interject. 'We need to see her urgently.'

'So do I,' said Katherine with a grimace. 'She borrowed my copy of the Chicken Debate and I want it back. But she went out on Saturday, and no one has seen her since.'

'She has been missing for *two days?*' cried Michael. 'Why did no one tell me?'

'Her retinue assure us that she often disappears for extended periods when she wants to pray,' shrugged Katherine. 'They were not concerned, so neither were we.'

'Did she say where she was going to do it?' asked Bartholomew.

'No, but she was last seen aiming for the town,' replied Joan. 'I was going to look for her myself as soon as the pea issue was resolved – her own nuns may not be worried, but she has been a little odd of late, and I would like to make sure she is safe and well.'

'Odd in what way?' demanded Michael.

'Fearful and unsettled. Probably because she stumbled across that corpse – Paris's.'

'Have you searched the priory?' asked Bartholomew, wondering if the Abbess's timely disappearance meant a killer had escaped justice.

'We have, but we will do it again.' With calm efficiency, Joan issued instructions to the women who had come to listen. Obediently, they hastened to do as they were told.

'May we see her quarters?' asked Bartholomew. 'If her belongings have gone, it means she . . . might have decided to make her own way home.'

He dared not say what he was really thinking, because he was unwilling to waste time on explanations that could come later.

'You may not!' objected Katherine, shocked. 'We do not allow men into our sleeping quarters. It would be unseemly!'

Most of the remaining sisters agreed, but Joan sensed the urgency of the situation and overrode them. She led the way to the tiny cell-like room that Isabel had chosen for herself – an austere, chilly place that showed the Abbess placed scant store in physical comfort. Her only belongings were a spare white habit and a few religious books. In the interests of thoroughness, Bartholomew peered under the bed. Something was there, tucked at the very back, obliging him to lie on the floor to fish it out. It was an ivory comb.

'That is mine!' cried Joan, snatching it from him. 'Or rather Dusty's. What is it doing in here? I thought Alice had stolen it.'

'Goda said she had,' mused Michael, 'although Alice denied it. Perhaps Alice placed it here in the spiteful hope that Isabel would be accused of its theft.'

'If she did, she is a fool,' said Joan in disgust. 'No one will believe that an abbess – and Isabel in particular – would steal a comb.'

'There is only one way to find out,' said Michael. 'Speak to Alice again. And this time, there will be no games. She will tell us the truth or suffer the consequences.'

He did not say what these might be, and Bartholomew gritted his teeth in agitation. How could they be wasting time on combs when the town was set to explode? Or *was* Isabel the killer, and the peculiar travels of the comb would throw light on why a saintly nun had turned murderer? Stomach churning, he followed Michael to the cellar, where the errant Alice had spent her last two nights.

Captivity had done nothing to blunt Alice's haughty defiance. She reclined comfortably on a bed in a room that was considerably larger and better appointed than Isabel's, and the only thing missing, as far as Bartholomew could tell, was a window. Clearly, nuns had a different view of what should constitute prison than anyone else.

'I will answer your questions,' she conceded loftily. 'But in return, all charges against me will be dropped and I will be reinstated as Prioress of Ickleton.'

Michael ignored the demand. 'We found the comb you hid in Abbess Isabel's room. However, your plot to see her accused of theft has failed. The comb was stolen from the Spital, but she has never been there. *You* have, though.'

Alice was unfazed. 'I have already told you: I did not take it. You will have to devise another explanation for how it ended up where it did.'

Bartholomew pushed his anxieties about the deteriorating situation in the town to the back of his mind, because a solution was beginning to reveal itself to him at last. He was sure Alice *had* stolen the comb, but was less certain that she had put it in Isabel's room to incriminate her, because Joan was right: no one would believe the Abbess would steal, and Alice would know it. The only other explanation was that Alice had *given* it to Isabel, and the Abbess had secreted it there herself.

'I believe you,' he said, speaking slowly to give his thoughts time to settle. 'You would have chosen a far more imaginative hiding place than under a bed.'

'Is that where she put it?' scoffed Alice. 'What a fool! She should be demoted, so that someone more intelligent can be installed in her place. Someone like me.'

'So you did give it to her,' pounced Bartholomew. 'Why?'

Alice folded her arms. 'I refuse to say more until you promise me something in return.'

'Very well,' said Michael. 'I promise to recommend clemency when you are sentenced to burn at the stake.'

Alice gaped at him. 'Burn at the stake? What for?'

'Buying cursing spells from a witch. Do not deny it, because we have witnesses. So what will it be? Cooperation or incineration?'

Alice's hubris began to dissolve. 'You misunderstand, Brother. The spell was only a harmless bit of fun – nothing malicious.'

'No one will believe you. Now, the comb: why did you steal it?'

Alice looked at Michael's stern, angry face, and the remaining fight went out of her. 'Because Isabel charged me to visit the Spital, find the comb and bring it to her. In return, she promised to get me reinstated.'

'You believed her?' asked Michael, sure Isabel would have done nothing of the kind.

'Not at first,' admitted Alice. 'But I was desperate, so I decided to take a chance.'

'Did she say why she wanted it?' asked Bartholomew.

'She refused to tell me. And then, when I was accused of theft and needed her to prove my innocence, she denied all knowledge of our arrangement. She betrayed me!'

'So you bought a cursing spell to teach her a lesson,' surmised Bartholomew.

'To make her confess to what she had commissioned me to do. I am *not* a thief – just the agent of one.'

Michael regarded her in disgust. 'You lie! If Isabel *had* told you to steal, you would have trumpeted it from the rooftops when you were accused. But you never did.'

Alice shrugged and looked away. 'I wanted to, but I am not stupid – I know who folk would have believed, and challenging Isabel would have done me more harm than good. But I am telling the truth now: she is the dishonest one, not me.'

'Then how unfortunate for you that she has disappeared,' said Bartholomew, feeling vaguely tainted by the whole affair, 'and can never corroborate your tale.'

'Disappeared?' asked Alice uneasily. 'Do you mean she has slunk off to pray in some quiet church? Or that she has run away?'

Michael glanced at Bartholomew. 'Perhaps Isabel *is* the killer. She brained Orwel, realised that Clippesby might have witnessed her crime, and rather than claim yet another victim – one who is a *real* saint in the making – she elected to vanish.'

'Leaving her possessions behind?' asked Bartholomew doubtfully, assailed by the sudden sense that their reasoning was flawed, and that pursuing Isabel as a suspect would lead them astray at a time when they could not afford to make mistakes.

'Leaving her spare habit and a few books behind,' corrected Michael. 'None of which are essential to a woman fleeing the law.' He glared at Alice. 'Regardless, she is not in a position to help you, so tell us more about your dealings with her.'

'But I have told you everything already,' whispered

Alice, her plans for vengeance and a triumphant return to power in tatters around her, 'other than that she was writing a report which she said would cause a stir.'

'What report?' demanded Michael. 'It was not in her room.'

'I think she left it with the Gilbertines. But do not ask me what it contains, because she refused to let me read it.' Alice's small faced turned hard again. 'However, if it is more evidence of my so-called wrongdoings, it will be a pack of lies.'

'Of course it will,' said Michael, regarding her with distaste.

Out in the yard, Joan was waiting to tell them that St Radegund's had been scoured from top to bottom, but Abbess Isabel was not in it. Michael nodded brisk thanks for her help, declined her offer to look for Isabel in the town, and left the convent at a run. When he and Bartholomew reached the Barnwell Causeway, they saw a smudge of smoke, grey against the blue sky. Was it someone burning old leaves? Or had trouble erupted already?

'Isabel's report will be about Alice,' predicted Bartholomew as they trotted along, 'because Alice continues to claim that she was unfairly dismissed – that Isabel exaggerated or invented the charges against her. No would-be saint likes being accused of dishonesty, so I suspect Isabel aims to expose Alice's unsavoury character once and for all.'

'Alice was asked to steal and lie, and she did,' mused Michael, 'proving how easily she can be corrupted. It is possible, I suppose.'

'Although if Isabel *is* the killer, why not just dispatch Alice, like she has her other victims? It would have been a lot simpler.'

'She would have headed our list of murder suspects if

322

she had,' shrugged Michael, 'and that sort of allegation is a lot more serious than defaming a nun whom no one likes. Unfortunately, her disappearance has convinced me that she *is* the culprit. I am sorry for it, as her crime will reflect badly on my Order.'

'But *why* would she dispatch Orwel? Or any of the victims, for that matter? It makes no sense.'

'I had high hopes of answers at St Radegund's,' sighed Michael wearily, 'but we should have stayed home and worked on quelling the trouble instead.'

Bartholomew was inclined to agree, and looked at the plume of smoke again. He tried to determine where it originated, stepping off the road to see if he could identify a church to give him his bearings. It was then that he saw a flash of white deep in the undergrowth. His stomach lurched.

'Oh, Lord!' he gulped. 'It is the Abbess!'

As he and Michael fought their way through the thicket towards the body, Bartholomew noted twin tracks where feet had been dragged backwards along the ground. There were also splashes of blood, suggesting that Isabel had been attacked on the Causeway, then hauled off it, out of sight. She was well hidden, and he would have missed her if he had not left the road to look at the smoke. He crouched next to her and was startled when her eyes flickered open – he had assumed she was dead. Michael dropped to his knees and took her hand in his.

'Abbess?' he called. 'Can you hear me?'

Isabel did not move.

'Head wound,' said Bartholomew tersely, wondering how long she been there. Since she had visited Margery two nights before? But no – she could not have survived her injury that long. Moreover, the blood was wet, suggesting a recent assault.

'And there is the weapon,' said Michael, nodding at the bloodstained stone that lay next to her. 'The same as Wyse and Orwel.'

'So we were wrong about her,' whispered Bartholomew. 'She is not their killer.'

'She is trying to speak! You listen – your ears are sharper. What is she saying?'

Bartholomew did his best, but still only heard half the softly murmured words.

'She does not know who attacked her,' he relayed. 'She heard footsteps behind her, but was hit before she could turn around. The first blow caught her shoulder, so she tried to fight back, but the second knocked her down. Her assailant kept his face hidden the whole time.'

He strained to decipher more, aware that Isabel's voice was growing fainter as the effort drained her strength. Eventually, he sat back.

'She wants a priest now. She says she refused to die until God sent her one, as it will help her case . . . her beatification.'

He moved away so Michael could perform last rites. Isabel's eyes shone with an inner joy when the monk pronounced the final absolution, then it faded and she stopped breathing.

'Such faith,' said Michael softly in the silence that followed. 'I wish I . . . But never mind. What else did she tell you?'

'That we should go to the Gilbertines, where she has left a full report, and that the comb holds the key to all we need to know about Paris and the others.'

'What did she mean?'

'I could not hear that part. She also said that Alice is irredeemably wicked, because even when she was pretending to be her – Isabel's – friend by "acquiring" the comb, she was still sending her deadly gifts. Her dying wish is for Alice to be excommunicated.'

Michael winced. 'But she charged Alice to steal, declined to tell the truth when the theft became public knowledge, *and* was plotting to see Alice ousted from our Order. That is hardly an example of good fellowship.'

'She did witness Orwel's murder,' Bartholomew went on. 'It frightened her so much that she fled to St Edward's, where she has been hiding ever since.'

'Orwel's body was taken there,' mused Michael. 'Its vicar is almost blind, and no one ever attends his services, because he tends to fall asleep in them. By luck, she went to the only church where she *could* lurk for days without being noticed.'

Bartholomew groaned suddenly. 'The next morning, I went there to re-examine Orwel, to make sure there was nothing I had missed. I thought I sensed someone watching me.'

'And you did not go to investigate?' demanded Michael, unimpressed.

'No, because I often feel I am not alone when I examine corpses. I assumed it was my imagination or . . . It never occurred to me that it would be a *living* person.'

Michael shook his head in disgust. 'We might have had answers days ago if you had bothered to search the place. So what caused Isabel to leave in the end?'

'Peas,' said Bartholomew helplessly. 'She wanted to know if they are better eaten with meat or fish. She was considering her own contribution to the question as she hurried along the Causeway, which is why she failed to notice her attacker until it was too late.'

'That means he struck not long before we passed this way ourselves,' said Michael uneasily. 'I do not suppose she noticed anything to help us catch him?'

'She claimed it was Satan, wearing handsome boots over his cloven hoofs and a fine brooch on his hat. She says she snatched it from him, although I think her mind was wandering at that point.'

'Are you sure? Because there is something shiny by her hand.'

Bartholomew peered into the grass and saw Michael was right. It was a pilgrim badge, like the one de Wetherset wore. The monk gazed at it in alarm.

'I hope she is not suggesting that the Chancellor attacked her!' He flailed around for a better explanation. 'She mentioned handsome boots. De Wetherset's are not noticeably fine, but Aynton's are.'

Bartholomew regarded him soberly. 'Aynton's are as ugly as sin – he is not the attacker. It *is* de Wetherset – he always wears this badge in his hat.'

'Then someone stole it to incriminate him,' argued Michael. 'The killer is trying to lead us astray – and he is succeeding if you think the Chancellor would kill a nun.'

'*Think*, Brother! We told de Wetherset that Isabel had witnessed Orwel's murder and could identify the culprit. But we delayed coming here, because *he* told you to go to the Jewry first, after which you wanted to release Meadowman. He must have dashed straight to St Radegund's to prevent Isabel from—'

'No! The other nuns would have mentioned a visit from the University's Chancellor.'

'They did not mention it because he never got that far – he saw Isabel trotting along this road first. He dispatched her in exactly the same way that he killed Orwel and Wyse, with a stone.'

'You are wrong! De Wetherset would not—'

'We know a scholar sat in the Griffin and waited for Wyse to leave, because witnesses described a portly man with a good cloak, inky fingers and decent boots. It is de Wetherset!'

'But why? *Why* would de Wetherset dispatch a harmless ancient like Wyse?'

'To stir up trouble between us and the town.'

Michael was becoming exasperated. 'That is the most ridiculous claim I have ever heard! No Chancellor wants his University in flames. What would be the benefit in that?'

'Because he cannot rule properly as long as *you* are Senior Proctor – you are too strong and hold too much influence. But you are responsible for law and order, so what better way to discredit you than to create a situation that you cannot handle? He wants everyone to clamour for your dismissal so he can reign alone.'

Michael regarded him askance. 'There are easier ways to remove a man from office than destroying the University and its peaceful relations with the town.'

'Yes – like ransacking your office in the dead of night, undermining your trade agreements, and appointing a lot of useless beadles in your name.'

'Hah! De Wetherset was not the driving force behind all that – Heltisle was. You are wrong about de Wetherset, Matt. He probably would like me gone, but he would never harm the University to achieve it. Heltisle, on the other hand, is ruthless, and exactly the kind of man to frame a friend to benefit himself.'

Bartholomew considered. Heltisle as the culprit made more sense than de Wetherset, who had always been the more reasonable of the pair. 'So you think Heltisle disguised himself as de Wetherset and came to kill Isabel?'

'I think it is easy to remove a badge from a hat, and Heltisle was also present when we claimed that Isabel could identify Orwel's killer. And while the Chancellor would *never* provoke a war between the University and the town to oust me, Heltisle might. Although this is a dreadful accusation to make . . .'

'And Heltisle is a dreadful man.'

CHAPTER 14

Michael paid a passing carter to take Abbess Isabel to St Radegund's, where she was received with grief, shock and dismay. Important heads of houses came to demand an explanation, so it was some time before he and Bartholomew managed to extricate themselves – although it would have been longer still if Prioress Joan had not intervened. Sensing their rising agitation at the delay, she ordered her colleagues to silence.

'They will tell us when there is more news,' she informed them briskly. 'Until then, I would rather they hunted Isabel's killer than stood around here chatting to us.' She turned to the scholars. 'So go – do your duty while we pray for this saintly lady's soul.'

Michael gave her a grateful nod, and he and Bartholomew hurried back to the town. Both were appalled by how many troublemakers from the villages were flooding in, eager to fight a foundation they had always resented, and the monk began to drag his heels.

'You do realise that someone may be manipulating us,' he said. 'That the killer *wants* me to accuse the Vice-Chancellor of a serious crime, so that we will be weak and divided when the crisis comes?'

'Then do not accuse him,' suggested Bartholomew. 'Just ask what he did after we said we were going to talk to Isabel. If he is innocent, he has nothing to fear.'

'It is not his fear that worries me,' muttered Michael. 'It is his indignation.'

They avoided the market square, which was almost certain to be thronged with angry tradesmen, and threaded through the maze of alleys opposite the butts instead. They were just walking up Shoemaker Row when they were hailed by Clippesby.

'There you are!' he cried in relief. 'Ethel told me that I would find you if I looked long enough, but I was beginning to think she was wrong.'

'What is the matter?' asked Bartholomew anxiously. He had seen that wild-eyed, frantic expression before, and it meant Clippesby was in possession of some troubling fact.

'Last week, Ethel – the College's top hen – heard Heltisle claim that Suttone had run off to get married. In other words, it was not fear of the plague that made him resign, but lust. Ethel did not believe it, so she wrote to Suttone, begging the truth. His reply arrived an hour ago. It is—'

'Not now!' snapped Michael, trying to push past him.

'Wait, Brother! *Listen!* Suttone explains everything. It was not the plague *or* a woman that made him go. He went because Heltisle *forced* him to. Here. See for yourself.'

Michael snatched the letter and read it, his face turning angrier with every word. Clippesby summarised it for Bartholomew.

'Heltisle threatened to destroy our College with lies unless Suttone did as he was told, and as Michael was away, Suttone had nowhere to turn for help. He bowed to the pressure, because he felt it was the best way to protect the rest of us.'

'Mallett overheard Suttone and Heltisle arguing the night before Suttone resigned,' said Bartholomew, recalling what the student had told him while they had tended the riot-wounded together. 'He thought Suttone was close to tears . . .'

'What in God's name did Heltisle threaten to do?' breathed Michael, staring at the letter. 'Suttone does not say.'

329

'Something very nasty,' said Clippesby, 'or he would have held his ground. But he crumbled, and Heltisle arranged for de Wetherset to be elected in his place.'

'So there we are,' said Bartholomew. 'Yet more evidence that Heltisle is less than scrupulous. We must stop him before he does anything else to further his ambitions.'

'He is at St Mary the Great,' supplied Clippesby. 'He *was* in his College, but a pigeon heard him tell a student that he wanted to keep an eye on de Wetherset.'

'We shall corner him there,' said Michael grimly, 'but let me do the talking, Matt. If you charge in and accuse him of murder, and it transpires that we are mistaken—'

'We are not mistaken,' said Bartholomew soberly.

Michael and Bartholomew hurried along the high street, acutely aware that everyone they passed was armed to the teeth. There was a good deal of vicious muttering, mostly directed against the French, who, it was rumoured, were poised to invade at any moment.

Bartholomew glanced up at the sky to gauge the time. They had spent much longer at St Radegund's than they should have done, and it would be dark in a couple of hours. Tradesmen were carting their wares to safer places, while homeowners nailed boards across windows and doors. Everywhere was a sense that now the day was nearly over, trouble was at hand.

'I fear Dick has given Leger an impossible task,' he said unhappily. 'Even under cover of darkness it will be difficult to spirit slow-moving ancients and children away from the Spital with no one noticing.'

'It will,' agreed Michael. 'But he *must* succeed. Failure is too awful to contemplate.'

'Perhaps we should help. They—' Bartholomew stopped walking suddenly and frowned his puzzlement. 'Look over there – Gonville theologians talking to candle-makers.'

'Yes, there will be a spat in a few moments. I could

intervene, but they will only pick a quarrel with someone else. It is not worth the time it would take.'

'No, *look* at them. They are not about to fight: they are having an amiable discussion.'

Michael narrowed his eyes. 'So what does that mean? That we are all friends again? Why, when only a few hours ago we were itching to kill each other?'

'I do not know, but it makes me more uneasy than ever.'

They reached St Mary the Great, where a number of Michael's beadles stood guard.

'The Vice-Chancellor *was* here,' said one. 'But then he and de Wetherset went out, taking a dozen of our lads to protect them. He promised to come back soon, though, and if you would like to wait inside, you can have a bit of our ale.'

'Thank you, Silas,' said Michael, heartened by the show of affection, as it meant the beadles would follow him when the crunch came. 'But we need to find him now.'

'Maybe Isnard knows where he went,' suggested Silas, eager to be helpful. 'Hey! Isnard! Have you seen Master Heltisle?'

'He was in the market square a few moments ago,' said Isnard, swinging towards them on crutches that were spotted with someone else's blood. 'But he left when I threw a stone at him. I wish it had hit the bastard! What he is doing to the trade agreements is—'

'Did you see where he went?' interrupted Michael urgently.

'Towards Tyled Hostel,' replied Isnard. 'But you two should go home and stay there, because there will be trouble tonight. We are going to find every Frenchman we can lay our hands on and hang them.'

'No, Isnard!' cried Bartholomew, shocked. 'You cannot—'

'We do not care if it is a townsman or a scholar,' interrupted Isnard, his usually good-natured face turned ugly with hatred. 'They will all die. Your own Heltisle just reminded us of the Winchelsea massacre, and it must be avenged.'

'So now we know the next stage of Heltisle's plan,' said Michael breathlessly, as he and Bartholomew ran towards Tyled Hostel. 'Uniting town and scholars in a purge against hapless foreigners. I will try to stop it, but I will fail in the face of such impassioned bigotry, and then he will demand my resignation.'

'There will be a bloodbath of innocents,' said Bartholomew, equally appalled. 'Look what happened to Bruges and Sauvage – I am sure they died just because of their names.'

'Heltisle has deployed the most insidious weapons of all,' panted Michael. 'Ignorance and intolerance. God help us all!'

Bartholomew was alarmed to note that it was not only the candle-makers and Gonville who had agreed to a truce for the purposes of fighting a common enemy. Trinity Hall's ranks were swelled with merchants, while several hostels had united with tradesmen from the market square. However, not everyone could bring themselves to do it, and King's Hall was engaged in a furious spat with a band of arrogant young burgesses. Heltisle had been fiendishly clever, thought Bartholomew, as when trouble did come, it would be impossible to know who was on whose side, thus exacerbating and prolonging the crisis.

They reached Tyled Hostel, where more of Michael's beadles had been allocated guard duty, although none were very happy about it. Their resentment intensified when some of Heltisle's Horde swaggered past, making the point that Michael's men were mere sentries while *they* could roam where they pleased. Michael homed in on the Horde's leader.

'You have no right to wear that uniform, Perkyn – not when I dismissed you for malingering. Moreover, why are you lurking down here? When the trouble starts, it will be on the high street or in the market square, so that is where you need to be.'

'Not according to Master Heltisle,' countered Perkyn, making no pretence of being under the Senior Proctor's command. 'He reminded us that Michaelhouse houses more Frenchmen than any other foundation in the University, so we are waiting to trounce them when they come out. They will not get past us to murder our women and children.'

Bartholomew suspected that Heltisle had given them tacit permission to assault anyone from the College, regardless of his origins. The Vice-Chancellor was attacking Michael on all fronts.

'We have exactly the same number of overseas students as Tyled Hostel,' Michael informed him curtly, 'and three fewer than Bene't. Now, enough nonsense. You will go—'

'Master Heltisle said you would try to order us away from your lair,' interrupted Perkyn insolently. 'And he told us to ignore you. So piss off!'

There was a collective intake of breath from the real beadles, which made Perkyn suddenly doubt the wisdom of taking on the Senior Proctor. Michael eyed the man coldly for a moment, then turned to his loyal followers.

'Arrest these fools. Heltisle is no longer in charge. *I* am.'

The real beadles cheered, then quickly rounded up the startled Horde and marched them towards the proctors' gaol. When they had gone, Michael hammered on Tyled Hostel's door, but no one was home except two elderly Breton scholars – the pair who Bartholomew had treated for a series of fear-induced nervous complaints a few days before. They tugged the visitors inside and closed the door quickly, both pale with terror.

'Heltisle came to collect de Wetherset's armour,' said one. 'And our students have gone to join the trouble outside. We tried to stop them, but they called us foreign traitors . . . They intend to fight when the trouble starts.'

'Where is Heltisle now?' demanded Michael.

'Gone to make sure Bene't is safe,' replied the second, close to tears. 'If you see Aynton, please ask him to come home. We are frightened here all alone.'

Bartholomew took them to Michaelhouse, where William, Aungel and Clippesby had already taken steps to defend the College from attack. Armed students patrolled the perimeter, and the gates could be barred at a moment's notice. One of the Bretons grasped Bartholomew's hand as he ushered the pair safely inside.

'I shall pray for you,' he whispered. 'You will need all the help you can get if you are to defeat the evil that has arisen among us.'

It was an uncomfortable journey to Bene't, as more than one person pointed out Bartholomew and Michael as men who hailed from a foundation housing foreigners. One was a patient, so Bartholomew stopped to reason with her, but Michael pulled him on. She had been drinking, which meant she was unlikely to listen.

Bene't was like a fortress, with students in armour stationed along the top of its walls and archers guarding its gates. Bartholomew was dismayed to note that several held weapons that shone with fresh blood. If they were willing to fight in broad daylight, what would the town be like when it was dark?

'Master Heltisle was here,' called a student, shouting down from the wall because he refused to open the gate. 'But then he went out again.'

'Where did he go?' demanded Michael, making no effort to disguise his exasperation.

'To rid the University of French infiltrators,' came the

belligerent reply. 'And to make sure that the town scum know their place – which is under our heel.'

'Now what?' asked Bartholomew, aware that last remark had been heard by several passing apprentices, so was sure to bring Bene't reprisals later.

'Back to St Mary the Great. Perhaps he went there while we have been chasing our tails out here.'

Heart pounding with tension, Bartholomew turned to run back along the high street. They passed Tulyet on the way, who reported tersely that Heltisle had refused to support another curfew on the grounds that scholars had a right to go where they pleased.

'But we would have a riot for certain if there was one rule for you and another for us,' finished Tulyet, his voice tight with anger. 'So now everyone has licence to be out tonight.'

'Have you heard from Leger?' asked Bartholomew anxiously.

'He sent a message to say that he will try to whisk his charges away as soon as darkness falls,' replied Tulyet. 'Pray God he succeeds, because I cannot help him.'

They went their separate ways, although Bartholomew paused for a moment to listen to Verious howling for all loyal Englishmen to destroy the enemy spies. The ditcher's face was bloated with drink, and Bartholomew doubted he was capable of distinguishing between an 'enemy spy' and folk he had known all his life. This was borne out when Isnard approached, and he would have been punched if the bargeman had not swiped irritably at him with a crutch.

Bartholomew felt as though he was in a nightmare, where every step took longer than it should, and St Mary the Great never seemed to be getting any closer. But they reached it eventually, and Michael aimed for the door.

'Heltisle *has* been here since we left,' said Bartholomew, suddenly hesitating.

'How do you know?' asked Michael uneasily.

'Because your beadles are no longer in place. I suspect he sent them away in the hope that this church will be attacked. It will be seen as a direct assault on the University, and will allow him to claim that you are incapable of defending us.'

'If you are right, then this is the last place he will be,' said Michael. 'He will not want to be inside when a mob marches in.'

'He knows nothing serious will happen until nightfall,' said Bartholomew. 'Until then, he will be busily gathering the documents he thinks he will need for when you have gone.'

The door was open, so they slipped inside. The church was empty, and not so much as a single clerk laboured over his ledgers.

'Good,' breathed Michael. 'They all have had the sense to hide.'

'Or gone to join the fighting,' Bartholomew whispered back. 'Now follow me quietly. I want to see what Heltisle is doing before we challenge him.'

He crept through the shadowy building to the grand room that had so recently been Michael's, and peered around the door. Then it was all he could do not to gasp in shock at what he saw. De Wetherset stood there with a stone in his hand, looming over someone who lay prostrate on the floor. The victim was Vice-Chancellor Heltisle.

CHAPTER 15

Bartholomew's insistence on stealth meant that he and Michael had several moments when they could see de Wetherset, but the Chancellor was unaware of them. He was muttering to himself, and the savage expression on his portly features told them all they needed to know about the identity of the killer. He had donned his armour, suggesting that he aimed to be in the thick of whatever happened that night, making sure it did not fizzle out before it had achieved what he intended.

'I cannot believe it,' breathed Michael. He was ashen, partly from shock that de Wetherset should be guilty, but mostly from knowledge of the harm it would do the University when the truth emerged. 'How *could* he?'

De Wetherset crouched next to Heltisle, peered at the wound he had inflicted, and raised the rock for a final, skull-crushing blow.

'Stop!' howled Bartholomew, not about to stand by while it happened, even if the victim was the detestable Heltisle. 'No more, de Wetherset. It is over.'

The Chancellor whipped around in alarm. 'Thank God you are here!' he cried in feigned relief. 'It transpires that Heltisle is a false friend. I asked why he had sent all the beadles away from our church, and his response was to race forward and stab me.'

Bartholomew was amazed that de Wetherset should expect them to believe it. 'The wound is to the back of his head, which means he cannot have been rushing at you. I suspect he was sitting at the desk when you hit him. Besides, you have no injury.'

'He missed,' said de Wetherset, eyeing him with dislike.

'Although not from want of trying – his metal pen was aimed right at my heart. Of course I defended myself.'

'With a stone that just happened to be to hand?'

'One I brought here to prevent documents from blowing around,' replied de Wetherset. He smiled at Michael. 'I forgot how draughty this chamber is. You may have it back, Brother, because I prefer the smaller one. I wish Heltisle had not insisted on uprooting you.'

'Do you,' said Michael expressionlessly.

De Wetherset shrugged. 'I made a mistake in appointing him Vice-Chancellor – his judgement is very poor. But I am sure you and I can work together to rectify all the harm he has done with his ambition and greed.'

Michael glanced at Bartholomew. 'You had better see if you can help Heltisle.'

Bartholomew stepped forward, but de Wetherset blocked his path.

'Stay back for your own safety,' he urged. 'He is a very dangerous man.'

'Let me see him,' ordered Bartholomew, trying to peer around de Wetherset's bulk. 'He may still be alive, and you do not want another death on your conscience.'

'I have nothing on my conscience,' objected de Wetherset indignantly. 'I cannot be condemned for defending myself against a lethal attack, especially from Heltisle. No one likes him, and it is common knowledge that his policies have done much damage.'

Bartholomew was disgusted that the Chancellor aimed to blame a friend for his own misdeeds, but supposed he should not be surprised. De Wetherset had always been ruthless.

'Then how do you explain *your* pilgrim badge clutched in the hand of a murdered abbess?' he demanded, and brandished the brooch aloft.

'You found it?' cried de Wetherset. 'Thanks be to God! It was stolen last night, and I thought it had gone for ever. Heltisle was the thief, of course, and you have just told me why – to see me accused of a crime I did not commit.'

He had an answer for everything, thought Bartholomew angrily, wishing Michael would just arrest the man so they could leave. He did not want to be in St Mary the Great when the inevitable mob marched in. Seeing Bartholomew did not believe him, the Chancellor turned to Michael.

'*You* know I am telling the truth, Brother. I heard a letter arrived from Suttone today. I imagine it revealed Heltisle as a bully who forced him to resign against his will. Yes?'

'Yes,' acknowledged Michael. 'Heltisle is no innocent. However, nor is he the mastermind behind the scheme to oust me and take control of the University. *You* are.'

'Can you prove it?' asked de Wetherset earnestly. 'No? Then I suggest you desist with these accusations and—'

'Why did you turn against Heltisle?' interrupted Michael. 'Were you afraid he would tire of being your henchman and claim the throne for himself?'

'I have already told you what happened,' snapped de Wetherset, growing exasperated. 'But we cannot stay in here quarrelling while the town seethes with unrest. We should leave. Then we shall say that Heltisle was killed by the rabble that will descend on this church at any moment—'

'Which is what you intended from the start,' said Bartholomew accusingly. 'That is why you sent the beadles away – so no one could ever testify that you were in here alone with him. But your accusation will ignite a brawl that—'

'Better a brawl than exposing our Vice-Chancellor as a criminal,' snapped de Wetherset. He addressed Michael again. 'You *know* I am right, Brother. Do not let

Bartholomew's asinine obsession with the truth destroy the University that you have nurtured so lovingly these last few—'

'There is blood on your boots,' interrupted Bartholomew.

'Of course there is – I have just been obliged to hit Heltisle in self-defence. There is blood on my tabard, too. See?'

'No – that is fresh. The spots on your boots are brown and dry. It is Orwel's blood. Or Wyse's. Not Isabel's – she is too recent as well. Now, let me examine Heltisle. He may be—'

'Stay where you are,' came a sharp voice from behind him.

Bartholomew whipped around and felt his jaw drop in dismay. It was Aynton and he carried a loaded crossbow.

Within moments, Aynton had propelled Bartholomew and Michael into the office and closed the door. Bartholomew was disgusted with himself. How could he not have predicted that the last member of the triumvirate would be to hand, and that he would side with the man who had given him his position of power? Aynton and de Wetherset were both members of Tyled Hostel, so of course they would be loyal to each other. Michael had been right to suspect the Commissary of unscrupulous dealings.

'They are mad, Aynton,' said de Wetherset. 'You should hear the nonsense they have been spouting about me. And then they killed Heltisle.'

Bartholomew blinked, hope rising. Did de Wetherset's words mean that Aynton was not part of the plot after all? His mind worked fast. How could he convince the Commissary that he was backing the wrong side? He glanced at Michael, whose face was full of grim resolve.

'Why did you embark on such a deadly path, de Wetherset?' the monk demanded. 'We could have

340

governed the University side by side, as we did in the past.'

'There was no deadly path,' said de Wetherset, flicking a nervous glance at Aynton. 'And we could never have worked together, because you would have turned me into another Suttone. Everyone agrees that you are too strong.'

'It is true, Brother,' said Aynton quietly. 'It is not healthy for one man to wield so much power, and nor is it right that the Chancellor is just a figurehead.'

De Wetherset smiled so gloatingly that Bartholomew felt his hopes fade. Aynton might not have been part of the plan to remove Michael, but he was clearly in favour of it. Meanwhile, Michael regarded the Commissary in stunned disbelief.

'So you are happy that de Wetherset's intrigues have set us against the town?' he demanded accusingly. 'And destroyed all the goodwill that I have built over the last decade?'

'The town does not want our friendship,' snapped de Wetherset. 'They cheat us at every turn, and it is time we put an end to it. Is that not so, Commissary?'

Michael was disgusted. 'So you aim to replace all the fair agreements I made with ones of your own – ones that will benefit us, but that will cause hardship in the town.'

'I make no apology for putting the University first,' flashed de Wetherset.

'Then you are a fool! You might win us a few weeks of cheap bread and ale, but resentment will fester, and we will lose in the end.'

'How?' asked Aynton curiously.

'Because no foundation can prosper in a place where it is hated. Our scholars will be murdered by those you have wronged, and new students will opt to study else-where. Gradually, we will wither and die.'

'I know why de Wetherset killed Wyse,' said Bartholomew,

more interested in their current problems than future ones. 'Because the trouble between us and the town was taking too long to blossom. He chose a helpless, frail old drunkard, then made sure everyone knew that a scholar had killed him.'

Was that a flicker of surprise in Aynton's eyes or had Bartholomew imagined it?

'He sat in the Griffin, making a great show of reading and flaunting his inky fingers,' said Michael, taking up the tale. 'Then he trailed Wyse to a deserted road and hit him. Wyse was only stunned, so de Wetherset callously shoved his head in the ditch and left him to drown.'

Bartholomew expected him to deny it, but the Chancellor glanced at Aynton, decided he had an ally, and shrugged his indifference.

'Something had to be done. We were stuck in a stalemate that benefited no one.'

Outside, there was a crash, followed by a cheer and a bellow of rage. The trouble was starting early. Bartholomew looked desperately at Aynton, hoping to see some sign that he wanted no part of de Wetherset's monstrous schemes, but the crossbow was still aimed at him and Michael, and it did not waver. He clenched his fists in impotent fury; it was hard to stand helpless while his town ripped itself apart.

'Then there was Orwel,' Michael went on. 'The Sheriff sent him to the Griffin to question witnesses, and what they confided allowed him to identify de Wetherset as Wyse's murderer.'

'I saw Orwel leaving this church once,' said Bartholomew, anxiety intensifying when he glanced out of the window to see dusk was not far off. 'I imagine he came to blackmail you.'

'He did,' said de Wetherset indignantly. 'And when I refused to pay, he arranged to meet the Senior Proctor and reveal all, although only in exchange for money, I

342

imagine. So I realised I had to shut him up permanently – for the good of the University.'

'But Abbess Isabel saw you,' said Bartholomew. 'Although she assumed you were the Devil, and was so frightened that she hid in a church for two days.'

'You said she could identify me, so I had to silence her, too. I had no idea how to do it, but then a miracle occurred – I spotted her walking through the Barnwell Gate. I caught up with her on the Causeway and . . .'

'Three innocent lives,' said Michael harshly. 'All ended with a heavy stone. Are you happy with that price, Aynton, or do you consider it too high?'

'It is more than three,' said Bartholomew when Aynton made no reply. 'It was de Wetherset who yelled the order to shoot at the butts. He planned all along for there to be trouble that evening, which is why he arrived wearing his armour – armour he has donned again tonight, which should tell you all you need to know about his intentions.'

Aynton's crossbow wavered for the first time. 'You provoked that brawl on purpose?'

'I regret the loss of life, but it was necessary,' said de Wetherset shortly. 'It proved that Michael cannot protect us from the town. And if he is unable to control a few spade-wielding peasants, how will he fare against the Dauphin?'

'So you hate the French, too,' said Bartholomew in distaste, watching Aynton regard the Chancellor uncertainly. '*You* stabbed Paris, the Girards and—'

'I did not,' interrupted de Wetherset. 'I imagine that was Heltisle's doing. I thought he was strong and able, but he proved to be a petty despot with no redeeming features.'

At that point, Heltisle astonished everyone by sitting up with a bellow of rage, and stabbing the Chancellor in the foot with one of his metal pens.

* * *

Outside in the street, it was growing dark. Some folk retreated inside their houses, praying the trouble would pass them by, but far more poured out to join in whatever was about to happen. In St Mary the Great, Heltisle's pen sliced through de Wetherset's foot and pinned it to the floor beneath. The Chancellor shrieked in pain and shock, and flailed at Heltisle with a knife. One swipe scored a deep gash across Heltisle's wrist, which began to bleed copiously.

'Stop!' roared Aynton, aiming his crossbow at them. 'You two did not act to strengthen the University against the town, but to benefit yourselves. You disgust me!'

'Thank God!' breathed Michael fervently. 'Now perhaps we can—'

'Of course we did it for the University,' snarled de Wetherset, his face a mask of agony. 'Or *I* did. Heltisle acted for himself.'

'Lies!' cried Heltisle. 'There is no blood on *my* hands. Everything I did was on his orders – hiring incompetent beadles, adjusting the trade agreements, antagonising the town—'

'And how willingly you did it,' sneered de Wetherset. 'You enjoyed every moment, and would have done more if I had not curbed your excesses.'

Heltisle gave him a look of disgust before addressing Aynton. 'Arrest these three idiots. None are fit to govern, so *I* shall assume command. Well? What are you waiting for?'

'Do you still have the key to this office, Brother?' asked Aynton. 'Good! We shall lock this pair inside, then set about mending the harm they have done.'

'No, you will obey *me*,' shrieked Heltisle, cradling his injured arm. '*I* am in charge. You heard what they said – Michael is so inept that he did not notice blood on a pair of boots, while de Wetherset is a murderer. You should have shot them the moment you arrived.'

344

'I am glad I did not,' said Aynton fervently. 'It took me a while to separate truth from lies, but my eyes are open now. Step away from the prisoners, Matthew. Do not even think of tending their wounds.'

'We cannot leave de Wetherset impaled,' said Bartholomew tiredly. 'And Heltisle will bleed to death unless I sew him up.'

'It is more important to tell Tulyet that we have identified the authors of all this mayhem,' said Aynton. 'Then peace will reign once more.'

'It is too late,' said Michael bitterly. 'The wheels of unrest have been set in motion, and nothing will stop us and the town from turning on each other now.'

'Good!' crowed de Wetherset. 'And when it is over, and you need a *strong* leader to crush what remains of the town, I shall lead the University to victory.'

'Actually, there will be no harm to us or the town,' countered Aynton, and looked pleased with himself. 'Because we have a common enemy – the French. I have spent the whole day telling everyone that the Dauphin is poised to invade, so we must stand together to defeat him. *That* is how we shall restore the harmony between us.'

'You have done *what?*' breathed Michael, aghast. 'Is that why some foundations have joined forces with townsfolk, making the situation more complicated than ever?'

'Yes, and it is a good thing,' Aynton assured him, beaming happily. 'It means no one will attack anyone else lest he hurts a friend. There is no French army waiting in the fens, of course. I just expanded on a false rumour that was circulating earlier in the week.'

'What false rumour?' asked Bartholomew uneasily.

'That the Spital is full of the Dauphin's spies. Do not look so worried, Matthew. It is not true. I met Warden Tangmer yesterday, and he assured me that no foreigner has ever set foot inside his gates.'

Bartholomew regarded him in horror. 'He was lying! There are women and children there – folk who are supposed to leave at nightfall.' He glanced at the window. 'About now, in fact.'

Aynton swallowed hard. 'But they cannot – they will be seen. Angry folk have been gathering there all afternoon, and the Spital is now surrounded by a sizeable mob. I assumed it would not matter – and better damage to a remote foundation than us or the town.'

'It looks as though I shall have my bloodbath after all,' said de Wetherset, and laughed.

Bartholomew refused to leave the Chancellor pinioned to the floor, so valuable moments were lost releasing him. Unfortunately, Heltisle had rammed the pen home with such force that it had shattered, and Bartholomew was far from sure he had removed all the fragments. Meanwhile, Heltisle stubbornly refused to let him tend his bleeding arm.

'I would sooner die,' he snarled defiantly.

'Send him home, Brother,' said Bartholomew, tired of trying to convince him. 'Tell his students to summon a *medicus* urgently or they will be looking for a new Master tomorrow.'

'Very well,' said Michael. 'But I am not doing the same for de Wetherset. He can sit in the proctors' gaol until I decide what to do with him.'

He had fetched beadles and stretchers while Bartholomew had been busy. Without further ado, Heltisle and de Wetherset were loaded up and toted away. The beadles made no effort to be gentle, and the faces of both men were grey with pain. When they had gone, Aynton turned to Bartholomew and Michael.

'Go to the Spital,' he ordered. 'I will stay here and help the Sheriff.'

'It should be me who stays,' objected Michael, sure Aynton would be of scant use to Tulyet.

'Please,' said Aynton quietly. 'I was an unwitting help-meet, but my conscience pricks and I must make amends. Besides, now de Wetherset and Heltisle are arrested, it means I am Acting Chancellor – a role I shall fill until you can arrange an election. Ergo, I outrank you. Now go – you have innocents to save.'

'Do you trust him?' asked Bartholomew, as he and Michael hurried through the now-dark church towards the door. 'He took a long time to choose a side – it should have been obvious that de Wetherset was guilty long before Aynton made his decision.'

'I have never trusted him. You are the one who thought he was harmless. But I sent Meadowman to Dick with a full account of what happened, and Dick is someone I *do* trust. He will keep Aynton in line.'

'Did you believe de Wetherset when he denied stabbing Paris and the others?' asked Bartholomew. 'I did – he confessed to the rest, so why baulk at those?'

Michael nodded tersely. 'The culprit is not Heltisle, either. He is a vile individual, but not one to poison children. Do we have any suspects left?'

'Aynton,' replied Bartholomew unhappily. 'But there is nothing we can do about him now. We must wait until we have rescued the *peregrini*, whose only crime was hoping to find a place where they could live free of fear and persecution.'

Night had fallen at last, and the high street and the alleys off it were full of whispers and bobbing torches. They added a tension to the atmosphere that did nothing to aid the cause of peace. Michael's beadles were everywhere, ordering scholars and townsfolk alike back to their homes, although with scant success.

'It is hopeless,' reported one in despair. 'The only good thing is the rumour about French spies at the Spital, as it has drawn many would-be rioters away. Even so, there

347

are hundreds left, and if we avert a battle, it will be a miracle.'

'Here is Dick,' said Michael, as there was a rattle of hoofs on cobbles and the Sheriff cantered up. Both he and his horse showed signs of being in skirmishes, and the knights who rode with him were grim-faced and anxious.

'For God's sake, tell no one else about de Wetherset,' he said curtly. 'If word gets out that a scholar orchestrated all this mayhem . . .'

'We have many bridges to repair,' acknowledged Michael. 'But it can be done.'

'I hope you are right. But do you really want Aynton to "help" me while you jaunt off to the Spital?'

'Not really, so keep him close, and do not turn your back on him for any reason.'

Tulyet regarded him askance. 'Do not tell me that *he* is the killer!'

'I do not know what to think,' said Michael tiredly. 'Just be careful. And do not forget that the Jacques might take advantage of the unrest to harm the town that killed their friends. They will be used to this sort of turmoil, given their penchant for insurrection.'

Tulyet nodded. 'And you be careful at the Spital. The *peregrini* will still be there, because Leger cannot have led them to safety with so many indignant "patriots" milling about outside. I wish I could help you, but my duty lies here.'

'So does mine,' said Michael wretchedly. 'Perhaps I should stay and let Matt—'

'Go,' interrupted Tulyet. 'But please come back soon. It will take every good man we can muster if we aim to prevent University and town from wiping each other out permanently.'

Michael dared not take beadles to the Spital, knowing he would be deposed for certain if it emerged that he had left the University vulnerable in order to rescue foreigners. He hurried to the proctors' cells and gave Heltisle's Horde a choice: to prove themselves worthy of the uniform they wore or to be charged with affray. Most sneered their contempt for the offer, obviously expecting Heltisle or de Wetherset to pardon them, but half a dozen accepted, one of whom was Perkyn.

'How do you know they will not turn on us?' asked Bartholomew, uneasy with such a pack trotting at his heels. 'Or refuse to obey your orders?'

'I do not,' replied the monk. 'But the sight of an angry Senior Proctor with six "trusty" beadles may make some scholars see sense. It is a forlorn hope, but it is better than nothing.'

They hurried through the Trumpington Gate, Michael wheezing like a winded nag. Then a familiar figure materialised out of the darkness: Cynric. Bartholomew was glad to see him, because Heltisle's Horde was growing increasingly agitated as they began to understand the dangers that lay ahead of them. Cynric was more likely to prevent them from bolting than him or Michael.

'You cannot stop what will happen there,' the book-bearer said, nodding to where the Spital was a pale gold smear in the distance, illuminated eerily by the torches of the besieging force. 'It will only end with a spillage of French blood.'

'I am not giving up,' rasped Michael. 'Not yet.'

They set off along the Trumpington road, cursing as they stumbled and lurched on its rutted surface. At the Gilbertine Priory, lights blazed from every window and the canons gathered at their gate, distressed by the tumult in a part of the town that was usually peaceful.

'Brother!' called Prior John urgently, his huge mouth set in an anxious grimace. 'I have some things you should see.'

'Not now,' gasped Michael. 'There is trouble at the Spital.'

'I know,' said John drily. 'At least two hundred scholars have stormed past, and we lost count of the number of townsfolk. All were howling about killing Frenchmen.'

'Please,' begged Michael, trying to jig around him. 'We do not have time to—'

'It concerns Abbess Isabel,' persisted John, grabbing his arm and shoving a letter at him. 'She compiled a report for the Bishop, and left it with me two days ago. She told me to read it if anything happened to her. Well, I heard she was dead, so . . .'

Michael looked from the missive to the Spital, then back again, agonising over what to do. His eyesight was poor in dim light, and it would take him an age to decipher what was written. Seeing his dilemma, Bartholomew took the letter and scanned it quickly.

'The first part is about Alice,' he summarised briskly, 'and contains hard evidence that will see her on trial for theft and witchery. The second half is about the killer.'

'Which killer?' demanded Michael. 'De Wetherset or the one who stabbed Paris and the others?' He lowered his voice. 'Who may be Aynton.'

'Isabel says the key to the mystery is a comb, which was lying next to Paris's body when she happened across it.'

'There was no comb at the scene of the crime,' said Michael. 'I would have seen it.'

Bartholomew read on. 'It was familiar, and when she realised where she had seen it before, she fainted in horror. When she came to, the comb had gone. She wanted proof before making accusations, so she charged Alice to steal it so she could look at it more closely. In return, she promised to get Alice reinstated as Prioress of Ickleton.'

'A promise she had no intention of keeping,' noted Michael, 'given the first half of her letter.'

'Which she justifies with the claim that Alice broke the terms of the agreement by sending her tainted gifts. But that is irrelevant. What matters now is that she says the killer is the owner of the comb.' Bartholomew looked up. 'She accuses Prioress Joan.'

'Then she is wrong,' said Michael firmly. 'Perhaps the comb *was* at the scene of Paris's murder, and someone did retrieve it while Isabel swooned. However, there is nothing to suggest that Joan is the culprit. It is more likely that someone left it there to incriminate her – someone like Alice, in fact.'

'That is what Isabel thought at first,' said Prior John, waving a second letter. 'Especially when she heard you say that Joan had an alibi for the Spital murders and has promptly promised to identify the murder weapon for you. So Isabel spent two days praying and reflecting in a church, and sent this addendum to her report today.'

Bartholomew read it quickly. 'She begs the Bishop's forgiveness for not speaking out at once, but she is now certain that Joan killed Paris and the others. She claims that Joan's alibi will not stand up to serious scrutiny and urges him to probe it rigorously.'

'What nonsense!' snapped Michael. 'We do not have time for—'

'I think Isabel might be right,' interrupted Bartholomew urgently. 'Goda and Katherine both said that Joan was horrified when she discovered the comb was stolen – more than either would have expected from a woman who cares nothing for trinkets . . .'

'She explained why,' barked Michael. 'Her horse liked to be groomed with it. Isabel was wrong. Why would Joan hurt Paris? Or any of the victims?'

'Perhaps she does not like Frenchies,' suggested Cynric, who had been listening agog. 'Like lots of right-thinking folk. However, I can tell you that she collected Dusty from our stables about an hour ago, and was very agitated while she did it. I got the impression that something was badly wrong.'

'It is,' said Michael tersely. 'She is in a town that is set to destroy itself and anyone in it. Of course she was agitated – she has her nuns to keep safe.'

'I saw her not long after that,' put in Prior John. 'She told me that she was off to Lyminster, and when I remarked that dusk was an odd time to begin such a long journey, she suggested I mind my own business. Then she galloped away like a whirlwind.'

'But why would she—' began Michael.

'We can discuss her motives later,' interrupted Bartholomew shortly. 'After we have prevented a massacre.'

'*If* you can prevent it,' said John grimly. 'Joan was staying at the Spital, was she not? I imagine she guessed that the "lunatics" are really Frenchmen in hiding, and I have a bad feeling that she has not finished with them yet.'

'And I have a bad feeling that you are right,' said Bartholomew.

CHAPTER 16

Bartholomew was glad when Heltisle's Horde was augmented by half a dozen Gilbertines, led by Prior John. The canons carried no weapons, so would be of scant use in a fight, but there was always the chance that the presence of priests would make a mob think twice about what it was doing. He glanced behind him, and noted that the six beadles were now down to five, as one had slunk away rather than face what lay ahead.

The glow from the Spital was brighter now, and he realised with despair that there were hundreds of torches – which meant hundreds of folk baying for 'enemy' blood. What could he, Michael, Cynric, five reluctant beadles and a handful of unarmed canons do against so many? Tulyet had been right: the Spital was already lost, and they should have stayed in the town, where they might have done some good.

'I still do not believe it,' Michael gasped as they hurried along. 'The culprit cannot be Joan. She is too bluff and honest for so sly a scheme. It seems to me that someone has gone to a lot of trouble to see her accused.'

'Katherine?' suggested Bartholomew. 'She is the Bishop's sister, and we all know how devious and ruthless he can be. Perhaps it runs in the family.'

As far as Michael was concerned, that was a worse solution than Joan. 'We only have Isabel's word that a comb *was* by Paris's body, and she was deceitful, as evidenced by her questionable dealings with Alice. Besides, there was no time for Joan – or anyone else – to reclaim the thing while Isabel lay insensible.'

'There was,' countered Bartholomew. 'When Isabel

swooned a second time – at the disturbing sight of a wantonly low-cut bodice – she was out for several minutes. If it was a repeat of her first episode, there would have been ample time for the killer to act.'

'I still do not believe—'

'And there is something else. We crossed Joan off our list of suspects because Goda said she could see Joan in the stables while she herself was in the kitchen. But did you check that is actually possible? I did not.'

'Nor did I,' said Cynric, who had been listening with unabashed interest. 'But I know the answer: you cannot see one from the other, because the chapel is in the way.'

'Goda lied,' Bartholomew went on. 'She did not mention seeing Joan when we first spoke to her – she only "remembered" during a second interview, by which time Joan had realised that she needed help.'

'There is a flaw in your argument,' pounced Michael. 'Goda claimed she could see the *shed* from the kitchen, too – which *is* possible, because I have a vivid recollection of a tray of cakes being carried from the kitchen when I was examining the burnt shed. But Goda made no mention of Joan slinking inside with a fancy French dagger – and remember that this was *before* anyone would have had a chance to bribe her.'

'Goda cannot have been gazing out of the door every moment that morning,' argued Bartholomew. 'At some point she would have looked away to put bread in the oven or fetch ingredients from the pantry. Or perhaps Goda did see Joan, but did not know it – she said the Girards "popped in and out". Well, one "Girard" may have been Joan in disguise.'

Michael remained unconvinced. 'But why would Goda lie? She cannot have known Joan well enough to warrant that sort of devotion.'

'She did not do it for friendship, she did it for money.

We know she was greedy – she coveted the dagger that killed the Girards, and she asked to be paid for answering questions. Joan capitalised on that avarice and bought herself an alibi.'

'He may be right, Brother,' said Cynric. 'Ever since the Spital murders, Goda has been flush with cash – new clothes, new shoes, new hair-frets. And that is suspicious, because the Tangmers are broke. She did not get her windfall from them.'

'No, she got it from the oils she stole from Amphelisa,' countered Michael.

'Not even the best oils would fetch the kind of money Goda has been laying out,' stated Cynric with great conviction. 'They—'

'But Goda began to sport these new purchases *before* Joan knew she needed an alibi,' Michael pointed out irritably. 'I repeat: Matt's logic is flawed.'

'Not so,' insisted Bartholomew. 'Hélène's milk was dosed with a soporific, and as I seriously doubt that Joan thought to pack some when she left Lyminster, it means she got it here – from someone with access to Amphelisa's supplies. I imagine Goda charged her a small fortune.'

'And may have blackmailed her about it after,' put in Cynric.

'Which means Joan knew that Goda would do anything for money,' Bartholomew went on, 'while Goda knew that Joan had deep pockets. A deal was made and we looked no further at either suspect.'

'Moreover, Goda *hated* the French,' said Cynric. 'I heard her say so several times. She would have had no problem looking the other way while Joan dispatched a few.'

'But people like Goda can never be trusted to keep their mouths shut,' continued Bartholomew. 'So Joan killed her, too. She is tying up loose ends, ready to return to her priory and her life as a servant of God.'

'What about Delacroix and his friends?' asked Michael archly. 'Are they to be forgotten in all this? I thought we had agreed that they were our most likely suspects.'

But Bartholomew was still thinking about Joan, and something else became clear to him. 'We have assumed it was Alice who told Norbert about the *peregrini* – that she guessed what they were on one of her visits to the Spital. But Joan and her Lyminster sisters also recognised them as displaced Frenchmen.'

'It *was* Alice!' snapped Michael. 'She betrayed herself by scratching.'

'Precisely! Joan knew that if she clawed at herself as she dispensed her treacherous news, everyone would assume that Alice was the guilty party. And we did.'

'Then what about the Rouen daggers?' pressed Michael. 'Joan said they were familiar. Why would she do that if she had been the one to wield them?'

'And has her testimony led us to the killer? No, it has not! What it has done, however, is make us think she is on our side, valiantly striving to dig solutions from her memory.'

'But why?' cried Michael. 'There has been no hint of Joan doing anything like this before. I would have heard if there were lots of unsolved murders around her priory.'

Bartholomew knew the answer to that, too. 'Because of Winchelsea. She was appalled by what she saw there, and Katherine said she is building a chantry chapel for the victims – a massive undertaking that reveals how deeply she was affected by the experience.'

'She was distressed by it,' acknowledged Michael. 'She mentioned it several times when we rode to the Austin Priory together. But—'

'She is avenging the victims by killing Frenchmen: Paris, Bonet, the Girards, Bruges and Sauvage. Although she made an erroneous assumption with the last two.'

'And tonight will see the remaining *peregrini* slaughtered,' finished Cynric. 'She will not even have to bloody her own hands, because our town will do it for her.'

When they reached the Spital and saw the baying mob outside, Bartholomew's heart sank. Spats sparked between the different factions – mostly scholars against townsfolk, but Maud's and Corner hostels were engaged in a vicious shoving match, while the bakers and the grocers harangued each other nearby. No one was listening to anyone else, and tempers everywhere ran high. There was no sign of Leger, and the scant troops Tulyet had spared to protect the place were under the less experienced command of a sergeant.

'I do not know where Sir Leger went,' the man said apologetically when Michael demanded an explanation. 'He just told me to take over.'

'He must have gone inside,' murmured Michael, and brightened. 'Maybe he has sneaked the *peregrini* out already.'

'Unlikely,' said Cynric. 'They would have been spotted.'

'Have you seen Prioress Joan?' Bartholomew asked the sergeant.

The man nodded to where the Trumpington road snaked south. 'She went that way an hour ago, like the Devil was on her tail. I called for her to stop – it was stupid, riding so wild with night approaching – but she ignored me.'

He hurried away when a quarrel by the gate resulted in drawn daggers. Perkyn watched him go with mounting alarm.

'I am not staying here to be cut down in my prime,' he gulped. 'I—'

'Stand your ground!' barked Michael, although the Horde had now dwindled from five to three. 'You will be quite safe as long as you follow my orders.'

'He will not,' whispered Bartholomew. 'There must be upwards of four hundred armed men here, all spoiling for a fight. You cannot reason with them, because they are long past listening, even if you could make yourself heard.'

'I disagree,' said Michael. 'They could have broken inside by now, but they hesitate out here. That means there is still a chance that we can persuade them to—'

'They are not "hesitating", Brother, they are thwarted,' countered Cynric, assessing the scene with a professional eye. 'The Spital was designed for this sort of situation – to repel folk who want to get at its lepers. The walls are high and the gates are sturdy, like a fortress.'

'So the people inside are safe?' asked Bartholomew in relief.

'Not safe,' replied Cynric. 'Just bought a bit more time. The defences *will* be breached tonight, and then the Spital and its inhabitants will burn.'

'But there must be something we can do,' said Bartholomew in despair. 'We cannot just stand here and watch innocents being butchered.'

'There is one thing,' said Cynric hesitantly. 'When I thought Satan was coming to live here, I made a thorough reconnaissance of the place, just to know what resources he would have at his disposal, like. There is a tunnel at the back . . .'

'A tunnel?' blurted Michael. 'Why would—'

'He just explained why,' interrupted Bartholomew shortly. 'The Spital was built like a fortress, to protect it from attack. Fortresses have sally ports, lest its defenders should ever need to slip out unseen.'

Cynric nodded. 'Unfortunately, the Tangmers cannot use it now, because the Spital is surrounded by hostiles. Anyone creeping out will be caught and killed.'

'Are you *sure* they did not leave earlier?' asked Bartholomew, hopefully. 'Before there were so many besiegers?'

'Quite sure,' replied Cynric. 'I can see one of them from here, watching us from the top of the wall. They are in there all right.'

'So if this sally port cannot help us, why mention the damned thing?' demanded Michael curtly.

'Because they *could* use it *if* we make sure they are not seen sneaking out,' explained Cynric. 'In other words, if we create a diversion for them.'

'Two diversions,' corrected Bartholomew. 'One for us to get inside so we can round them up, and one to bring them out and spirit them away.'

Cynric gaped at him. '*We* cannot go inside! What if the defences are breached while we are in there? We would be torn to shreds.'

'It is a risk we must take,' said Bartholomew. 'How else will we explain the plan?'

'But they are French, boy,' objected Cynric. 'The villains we fought at Poitiers.'

'We did not fight women, priests and children,' argued Bartholomew. 'Or the Tangmer clan, whose only crime was to offer sanctuary to people in need.'

'You may have fought the Jacques, though,' muttered Michael acidly. 'Unless they were too busy rebelling against their aristocratic overlords to defend their country at Poitiers.'

'Jacques?' pounced Cynric, his eyes alight with interest. 'Some are *Jacques*? Why did you not say so? I have no problem helping brothers who stand against oppression.'

'Good,' said Bartholomew, too desperate for Cynric's help to confess that the Jacques were no longer in there. 'Now, show us this tunnel before it is too late.'

As Cynric led the way cautiously through the shrieking besiegers, Bartholomew saw the Welshman was right to predict that it was only a matter of time before the Spital's defences were breached. At the front, a determined but inept gang of townsmen was trying to set the gates alight, while all along the sides were folk wielding axes, picks and hammers. At the same time, a number of resourceful scholars were busily constructing makeshift ladders, ready to scale the walls.

Then they reached the back, and Bartholomew felt hope stir within him. No one was there, because the whole area was choked with brambles, so that reaching a wall to batter at was impractical. But even as he drew breath to point this out, a mass of bobbing torches signalled the arrival of more rioters, all eager to find a hitherto unoccupied spot where they could stand and howl abuse.

'Stupid Tangmer!' spat Cynric, as the newcomers began to bellow at the strangers inside. 'He could have made it out earlier, but it will be ten times harder now that Isnard and his friends have arrived.'

Bartholomew peered into the gloom and saw it was indeed the bargeman and his cronies who had laid claim to the back wall. All had drunk themselves into a frenzy of hatred, and the vile words and threats that spilled from their mouths shocked him to the core. He wondered if he would ever see them in the same light again.

He glanced behind him, and saw that the last of the Horde had vanished, leaving just him, Cynric, Prior John, Michael and the six canons. His stomach churned. The plan's success depended on no one noticing what he was about to do, which would be all but impossible with so few helpmeets. If just one man looked across at the wrong time . . .

'Right,' whispered Cynric, stopping near a particularly dense thicket of brambles. 'Tell us the plan. I hope it is a good one, or your Frenchies will die and the Tangmers with them.'

Everyone looked expectantly at Bartholomew, who scrabbled around for inspiration.

'The canons must holler that they have spotted a spy, then make a show of running after him,' he said, thinking fast. 'The mob will scent blood and join the chase, leaving the rest of us to slip into the tunnel unseen.'

There was silence as the others regarded him in consternation. He did not blame them. There was a lot that could go wrong, and he was not happy with it himself, but it was all he could devise on the spur of the moment.

'But no one will believe us!' gulped John. 'We are men of God – the rioters will know we are not in the habit of flying off after some hapless soul like a pack of savages.'

'You are not,' agreed Cynric, eyes narrowed in thought. 'But Isnard is. Make sure he hears when you raise the alarm, and he will do the rest.'

'Yell as loudly as you can,' Michael instructed the Gilbertines, his voice unsteady with agitation. 'It would have been better with more men to help, but . . .'

'Do not worry, Brother,' said John, grimly determined. 'We know what is at stake. You can rely on us to do what is necessary.'

'Then let us begin,' said Cynric.

Bartholomew had no real hope that the diversion would work, because John was right: who would believe that the gentle, kindly Gilbertines would bay for the blood of strangers? But Cynric had the right of it, and bigotry saved the day. Isnard was livid at the notion that the enemy might be escaping right under his nose, and his bellows of rage drowned out all else. Within moments, the canons were leading a demented, screaming mass of drunken zealots over the fields at the back of the Spital, Isnard swinging after them on his crutches.

'Now, follow me,' Cynric hissed to Bartholomew and Michael when they had gone.

He ducked into the brambles and was immediately lost from sight. Bartholomew did likewise, Michael at his heels.

It was almost pitch black without the rioters' torches, but they could just make out a rough, winding path through the foliage.

'Someone has used this today,' whispered the book-bearer, although how he could tell in the dark was beyond Bartholomew. 'Sir Leger on his horse probably, which means he *is* inside, waiting for the best chance to lead his charges out. Good! Let us hope he has them assembled, so they will be ready to go at once.'

'I think we might have made a tactical blunder by sending the rioters across the fields,' blurted Michael suddenly. 'Because they will be coming back – empty-handed and furious – in exactly the direction that we will be taking the *peregrini*.'

'There is a concealed track,' whispered Cynric. 'Leger must have used it safely today, or someone would have noticed him riding back here and disappearing – and the Spital would be in flames already.'

They reached the wall, where a short, steep slope led down to an arch that was almost invisible in the gloom. Cynric slithered towards it and began to wrestle with a gate. Bartholomew followed, helping the less-agile Michael and marvelling that Leger had convinced a horse to make the journey.

'How did you find it?' he whispered, thinking that it would never have occurred to *him* to explore briar thickets in search of hidden entrances.

'By being thorough,' replied Cynric, 'which was important when I thought Satan was going to live here. But we can discuss this later. Now, get inside. Hurry!'

'You first,' said Bartholomew, regarding the gate and the passage beyond uneasily. He could see nothing but blackness. 'You have done it before.'

But Cynric shook his head. 'I had best stay here, ready to create the second diversion, which *must* be done properly, or you will all be killed as you come out. Prior John cannot do it, because even Isnard will be suspicious if he tried the same thing twice.'

It was a good point, although Bartholomew was dismayed to learn that Cynric would not be there when he ventured inside the Spital. The book-bearer was much better at anything that required sneaking around in the dark than him or Michael.

Heart pounding, and expecting at any moment to hear a screech to say they had been discovered, he stepped into the tunnel, one hand on the wall as he made his way along it. It was damp and stank of mould. The ground descended sharply, then began to rise again as they passed under the wall's foundations. Then his groping hands encountered another door. He grasped the handle and pushed. It opened, and fresh air wafted around him.

He emerged behind a compost heap, near the blackened rubble of the shed. Cautiously, he peered around, hoping desperately that the *peregrini* would be waiting there, but nothing moved.

'It should have been me left behind to handle the second diversion,' grumbled Michael, brushing dirt from his habit. 'I am not built for creeping about in underground passages. I am not a ferret.'

Bartholomew motioned him to silence, then crept forward cautiously. Two lamps burned near the gate, while more were lit in the chapel, but other than those, the Spital was in darkness. Moreover, there were no sentries on the wall or patrolling the grounds to raise the alarm in the event of a breach.

'The Tangmers were standing guard when we arrived,' he whispered. 'Cynric saw one of them. Now they are not. Does it mean they escaped while we were walking about outside?'

'I think we would have seen them,' said Michael worriedly. 'But look how many lamps blaze in the chapel. I have a bad feeling that they aim to claim sanctuary.'

'But they will not get it!' gulped Bartholomew in alarm. 'In Winchelsea, the parish church was set alight with dozens of people locked inside – the *peregrini* and the Tangmers will suffer the same fate if they are caught in there. We have to get them out!'

He began to stumble across the uneven ground towards it, Michael at his heels. They reached the hall and aimed for the chapel's main door, but it was locked. No one answered their frantic knocking, so they hurried to the side entrance in the hope of making themselves heard there. It was open. Bartholomew stepped inside and immediately smelled burning. He grabbed a lantern and ran into the chancel, coughing as smoke swirled around him.

'Where are they?' demanded Michael, peering around through smarting eyes. 'And what is on fire?'

'Amphelisa's workshop,' rasped Bartholomew as he started down the nave. 'I told her the chapel was not a good place for it. It is too close to those great piles of firewood.'

'*Unseasoned* firewood,' rasped Michael, 'which is why there is so much smoke. We—'

He faltered when a figure appeared through the swirling whiteness. It was a large Benedictine nun with a wet scarf over her nose and mouth. She had exchanged her black cloak for Amphelisa's old burgundy one, which was so impregnated with spilled oils that Bartholomew could smell them even over the stench of burning.

Behind her were three men, all armed with crossbows. Their faces were also masked, although Bartholomew recognised Leger's fair hair, and thought the other two were knights from the castle.

'Why could you two not have minded your own business?' growled Joan crossly. 'I suppose you used that wretched tunnel to sneak in.'

'How did you know about—' began Michael.

'I had a good look around when I was billeted here,' replied Joan briskly, and shook her head in exasperation. 'I had no wish to kill you, but now I have no choice.'

'I will do it,' offered Leger helpfully.

CHAPTER 17

There was silence in the chapel, then Bartholomew leapt at Leger, in the hope that a swift assault would give him a vital advantage. It was a mistake. With indolent ease, Leger twisted away, and Bartholomew went flying from a casual blow with the crossbow. It did him no harm, but he landed in a place where the smoke was much thicker, simultaneously blinding him and rendering him helpless from lack of air.

'Put them with the others,' he heard Joan order. 'Quickly now.'

'Why?' demanded Leger. 'I can shoot them down here.'

'It is a chapel,' snapped Joan. 'A holy place. Now do as I say. Hurry!'

Bartholomew tried to scramble away when the knights came, but they knew how to handle awkward prisoners. He and Michael were bundled through Amphelisa's smouldering workshop and up the steps to the balcony. As the door was opened, an almighty racket broke out. Children sobbed, women screamed for mercy, and old men wailed in terror. Bartholomew and Michael were shoved inside so roughly that both fell. The clamour intensified.

'Silence!' roared Joan. 'Or you will be sorry.'

'*This* is a holy place, too,' Michael reminded her as the din petered out. 'Part of the chapel. If you spill blood up here, you will be damned for all eternity.'

'Who said anything about spilling blood?' asked Joan shortly.

Bartholomew sat up, acutely aware of the snap and crackle of the fire below. Smoke oozed through the floor-boards. He blinked tears from his stinging eyes, and saw the *peregrini* and staff huddled at the far end. So were the Jacques.

'You think burning people alive is acceptable, but shooting them is not?' breathed Michael. 'Please, Joan! Think of your immortal soul!'

'I *am* thinking of it,' snarled Joan. 'Which is why I must avenge Winchelsea. It would be a far greater sin to pretend it never happened.'

'It is not for you to dispense justice!' cried Michael. 'It—'

'Who will, then?' she demanded tightly. 'The survivors of Winchelsea? All the fighting men are dead. The King? He is too busy with his war. Mother Church? She brays her horror, but her priests lack the courage to act.'

'Not them – God,' said Michael. '*He* will punish the guilty.'

'Quite,' said Joan. 'And I am His instrument, doing His will.'

'He does not want this!' Michael was shocked. 'And your actions will only compound the atrocity. Murdering more people will not make it better.'

'On the contrary, those whose loved ones were butchered by French raiders will take comfort from it. They said so as I helped them bury their innocent dead.'

Michael indicated the *peregrini*. 'They also lost loved ones that day. Delacroix's brothers were killed defending Winchelsea.'

'They are spies,' stated Joan uncompromisingly. 'They wrote to the French, advising them when best to attack Winchelsea. The Mayor told me personally. It is *their* fault the slaughter was so terrible and they will pay for their treachery today.'

Her eyes blazed, and Bartholomew knew Michael was wasting his time trying to reason with her. Meanwhile, the smoke grew denser with every passing moment, and her prisoners were already struggling to breathe.

'You cannot be party to this, Leger,' shouted Michael, snatching at straws in his desperation. 'You are a knight – your duty is to protect the weak.'

'My duty is to protect England from the French,' countered Leger. 'Which is what I *am* doing. Besides, you may have forgotten Norbert, but I never shall.'

'Norbert?' blurted Michael. 'What does he have to do with it?'

'He was murdered in that skirmish by *foreign* scholars. And since Tulyet refuses to take a stand against them, I have joined ranks with someone who will.'

He nodded to his fellows and they prepared to leave. Bartholomew was in an agony of tension. He *had* to stop them! Once the door was locked – and he was sure Joan would have the only key – their victims' fate was sealed. There would be no escape from the flames.

'Joan *used* Norbert,' he yelled, hoping Leger would turn against her if he knew the truth. '*Deceived* him. It was not Alice who told him that the Spital harboured French spies – it was Joan. She deliberately misled him by aping Alice's scratching.'

'But French spies *are* hiding here,' shrugged Leger. 'And Norbert would not have cared which nun the information came from – just that she was right.'

'You will not live long once you leave,' warned Bartholomew, opting for another strategy. 'Like Goda, you will be stabbed to tie up loose ends. And if you want proof, look at Joan's shoes – stained with the oil that spilled as she chased Goda around this—'

Eudo tore at Joan, bellowing his rage and grief. Leger shot him. The big man thudded to the floor and lay still.

'I did chase her,' admitted Joan, regarding the dead man with a chilling lack of emotion. 'But I did not kill her – she had grabbed a knife from the kitchen and she fell on it as we raced around. Her blood is not on my hands.'

'Paris,' said Michael, declining to argue semantics with her. 'You killed him for—'

'For being French,' spat Joan. 'And his death is *your* fault – I would not have known he even existed if you lot had not made such a fuss about him stealing someone else's work. And as for that spicer – well, he had to die after he had the audacity to inform me that the Dauphin only did in Winchelsea what English soldiers do in France.'

Most of the prisoners were on their knees or lying down, gasping for air. Only Delacroix remained stubbornly upright, glaring defiance through streaming eyes.

'And the Girard family?' asked Michael. 'I assume you could not bring yourself to knife the little girl, so you put a soporific in her milk.'

Joan winced. 'It was cowardly of me.'

'Yet you helped to rescue Hélène. Were you not afraid she would identify you?'

'One nun looks much like another to children. And as for pulling her from the shed . . . well, suffice to say that I was caught up in the moment.'

'How did you stab four adults with such ease?' asked Michael, casting an agonised glance at Bartholomew, begging him to act while he kept her talking. 'Two were Jacques – experienced fighters.'

'Experienced fighters who turned their backs on a nun,' said Joan shortly. She opened the bag she carried over her shoulder and began to rummage about inside it. 'Now, enough talking. I am—'

'Bruges and Sauvage were next, even though neither was French,' persisted Michael.

'I pray that God will forgive my mistake.' Joan pulled two daggers from the bag and dropped them on the floor, where they joined a number of others already lying there. 'I collected these after Winchelsea, when I vowed that a French life would pay for every English one. Today will see that oath more than fulfilled.'

'You only found one of the batch she left when she dispatched the Girards,' put in Leger gloatingly. 'You might have had answers a lot sooner if you had been more thorough.'

Michael ignored him and continued to address Joan. 'And when these weapons are found, I suppose you will have a flash of memory, which will "prove" that the *peregrini* killed Paris and the others.' His expression was one of deep disgust.

Joan inclined her head. 'Although your Junior Proctor will have to act on my testimony now, given that you will not be in a position to do it.'

'Wait!' shouted Michael desperately, as she turned to leave. 'You cannot do this!'

Joan paused and regarded him thoughtfully. 'Before I go, answer one question: how did you guess it was me? Not from that stupid comb I dropped when I dispatched Paris? I had a feeling that Abbess Isabel recognised it before I managed to reclaim the thing. Is that why Alice took it from my bag? To give to her, so she could be certain?'

'Yes, and Isabel has told everyone her suspicions, so you can never return to Lym—'

But Joan was already sweeping out, Amphelisa's cloak billowing around her. The soldiers followed, and the door slammed shut behind them.

For a moment, the only sounds were the growing roar of the flames below and footsteps thumping down the stairs. Then the Jacques released bellows of rage and ran at the door like bulls, kicking and pounding on it with all their might. But the wood was thick, and Bartholomew knew it would never yield to an assault, no matter how determined. The other adults began to wrap cloaks and hats around their faces and those of the children.

'Tangmer!' shouted Bartholomew. 'Is there another way out?'

'No – we never imagined one would be necessary,' gasped the Warden, his face ashen.

'We lied,' whispered Father Julien, who was on his knees, hands clasped in prayer. 'And this is God's judgement on us.'

'Lied about what?' demanded Michael.

'The dagger that killed the Girards,' said Julien. 'Of course we recognised it – they are made all around Rouen. But if we had admitted it, you would have accused us of murder . . .'

It was no time for recriminations, so Michael went to help with the children, while Bartholomew conducted a panicky search of the balcony. But Tangmer was right: there was only one way in or out, and that was locked. Three of the walls were solid stone, while the fourth was the wooden screen designed to keep lepers away from the healthy. The screen was sturdy, and would not be smashed without an axe – which they did not have.

Yet it did flex when Bartholomew thumped it in frustration. He examined the way it had been secured to the wall, and saw someone had been criminally miserly with the nails. There were plenty to anchor it in place where it met the knee-high wall at the bottom, but there were only a few at the sides, and none at all along the top.

'Help me!' he rasped, kicking it as hard as he could. The Jacques joined in and so did Tangmer, but their efforts were more frantic than scientific, and were aimed at the wrong spots entirely. Then Michael approached.

'Stand back!' he shouted.

He trotted to the back of the balcony, lowered his shoulder and charged, gaining speed with every thundering step. He struck the screen plumb in the middle, so hard that Bartholomew flinched for him. There was a screaming groan as the wood tore free at the top and sides, although the bottom held firm. Then the top flopped forward in a graceful arc to land with a crash on the nave floor below.

Michael was moving far too fast to stop, so his momentum carried him over the wall and out of sight. Horrified, Bartholomew darted forward to see that the screen now formed a very steep ramp, down which Michael was dancing, arms flailing in alarm. The monk reached the bottom and staggered to a standstill.

'I meant to do that,' he lied. 'Now bring everyone down. Hurry!'

No one needed to be told twice. They slid and scampered down the screen like monkeys, grateful that the smoke was less dense below. Confident no one would escape, Joan had not bothered to lock the side door, so everyone was soon outside, coughing and gasping in relief. The Jacques began to scout for signs of their would-be killers.

'We can douse the flames,' rasped Tangmer. 'Save our chapel.'

'No,' barked Bartholomew. 'You must leave *now* or the rioters will—'

He faltered when there was an urgent yell from Delacroix. The townsfolk had finally succeeded in setting the gates alight, and were hammering through the weakened wood with a battering ram.

'To the tunnel!' shouted Bartholomew, hoping Cynric would be able to stage a second diversion with very little warning.

He began to lead the way, aware that the besiegers' howls had changed to something harder and darker now that victory was within their grasp. He had no doubt that anyone caught inside the Spital would be cut down, regardless of who they were. There would be regrets and shame later, but that would not help those who were dead.

Then there was a crash, and the gates fell inwards. The

372

rioters poured across them, screaming for blood. In the vanguard were Heltisle's Horde, their faces twisted with hate. The *peregrini* children whimpered in terror.

Bartholomew stopped running and turned to face them. It was too late to lead anyone to safety now. He picked up a stick from the ground and prepared to fight. Michael came to stand next to him.

'We nearly did it,' the monk whispered, his voice heavy with regret. 'Just a few more moments and we would have been away.'

Suddenly, there was a rumble of hoofs, and Joan emerged from the stables on Dusty, the three knights at her heels. Their appearance through the drifting smoke was distinctly unearthly. All wore cloaks that flapped behind them and masks that hid their faces. Seeing the gate down, and knowing it would be easier to escape that way than coaxing their nervous mounts back along the tunnel, they thundered towards it.

'Like the four horsemen of the apocalypse,' muttered Bartholomew, sickened to know they would never face justice.

'With Joan as Death,' said Michael. 'It is an apt analogy.'

But as the Prioress approached the gate, a spark from the burning chapel landed on the cloak she had taken from Amphelisa. There was a dull thump as the oils in it ignited. Suddenly, she was no longer a person, but a mass of bright, leaping flames. She screamed in horror and pain, and Dusty, terrified by the inferno that raged so suddenly above him, took off like an arrow. Those in his path scattered in alarm.

Then there came an unmistakable voice from behind them. It was Cynric, who had grown increasingly alarmed by the length of time Bartholomew and Michael were taking, so had come to find out what they were doing.

'Satan!' he howled. 'It is Satan, straight from Hell!'

'He is right,' yelled Isnard. 'Margery said he was coming to live here. Well, here he is!'

'Run!' screamed Cynric at the top of his lungs. 'He wants our souls!'

Joan was burning more brilliantly than ever, and gave a shriek of such agony that it did not sound human. Heltisle's Horde turned and raced back through the gates. Their panic was contagious and within moments the Spital was empty, scholars jostling with townsfolk to hare towards the safety of home.

In the distance, louder and shriller than the wails of the mob, was Joan's voice, as Dusty bore her in the opposite direction. Bartholomew ran to the gates and looked down the road after her. She blazed for what seemed like a very long time before the flames finally winked out of sight.

EPILOGUE

It was surprisingly easy for Michael and Tulyet to restore the peace following the events at the Spital. Word spread fast that Satan had appeared in the form of blazing Death, and most people fled to the churches, where their priests urged them to pray for deliverance.

Once they had begged the Almighty for mercy, few felt like risking His wrath by indulging in another skirmish. They emerged subdued when dawn broke the following morning, and most went about their business quietly, lest they attracted the wrong kind of attention. A few hotheads declined to give up, but Michael's beadles and Tulyet's soldiers quickly rounded them up and locked them away until their tempers cooled.

As soon as it was light enough to see, Bartholomew and Michael went to look for Joan, to retrieve her body before anyone guessed the truth and decided to resume the assault on the Spital. They found her by the side of the road, still smouldering, but identifiable by her size and the Lyminster ring-seal on her finger. They also found Dusty. The horse had managed to throw his rider before she had done him any serious harm, after which he found a quiet woodland glade and began to denude it of grass.

Joan's nuns collected her charred remains, and arranged to take them home. Michael could not imagine how they would explain what had happened to her in their official report – he was not sure what to say in his own. Magistra Katherine assumed command, and seemed much more comfortable in the role than Joan had ever been.

Leger and his two cronies did not get far either. Their

plan had been to ride straight to the King and denounce Tulyet as a traitor, but the road south was so badly rutted that they were forced to dismount and walk. The call to arms meant the whole country was alert for suspicious activities, and three warriors slinking along in the dark shocked the villagers of nearby Trumpington into action. The next day, they presented a trio of arrow-studded corpses to Tulyet, and informed him that the French army was now minus three of its spies.

Bartholomew returned to his teaching, determined his lads would learn all they could humanly absorb in the last few weeks of term. At the end of one busy day, he went to the orchard to read his lecture notes ready for the following morning. An apple tree had fallen years before, and provided a comfortable bench for anyone wanting peace and quiet. The sun was low in the sky, sending a warm orange glow over the town, and the air smelled of scythed grass and summer herbs. Michael joined him there.

'I am keeping Dusty,' the monk announced. 'He should have a rider worthy of him.'

'I suppose he deserves some reward for carrying "Satan" away from the Spital,' said Bartholomew. 'Cynric adores him for it, so he will certainly be well looked after here.'

'Yelling that Joan was the Devil was impressively quick thinking on his part,' said Michael. 'Such a ruse would never have occurred to me. It saved our lives.'

Bartholomew laughed. 'It was not a ruse – he believed it. Thank God for superstition!'

'I had a letter from Father Julien today,' said Michael, closing his eyes and tipping his head back to feel the setting sun on his cheeks. 'The nuns of Ickleton were delighted to accommodate him and his flock in exchange for me ridding them of Alice. The *peregrini* are safe now.'

'But for how long?' asked Bartholomew worriedly. 'Perhaps another mob, buoyed up by ignorance and misguided patriotism, will assemble, and they will be forced to run again.'

'Ickleton is well off the beaten track, and no one ever goes there. They will live dull but peaceful lives eking a living from the land. Julien says they are all grateful and very happy.'

'Even Delacroix? I cannot see him being content to wield a spade for long.'

Michael smiled. 'He also mistook Joan for Satan and plans to take the cowl – to make amends for all the vile things he did in the Jacquerie. Incidentally, it was conscience that brought him and his friends back to the Spital that night – they realised it was wrong to leave the others alone, so they returned to help them.'

'The Spital,' mused Bartholomew. 'What will happen to it now? It is only a question of time before someone decides to punish Tangmer and his family for hiding Frenchmen.'

'The Tangmers have made their peace with a public apology and an offer of free treatment for all local lunatics. As no one knows when such a boon might come in useful, both the town and the University have promised to leave them unmolested.'

'A public apology?' echoed Bartholomew in disgust. 'For offering sanctuary to people fleeing persecution? We should commend their compassion, not force them to say sorry.'

'It was an expedient solution, Matt. Besides, Tangmer's motives were not entirely altruistic. It transpired that he charged the *peregrini* a fortune for the privilege of hiding with him, although Amphelisa still labours under the illusion that they paid a pittance.'

They were silent for a while, thinking about Joan and the havoc she had wrought with her warped pursuit of vengeance. Eventually, Bartholomew spoke.

'So she stabbed Paris, Bonet, the Girard family, Bruges

and Sauvage with blades left behind after the raid on Winchelsea, although Bruges was from Flanders and Sauvage just happened to have an unlucky name. Then she dispatched Goda to ensure her silence, and aimed to murder the *peregrini* and the entire Tangmer clan in the chapel.'

'And de Wetherset brained Wyse to "prove" that I am incapable of keeping the peace. Orwel guessed it was him from what he learned in the Griffin, so de Wetherset murdered him as well. And I sealed poor Abbess Isabel's fate by claiming that she could identify the culprit.'

Bartholomew winced. 'His actions beggar belief! What will happen to him?'

'I sent him to Ely, to face an ecclesiastical court. Unfortunately, he hit Meadowman over the head with a stone and escaped en route.'

Bartholomew regarded him in dismay. 'Meadowman is dead?'

'No, thank God – just very embarrassed. I imagine de Wetherset will flee the country now. It is unfortunate, but at least his exploits will never become public, as they would with a trial. The town would go to war with us in a second if they ever learned the full extent of what he did.'

'And Heltisle is dead, of course. He bled to death after de Wetherset slashed his arm. I could have saved him, but he refused to let me.'

'You were right about Aynton, much as it irks me to admit it. Since the crisis, he has worked tirelessly for peace, and has done much to soothe ragged tempers.'

'Will you summon Suttone back now? His resignation must be invalid, given that Heltisle forced him out by sly means.'

'I offered to reinstate him, but he wrote to say that he is happier away from the turbulent world of University politics. He told me the nature of Heltisle's threat, by the way: a promise to fabricate evidence "proving" that Michaelhouse is full of heretics.'

Bartholomew was bemused. 'Why did either of them think people would believe such an outrageous claim?'

'Because Heltisle intended to base his allegations on your controversial approach to medicine, Clippesby's mad relationship with animals, William's worrisome fanaticism, and my association with a bishop of dubious morality. It would have been extremely difficult for us to refute his charges, given how cunningly he aimed to weave truth with lies.'

Bartholomew winced. 'I see.'

'But as regards a new Chancellor, Aynton has agreed to take advice from me, so I have arranged for him to be elected next week. I think he and I will do well together.'

Bartholomew was torn between amusement and despair. They had been through hell because some scholars felt Michael had accrued too much power, and now there was to be yet another of his puppets on the throne. Nothing had changed except some new graves in the churchyards. It all seemed so futile.

'Will you appoint a new Junior Proctor to replace Theophilis?' he asked.

'Eventually. I suppose I should have been suspicious of someone with such a glorious name. "Loved by God" indeed!'

'Aungel thinks he chose it himself,' said Bartholomew, recalling a conversation held when the Junior Proctor had been writing down other scholars' opinions about Clippesby's thesis, almost certainly with a view to passing them off as his own.

'Aungel is right – Theophilis' real name is John Clippesby, and – irony of ironies – he changed it because he did not want to be confused with a lunatic. But in his defence, he did not steal the letter you wrote to me outlining Norbert's confession, and he was innocent of betraying me to the triumvirate.'

'So who did take the letter?'

'No one – it had fallen behind my desk. But trying to filch Clippesby's ideas was a low thing to have done, like snatching sweetmeats from a baby.'

'Not entirely. It transpires that Theophilis is the one who was taken advantage of – every time Clippesby mentioned a text that he thought might be relevant, Theophilis raced off to read it. Then he reported back on what he had learned, thus saving Clippesby the trouble of ploughing through it himself.'

Michael laughed. 'And Clippesby certainly bested Heltisle over selling his treatise. Bene't College insists on honouring the contract, in the hope that we will overlook the fact that their erstwhile Master tried to cheat the University's favourite genius.'

They were silent for a while, each thinking about the events that had so very nearly destroyed the University and the town that housed it. Then Bartholomew brightened.

'I had a letter today. Matilde and my sister are coming home tomorrow. I have missed them both.'

Michael smiled contentedly. 'So all is well at last. You are to be reunited with your loved ones, I shall soon have another malleable Chancellor, all the nuns have gone home, I now own a magnificent horse, and Michaelhouse prospers beyond its wildest dreams.'

'It does?'

'The Pope has given the Chicken Debate his seal of approval, so the demand for copies will soar. Not only will we be paid every time one is sold, but we are on the verge of international fame. It is high time – our College is a good place, and I am glad its future is assured. You may be leaving us, but we will survive.'

Bartholomew was delighted to hear it.

* * *

De Wetherset was not really equipped for life as a fugitive in the Fens. He had grown soft and fat from easy living in the University, and hated sleeping in the open like a beggar. But it was better than being paraded as a criminal, as he was sure that Michael had amassed more than enough evidence to see him convicted by the Bishop's court.

He grimaced. He had been right to try to claw power back from the monk, although he realised now that he should have done it gradually, rather than racing at the problem like a bull at a fence. But he had been impatient for change, and ever since his pilgrimage to Walsingham, he had been imbued with great energy and ambition.

Now all his plans lay in ashes, and he was not sure what to do. Every fibre of his being screamed at him to avenge himself, but he had no idea how to go about it. Should he slip back to reignite the trouble between University and town that he had so carefully stoked up? Or go to Avignon, to give the Pope his own version of events?

He winced as he moved the foot that his so-called friend Heltisle had stabbed. He had refused to let Bartholomew examine it again, preferring instead to hire Doctor Rougham. Bartholomew had warned Rougham that slivers of the pen might still be in the wound, but Rougham had scoffed his disagreement. Unfortunately, Bartholomew had been right, because the wound was festering and it hurt like the Devil.

That night, de Wetherset fell into a fever, and when a Fenland fisherman found him two days later, he was gibbering in delirium. The fisherman had heard that the Spital took local lunatics in for free, so he carried him there on his boat. Tangmer and Amphelisa accepted the new arrival politely, and rewarded the good Samaritan with a bowl of stew and a penny. The fisherman went away, happy in the belief that he had done the right thing.

'Well?' asked Tangmer, staring down at the writhing,

gabbling ex-Chancellor. 'Here lies the author of all our troubles. Should we help him or let him die?'

'We should help him,' said Amphelisa. 'But he will never fully recover from the madness that afflicts him now, so we shall instal him in our most secure cell. Later, when his fever abates, he will doubtless claim that he is sane, but all lunatics do that, do they not?'

Tangmer blinked. 'You mean we should keep him here for ever? Locked up like a dangerous madman?'

'He *is* a dangerous madman. Why else would he have killed Wyse, Orwel and Abbess Isabel, or stirred up hatred between his University and the town – hatred that almost saw us destroyed? This is the best place for him, husband, and we shall keep everyone safe from his wicked machinations for as long as he breathes.'

'Well, then,' said Tangmer softly. 'Let us hope he lives for a very long time.'

HISTORIC NOTE

The Hundred Years War was an uncertain time for England and France. The Battle of Poitiers in 1356 had dealt the French a serious blow – their king was captured and carried back to England as a prisoner – but the resulting peace was uneasy. To show England that France was not yet ready to concede defeat, part of the Dauphin's army staged lightning raids on the English coast. Two of these targeted Winchelsea, which was much easier to reach from the sea in the fourteenth century, although it is inland now.

The first attack was in 1359, while townsfolk were at their Sunday devotions. The church door was locked and the building set alight, an act of savagery that became known as the St Giles' Massacre. The second incursion came a year later, when some two thousand men, according to some sources, slaughtered the port's inhabitants, and looted and burned its buildings. Robert Arnold was Mayor of Winchelsea at about this time, and Valentine Dover was a burgess.

This second raid sent alarm rippling through England. There was an immediate call to arms, where every male aged between sixteen and sixty was ordered to prepare himself for war. Meanwhile, the regular English army marched south to Paris, leaving a trail of death and destruction in its wake. This campaign ended with the Treaty of Brétigny in July 1360, although that was by no means the end of hostilities, which rumbled on for the rest of that century and half of the next one.

The war with England was not France's only problem. In 1358, there was a popular uprising known as the

Jacquerie. It was disorganised and chaotic, and fell to pieces when its leader was captured and executed. After his death, the aristocracy embarked on a programme of vicious reprisals that displaced a huge number of people, many of them hapless innocents. Some doubtless did try to find safety across the Channel.

Thomas de Lisle, Bishop of Ely, was in self-imposed exile at the time. He had been accused of several criminal acts, including murder, kidnapping, theft and extortion, and rather than risk conviction in a court of law, he had legged it to Avignon, where he threw himself on the Pope's mercy. There was a Katherine de Lisle who became Prioress of Lyminster some time before 1370, but her relationship with the Bishop is uncertain. Her predecessor was Joan de Ferraris, who last appears in the records in April 1360.

The Bishop's incumbency was marked by a number of unsavoury disputes. One was with Alice Lacy, Prioress of Ickleton, and followed a visitation by Isabel of Swaffham Bulbeck (Isabel was actually a Prioress, but I promoted her to Abbess to avoid too many nuns holding the same title; similarly, Katherine de Lisle was never *Magistra*).

Isabel discovered 'various enormous defects' and evidence of loose morals at Ickleton, and her report to the Bishop saw Alice immediately deposed. However, Alice did not go quietly. She returned to her priory in a terrible rage, breaking down its doors and helping herself to its treasure. When the Bishop's agents tried to stop her, she threatened to cut off their heads. She was eventually excommunicated.

There was no *conloquium* of nuns in Cambridge in 1360, although there was a Benedictine convent called St Radegund's on the road known then as the Barnwell Causeway. Remnants of the foundation can still be seen in Jesus College today.

Other people in *The Sanctuary Murders* were also real.

Richard de Wetherset did return for a third term as Chancellor in 1360. He was succeeded by Michael de Aynton (or Haynton). The Master of Bene't College was Thomas Heltisle, and other scholars in the University at this time included Baldwin de Paris, Jean de Bruges, Walter Foxlee, John Smith and William of Koln (Cologne). William Shropham was Warden of King's Hall, and William Pechem was Prior of the Franciscan convent.

By 1360, Ralph de Langelee had stopped being Master of Michaelhouse. Evidence is sketchy, but it seems Michael (de Causton) took his place. Other Michaelhouse Fellows in the mid-fourteenth century included William (de Gotham), John Clippesby and Thomas Suttone. There was also a William Theophilis, who had arrived by 1369, when he also became a proctor. John Aungel, Thomas Mallett and John Islaye were later members of the College.

There were three hospitals in the Cambridge vicinity. One was the Hospital of St John the Evangelist, which later became St John's College. Another was the Hospital of St Mary Magdalene of Stourbridge, the chapel of which still stands today. And the third was the Hospital of St Anthony and St Eloy, or Eligius, which stood on the corner of Trumpington Road and what is now Lensfield Road. It was founded in 1361 by Henry Tangmer (who had a kinswoman named Amphelisa), and although it was technically a 'lazar house', leprosy was in decline by the fourteenth century, so the likelihood is that it was for people with a variety of skin conditions, or perhaps even those with mental health problems. Regardless, its relatively isolated position suggests that the residents were kept apart from the general populace. It was often referred to as the Spetylehouse or Spital. It later became an almshouse, and was only demolished in 1837.

THE BARTHOLOMEW SERIES

 SUSANNA GREGORY — A PLAGUE ON BOTH YOUR HOUSES

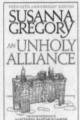 SUSANNA GREGORY — AN UNHOLY ALLIANCE

 SUSANNA GREGORY — A BONE OF CONTENTION

 SUSANNA GREGORY — A DEADLY BREW

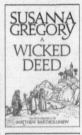 SUSANNA GREGORY — A WICKED DEED

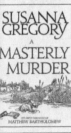 SUSANNA GREGORY — A MASTERLY MURDER

 SUSANNA GREGORY — AN ORDER FOR DEATH

 SUSANNA GREGORY — A SUMMER OF DISCONTENT

 SUSANNA GREGORY — A KILLER IN WINTER

 SUSANNA GREGORY — THE HAND OF JUSTICE

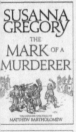 SUSANNA GREGORY — THE MARK OF A MURDERER

 SUSANNA GREGORY — THE TARNISHED CHALICE

 SUSANNA GREGORY — TO KILL OR CURE

 SUSANNA GREGORY — THE DEVIL'S DISCIPLES

 SUSANNA GREGORY — A VEIN OF DECEIT

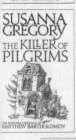 SUSANNA GREGORY — THE KILLER OF PILGRIMS

 SUSANNA GREGORY — MYSTERY IN THE MINSTER

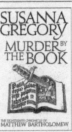 SUSANNA GREGORY — MURDER BY THE BOOK

 SUSANNA GREGORY — THE LOST ABBOT

 SUSANNA GREGORY — DEATH OF A SCHOLAR

 SUSANNA GREGORY — A POISONOUS PLOT

 SUSANNA GREGORY — A GRAVE CONCERN

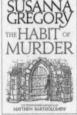 SUSANNA GREGORY — THE HABIT OF MURDER

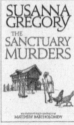 SUSANNA GREGORY — THE SANCTUARY MURDERS

The Chaloner Series

A. THOMAS CHALONER MYSTERY

SUSANNA GREGORY

Deception & Deceit in Restoration London

A Conspiracy
of Violence

A THOMAS CHALONER MYSTERY

SUSANNA GREGORY

Chaloner's Second Exploit in Restoration London

Blood on
the Strand

SUSANNA
GREGORY

The Butcher
of Smithfield

*A Thomas Chaloner Adventure
in Restoration London*

SUSANNA
GREGORY

The
Westminster
Poisoner

A Thomas Chaloner Adventure

SUSANNA
GREGORY

A Murder on
London Bridge

A Thomas Chaloner Adventure

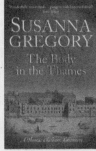

SUSANNA
GREGORY

The Body
in the Thames

A Thomas Chaloner Adventure

SUSANNA
GREGORY

The
Piccadilly Plot

A Thomas Chaloner Adventure

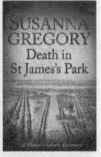

SUSANNA
GREGORY

Death in
St James's Park

A Thomas Chaloner Adventure

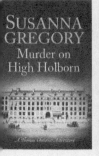

SUSANNA
GREGORY

Murder on
High Holborn

A Thomas Chaloner Adventure

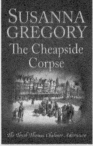

SUSANNA
GREGORY

The Cheapside
Corpse

The Tenth Thomas Chaloner Adventure

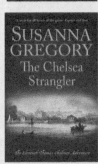

SUSANNA
GREGORY

The Chelsea
Strangler

The Eleventh Thomas Chaloner Adventure

SUSANNA
GREGORY

The Executioner
of St Paul's

The Twelfth Thomas Chaloner Adventure

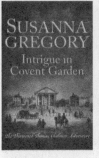

SUSANNA
GREGORY

Intrigue in
Covent Garden

The Thirteenth Thomas Chaloner Adventure

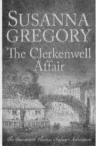

SUSANNA
GREGORY

The Clerkenwell
Affair

The Fourteenth Thomas Chaloner Adventure

A THOMAS CHALONER MYSTERY

SUSANNA GREGORY

Decadence & Deceit in Restoration London

A Conspiracy
of Violence

The dour days of Cromwell are over.

Charles II is well established at White Hall Palace, his mistress at hand in rooms over the Holbein bridge, the heads of some of the regicides on public display. London seethes with new energy, freed from the strictures of the Protectorate, but many of its inhabitants have lost their livelihoods. One is Thomas Chaloner, a reluctant spy for the feared Secretary of State, John Thurloe, and now returned from Holland in desperate need of employment.

His erstwhile boss, knowing he has many enemies at court, recommends Thomas to Lord Clarendon, but in return demands that Thomas keep him informed of any plot against him. But what Thomas discovers is that Thurloe had sent another ex-employee to White Hall and he is dead, supposedly murdered by footpads near the Thames.

Chaloner volunteers to investigate his killing: instead he is dispatched to the Tower to unearth the gold buried by the last Governor. He discovers not treasure, but evidence that greed and self-interest are uppermost in men's minds whoever is in power, and that his life has no value to either side.

*

'Pungent with historical detail' *Irish Times*

This book is for Siobhán and Alexand[...] [...]f Ireland at the same age—though with [...] [...]em in the hope they will long continue to love and re-visit a part of the world which is also a part of me.

Acknowledgements

Many more people than may realize it helped in the writing of this book: casual acquaintances met in hotels and pubs whose enthusiasm when they found I was working on the west of Ireland was instantly shared by way of anecdote or minor correction to prevent me putting my foot too deep into it! I was at times quite overwhelmed as people went out of their way to answer questions and give directions. In particular, the guides at the west's historic sites I visited consistently demonstrated a standard and courtesy of which they should be really proud. To give one small example: Phonsie O'Brien, the caretaker at Lough Gur, stopped what he was doing at home, drove to the site, opened it specially for us—in mid-January—and spent more than an hour carefully showing us what we wanted. Mrs Ollie Grey at Kylemore Abbey, whose husband Shane runs Scuba Dive West, was extremely helpful answering questions about the abbey and the area and its history, and I lost count of the number of times I phoned Clodagh Coyne on Inishbofin to check something with her or ask a question.

In Limerick, the Irish horseman, Aiden O'Connel, was such an enthusiast for his sport and his county that it changed my whole view of that area and Bryan Murphy, who presides over the Dunraven Arms as a benevolent and gracious dictator, was kindness itself. I could list dozens of names, but most would think their help was just a normal part of their daily lives—it is the way of people all over Ireland, particularly in the west. I must declare one family interest: in Connemara, Joe Rafferty of Roundstone is what we Irish call a 'connection by marriage' of mine, that is to say a cousin! His enthusiasm for this work and his unfailing help at all hours of the day and night went way beyond what any cousin has a right to expect. He read the manuscript and helped with emendations and guidance for which I am very, very grateful. Someone else who read the text was Mairie O'Connell, previously an inspector with the Irish Tourist Board, and her advice and encouragement needless to say thus took on an added importance.

The west of Ireland is at the moment particularly well served with books, pamphlets, videos and the like about the history, social, political and cultural life of the area. I have now many more books on Ireland than I had when starting to write this work! Seamus Caulfield's pamphlet on the Ceide Fields and the small booklet which Foxford Woollen Mills have produced about their foundress Agnes Morrogh-Bernard are two which spring immediately to mind, but there are dozens, maybe hundreds of others of equal value.

I would like to thank Aer Lingus and the Irish Tourist Board in London for their help in getting us there and back and around the west of Ireland. Editor Polly Phillimore was extremely patient and painstaking, for which I extend her many, many thanks. And to Alexander, now aged seven, thanks too for his (almost!) unflagging good humour and enthusiasm for funny-shaped rocks, prehistoric golf courses, ruined abbeys and of course for giving his crucial imprimatur to so many restaurants.

Finally to Karolyn, my partner and co-author, I cannot really express adequate thanks. When this venture was first mooted and the idea of including restaurants and menus arose, I had no doubt that she would be a great help. Little did I know that she would become co-author in every sense. Her experience and her refusal to accept my hurried assumptions and sometimes rather eccentric approach to writing have, I know, saved me from making mistakes I would have come to regret. It is a rather pathetic understatement to say that without her this book would never have got past page one. I am so grateful to her and appreciative of her work that this acknowledgement is the only section I have done *completely* on my own, and then only in order to say thanks and here's to the next one!

Henry Kelly
in the West of Ireland
with Karolyn Shindler

Cadogan Books plc
Cadogan Books plc
London House, Parkgate Road,
London SW11 4NQ, UK

Distributed in the USA by
The Globe Pequot Press
6 Business Park Road, PO Box 833,
Old Saybrook,
Connecticut 06475–0833

Published in the Republic of Ireland by
WOLFHOUND PRESS Ltd
68 Mountjoy Square, Dublin 1

Cover illustration by Marcus Patton
Cover and book design by Animage
Maps © Cadogan Guides, drawn by Map Creation Ltd

Series Editors: Rachel Fielding and Vicki Ingle
Editing: Polly Phillimore and Dominique Shead
Proofreading: Fiona Clarkson Webb
Production: Rupert Wheeler Book Production Services

ISBN 0–1–86011–080–0 (UK/US)
ISBN 0-86327-533-8 (Ireland)

A catalogue record for this book is available from the British Library
Printed and bound in the UK by Redwood Books Ltd, .

The authors and publishers have made every effort to ensure the accuracy of the information in the book at the time of going to press. However, they cannot accept any responsibility for any loss, injury or inconvenience resulting from the use of information contained in this guide.

Introduction

To be honest, there is no such place as the 'west of Ireland'. For some it is an evocation, for others an idea, a dream, a vision of extraordinary scenery and absolute tranquility. It is all those things for me—and more. While your spirit is inspired by nature, and your mind by some of the most astonishing archaeological sites in Europe, your more basic senses can indulge in some of the best food, drink and good companionship that you will encounter anywhere.

When I was asked to write this book, it was left to me to come up with my own definition of the west of Ireland. There is what I believe to be a natural sweep which begins in the Shannon area—essential because that is where there is a first-class and very useful airport—continues on to take you through Limerick, a county of which I knew little and have now come to adore, then through Clare with its unique and extraordinary landscape, Galway and its heart-land of Connemara, Mayo with its terrible history of famine and its stunning beauty as varied as a patch-work quilt of colour and light and shade, and finally Sligo, where the poet William Butler Yeats was more inspired than anywhere else in his worldwide travels and where you may actually dip your toes, should you be so inclined, in the very waters that inspired his poetry.

I suppose it is not unusual for different areas of any country in the world to have distinctive and varying features, yet the contrasts in the west of Ireland are quite startling. Limerick is gentle and green, with a glorious prehistoric site that was a focus of mystery and legend long before the Stone Age remains there were discovered. It is also a mecca for golfers and huntsmen and is generally accepted as the home of the limerick—the nonsense poems made famous by Edward Lear and others. How they started is open to debate, but it may well have been as humourous drinking songs with verses of five lines written by a group of poets, who were known as the Maigue poets after the river that flows through the county.

When you drive north into Clare and enter the Burren, you will imagine you are, like John Keats when he wrote 'On First Looking Into Champan's Homer', 'silent upon a peak in Darien'. For the Burren is a remarkable natural phenomenon—mile upon mile of limestone pavements, down to the shore and embracing the hills, with flowers and plants flourishing in every cranny. Under the Burren is a network of caves; on top are remains of homesteads and graves of prehistoric man. It is literally breathtaking and I envy those about to see the Burren above and below ground for the first time.

Out of Clare and on to county Galway and Connemara in the far west and the landscape changes yet again: this time to a combination of bog and rock, through which narrow but serviceable roads will take you to the very edge of the west's most famous mountains, The Twelve Bens: a series of mountains which follow each other into the middle distance, now covered in a typical Irish mist and now sparkling clear in bright sunshine. Here too, as so often in the west of Ireland, are sweeping beaches which are pretty empty even in high summer. The sea is clear, and swimming and fishing are among the finest in the country. From the village of Cleggan in Connemara you may travel by a short ferry route to the island of Inishbofin. History has poured itself over every inch of this place, leaving its historic sites and ruined castles for our exploration. Not to be outdone, nature has provided a setting of exquisite beauty. A day is never enough on Bofin.

Through north Connemara you head for county Mayo to which the Irish themselves may often add 'God Help Us', for nowhere suffered more through Irish history and particularly through the terrible 19th-century potato famines than this huge county. Now it is a wonderful, thriving, exciting place, a tribute to its people. Yet between the years 1845 and the turn of the century, thousands of them died or suffered the pain of enforced emigration to north America in great poverty because of the famine. Mayo's loss was not over then and the 20th century only gave it more hardship, more unemployment, more emigration. Whole towns literally closed and the late great Irish journalist and writer, my dear friend John Healy, when he wrote passionately about his own home town Charlestown, which for years lay boarded up and almost totally empty, called his book simply: *No-One Shouted Stop—The Death of an Irish Town*. Today it is a different Mayo that presents itself to the tourist: it is sophisticated and well-organized, with some of the finest salmon fishing and game shooting in Ireland, stunning scenery and a huge cliff-top Stone Age site which was preserved for 5000 years under blanket bog.

Sligo, where the Nobel prize-winning poet W.B.Yeats found so much inspiration, is so small you feel at times it is a pocket county compared to Mayo! And in a way it is: its charms are compact, easily reached but no less readily enjoyed. Sligo will give you beauty and history, outdoor sports and indoor relaxation in about equal measure. It will let you walk the strand at Rosses Point or wander through the prehistoric cemetry at Carrowmore, or delight in one of the finest views in Ireland from the top of Carrowkeel with its cluster of Stone Age passage-graves. It will also nudge you towards quieter walks and contemplations along lakes where gentle waters lapping in the light of the setting sun across pebbled beaches will make any man or woman with a soul feel they too might be a poet.

A holiday for me is about relaxation, recreation and rejuvenation. I have never been one for lying by a swimming pool; my enjoyment comes from a gentle exploration of places and people—present and past.

And this is a place for great and unexpected conversations. The thirst for education in rural Ireland stretches back into history and has never diminished. These traditions are from hedge schools where children learned reading, writing and their tables in secret because of oppressive anti-catholic laws. This is a people whose forefathers were, as my father liked to tease his British friends, 'speaking Latin and Greek and writing poetry and translating the gospels while the English were still covering themselves in woad!' It is probably the thirst for knowledge and the eagerness to learn which to this day gives the Irish the interest in, and sometime gift for, communication at every social level. I have discussed the current political situation in Ireland, Britain and south-east Asia far into the night in tiny pubs in Galway with men who may have left school at 14 years of age to help on the farm but whose self-education has never stopped. The next night we have talked of cricket, classical music and whether or not priests should be allowed to marry. These were not merely pub chats where prejudice masquerades as opinion: should you be so inclined, you will have your intellect stretched, teased and amused more often in a day in the west of Ireland than at a dozen seminars! On a more serious note, for all the seats of learning and universities that stretch the length and breath of Ireland I must add another: it is the unofficial one formed by mothers, fathers, grandmothers, grandfathers and relatives who, whether coming from small holdings or decent-sized houses, declared that they would educate their children and their children's children so that past mistakes would not be repeated and famine and injustice and abject poverty, the three horrors of the 19th century, should not be visited upon them again.

Communication gifts and awareness are not of course unique to the Irish but they do seem to be the stock-in-trade of most westerners you meet. Coupled with a gentle philosophy and a tremendous sense of fun, they make for a warm, witty and welcoming people.

Give yourself time and relax in the west of Ireland. You will not be disappointed. We have tried to point you in the right directions but remember they are personal choices. These are our 20 days. You don't have to cover them in 20 days and indeed you should take them in your own time. Nor have we covered everything: how could we in such a huge area? We have suggested restaurants that we have enjoyed, and we recommend them with enthusiasm. We have added a recipe from each place so that in the dark days of winter at home you may make something yourself and remember John Roche's Rock Glen Hotel, or what you had in Rory Daly's at Leenane and, oh! wasn't that lunch in Monk's in Ballyvaughan great, and tomorrow night maybe we will pretend we are at the Dunraven Arms in Adare and use their recipe! All the suggestions are ours, all the choices are yours.

For the traveller, the West of Ireland is a great natural playground where history and beauty mingle as easily as oysters go with Guinness. There are few if any motorways: roads vary but they are not designed for those in a hurry. The infrastructure indeed seems almost to have the perfect balance: it does not get in the way of commerce and it lets the tourist have a good time.

Our maps and 'guiding' are meant as references. Take your own maps, remember that nearly all the places you visit have little pamphlets or booklets which may add to your knowledge and that local people all over the west of Ireland are not just prepared to help but are positively enthusiastic. Your big problem may be getting away from someone on the road to whom you have simply addressed a basic question!

I was born in Dublin and my family moved almost immediately to Athlone in the heart of rural Ireland. It was a loving, quiet childhood but hardly spoiling. Food was rationed in the aftermath of the Second World War, treats were few, pleasures simple but wonderful: country walks, rabbit-chasing, fishing, boating on the Shannon, watching my relations duck-shooting and pheasant-shooting. Growing our own vegetables, being amazed at the arrival of the first double-decker bus I had ever seen, walking to school—even at the age of five—gathering fresh field mushrooms one morning, and the next going to collect fuel from the cut turf on the side of the Bog of Allen which sweeps through the Midlands of Ireland. Looking for the names of my father and mother in the *Westmeath Independent* if they had attended the annual dinner dance of the Irish Army Western Command or a golf club bash or hunt ball. The stuff of rural communities everywhere the world over. All this has remained but now, having lived outside Ireland for more than 20 years and having often been infuriated to the point of public anger by certain attitudes, I have to say that in the last 10 years Ireland has taken itself by the scruff of the neck and decided that old attitudes such as what my English teacher used to call the 'twill do attitude'—'it's not right but 'twill do'—have all but disappeared.

This I am sure has a variety of explanations: emigrants returning for holidays from around the world have seen nothing attractive in grubby hotels or restaurants, poor service and indifferent food. The message has got through and the Irish tourist authorities have worked all over the country to encourage and improve standards. And this applies at all levels. Now you are almost spoilt for choice from excellent bed and breakfast places, hotels, restaurants and pubs. Archaeological and historical sites too are now largely well looked after, not in a gimmicky way, but one that lets you understand their significance. And surrounding it all, of course, is a landscape whose beauty is, to my mind, unparalleled. Enjoy these 20 days in the west of Ireland. I did and always have and, if you will excuse me, I am about to do so again!

Henry Kelly
Karolyn Shindler
January 1996

History

I sometimes feel that the west of Ireland is one enormous prehistoric site, for in every county, Neolithic—and later—remains are being discovered, and you begin to wonder whether every curiously shaped rock, or pattern of stones on the ground is perhaps of man's design, rather than nature's. Although there is evidence that many of the Stone Age people who lived here 5000 years ago led peaceful lives, the same—as you have probably noticed—cannot be said for Ireland's later history. About the only people not to invade Ireland were the Romans!

An old history teacher of mine once said that you ought to be able to sum up the 'whole business of Irish history in a few paragraphs—or else you will find you need a few million.' He has a point. The history of Ireland is the history of England, of France, of Spain, of North America and even further afield. Emigrants and exiled prisoners helped to found Australia, rebels fled justice or the lack of it to Canada and the United States. The Irish diaspora reached its height in the middle to late years of the 19th century after the terrible Famines and continued for political and economic reasons with ebbs and flows until the mid-1950s. It has meant that today you could not possibly, for certain, establish accurate numbers of native-born Irish people (not to mention second and third generation Irish) living outside their tiny island.

As you travel through the west of Ireland, the very fields, the stone remains of our ancestors, the crumbling castles and ruined houses, even the landscape itself, bears testimony to the nation's history. In all the counties you visit, you can trace the past from the Stone Age, through the turbulent Celtic era with its legacy of internecine wars and its wonderful legends, to the arrival of Christianity which officially came with St. Patrick in AD 432. In the following 300 years, Ireland became renowned as the 'island of saints and scholars'. For a short space there was peace and tranquility and the island came as close as it ever would to being the ideal of a land flowing with milk and honey and wisdom.

It ended about AD 800, when the Vikings invaded with their customary violence, and the powerful families along this west coast—as elsewhere in Ireland—could conceive of no other way of life than fighting each other. In 1169, the first Normans invaded Ireland—at the invitation of the deposed King of Leinster, Dermot MacMurragh, who had fled to England to ask for help. Dermot got his throne back and the following year his daughter Aoife married the most powerful of the Norman invaders, Richard Fitzgilbert de Clare, otherwise known as Strongbow. The ceremony, in Christ Church Cathedral in Dublin, was splendid and it seemed that peace was at hand. In 1175, the Norman triumph appeared complete when Henry II of England also became King of Ireland. Today you can still wander around the very stones upon which Strongbow and Aoife knelt to pledge their vows in Christ Church, though the passage of ecclesiastical time and religious changes have seen to it that the cathedral is now Protestant.

Anglo-Irish feuding and treachery however were never long out of the picture, with each side blaming the other for any breaches of treaties, betrayals and dishonesties. It is really best not to get involved! It is safe enough to know that all these centuries will unfold before your eyes as you go from Limerick in the southwest to Sligo in the north-west. There is not a corner untouched by the passage of history and few corners where that history is not visible and preserved for the modern tourist. The Reformation and the suppression of the monasteries in 1536 by Henry VIII did nothing for Anglo-Irish relations, and when Spain and other enemies of England began to think of Ireland as a useful backdoor into England—particularly the west coast—Elizabeth 1, Henry's daughter, tried to bring Ireland under her control but succeeded only in enflaming passions for an Irish Ireland. The west coast became notorious for its strongholds of insurrection against the English, the warring families such as the O'Malleys using the Spanish or French for their ends as much as they in turn were being used! This cycle of insurrection, invasion, massacre, insurrection continued under Oliver Cromwell in the 17th century. And so it went on, through the victory of the Protestant William of Orange at the Battle of the Boyne, the siege and defeat of the Catholic army at Limerick and the introduction of draconian laws against practising Catholics.

The last foreign invasion was by the French in 1798 at Killala Bay in County Mayo. This failed rapidly when promised support by Irish rebel leaders failed to materialize.

By 1800, sufficient forces had combined in Ireland and England, and enough blood and sweat and tears had flowed under enough bridges, for an Act of Union to be passed, which came into effect in 1801. It meant that Ireland was now part of Great Britain though it did not put an end to nationalism and the idea that the Irish either could or should be allowed to govern themselves. Native Irish politicians sat in the British Parliament at Westminster, where they often exercised strong influence on British policy, particularly towards Ireland. The Penal Laws which in previous years had effectively reduced Catholics to non-persons were abolished and the Catholic Emancipation Act of 1829 meant Catholics could now sit as members of Parliament. Moves for Home Rule with a Dublin Parliament began and, as so often, God or fate, depending on your point of view, took a hand.

The potato famines from 1845 highlighted the enormous economic problems of Ireland. Not all landlords and their agents in Ireland were the monsters they have been portrayed as by any means, but many undoubtedly were. The everyday poverty of so much of the population was intense and it was made worse by landlords in other parts of Ireland removing unwanted tenants and dumping them in the west. Even in these coastal counties, with seas and rivers full of fish, the potato was the staple food, providing essential nutrients. Some attempts were made to try to persuade people to grow other foods, particularly after the loss of potato crops earlier in the century, but most were reluctant to. The potato was what they were used to; it would grow in the thinnest soil and needed little care, and if you were a labourer working for a farmer, there was little time to tend your own crops. There was also the fear that if any improvement was made to even the meanest patch of land it could lead to an increase in rent, and if that could not be met eviction would follow. The consequences therefore in succeeding years of the loss of the potato crop were devastating, and the population of Ireland, through starvation, disease and emigration, fell from the eight million recorded in the census of 1841 before the famine to about six million in 1851. In these five western counties, one in four of the people died. The government may have been slow to react, but as you travel through the west of Ireland, you will find in every county stories of those who worked to help the poor, in some cases bankrupting themselves.

By the end of the 19th century, politics, part nationalist, part desperation hardened by the fury of what had happened in the preceeding 50 years, again took an ugly turn, culminating in the ill-starred Easter Rising of 1916. This rebellion against English rule in Ireland was to turn the population from bemused onlookers of something they hardly understood into saddened and angered retrospective supporters of nationalism. The English executed the leaders of an uprising which initially had little support, was not officially sanctioned even by all its leaders, and lasted less than a week.

At the time of writing, Irish history has taken another turn—and as usual its outcome is unpredictable. The reasons for the emergence in the 1960s of a civil rights movement in Northern Ireland, the six counties traditionally claimed as theirs by the Republic but constituted in fact as a separate state within the United Kingdom following the Government of Ireland Act in the early 1920s, are too varied and complex to be debated here. Enough to say that by 1968 the Northern Ireland state was crumbling at the edges and massive street protests were to lead to more than a quarter of a century of serious unrest. Again as so often before in Irish history, when good, decent men and women on both sides tried to calm situations their voices were drowned by forces which, initially finding their roots in non-violent protest, in turn found themselves brushed aside by more extreme activists. The slumbering remnants of Irish ultra-Republicanism, almost dormant since the ill-starred 1916 uprising, seized what they thought was a golden opportunity to 'right Ireland's wrong' for once and for all. What followed was 25 years and more of bloody civil disturbance, urban guerilla warfare and all that it involves by way of random acts of violence, which even by late 20th-century standards fair took one's breath away. The Provisional IRA held sway for most if not all of this quarter-century, in many cases dictating matters to the politicians by the ferocious nature of their activities, claiming as they did to represent a combination of Catholic oppression and pan-nationalist ambition. On the other side of Ulster's sectarian divide, extreme Protestant paramilitary organizations found no contradiction at all in carrying on their war against the IRA while ignoring London's pleas to keep out of the equation and let the security forces deal with terrorism. A ceasefire agreed by all sides, initiated by John Hume, Northern Ireland's leading Catholic politician, and brokered at a distance by Dublin and Washington lasted—and is still going—for longer than many would have believed, and what has come to be known as the 'peace process' was given its ultimate boost with the visit to Belfast, London and Dublin in late 1995 by President Bill Clinton, whose behind-the-scenes persuasion and remarkable public utterances which softened even the hardest of hearts and touched even the most cynical of souls, suddenly seems to have presented Anglo-Irish relations with its best opportunity for decades—some would say centuries—to solve an age-old problem: the problem of peoples occupying one small island, claiming as at one and the same time, 'old enemy, old friend'.

As you travel through the west, should you wish to discuss this or any other aspect of Irish history some evening in a pub, there will be no shortage of willing participants! And the best indication you will get of the impossibility of arriving at 'conclusions' about Irish history is that if, say, you have half a dozen conversationalists in your group trawling through Irish history, then be absolutely certain you will also have half a dozen different opinions! Perhaps that is the healthiest thing one could say about the state of any nation.

Limerick
Adare

If I had to pick a spot in the county where I would be happy to say the heart and soul of Limerick beats, the beautiful village of Adare would get the vote. Here are no rolling hills and few rushing waters, but the quiet solitude of the Irish countryside broken only seasonally by the shouts of huntsmen and the baying of fox hounds. It is a village which begs you to relax and take it and yourself easy, to meander, to wander in what with good reason has been called the prettiest village in Ireland. You will find perfectly preserved and working churches which date back centuries, crumbling ruins which yet merit a visit, the gentle river Maigue slipping through swaying woods and, for good measure, two of the finest hotels in the west of Ireland and a restaurant that would stand comparison with any in Europe.

Getting there

Adare is about 10 miles south west of Limerick city on the N20, and driving into it you would be forgiven for thinking you were driving into a little village in the English countryside. The roofs are thatched, roses grow round many a door and the main street is surprisingly wide. It is a neat, clean, tidy place—what else for a winner of the Irish Tourist Board's 'Tidy Towns' competition!

Adare's Irish name is Ath Dara, 'ford of the oaks', as the settlement grew in this beautiful wooded place where the river Maigue could be forded. It is thought the village was founded in the 11th century AD, and the thatched cottages,

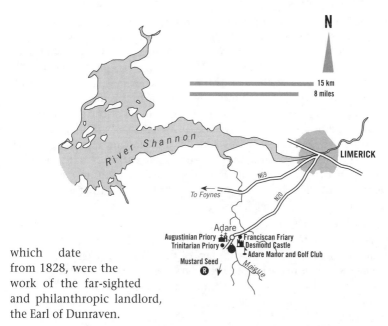

which date
from 1828, were the
work of the far-sighted
and philanthropic landlord,
the Earl of Dunraven.

For its size, Adare has a disproportionate amount to offer: two priories, both restored from semi-ruined states and operating as places of worship; a friary, which stands in a setting so wonderfully bizarre it really does have to be seen to be believed; a fine but crumbling castle; Adare Manor, the former home of the earls of Dunraven, now a hotel; and a washing pool once, doubtless, the hub of village gossip. It was the great botanist and traveller, Robert Lloyd Praeger, who wrote in his now sadly out-of-print work on Ireland, *The Way That I Went* (published in Dublin in 1937) that Adare was an 'architectural museum'. It is certainly that, and a bustling, lively one. There is a fine heritage centre here, half-way down the main street, with an excellent audio-visual guide to the sites you are about to visit and it is well worth your while first spending half an hour here.

The **Trinitarian Priory**, the oldest of the three religious houses in Adare which were all founded by the Earls of Kildare, is just down the road from the heritage centre. It is a great grey-stone building, rather solid-looking with a square, crenellated tower. It was founded in about AD 1230 for the Trinitarian Canons of the Order of the Redemption of Captives, who worked to raise the ransoms necessary to free Christian captives during the Crusades. This was the only house of their order in Ireland and they ran a hospital, treating patients with herbs which they grew in the gardens. In 1539, following Henry VIII's break with Rome, the priory was suppressed and the 45 friars killed. For more than 250 years this huge building stood empty, gradually crumbling away. Then in 1811, part of it, including the tower, was restored by the first Earl of Dunraven who gave it to the people of Adare as their Catholic church, which it is to this day. It was further restored and enlarged in 1852. One feature in the priory gardens which you should not miss is the dovecote. It is a circular building, with walls nearly three feet thick. It was actually used to house pigeons, which formed a large part of the monks' diet. There is, incidentally, an early theory that this was a pagan vestal fire house, though no records exist referring to young Adare ladies in long white robes pouring water out for their lordships from stone jars!

Across the road from the Trinitarian Priory is the **Washing Pool** and watering place for horses, which was restored about 20 years ago. It is a shallow pool fed by a little tributary of the Maigue, the Drehideen. The stone walls on either side have been repaired, as has the floor of the pool. The women of Adare would wash their clothes on washing stones, placed in the pool, no doubt exchanging gossip as they washed their dirty linen in public.

The **Augustinian Priory**, originally known as the Black Abbey, is just a few minutes' walk away, down by the bridge over the Maigue. On your way you pass the Dunraven Arms—hotel, pub and restaurant combined and well worth a detour. The priory was founded in 1315 but little is known about it until after the suppression of the monasteries. It too is built of grey-stone, but is a more beautiful building than the Trinitarian Priory. Through the idiosyncratic nature of Anglo-Irish history, the Augustinian Priory is now a Church of Ireland place of worship. It has some rather fine stone carvings, dating from the 14th century, of foliage, animals and human heads and cloisters which are some 30 feet square.

From the Augustinian Priory it is only a few yards to the **bridge** which, in spite of being built in 1390, still carries the main Limerick road. Very narrow, 'V'-shaped recesses were built into it to protect pedestrians from passing carts and horses. This feature is so unusual that when the bridge was widened in the 19th century the builders were instructed by the Earl of Dunraven to preserve the recesses. From here there is a fine view of the 13th-century Desmond Castle, originally built by the Earls of Kildare, looming above the river Maigue. Now it is ivy-covered and in a state so precarious that this is about as close as you can get.

My favourite site of all those on offer in Adare is the **Franciscan Friary**. Not only is it a wistfully beautiful ruin, but it stands, almost surreally, between the 14th and 15th greens of Adare Manor Golf Club. I should like to think the golf club had a neat sense of history by clasping the abbey to its bosom with holes that match the centuries in which the religious houses flourished, but that would be far-fetched even for me.

There is a public right of way to it from the main road even though it is through a privately owned golf course. Do, of course, watch your step if there are golfers on the course. If you plan to have tea or you are staying at the Adare Manor Hotel, there is a lovely walk along the Maigue from the hotel to the Friary. The last time I was there I walked towards it in a burst of bright sunshine when it fairly gleamed and glinted a mellow gold. Within seconds, as a rain cloud came over to block the light, the ruins took on an eerie, haunted appearance.

It is the youngest of the three religious houses, founded in 1464. In 1646 it was sacked and burned by Cromwellian soldiers, that terrible time indelibly marked in the blackened stones around the upper windows. Although roofless, there is enough of the Friary still standing for it to rank as an excellent example of a 15th-century Irish monastery, with nave, chapels, cloisters, tower, refectory and outbuildings. The dormitories were in the no longer extant upper storey. It is an elegant, graceful building, with the fine stonework of what is left of the soaring windows testimony to the original workmanship. You can wander through the nave to the remains of two chapels, which still contain tombs. Enough of the cloisters still stand for you easily to imagine them silent except for the soft rustle of parchment as some meditating friar turned a page. About twenty of them lived here at any one time, leading simple lives of prayer and preaching. A mill stood near the Friary, where they ground corn. Inside the ruins, the

Franciscan friary

quietness of the place is broken only by the occasional smack of ball on iron, or a cry of 'Fore!'. A little sign pointing through the Friary indicates to golfers where the next tee is, and when you walk down a small passage at the back of what would have been the high altar and emerge again onto the golf course you are confronted with a white sign which reads: 'Hole Number 15, Par 4: Stroke Index 6. Sponsored by Carlsberg Lager'.

An elderly friar is alleged still to wander dreamily down to the river to catch a salmon from the waters with his bare hands for the Friary supper; I wonder what he would make of this! If you are in any doubt, by the way, as to what he looks like, look no further than the western wall of the Friary where there is carved the small figure of a Franciscan monk.

If you have the time, walk around the grounds of the Adare Manor Hotel on your way out. Dinner tonight is at a restaurant which for a decade was a focal point for serious food-lovers in the village—the Mustard Seed—but use this as an opportunity to get acquainted with the Manor, because you will be back here to eat another night.

Dinner at the Mustard Seed

The Mustard Seed at Echo Lodge, Ballingarry, Co.Limerick
℡ *(069) 68508*

Open daily all year for dinner, except Sundays. Set dinner menu: IR£26–29 inc. tax.

The Mustard Seed is really a must! It is owned and run by Daniel Mullane, who seems to have found just the right formula. For the last decade it has occupied a rather quaint cottage on the main street, just beyond the gates of Adare Manor, but from March 1996 it is moving to a former convent called Echo Lodge about 8 miles away—a mere bagatelle in view of the food they produce. The new Mustard Seed at Echo Lodge will overlook the village of Ballingarry and have 12 bedrooms, so you need stagger no further than upstairs when you have finished feasting. Echo Lodge was built in 1884 as a family house and it still has the original shutters and polished floorboards. Warmth and a rather cosy comfort was the hallmark of the Mustard Seed in Adare; Dan Mullane says the new place will be just as cosy, but more stylish and on a larger scale, with three open fires and as full of eclectic memorabilia as the original restaurant. The dining room will be two interconnecting rooms hung with gilt-framed mirrors. Where it matters (in the kitchen, of course!), there will be no change at all, as all the staff are moving to the Mustard Seed at Echo Lodge, taking with them their skills at producing food which is a sybaritic blend of the best local produce with modern, imaginative and beautifully presented dishes.

Dinner at the old Mustard Seed was hugely enjoyable. Over champagne and canapés of creamy smoked salmon paté in the little bar downstairs, with its fire and Victorian memorabilia, you read through the menu and decide you would like it all! The four-course dinner menu has a choice of six starters, followed by either a soup, sorbet or salad. There are also six main courses to agonize over, including a vegetarian dish. You will undoubtedly be seduced by the rich, dark, wonderful Irish bread and beautiful creamy butter, but restrain yourself.

For a starter you can choose from baked goat's cheese with a herb crust on a nest of leaves with balsamic vinegar and olive oil, or perhaps a roll of smoked Irish salmon and trout *rillette* with a sharp *beurre blanc* and new potato salad. If it is on the menu, try the money bag of prawns: big, fresh, seriously garlicky prawns in a bag of filo pastry tied together with the finest threads of caramelized onion, and served on a bed of frisée and radicchio. Follow that with a carrot and ginger soup, a rhubarb and citrus sorbet or a light salad with a wonderful honey and lemon dressing. For a main course, choose between panfried Irish beef with oyster mushrooms and a green salsa, or a leek and cheese soufflé on couscous and cannelini beans with a spring onion cream sauce. If you are a fish fanatic, there is beautiful, meaty John Dory in a wonderful, rich but well-balanced langoustine sauce, simple black sole, perfectly cooked, and, of course, wild Irish salmon.

The vegetables are equally good. The colcannon—a mixture of cabbage and potatoes flavoured with herbs—was simply the best I have ever had. Carrots were sweet and still nicely crisp while the spinach had that 'just picked' flavour.

The puddings are so good that you could, perhaps, skip what comes before and just indulge in those—but then think what you would have missed! I compromised and had three puds on one plate: light and creamy bread and butter pudding with a satisfyingly crispy brown top, the most amazing brandy snap ice cream in a little basket of brandy snaps, and a chocolate mousse with a little tiny cap made of the lightest pastry on top, dusted with icing sugar and sitting in a little tiny pool of dark chocolate. It looked and tasted absolutely fantastic and I am afraid I have to tell you I ate all of it.

Rich dark and white chocolate truffles come with the coffee, though you will not be surprised to learn we could not do justice to those.

The food was great, the service good and the prospect of a small child dining in the evening phased them not one jot—in fact he was warmly welcomed and every dish was made child-friendly!

Honey and Lemon Salad Dressing
from the Mustard Seed

Ingredients:

Juice of 2½ lemons

8oz/225g clear honey

Sunflower oil

Water

Salt and pepper to taste

Method:

Put the lemon juice and honey into a bowl and whisk them together slowly. Then add the oil, a little at a time until you achieve the thickness and taste required. If you find it is too thick, thin it down with a little cold water. Adjust the seasoning to taste. This goes beautifully with most salad leaves, and particularly the slightly bitter ones, such as frisée and radicchio.

Limerick
Lough Gur

Now why does Lough Gur, which could be described as just another lake in the west of Ireland, and the only lake in Limerick, deserve at least a whole day to itself? Quite simply because it is an archaeological treasure house of enormous richness and beauty, breath-taking and eerie at the same time. Until my first visit I had never, to my shame, heard of it but since that day I cannot wait to go back. Man has lived here for nearly 5000 years and for miles there are wedge-shaped tombs, stone circles, Neolithic house sites, stone forts and even a crannog—a sort of fortified dwelling—in the lake. Like so much else in Ireland, it has layers of over-lapping history and legend.

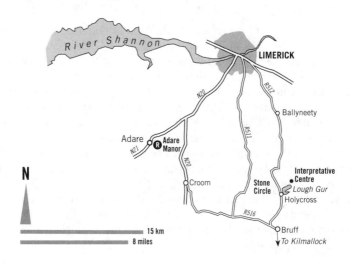

Getting there

On the morning we decided to head for Lough Gur from our base in Adare, the nice young girl in the Heritage Centre told us that we should head back towards Limerick, then when we got to Punch's pub on the left we were to turn right onto the Dublin–Waterford Road and after 'about three roundabouts or so' there would be a turn for Lough Gur! The more conventional directions are to take the N20 from Adare to Limerick and Lough Gur is about 11 miles south of Limerick city, off the R512 road to Kilmallock.

The entrance to **Lough Gur** is guarded by the remains of two castles built by the Earls of Desmond. One of the more vivid legends is that the last of the Earls Desmond is meant to hold court under the waters of Gur and emerge fully armed at daybreak on the morning of every seventh year until the silver shoes of his horse are worn away. Only then will the spell be broken and the earl free to return to earth and regain his estates. The lake itself, to give a nudge to the legend, is clearly shaped like a horseshoe. In the early 19th century attempts were made to drain the lake and convey the water into ground lower than the present bed. Alas! the man in charge of the operation, one Stackpoole Bayley, was killed one night in a fall from his horse as he came home from dinner, an event which the locals to this day attribute to an encounter with the wandering earl who was displeased, to say the least, that anyone should want to alter the waters of his court.

Another eerie legend suggests that for centuries no farmer could cultivate even an acre along the borders of the lake. As soon as the shoots of corn or grass showed green above the earth, they would be eaten overnight by some unseen and unknown animal. A local determined to keep watch one night and swore he saw a fine fat cow followed by seven heifers walk from the water and enter his field. He rushed to close the gate and stop them from escaping back to the Lough, but the old cow was too smart for him and rushed past him to the water before he had the gate fully closed, leaving him the surprised and proud owner of the seven calves. Unfortunately one night he left the gate open and in the morning the whole herd was gone, leaving him with nothing as before. No less an authority than Sir Walter Scott, who had land and a dwelling not far away at Abbotsford, tells of hearing this same legend from locals during his time there and wondering whether maybe the creatures from the deep were not cows, but a herd of hippopotami.

The botanist Lloyd Praeger said that apart from Lough Gur Limerick had little to offer, and while I would not wish to be quite so dismissive of the county since I want to go back again and escape with my life, there is a mesmeric quality about the Lough which is simply unique.

When you get there, park in the car park. As you enter it you will see on the hillside on your right-hand side two linked 'Neolithic' houses, one round, one rectangular, in a perfect state of repair. That is because they are the visitors' centre, or **Stone Age Interpretative Centre**. Start here, as its audio-visual guide is invaluable in helping you interpret the wonders outside. On show are models of life in prehistoric Lough Gur, and a number of artefacts found there—axes, pottery and objects in bronze, bone, stone and flint. The houses themselves are also worth looking at, with their thatched roofs and wattle and daub walls on stone foundations, the main difference from the prehistoric originals being that these are suitably insulated and fire-proofed for 1990s' requirements. The guides will explain their structure and be happy to give you any additional information.

Once outside, there are information sites and plaques which describe in detail and with great insight what lies around you. Armed with this you can walk in the footsteps of the folk who lived here around 3000 BC. The first men and women here cleared the forests and built the stone houses; they planted crops in the fields, and there is clear evidence that they herded cattle, sheep, pigs and as a bonus hunted on the nearby hills. Then came metal, bronze, iron and, as their lives changed, the lough which dominated their lives became sacred. Some say the conversion to Christianity came after the people, having thrown their man-made weapons and iron-work into the lough to appease or flatter their gods, received little in return from the supposed dwellers of the deep and decided to try their luck with the newer religion.

You can actually walk around the lough but it is quite a step and I would

Great Stone Circle of Grange

settle for a good canter to the far right-hand corner, beyond the Interpretative Centre, and a brief skip up one of the little hills. A stunning view of the lake will present itself to you. Pause as you reflect on this beauty and what has been here before you: it is quite a humbling experience. When you have drunk sufficiently of the view, return to the main site: you have the whole day, and there is much to see. Remember, though, that this is a *working* archaeological site and not all the forts, dwelling sites and stone circles are open to the public. Those that are open are clearly marked.

Crannogs, or small defended lake dwellings, are common in the west of Ireland. They are made largely of wood—their name derives from *crann*, the Irish word for a tree. The Bolin Island crannog, which is not too far from the Interpretative Centre, was built by the people who farmed round the lake sometime between AD 500 and 1000. The terrors of the time are easy to imagine, as this little island, some 30 feet or so across, is just big enough to have supported and protected one household from marauders, human and animal.

To the right of the Interpretative Centre on a natural platform is a small undefended early Christian site known as **The Spectacles**, dating from about AD 400–1200. You can stand there and gaze on the foundations of small stone houses and neat, well-laid fields where men, women and children lived and worked 1500 years ago. Artefacts found on the site—iron knives, pins made of bronze, glass beads, a bone comb—suggest a people of simple sophistication who themselves unearthed Neolithic pottery, flint scrapers and other fragments.

If the weather is fine, Lough Gur is one of the most perfect places for a picnic, and depending on how energetic you feel after lunch you can either walk or drive to the sites further round the lough. The first you come to is a huge **wedge-shaped tomb**. The megaliths—the enormous slabs of stone— were originally covered by a mound of smaller stones which time and somewhat unofficial local building requirements have dispersed. Locally it was known as the Giant's Grave. Alas, it was built for no mythological creature: the bones of at least eight adults and four children were found here, together with other bones which clearly had been cremated.

Nearby is the so-called '**New' Church**, or Tempall Nua. Built in the 15th century by the Desmonds so that their lordships did not have to travel to the Parish Church for Mass, it declined with their fortunes and by the 17th century was a ruin. It was rebuilt in 1679 and, because its services were then Protestant, it became the 'New' Church. To get to the church from the road, you wade through long grasses and wild flowers. Walking inside the ruined, roofless walls, the atmosphere changes in the most extraordinary way. It is as if you had walked into a flourishing church with roof and altar. The change is haunting and yet there is nothing here except ivy-covered walls, a few tombs and a wonderful view of trees through the Gothic windows. Above the door is a small icon of the Virgin, still with traces of blue on her robes.

The last essential site to visit round Lough Gur is in many ways the most impressive. Drive from the New Church to Holycross crossroads, turn right and take the Limerick road to the **Great Stone Circle of Grange**. It is the largest and most spectacular stone circle in Ireland, and dates from about 2000 BC. It stands protected from the road, with farmland all around. (Limerick is renowned for its pastures and its cows, and you may feel that 90 per cent of them are here!)

There is a convenient parking area, and do not forget to take your wellies. In autumn, winter or when the weather is wet it will be seriously muddy. Key details about the circle are displayed on an excellent information board just as you enter the main field. Do read them; the more you know about the stone circle, the more extraordinary it becomes. To reach the circle, walk through a gate up a steep man-made embankment of earth, small stones and turf, which is the outer ring of the stone circle. As the first stones come into view, I defy you not to gasp. The stones are very close together and unlike, say, Stonehenge, there are no great dolmen, rather upright stones of varying sizes. There are 113 of them; some are huge, some hardly there at all, some covered with moss, some not at all. On wet days, you almost have to slide down from the top of the embankment—or if you are a skier you might find a couple of parallel turns useful!

The interior of the circle, which to the eye at least resembles a perfect circle, is an artificial floor, which is why it is so flat. It is made of gravelly earth to a depth of about 28 inches above the original ground level and is about 50 yards in diameter. A few trees grow round the perimeter. One tree is so close behind a stone that they have become almost as one, the moss-covered stone now seemingly integrated into the living trunk. The wind through the trees is wistful and eerie. This is not a place to be alone on a moonlit night, even less if there is no moon at all!

The great question, of course, is what is it for? Directly opposite from where you enter the circle from the road, there is a narrow gap in the stones. It leads to a similarly narrow entrance pathway, lined on either side with retaining stones. Presumably this is a religious site but all that is known, as with so many other stone circles, is that at dawn on mid-summer's morning, as the sun rises, its rays shine directly through the entrance pathway and into the centre of the circle.

In three places within the circle, archaeologists have found fragments of human bones. The circle is evidently not a grave, but current thinking is that these may have been part of some funeral rites, and the bodies left to rot before burial.

Turn your back now on the circle and look across the fields, hills and fertile plains where the Bronze Age lake-shore farmers lived. Although we know that they worked the land, built the houses we have seen at Lough Gur and buried their dead in wedge-graves, the door to their rites, their beliefs and the nature of their society is still closed.

I will be the first to admit I did not expect to find such riches in rural Limerick. But then the more you go through this county the more you think its Irish Tourist Board slogan should be 'County of Surprises'. You have spent a day in an area not much bigger than half-a-dozen football pitches, yet you have crossed not just centuries but millennia. There is only one fitting end to this extraordinary and rewarding day and that is some of the Lucullan delights and Bacchanalian pursuits for which the Irish have been famous, I dare say, since Bronze Age man first asked Bronze Age woman if she fancied a quick drink before dinner. Adare Manor, here we come!

Dinner at Adare Manor

Adare Manor, Adare, Co.Limerick
℡ (061) 396566

Open for lunch and dinner all year. Set dinner: IR£32.50 plus service charge.

The great, grey, Gothic pile that is Adare Manor stands on the banks of the river Maigue. For two centuries it was the home of the Earls of Dunraven. It was the second Earl, and his wife Caroline, who built the present house. They are also responsible for the pretty thatched cottages along the main street of Adare. The Manor was started in 1832 and finally completed by 1876. The building work was given to a local man, James Connolly, and for 21 years he worked on the Manor, using local labour and materials wherever possible. Carved into the stone south parapet of the building is the legend: 'Except the Lord built the house, then labour is but lost that built it.' The staircase, the minstrel's gallery, the fine panelled walls and ceilings of the dining room and several of the marble chimney pieces were designed by Augustus Welby

Pugin, that obsessive champion of Gothic architecture who had so much influence as the designer of the Houses of Parliament in London.

The Manor is now owned by a quietly spoken American, Tom Kane, who bought the place in the mid-1980s and has turned it into a luxury hotel with a golf course designed by Robert Trent Jones.

Tonight we are concerned with the restaurant. Bronze Age man and woman might have felt a trifle uneasy having their drink in the drawing room at Adare Manor, but we didn't! It is a long, high-ceilinged room with a huge chandelier, comfortable chairs and a skilled barman. Take your time reading the menu, where you have a choice of *table d'hôte* or *à la carte*. A light scallop mousse coated with a white wine cream sauce enhanced with ginger, scallions and tarragon might tempt you. But so might roast breast of pigeon on a purée of turnip spiked with black peppercorns. In winter, try little slivers of air-dried venison on a purée of the most sublime mashed potatoes and poached quail's eggs. My choice was the softest, mildest, smoked wild Irish salmon surrounded by a sauce of pure cream scattered with chopped fresh chives.

To follow that, you might have a sorbet of lemon and thyme, a soup of courgettes with garlic, or a quite wonderful prawn bisque. For a main course, the fish here is excellent, but so too is the meat. You could try chargrilled fillet of salmon on a warm celeriac, shallot and mussel vinaigrette, or a poached medley of seafood with a light caviar sauce. Or perhaps a plate of three meats—lamb, beef and veal—with caramelized shallots on a beautifully reduced *jus*. There is always a vegetarian dish, perhaps a quiche of vegetables topped with Gubbeen cheese and a fresh tomato sauce. The produce is largely local, and some of it grown in the Manor's 900 acres.

As for puddings, just throw away any good resolutions. Rich chocolate *marquis* garnished with a compote of mandarins vies with a smooth, rich chocolate and coffee terrine. A glazed exotic fruit salad is topped with lime sorbet, while a marvellous, spicy cinammon cream melts gently into warm apple strudel. If none of that tempts you, there is a board of Irish cheese with home-made biscuits.

The dining room is a fine setting for chef Gerard Costelloe's offerings. It is splendid and finely panelled, with classic white table linen and crystal to complement it. The service was professional and friendly and our small son was given an appropriately sized knife and fork without our saying a word. Coffee and *petits fours* are taken in the drawing room or darkly comfortable library.

Gerard Costelloe's Prawn Bisque
from the Adare Manor Hotel

The intensity of flavour of this marvellous, creamy, smooth bisque is achieved not by using the flesh of the prawns but their shells. Use the prawns for another dish, or smile sweetly at your local fishmonger.

Ingredients: *Serves 6–8*

1½lb/700g shells of Dublin Bay prawns

2oz/50g tomato purée

1 pint/½ litre double cream

2oz/50g peeled and chopped carrots

2oz/50g peeled and chopped onions

2oz/50g washed and chopped leeks

2oz/50g peeled and chopped celeriac

2 cloves garlic and 1 bay leaf

4oz/100g whole tomatoes, halved

½ teaspoon ground star anise

1 pint/½ litre fishstock, home-made preferably but fish stock cube will do

4 tablespoons brandy

4 tablespoons white wine

1 tablespoon Pernod

A few whole prawns for garnish (optional)

Method:

Crush the shells. You can do this by covering them with clingfilm and banging them with the base of a frying pan. Remove the clingfilm and put the crushed shells into a large saucepan with all the vegetables. Pour on the brandy and flame them as if you were flaming a Christmas pudding. When the alcohol has burned off, add the tomato purée and all the other dry ingredients, stir together, then pour in the white wine and fish stock. Bring to the boil then simmer gently until the liquid has reduced by a third.

Add the double cream and cook gently for 45 minutes. Pour the bisque through a fine sieve into a clean saucepan, stir and season and reheat gently. Finish with the Pernod and garnish with a few whole prawns.

Limerick
Glenstal Abbey and the Clare Glens

For millions of television viewers throughout Europe, watching the 1995 Eurovision Song Contest threw up an unexpected and almost unbelievable surprise. It was the sight and sound of monks from a Benedictine Abbey, Glenstal, taking part with pop groups and a light music orchestra in the interval of that great media extravaganza. It was a demonstration of singing which their medieval founder would hardly have envisaged as part of their strict daily routine! If you time your arrival at Glenstal Abbey correctly on any day, you can see and hear these self-same monks singing their daily office or chanting during the celebration of the Roman Catholic Mass with a purity and beauty that is surely intensely moving whatever your beliefs. And when you leave the Abbey, drive the short distance to the green and shimmering Clare Glens, a place renowned for its natural beauty for 150 years. Between these two you will spend a hugely fascinating day, enriched by a sense of awe at both the scenery and the peace and tranquillity of the Abbey.

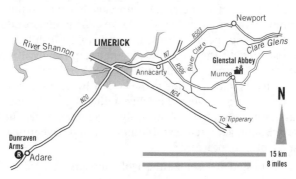

Getting there

From your base in Adare it is an easy drive to the little village of Murroe in the heart of the Clare Glens. Leave Adare as if you were going back to Limerick and when you reach the city take the signs for Dublin. After half a dozen miles or so on the main Limerick–Dublin road, the N7, you pass through Annacarty and soon after is a sign for Murroe. Shortly before the village itself there is another signpost for Glenstal, the abbey, and the Clare Glens.

The name **Glenstal** literally means 'the Glen of the Stallion' and though these days everyone pronounces it with a long final 'a' as in 'stall' you can meet older monks and natives of Murroe who will use a short 'a' as in 'stag'. Help yourself to whichever you prefer. There is evidence that man has lived here since about 3000 BC. Bronze Age tools have been discovered which are now in the National Museum in Dublin, while in a field above the abbey there is a passage grave.

Glenstal is no conventional abbey. It is actually a castle, Norman in appearance, with a round tower that looks a bit like Windsor Castle. On the turret is the inscription *Bardwell me fecit* and a date that looks very like 1139. In fact, the castle was built in the 1830s and designed by William Bardwell, an English architect, who wanted everyone to believe this was a genuine 12th-century castle. He was commissioned to design it by Sir Matthew Barrington, whose ancestors had been Norman, and Barringtons lived in the castle until the civil war of 1922–3.

The last Barrington to live there was Sir Charles. In 1921 his daughter Winifred was out driving with an officer from the Black and Tans, apparently wearing his cap. It was just before the Irish Civil War and the couple were ambushed and shot at, aim of course being directed at the Black and Tan cap. Winifred was killed. The death of his daughter, coupled with the difficulties of living in an increasingly unstable Ireland and the enormous cost of running the castle, led Sir Charles to close it and abandon Ireland for his estate in England. He offered the castle to the Irish Free State as an official residence for the President, but not surprisingly it was felt the castle was too far from Dublin. In 1926, however, for the sum of just £2000, Sir Charles sold the castle to the Benedictines. St Benedict intended that no two monasteries should be alike, rather that each should have its own ways and traditions. Perhaps only a monastic order such as this, living by wisdom, good sense and firmness, could have turned a secular castle into a place of peace.

As a university student—some time ago!—and although not educated by the Benedictines, I regularly attended Easter weekends each year at Glenstal. Ostensibly for minor religious renewal though without any hint of aggressive dogmatism, the weekends afforded tired students and businessmen from all over Ireland the chance to be peaceful and quiet for a few days. A day might begin with Mass, or with an even earlier rising with the monks for matins, sung often before dawn. There were chances to hear quiet talks from wise men on matters of faith and morals and, as afternoon drifted into evening, you could walk in the grounds discussing questions of social, religious and political moment which were either taxing the mind or, on a more mundane level, happened to be in that day's newspapers. The evenings invariably included a walk to the one village pub (surely a record for Ireland) for some Guinness.

Little has changed in the 30 years since I first visited Glenstal except that the church, which was built in the 1950s, has since been given the most astonishing interior, of which more later.

The avenue of Glenstal winds upwards from the main road through grounds that are now a wildlife sanctuary and full of surprises. You may well see a couple of swans where you would have expected deer, sedately walking across the grass and grazing. More predictably, others can be seen floating with grace across the five artificial lakes.

In the 19th century, the gardens were planted with a great variety of trees and flowers. The most spectacular must be the rhododendrons, huge bushes of them, sweeping in massive banks of every imaginable colour and embracing trees in their path. They are superbly maintained by the monks and their gardeners. Take extra film for your camera when you come here.

For the last 60 or so years, this place has also been home to one of the more respected public schools in Ireland. Two huge circular towers support an arched gateway which sweeps gently towards the school buildings on the left and the marvellous church on your right.

There is a peace about Glenstal which, as the west of Ireland man said, is a bit like sunshine: it is easy to recognize but hard to describe. Plan your journey to arrive with plenty of time to spare before one of the monks' services so that you can have a good look around the grounds and the church, dedicated to St Joseph and St Columba. Please check with the monks' visitor centre about parking. Service times may vary but there is generally a Mass just after midday every weekday where the monks process to the choir on either side of the high altar to take their places in the stalls. Some stand, some lean, older priests may sit down. If you have heard Gregorian chants—an increasingly popular form of singing which has captured the imagination of a material Western world over the last few years—then I assure you that what you hear in Glenstal is streets ahead of anything else in its genre.

The monastic church is big, bare and direct. There is a simple high altar flanked at the back by the choir stalls and there is little ostentation in what I will, with some irreverence, call the fixtures and fittings. But it is the colour which will fair take your breath away: the walls are a simple white, but the ceiling is painted in brilliant waves of bright red, green and blue; even the organ pipes are similarly decorated. One not wholly convinced Benedictine monk described the effect to us as psychedelic. But when you add to this the mixture of white and red worn by the monks and sit listening to the chanting, you will begin to understand St Benedict's phrase which is the maxim of the monks at Glenstal: *Ut in omnibus glori Deus* (That in all things God may be glorified).

When you leave Glenstal, making I am certain a vow (you are allowed to in a monastery!) to return whenever you have the chance, drive back towards the main road and follow the signs for the **Clare Glens**. This is another day to opt for a picnic lunch. There are a few pubs in the neighbourhood where you can get rid of the morning's thirst but you have a treat in store now as you head towards the Clare River, which divides the counties of Limerick and Tipperary. It has been a well-known beauty spot for more than 150 years. The land was owned by the Barrington family who in 1927 gave it to the counties of Limerick and Tipperary as a public amenity and so it has remained.

Watch carefully for the road signs as you drop down towards the car parks which straddle the road. Just inside the entrance to the Glens there is a notice board with excellent plans illustrating the two marked trails you can follow. One is an adventure trail which is about two miles long and not really suitable for the elderly or very young, and the other, which can be enjoyed by everyone, is about a mile long. Wear proper walking shoes or trainers with good treads as even the shorter trail, which we took, can have its precarious moments whatever the weather.

The Glens are really a sandstone gorge, through which the Clare River plunges in a series of waterfalls, though when you start your walk the water looks like one gently sloping waterfall. You walk through green glades of oak, ash and conifers, the river rushing downwards to your right. As the path winds around the gently sloping hills the water disappears and re-presents itself as you progress. Huge rocks fill the gorge, creating both

Clare Glens

little pools and waterfalls of every size. The speed and ferocious pitch of the water creates white water rapids. At times you feel you are in the middle of a picture spread in the National Geographic Magazine.

Take great care, particularly if you have children with you, though they will adore this adventure. The path takes you up and up and, just as you are wondering how you are ever going to get down, it bends to cross a little bridge fording the gorge. Stand on this bridge and let your eyes feast: downwards there are the magical waterfalls and beguiling pools, upwards misty trees and the plunging river. The path back down to the road winds along the opposite bank, high above the river, but it takes you back down more quickly than you would have thought possible.

It is really well worth taking hours over this trip. The opportunities for photographs, videoing and sketching are limitless. It is as if you are trapped in a great green cavern; the overhanging trees and surrounding vegetation give an almost tropical atmosphere (though not temperature!) to the whole place. If there are forty shades of green in Ireland, and there probably are, they are here in the Clare Glens. The fascination and contentment that Ratty and Mole felt for the river in *The Wind in the Willows* are doubled here. At every hand's turn are moss-covered rocks, maiden hair fern growing wild and wonderful, bulrushes that seem to have bolted beyond their normal height and, in small pools of calm on the river, flowers like little islands of peace after the roar and activity of the rushing falls.

This is a wonderful adventure for both adults and children. Our six-year-old, well-equipped and shod and with a rucksack on his back containing necessary sustenance, absolutely loved the few hours we spent in the Clare Glens. On the journey back to Adare we were silent, full of the beauty of the day, but as we got nearer, we all wanted to share what we had seen, and where better than at the Dunraven Arms.

Dinner at the Dunraven Arms, Adare

The Maigue Room Restaurant, Dunraven Arms Hotel, Main Street, Adare, Co.Limerick
✆ (061) 396633

Open daily for dinner and for Sunday lunch all year. Set dinner (inc. coffee): IR£22.95 plus service charge.

Walking into the Dunraven Arms Hotel is like pulling on your favourite snugly sweater—instantly you feel cosseted and at ease. It is a most welcoming place, comfortable, casual and hospitable. For those addicted to fox-hunting, the hotel is heaven. The staff will arrange for you to hire a horse and join a local hunt—the County Limerick Foxhounds, the Galway Blazers, Stonehall Harriers, Scarteen Hounds or Golden Vale Hounds. In fact you can go out with a different hunt pretty well every day in the season. And each night in the winter it is not so much golf clubs or tennis racquets you see being put away, but riding gear and boots covered in mud being whisked off to be cleaned. Summer or winter, the boss himself, the never-to-be-forgotten Bryan Murphy, will be there, either organizing the hunt or golf for the following day or fielding phone calls from people who want information on one or other or both.

If you book into the hotel for a riding holiday, you will be asked such questions as 'How tall are you?' and 'What weight are you?' I should not be coy about this, as the food at the Dunraven Arms is of the kind to ensure you will not go home any lighter!

The bar is big, pubby and comfortable and is very much a local meeting place. It overlooks the hotel's very pretty garden, where they grow many of their vegetables. The food they serve at lunchtime is excellent and so was our dinner in the hotel's main restaurant, the Maigue Room, named after the river that ambles through Adare. The dining room itself is comfortable and traditional with crisp white linen and nicely spaced tables. Fish and game are specialities here, and the chef, Mark Phelan, deliciously combines traditional dishes with modern ideas.

Sit by the fire in the bar and make your most difficult decisions of the day.

Will you have slices of pan-fried black pudding with the crispest, lightest apple fritters on a confit of red onions? Or perhaps tagliatelle of wild mussels and smoked salmon scented with basil? I had something unique to the hotel: whiskey-barbecued salmon served with avocado pear and cherry tomatoes in a lemon vinaigrette. The salmon was succulent with a dense texture, and a marvellous flavour. It is smoked specially for the hotel up in Connemara. Choose then from a consommé with slivers of red pepper, tossed seasonal salad with a pleasantly sharp dressing flavoured with pink peppercorns, or a fresh fruit sorbet.

For a main course, the roast prime rib of beef carved from the trolley was pink and perfect. It was served with Dunraven pudding (otherwise known as Yorkshire pud!) and a light *jus*, which I would not insult by calling gravy, and a creamy horseradish sauce. But you could also revel in a pan-fried darne of local salmon and brill, with stirfried vegetables and a delicate soya sauce, or a grilled fillet of John Dory with black tagliatelle and huge prawn tails in a rich, deep, creamy seafood sauce. There is always a vegetarian dish, perhaps lightly steamed vegetables and pasta strands in a lemon and ginger sauce. The bread is dark, Irish and very morish.

Puddings are a delight: perhaps a lemon tartlet made of light, crisp pastry surrounded by a strawberry *coulis*, or a frozen chocolate terrine with two contrasting sauces: one a lovely sharp orange sauce, the other a rich dark chocolate, the whole decorated with a couple of little

Dunraven Arms

slices of orange. The ice creams are homemade, served with a *coulis* of raspberries, and there is of course a fine board of mature Irish cheese. Choose from a perfectly ripe Cashel Blue, a sliver of Gubbeen or a golden round of St Tola's goats' cheese. What is on the cheeseboard depends on what is in the best condition.

Child-sized portions were provided without a murmur, and when these had disappeared a demonstration was offered (unasked) to said child of the intricacies of the saddle—in the hall, I hasten to add, not in the dining room.

Frozen Chocolate Terrine
from the Maigue Room at the Dunraven Arms

This is wonderfully easy to make, and very, very impressive.

Ingredients:
Serves 8–10

> 7oz/200g chocolate and hazelnut spread
>
> 11oz/300g milk chocolate, melted and cooled
>
> 2 tablespoons Kahlua liqueur
>
> 6 eggs, separated
>
> 10floz/300ml double cream, whipped
>
> 2 tablespoons caster sugar
>
> 5oz/150g dark chocolate, grated

Method:

Into a bowl put the chocolate and hazelnut spread, the melted and cooled milk chocolate, the Kahlua and the egg yolks. Beat it all together vigorously, then fold in the whipped cream. Whisk the egg whites in a separate bowl until soft peaks form, and gradually fold in the sugar. Beat for another 2 minutes. Fold the egg whites and the grated dark chocolate into the milk chocolate mixture and mix gently until it has all combined. Line a loaf tin with clingfilm and pour in the mixture. Cover and leave in the freezer for at least two hours until it has set absolutely firm. To serve, carefully turn out the terrine onto a pretty dish and serve in slices with a little cream. You can if you like decorate this with a few orange slices, with all the pith removed.

Limerick/Clare
Foynes and Bunratty Castle

It is hard sometimes to remember what a romantic adventure flying once was, when you are cooped up with two or three hundred others in an aeroplane which seems just as functional these days as a bus. But go to Foynes on the shores of the Shannon estuary and envelop yourself in the nostalgia of those heady days of transatlantic flying boats, when a small port became the focus of air travel between the United States and Europe. And when you have had your fill of modern adventure, follow the estuary round through Limerick and out again towards that other famous (but still functioning!) airport, Shannon, cross the border into County Clare and go even further back in time in the extraordinary Bunratty Castle and Folk Park. Some dismiss this as a great cliché and a tourist trap, but I think it is one of the most imaginative historical sites in the Republic and sheer magic for children.

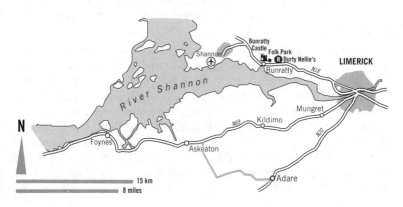

Getting there

To get to Foynes from Adare, you can wriggle your way across country, following the signs for Ashkeaton. You then join the N69 and head west for Foynes. Pretty and rural though this way may be, it is easy to take the wrong turning. The foolproof way is to head back to Limerick city from Adare, and take the N69 through Ashkeaton to Foynes. This route also takes you through the area around Mungret, an early monastic site and now the seat of a prominent Jesuit school. If you are interested in horse-racing, and if the village of Kildimo, through which you also pass, sounds familiar, it did indeed give its name to a famous racehorse who was often tipped for the Grand National, but never quite made it.

The day we arrived in **Foynes** could fairly be described as a 'soft old day'. The clouds were low and grey, the rain drifted mistily across the harbour. It was easy to imagine the flying boat passengers of 60 years ago anxiously waiting for the skies to clear. The first transatlantic flight was made from here in 1937. The runway was the calm stretch of the Shannon between the mainland and Foynes Island. On board the aircraft, passengers were served lavish meals, often seven courses, with the finest linen in a proper dining room. Afterwards they could stroll round the internal promenade deck and enjoy the view. At the rear of the plane there was even a honeymoon suite! This was exclusive travel. The planes were built to take 60 passengers, but the weight of fuel for the Atlantic crossing meant that, in practice, only between 20 and 35 flew. The cost, one way, was $337 which in today's money is just $4200.

But in a way this was superficial luxury. Flying was in its early days, and though the flying boats had four engines, the journey to St John in Newfoundland took 12 hours, and bad weather often meant the aircraft had to turn back.

Thus it was, so legend has it, that one of the great drinks of Ireland came to be invented. Irish coffee is a happy mixture of coffee, sugar and whiskey with thick cream on the top which gives the visual effect of a half pint of Guinness. It seems to be the case that the man responsible was a barman at Foynes called Joe Sheridan. When bad weather forced an aircraft to return to Foynes with its cold and frustrated passengers, our man thought they were in need of something a little more reviving than a simple hot coffee, so he laced it with whiskey and some sugar. With no milk to hand, he dropped a generous spoonful of cream into it and discovered, to his amazed delight, that the cream floated deliciously on the surface and filled the glass perfectly. Thus was one of the world's most famous drinks created, though why, in fairness, we don't call it a Sheridan is beyond me.

During the Second World War, Foynes was essential as a link between America and Europe. Although Ireland was a neutral country, most passengers coming through Foynes were top level military and diplomatic personnel, many on active duty and travelling with false passports. In spite of a news black out, there were persistent rumours of American military uniforms being seen at Foynes. By the end of the war, the huge technological advances in aircraft design spelled the end of the flying boats. In October 1945 the last of them left Foynes, leaving what memories! For a few crucial years, Foynes had enjoyed a role of real international importance, the flying boats bringing more than a touch of glamour to this small west coast town.

And now what is left? Well, every August Foynes hosts an Irish Coffee Festival with a competition to find the champion Irish coffee maker. Imagine being a judge at that! But what you must visit is the Foynes Flying Boat Museum, on your left as you enter the town from the Limerick side. It has exhibits, photographs and an audio-visual show that sweeps you back to those early, brave days of long-distance flying. In this age of satellites and instant computer communications, you can only be amazed at the radio and weather room with its original transmitters, receivers and morse code equipment. These days, alas, the magic and mystery of the flying boats in the harbour has been replaced by the bustle of what is now Ireland's fourth largest commercial port, through which most frozen Irish beef is exported.

I stood late one afternoon on the quayside, in glimmering but fast-disappearing light and with a gentle mist swirling, and tried to imagine what it might have been like here 50 or 60 years ago as planes carrying glamorous and important people, many essential to the war effort, took off or landed in a swirl of spray and headlights emerging from the dark. Legends and folklore in Ireland do not need to be centuries old. In Bunratty Castle however, they certainly are!

> *To get to Bunratty, go back to Limerick on the N69, then out towards Shannon airport on the N18. Here you are just over the boundary in County Clare. It is an easy, well sign-posted journey and you should arrive nicely in time for lunch at one of the institutions of the area, Durty Nellie's (see below). Not that it matters if you are late; lunch seems to be available throughout the afternoon.*

Bunratty Castle looms massively over the landscape as you approach it, a 15th-century tower house which has been meticulously restored. It stands in a folk park which should really be called a living museum: reconstructed homes, farms, shops and streets of a century ago.

Until the 18th century, Bunratty was a fortress and stronghold of the powerful O'Brien family, the Earls of Thomond. That they managed to keep the castle so long is probably due to innate political cunning. In the 17th century, it was said of Barnaby, the sixth Earl, that he managed to be Royalist, Rebel and Roundhead, yet still managed to end his days seemingly loyal to the king, and still in full possession of his estates! The O'Briens then moved to Dromoland, and Bunratty was occupied by a series of Anglo-Irish families. The last of these, the Studdarts, built Bunratty House in the grounds. Originally intended as temporary accommodation, it proved so much more convenient to live in than the big draughty castle that they stayed there, and the castle was left empty and neglected. By the 19th century, it was a ruin and eventually the roof of the Great Hall collapsed, a matter of great local concern.

In 1956, Bunratty was bought by the late Lord Gort, whose ambition it was to restore the place. Over the years he rebuilt the castle and filled it with a marvellous collection of 15th- to 17th-century furniture.

The castle is a wonderful place to explore, and it is full of the gruesome things guaranteed to send shudders down the spines of young and old. There is a dungeon about 15 feet deep into which the prisoners were thrown. Above the entrance is a 'murder hole' from where boiling water or tar could be hurled on invaders' heads. As for the narrow spiral staircases, who knows what shadows of the past might suddenly appear here? In the Great Hall on a dais is a table some 22 feet long, behind which is a great Chair of Estate. Check first with the guides, and if they allow you to try it for size, you can, for a few moments, imagine yourself as the great and powerful Earl of Thomond!

From the ornate guests' apartments in the south solar to the Earl's private kitchen, the castle is full of exhibits, displayed as they would have been used. Early cooking pots are arranged on a 17th-century table, a 15th-century bed dominates what was the Earl's bedchamber. The lower chapel has a fine stucco plaster ceiling, dating from the 16th century, while a 15th-century carved figure of St Sebastian stands in a window alcove. In the robing room is a vast Flemish clothes cupboard, carved from oak, while to the right of the entrance there is a 12th-century chest.

Take your time as you walk around; the quality of so many of the pieces deserves close study.

In the north solar, high up in the castle, the oak panelling dates from about 1500, while the table here is said to have been salvaged from a Spanish galleon wrecked off the Clare coast at what is now called Spanish Point. Follow the staircase up through the Earl's pantry and up again round a narrow, difficult spiral staircase. The effort is worth it as you emerge onto the battlements of the northeast tower and are confronted by a magnificent view which blurs the centuries: the remains of great houses, Limerick City in the misty distance, and to the southwest the runways of Shannon airport.

When you have had your fill of the castle, spend some time in the **Folk Park**. The buildings are faithful copies of their originals, except the Shannon farmhouse which *is* original—it once stood on the proposed site for the main runway of Shannon airport. It was demolished and re-erected in the folk park, the first building to be constructed there.

Not only are there farms, a fisherman's house, a blacksmith's forge, shops, a byre and all the other necessities of 19th-century rural Irish living, but turf fires burn in the grates, chickens wander in and out, cows queue patiently to be milked and pigs snuffle noisily as they are fed. The smell of baking bread makes you think it must be time for tea, and you can watch the butter to spread on it being churned. If you wander down the village street, the shops have been set out as they would have been 100 years ago.

The draper's shop is full of linen, poplin and wool, as well as ready-made clothes of the time. The grocer's has a wonderful, cluttered air that makes you long for the days before pre-packaged, cook-chill food, and there is, of course, a pub. In the Talbot Collection you can see a fine array of farming implements, together with an audio-visual show.

Bunratty is good fun as well as telling you, in the nicest possible way, a good deal about the social history of Ireland. It all becomes very real as you drive down to Loop Head (*see* Day 5), through wild and barren scenery to the furthermost point of County Clare.

Lunch at Durty Nellie's, Bunratty

Durty Nellie's Oyster Restaurant, Bunratty, Co.Clare
✆ (061) 364861

Open for lunch and dinner all year. Lunch (inc. tea or coffee): approx. IR£10 per head

Durty Nellie's is a rambling place right beside Bunratty Castle. It has been serving food and drink in vast quantities since 1620 in two restaurants and a bar. The Loft Restaurant upstairs is open only in the evenings, but the Oyster Restaurant on the ground floor is open just about all the time. It is a great place, dark, cosy, bustling and atmospheric. There is linen on the tables and sawdust on the floors. I would not recommend that you go so far as to get down on your hands and knees and study the floors, but they are covered in flagstones from Liscannor, further north near the wonderful Cliffs of Moher. There is a marvellous story that an MP from the area bet a government minister that he could build a wall one mile long, one and a half inches wide and six foot high without it falling over. The prize, if he won, was to be one of Her Majesty's (in this case Queen Victoria's) warships. The bet was accepted, and amazingly, the MP won. He used Liscannor flagstones, which are eight foot high and one and a half inches thick. He dug a mile of foundations, two feet deep, placed the flagstones in them, and lo and behold, a perfect wall, of the exact measurements, which did not fall down. He then used his prize warship, so it is said, to transport Liscannor flagstones to the most profitable markets.

Lunch at the Oyster Restaurant is very good and very reasonable. The food is a happy mix of local ingredients made into both traditional and international dishes. The smoked salmon is Irish, smooth and plentiful; plump mussels steamed in garlic fill a huge bowl. Wonderfully fresh crab surrounded by slices of grapefruit go very well together, and there are crisp, juicy mushrooms in a garlic sauce. The main courses are an eclectic mix of Irish, Chinese and Italian, with just about everything else in between. Stir-fry pork with rice, veal steak Bearnaise or roast duckling with a Cointreau sauce are available, but so are cold platters spilling over with seafood, or prawns and smoked salmon or chicken. The poached salmon can only be described as perfect, while the small portion of spaghetti Bolognese received total six-year-old approbation! The fish of the day when we ate there was codling, a succulent white fish, lightly grilled with lemon—simple and delicious. Puddings include peach melba, pear Belle Hélène and a gooey homemade cheesecake.

Poached Salmon with Balsamic Vinegar
from the Oyster Restaurant, Durty Nellie's

Ingredients:
Serves 4 as a starter

8oz/225g fresh wild salmon fillet

2floz/50ml dry white wine

1 bouquet garni

Some mixed salad leaves

For the dressing:

2floz/50ml olive oil

½floz/15ml balsamic vinegar

½floz/15ml water

½oz/15g fresh chopped chives

Method:

Put the salmon into a large pan with the water, wine and the bouquet garni. Bring to the boil then turn the heat down immediately and poach gently for 10 minutes. To make the dressing, in a food processor or blender or in a bowl with a whisk, blend together the oil and balsamic vinegar. Add the water and chives. Drain the poached salmon and divide it into four. Arrange some mixed salad leaves on four plates, put the salmon on top and pour over the dressing.

Clare
From Loop Head to the Cliffs of Moher

This is a day of awesome scenery and strange tales, of huge cliffs and leaping hags, and an innocent man hanged for foul murder. From the soft greenness of Limerick, suddenly you are in the barren loneliness of the west of Ireland, where until just a few decades ago everyday life was about survival. Travel a few miles further, and you will be confronted by a sweep of golden sand and a holiday resort that was *de rigueur* for summer vacations. On a few more miles and watch the huge Atlantic waves sweep over the wrecks of Spanish galleons, overwhelmed here after the Armada. And at the end of the day, you may well be silenced by the Cliffs of Moher and your first glimpse of the Burren.

Getting there

You can drive to Clare by following the route you took for Bunratty Castle, but that is long and there is a much more interesting (and shorter) journey. From Tarbert, which is just over the border from Limerick in county Kerry, to the village of Killimer across the Shannon estuary in Clare, there is a regular ferry service. When you leave Adare, drive up the main street away from Adare Manor and follow the signs at the top of the town for Rathkeale. There you turn right for Askeaton. If you have a golfer with you, I should, at this point, blindfold him (or her) as you will see signs for a town in Kerry called Ballybunion, which contains what the great American golfer Tom Watson describes as 'the finest and most enjoyable links golf course I have ever played'! When you reach the N69 at Askeaton, continue through Foynes and Glin until you reach Tarbert. The signs for the ferry are clearly marked. There are hourly sailings at half past the hour throughout the year, though it is always best to check. The ferries are basic, but they do the simple job required of taking you across the Shannon to southern Clare in about 20 enjoyable minutes, saving a long trip by land.

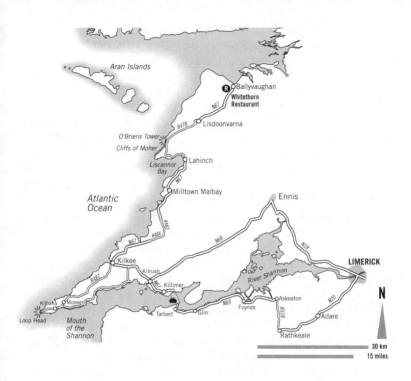

Ahead of you directly is southern Clare and on a clear day, you can see down the peninsular towards Loop Head. When you leave the ferry at Killimer, take a few minutes to visit the local churchyard and see the bronze monument to Ellen Hanley, the Colleen Bawn, or 'Shining Girl', whose short life inspired a play, a novel and an opera, all hugely popular in the 19th century.

Ellen was born in 1803 in county Limerick and at the age of just 15 she married in secret a local landowner's son, a former Marine Lieutenant called John Scanlan. The following year, in the summer of 1819, they were crossing from Clare to Glin in Limerick together with Scanlon's servant and boatman, Sullivan, and a few other people, when a storm forced them to land further down the coast on the shores of Kerry where they stayed the night. The next day the other passengers continued their journey to Glin by road, but nothing more was heard of poor Ellen until her body was washed ashore in September. Sullivan too had disappeared. Her husband was charged with her murder, though he continually protested his innocence. The alleged motive was that her low birth might embarrass his middle class family. No less a person than Daniel O'Connell, the great fighter for Catholic Emancipation, defended Scanlan, but he was convicted and hanged. Although Sullivan's disappearance was considered suspicious, it did not affect Scanlan's trial, or his punishment. A few weeks later Sullivan turned up and confessed to the crime. He too was tried, convicted and hanged, his claim that he was loyally carrying out his master's wishes falling on deaf ears. But from such misery came inspiration and immortality. Dion Boucicault, the Irish playwright, turned the story into a play, *The Colleen Bawn*, the Irish writer Gerald Griffin wrote a novel, *The Collegians*, and the composer Julius Benedict made it into an opera, *The Lily of Killarney*, all of which were great 19th-century successes.

When you leave Killimer, follow the signs for the busy little town of Kilrush, on the N67. From there, you follow the coast road that twists westward along the Shannon estuary. When you reach Kilbaha you are almost at the very edge of Clare. In the parish church of Moneen is a little wooden hut on wheels—the 'Little Ark'. After Catholic Emancipation in 1829 some landlords still would not recognize the right of Catholics to practise their faith, and forbade priests from saying Mass on their land. Furthermore, tenants were warned that if they allowed Mass to be said in their homes, they would be evicted. But this was an area of strong faith, led by a strong and enterprising local priest, Father Michael Meehan. The one place in the parish that was outside the landlord's jurisdiction was the beach between high and low tide. Standing on soggy sand in weather that was often wet and mostly windy was clearly not practical in the long term. Inspiration came to Father Meehan while he was riding on the local horse-drawn omnibus, a vehicle raised off the ground, with steps at one end, obviously mobile, and with a roof. With £10 that he could hardly spare, he went to the village carpenter and asked him to build this strange thing rather like a large bathing machine and within two weeks it was done. Through the windows and doorway, the altar could be seen at the far end. When the tide was right, the hut would be pulled down to the beach and there, on the shore between high and low tide, he would celebrate Mass, just as if he were in his own church.

Behind the cliffs and the magnificent coastal scenery of the peninsula, the land is bleak, housing is scattered and even the growth in holiday homes in recent years has not touched the loneliness. The land is divided into small fields, partitioned not by recognizable dry stone walls, but by thick, shaggy overgrown banks. A few abandoned houses still stand, and occasionally you can see a mildewy thatch on a roof, with remnants of the rope used to tie it down against the high winds. In normal times, the people who once inhabited these houses lived principally by fishing, with potatoes as their other essential food. Turf was cut to sell or exchange for goods; the men would take it in laden boats up the Shannon, selling the fuel wherever they could. In the late 1840s, in the few square miles between here and Kilkee, 4000 people died as a consequence of the potato famine and eviction by absentee landlords. The sea may have been full of fish, but starvation caused by the total failure of the potato crop in 1846 and a fever which affected one family in ten meant the men simply did not have the strength to take their boats out to sea. For many communities, the only help they received was from extraordinary and saintly priests like Father Meehan.

From Kilbaha it is just a few minutes drive to **Loop Head** itself. Celtic legend has it that the great hero, Cu Chulainn, was being pursued (something which seems to have occurred quite frequently) by a distinctly unlovely woman, named, rather aptly, Mal. When he reached the cliffs, he leapt with that lightness and prowess for which he was renowned, some 30 feet out into the sea onto a rock to escape her. The ugly hag tried to follow, but crashed down into the wild sea and was drowned. Her body was later washed up further along the coast at Mal Bay by Spanish Point. Ever afterwards, this most south-westerly point of Clare has been known as Loop (or leap) Head.

Stand on Loop Head, leaning into a wind of salty strength with the Atlantic crashing below, and you can easily understand all the myths and legends. To your left, below the waters of the Shannon, is a legendary city, whose spires and towers, so the story goes, cause the great waves at the mouth of the estuary. Every 7 years, the entire city is said to be visible, a sight fatal within a month to all who see it! It is an invigorating place—last night's cobwebs do not stand a chance—and if the weather is clear there are marvellous views across to Kerry and northwards up towards Galway.

From Loop Head, go back to Kilbaha but this time take the R487 for Kilkee, not the coastal road to Carrigaholt. On your left are the great waves of the Atlantic and mighty rocks. Look out for the Bridges of Ross, where the cliffs point out to sea. Erosion has worn away the rock leaving a natural bridge, famous since the 18th century. Then there were two bridges, now only one remains intact.

When you arrive at Kilkee, the contrast with the bleakness of Loop Head is startling. Suddenly you are in one of the busiest resorts in the west of

Ireland. Since the early 1800s, Kilkee has been popular as a seaside resort and it developed, according to newspapers from the last century, as 'this fashionable bathing place.' It attracted notable visitors from all over Ireland and also from Britain. The poets Tennyson and Sir Aubrey de Vere came here, while Charlotte Bronte the novelist spent her honeymoon in the town in 1854. The Crown Princess of Austria came in 1896 and the author Rider Haggard holidayed here, as did the Irish novelist Gerald Griffin of 'shining girl' fame. The popularity of the town increased even more when the West Clare Railway was opened in 1890 linking the county town of Ennis with Kilkee. In your hotel some night in the west of Ireland see if you can prevail upon a local to sing you the immortal ballad by the song-writer Percy French 'Are You Right There Michael?'. A poignantly funny song about the delights and chaotic inadequacies of the railway link, it brought reactions in equal measure of hysterics from those who knew what it says to be true and others, more stony-faced, who thought French was laughing at the Irish. For the rest of us, we just sing it and enjoy! It was a sad day for the town when the railway link finally closed in 1961.

In the late 1950s, when I was a child, Kilkee was *the* place for holidays. Familes would come for the whole summer. Fathers would leave their offices in Dublin or Galway and come for perhaps a fortnight in August, joining the families the rest of the time at weekends. I still remember the awful feeling one year of being the only boy in our road not going to Kilkee. Our family were going for three weeks to somewhere called the Isle of Man!

If the weather is fine, take half an hour to walk along the huge beach or just sit and admire the sweep of the bay. Even today, with competition from international resorts and cheap package holidays, Kilkee remains popular.

From Kilkee continue along the coast on the N67 towards Milltown Malbay. The sand dunes along this road are huge and grass covered. As you approach Milltown Malbay there is a huge sweep of beach ahead of you and the Atlantic rolls into the bays in enormous waves providing some of the best surfing in Ireland. A large notice urges bathers to exercise extreme caution at all times. It is here, off Spanish Point, that part of the Spanish Armada was wrecked in 1588. The sea-shore here looks back on your left towards Loop Head in the distance and to your right northwards across the surf to one of the great places in the west of Ireland, the **Cliffs of Moher**.

As the road sweeps round Liscannor Bay towards Lahinch, there are sign-posts directing you to the cliffs and to the car park near the visitors' centre there. Ahead of you the cliffs loom, rising up 700 feet straight out of the sea. They are dark, beautiful, intriguing. For 5 miles they process up the coast, home not to legendary heroes, but to kittiwakes, puffins, guillemots and razorbills. There are well-kept walks and protective railings along the cliff-top with good reason, as the edge of the cliff can crumble away without warning. Follow the path to the highest point of the cliffs, to O'Brien's Tower built in the middle of the 19th century by the eccentric MP Sir Cornelius ('Corney') O'Brien. From here you can see the whole majestic sweep of the cliffs standing against the sea. Over thousands of years the Atlantic has eroded the cliffs, as if wilfully it had taken huge random bites, creating little bays and inlets which it then fills with dramatic waves, sending mist and spray high up the rock face. On a clear day you will easily see all the way south to Loop Head; out to sea are the Aran Islands, and to the north there is Connemara.

Cliffs of Moher

This is a spectacular way to spend a few hours. One fine summer's day, I persuaded a local boatman to take a group of us out on the sea here. We stayed hundreds of yards away from the cliffs, but that mattered not at all. Towering giddily above us was sheer rock-face, revealing in the coloured bands of shale or rock the different eras of the earth's formation. Every now and again, a flock of birds would rise from some unseen ledge, swoop above the waves and then settle back into the cliffs. All the time there was the sound of the Atlantic crashing endlessly against those mighty rocks. Never had we felt so vulnerable and insignificant.

A place of such drama scarcely needs myths to enhance it (though maybe it does to explain it!), but from the Cliffs of Moher, up the west coast to Donegal, the ancient bards tell of a vast, rich and fertile island lying under the ocean. This has been called Hy Brazil or Brasil, a land of perpetual sunshine with rivers, forests, mountains and lakes. Castles abound and palaces too, gracing river banks or mountain stretches where they vie for attention with the lushest and greenest of pastures and fine lands. In such a fantastical paradise, what else could its inhabitants be but perpetually young and happy!

That description may not quite fit all of us, but there is something revitalizing about the beauty and power of these cliffs. And, in a way, they will have begun to prepare you for one of the world-renowned great sights of Ireland—that extraordinary phenomenon known as the Burren.

Head north on the R478 to Lisdoonvarna and then on the N67 to Ballyvaughan, a small, popular town with this area of outstanding natural beauty and immense historical and botanical interest right on its doorstep. On your way to Ballyvaughan you will drive by it, mile on mile of limestone pavement at once awe-inspiring and confusing. In the setting sun, the colours change constantly, battle-ship grey, a glow of yellow or red, and as the sun sinks, the rock acquires a luminosity of almost fairylike enchantment. Maybe those stories of sunken islands where no one grows old are not so far-fetched after all!

Dinner at the Whitethorn Restaurant, Ballyvaughan

The Whitethorn Craft Shop and Restaurant, Loughrask, Ballyvaughan, Co.Clare

℗ *(065) 77044*

Open for lunch and dinner March–October. Tourist menu (three courses and coffee): IR£12.

A restaurant built in a converted fish factory does not sound the most tempting of locations, but that is exactly what the Whitethorn is. It perches right on the edge of the sea, overlooking Galway Bay and Connemara beyond. A huge picture window brings the scenery inside. Behind the restaurant are the limestone hills of the Burren. This used to be the coastguards' station and their boathouse next door is now used for storing currachs. Any whiff of the fish factory has long since been expunged! Converting the place was the excellent idea of Leonard Culligan, a dentist from Ennis who opened it about 6 years ago. It is run by his daughter Sarah in the kitchen and his son-in-law John McDonnell front of house.

The Whitethorn is more than a restaurant. It is also a bar, a café and a craft shop. As you enter the building, you walk into the well-stocked craft shop which sells a range of goods, from little Irish mementoes to clothes and original pieces in pottery and wood. This opens onto a very pleasant self-service café-restaurant which serves food all day and every day during the season—home-made and imaginative. You can also eat outside on the terrace overlooking the bay. The bar is comfortable and has a piano which is put to good use until very late on!

Three or four times a week, they open a more formal restaurant for dinner. This is a very pretty room, all soft greens and deep pinks, more like a country house dining room than a seaside restaurant, with linen table-cloths and a wonderful view of the sun setting behind the mountains of Connemara.

There are two menus to choose from, a tourist menu and *à la carte*. Beneath each dish is a suggested wine to complement it. John McDonnell went walkabout in Australia for four years, during which time he did a wine course. His love and knowledge of wine is apparent, with not surprisingly an emphasis on Australian vintages. The dishes are simple, a comfortable mix of excellent local produce and dishes familiar to a passing tourist trade. To start, there are mussels poached in white wine and cream, locally smoked chicken with a leafy salad and raspberry dressing, smoked salmon—also local—with a yoghurt cream dressing, and a soup of the day. The night we were there it was a smooth sweet carrot soup with a lovely bite of fresh ginger. The crab claws baked in garlic and herbs are wonderfully meaty. For a main course, such stalwarts as duck and sirloin steak are imaginatively served with a good rich fruit-filled sauce for the duck and a creamy sauce with a generous splash of Irish whiskey for the steak. The fillet of plaice stuffed with crabmeat and served with an orange butter sauce is full of cream and flavour and quite delicious, the orange balancing the richness of the crab very well. You could also choose an escalope of salmon with a lemon sauce or perhaps a vegetable and nut Strogonoff with herbed rice. Puddings are creamy or fruity—or both! A well-filled apple pie, a light pavlova or perhaps a goblet of ice cream. The cheeses are marvellous, and made just a few miles away in Corofin in the middle of

Clare. Both cow and goat cheeses are flavoured with peppercorns, or herbs and caraway seeds, or left plain. The cheeseboard is beautifully presented and the bread, needless to say, home-made.

The service is good and the McDonnells very friendly and helpful. Children are welcome.

Carrot and Ginger Soup
from the Whitethorn Restaurant

Ingredients:

Serves 6

5oz/150g onions, peeled and roughly chopped

1lb/450g carrots, peeled and roughly chopped

Generous ½oz/15g fresh root ginger, peeled and grated

Salt and freshly ground black pepper

2oz/50g butter

2½–3 pints/1.5–1.8 litres vegetable stock (stock cube will do)

2–3 tablespoons pouring cream

Method:

Melt the butter in a large saucepan and add the carrots and onions. Cook gently until the onions are soft, but do not let them brown. Add the stock, bring to the boil, then simmer gently for about 10 minutes until the carrots are soft. Take the pan off the heat. In a food processor or liquidizer purée the soup. Add the grated ginger while the soup is being puréed. Season to taste with salt and freshly ground black pepper. Pour the soup back into the saucepan and add the cream. Re-heat gently and serve at once.

day six

Clare
The Burren

There is nowhere quite like the Burren. The word comes
from the Irish *boireann* or rocky land. It has minor outposts
on the Aran Islands in Galway Bay and in southern
Connemara, but they are nothing like as dramatic as here in
northwest Clare. In a bizarre sense the Burren is hardly Irish
at all. There are no bogs, no meadows, nothing in fact but a
moonscape of limestone pavements called clints, dissected
by deep, narrow crevices known as grykes. Year after year
the Burren draws me back. No matter that you read the
scientific explanations of how it was formed, that you know
that once forests of pine and yew and hazel covered the
hills—the sight of those endless, pale, limestone slabs dropping down to the sea or embracing the hills silences and
enthrals you. It is almost impossible to believe that 5000
years ago man lived and farmed here, but the evidence is all
around—more than 100 prehistoric tombs and 500 ring
forts, which are now thought to have been homesteads. It is
a magnificent place, and the deeper into, and indeed under,
it you explore, the more rewarding it becomes.

If you are a walker, the **Burren Way** is for you. It is a path of some 22
miles from Ballyvaughan in the north to O'Brien's Bridge, near Liscannor,
in the south. Of course you do not have to walk it all and there are places
to stay, for example in a 500-year-old farmhouse at Lismactigue high in
the heart of the Burren. Open the curtains in the morning and in front of
you stretches nothing but a glowing pink sky, creamy-white limestone
and a day spent walking in some of the finest scenery nature and prehis-
tory can offer.

I prefer to mix driving and walking. If this is your first visit to the place,
rather than immediately going off to see the various megalithic sites, take

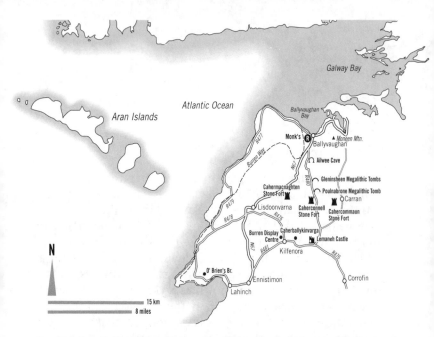

time to absorb those amazing rocks. Drive westward out of Ballyvaughan on the coast road. Where the Burren sweeps down to the side of the road like a sort of dry sea, stop and just walk on the surface. There you can see close up the symmetry of the rock structure, clints which range in size from a few inches to half a tennis court and grykes which run unnervingly straight, dividing the slabs. Where else have you been where to reach the sea you cross vast rock surfaces, huge swathes that sweep towards cliffs which in turn drop dizzyingly down to the water below? Further on, you can walk to the shore itself and on the way come across tiny pools of sea-water with the attendant flowers and perhaps the odd crustacean nestling on the edges.

Although from a distance the rock looks bare and barren, it is quite another matter when you are standing on it; it is full of life. In the tiniest fissure and hollow, flowers and plants bloom. It has been called the finest natural rock garden in the world, and that is easy to believe. At any time of the year, but particularly in May and June, the plants are magical. Of the 1500 species of plant in Ireland, 1000 of them are here. Some are rare, others not. Most surprising of all, plants from the Arctic and the Alps grow side by side with those more commonly found in the Mediterranean: starry white spring sandwort, gentians of intense blue, delicate saxifrage on its cushion of foliage, the bee orchid, the pure white Dactylorhiza o'kellyii (*sic*), which looks a little like a white hyacinth. They almost seem to grow out of the rock itself.

Climatic change, the Gulf Stream, warm rain and an almost total absence of frost have all been given as reasons for this *mélange* of plant life. The warm Gulf Stream is certainly responsible for another very curious phenomenon. If you are driving through the Burren in winter, you may be surprised to see cattle grazing high on the hills, apparently on bare rock. In every other temperate country, cattle are brought down from the hills in winter to shelter in the warm valleys. Here, because of a climatic quirk known as reverse temperature curve, they are sent *up* into the hills early in November and stay there until April. The limestone absorbs and retains the heat from the sea, the grass grows abundantly and the cattle are well fed. Although from below the rock looks barren, there are in fact terraces up there which form little pastures for the animals, and for hundreds of years this has been the pattern of farming in the Burren.

When you have wandered enough, return to Ballyvaughan for lunch.

Lunch at Monks, Ballyvaughan

Monks Pub and Restaurant, Ballyvaughan, Co.Clare
℡ (065) 77059

Open for lunch and dinner April–October and Christmas. Closes at 6pm November–March. You can eat very well for around IR£6 each.

Just across the road from the quayside in Ballyvaughan is Monks pub and restaurant. It is a pretty, white-washed building, with flowers outside and a little courtyard where you can eat if it is warm enough. In summer the pier across the road seems to act as an *ad hoc* eating place. The view across the bay is lovely, and after lunch you can wander over to the pier and watch the fishermen mending their nets.

Inside is a series of interconnecting rooms with wooden tables and chairs. In the main room is an open fire with a low table and chairs placed snugly round it. If this is the table you would like, get here early—everyone else does. At the back is a wide bar. If you just want a drink, that is fine, but Monks serves a gorgeous array of sandwiches, soups, salads and light dishes, all home-made and served with their own very tempting soda bread. The food is simple, the ingredients local and Monks' reputation is deservedly high.

The seafood chowder is full of fish, shellfish and little fresh pieces of vegetable. What is in it depends on the catch of the day. Oysters have not travelled more than a few miles to arrive on your plate, while the fish cakes will make you quite rethink your school view of the dish. The seafood platter is of a size which you may think is enough for two; salmon, crab, prawns, mussels, even oysters may be heaped on it. The open crab sandwich anywhere else would be called crab salad with scrummy home-made bread. It is served with crisp lettuce sprinkled with fresh parsley and decorated with slices of tomato and fresh orange. A mild salad onion adds to the flavours. I cannot remember when I had fresher, sweeter crab. The prawn cocktail really is made from prawns, not shrimps, and the toasted sandwiches arrive hot, crisp and full of filling. If you have time for pudding, try the apple pie, home-made and, if you want it, covered in cream. Monks is a lovely, bustling place with friendly, enthusiastic service. Children's portions are available.

From Ballyvaughan you can drive to specific prehistoric and Christian sites, but arm yourself first with information and a map. Start your tour of the Burren at the **Burren Information Centre** in Kilfenora. Take the N67 from Ballyvaughan to Lisdoonvarna, then turn left onto the R476 for Kilfenora. The staff are extremely helpful, you can buy detailed maps and there is also an audio-visual display. Some, but not all, of the major sites are clearly signposted; some are on private land where farmers do not always allow access. The guides at the centre will tell you exactly where the sites are, which of the unsignposted ones farmers will allow access to and which not.

Kilfenora itself is a tiny village with a population of barely 200, but it has a unique status: as a result of a dispute in the 19th century, the Roman Catholic population discovered it had no official parish priest. The Vatican therefore took it over and has technically controlled it ever since. Thus can this small Clare community boast of having the Pope as its Bishop! Here, next door to the Burren Information Centre, there is a small and ancient cathedral on the site of a monastery founded by the town's patron saint, St Factna. The stone carvings here are breathtaking, particularly the 600-year-old representations of bishops, and the very fine 12th-century stone crosses. In the graveyard there is the Doorty Cross—a monster of a construction which seems to glower down at you and shows three different bishop's croziers: Irish, continental and a tau cross. On the

other side there is a representation of the entry of Christ into Jerusalem. In the field next to the church and graveyard there is another great cross with a crucifixion scene and elaborate geometric motifs.

About a mile and a half outside Kilfenora, going eastwards on the R476, is a large stone fort. There are about 500 stone forts or *cahers* in the Burren, some now just faint outlines, others substantial and impressive. Most of them, it is thought, were not defensive structures but homesteads from where people farmed, hunted and bred cattle. It is astonishing when you look now at the emptiness of the Burren that the thin coating of soil which once covered the limestone could have supported so many people. This fort, near Kilfenora, is Caherballykinvarga, and unusually does seem to have had defences. It is surrounded by vicious spikes of stone, known as *chevaux de frise*, which have been set in the ground as a rather nasty barrier against unwanted visitors.

From here, continue east along the R476 until you come to a wonderful ruin of a house, four storeys high with surprisingly large windows and a tower house attached. This is **Lemaneh Castle**, an O'Brien Tower House built in about 1480, to which was added a larger house in the 17th century. It must once have been splendid. There are those who claim that they have been able to sense the presence in the tower of one Maire Ruadh (Red Mary), wife of Conor O'Brien. When her husband was killed in a skirmish with Cromwell's men, she is said to have leaned out of a window in the tower when the body was brought home and told the men to take it away. *She* would have no dead men here! She then promptly married one of Cromwell's officers, thus avoiding the confiscation of her lands. It is also rumoured of her that she subsequently disposed of him through a rather high window. In charge of the Cromwellian army in the skirmish that killed the unloved Conor was General Ludlow, immortalized for his classic description of the Burren: 'Here, not enough earth to bury a man, not enough timber to hang him and not enough water to drown him.'

Turn left now by Lemaneh onto the R480 towards Ballyvaughan. It is along this road that you can see the most famous sites, all of which are easy to get to. The first sign you come to is for Caherconnell, a massive stone fort with concentric walls, visible to your left from the road. It stands on a little hill. You get to it through a farmyard, and access to it was smilingly given to us. The stones are dark grey and of an even size. The wonder of it is that the stones were not removed over the centuries for building, though in many cases it was superstition and fear of the evil that might befall that has allowed so many of these forts to survive.

It is not just evidence of where he lived that early man left behind here, but of where he is buried. Just a little further on up the road on the right is probably the most famous of all the prehistoric remains in the Burren— the **Poulnabrone Megalithic Tomb**. Climb over a stile and it is a short walk across rock. The top slab or capstone of this dolmen probably weighs 10 tons and measures 12 feet by 7. It is hard to imagine how that slab was pushed into position 5000 years ago. What you see standing there now is just the skeleton of the tomb. When it was built it was covered with a vast cairn of loose rocks and soil, though it is possible the capstone may have been left uncovered. It was excavated in 1986, and there is evidence that around 30 people, men, women and children, were buried there.

Portal tombs like Poulnabrone are very rare here, but the next set of tombs you come to a little further up the road are wedge-shaped and date from about 1500 BC. There are at least 130 of these in the Burren. They are table-like structures, which always face to the west and taper down towards the east. Here at **Gleninsheen**, where there is a small group of them, one of the greatest artefact finds in Ireland was made: a gorget, probably a neck ornament, made of the finest gold and patterned in seven roughly concentric ridges with a delicate rope pattern in between. At each end is a disc decorated with little concentric circles surrounding a small conical spike. It was made in about 700 BC. Like the flowers of the Burren, the patterns on this ornament show influences from the Baltic in the north and the Mediterranean in the south. But if you want to see it, you must go to the National Museum in Dublin.

From here it is an easy drive back to Ballyvaughan. You know now what the Burren looks like on top—but what lies underneath?

Seafood Chowder
from Monks

You can make this from a combination of white fish, smoked fish, salmon and shellfish in whatever proportions you fancy. It is more of a stew than a soup.

Ingredients:

2lb/900g of a combination of white fish, mussels, salmon, smoked salmon, trout, smoked trout, prawns, crabmeat

1½ pints/900ml fish stock

1½ pints/900ml pints milk

1 onion, peeled and finely chopped

6oz/175g potatoes, peeled and finely chopped

1–2 tablespoons flour

2 sticks celery, cleaned and finely chopped

Salt and freshly ground black pepper

2oz/50g sweetcorn kernels

6 pink peppercorns

1 glass white wine

2 tablespoons single cream

1 teaspoon chopped fresh or freeze-dried tarragon

Method:

In a large saucepan, bring to the boil the fish stock, milk, onion, potatoes and celery. Simmer until the vegetables are just soft. Whisk in a tablespoon or two of flour to thicken the liquid. Season to taste, but go easy on the salt if you are using smoked fish. Add the peppercorns, sweetcorn, white wine and tarragon, bring back to the boil, then reduce to a simmer. Chop the fish into small pieces roughly the same size. If you are using a few mussels, clean thoroughly. Add the fish to the pan and simmer very gently for about 4 minutes until the mussel shells have opened and the fish is opaque. Add the cream, stir very gently so you don't break up the fish and serve with warm crusty brown bread.

day seven

Clare
Under the Burren

The caves of Clare contain many secrets. Not just the wondrous shapes created by the action of water on limestone, but the bones of animals—bears in abundance, wolves, foxes, Irish elks and Arctic lemmings. Most of the caves under the Burren are strictly for experienced potholers and speleologists. The approach is down a pot-hole or swallow hole and, when you get down there, streams run along narrow passages making progress wet and dangerous for any except the expert. Many fill with water when it rains. There is, however, one cave system which is open to the rest of us, and for me it was an introduction to a totally new underground world. This is the Stygian darkness of the Ailwee Cave, millions of years old. Here, down more than a mile of passages, with handrails to help you, lights to penetrate the blackness and show you the way and guides to both lead and explain what you are seeing, you can experience a world normally reserved for the very few.

Getting there

The Ailwee Cave is a couple of miles outside Ballyvaughan, off the N67. There are plenty of signposts. The access road winds up the hillside, and all you can see is Burren. As it winds round again, it opens out into a car park and nestling into the hillside is a semi-circular building so sensitively designed it blends into the background. The entrance to the cave is no longer down wet, dangerous crevices, but through the building.

The story of **Ailwee Cave** is a remarkable one. Millions of years ago, streams on Ailwee mountain sank underground, found the weakest parts of the limestone and began to dissolve it. Successive ice ages, alternating with warmer periods, began to form the caves we see today. As the climate

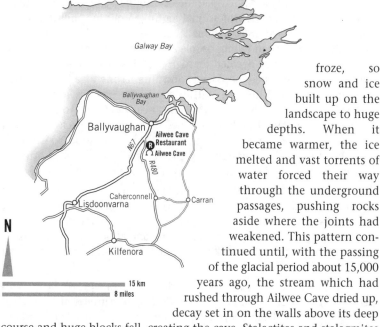

Galway Bay

Ballyvaughan Bay

Ballyvaughan

Ailwee Cave
Restaurant
Ailwee Cave

N67

R480

Caherconnell
Lisdoonvarna

Carran

N

Kilfenora

15 km

8 miles

froze, so snow and ice built up on the landscape to huge depths. When it became warmer, the ice melted and vast torrents of water forced their way through the underground passages, pushing rocks aside where the joints had weakened. This pattern continued until, with the passing of the glacial period about 15,000 years ago, the stream which had rushed through Ailwee Cave dried up, decay set in on the walls above its deep course and huge blocks fell, creating the cave. Stalactites and stalagmites started to form from crystals of dissolved limestone known as calcite, and the cave began to look as it does today. For thousands of years, its development proceeded unseen. The constant temperature in the cave, around 50°F/10°C, proved attractive to animals as a lair or refuge. Unlike some caves, man does not seem to have come near the place until very recently.

The story of how the cave was discovered is almost like something out of a Disney movie. In 1944 Jacko McGann, a native of Ballyvaughan, was out on the Burren with his dog. The animal suddenly disappeared into a small hole in the rock and the concerned Jacko followed him. As in all the best adventure stories, he happened to have a candle in his pocket. With the aid of its light, he gazed, presumably astonished, at what he saw. He explored much of the cave and had the good sense of history to leave his initials where they can be seen to this day at the base of the 'frozen' cascade. Nothing more happened until 1973, when a group of students from Bristol University touring the Burren were told by Jacko of the cave in Ailwee mountain. They in turn explored it as far as they could but a huge rock fall had more or less closed the cave after about 220 yards.

In 1975 serious work began to open the cave to the public and try and put the whole operation on a professional footing. A mining engineer, Roger Johnson, and his wife Susan bought the land from the local farmer. Although they had been telling people about the caves for years, nothing had happened, so they decided to open it themselves. Roger had a colleague who was an experienced caver and another friend, a local teacher, completed the initial line-up. Within a year the cave was open to the public, and the original tiny muddy entrance which had to be crawled through was enlarged by blasting. Since l976 intensive excavation and development has extended the tour deep into the hillside. In 1991, to make the tour circular, a passageway 230 yards long was blasted through the rock to form an exit tunnel, the only man-made section of the caves.

The tour inside the cave lasts for about half an hour and has to be taken with trained guides, for reasons which become obvious the minute you set foot in Ailwee. The journey takes you through caverns and chambers, the floors of which can be uneven and slippery, and at one point you cross a narrow bridge high up the rock face. Your journey under the earth is an extraordinary experience.

Not far inside the cave you can see the claw marks of a brown bear (*Ursus Arctos*), long extinct, whose bones were found here. Through the Mud hall with its knobbly stalagmites you come to what looks like a frozen waterfall, a petrified cascade of calcite that has spread over the rock face. Look up and around you as you go. Fine, straw-like stalactites hang from the ceiling. From the side walls, breathtaking growths reach to you: calcite-shaped like a wasp's nest, and of a size you would only expect to see in a horror movie. Elsewhere is a formation eerily resembling praying hands. Stalactites bunch together like pale, ghostly carrots. There is even a column which has been formed by a stalactite and stalagmite joining to link the floor to the ceiling. Easily the most spectacular sight in this strange world is the waterfall, which was created by diverting an underground stream. It cascades mightily down the rock face, occasionally sending a fine spray of water over spectators. The only way through this cavern is over a narrow bridge built in 1989 which hugs the rock face opposite the waterfall. The journey back to the real world through the exit tunnel is strange in itself. The tunnel is very long and straight and you are suddenly aware that 5000 tonnes of solid limestone were removed so you can walk here.

The visitors' centre has craft shops full of mineral specimens, crystals, fossils and various souvenirs. You can watch cheese being made in the dairy,

see honey dripping from combs in the apiary, while in the kitchen, fudge, chutney or jam is produced. There is also a dovecote, built in 1990 and full of fan-tailed pigeons. After all that, you really have to have lunch here, and that is no hardship.

Lunch at the Visitors' Centre, Ailwee Cave

Ailwee Cave (Tourist Amenity), Ballyvaughan, Co.Clare
© (065) 77036

Open 10am–5.30pm March–November. Prices are reasonable: IR£3.95 will buy you the soup of the day with brown bread and butter, smoked mackerel and salad and coffee.

The self-service restaurant is upstairs. It is semi-circular in shape and the walls are hung with pictures of the flowers of the Burren. The windows look out over Galway Bay, either glittering and blue with Connemara in the distance, or grey, misty and enclosed. The tables are dark wood and the smell of fresh bread draws you to the counter. The menu is simple and delicious, the produce local and fresh. The smoked trout and smoked salmon come from Lisdoonvarna, the free-range chicken is local, while the fresh crab comes up the coast from Doolin. The quiches Lorraine, seafood or vegetarian are baked in the Ailwee kitchens. Salads to choose from include green leaf, potato, bulgur wheat, tomato or coleslaw, crisp and tasting of cabbage and carrot, not salad cream. The salads are served with freshly made herb vinaigrette or mayonnaise which you help yourself to from little bowls on the counter. Home-made soup is served with their wonderful bread. The cheese in the ploughman's lunch is Burren Gold, made in the dairy from unpasteurized milk. It is a rich yellow cheese, a little like Gouda. You can have it plain, or flavoured with black pepper or chives and garlic. Home-made brown bread and pickles and a chunk of apple complete the dish. The one exception to this admirable home cooking is the whole honey-baked ham, which is baked locally by a man who Susan Johnson resignedly admits can simply bake it better than anyone else she knows. Dotted with cloves and crisp and crunchy on the top, it is pink and succulent inside. There is just one hot dish on the menu, and that is Guinness stew—beef marinated in Guinness, then simmered slowly in the oven with carrots and onions. It is served with jacket potatoes and, of course, their own brown bread.

The coffee is fresh and smells it. Instead of pudding, try a creamy cake or a little gingerbread, which has to be quite the stickiest I can remember. If you feel like a drink, they do have a licence for wine. If the weather is fine, take your coffee out onto the terrace, enjoy the views and lose yourself in the tranquillity.

After lunch, take the gentle climb above and beyond the cave itself so that you walk over what you have just walked under. Climb as high up the hillside as you can, though watch your footing on the grykes. The views from here over Galway Bay are stunning. You may also find flowers here that you have not see before. No part of the Burren is exactly like any other. When you leave Ailwee, shortly after you rejoin the main road, you will see signs for 'An Rath'. It is an earthen ring **fort**, very rare here because of the thin soil covering and well worth seeing. Climb over a stile and the fort is a short distance away past the trees.

There is one other feature of the Burren you really must see before you leave the area, one which could not exist without those underground caves and tunnels. Over the centuries it has added to the mystery of the place. *Turloughs*, or disappearing lakes, can spread over many acres or be quite small. Some have a permanent show of water, others can be grassy hollows in the hillside until heavy rainfall fills them with water, and then, mysteriously, after a matter of hours (depending on their size) they empty again. What actually happens is that the underground passages through the rock under the *turloughs* overflow with water in wet weather and then they drain when it is dry. One of the best *turloughs* is near the little village of Carran. Drive south down the R480 until shortly after Poulnabrone, where you will see a left turn for Carran. It is a narrow, twisty road. When you get to the small cluster of houses, look behind them and there, in a little valley, is a lake, or should I say there *might* be a lake. This is the **Carran Depression**. In winter it is a wide lake eight feet deep, in a hot dry summer it is a stretch of reed-covered earth with a little pool of water in the middle.

About a mile and a half south of Carran is the stone fort of **Cahercommaun**. It is, from all accounts, an extraordinary and majestic place, perched on the edge of a ravine and not visible from the road. It is a National Monument but at the moment there is no public access to it, though hopefully that may change; the Burren Centre at Kilfenora should be able to advise you. The Burren landscape round here, however, is breathtaking, and more than a little compensation for not being able to see Cahercommaun. Drive round the Carran Depression and continue through the limestone hills until you find a parking place off the road. This is some of the wildest, most beautiful Burren scenery. The stones you walk over are carved into strange patterns by wind and water and the views over valleys and onto the next limestone-clad mountain are quite spectacular.

As you drive back towards Carran and then to Ballyvaughan, with the dipping sun again turning the limestone into a magical wonderland, or, if it is raining, into a landscape almost primeval in its grey desolation, you are keenly aware that this is an extraordinary place in every sense. These wonders of the Burren, however, are just a beginning. Next (*see* Day Eight) we leave Clare for Galway and what I believe to be the most beautiful place imaginable, Connemara.

Sticky Gingerbread
from Ailwee Cave Visitors' Centre

Ingredients: *Makes approx. 24 slices*

8oz/225g margarine
8oz/225g brown sugar
8oz/225g golden syrup
1 pint/½ litre water
1½lbs/700g plain flour

2½ teaspoons bicarbonate of soda

2½ teaspoons baking powder

2½ teaspoons ground ginger

2 eggs

Method:

In a large heavy-based saucepan melt together the margarine, sugar, golden syrup and water over a gentle heat. Remove from the heat and allow to cool. Mix together the flour, bicarbonate of soda, baking powder and ginger in a large bowl. In another bowl, beat the eggs together and then add them to the syrupy mixture a little at a time. Add the dry ingredients gradually, stirring all the time, and mix together until everything has been combined and the mixture is smooth, thick and rich.

Pour into a greased baking tray, about 30cm by 23cm. Bake in a preheated oven, 375°F, 190°C, gas mark 5, for about 30 minutes or until firm to the touch. Remove from the tin, allow to cool and cut into slices.

day eight

Galway/Connemara
From Clare to Clifden

Today is as much for the soul and the heart as for the eyes. From the wonders of the Burren we head for Galway and Connemara. It is by a long shot my favourite place, not just in Ireland but in the world. Beware, therefore, of my superlatives. I will do my best to be even-handed but, having been brought up in rural Ireland, the delights of Connemara where many of my childhood holidays were spent are still vivid memories, topped up in recent years by eagerly awaited return visits. I have lost count of the number of friends I have kept up until late—or even early—hours urging them with all my available powers to make Connemara a must in any Irish holiday.

The route takes you from Ballyvaughan to Kinvara, with its memories of the poet William Butler Yeats and the marvellous Lady Gregory. Then on to Kilcolgan and Clarinbridge for lunch and some of the best oysters you will find anywhere. By-passing Galway city, drive through Oughterard, Maam Cross and Recess and so to Clifden in the heart of Connemara.

Getting there

From Ballyvaughan to Clifden is a distance of around 140 miles. A word of warning: don't rush and don't expect to cover these miles as if you were on a motorway. The whole point of being in the west of Ireland is that there are no motorways. There are excellent roads: indeed the popular notion that every road outside the main cities is really only a sophisticated dirt-track is long gone, but in the west the roads are still basically single carriageways and, as I have known to my cost, if you're unlucky a journey of 30 miles that should take the same number of minutes can be doubled.

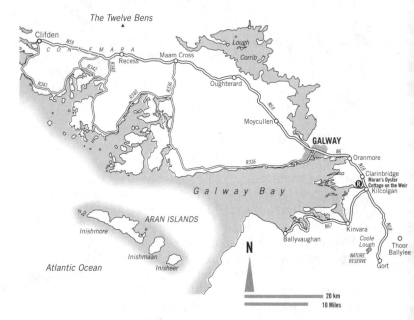

If the weather is fine and the day clear as you leave Ballyvaughan and head towards Kinvara, there are fantastic views towards southern Galway and further left to Connemara, while far out in Galway Bay are the shadowy humps of the Aran Islands. Clare is now behind you. This is County Galway.

Kinvara is a pretty fishing village with a splendidly restored 16th-century castle, which puts on medieval banquets, accompanied by readings from Irish literature. It was near Kinvara that William Butler Yeats met **Lady Gregory** in 1897 while he was on a tour of Gort and Connemara. She was a young widow, small, apparently nice-looking but not beautiful, with a first-class mind and a great desire to nurture and promote Irish literature and culture. He was dark, intense and passionately in love with someone else. But such was their instant rapport that at that first meeting the idea was born for the Irish Literary Theatre which subsequently became the famous Abbey Theatre in Dublin. Isabella Augusta Gregory, known as Augusta, lived at Coole near Kinvara in a Georgian mansion. Here, and in the tranquil grounds with their Seven Woods and the lake where he first saw the 'nine and fifty swans', Yeats found the peace necessary to write. When he was ill or depressed, he would come here. Lady Gregory organized his life, not interfering but ensuring he ate when necessary, being there when he needed to talk and making sure no one interrupted when he wanted solitude. Later Yeats wrote: 'I cannot realize the world without her. She had been to me mother, friend, sister and brother. She brought to my wavering thoughts steadfast nobility—all night the thought of losing her is a conflagration in the rafters.'

Over the years, the money she freely loaned him meant he could concentrate on his writing and did not have to worry about paid employment. It is arguable that without her the Nobel Prize for Literature which he was awarded in 1923 simply could not have happened.

In her own right, though, she was formidable. She was born into a comfortable but not particularly intellectual family at Roxborough House, about 10 miles from Coole, and at 27 had married a man much older than herself, a retired Colonial civil servant who had spent most of his working life in India. Following his death, she inherited considerable wealth. If that chance meeting with Yeats had not taken place, I often wonder how the Irish literary revival would have developed, because Lady G (as everyone who knew her referred to her) had, even before she met Yeats, taught herself Irish, collected Irish folklore and stories from the neighbourhood and written poems, plays and short stories. In 1909 she published her *Seven Short Plays* (Maunsel & Co. Ltd, Dublin) with this Dedication: 'To you, W.B. Yeats, good praiser, wholesome dispraiser, heavy-handed judge, open-handed helper of us all, I offer a play of my plays for every night of the week, because you like them, and because you have taught me my trade.'

At Coole she created a literary salon with the writers who were at the heart of the Irish literary renaissance, which began towards the latter half of the 19th century and continues to flourish to this day. It is something of which the Irish are justly proud. George Bernard Shaw, J.M. Synge, Sean O'Casey, John Masefield and the painter Augustus John came here as well as Yeats. It was a literary salon in quite exquisite surroundings and is seared into every Irish school-boy's education. Today it can become part of your adventure. I have left it until now to tell you that Yeats's great sanctuary was pulled down in 1941 for its valuable stone. Not the worst, but certainly not the finest moment in Irish rural redevelopment. Yeats himself tells us a little of what it was like:

> *Beloved books that famous hands have bound,*
> *Old marble heads, old pictures everywhere;*
> *great rooms where travelled men and children found*
> *Content or joy...*

Coole Park and Ballylee, 1931.

65

One of those children was Lady Gregory's grand-daughter Anne, who in her delightful memoir called *Me and Nu: Childhood at Coole* (published by Colin Smythe Ltd, Gerrards Cross 1990) describes the drawing room as '...a lovely big room. It had an enormous big bay, the whole width of the room, with three separate great windows reaching from floor to ceiling. Grandma's desk was in the middle, out in front of the centre window, and in the window was a large white marble figure of Andromeda as large as life, sitting on a great marble rock. Sometimes if we lay on the floor in front of Grandma when she was writing, and got in exactly the right place, it looked as though Grandma had two heads—her own and a white marble one growing out of the top of hers...'

All that remains of the house now is a low grassy platform, a mute indictment of those who allowed its destruction.

Happily the surrounding parkland has been much restored and is now a wildlife park, open to all, so at least something of the glorious place has been preserved. The avenue of huge holly trees that led up to the house still stands and so does something of real historical, literary and cultural interest: the so-called 'autograph tree', a vast, spreading copper beech upon which Lady Gregory's famous guests cut their initials over the years. The tree is protected now by eight-foot-high iron railings to stop a practice prevalent when I first went there, of every 'ordinary' visitor adding their name to the overcrowded bark. A little diagram by the tree shows you where the most famous signatures are, and what they look like. Most are still perfectly distinguishable: A.E. (George Russell the painter), Sean O'Casey, W.B.Y. and G.B.S. You will not of course be able to see my attempt at carving H.F.K. there, but I assure you that in 1956, when a mere babe of 10 years armed with a pocket-knife I had been given for my birthday, I did indeed violate the sacred bark!

About a mile from where the house used to stand is Coole Lough, of which Yeats wrote that he knew 'the edges of that lake better than any

spot on earth...' Stand where Yeats did when he saw the great birds that inspired the poem, 'The Wild Swans At Coole'. If the Burren already feels far behind you, Coole Lough will bring it back. It is a *turlough*, though one that always has some water in it. The water level rises and falls depending on the time of the year. My parents told me that when they came here for their first holiday after the Second World War in 1945 they had the delight of seeing the lake go from almost empty to brimming in a matter of weeks.

When you leave Kinvara, digress a little and head south towards Gort. Just before you get to Gort you will see the signs for **Thoor Ballylee**. It is a tower house which Yeats bought for IR£35 just after the Dublin Easter Rising of l916 and with still two years to go of the Great War. It was to be a spiritual and peaceful place for him—a haven from the dangers of the new emerging Free State in the 1920s when Yeats, by then a Senator in the new Irish Parliament, had to have a bodyguard. A Norman keep originally, Yeats restored it for his wife and two children, and to this day it remains an extraordinarily tranquil place, quite remote, with water lapping around it. Many of Yeats's last poems were written here including 'The Tower' and 'The Winding Stair'. He lived there until 1929. It has since been restored again, and you can climb the winding stair, up through the dining room, drawing room and bedroom to the battlements for an inspirational view over the countryside. There is an excellent and witty audio-visual presentation by the Yeats scholar Augustine Martin, a well-stocked bookshop and a tearoom. It is well worth a diversion on your way to lunch.

Leaving Thoor Ballylee, ignore the signs for Loughrea and take the N18 north towards Kilcolgan and Clarinbridge, where lunch in one of the best pubs in the west of Ireland awaits.

Lunch at Moran's Oyster Cottage on the Weir

Moran's Oyster Cottage, The Weir, Kilcolgan, Co.Galway
℗ *(091) 796113*

Open for lunch and supper all year. Even if you eat a lot, the bill for food is unlikely to be more than IR£15, and you can eat very well for considerably less.

The sign for Moran's Oyster Cottage on The Weir comes just as you leave Kilcolgan for Clarinbridge. It is very easy to miss it so be prepared to turn round and drive back again! Everyone refers to Moran's of Clarinbridge but, confusingly, it is actually Moran's of Kilcolgan, though it is mid-way between the two places. The pub has been famous for its oysters since it was founded in 1760 and, if you drive too far and enter Clarinbridge, you will see the signs proclaiming that Clarinbridge is 'The Home of the Oyster'. Who says the Irish exaggerate? But the area is bliss for crustacean-lovers. When you have found the signpost for Moran's, turn left and follow the road round for about a mile until it widens with the pub on your right and the water to your left.

Last time I went to Moran's it was just eleven o'clock in the morning on New Year's Eve. I was not even sure the pub was open. It was, just. We were warmly welcomed by a few members of staff who were busy putting finishing touches to the night's preparations, when they were expecting around 90 revellers for dinner. We asked for oysters. No trouble and what would you like with them, Guinness? Coming up. Our six-year-old opted for a toasted cheese sandwich which he declared quite delicious. The oysters were served with bread that was still warm from the oven. This was not the day for sitting outside Moran's and enjoying the weir and the lapping waters across the road, but in summer the place is alive and there is nowhere better for lunch.

Moran's is a truly great Irish pub: full of good food and drink and conversation that does not end until the last person leaves. Even the fixtures and fittings ensure you are entertained. My own favourite is a poem by a Moran's devotee that has been neatly framed and hung on the wall:

> *There is no better oyster than one eats in Moran's bar*
> *And people always come back here from foreign lands afar*
> *Their oysters are tremendous and their other shellfish too*
> *But try some Irish coffee which can do such good for you.*
> *Then after all these oysters and whiskies you drink here*
> *You also might see mermaids gently swimming in the weir!*

You can have lunch either in the little bar with its wooden tables and benches and view over the weir, or in the dining room with its checked tablecloths. It is all too easy to be persuaded away from your good intentions of a one-course lunch. As the poet said, their oysters are tremendous and their other shellfish too. The prawns are big and meaty and complemented by a creamy sauce. The seafood cocktail has identifiable lumps of crab, prawn and whatever else came in with the day's catch, while the garlic mussels are stuffed with a wonderful garlicky, bread-crumby stuffing. Other starters include seafood chowder, egg mayonnaise and fresh, creamy vegetable soup. Delectable local oysters (IR£9.50 a dozen) await you between

September and April; the rest of the year Gigas oysters (IR£8 a dozen) are on offer, also locally grown and jolly good.

To follow, if you love seafood, you must try the seafood special, a marvellous platter of smoked salmon, crab, prawns and crab claws, served with home-made brown bread. Alternatively, there is a plate of wild smoked salmon on its own, or with prawns or crab. Or you can just have the very good local crab, served with brown bread. And after all that, if you would still rather have a sandwich, well, you can have a plate of those too. Puddings are simple and fresh—apple pie, cheesecake or home-made ice cream. If you are not driving, Moran's serves some of the best Irish coffee in the business.

Incidentally, every town in Ireland that produces or sells oysters boasts that theirs are the best, but in Galway, and around Kilcolgan and Clarinbridge especially, the combination of waters, a mixture of fresh and salt, gives the oyster a fine texture and a special taste. While my own personal choice of oyster haven has always been Moran's, I should tell you that in the main street in Clarinbridge the equally famous Paddy Burke's pub has excellent food and drink, and is the focal point for the September Oyster Festival which attracts visitors from around the world. When I was a young reporter on the *Irish Times*, I was once sent there to cover the 'celebrity' opening. Mercifully I was advised by an old colleague to write and send my report *before* I started on the oysters or Guinness. Happily I did, as it was another four days before I arrived home!

After lunch and a final look at the weir, drive back to the main road, turn left and head towards Galway city. The road will take you through Oranmore and round the bay towards the city. What you are looking for though are signs for the by-pass, not the city centre, and keep heading for wherever it says Clifden.

Once you are round Galway city, the N59 will take you past the shores of Lough Corrib. The views are spectacular—little tree-clad islands and a huge expanse of sparkling blue water. The road continues through Moycullen, and on to Oughterard. Here a strange thing happens. The town itself is pleasant and bustling. You drive westwards out of it through pretty, tree-lined streets with a small bridge over a gently flowing river.

Almost immediately, as you leave Oughterard, you begin to enter **Connemara** proper. The landscape changes from gentle green. Up on the hillsides, in places, you can see a pattern of walls, the last remains of land that was once farmed. Little loughs dot the landscape, there are patches of trees and quite a lot of afforestation. Piles of cut turf are heaped along the roadside.

Through Maam Cross, the loughs are close by the road, many covered with waterlilies throughout the summer months. On now to Recess and ahead of you the misty Twelve Bens, the famed mountains of Connemara.

This is the last leg of your journey to Clifden and you are about to enter a truly magical place. You have reached the land of bog and bare mountain, of wild sea-shores where man has lived, fished and hunted for thousands of years. Alcock and Brown landed here after their historic trans-Atlantic voyage. Every summer horse traders from all over Ireland and Britain and western Europe arrive here for the Connemara Pony Show, and here, if you are lucky, as you drive along Clifden's glorious Sky Road, you may spot a porpoise in the bay.

You are entering a huge nature reserve, the beauty of which can reduce even the Irish to silence. And as a bonus, there is great food, first-class hotels, the best of drink and laughter that the west can offer you, and people whose ancestors fished and farmed, who know how to enjoy themselves and make every visitor feel special and welcome.

As I write I envy the people who are entering Clifden and Connemara for the first time.

Garlic Mussels
from Moran's Oyster Cottage on the Weir

Many large supermarkets now sell fresh mussels ready-cleaned, which saves you scrubbing off the 'beards' and so on. Of course, if you buy from a fishmonger, you may still have to do some work! But even if you buy ready-cleaned mussels, it is still sensible to check them.

Put them into a bowl of cold water and make sure there are no cracked shells, or any mussels that are open. If the shells are loose, tap them lightly. If they do not close at once or they are open, throw them and the cracked mussels away. It is not worth taking any risks.

Ingredients:

Approx. 2 dozen mussels

For the stuffing:

8oz/225g fresh breadcrumbs

8oz/225g butter, softened

1–2 cloves garlic

A little salt and freshly ground black pepper

1 teaspoon Pernod

2 teaspoons mixed herbs

A handful of fresh chopped parsley

Method:

Put the mussels into a large saucepan and just cover them with water. Bring to the boil, put the lid on and cook over a fierce heat for about 5 minutes, shaking the pan occasionally. When the mussels are open, they are ready. Drain them and put to one side. To make the stuffing, crush the garlic and stir together with all the stuffing ingredients in a large bowl until thoroughly mixed. Pre-heat the grill to maximum. Take off the empty half of the mussel shells and throw away. Carefully spread a layer of the stuffing over each mussel, and if you like, dot with a little butter. Put the stuffed mussels under the hot grill for about 4 minutes until the coating is brown and crispy, but be careful not to burn them. Sprinkle with a little fresh parsley and serve immediately.

Galway/Connemara
Clifden and Environs

I am about to take you where my own heart lies and where you will, I have no doubt, lose yours. Connemara has been visited over the centuries by the famous and the ordinary, by poets and landowners, by the rich and the poor. It also draws to itself the Irish and those who would like to be, and Irish men and women who have gone from this desolate place but who can never pass a day, whether in Manhattan, Manchester or Madrid, without momentarily yearning for the peace they have left behind. Writers and poets over the ages have sung and written of Connemara. Botanists and those seeking to wander among bogs and grasslands collecting wild flowers and the flotsam and jetsam thrown

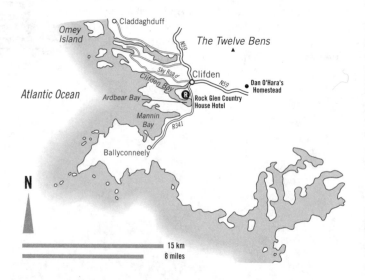

up by the Atlantic Ocean have come here on holiday and simply stayed, settling down and becoming probably more Irish than they had ever intended.

Make your first day one of gentle contrasts. Start with a wander round Clifden itself, then visit a heartbreakingly historically accurate heritage centre, where there is also a newly discovered prehistoric site. Just a short drive from Clifden along fuchsia-lined roads, there are long, golden, empty beaches or strands (*tra* is the Irish word for beach or strand and you will see it on signposts all over Connemara)— Mannin, Clifden or the Coral Strand are quite near the town, but I suggest you go a little further to the quarter of a mile stretch of sand, visible only at low tide, that divides the island of Omey from the mainland. Before you go, make sure, however, that the tide will be out. When you return at sunset to Clifden, drive up the wonderfully named Sky Road until the sea and the land are spread shimmeringly below you. And, as an added bonus, there is what in Irish is called *nua gac bia agus sean gach di*, which roughly translates as the very best of new food and old drink.

Getting there

The main road from Galway, the N59, leads directly into Clifden and then continues out the other side northwards to Mayo. We made the town the centre of our stay here, for all of Connemara is within easy reach of it.

Here in Connemara you can taste several seasons in one day as first the sun sparkles over sea and lakes, and then a sea-mist or light rain wanders in from the Atlantic like a spirit come to see what is going on, lingers for perhaps 20 minutes or so and then moves gently on, leaving the land glittering again under the returned sun. Here too, as you drive along, you will see the occasional turf cutter at work. Not so very long ago he would carry the turf home on a donkey, the reed baskets slung on either side fully loaded with fuel for the winter. Now he is more likely to use a tractor, though occasionally donkey transport can still be seen. Some of the most memorable conversations I have ever had have been at the side of a bog road, talking—sometimes in Irish since there are a few folk left here to whom English is a second language—about the day, the turf, the sheep and cattle that roam the hills, the tourist season, Irish politics, American politics, English cricket, the troubles of the European Community and much besides. The tradition of learning and education in rural Ireland goes very deep.

Clifden is the largest town in Connemara, and its unofficial capital. It is pretty nearly surrounded by small mountains except to the west where it is open to the sea, the reason Clifden was built in the first place. It was founded by a local landlord, John D'Arcy, in about 1812, the torch being carried on through the l9th century by his son, who rejoiced in the name of Hyacinth. Its Irish name is *an Clochan*, or stepping-stones. The port was deep enough for ships of 200 tons, and its major trade was the export of corn, which continued even while the population of Connemara was dying of starvation in the potato famines of the 1840s. Like many landlords in the west, D'Arcy was dependent for his income on rents from his tenants. Those rents ceased because of the famine and by 1850 D'Arcy, who had worked so hard to try to help his devastated people, was bankrupt and forced to sell the estate. He then entered the church and became rector of Omey until his death in 1874.

With the coming of the railways, the importance of the port declined, but by 1935 the railway too had had its day and the line was dug up and sold for scrap. Clifden today thrives on its tourist and service industries and, in place of sea-traders, there are now sea-anglers and dinghy sailors. Tourism

Clifden

has its price, and parking in the town in the high season is a nightmare. A few years ago, much against local feeling, a one-way traffic system was introduced which just means that an increasing number of cars go round in circles rather than straight lines, and since every now and then you come across a local who has unilaterally opted not to join the system, it can be quite hilarious. Unless you are actually staying in Clifden, take a taxi, or ask your hotel or guest house to give you a lift and call back for you later.

Dominating the skyline as you enter the town are Clifden's own twin peaks—the two churches, one Catholic, one Protestant. The Catholic church with its superb rose windows was built in 1830. The Protestant church, built 10 years earlier, is a simpler affair at the other end of town and has a copy of the historic Irish Cross of Cong. There is a monument to founder D'Arcy in the town, excellent shops, art galleries and, when I last counted, nearly 20 pubs! If you have had a successful day fishing, your landlady or chef wherever you are staying will surely not mind if you bring your catch back for them to cook for your supper. Be warned though: they may well have an even finer fish already on the menu. A few minutes walk from the centre of town is the Owenglen Cascade, where you may see salmon leaping. In the 30 years since I started coming to Clifden, I have seen their numbers dwindle from dozens to a very few, but you may be lucky.

About three miles outside Clifden, on the Galway road, is the **Dan O'Hara Homestead and Heritage Centre**. It is a pre-1840 farm, lovingly and painstakingly restored. The census figures for 1841 suggest that the population of the whole of Ireland was just over 8 million, divided almost perfectly between men and women. With the dreadful potato famines that started in 1845 and were to continue on and off in various harrowing degrees for 20 years, together with evictions by absentee landlords, the population through death and emigration to North America was effectively halved. In addition, the bald statistics of official emigration do not take account of voluntary passage away from famine of those who still had strength and the money to leave of their own accord; nor of the population shift which saw Connemara people and particularly those from Mayo and Donegal drift towards Dublin and over to Liverpool in search of a better life. The Heritage Centre should be the first stop on your Connemara journey, because nothing will better put the area into context.

The centre is in three parts. Park in the main car park and start your exploration back towards the entrance at the *crannog*, a pre-historic lake dwelling. This circular, close-thatched reconstruction is perfect, showing us how, thousands of years ago, the families who occupied these lands built their homes on make-shift stilts in water, with portable and retractable bridges to the land. Thus, once safely at home after a day's hunting, the family was almost impregnable from raiders or the wild animals which roamed the countryside. Walk across the little wooden bridge and go inside the *crannog*. It is surprisingly large, with a turf fire burning in the middle. Although some smoke escapes, for modern man the smoke that remains inside is too oppressive to cope with for more than a few moments and you wonder how the lungs and eyes of those *crannog*-dwellers fared.

The homestead itself is reached by a path that climbs up the hillside, and it is named after the famous and moving ballad of Dan O'Hara. He, so the story goes, was once a tenant farmer, perhaps more prosperous than most (though that word is relative in Connemara). He worked the land with his family, growing potatoes and other vegetables, with a few chickens, a pig, perhaps a cow and a goat or two, and a horse. As long as the rent was paid in full and on time, there was no trouble from the landlord—probably an absentee living in England. The land was good, and potato blight was a horror to come. Dan O'Hara's downfall was not the failure of the potato crop, but his own success. The cottage, according to legend, was very dark, and he wanted to enlarge the windows and glaze them. But no sooner was this done, than the landlord demanded an increase in rent for the improvements. O'Hara could not afford to pay, and he, his wife and their seven children were summarily evicted.

The family, so the ballad continues, took passage to America, but during the voyage his wife and three of his children perished. The surviving children were put into homes when they arrived in America, and Dan himself was left alone and ill, a hopeless, broken man selling matches on the streets of New York and praying for death to let him rejoin his wife and family. This may be a ballad, but the tragic story of Dan O'Hara was reflected many times over in the lives of thousands of people who suffered so gravely. We sat in the little cottage one morning, looking out of those glazed windows across the ridges that marked where the potato fields had been and listened to a soft-spoken man recounting the story of the cottage, the surrounding farm and the trials and eventual fall of the O'Hara family. He then sang a few verses from the 'Ballad of Dan O'Hara' and there was no one in that little room who remained dry-eyed as his lilting voice pleaded, on behalf of the match-selling west of Ireland émigré:

A cushla geal mo chroi
Won't you buy a box from me
And you'll have the prayers of Dan from Connemara?
I'll sell them cheap and low
Buy a box before you go
From the broken-hearted farmer Dan O'Hara.

The words '*a cushla geal mo chroi*' pronounced as '*a kushla gal mo cree*' roughly translate from the Irish as 'dear man/woman/loved person, hope of my heart'.

Inside the cottage you marvel at how a family of seven, in some cases even 10 or 11, lived and slept and ate. Preserved here and restored are the small items of furniture which would have been in everyday use 150 years ago. In the living room is a simple, wooden dresser, a sure sign of prosperity. Under the window is a small table, and there are a couple of chairs and a stool. A pot and a kettle are by the fire. The older children slept in a curtained alcove in this room, while the babies slept with their parents in the bedroom next door. Tiny outhouses show where perhaps a few chickens, goats or sheep would have been kept, and there are some for you to see today, alive and noisy. On a bend in the track leading to the cottage is a sty, which has a large, grunting occupant, and next to it a rough stable in which a very patient horse resignedly submits to the tentative pats of children. The farmer might also have had a donkey, for turf-gathering from the bogs around.

Above and beyond Dan O'Hara's cottage, a Neolithic grave site around 4000 years old has been discovered. One tomb so far has been uncovered and it is thought there are several more. When archaeologists are working there the site is marked out with white lines, white tape and small flags of different colours, causing our six-year-old to exclaim: 'Look, a prehistoric golf course!'

The views as you walk back down to your car from here are wonderful: a rolling green landscape set with countless tiny loughs, with misty blue hills in the far distance. Go back into Clifden and head north on the Westport road (N59) for about six miles or so until you come to a junction with signs for Claddaghduff. Here you turn left for Omey and continue until you come to a large grey church, which is Claddaghduff church. Turn sharp left and the road goes straight down to the strand with **Omey** *opposite. When the tide is out you can drive from the mainland across the sands. The firmest path is marked by poles and there is a narrow road on the island itself. You must check the times of the tides or you may be stranded on the island.*

My personal preference is to park and walk across to the island. The quarter of a mile of sand is firm and golden, broken here and there by little miniature mountains of rock formations containing tiny warm pools of Atlantic water with crustaceans clinging to their sides and with seaweed and a huge variety of plant and miniature fish life just below the surface. The walk across can take ten minutes at a brisk pace but the last time I went it took a good hour, so fascinating were the sights on the way. The strand is vast, spotless and safe (provided the tide is not on the turn) and a wonderland for children. Ours was totally absorbed by the 'tiny swimming pools' as he called them and the prospects that we might catch some form of fish.

Across on the island the graveyard is the first thing you come to. It is right on the shore and has an eerie fascination. This is a place not only for the dead of the few resident families who to this day occupy Omey, but also for the whole area, the funeral cortege driving across the sand at low tide from the mainland. The tall Celtic cross marks the grave of mackerel fishermen who drowned in the local tragedy known as the Cleggan Disaster on 27th October 1927. Of the four boats that went out from the little village of Rossadillisk in Cleggan Bay that night, three were overwhelmed by a sudden storm and sixteen men died. Their names are engraved on the cross. As with so many other graveyards in Ireland, you can find here gravestones of men and women with addresses in the United States, Canada and Great Britain, brought home to be buried on the island they or their ancestors left under the twin pressures of unemployment and the desire to see another world.

The few who still live on this fertile, tranquil island farm the land. About 7000 years ago it had a thriving population. One of the oldest artefacts unearthed in the west of Ireland was found here a couple of years ago, a ceremonial battle axe. There are also kitchen middens here, where Neolithic man dumped his kitchen waste, and an extensive Bronze Age settlement.

You could easily spend a day or more on Omey and, if you get one of those wonderful, warm, sunny Connemara afternoons with a gentle breeze and not a cloud in a clear blue sky, you really will not want to leave. Whether you walk or drive, stick to the island's only road for your explorations. There are no signposts on the island to guide you to the prehistoric sites or indeed to the remains of a 14th-century church buried in the sand; either take a large-scale map with sites clearly marked and a lot of determination and patience, or contact Connemara Walking Tours at the Island House in Clifden where *the* archaeologist of the region, Michael Gibbons, organizes archaeological walks and tours, not just to Omey but all over Connemara. If you are here simply for peace and beauty, then wander at your leisure. Some of the fields are fenced off, but there is still plenty of empty, open and flower-filled space. And if you have the time, walk some way round the island on the sand. I have never seen so many varieties of seaweed and there are countless different shells.

When you get back to Clifden, if it is a fine summer's evening, do what everyone else does: sit outside one of the many pubs with a drink, and watch the world wander by, the bikers from every country imaginable, the buses with their students, individual travellers like yourself taking time in Connemara to stand and stare. But before the sun finally disappears, there is one more delight for you, a visit to the **Sky Road** just outside Clifden. To get to the Sky Road you simply follow the signs at the west end of the town. The road winds steeply upwards, lined with bushes of delicate fuchsias. This journey is tough on the driver, not because the road is particularly difficult, but because the views are so breathtaking that his (or her) passengers are continually urging him to 'look at that', when he cannot! There are a few houses on the way; one, now painted white, is still known to generations of natives and tourists as the Pink House, which once, many years ago, it was. Below the road on the hillside is a large red building, once the old coastguard station, now apartments.

Just when you think the road cannot possibly go any higher, it widens out, inviting you to stop. Behind you the hillside is covered in brilliant yellow gorse and deep purple heather. Before you and below you is the vast Atlantic Ocean, stretching away to America in the west, breaking round islets and flooding into the inlets of Ireland. The setting sun catches the rocks, the hills and maybe the occasional fishing boat nosing in or out of the bay. A glint of gold betrays the buoys marking lobster pots some 15 fathoms deep and another shaft of light illuminates a tiny strip of sand from a beach on the other side of your vantage point. If the day has been warm, you may be able to spot porpoises in the bay, chasing a shoal of fish. As the sun sets, the colours turn from pink and gold to a silvery, shimmering, misty grey. Great stuff, that of which dreams and memories are made. Wordsworth believed that nature never did 'betray that heart that believed in her'. In Connemara, on the Sky Road, drink deep of nature: the memory will reward you when you need to fashion some moments of tranquillity in a hurly-burly life.

Dinner at the Rock Glen Country House Hotel, Clifden

The Rock Glen Hotel, Clifden, Connemara, Co.Galway
℡ (095) 21035

Open daily for lunch and dinner April–October. Set dinner: IR£22.

Tonight your dinner is in a hotel so relaxing, peaceful and with such good company, food and drink that there is a selfish part of me reluctant to share it with anyone else.

The Rock Glen is a converted 19th-century shooting lodge, built in 1815 for John D'Arcy, the founder of Clifden. It is just a mile and a half from the town, on the Roundstone road. John and Evangeline Roche created this wonderful haven more than 20 years ago. Their daughter Siobhan now runs the restaurant, son John runs the bar and their younger daughter Roisin makes up the family team. The house is set between the Twelve Bens and Ardbear Bay, with just a gentle stroll down to the water's edge.

It is more like a country house than a hotel, with deep comfortable sofas, open turf fires and friendly and efficient staff. One of life's greatest pleasures is to sit in the conservatory overlooking the bay, glass in hand, a dish of golden brown home-made potato crisps in front of you, and the menu. John Roche runs the kitchen, using the best local ingredients—lobster, oysters, prawns, wild salmon fresh and locally smoked, trout, Connemara lamb, pink and tender, free-range chickens, local cheese.

The dining room is comfortable and traditional—soft reds and white, a big chandelier, lots of mirrors. The tables, covered in crisp linen, are nicely spaced and those by the windows are much coveted. In summer the day is reluctant to leave. It is not until about 9.30 in the evening that the hills across the bay turn blue, then purple then grey, and then they are gone.

The *table d'hôte* menu with its choice of six dishes for each course changes daily, or you can choose from the *à la carte*. Oysters are served *au naturel*, on crushed ice, or perhaps lightly grilled on spinach and gratinated with a white wine butter sauce. The oak-smoked Connemara salmon has a deliciously robust flavour, while the traditional avocado pear and crabmeat salad is transported by the sweet, delicate flavour of the local crab. Chicken liver paté with garlic toast is smooth and well-flavoured, while for vegetarians the deep-fried slice of Brie wrapped in filo pastry on a bed of lettuce and served with hot Cumberland sauce is a lovely combination of flavours.

To follow there is a choice of soups or sorbets: rich beef consommé with sherry, creamy celery and Stilton soup or refreshing chilled tomato and cucumber soup, or you may prefer an orange and mango sorbet (probably the most sensible decision, as the portions here are not small). For a main course, the black sole fillets with a light wholegrain mustard sauce are wonderful, the firm, well-flavoured fish complemented by the bite of mustard. The roast sirloin of beef with a light Burgundy *jus* is served as rare—or otherwise—as you like it. Sautéed pigeon breasts with a redcurrant *jus* are nice and gamey. John Roche's *jus*, by the way, has a wonderful depth of flavour. There is roast rack of lamb with rosemary and mint, or loin of veal grilled with fresh asparagus and Emmental cheese, served with a red wine *jus*. The wild Atlantic salmon with lemon butter is as tender and succulent as I have ever had it, while the raywing with brown butter and capers is a delicious French dish, classically presented and cooked.

The puddings are of the 'you only live once' variety—blueberry crème brûlée, open apple tart with vanilla ice cream *and* cream, perhaps bread and butter pudding with an apricot glaze, or a light pastry tulip filled with home-made ice cream and toffee sauce. Wonderful. There is also a selection of Irish cheeses, served with apples, celery and grapes. The service is friendly and helpful and children are welcomed.

You can help yourself to coffee in the drawing room; it is laid out on a table and constantly replenished. Or, and this is what makes the Rock Glen so very special, do what many of the guests do and order your coffee—Irish of course—in the bar. There in front of the fire, as the evening turns to night, the singing is likely to start. You will probably be among businessmen, politicians, lawyers, all pillars of society and different nationalities, but as the first note is struck on the piano, someone will start to sing—'The Ballad of Dan O'Hara', 'Are You Right There Michael', 'Slattery's Mounted Foot', 'Danny Boy'. And everyone joins in. It is a spontaneous happening; if you tried to force it, it just would not work, but this, as they say in Ireland, is great 'crack', which translates as fun, a great laugh, a great time—you get the drift. Perhaps it is something John Roche adds to the soup, but I think it is simply that the place puts you so at ease that pretty well anything can happen.

Loin of Veal with Asparagus and Emmental Cheese, Served with a Red Wine Jus

from the Rock Glen Country House Hotel

This is a proper grown-up recipe, one you have to take a little time over, though nothing you have to do is difficult. The result is wonderful, and you will also have learnt how to make a *jus* like John Roche!

Ingredients:

Serves 6

6 loin of veal cutlets (ask your butcher to remove the bones and fat)

8oz/225g Emmental cheese, thinly sliced

12 fresh asparagus spears, or good tinned ones

Salt and freshly ground black pepper

For the jus:

10floz/300ml red wine of good colour

2floz/50ml red wine vinegar

1 shallot, peeled and finely chopped

6oz/175g butter

1 pint/½ litre chicken stock

Method:

If the asparagus is fresh, trim the white tails and peel the outside of the stalks with a vegetable peeler. Place them in a saucepan of boiling water until slightly softened (test them with a fork). Take them out of the pan and put into cold water to stop them cooking any further. Drain when cold. If you are using tinned asparagus, open the tin and drain contents.

In a large saucepan boil together the red wine, vinegar and chopped shallots until the liquid is reduced to just 2 tablespoons. Beat in the butter bit by bit. In a separate pan, boil down the chicken stock until you have about a quarter of a pint left, then add it to the reduced wine and butter.

Season the veal cutlets with salt and freshly ground black pepper and sear quickly in a very hot pan until browned on both sides. Place the cutlets on a rack in a grill tray and place two asparagus spears on top of each and a thin layer of sliced Emmental to cover the cutlet. Put a little water in the tray under the cutlets and place under a pre-heated medium grill until the asparagus are hot through and the cheese has melted. The meat should be medium-cooked at this stage. Carefully put the cutlets onto a serving plate and keep warm. Drain the juices from the grill tray into the red wine sauce and re-heat quickly if necessary. Serve with the red wine *jus* and garnish with a sprig of fresh parsley.

day ten

Galway/Connemara
Across the Bog to Roundstone,
Gurteen and Dog's Bay

How would you like to stand above a sweep of two bays,
with almost empty sandy beaches stretching for as far as the
eye can see on either side and the Atlantic swirling in front
of you and beside you? How would you like to wander
slowly along the sea-shore, searching for your ancestors'
discarded kitchen waste? Waste discarded, incidentally,
maybe 4000 or 5000 years ago. And how would you like to
wander into a small workshop and watch the traditional
Irish drum being carefully made by hand, and then have a
go at playing it? And to reach this gentle place, the pretty
town of Roundstone, how would you like to drive 12 miles
across flower-strewn bog set with tiny lakes and streams
where the only chance of being held up is by the traffic of a
slow-moving flock of sheep? Where you can, if the mood so
takes you, stand on a rock in the middle of a field not 10
yards from the roadside and pretend to be a sheep? And
along the way you can view the exact spot where Alcock
and Brown landed after their historic transatlantic flight
and see the memorial to them and their achievement.

Getting there

*Leave Clifden on the Ballyconneely road (R341). The roads around here are very
well signposted and there are also smaller brown and white signs which direct
you to hotels, places of interest and beaches. Along this road you will quickly
pass a pottery on your left and signs for the Rock Glen Country House Hotel on
your right. After a few minutes, the road crosses a small bridge, not over a river
but over a tiny inlet of the sea, a finger of Ardbear Bay. If the tide is high the
water surges noisily under it; if it is out seaweed-covered rocks stretch out so far*

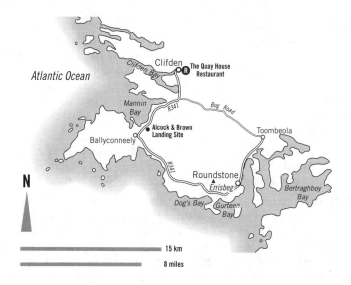

Atlantic Ocean

Clifden
The Quay House
Restaurant

Clifden Bay
R341
Mannin
Bay
Bog Road
Toombeola
Alcock & Brown
Landing Site
Ballyconneely
R341
Roundstone
Errisbeg
Bertraghboy
Bay
Dog's Bay
Gurteen
Bay

N

15 km
8 miles

*you wonder if the sea is ever coming back. After a few more miles you will come to a junction offering you the Bog Road to Roundstone or the road to Ballyconneely. Take the Ballyconneely Road and then follow the signs for the **Alcock and Brown Memorial** higher up on your right.*

The stone memorial is shaped like the tail-fin of an aircraft and commemorates the day in June 1919 when John Alcock piloted a Vickers Vimy biplane, with Arthur Whitten-Brown as navigator, 2000 miles across the Atlantic from St John's, Newfoundland to this bit of bog in the west of Ireland. It was an extraordinary achievement, this first non-stop flight across the Atlantic. It took just over 16 hours at an average speed of 120mph, and brought them, in addition to enduring fame, a prize offered by the London *Daily Mail* of £10,000, a considerable sum in 1919. From the memorial you can look across the bog to the exact spot where they came down. In the middle of the bog far down in front of you is a huge white cairn shaped like an egg.

To reach it, go back to the main road and cut straight across down a narrow track. This is only suitable for cars for a short distance; walk the rest. The cairn is by the remains of the Marconi station on a high point of ground, with the landing site itself another 500 yards further on. Now it is possible to understand why, instead of a dignified return to earth, they crash landed. At 8.40 in the morning, they sighted the Irish coast and tried to land near the Marconi telegraph station. Spotting what they thought was flat firm ground they came in to land—and plunged into soft, soggy peat, nose first and tail high in the air. The Marconi station, which incidentally is from where Guglielmo Marconi sent the first wireless signals across the Atlantic in 1907, telegraphed London with the news. All that is left now of the station is its outline in concrete. It was a sizeable building, but what an isolated existence those radio pioneers must have had.

Both men were knighted for their achievement. Alcock died shortly afterwards in a flying accident but Arthur Brown lived until 1948. You can see their plane in the Science Museum in London.

From the cairn, return to the main road, go back to the previous junction and take the right turn for the **Bog Road** to Roundstone. The bog in question has been described as the finest bog in the west of Ireland and indeed one of the finest anywhere in Europe. Writers have long eulogized over it and little wonder. Here, on either side of the narrow road, lies blanket bog for as far as the eye can see, with the occasional lake and tiny streams and little rivers darting in and out of the turf. There are lay-bys where you can leave your car, but make sure you have walking shoes, even in summer. The bog is rock hard at one step and at the next you could sink in over your ankles or even further. A walking stick to test the ground would not come amiss.

The great botanist and writer Lloyd Praeger tells in his book, *The Way That I Went*, of a bizarre incident on a wet day in August 1935 when he and a group of distinguished botanists met in Roundstone, among them a Dane called Jessen and a Swede named Osvald. 'The occasion was a kind of symposium on bogs, held in the middle of one of the wettest of them… We stood in a ring in that shelter-less expanse while discussion raged on the application of the terms soligenous, topogenous and ombrogenous. The rain and wind, like the discussion, waxed in intensity and under the unusual superincumbent weight whether of mere flesh and bone or of intellect, the floating surface of the bog slowly sank until we were all half way up to our knees in water. The only pause in the flow of the argument was when Jessen or Osvald, in an endeavour to solve the question of the origin of the peat, would chew some of the mud brought up by the boring tool from the bottom of the bog to test the presence or absence of gritty material in the vegetable mass!'

I would recommend that you look at the bog, walk on the bog, but I would not recommend it for lunch! But the fascination that the bog held for those academics of 60 years ago is just as true today. The landscape is covered in heathers and moss and bog cotton which looks just as you would expect: little balls of white fluff hanging precariously from sticks in the middle of the peat. There are also, if you know where to look, pansies growing wild, orchids similar to those of the Clare Burren and, in the more remote places, dozens of other varieties which make this a botanist's delight but which may be difficult for the casual visitor to spot. If you are interested, there are plenty of pamphlets with details of the flora to be found in the bog and surrounding areas.

You will, most likely, see a turf cutter on your journey, working away as his father and grandfather did before him, harvesting fuel from the top layers of the bog. Turf-cutting is a very precise art, largely passed on through the generations. The right tool—a *slean* in Irish, which looks like a narrow spade—is essential, and you must be strong with plenty of stamina. Other than that anyone can do it. One section of bog is worked at a time, creating straight-sided trenches. Those no longer in use soon begin to merge back into the surrounding bog. Sometimes you will see cutting right up to the edge of the road but more often than not the cutting will be done deep in the bog and the turf brought to the roadside in large sods. They are placed side by side and on top of one another to assist drying, and added to until there is a substantial mound of turf. The cutter will return to turn the sods around in the sun until he feels they are ready to be brought home. Even in winter you will see turf on the road-side, often covered in a tarpaulin to protect it from the rain. The smell of burning turf is unmistakable and unforgettable, a wonderful peaty smell. For the local population, there is of course no choice: peat is the main source of heating. It burns quickly and good supplies are essential. Although lorries are more often used to transport the turf, the sight of a turf cutter and his donkey laden with panniers of turf slowly going home across the bog is still quite common.

When you reach Toombeola, the road turns right for **Roundstone** where you arrive after a mile or so. This is my favourite approach to the town, though there are those who will argue fiercely that the prospect from the coast road is better. You will see in many local art galleries representations of Roundstone from every vantage point. It is a lovely, thriving town. While other tourist resorts have lost their heads and much of what made them special in the thrust for commercial profit, Roundstone has not followed that path, yet it serves the visitor well with its pubs and restaurants. It has a fine though small harbour which faces across a few miles of water to Bertraghboy Bay, a number of fish restaurants, and a wide, gentle, principal street which is a delight to wander along at any hour of day.

The harbour, and indeed the existence of the town itself, is due to Alexander Nimmo. He was a Scot who arrived in Ireland in 1822 to take up a post as Surveyor to the Commissioners, charged with reclaiming Irish bogs. An engineer by profession, he was mainly responsible for about 30 stone piers built along the west coast and for the building of some of Connemara's principal roads, the bases for today's main routes in the area. Roundstone did not exist then, apart from a small quay. Once Nimmo had designed the harbour, he organized the purchase and sale of plots of land for house-building around it. A number of other Scots settled here and the Franciscan order of monks came in 1835 and remained until the last monk retired to Clifden in l974.

On the site of the monastery is Roundstone Park, a cross between an industrial enterprise park and a cultural centre, which is dedicated to the memory of the late Michael Killeen, the outstanding former chairman of the Irish Industrial Development Authority and a frequent visitor to the area. You can see traditional Irish instruments being made—and try them and buy them—as well as fine local pottery and the inevitable touristy knick-knacks. If you get the chance, watch the *bodhran* (pronounced 'bow rawn'), the traditional Irish hand-held drum, being made and hear it played. It is made by stretching goat skin over a circle of light wood, usually birch. The haunting sound it makes is achieved by striking the *bodhran* with a bone or bone-like stick, the beater, held in one hand, while the other hand is underneath the skin, pressing and moving it to vary the depth of sound. There are many pubs in Connemara where you can watch and listen to a *bodhran* player. The Irish dramatist, John B. Keane, used this unique sound eerily in his seminal work about the death of a young Kerry girl forced into marriage against her wishes to a sweaty octogenarian. The play, *Sive* (pronounced like the English word 'sigh' with a 'v' sound in the middle), caused a sensation when first produced nearly 40 years ago and is a hardy annual to this day on the drama circuits all over Ireland. If you want to hear *bodhran* at its best go to a pub where there is a player and ask to hear Carthalan's curse from *Sive*: you will not be disappointed, though your hair may stand on end.

From wherever you are in the town, Roundstone is dominated by Errisbeg, variously described as a small mountain or a large hill. If the weather is good, it is well worth climbing for rewarding views over the Atlantic. Look

down from the mountain and you will see, just outside the town, the two splendid beaches of **Gurteen** and **Dog's Bay**, separated by a narrow spit of land. From the mountain they simply emerge as little lines of white, washed by the Atlantic blue waves as they lap towards the shore, and they are wonderful places to explore.

The bays are just a mile or two from the town and in summer, if the weather is fine, it may be a good idea to walk to them as there can be traffic problems in and around the area. The approach road down to the sea-shore and car park is narrow and you can easily regret your laziness as you go back and forwards trying to squeeze past other cars. Whatever the minor chaos on the roads though, the beaches are huge enough to make you feel you are quite on your own. When you first see the sweep of these two bays, you understand why there are fierce arguments about which road to Roundstone is the better one.

The two bays curve round like scimitars, separated by a long thin sandspit sticking out to sea with a mile-long hump of rock on the end, which looks as if it should be, and probably once was, a tiny island, separate from the mainland. My favourite of the two bays is Dog's Bay, though both are lovely. The water is the clearest you can imagine and the sand is an almost perfect shining white, with no hint of the gold or brown which most sea sand has. The reason is that the sand here is not formed from quartz grains but from minute shells known as *foraminifera*. You are quite likely, as you wander along the beach, to see someone with a magnifying glass lying flat out and peering earnestly at the ground, examining closely the make-up of the sand.

There are other shells here, however, whose history I find extraordinary. Wandering along the little dunes above the beach one day, we found, a good 500 yards from the sea in a flattish place on some rock, a thick layer of shells. Part of the rock was a browny-black. It seemed unlikely that the shells had been deposited here by even the highest of high tides, and even more unlikely that passing seabirds had dropped hundreds of shells in exactly the same place.

On enquiry, we learned that these were in fact rubbish tips from pre-history, known as **kitchen middens**. These are sites of tremendous interest and are made up of layers of sea-shells. If you come across a single midden you are staring at thousands of years of history in a small rectangle of space on an Irish beach. Look out for them some distance from the shore, and in sand dunes. Over the millennia the sea and wind have caused the sand to shift, dunes have formed from this movement and in the hollows that were thus created the remains of our ancestors' shell-fish suppers were preserved: cockles, oysters, winkles, limpets and more. Even Stone Age axes and Bronze Age artefacts have been found in some middens, more of which, by the way, you can find on the island of Inishbofin. Some of the stones that lie here are the remains of the ancient fishermen's homes. Every now and then you will come across a huge piece of flat rock and spend an age trying to figure out why it is lying just where it is. Is it part of nature, or is it perhaps the relic of some lost prehistoric rite?

As you sit and let the day slip into evening and reflect on the experience of Roundstone, let me give you one memory which I think will sum up my feelings about the place. One evening a few years ago, we were sitting with a dear friend and Roundstone native, who had spent many years as an executive with a major international oil company before coming back here. Surely, we wondered, in this remote place he must sometimes miss the buzz and challenge of his businessman's life? Our friend was sitting with his back to the sublime view across the green slopes towards the Atlantic and the evening sun glinting on Gurteen and Dog's Bay which we had been delighting in. He leaned towards us and simply said, 'Look over my shoulder, ask me that question again and you already have the answer!'

Dinner at The Quay House, Clifden

The Quay House Restaurant, Beach Road, Clifden, Co.Galway
℗ *(095) 21369*

Open for lunch and dinner April–October. Starters: IR£4.95; main courses: around IR£12; puddings: all IR£2.50.

Drive back over the Bog Road to Clifden, and then down to the quay. Overlooking the water is an elegant, cream-painted, three-storey building. Built in about 1820, it was originally the Harbourmaster's House, then the Convent of Mercy, then a Franciscan Friary and in the early 1900s it became a hotel. Now it is a restaurant—with rooms—owned by Paddy and Julia Foyle, who also run a country house hotel a few miles away, Rosleague Manor, and a bright, cheerful restaurant called Destry's in the middle of Clifden. Somehow they have also found time to create this new venture, the Quay House. The original house has spread sideways. On one side there is now a plant-filled conservatory, while the restaurant itself starts in the house and then expands comfortably into the building next door. For all the elegance of the façade, inside it is disarmingly chaotic with more than a touch of the idiosyncratic. For no apparent reason, one of the set of prints hanging in the hall is upside down. The walls of the corridor leading to the kitchen are crowded with horned examples of a taxidermist's skills and there is also a vast tiger skin which, says Julia Foyle, belonged to a beast shot in Bengal in the 1930s after consuming at least seven ladies.

Pre-dinner drinks are taken in the conservatory or in the drawing room, full of deep sofas. The dining room is actually two rooms, opened out into one and painted the colours of the Atlantic on a clear Connemara day—aquamarine, a deep misty blue and a dazzling white. The windows look out over the quay, where on a still day Clifden is perfectly reflected in the water—half the time, that is; the tide goes out so far that what you see then is sand, rock, seaweed and the masts of beached boats. Half way up the far wall is a triangular-shaped fireplace, while candles flicker on every table. It is eclectic, attractive and welcoming—and so is the menu.

Smoked salmon, crab, mussels all appear as starters, but turned into highly individual dishes. The tagliatelle of smoked salmon is served with chorizo—a spicy sausage—and the warm salad of mussels and smoked bacon has a dressing of anchovy and soya. Crab is turned into a wonderful mille-feuille with spinach and served with an apple and apricot chutney and mango-flavoured mayonnaise. There is chowder, not the ubiquitous seafood variety, but a delicious combination of smoked salmon and lentils. The main courses are equally inventive. The stuffed cushion of veal has a marvellously smokey taste from the ham it is wrapped in, and it comes with a leek and mushroom samosa. Breast of chicken is coated with herbs, and then married to a coconut and lime hollandaise. Wild salmon is grilled and served with a lime and vermouth sauce, while the rack of Connemara lamb is served simply with garlic and thyme. The star of the pudding menu is the well-named Lethal Chocolate Pudding, though the lemon tart with a vanilla and fruit *coulis* ran it pretty close. The ice creams are home-made, or you might try the iced nougat and mango parfait. If you can still lift a knife, the cheese board is excellent.

The service is friendly and attentive and children are welcome. The wine-list, unusually, also has a simple pricing structure—either IR£9.95 or IR£11.95, with just a few individually priced. At the bottom of the wine list the Foyles have noted: 'Prices include duty and government rip-off tax of 21%'!

Crab and Spinach Mille-Feuilles with Apple and Apricot Chutney and Mango Mayonnaise

From The Quay House

Ingredients:

Serves 4

8oz/220g white crabmeat

4 tablespoons mayonnaise

Salt and freshly ground black pepper

Juice of half a lemon

1 sheet filo pastry

1oz/25g butter, melted

2 handfuls of fresh spinach

For the mango mayonnaise:

2 tablespoons mango purée or 1 fresh mango, juice of half a lemon and scant half teaspoon of sugar

1 tablespoon mayonnaise

For the chutney:

4floz/120ml apricot purée

Half an apple, peeled and diced

Half each red and green pepper, diced

Half a nectarine, peeled and diced

2 shallots, peeled and diced

1–2 tablespoons sunflower oil

Salt and freshly ground black pepper

Quarter of a teaspoon ground cumin

Method:

To make the chutney, heat the oil in a heavy-based pan and add the diced apple, red and green peppers, shallots and nectarine. Sweat them gently until soft, but do not let them brown. Add the apricot purée, bring to the boil and let it bubble until reduced by half and the texture is like jam. Stir occasionally so it does not stick to the pan. Season with salt, pepper and cumin and allow to cool.

Cut the filo pastry into 12 rounds with a biscuit or scone cutter (each mille-feuille needs three rounds) and put them onto a greased baking tray. Brush each round with a little melted butter and bake in a pre-heated oven, gas mark 6, 400°F, 200°C for just 3–5 minutes until crisp and golden brown. Watch them carefully as they cook very quickly. Allow to cool.

Remove any stalks from the spinach, wash thoroughly and blanch in boiling water for 1 minute. Drain and refresh in ice-cold water and drain thoroughly.

If you cannot find mango purée in the shops, peel and chop a ripe mango and blend it in a food processor or liquidizer with the juice of half a lemon and a very little sugar. Add the tablespoon of mayonnaise and blend for a few seconds more until smooth.

Mix together the crabmeat and four tablespoons of mayonnaise, and season to taste with the lemon juice, salt and freshly ground black pepper.

Assemble each mille-feuille as follows: put some spinach onto a pastry round so it just covers it, then some crab, then a layer of chutney, another pastry round, then more spinach, crab, chutney and top with another pastry round. Carefully place each mille-feuille on a plate with a dessertspoonful of the mango mayonnaise and serve.

day eleven

Galway/Connemara
Inishbofin—The Best Day Ever!

A tiny island covered in flowers and enchantment and
named after a cow does not sound a very likely
combination, but Inishbofin is one of the most entrancing
places you are ever likely to visit. At the end of a day spent
there recently, my family declared it to be 'the best day ever
in the west of Ireland'. That day had been spent walking
through time—past a medieval abbey, prehistoric fields and
house sites which go back some 5000 years, and a star-
shaped fort built by Oliver Cromwell's forces in the
17th century. With the tide fast receding, we watched a
duck leading her brood of 10 unsteady ducklings across the
sand to a swimming lesson. We walked by golden sand
dunes and green fields, a lake of blue water covered with
countless water lilies of palest pink, up little hills carpeted
in yellow, mauve and white, and gazed on incomparable
views over the glittering sea back to the mainland. We also
had an extremely good lunch.

Getting there

*The ferry for Inishbofin sails from Cleggan, about 10 miles north of Clifden off
the Westport road. Boats leave regularly, but it is a wise traveller who checks the
times and makes a firm resolution to get to Cleggan as early as possible in the
morning—there will be fewer people queuing and you will have longer on the
island. There are a couple of carriers which vie with each other for your business.
This operation starts about half a mile away from Cleggan, where small boys
will rap on the window of your motor-car and shove leaflets at you claiming
theirs to be the 'Best/most modern/cheapest boat to Bofin'. They may also try to
sell you a ticket. It is perfectly valid, but we preferred to have a look at the boats
before we bought our ticket from the ticket office. To be honest, they are much*

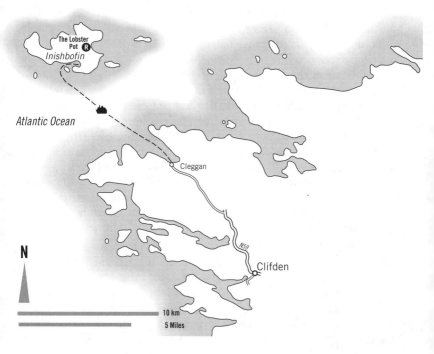

*the same and provide pretty much the same service, the only difference being that
the more modern boats knock a few minutes off the journey.*

The boat trip to **Inishbofin** on a fine day is wonderful; that really is the
only word to describe it. Your fellow passengers may be a group of nuns
on their way to see the early Christian sites, visiting American film stars
looking cool in dark glasses, families on holiday, and very often archaeologists and botanists full of excitement at the prospect of this
treasure-house. The journey takes about 45 minutes, which is happily
spent looking at the curious wave patterns created by the tides, watching
for fish and of course the approaching island.

From the mainland, the island appears as a soft, dark shape rising from the
sea, with magical legends surrounding its name. Inishbofin is known variously as *Inis Bo Finne* or, to closer natives, simply as Boffin or Bofin.
Translated from the Irish this means literally the 'Island (*Inis*) of the White
Cow (*Bo Finne*)'. It was invisible, so the legend goes, to early man,
shrouded in mists and appearing and disappearing at will. Then two fishermen, lost in fog, chanced upon an island where none before had existed.

They landed and lit a fire so they could cook some fish. The smoke caused the mists to disperse and for the first time they could see where they were. In front of them was an old woman driving a white cow. On seeing them, the woman ran off. One of the men chased the cow and caught it by the tail, whereupon the tail broke off and the cow turned into a statue of white quartz. Meanwhile the other had pursued the woman but, when he reached her by the shores of a lake, she stopped and faced him and he too was turned to white quartz, while she plunged from sight into the lake. Until about 100 years ago, there were, apparently, two white quartz standing stones near a lake on Inishbofin, but there is no trace of them now. The legend ends with the warning that in times of distress the white cow and the old woman appear. I have never been able to work out whether if they appear, distress has already arrived or, if there is distress already and they have not yet appeared, I should hang around the island in the hopes of seeing these two strange creatures!

As your boat slows down to ease its way into the harbour, above you on the rocky promontory is a great fort which seems to rise out of the rocks. A castle once stood there, built by Don Bosco, a Spanish pirate. He was a chum of the fierce O'Malley clan, who had seized control of the island in the 14th century. Their castle was on the other side of the harbour and by slinging a chain boom from castle to castle across the harbour mouth they could, by pulling the chain tight, either capture treasure ships or keep out unwanted intruders, government forces and so on. Built on the site of the Spaniard's castle, or very close to it, the ruin that you sail beneath is a star-shaped fort, known as Cromwell's barracks. It is hard to believe that this little blob of an island actually played some part in that great struggle between Cavaliers and Roundheads in 17th-century Britain, but it did. The Royalists who had fled to Inishbofin were the last on the west coast to surrender to the Parliamentarians, and this they did in 1653. Cromwell's men built a new fort and for a time it was used for imprisoning Catholic clergy found guilty of high treason because of their religious beliefs. It was not death that awaited them, but deportation, often to work on plantations in the West Indies. For some years the fort was also useful as a defence against French pirates and marauders but finally, in the early 18th century, it was abandoned. If you want to have a closer look at the fort, it is a 20-minute walk over the hills. At low tide you will also then be able to see the remains of a medieval harbour which is otherwise underwater.

If you have been wondering why this remote island has had such an active past, you will begin to understand as your ferry rounds the point on which

Cromwell's Fort

the fort stands. The harbour is big and very safe and sheltered from the Atlantic storms, a natural haven for all comers. When you have disembarked, leave the pier, turn right and start walking eastwards along what is the Low Road, with Cromwell's Fort now away to your right and behind you. The island is only about three miles long and one and a half miles wide and you are now about half way along it. This little road will take you to the medieval ruin known as St. Colman's Abbey, through glorious scenery, and to lunch about an hour's walk away. There are a few cars on the island and a large number of bicycles, but when we were there in August, for a large part of our walk we saw no one at all.

Before you have even left the harbour area, you come to a big grey-stone church. Christian worship here goes back to St Colman who arrived on Bofin in about AD 664. The present **church of St Colman**, (this, as you have probably guessed already, is not St Colman's Abbey!) was started in about 1910. The building was finished in 1914, and Mary Lavelle's pamphlet, 'A Brief Guide to Inishbofin', contains some lovely local snippets of information about how much it cost. The church itself was just £1400. All the workers, 23 in total, were local men, though the man in charge of the operation, Michael Gilooly, travelled from Galway to Clifden then to Cleggan and across to the island to supervise the works. His expenses for this were four shillings and twopence for the train from Galway to Clifden and five shillings for the car to Cleggan. Wages for the men were between nine shillings and 12 bob a week.

Years ago, though it is gone now, there was a plaque inside the church to a chieftain from County Leix, Rory O'Moore, which read: 'In memory of many valiant Irishmen who were exiled to this Holy Island and in particular Rory O'Moore, a brave chieftain of Leix who, after fighting for Faith and Fatherland, disguised as a fisherman, escaped from this island to a place of safety. He died shortly afterwards in about 1653, a martyr to his religion and country. He was esteemed and loved by his countrymen who celebrated his many deeds of valour and kindness in their songs and reverenced his memory so that it was common to hear the expression; "God and Our Lady be our help, and Rory O' Moore!'" In the 80 or so years since the church was built, the population of the island has declined from about 900 to around 180.

Day's Bar and Hotel is a few yards further on. Until 1916, this was Bofin House, where the landlord lived. The last landlord of the island was Cyril Allies, whose father had acquired Bofin in lieu of a financial debt. At the end of the 19th century the island was suffering deeply from the effects of the famine and emigration and Allies put much of his own money into projects to rebuild the fishing industry, such as the new pier, a new lighthouse and fish curing stations. He died in London.

Past Day's, the road heads east towards the far end of the island. The low hills to your left are inviting and an easy climb. The view is simply glorious and the flowers that cover them a botanist's delight. You may also see rabbits—the east end of the island in particular has them in abundance—and in the fields there may well be a few cows, or perhaps a solitary horse, standing knee high in grass thick with yellow flowers.

It is in such a field that you see a ruined, roofless church. This is **St Colman's Abbey**, or to be exact, the ruins of a church built probably in the 14th century over St Colman's 7th-century place of worship. History tells us that after the Synod of Whitby in AD 664 it was decided that the Roman date for Easter should be adopted instead of the Celtic Church's, which had previously been in use. The then archbishop of Northumberland, Colman, left England in disgust and headed with a band of dissident monks first for Mayo and then for Inishbofin where he founded this monastery. His church survived until the 14th century, when it is generally accepted that it was ransacked and destroyed by a fellow named John Darcy, a Lord Justice, believe it or not, who sailed the west coast of Ireland looting, plundering and burning all he could lay hands on. In the graveyard which lies beside the ruined church there are two holy wells, St Colman's Well and Tobar Flannan, literally the Well of St Flannan. Flannan probably pre-dated Colman on the island but we cannot be certain of this. There are also several 7th-century gravestones.

Not far from the ruined chapel is the exquisite, tranquil Church Lake. Here the gentle lapping water is home to flowers, reeds—and weeds—similar to those you may have seen on the Burren. The flowers are yellow, blue, white. You can see so many almost at a glance that it is like being in a huge natural garden centre. Great green lily pads float on the water, and the pale pink lilies simply cover the whole lake. We did not see Jeremy Fisher, but pond insects were hopping happily from pad to pad. Bird-watchers have a great time spotting and listening to a wide variety of species: coots, moorhens and mallards among others. In the fields around the lake you may spot some of the nesting birds including skylarks and pipits.

If you walk on a little further past the abbey towards the bay opposite the nearby little island of Inishlyon, in the far righthand corner of the bay are kitchen middens which may be around 6000 years old. This is a sandy beach with good swimming, but I suggest you go back to the road and head on towards East End Bay, where lunch at the Lobster Pot awaits.

Lunch at The Lobster Pot

The Lobster Pot, Inishbofin

Sample prices: potato cakes are IR£1.25, a crab open sandwich IR£3.95 and children's sandwiches about 80p.

The bathing in East End Bay is good too. There is a wide sandy beach and clear water so if it is warm enough and you have the inclination, have a swim before lunch. The Lobster Pot is a small restaurant specializing, needless to say, in fresh fish, salmon, lobster, cray fish, crab and associated goodies such as warm Irish brown bread and what have to be the best potato cakes in Ireland. It is owned and run by Clodagh and Augustine Coyne. She is the chef, he does much of the fishing and lobster catching and they grow all their own vegetables and herbs. They started the restaurant nearly 25 years ago, catering for what was then a small but steady trickle of tourists. Since then, numbers have grown, as the reputation of their restaurant has spread—not through advertising, but through word from its faithful devotees, of which I am happily one.

Only 28 people can sit inside, but in fine weather tables and chairs are put outside, according to demand. If they are full when you arrive, just let them know you would like a table and simply enjoy the bay, walk along the sand or out along the quay to the curing station. Inside, the restaurant is simple: yellow-covered tables and on the wall a large Admiralty chart of Inishbofin which you instantly think you cannot do without. There is also a fascinating moon calendar—what else in a place where life is dictated by the phases of the moon?

The menu is short and tempting and very fresh. There is a soup of the day, perhaps vegetable, and seafood chowder. Open sandwiches served with salad predominate: fresh wild salmon, crab, chicken and avocado, cream cheese and cucumber, egg mayonnaise or cheese, fruit and nuts. Inishbofin mackerel is served either fresh and lightly fried, or smoked, both with salad and brown bread, or there is ratatouille with noodles. What you must have here are the potato cakes. Clodagh Coyne has turned this simple dish into an art form. Her potato cakes are crisp, golden, piping hot and as light as can be inside. They may be served with butter, but they are cooked in a pan which has only been lightly greased with oil.

Children are very well looked after here, with small portions and sandwich fillings of banana, peanut butter, chocolate spread or honey. Home baking dominates the pudding list with rhubarb tart and cream, chocolate fudge cake, Gaelic coffee cheesecake, Bakewell flan or perhaps fruit crumble. There is a wine licence, but the home-made lemonade and the barley cup were delicious. There is also fresh coffee and a wide variety of teas or hot chocolate with cream and chocolate flakes. Service is helpful and friendly and if you have any special dietary requirements, such as soya milk, they have that too.

For your return to the pier, simply retrace your steps from the Lobster Pot. There is another road, the High Road, but it takes you past Inishbofin's generating station and that is not what you came to the island for!

Back at the pier, head westwards and soon on your right you will come to the Doonmore Hotel, originally dating from 1908 when it was the Murray family home and now, still in the same family, a hotel. The building was added to gradually over the years but parts of the original still stand. The rocky sea-shore opposite is lovely and you may well find an artist or two or perhaps a photographer busy at work. As a drink by now would probably be welcome, take a few minutes to sit on the wall, or perch on the steps leading down to the rocks and enjoy the view.

In the evenings this is a favourite location for bird-watchers, with terns, fulmars, petrels, gulls and dozens of others. If you are really lucky, Bofin might just give you a treat: it is one of the few places left where the corncrake can still be heard, although like everywhere else the numbers are in sad and rapid decline.

If there are still two or three hours left before the last ferry leaves, or you are planning to spend a second day on the island, go on walking west. The road will take you past the Doonmore Hotel and towards Cnoc Mor and the Promontory Fort, though after a bit it is no longer paved. The fort is about one and a quarter miles from the Doonmore Hotel, which in turn is about half a mile from the pier and your ferry, so if you have the time this is your chance for some amateur archaeology. Inishbofin has been extensively investigated over the past 20 years or so by experts, who reckon that there was a fairly large population here about 2000 years ago. They have discovered field systems, terraces, hut sites and kitchen middens similar to those elsewhere in the west. They have also found ancient cooking sites, in Irish *fulachta fiadh*. Unless you know what you are looking for, these can be quite easy to miss. Generally speaking, they can be found by streams or marshy ground. They are horseshoe-shaped grassy mounds, with a hearth in the middle. Close by is a bath-shaped trough dug in the ground. It is thought that the trough, which would have been lined with wood or stones, filled with water which seeped from the stream or marsh. Stones were heated on the hearth until red hot, then dropped into the water until it boiled. Christy Lawless, an amateur archaeologist in county Mayo who drives the library bus for a living, has found around 140 *fulachta fiadh* in Mayo. He built an exact replica and set out to cook a joint of meat the Bronze Age way. He heated stones in the fire until red hot, and then dropped them into the water. While the water came to the boil, he

wrapped a joint of meat in straw to protect it from dirt and grit and then lowered it into the boiling water. He kept it boiling by adding another red hot stone every 10 to 15 minutes. In all he needed 60 stones. The joint took 30 minutes to the pound (450g) plus 30 minutes until it was well done. What an insight into Bronze Age life that must have given to Christy Lawless.

On the north side of the little hill of Cnoc Mor (so you need to walk round it, not up it) you can see evidence of a field system and ancient house sites, probably around 4000 years old. What is left of the houses is a circular shape on the ground, about eight feet across. The fort, **Dun Mor**, is a little further on, along the narrow promontory. It is visible as a pile of stones, all that is left from the original walls. The site is wild and dramatic and you get the best view and impression of what it may have been like by standing back a little and observing from a distance.

There is plenty to explore in and around Dun Mor, the fields on either side of the track, the sea-shore itself and the rocks. I have never seen seals or porpoises here or even puffins, but the islanders will tell you that if you have patience it will be rewarded. It is possible to walk round the island but there are only a limited number of miles of paved road, the rest being unpaved or narrow tracks and little paths, and it will probably take you longer than you have time for if your stay here is just one day. If all this has left you eager for more, there are pamphlets and leaflets which concentrate on nothing but the archaeology and natural history of Inishbofin. And if you were minded to, the island plays host every year to a summer school which is devoted to these topics, with lectures from the acknowledged experts. Details are readily available from local tourist information centres. If you simply want to spend more time here, there are two hotels, guest houses, and houses for rent on a weekly or monthly basis. I have met people who have been coming to Bofin for 15, 20 years and would never think of going anywhere else for their vacations. It is easy to understand why.

Your departing boat for Cleggan lets Cromwell's fort slip past you now on the left. The retreating island always leaves me with pangs of regret and an almost instant longing to return to this place of peace, beauty and tranquillity. Now out to sea and with the mainland and Cleggan quickly in sight, your ferry rises and dips to a gentle evening swell. Will this be the evening when porpoises or seals shyly appear? After such a perfect day, why would they not?

Potato Cakes
from the Lobster Pot

You need a good all-purpose potato for this—a floury type that mashes well.

Ingredients:

Makes about 12

1lb/450g potatoes, peeled and chopped

A knob of butter

Salt and freshly ground black pepper

2oz/50g flour (approx)

Half a teaspoon baking powder

1 egg, beaten, free-range if possible

Method:

Boil the potatoes in plenty of salted water until soft, then drain and mash them. While they are still hot, pop in a small knob of butter to help bind them. Add the salt and pepper. When the mash is cool enough to handle, sieve in some of the flour with the baking powder and the beaten egg. The amount of flour will vary with the type of potato. Work in the flour and egg to bind the potato to a fairly firm dough and knead lightly until smooth. Turn the mixture out onto a board and flatten to about half an inch thick. Cut into rounds with a scone cutter, or into triangles. If you prefer, just halve the dough and shape it into two rounds.

Grease a pan with oil and when it is hot add the potato cakes. Cook until they are golden brown underneath; check after 2 or 3 minutes, and when a good even colour turn and cook the other side. Serve hot with butter.

day twelve

Galway/Connemara
The Twelve Bens

Connemara is so full of delights that it is tempting to try to see everything. That, however, is probably a lifetime's work, so this last day in Connemara is about contrasts—from unmarked roads leading to the remote foothills of the region's mountains, the Twelve Bens, to a visit to the Irish-speaking area, the Gaeltacht, in the south, where the youth of Ireland are still sent on holiday to learn their language and culture. It is a strange, barren part of Connemara, covered not with bog or grass or trees, but with huge rocks and boulders. In the late afternoon, on to a walk beside a glorious salmon river, through acres of woodland in the grounds of Ballynahinch Castle, which has links with a buccaneering woman, Catholic emancipation, animal welfare, royalty, the League of Nations, first-class cricket and which, on top of all that, now offers first-class food.

From wherever you are in the region, you can see the Twelve Bens, *Benna Beola*, gently embracing Connemara. From a distance they are misty and blue; close to, they are soft browns, mauves and greens.

Getting there

Leave Clifden on the Galway road (N59) and drive past the Dan O'Hara centre on your left, then past the entrance to Ballynahinch Castle which is on your right. Continue for about another two miles until, on the left, you come to a road signposted 'Canal Connemara Ponies 1km'. This has nothing to do with where you are going; the signpost simply indicates the road to take. There is a house on the corner and for the last few years some elderly-looking buses have been parked here.

The road is asphalted and quite good, though the tufts of grass growing happily down the middle indicate this is not the most travelled road in the region. It snakes up towards the mountains, and after just a quarter of a mile the views start to be spectacular. What you seem to be doing is driving into a half saucer formed by the great mountainous ring of the **Twelve Bens** in front of you and the bog and the distant sea on either side and behind you. Suddenly you are so close to the mountains that you can touch them. From here they look an easy, gentle climb, but they are deceptive and can be dangerous unless you are an experienced climber and properly equipped. Hidden in this saucer is a scattered community, just a few houses, neatly kept and painted. There is also a sizeable population of sheep, with distinctive local markings of dyes rubbed into the fleece as a sort of registration mark for their shepherds. On either side of the road is bog, neatly cut and probably drying a bit more quickly than the Roundstone bog by virtue of the combination of wind and sun which drench it each day in alternating gestures of help.

Stop where you can and walk over the springy turf. The air is pure and exhilarating and the scenery so unspoiled you wonder if you should be there at all. The only concessions to what we laughingly call civilization are the marching telegraph poles carrying messages and power to the scattered families, and the odd car or tractor outside a smallholding. Yet despite signs of life and the historical fact that this area has been inhabited for centuries, there is an eeriness, a sense of isolation in this saucer of the Twelve Bens. Even the rain is strange. Here it falls not aggressively, but like a soft watering on your face, and it is made all the more romantic by the fact that you can see it coming. We have stood for minutes up here, watching from a distance as rain fell from small clouds drifting gently towards us through the clear air.

As you drive back down away from that awesome ring of mountains, the land below you shimmers silver from myriad lakes and streams, the bog a palette of misty colours in the pure light. If you felt removed from time in the shadow of the Twelve Bens, where you are now going is a part of Ireland which hangs on tightly to the past. Back on the main road turn left and follow the main Clifden–Galway road taking the signs for Recess and Maam Cross. You are heading south for the Irish-speaking part of Connemara, in Irish, the **Gaeltacht**, pronounced gael-tocht. There are now few, if any, people left for whom Irish is their only language, but every child in Ireland has to learn Irish as part of the curriculum. For most of us, Irish is our native language, and English our mother tongue. My father and I spoke Irish at home simply for the pleasure of it. My mother spoke it not at all, and the rest of my family had a few words which really amounted to 'hello', 'good-bye' and 'which way to the church'! Yet from my earliest days I was fascinated by this extraordinary tongue: a language so rich in descriptive words and meanings that it is little wonder we Irish have superimposed a flowing loquacity onto the main English language causing us to use a dozen words where six would do.

The road from Recess leads straight into Maam Cross, where you take the right turn onto the R336 for Screeb. There are also signs for Rosmuck and Pearse's Cottage, which is where you are headed. The countryside in south Connemara is very different from Clifden and Roundstone: it is an austere, almost barren landscape, with bare limestone hillsides in places reminiscent of the Burren. Huge boulders litter the place and you wonder how anyone could possibly eke out a living here. When you get to Screeb, turn right on to the R340 and follow the signs for **Pearse's Cottage**. It is a small, white-washed, thatched cottage, standing peacefully on its own on a little hill overlooking an inlet of the sea. Pearse was one of the leaders of the ill-fated 1916 Rising in Dublin, executed by the British and revered (with mixed feelings) by the Irish to this day. He was a decent man, a school teacher by profession, who set up his own school, St Enda's, to put

his ideas on education into practice. He was also a poet and playwright who directed his own plays at the Abbey Theatre. This cottage was a summer retreat, where he improved his Irish, took school children for holidays and discussed well into the small hours his vision of an Ireland that would be 'not only free but Gaelic as well'. It was a wonderfully romantic, sad, and in its own way beautiful vision, so much so that Yeats, who knew Pearse well, was moved to speak of the Rising which Pearse inspired as 'a terrible beauty'.

The cottage has been restored; after Pearse was executed it was burned out during the War of Independence by the Black and Tans, a unit of the British Army who got their name from a combination of their uniform which was soldier tan and police black. The cottage is very simple, just a couple of rooms which have been furnished with a dresser, a table, a little desk and so on—the sort of things Pearse might have used. The children camped outside. There is a guide and the cottage is open throughout the summer.

There is a little personal footnote to the story of Patrick Pearse. When my late father worked as a civil servant just after the foundation of the Irish Free State in the early 1920s, one of his tasks was to sort through box after box of letters which had been sent by members of the general public to the outgoing, that is, Imperial or British civil service. Most of them were meaningless and totally irrelevant applications or supplications for this, that or another favour, but one day my father came across a letter on headed note-paper from St Enda's School in Dublin. Curious, he read the hand-written letter, which turned out to be a most courteous note from Pearse to the equivalent of a tax inspector, thanking him for his assistance in the financial affairs of the school. There was nothing untoward in this note, but my father was intrigued at the notion of a man who was later to be executed by the British being so mannerly to His Majesty's officials. He kept the letter, perhaps stole is the appropriate word, rather than filed it and when I grew up, confessed all to me. The letter is now in the museum in Clongowes Wood College in County Kildare, to which we gave other papers and notes of my father's time in the civil service.

As Patrick Pearse did, you will find plenty of native Irish speakers here and in the surrounding area. Many men and women now in their sixties or seventies in this neighbourhood will remember from their childhood older people, probably their own grandparents, who spoke no English.

> *If you follow the road down to Rosmuck, you will simply have to drive back again as it goes no further, though the compensation is some beautiful empty beaches. Drive back to the main road, but instead of turning right and heading back to Maam Cross, turn left onto the R340 and start heading round the coast for Kilkieran, Carna, Glinsk and Gowla, passing along the edge of Cashel Bay and on to your eventual destination, Ballynahinch.*

The rock-filled terrain here is so strange, so alien, it is hard to believe you are in the same country, leave alone county, as Clifden. As you round the point of Kilkieran Bay and start to head north, in clear weather you can see the biggest of the Aran Islands, Inishmore, in the distance. In the middle of June on Ascension Thursday, the islanders hold a torchlight procession, and this can be seen from here—in clear weather—as a moving train of lights, without visible means of support, seemingly suspended above the sea. It is a wonderfully eerie sight.

Past Carna, with its bay full of little dark islands floating on a silvery sea, and on towards Glinsk, the land begins to take on the more familiar colours and textures of western Connemara. Look across Bertraghboy Bay, and there is Roundstone, with Gurteen and Dog's Bay. You begin to feel you are coming home! This is not a long journey and you soon turn left and rejoin the main Recess to Clifden road and follow the signs for Ballynahinch Castle.

Over the years **Ballynahinch** has been associated with myth, legend and even fact. The road runs past a lake surrounded by dark woods, and in the middle of the lake floats a small island with a romantic, ruined ivy-covered castle on it. That is the original castle. It was said to have been built by Donal of the Combats O'Flaherty, an Irish chieftain from these parts who was married to Grace O'Malley, the notorious Irish pirate queen. According to local tradition, bad luck would befall him because he built the castle with stones from a friary his ancestors had founded at nearby Toombeola. And so it did, and pretty permanent bad luck too—he was murdered by another war-like family, the Joyces from Galway.

In later years Ballynahinch was the home of the man fondly known as Humanity Dick Martin, or more formally as Colonel Richard Martin, Member of Parliament. He was famous for his kindness to animals and his habit of locking up on the island in the lake anyone on his estate who mistreated them. It was his bill in the House of Commons which led to the founding of the Royal Society for the Prevention of Cruelty to Animals. Humanity Dick was a lawyer, a duellist, and a colourful, larger-than-life character. By birth a Catholic, he was brought up as a Protestant and became a fierce champion of Catholic emancipation. He lived between 1754 and 1834 at a time when the laws of the land, if strictly applied, prevented a Catholic from going to school or university; nor might a Catholic bear arms, sit in Parliament, own a horse worth more than £5, study abroad, follow a profession, marry a Protestant or possess land. Humanity Dick was a fierce opponent of such laws, and in 1812 persuaded Protestants in the city of Galway to pledge themselves neither to seek nor accept public office nor to help others to do so until Catholics were allowed the same privileges as Protestants. It was a courageous step and did not totally endear Humanity to every politician in Ireland or England. He lived briefly at Ballynahinch, but he was so eccentric and careless with his friends and money that his was not a very successful tenure of this fine estate with its estimated 35,000 acres of shooting land, its river, its lush grounds and its own railway station.

The Martins' tenure of Ballynahinch was succeeded by another who is still remembered with great fondness by local people—and tens of thousands of others. What will strike you at once as you enter the hotel's main reception area and look towards the bar is the picture of an Indian prince in full traditional costume. This man is probably the most famous of all owner/residents of Ballynahinch. To give him his full title he was Colonel His Royal Highness Shri Sir Ranjitsinhji Vibhaji Maharaja Jam Saheb of Nawanagar, otherwise known as Ranji. Ranji was a diplomat, representing India at early meetings of the League of Nations, and a great cricketer, for which, outside India, he is perhaps better known. He played for Cambridge and England and was regarded as one of the greats of his generation. His *Jubilee Book of Cricket* and a series of cricketing articles he wrote at the turn of the century are still seminal works on the game. He was also a hunter and fisherman; indeed he once told friends that he lived for fishing. He was living in London in semi-retirement in 1924 when he heard that Ballynahinch was on the market. He sent a man to inspect it and when a favourable report came back Ranji first rented and then bought the house. What is now the main bar used to be the billiard room and once a year it was turned into a dining room for the estate workers and servants whom Ranji treated superbly. Indeed he was in many ways the saviour of this part of Connemara and is still spoken of with great affection.

A few years back I managed to interview the last surviving worker from the estate, Martin Halloran. His affection for Ranji and his pride in having worked for him were very evident as he told me that it was not uncommon for Ranji to 'keep us on the river all day and into the dark of the evening, fishing, fishing, fishing!'

His generosity, as Martin says, was legendary. He would bring a couple of cars with him every year when he came, normally from April to October, when he might go back either to India or to Britain. When the time came for him to leave he would present the cars, which might well include a Rolls Royce, to local people: one maybe to a clergyman or a doctor or someone he felt needed it for their work. He always arrived at the house by special train from Galway, and when local people knew of his impending arrival they would put lighted candles on the track side to welcome him. You can still see the little station on the estate, though it is now defunct as the railway no longer operates in Connemara. With Ranji's arrival, Bally-nahinch and surrounding villages got a huge new lease of life and at one stage more than 60 men were employed on the estate. He would tour other villages and where he saw poverty would set people to work building huts and seats and shelters along the shores of lakes, bridging rivers and improving roads. He paid for all this out of his own pocket which, together with the staggering sum of £30,000 which he spent buying the castle and grounds, made him one of the great benefactors of an Ireland that desperately needed economic support after the Great War, the l916 Rising, the War of Independence and then the terrible Civil War.

One story in particular illustrates what Ranji meant to the people and they to him: when preparing for his first tenants' dinner, it was put to him that there should be no loyal toast to the King of England since local feeling among farmers, estate workers, fishing ghillies and others was fervently anti-British. 'Very well,' said the Jam Saheb, 'no toast, no dinner.' But there was a dinner and when Ranji rose to propose a toast his local advisers feared there might be a riot. They reckoned without Ranji's diplomatic skills: 'Gentlemen,' he began, standing with glass in hand, 'we have a custom in the country from which I come. It is an old custom and one very precious to me, and I am going to ask you to observe it. I want you to stand with your glasses and drink to the health of…the Emperor of India!' Whether all or any of his listeners put two and two together and realized that the Emperor of India and the King of England were one and the same person is irrelevant. The dinner, toast and all, was a great success.

He died on 2 April 1933 in India. By a cruel twist of fate, when news reached Ballynahinch and Clifden that their beloved Ranji had passed away, it was thought he had died on 1 April and with that date in mind some locals refused to accept his death, thinking it must be a joke. When the sad news was confirmed, as Martin Halloran told me himself with tears in his eyes, 'almost everywhere you went for weeks, even months, people couldn't stop crying for Ranji.'

This then is the house you are in. Outside is a tennis court and croquet lawn. The cricket nets are hardly used since the days Ranji would have had first-class players from England over for weekends. For the active tourist there is salmon and sea-trout fishing, woodcock shooting and within easy reach there are three first-class golf courses. You can hire bikes from the hotel and explore the estate or just wander in the 350 acres of grounds where not only is there the beautiful river but a boating and fishing lake, the old railway station and various shooting lodges. What could be a better way of spending your last afternoon in Connemara, before returning to the hotel and dinner?

Dinner at Ballynahinch Castle

Ballynahinch Castle Hotel, Recess, Connemara, Co.Galway
℡ (095) 31006

Open for lunch (at bar) and dinner all year except 3 weeks in February. Set dinner: IR£23.00.

When you drive up to Ballynahinch, you see extensive grounds, the solid Victorian building and, inside, big comfortable rooms with deep sofas and open fires burning wood or turf. What you do not immediately see is the river. It runs close behind the hotel, which stands high on the bank above it. The views are incredible and that is why, before you set foot in Ballynahinch, you should ring them up and book a table by the window as the dining room overlooks the river. Before you sit down to your pre-dinner drink, look around a little. There can be no doubt about the main function of the hotel—a rack full of fishing rods stands just off the hall, and if the staff are not too busy ask at reception if you can see their fishing book, which records the weight and numbers of salmon caught over the years.

The main bar is more of a pub—flagged stone floor, small wooden tables and chairs—and is popular with the locals as well as hotel guests. If you wish to concentrate on the menu, the fireside sofas in the main hall and drawing room offer the quiet comfort necessary for such important business. The dining room itself is spacious, the lights reflecting off silver and crystal.

The set menu offers four courses with lots of choice, mostly uncomplicated dishes which rely on good, fresh, local produce and make the most of them. Crab claws with garlic butter are a tender, meaty starter, in which neither butter nor garlic are in short supply. Avocado and dessert pear with Parma ham and sour cream dressing is a contemporary version of an old favourite, and a lovely combination of flavours. The smoked salmon is everything it should be, pink, succulent and almost overflowing from the plate, or you might prefer a deep-fried selection of cheese with Cumberland sauce. A soup of the day follows, carrot and ginger or maybe potato and leek, or a sorbet if you prefer, or perhaps a salad with a choice of dressing—poppy seed, blue cheese or French. You feel a sort of duty to choose salmon for your main course, grilled with a Béarnaise sauce, or perhaps baked with mushrooms, onion, tomato, herbs and white wine. But the peppered fillet steak with brandy sauce is thick and tender, the rack of lamb with rosemary and thyme sauce full of flavour, while for vegetarians there may be a dish of aubergines with tagliatelle and tomato sauce or courgettes with curried mushrooms. There is also a fish of the day—a plain grilled sole, or perhaps what they call a symphony of the sea, consisting of succulent pieces of brill, halibut and salmon in a light, delicate saffron sauce.

You could skip pudding and go straight on to coffee, but if you did you might miss a hot orange soufflé, or strawberries with lemon ice cream topped with champagne and curaçao. If that does not tempt you, there is ice cream layered cake with hot fudge sauce, or (my weakness) apple pancake with hot vanilla sauce and Calvados. There is also a selection of Irish cheeses. I cannot tell you what the filter coffee is like, but the Irish coffee is excellent! The service is friendly and attentive and children are welcomed.

Symphony of the Sea with Saffron Sauce
from Ballynahinch Castle

This is very quick to make; the fish only takes 5 minutes to cook, so get everything else ready first.

Ingredients:

Serves 4–6

4oz/100g fresh salmon
4oz/100g crab claws
4oz/100g monkfish
4oz/100g prawns
4oz/100g cod
A few chives, lemon and tomato slices for garnish

For the saffron sauce:

1 tablespoon sunflower or safflower oil
1oz/25g shallots, peeled and finely chopped
3floz/100ml white wine
5floz/150ml fish stock
A few strands of saffron
8floz/250ml double cream
Salt and freshly ground black pepper

Method:

Make the saffron sauce first. Heat the oil in a large saucepan, then sweat the shallots and saffron for a few minutes. Add the wine and fish stock, bring to the boil and let it bubble away until reduced by half. Add the double cream (which will not curdle if you boil it) and reduce again until the sauce is thick and shiny. Strain and correct the seasoning.

Cut the salmon, monkfish and cod into 3-inch pieces. Put the fish, the prawns and the crab claws into a large pan with enough water just to cover the fish and shellfish, bring to the boil, then immediately reduce the heat and simmer very gently for just five minutes.

To serve, pour some sauce into the middle of each plate—which you have warmed—and arrange the fish on it. Decorate with a criss-cross of chives, a tomato rose if you can manage it, otherwise a few thin tomato slices and a slice of lemon.

Mayo
The Road from Clifden to Louisburgh

It is very hard to leave Connemara, but the road north to Mayo goes through wonderful countryside. It takes you through the Connemara National Park, past the Gothic extravagance of Kylemore Abbey, through woods and by mountains to the long narrow inlet of Killary harbour with its marvellous scallop and mussel beds and the little town of Leenane. Shortly after leaving Leenane, the road enters County Mayo and follows a lonely route through bog and mountain, past Doo Lough with its tragic history. Then slowly the land begins to change, to soften, browns turn to green and ahead of you is the welcoming town of Louisburgh.

Getting there

Leave Clifden as early as you can—there is a lot to see. Take the main Westport road out of the town, the N59. The road you are on winds upwards out of Clifden and after a mile or so gives you a splendid view of the town with its twin spires. It is a very pretty journey through Moyard and Letterfrack and past the 5000 acres of wood, lake and mountain of the Connemara National Park. To your right are the Twelve Bens. The Abbey is signposted left, and at your first sight of it, you are tempted to stop.

Kylemore Abbey lies in a perfect setting on the shores of Fannon Pool, its white granite and pale grey limestone walls luminous against the green of the wooded hillside rising precipitously behind it. It is an extraordinary piece of mock-Gothic architecture built around 1865 by Mitchell Henry, a surgeon and businessman who had homes in Manchester, Liverpool and London. He married a girl called Margaret Vaughan from County Down and they decided to spend their honeymoon in Connemara. The story goes that on a picnic one day they fell totally in love with the enchanting

valley of Kylemore. On the side of a hill they spotted a tiny house and thought it would be idyllic to live there.

Back in England, Mitchell Henry set about finding the owner of the dwelling and discovered that there were nearly 10,000 acres of bogland, water, woods and moorland attached to the smallholding. He bought the lot and gave instructions to build the fantastic castle which you are now visiting. The construction of Kylemore took seven years. It had 70 rooms including 33 bedrooms, a ballroom, billiard room, library and reception, morning and dining rooms. Nothing was spared; it even ran to a Turkish bath. Outside there were walled gardens, staff apartments, and heated glasshouses for rare plants. Some say Henry was influenced in his choice of architecture by the contemporary popularity of the novels of Sir Walter Scott, evoking nostalgia for the romantic times of earlier centuries. He also built a Gothic church in the grounds, a replica of Norwich Cathedral.

The couple had nine children and spent much time at Kylemore, and Mitchell Henry also sat as Member of Parliament at Westminster for County Galway. But their idyll in Kylemore Castle did not last long. On a visit to Egypt with a friend, his wife caught a fatal disease and after just a few days died in Cairo. Mitchell lost interest in Kylemore, and the estate was sold. The next owner was a Chicago businessman who bought it for his daughter when she married the then Duke of Manchester. In 1903 it was rumoured that King Edward VII was interested in buying a place in Connemara and Kylemore was mentioned, but nothing happened other than that the King and Queen Alexandra were entertained to tea there. The Benedictine nuns who eventually moved into Kylemore in 1920 came from Yprès in Belgium, from where they had fled during the First World War with as many of the convent treasures as they could carry.

Today this impressive abbey is visited during the high season by an estimated 1000 tourists a day, so you will see at once why I recommended an early start! In winter, however, you may be the only visitors, as we were. It is a functioning, flourishing Benedictine community of nuns, who also run a girls' school with more than 200 pupils, some day-girls, some boarders. Despite all the visitors in the summer, the nuns still carry out their religious duties on a daily basis. You are allowed into the Abbey to see the hall, which houses some of the original treasures the nuns brought with them from Belgium. You can wander freely round the grounds, past the beautiful reed-fringed lake to the Gothic church about half a mile beyond the Abbey. It is small, with intricately carved stonework and, inside, columns of Connemara marble. It has been superbly restored and renovated after 20 years' work and was re-opened in March 1995 by the President of Ireland, Mrs Mary Robinson. I have watched progress on the renovation over the years and much of it has been painstakingly difficult—eradicating damp, replacing roof beams, broken stained-glass windows and damaged stonework.

The nuns have shown commendable commercial instincts in building a visitors' centre, a cafeteria and a large craft shop which sells Irish crystal, china, clothing and pottery, including their own, which you can only buy here. Making their own pottery is a comparatively recent idea, and it happened in the mid-1970s when the nuns sent one of their members to Youghal pottery in County Cork to learn the craft. You can see into the pottery itself through a glass window; the place is too small for visitors.

If you are fit and energetic, high above the Abbey on the rocky hillside, visible from far away, is a Christ figure. There is a path, but it is several hundred feet up the hill. The views, I am told, are spectacular.

When you leave Kylemore, turn left now onto the main road and you will have another chance to admire that wonderful view as the road cuts a swathe through the lake. We, and probably most other visitors, have countless photographs of the Abbey taken from here, the same view as all the postcards!

The road from Kylemore to Killary Harbour is one of my favourite drives in all the west of Ireland. To your left, dense woods occasionally part to let you see or at least hear a waterfall, while to your right the lake water laps to the road's edge and has been known to flood across it in bad weather. One moment this is desolation of a kind to make you shiver: hardly any houses on the bleak hillside across the lake, a few sheep clinging precariously to the mountainside and a chill wind that smacks through the valley. But the next moment the wind will drop, the clouds will change from an ominous grey to wisps of white like the cotton shrubs of the bog, and what might have been angry rain has turned to soft gentle drizzle soaking into the land. The bog here has been cut down and down for turf so that it is now almost level with the road and probably six feet lower than it was some years back.

You are now heading away from Kylemore towards Leenane, with the Maumturk mountains away to your right. About 15 minutes after leaving Kylemore, there is a turning to your left marked 'Scubadive West'. If you feel like a swim before lunch, or simply a walk along a remote, beautiful beach, go down this road. It is quite narrow and pot-holed in places and winds a bit, but just follow the Scubadive West signs and you will get there. The scenery is wild and spectacular, with areas of red sandstone, sculptured by the wind. When you reach it, the beach is wide, golden and sheltered. It is called **Glassilaun**, which means green island, and there in the bay are tiny little green islands. To your right, tucked away by its own little beach, is Scubadive West, and beyond that is the deep quiet inlet of Little Killary. If you have the time, this really is a detour well worth making. There is no road round the point to Killary Harbour itself, so you must retrace your route back to the N59 and on to Leenane.

The road curves round until it is running alongside **Killary Harbour**, which, as every Irish schoolchild knows, is Ireland's only fjord: shallow at the mouth and deep within, it cuts in towards Leenane and provides glorious views all the way along. A fjord is basically a submerged river valley which over thousands, millions of years has been greatly deepened by ice-action. It is 10 miles long, about half a mile wide and at its deepest more than a dozen fathoms. In effect it divides Mayo and Galway, with Leenane marking the last part of Galway.

As you drive with Killary Harbour on your left, look over to the other side of the fjord where there are examples of potato ridges: the almost geometrically perfect lines of raised, grass-covered earth which are sad, blunt testimony to the desperation of the peasantry in this and other areas in the 1840s—the skeletons of memory, I have heard them called. The potato was the staple food here in the last century, and when the blight, which was a fungus called *phytopthera infestans*, rotted the potato crop almost overnight, they were simply left in the ground and the fields abandoned.

Growing up in Dublin many years ago I was fortunate to have as my next-door neighbour one of the world's leading authorities on the potato and potato blight and famine, Dr Austin Bourke. Austin died in August 1995, but a few weeks before his death I consulted him about these ridges and he told me that they were also prevalent in parts of the north of England. Known also as 'lazy' beds, from the French *laisser*, to leave or leave alone, the beds marked a system of potato planting favoured in the middle of the 19th century in Ireland. What happened was this: the seed potatoes were laid at intervals in long straight lines on the top of the ground and then soil was heaped upon them from either side. Thus channels were formed on the sides and a sort of triangle effect was created. Looking from a distance, you can see exactly the ridges formed by this operation. Dr Bourke went to Chile in the mid-1950s on behalf of the World Health Organization because a blight similar to that which occurred in Ireland in the 1840s was feared. He had some fascinating information about the potato itself: 'A very strange, peculiar plant,' he said, adding: 'It is two months after it is put in the ground before the leaf appears and then a further six weeks before the tubers and roots begin to form beneath the ground. Then when the flower comes you know very quickly whether the plant is healthy or not. Of course this meant that in our Famines, it would be impossible to tell for about three months or so after planting whether the crop would be a success or not.'

Towering over all this on the Mayo side is Mweelrea mountain, which reaches a height of more than 2600 feet, making it easily the highest in the region. At the apex of Killary Harbour is **Leenane**, a pretty little town which today boasts on the walls of its pubs and hotels the photographic evidence that it has been the setting for major motion pictures, including

the movie version of the play *The Field* by John B. Keane (author of *Sive*). The town is small, and sensibly provides a car park just outside it which I suggest you use.

From there, it is a short stroll through the town to the Leenane Cultural Centre, a long low building facing straight up Killary Harbour. It is a great place. Mainly a centre for recording and demonstrating the history and traditions of the sheep and wool industry in Ireland generally, the emphasis is on this part of the west and Connemara in particular. History comes to you in the form of video, photographs and live activity. Go into the wool museum and you can see a lady demonstrating on a wooden spinning wheel all the ancient crafts and skills such as carding, spinning and weaving itself. She is used to questions about spindles and Sleeping Beauty! Here too you can see how natural plant dyes from the flora of the neighbourhood are used to colour the wool. Some of the results are quite breathtaking and are for sale with other knitwear in the craft shop.

When you leave the Centre take a few minutes to wander across and look over Killary Harbour to the sea, the mountains and the sheep. Sheep play and always have played a crucial part in the life of these rural communities in Connemara and they are pretty nearly all what are called Blackface mountain sheep, originating from Scotland in the 19th century. Judging by the finished product, the wool they produce is excellent. These are tough customers who can exist on the scant food available to them on bog and mountain, and if you thought that sheep only ate grass, look closely at the sheep grazing down on the shore at low tide. That is not grass, it is seaweed. And if the sight of sheep eating seaweed reminds you it is lunch time, head back through the town to the Portfinn Lodge. It is just above the road, and well-signposted.

Lunch at Portfinn Lodge

Portfinn Lodge Seafood Restaurant, Leenane, Co.Galway
☏ (095) 42265

Open daily for dinner Easter–end October; open for lunch and dinner July and August. Starters: around IR£5.50; main courses IR£12–IR£13, apart from the Portfinn Special which is IR£20; puddings: about IR£3.00.

Portfinn Lodge is a low, modern, white building, a restaurant with rooms, and it commands a wonderful view over Killary Harbour—almost as if it were keeping an eye on the source of the marvellous shellfish on offer here. It is a family concern, run by Brid and Rory Daly and their daughter Maeve. Rory is a big jovial man with the sort of looks you associate with the archetypal chef and culinary skills most can only aspire to. The dining room is simply decorated—white walls, white table linen. It needs very little for it is dominated by the big windows which look westwards over the Killary. Bread baked with sunflower seeds arrives at the table when you do, and it is surprising how much you manage to nibble as you read the menu. The dishes are predominantly fish and shellfish with a scattering of southeast Asian dishes, a couple of offerings for carnivores and a vegetarian dish of the day.

The starters are straightforward: wild smoked Irish salmon, marvellous prawn and crab cocktail, a garlic and liver paté, half a sweet melon with port or a seafood bisque. The main dishes made us think seriously about spending a few days here: turbot in champagne, fillets of brill with crab and Pernod, a vast steak of wild Irish salmon simply grilled and served with a garlic, lemon and herb butter. If you are deeply serious about seafood, then the Portfinn Special is for you: half a lobster served with a combination of scallops, salmon and monkfish, and you can choose the sauce. I had what I have to say are simply the best scallops I have ever eaten anywhere. In front of me was placed a large glossy black plate, encircled by the whitest, plumpest, sweetest of scallops. The sauce was champagne and cream and I wanted to stay there forever! The oriental dishes were a selection of fish in a coconut, curry and yoghurt sauce, served with spiced rice and chutneys, or marinated goujons of seafood, stir-fried with vegetables and served with basmati rice, poppadams, chutney and a satay sauce. Grilled sirloin steak or roast duck with an orange and Grand Marnier sauce are also on offer. Puddings are of the sticky, creamy variety or there are Irish cheeses. The service is good and children are welcomed.

My late mother and father spent many happy holidays in Leenane and my father particularly told me of the sheer pleasure of walking away from Leenane with the Killary on your left and behind you and heading on foot into County Mayo. After lunch at Portfinn Lodge, that is probably what we should have done.

Shortly after leaving Leenane on the road to Louisburgh, you drive by the river Erriff and the very pretty Aasleagh Falls. You can walk right down to the water's edge there, across a little stile. For the first few miles as you move away from Leenane you are on the opposite side of the Killary, facing towards the open sea. The road then bends northwards and you pass a small place called Delphi which Prince Charles visited briefly in 1995. The original name of the place was Fionnloch, or 'white lake'. The name was changed after its owner, the Marquis of Sligo, who had been a friend of Lord Byron's at Harrow school, visited Delphi in Greece. Lord Sligo was so impressed with the similarities between it and this Mayo landscape which he felt had a Delphic air of peace, with birdsong and lapping water adding to the atmosphere of wisdom, that he changed the name.

On your way to Louisburgh you will pass two other lakes, Glen Cullin, the lake of the holly tree glen, and **Doo Lough** or 'the dark lake'.

This route through the mountains is wild, desolate and at times eerie, but when the sun shines you can get stunning views over the lake and river and beyond to Mweelrea, and back along the road towards Leenane. On a dark west of Ireland day with rain and wind sliding off the mountains it seems a place hardly fit for the poor sheep who munch their huddled way along the mountain-sides, never mind for man. There is little habitation here but around Doo Lough itself there is much from 19th-century Irish history to stop you in your tracks. It was here that one of the most heart-breaking tragedies of the famine of 1849 occurred, and by the side of the road stands a simple bare stone cross in memory of those who died. Starvation was everywhere in this part of Galway and Mayo. The potato crop had failed yet again, rents could not be paid and evictions were the order of the day. Contemporary descriptions of wretched families huddled by the roadside with a few belongings bring tears to the eyes even in a 20th century almost inured to terrible human suffering.

Against this background, picture if you will local landlords or agents of absentee landlords: men who lived, for example, in London or Manchester and owned large estates in the west of Ireland where the rent was collected on their behalf by the agents. The peasants, the worst victims of the failed crops, had no representation whatsoever and would depend on kind and humane agents and landlords, of whom it must be stressed there were many, for either putting back payments or trying to solve what was an insoluble problem in the best way they could. Hundreds of people in Louisburgh (our ultimate destination for today) were quite literally starving. The rumour spread, which quickly became a strong belief, that there was food in good quantities at Delphi and there too some of the local dignitaries and agents were gathered. A group of between 400 and 500 men, women and children set out from Louisburgh to walk to Delphi, a round-trip of perhaps 40 miles and not on the road surface we are driving upon these days but across at best horse-tracks or a few well-trodden paths. Many people died on the journey to Delphi and were buried hastily at the side of the road. Those who made it waited in vain all day at the house where the worthy locals were meeting, only to be told there was no food for them, no places in any of the workhouses which might have afforded them some shelter and meagre rations, in fact nothing. They turned for home and headed back to Louisburgh past Doo Lough as evening fell. The weather was atrocious and when they reached the point where they had crossed the river on the outward journey, it was now in such a torrent as to be almost impassable. Weak with hunger, in rain, wind and darkness they nevertheless tried to cross. More perished now, swept aside like match-sticks by the flood and though there is no accurate account of numbers, to this day you will find the popular local belief that more than half, probably two-thirds, of those who set out from their home town never made it back to Louisburgh.

I have always travelled the first few miles after Doo Lough towards Louisburgh in comparative silence. You need a few moments to digest what you now know; the bleak Sheefrey Hills to your right, with almost certainly a sweep of Irish mist coming from them, seem a sort of mute witness to your own emotions.

As you head towards Louisburgh with the lough now slipping away behind you there are some beautiful almost miniature views to your left. The ever-changing colours now are soft reddish browns, light and dark green, and black. There is some afforestation of the Highland Spruce variety. You can continue along this main road to Louisburgh, but there is a pretty secondary road you can take which runs down near the sea. Turn left at the sign for Kiladoon. The road runs through soft, pretty country-side, with hills covered in purple heather. At the village of Killeen there are cross-roads. Ahead of you is the road down to a splendid beach well over a mile long called Silver Strand, where the Atlantic rollers crash onto the shore—a joy for surfers. Far out in the bay is lovely Clare Island, once the stronghold of Grace O'Malley. Turn right onto the road which will take you into Louisburgh. Just before you get into the town you will see signs for Roonah Quay, from where, if you have a day to spare, you can take the ferry over to Clare Island—a journey of just 15 minutes.

Rory Daly's Fillets of Brill with Crabmeat Sauce
from Portfinn Lodge

Ingredients: *Serves 4*

2½lbs/1.25kg brill fillets, skinned

1½ pints/900ml fish stock

4oz/100g butter

Half a shallot or 2 spring onions

2–3 tablespoons olive oil

1 clove garlic, crushed

½ cup flour

½ cup Gruyère cheese, grated

½ cup cooked white crab meat

½ cup puréed tomatoes, fresh or tinned

1 tablespoon chopped fresh basil

¾ cup dry white wine

Salt and freshly ground black pepper

½ cup double cream

Method:

Bring the fish stock to the boil. In a separate saucepan, melt the butter and stir in the flour. Mix to make a roux. Add the boiling fish stock, stirring all the time until you have a smooth, creamy mix. Pour in the wine and cook for 3–4 minutes, stirring often. Set aside.

Peel and chop the shallots or spring onions and fry gently in one tablespoon of olive oil until translucent. Add the tomatoes, crushed garlic, basil, salt and pepper to season and cook fast for 1–2 minutes. Add to the wine and fish stock sauce, together with the crab meat and Gruyère cheese.

Lightly dust the brill fillets with flour. Heat the remaining olive oil in a large frying pan and seal the brill very quickly in the oil, just half a minute each side. Remove from the pan and place the fish on a baking sheet. Bake in a pre-heated very hot oven for 3–4 minutes, testing that the fish is moist. Do not overcook.

Gently heat the sauce and when it is simmering, *not* boiling, add the cream.

Pour the sauce on top of or under the fish as you wish. Garnish with lemon slices and parsley and serve with new season potatoes and a mixed salad.

day fourteen

Mayo
Louisburgh, the Granuaile Centre and Old Head

Louisburgh, pronounced Lewisburgh, is a great town in which to base yourself. Not only are most of the places you will want to visit in Mayo within easy reach, but the town itself is peaceful, neat, with tempting little shops. Just a few miles from here is a beach covered in shells, rock pools, a huge sweep of sand and a little quay perfect for some amateur fishing, while in the middle of the town is an interpretative centre devoted to the life and swashbuckling times of the amazing Grace O'Malley, otherwise known as Granuaile, Grace of the Islands.

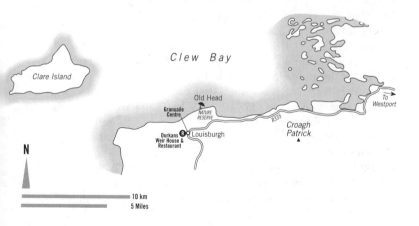

The **Granuaile Centre** is just off the main cross-roads in the middle of Louisburgh and well-signposted. Grace O'Malley, the 'Pirate Queen', was one of the most notorious figures in 16th-century Ireland. She dominated the west coast and there are countless legends and stories about her. The centre illustrates her life and times through pictures, artefacts, replicas and video. Most of what is known about her mingles historical and incontrovertible fact with legend and some Irish wishful thinking. She was born it is thought around 1530, the only daughter of Owen O'Malley, chief of the O'Malley clan which ruled the west coast from Achill Island to Inishbofin. The family motto, suitably, was '*Terra Marique Potens*', powerful by land and sea. At 16 she married Donal O'Flaherty, son of the clan that dominated the southern lands around Connemara. You have to try and imagine a sort of seafaring version of city business transactions, except with ships, blunderbusses and men and women taking the parts of polite dealings in stocks and shares. Land was for ever being raided and plundered and Grace was fearsome in such activity and by all accounts fearless in battle. Land-grabbing piracy and cattle-rustling were the order of the day and on one such raid Grace's husband was murdered by the Joyces from Galway. Some women—and men—might have capitulated. Not Grace. She rallied the O'Malley clan and sailed to Clare Island, which she made her permanent base.

From here she created a ring of forts along the mainland. When the time was ripe, she would launch her small fleet of almost Roman-type galleys powered by oars and sails, attack ships sailing from Scotland, Spain and France and plunder their cargoes. In 1566 Grace married again, this time to Richard Burke, who came from another local family and whose plundering instincts were much akin to the O'Malleys, and her swashbuckling lifestyle thus continued. About this time one of the more outrageous stories about Grace is said to have taken place, though it could perfectly well be true. At the age of 45 she gave birth to a son—while she was at sea and taking part in a battle. An hour after the birth, the enemy, who were Turkish pirates, managed to board her ship. Her sailors were on the point of being overwhelmed, when Granuaile suddenly appeared on deck wrapped only in a blanket, blunderbuss in hand, and shot the enemy captain. Her men rallied, captured the Turks and hanged the lot of them. She must by now have seemed unvanquishable but in 1577, during a raid on a castle, she was captured and flung into Limerick jail where she remained for 18 months. The condition of her release was the promise that she would end her marauding ways.

Her energies seem then to have been diverted from piracy to patriotic action against the English occupation. The violent suppression of the Irish by the Governor of Connacht, Sir Richard Bingham, in his attempts to

Clew Bay

enforce English rule in Ireland, roused Grace to extraordinary action. She determined to appeal directly to Queen Elizabeth I and, aged 63, set off to sail from the west coast of Ireland to London, eventually sailing up the Thames to confront the Virgin Queen. Amazingly, in September 1593 she was granted an audience (I have always wondered what might have happened if Elizabeth had granted such a thing to Mary Queen of Scots, whose admirers maintain that had they met, Elizabeth would never have signed Mary's death warrant). Elizabeth, so the story goes, at first offered Grace a title and was taken aback when Granuaile abruptly rejected it on the grounds that she was already a queen in her own right. How I should love to have been at that meeting. A deal was eventually struck. Grace kept her lands and her freedom, renounced her warlike ways and indeed helped to stamp out piracy along the very coast where she had ruled with such fearsome authority for so long. Thus did yet another Irish poacher turn game-keeper! She died in 1603, the same year as Elizabeth I.

The Granuaile Centre tells the story vividly and if your appetite is whetted, the craft shop sells biographies of the lady. The centre also has an exhibition on the Famine.

Just a mile or so northeast of Louisburgh is the beach at **Old Head**, which is a great place to spend the afternoon. Beaches in this part of County

Mayo are rarely, if ever, crowded; they are clean, generally safe and go on for miles. This is a wonderful sandy bay, and when the tide is in, fishing smacks and amateur fishermen with hired equipment can move out from the small pier in search of mackerel, various white fish and perhaps even sea-trout. When you look down into the clear, clean water, you have a perfect view of crabs scuttling around on the seabed, and shoals of little fish darting through the seaweed. You can, of course, sit on the end of the pier and have great fun with just a crab line plucking these little fellows from the tide. The last time we were there a small boy and his father were catching enough mackerel to dine off for a week. You may also see a few lobster-pot boats and their crews. The beach itself is a delight, full of pretty stones, shells and rock pools if the tide is right, and the sand is, I am assured, perfect for sandcastles. It is also a wonderful place for a stroll: over a mile of sand, Clew Bay in front of you, framed by Croagh Patrick and attendant hills.

Back in Louisburgh, take some time to wander in the town itself. There are two or three antique shops and a chemist which sells everything from cough mixture for people to liniment for horses, via china, calculators and novels. The local bakery, in a wonderful gesture against the excesses of modernity, does not open until 10 o'clock in the morning and supplies home-made bread and cakes whose smells will set your nose twitching. If you are in the town in July, there is a week-long summer festival with a vintage car rally, sumo wrestling, a heritage day, curragh races and a host of other goodies.

Dinner at Durkan's Weir House

Durkan's Weir House Hotel and Restaurant, Chapel Street, Louisburgh, Co.Mayo
℡ (098) 66140

Open for bar lunch and supper all year; restaurant open daily June–September, Friday and Saturday nights only October–May. Set menu (inc. soup course): IR£17.50; à la carte main courses: around IR£12.00.

Just off the main street (actually called Main Street) in the middle of Louisburgh is a largish building painted cream and blue in a not very prepossessing site; in fact I confess I was not sure we were at the right place. However, do not be put off. Durkan's is owned and run by John and Eileen Durkan and it is both a pub and a restaurant. Set back a bit from the road, there are a few tables outside and you can sit there in the summer and have some of their splendid bar food. It has two bars, one the pub, the other more of a bar where you have your pre-dinner drink. The restaurant itself is very pretty—soft greens, sweeping curtains, two fireplaces and it is wise to book.

John Durkan, who is passionate about food and adores cooking, worked his apprenticeship in first-class restaurants. The food is as fresh as it can be. The mussels and scallops come from the Killary, and the rest of the fish—monkfish, brill, sole, halibut, turbot—he collects from the local fishing boats, so you have a fair chance of eating fish that was still in the sea that very afternoon. In the summer, they fatten up their own animals. Vegetables and herbs, which he uses to great effect, they buy from local producers.

When we were last there we had a bit of a debate about Irish stew, on the thorny question of whether or not you put carrots in it. I was brought up to believe it was heresy for the dish to contain anything other than lamb, potatoes and onions, salt, pepper and water and that was it, though now I add stock and a bouquet garni. It is cooked long and slow so the meat is succulent and melting, the potatoes have almost disintegrated, as have the onions, and they form a wonderful fresh, naturally flavoured, thick sauce. John Durkan, in the Irish stew he serves in the pub at lunch time, not only adds carrots, but also broccoli, cauliflower and whatever fresh vegetables he happens to have. You have wonderful succulent lamb and melting potatoes, and then you unexpectedly bite into fresh, crisp vegetables which he pops in at the last moment, switching the stew off and leaving it to settle for 10 minutes or so; in those 10 minutes, the vegetables cook in the heat of the stew. I freely admit it was delicious, but was it *Irish* stew?

The menu for dinner combines adventurous dishes with excellent produce cooked as simply as you like. To start with there are Killary mussels in a white wine sauce, or warm salad with home-made black and white pudding with chutney. There is a fresh salmon mousse with a *coulis* of leek, or breast of wood pigeon with a port and grape sauce; also, of course, smoked Irish salmon, or half a melon with port. That is followed by the fresh catch of the day served with a champagne sauce or however you want it, or pink, succulent rack of lamb flavoured with rosemary and surrounded by a perfect lamb *jus*. There is Dover sole off the bone stuffed with a seafood symphony (a mix of fish and shellfish), or perhaps beef casserole in

Guinness with herbs, a marvellous, rich dark dish with the tenderest pieces of beef and melting vegetables. For pudding, you can choose from a delectable and totally wicked bread and butter pudding, or a raspberry mousse made with their own raspberries. Crème brûlée is available, and so is a light pavlova filled with cream and fresh fruit and served with a *coulis* of strawberries, raspberries and blackcurrants. The coffee is good and there are herbal teas. The service is excellent and children are welcomed.

Beef Casserole with Guinness and Herbs
from Durkan's Weir House

Ingredients: *Serves 6*

1½lbs/700g best chuck beef

2 dessertspoons oil

1 clove garlic, crushed

3 medium carrots, peeled and chopped

3 sticks celery, trimmed and chopped

2 leeks, trimmed and finely chopped

1 large onion, peeled and finely chopped

1 small turnip, peeled and chopped

2 medium parsnips, peeled and chopped

12 small to medium potatoes, peeled

3oz/75g flour

4 ripe tomatoes, roughly chopped

1 dessertspoon tomato purée

1½ pints/900ml vegetable stock, fresh if possible

2 tablespoons double cream

3floz/75ml Guinness

1 dessertspoon each fresh chopped thyme and basil

1 bay leaf

Fresh chopped parsley and chives to decorate

Method:

Cut the beef into small cubes, not more than half an inch. Heat the oil in a large pan and fry the beef for about 10 minutes, turning so it browns on all sides. Add the chopped tomatoes, tomato purée, flour and crushed garlic and stir well to prevent burning. Simmer the mixture gently for 5 minutes. Add the carrots, celery, turnip, parsnips and the thyme, basil and bay leaf, then add the potatoes (chop them in half if they look too large), vegetable stock and Guinness and bring it all to the boil. Turn the heat down and simmer gently for 20–30 minutes until the meat is tender. At the end of this time, add the finely chopped onion and leeks, stir, then turn the heat off and leave the stew to stand for about 10 minutes. The onion and leeks will cook in the heat from the stew. To serve, add the cream and sprinkle with fresh chives and parsley.

day fifteen

Mayo
To Be A Pilgrim

Every year, thousands of pilgrims of all ages and degrees of
fitness climb Croagh Patrick, Ireland's holy mountain
sacred to St Patrick, and today you can be one of them.
Even if you only manage part of the climb, the views down
over Clew Bay are worth every aching muscle. When you
come down, visit Murrisk Abbey, the traditional starting
point for the ascent of Croagh Patrick, and then drive to the
newly restored and re-opened Ballintubber Abbey, known as
'the Abbey that refused to die' and which was nearly 'the
Abbey that never was'!

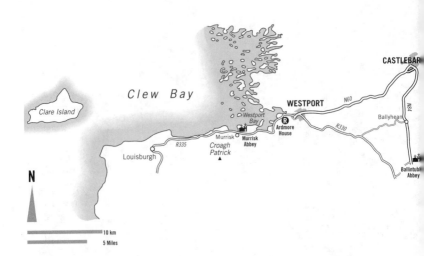

Getting there

Leave Louisburgh on the main Westport road, passing the police station on your left at the top of the town. Very soon, if there is no mist, you will start to get superb views of Croagh Patrick, towering to your right and easily the dominant physical feature of the neighbourhood. As you head for Croagh Patrick, Clew Bay is all along your lefthand side, a wonderful sweep of bay with Clare Island in the middle-distance and fine clean beaches everywhere, most of them empty.

Recently there has been some minor controversy due to the fact that what looked like gold deposits where found on the Lecanvey side of the mountain, the bit you see to your right travelling from Louisburgh. Debate raged about its exploitation but eventually economic uncertainty and the natural disinclination of local people to welcome the disruption, not to mention their anxiety about disturbing what, after all, is a holy place, put a halt at least for the time being to further excavations.

For miles around in this part of Mayo you can use the 'Reek', as it called, as a landmark: that is, when you can see it. Being high enough to dally with the clouds, the top of **Croagh Patrick** is often hidden in mist but on clear days it is possible to see with the naked eye the summit and the church where pilgrims attend mass. It is relatively easy to climb and with its distinctive cone shape has been a focus of religious worship for thousands of years. The present church was built in 1905, all the materials being lugged the 2510 feet to the top by pilgrims. It took a year to build and for many of those months the carpenter, stone mason and builder lived in a tent on the summit—a damp, cold, windy and foggy experience for much of the time.

There are a variety of traditions which local people will tell you about climbing Croagh Patrick. Some climbers set off in the early evening in fine weather in summer and hope to reach the summit just before or around nightfall—if you are fit and the mountain is not crowded it takes around two hours. A few hours' sleep and you awake, hopefully, to fine weather and an astonishing view over Clew Bay, where legend claims there is an island for every day of the year. Another tradition is that no matter what the weather, there will always be at least one person doing the pilgrimage every day, summer or winter. Indeed in the old days hardy Mayo men would take it in turns in the harshest of weather to go onto the mountain and up to the summit so that the old tradition was maintained. The last Sunday in July every year is officially designated 'Reek' Sunday and sees the single greatest concentration of pilgrims, sometimes as many as 60,000.

Croagh Patrick

My advice is to get to Croagh Patrick early in the morning and at least give it a go. There is a car park at the foot of the Reek so if it gets too much your vehicle is at hand. You do not have to be an experienced climber, but this is a climb which requires good walking or even climbing shoes or boots, a stick and a healthy constitution. It can be tricky in places and demands your attention the whole time. It is a thoroughly enjoyable way to spend your day, but it is not a leisurely stroll up a hill.

When you leave the car park, the first hundred yards or so are deceptively simple and the statue of St Patrick seems to beckon you on. Soon you will pass a large blue and white sign which details for you the benefits, according to the Roman Catholic tradition, of climbing the mountain. Making the climb on St Patrick's Day (17 March) or in June, July, August or September and attending religious services in the summit chapel makes a soul worthy of what is known as a plenary indulgence: a belief Catholics have that for good works on earth all their sins are washed away at the time of their death and the prospects of eternal rest in Heaven are considerably increased.

You will also see on this sign the three 'stations' or designated places and methods of worship which a pilgrim should follow; these involve walking around the various points of pilgrimage, normally seven times, and reciting prayers. Some of these beliefs may seem strange towards the end of the materialistic 20th century, but they are strongly adhered to by millions of Roman Catholics and you could never doubt the devotion of the pilgrims you will see on Croagh Patrick. When you leave this signpost the climb starts to get gradually more difficult; beware of slipping stones and the ground underfoot especially if there has been rain. If there is a crowd of people on the Reek, there is no point in getting impatient: the mountain has been here since long before St Patrick and it will wait for you.

Tradition has it that St Patrick spent the 40 days and nights of Lent here in fasting and prayer. For this he supposedly got a promise from God that the Irish would never give up the Christian faith Patrick had brought them. Some pilgrims for penance and self-mortification follow literally in Patrick's steps and climb the mountain barefoot, a very real penance when you realize that the quartzite, which forms the mountain, breaks up all over the place into sharp-edged pieces. For about the last third of the way, the path is steep and strewn with loose stones and rocks, and it is not unknown for the less sure-footed to finish the climb on hands and knees. However you get there, it is a wonderful sensation to be on the top. I have hardy friends who climb the Reek regularly just for the view, never mind the pilgrimage.

Even if you have no religious interest, have a look at the little chapel. It is small and simple and what a congregation it has. When you walk to the far side of the chapel, the views stretch as far back as Leenane and Connemara. On a good day, you can see the whole of Connacht.

At the end of your journey back down the mountain, take some refreshment in the handiest pub around: it is right at the foot of Croagh Patrick.

With lunch finished (or maybe it was afternoon tea if the mountain was hard on you) you can decide whether to walk or drive the short distance to Murrisk and its Abbey, the traditional starting point for the pilgrimage, signposted just opposite the pub, which is called the Campbell. Murrisk is a tiny bay with an attractive beach and a small quay where one day during a holiday I met a lobster fisherman and his son back from gathering their catch. They complained that the catch very often was poor, and that was why lobster was so expensive. The reason, they said, was that too many fishermen—cowboys, they called them—were catching female lobsters and not throwing them back, with the result that future lobster stocks were being jeopardized for short-term gain and already there were far fewer of them.

There is plenty of room to park at **Murrisk Abbey**, a rather sad and lonely ruin on the shores of Clew Bay. It was built for the Augustinians in the 15th century, and destroyed a century later by the English. Like many other ruined churches and abbeys in the west of Ireland, the church may have been destroyed, but the graveyard is still consecrated ground and still used for local families.

On one stone set into a wall the following is inscribed, giving a clue to the recent history of Murrisk: 'AD 1942. On the 11th August after a lapse of nearly four centuries since the destruction by heretics of Murrisk Abbey, the Holy Sacrifice of the Mass was again offered for the first time in this oratory by the Reverend J. O'Malley Campbell, the Parish Priest of Achill Island, and the Reverend William Hastings, both natives of this parish. The people of Murrisk in gratitude to Almighty God erected this memorial: *Laus Deo.*'

And that is pretty well that, though the delicate stonework of a window indicates this was once a fine building. The little oratory where the 1942 Mass was most likely celebrated is locked. Through the iron bars into the dimness you can see what looks like the high altar, dripping wet from the damp atmosphere all around. There is what could even be another church but it looks a bit like a gravel cave.

Inside there is a memorial stone which reads: 'To the memory of Owen Campbell of Murrisk, who died on June 9th 1928 aged 81 years and his wife Mary Campbell, July 6th 1904 aged 52.' When we went back to the pub, it was to discover that the present landlord is the third Owen Campbell to run the place.

If you have the energy and inspiration to go on, there is one more point of pilgrimage to be made, though you could leave it until another day, and that is to visit **Ballintubber Abbey**. It is an easy journey by car, and is also the starting point of a 22-mile-long pilgrim's path to Croagh Patrick which is still walked today. (No, I am not suggesting you walk it now!)

> To get to Ballintubber by car you leave Croagh Patrick and Murrisk and head for the sizeable town of Westport. From there you can take the little road across country to Ballyhean and then go south on the N84 for a little way until you reach the Abbey; but the more foolproof way is to follow the N60 from Westport to Castlebar, and then go south on the N84. The Abbey is well-signposted and there is a car park opposite it.

Ballintubber is known all over Ireland as 'the Abbey that refused to die' because of its long and successful struggle to maintain Christian worship against all odds since its foundation in 1216. The Abbey church is 29 years older than Westminster Abbey in London and, to put it in perspective, it was 300 years old when Columbus discovered America. It is 300 years older than St Peter's in Rome, it had been in use for 350 years before Shakespeare was born, and it is roughly a contemporary with cathedrals at Notre-Dame, Chartres and Rheims.

There is a lovely story about the building of the Abbey. In about 1162 a boy and his mother came looking for shelter to a man called Sheridan, who was in charge of a deteriorating old church or abbey. The boy was fleeing from his stepmother, a local queen, who wanted to kill him. Sheridan gave them shelter and protection and the boy grew up to be Cathal O'Connor, King of Connacht. Back he came as king to Sheridan and asked if there was anything he could do to thank him for saving his life. Sheridan suggested he rebuild the church and the king agreed and sent his masons to Ballintubber. Six years later he called on Sheridan again and asked how the new church was and to his astonishment Sheridan asked: what church? The king now sent for his masons only to discover they had indeed built an abbey at Ballintubber but at the wrong Ballintubber, one near a place called Castlerea. 'The Abbey that refused to die' was looking now like 'The Abbey in the wrong place', but the King agreed to correct the mistake and as compensation instructed that Sheridan's Ballintubber should be built seven times bigger than the original plans. Not only that, but because the Abbey and its environs were a starting point for pilgrims on the road to Croagh Patrick, King Conor

brought Canon Regulars of St Augustine from France to look after them in the Abbey and on the Pilgrims' Way, the *Tochar Phadraig*.

You can still march that route, on your own or with a group organized through the Abbey. The path is marked on most Ordnance Survey maps. I am sure if you wanted to do it and had good tough shoes, a stick and the sort of heart and equipment you need to climb Croagh Patrick when you get there, you would manage the trek in a good day. It is about 22 miles from the Abbey to Murrisk and I have always reckoned three or four miles an hour is reasonable going for a good walk. Assuming you take this route make sure you have an arrangement at the other end to get back to where you have left your car! At the beginning of the Pilgrims' Way you will see a thoughtful inscription on a stone, taken from the Book of Lismore. It reads: 'Going on pilgrimage without change of heart brings no reward from God. For it is by practising virtue and not mere motion of the feet that we will be brought to Heaven.'

If you simply felt like testing the Pilgrims' Way by going a few miles, then get one of the Abbey guides to point you towards Derryhondra, about two miles away from the church itself, where there is a famine grave. You would hardly know what it was: a slight mound, with small rock-like stones for headstones, no names or details, just a crude, hastily made last resting place for the victims of the blight.

In the Abbey grounds you can see the remains of the original route, which started out as probably a druidic roadway going back to about AD 350, 90 years before Patrick brought Christianity to Ireland. The roadway was made on a foundation of oak beams which rise through today's grass and moss. Also in the grounds and sheltered by a surround of low brick wall is St Patrick's Well, where it is said he baptized people in AD 441.

Ballintubber had a bare 50 years of peace before part of it, the nave, was burned. It was rebuilt in 1270 and some of the carved stonework you see in the chancel today is part of the original. The baptismal font, which is still in use, dates from AD 1200 and is believed to have come from Sheridan's original church. Needless to say, in this area you cannot get away from Grace O'Malley. Her son Sir Theobald de Burgos (presumably the one born on board ship in mid battle) who was murdered in 1629 is buried here. He was the first Viscount Mayo. In 1653, Cromwell's men tried to destroy the Abbey and managed to raze the monastic buildings, dormitories and domestic quarters, but the church somehow survived.

Restoration attempts in the 1840s were brought to a halt by the Famines, and in 1846 monies set aside for restoration were spent on relief and what food could be obtained for the poor and starving. Before the Famines Ballintubber had a population of nearly 7000; after them it had fallen to below 3000, most dead from starvation and typhoid. A further 500 went to America and Britain.

Probably more people would have died but for an extraordinary intervention by Mammon on behalf of God! In 1846 G.H. Moore of Moore Hall had a horse called Corranna which won the prestigious and valuable Tradesmen's Cup, now the Chester Cup, and with it a prize of more than 300 sovereigns, a substantial sum of money. The horse, trained by a Mr W. Boyce and ridden by a young man called Frank Butler, started with odds of 40–1 and between prize money and his wager Moore made £10,600 total profit and gave all the money to the relief of starvation in and around Ballintubber. It is said that before the race he said to the young jockey, a local lad: 'You are not riding against other horses but against the Four Horsemen of the Apocalypse: death, disease, hunger and famine. You must win.' The boy and horse duly obliged and later Moore was to say that his other horses would surely run better with the blessings of the poor. Moore's son, incidentally, was George Moore, the writer and critic who was an integral part of Lady Gregory's circle, and was also at the receiving end of some of W.B. Yeats's most malicious, but very funny (to us, anyway!) writings.

Even during Famine days and when the Abbey was roofless, Mass was still celebrated, and I remember seeing an interview on Irish television in the early 1960s with a 90-year-old woman who well remembered attending Mass when there was no roof on the Abbey. She told the interviewer that the remarkable thing was that even on cold, windy days and with maybe snow coming in through the roof, the candles would never blow out until they were quenched after Mass by the altar boys. Restoration work began again in 1889 and the north transept was re-roofed and restored. In 1965 what was to be almost exactly 30 years' work to rebuild the Abbey church began. It is now a place of peace, very plain, with simple white-washed walls. It can never be just as it was in 1216; relics of later centuries are everywhere. The west doorway and window in the nave are 15th-century; the small clerestory windows are 13th-century; the roof is Irish oak *c.* 1965, a replica of a 15th-century roof; the figure of Christ on the crucifix over the altar is probably 17th-century; the stone altar near the east end of the chancel is largely the original. And so on. But the whole is a remarkable testimony to a community who would not give up, who were bound together over the years by one overriding goal, that the Abbey should not die.

Dinner at Ardmore House, Westport

Ardmore House Restaurant and Bar, The Quay, Westport, Co.Mayo
℗ *(098) 25994*

Open for dinner daily (except Sundays) all year; closed one week in November and one week in February. Set dinner: IR£17.95; à la carte main courses: around IR£12–£13, except the lobster which is IR£19.50 for 1–1½lbs.

After the exertions of the day, an evening of quiet relaxation and quite a lot of good food are probably very necessary. On a little hill just outside Westport, overlooking Clew Bay, is Ardmore House. Since 1978 it has been owned and run by Noreen and Pat Hoban, she in front of house, he in the kitchen. It is open for dinner only, though they do serve bar snacks from 4pm into the early evening. When your restaurant is just a few yards from Clew Bay, seafood is bound to be the house speciality. The lobsters come from the part of the bay in front of the restaurant, the fish from not much further (actually from Achill Island). Pat Hoban might get a call to say a boat is coming in, and from it he takes the pick of the fish—brill, turbot, sole and, in summer, wild salmon. Mussels come from Killary—where else?

A table by the window is a must here, if you can get one, for the view over Clew Bay with the setting sun is just glorious. The restaurant is divided into nooks and corners with little pine screens; the table linen is pink and white. There is both a set menu and *à la carte*. To start, there might be pan-fried black pudding with oyster, apple and onion in a light mustard sauce, or crispy fried mushrooms with garlic mayonnaise. The Killary mussels are cooked *à la marinière*—steamed in white wine with garlic and a bay leaf or you might try warm salad of chicken and bacon with toasted pine kernels. There are also simple starters—home-made paté with redcurrant jelly, melon with a strawberry *coulis* or a mixed leaf and tomato salad. That is followed by a fish and shellfish soup, or a purée of vegetable soup.

If you are a lobster fan, then the Clew Bay beauties are cooked simply, with lemon or garlic butter on the side. The brill, turbot and sole are also cooked simply—*meunière*, pan-fried with lemon butter or grilled. As they have only just swum out of the sea, what more do they need? If you prefer sauces, there is turbot in a champagne-flavoured sauce, fillets of sole Marquery, cooked with mussels and prawns in a white wine sauce, or perhaps plump Killary scallops with a wicked sauce flavoured with Irish whiskey. The seafood platter has it all—mussels, oysters, salmon, crab claw and white fish. The rack of lamb is served with a rosemary-flavoured gravy, the wonderfully tender medallions of beef come with intensely flavoured wild chanterelles and shallots, or there are fillet or sirloin steaks, served with a choice of sauces. If you like your food seriously rich, then the breast of chicken filled with smoked salmon and cream cheese in a lightly flavoured tarragon sauce is for you.

For pudding, you could indulge in Ardmore brown-bread ice cream, or perhaps a rhubarb tartlet with vanilla ice cream and a fruit sorbet, an Irish Mist soufflé with a crème de menthe and chocolate sauce, or simply a summer fruit plate with fresh cream.

The service is efficient and children are welcome.

Pat Hoban's Turbot with Champagne Sauce
from Ardmore House

Ingredients:

Serves 4

4 x 6oz/175g fillets of turbot

Salt and freshly ground black pepper

1 teaspoon chopped fresh fennel

For the sauce:

> Bones from the turbot, roughly chopped (ask your fishmonger for them)
>
> 4 shallots, peeled and finely chopped
>
> 2oz/50g butter
>
> 1 small leek, washed, trimmed and chopped
>
> 1 bay leaf
>
> A sprig of fresh parsley
>
> ½ pint/300ml champagne
>
> ½ pint/300ml double cream

Method:

To make the sauce, melt the butter in a pan and sweat the shallots and leeks gently without colouring, then add the fish bones and sweat for a further minute. Pour in the half pint of champagne, add the parsley and the bay leaf, bring to the boil, skim and let it bubble until it reduces by half. Add the double cream and simmer for 10 minutes. Strain the sauce, return it to the heat, whisk and season. Keep in a warm place. Preheat the oven to gas mark 4, 180°C, 350°F. Place the turbot fillets on a large sheet of foil and sprinkle with the teaspoon of chopped fresh fennel and season with salt and pepper. Bring the edges of the foil together so it forms a loose packet around the fillets, but make sure the edges of the foil are tightly closed. Bake in the oven for 10–15 minutes. When the fish is cooked, lift each fillet onto a hot serving plate, coat with the champagne sauce and serve at once.

day sixteen

Mayo
Westport and Foxford

I should like to think that in your time in the west of Ireland you will have clear blue skies, uninterrupted sunshine and moderate to fresh breezes which will keep you warm and comfortable. In all honesty you are bound to get some rain, so what I am suggesting for today is enjoyable whatever the weather. It combines shopping in Westport, a drive round the northern shore of Clew Bay with its fine beaches, brilliant fuchsia hedges and haunting ruins, and a visit to the Foxford Woollen Mills. These were founded by a woman—a nun—whose energy and determination would have shamed Grace O'Malley and who changed the lives of the people of Foxford. The drive from Foxford to the wonderfully idiosyncratic place for tonight's dinner encircles that brown trout and salmon fishers' paradise, Lough Conn.

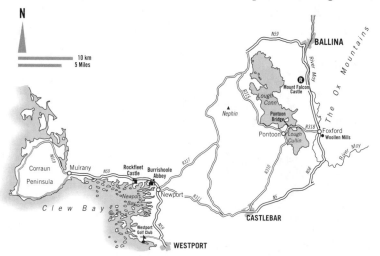

But first to **Westport**, one of the busiest towns in the west of Ireland. It is an unusual town for Ireland in that it did not grow piecemeal, but was planned almost down to the last detail for the Marquis of Sligo by the great Georgian architect James Wyatt. Wyatt put in broad streets, and along the banks of the River Carrowbeg at one end of the town created a mall effect on either side with overhanging trees: a lovely sight on a fine day or even when soft rain drizzles from the leaves. A rather alarming legend warns that a well called Poll an Chappell in the old part of the town will one day flood and drown Westport and its citizens.

The shops in Westport are as good as anywhere in the west. There are excellent clothes shops with locally and nationally produced garments that range from the functional to the very stylish. Irish designers have wisely started to make sure their products are available in smaller, busy towns and not just in the main cities, and the choices here are very good. There are some excellent art galleries, antique shops and one of the best-stocked bookshops in Mayo, with a most knowledgeable and helpful owner, which specializes, though not to the exclusion of other titles, in books of Irish interest and those relating to the history of Mayo and surrounding counties. Visit Westport in June and you will run into the two annual events which start the summer season for the town, the International Sea Angling Festival and the Horse Show. If you go in July, the annual Street Festival is as it sounds—a knees-up of music, art, song and dance in the streets. In the summer months it is impossible to find a pub that does not have a traditional evening of songs, ballads and music. In September there is the Westport Arts Festival and in October a hill-walking festival.

For the golfers among us, a few miles out of town is Westport Golf Club, one of the finest in the whole of Ireland. This is a course where your local caddie will tell you to 'aim for Croagh Patrick, sir, but just a bit right of the church on the top', for the Reek dominates the course and is an added distraction to your game as one minute it disappears in a mist and the next appears in all its glory bathed in bright sunlight. This is a tough test of golf but hugely enjoyable, and at one stage requires you to drive your ball out over Clew Bay and back to dry land again. (Not the whole bay of course, but enough to intimidate the unwary.)

When you leave Westport, take the road going north signposted Newport and Mulrany (N59). Not far out on the Newport road, in the northern corner, as it were, of Clew Bay (which is here called Newport Bay), you come to the 15th-century **Burrishoole Abbey** which was founded for the Dominicans by Richard Burke. Now it is an elegant, beautiful ruin, lapped almost all around by the sea though always accessible. A little further on you come to **Rockfleet Castle**, also known as Carrickahooley Castle, though it is little more than a tower. It is built on the rocks with a totally commanding view over the whole of Newport Bay and Clare Island. This of course is Grace O'Malley country and if you recognized

the name of the founder of Burrishoole Abbey, yes, that was one of her relatives. Rockfleet Castle was also built by the Burkes in the 15th century and it passed to Grace, so the story goes, by means of a little subterfuge. When she married Richard Burke in 1566, she did so on the understanding that either of them could end the marriage after one year by means of a simple declaration. She used the year to garrison the castle with her own men, and at the end of the year declared the marriage over. Poor Burke found himself in no position to ask, 'Please may I have my castle back?'

The tower has been restored and you can go into it, up first wooden steps and then a spiral staircase. As you will see, the price of a buccaneering life is not untold space and luxury, but a home where defence is the main priority.

The road between here and Mulrany sweeps you round the north side of Clew Bay and everywhere there are glimpses of tiny beaches which seem to wink at you and invite you down for a swim, a paddle or even a walk. Be sure to take at least one offer, unless you decide to wait and walk the biggest strand in the area, at Mulrany itself. The temperate climate and soft rains and sunshine throughout the year encourage a great profusion of fuchsias and rhododendrons here, and in spring and summer the countryside is ablaze with colour. If the weather is good and you are tempted to drive further, take the single track road round the hilly Corraun peninsula, a sort of thumb of land about six miles across, appended onto Mulrany's hand that juts out to the very end of Clew Bay and has some terrific views. Just follow the road round and it will take you back to Mulrany, and then follow the signs for Castlebar. Foxford is your destination, north of Castlebar and well signposted.

Foxford lies between the Ox mountains and Nephin mountain, which is a little higher than Croagh Patrick and was formed from a whitish quartzite which can make it look as if it has a perennial cap of snow.

When we first went to Foxford, we knew a little about the woollen mills, but nothing about the extraordinary woman who founded them. The town looks so prosperous now and is a magnet for fishermen drawn to the salmon and trout in the river Moy, Lough Conn and Lough Cullin. Foxford lies on the Moy and as well as being popular with anglers it is a decent-sized, pleasant market town with the usual thriving pubs and a few hotels and restaurants. At its heart, however, are the **Woollen Mills**, founded in 1891 by a young nun, Agnes Morrogh-Bernard who, with the help of an Ulster Protestant Freemason called John Charles Smith and against incredible odds set up the mill to try and stem the flow of emigration and create much needed local employment. The same order of nuns continued to run the mill until the late 1980s. It is now privately owned but still produces the products which made their appearance more than a century ago: fine quality blankets, tweeds, scarves and even some of the blue serge which is used for the uniforms of the Irish police force, the Garda Siochana, literally 'Guardians of the peace'.

Parking can be tricky in Foxford. There is a small car park near the mills but it fills very quickly and one bad piece of on-street parking followed by the arrival of a tour bus and the town comes to a standstill. I know, it has happened to me! Your best chance is to take whatever spot you can find where it is legal to park and walk the few hundred yards to the mill.

On your left as you go in the mill is a very substantial shop selling the tweeds and woollens produced here, as well as a good range of clothes from Irish designers. There is also crystal, china and the more usual things you would expect to find in a well-run arts and crafts shop. Upstairs there is an art gallery and a café with good home-made fare and excellent coffee. Leave all this until later. The visitors' centre offers a tour which tells the story of Mother Morrogh-Bernard and Foxford in dramatic audio-visual tableaux; it takes you through the schoolroom, the old mill, even a public meeting with life-like models and sound effects bringing it all rivetingly to life. You can follow that with a tour of the working mill itself. Every now and then you get a glimpse through the windows of the river, the ultimate source of Agnes Morrogh-Bernard's inspiration and the strength that has sustained Foxford over the decades.

Agnes Morrogh-Bernard was born in Cheltenham in Gloucestershire in February 1842. A detailed account of her life and work can be found in an excellent pamphlet locally researched, written and published. Her father John was from a prominent Cork family, the Morroghs of Glanmire, but had gone to school in England. Agnes's mother, Francis Mary Blount, was from an old English Catholic family and she had met John Morrogh when she was living in Cheltenham. He was at school not far away in Bath and spent his holidays in Cheltenham with his maternal grandmother, Mrs Bernard, who owned estates in Kerry. The couple were married in 1841 and returned to Cork to set up home. Mrs Morrogh went back to Cheltenham to be with her family for the birth of her first child, Agnes. When John Morrogh's grandmother died in 1849, he inherited the extra name along with the estates.

Shortly after the birth, mother and baby returned to Cork where the family lived until 1849 when, with his new inheritance, Agnes's father moved his family to Kerry. By all accounts a decent and kindly landlord, he was now faced with raising a daughter in famine-wracked Ireland. He grew flax on the land to provide local employment and the young Agnes would have seen from childhood her mother and father trying to help the poor and the destitute who gathered in increasing numbers as starvation swept the land. Agnes had a thorough education at convent schools, and was a good horsewoman and musician. But as the years passed, she set her heart on becoming a nun—not a recluse, but one who combined a religious life with active help for those in desperate need. Her father was heartbroken that his daughter, his pride and joy, wanted to become a nun and when he accompanied her to enter the convent of the Sisters of Charity in Dublin in July 1863, other nuns remarked that they had never seen a more heartbroken parent.

Agnes chose as her religious name Sister Mary Joseph Arsenius. She was professed as a nun in 1866 and having worked for some time in Dublin in various schools she came to Ballaghaderreen in County Roscommon in 1877. Her ideas, and her ability to implement them and organize and enthuse others left every place she worked at energized and thriving. In 1890 it was decided that Foxford and the surrounding area, which had been devastated by famine and emigration, would benefit greatly from the work of the Sisters of Charity, with Agnes as Rectress. Almost immediately a thought struck her: surely something could be done with this wonderful river that raced through the town? At Ballaghaderreen she had supervised a small spinning and weaving centre, but at Foxford the possibilities were so much greater with the power of the river to drive the machines. It is tempting, but true, to say the rest is history.

The Sisters of Charity lived by the rule that you should not rely on God's providence alone; you had a duty to meet it half-way. So after failing to get local support, Agnes eventually wrote to John Charles Smith of Caledon Mills, in County Tyrone, described to her by a friend as 'the most practical man in Ireland'. Agnes got a reply from Smith which read: 'Madam, are you aware you have written to a Protestant and a Freemason?' Agnes paid no attention to this, nor did Smith to the fact that she was a Roman Catholic nun. When they met, Smith at first poured scorn on her plans, but Agnes said she was going ahead anyway. He looked across the room at this determined lady and replied calmly: 'Very well then. I place myself and my experience of 20 years at your disposal.' The plan was off and running. Mother Morrogh-Bernard not only trained people to work the mill, which she named Providence Woollen Mills, she also organized a training plan in sewing, knitting, cookery, laundry and dairy-work. Success would only come if they could sell the cloth, and Agnes herself went to the buyers of the larger shops with samples of their material.

Grants were squeezed from initially reluctant authorities but with increasing ease as the mill began to take shape, and by the turn of the century it was a flourishing and profitable business. Agnes was ahead of her time as an early communications and public relations genius: she made sure that Anglo-Irish nobility with influence knew about Foxford, came to visit and helped promote the product. She organized the building of schools. She set up the re-training of peasant-farmers in a 5-mile radius from Foxford in all aspects of farming, and to a peasant population used to tilling what land was available to them, she introduced the notion of weaving, spinning and dealing with production lines for a commercial product. With money donated through charity, she even started a road-building project. In 1907 a terrible fire did much damage, gutting part of the mill and a school. Both were rebuilt and Agnes had a water-sprinkler system installed and switched the power source from gas to electricity. Providence giving and being given a hand, indeed!

All this is but a summary of an extraordinary woman whose achievements can still be seen all over Foxford, such as the music school she built in

1923, and the convent chapel completed in 1925. Even up to her death, aged 90, though stooped with age, she was still working on new ideas and projects. The continued existence and success of the factory is a tribute to a woman's efforts in an age when women did not have the vote, when a starving and destitute population fell to its knees and struggled for decades to arise, and when the modern channels of communication, technological developments and ease of transport simply did not exist. Against those odds, some of this remarkable woman's achievements slip astonishingly into perspective.

Foxford is only a few miles south of the Mount Falcon Castle, which is where you will have dinner, but if you go straight there you will deprive yourself of one of the most beautiful and spectacular drives in Mayo. If you have the energy after your trip to the mill then I urge you to take the Pontoon road, signposted in Foxford, and drive south, then around **Lough Conn**. Pontoon's name, you will not be surprised to learn, derives from the pontoon bridge which once crossed between Lough Conn and Lough Cullin, joining the Castlebar–Ballina road. There is now a permanent bridge. The Lough, about nine miles long and from two to six miles wide, has little bays, is full of tiny islands as well as wonderful salmon, and from the eastern shore there is a marvellous view to the west of Nephin rising from the waters.

Dinner at the Mount Falcon Castle

Mount Falcon Castle, Ballina, Co.Mayo
℗ *(096) 21172*

Open daily for dinner all year except February and March. Dinner: IR£20.

The Mount Falcon Castle is about four miles south of Ballina on the main Ballina to Foxford road and is well-signposted. The gates lead you into perfect parkland. There are about 100 acres of it, stretching down to the salmon-full river Moy. A sign on the largish hut on your left as you go up the drive says 'Fisheries Office', leaving you in no doubt that this is a serious place. When the grey-stone, creeper-clad building comes into view, it is revealed as not so much a castle, more a crenellated hunting lodge, and during the game season you may be greeted by the sound of shooting, while in the hall horned trophies from earlier times hang on the walls. It is not like being in a hotel at all, more like being in someone's home, which is exactly what it is. It is owned and run by Mrs Constance Aldridge, who for a generation has welcomed visitors here. In 1932 the house was about to be demolished when she and her late husband, Major Robert Aldridge, bought it for £4000. Archaeology and fishing became the Major's life and he discovered about 30 megalithic tombs and monuments in Mayo.

Mrs Aldridge runs a small farm in the grounds. The milk comes from a Jersey cow, eggs from the most free-range hens you ever saw. Children are not only welcomed here, they are swept off to be introduced to the disappearing art of milking by hand and collecting eggs in a basket for that morning's breakfast. There are also three wonderful floppy spaniels, who adopt you as a chum and try to take you for a walk—you are encouraged to obey.

Pre-dinner drinks are taken in a chintzy drawing room with a big open fire and Constance Aldridge, the marvellous hostess. She presides over everything: supervising the kitchen, hosting dinner and sitting in the centre of after-dinner conversation in the drawing room, making every guest feel genuinely welcome.

Your fellow guests are as likely to be American academics or oil men as Dublin lawyers or artists, British doctors or German businessmen. About 10.30pm on the night we were there, the door bell rang and three middle-aged Frenchmen, whose clothes proclaimed them to be experienced huntsmen, sort of exploded in, embracing Mrs Aldridge and overflowing with Gallic apologies for being late for dinner. They can only be described as Mount Falcon recidivists, returning here decade after decade for the hunting season. The reason for this interest in the other guests is that this is the moment to tell you that there is no menu, and everyone sits round a huge mahogany dining table which can seat 22 or shrink to accommodate 6. Dinner is at 8pm, you sit where Mrs Aldridge tells you, and it is exactly like being at a country-house party, with wonderful food. Much of it comes from the Mount Falcon farm, garden and river, and local suppliers. The cooking is traditional country-house, straightforward and very good.

The dining room has simple white walls, red curtains and a red-patterned carpet. The table, laid for 22, looks superb: ranks of white table napkins, rows of glasses and sparkling silver. There is no real choice of food, but if there is something you do not like you have only to say. On the night we were there, to start with there were a dozen oysters. The offer to make it 18 was a bit much even for me, but we compromised at 15. Then came a deep, rich golden brown turkey soup which Mrs Aldridge, who of course sits at the head of the table, herself served from a huge tureen, with an enormous silver ladle. That was followed by the pinkest, rarest roast beef, spinach from the garden, mashed potatoes, cauliflower, gravy, horse-radish, all superb. A board of Irish cheeses in prime condition was then passed round, and then round again. Pudding was either a pavlova with apricots or a lemon soufflé with cream, which just floated off the plate.

Coffee, filter or Irish, is taken in the drawing room. The chintzy chairs are pushed back, extra chairs are brought in and all 22 or so guests, with Mrs Aldridge in the middle, sit and chat round the fire. It is just like a house party, or the Rock Glen at Clifden without the singing. As someone kept whispering to me, 'This is great crack!' And it was.

The service, by local girls trained by Mrs Aldridge, is excellent.

Lemon Soufflé
from Mount Falcon Castle

Ingredients: *Serves 6*

6oz/175g caster sugar

3 eggs, separated

Grated rind and juice of 2 lemons

½oz/15g powdered gelatine

3 tablespoons water

6floz/175ml whipping cream

Method:

Prepare a one-pint soufflé dish by slightly oiling it. Whisk the sugar with the egg yolks in a basin until light and fluffy. Add the juice and rind of the lemons. Put the basin over simmering water and whisk until the mixture is smooth and creamy. Take it off the heat and whisk again for a minute or two, then allow the mixture to cool. Dissolve the gelatine in the 3 table-spoons of water in a bowl over hot water. Add it to the mixture slowly in steady, thin streams which prevents the gelatine from turning stringy. Whip the cream lightly and fold gently into the mixture. Whip the egg whites until stiff and fold those into the mixture gently. Pour the lot into the oiled soufflé dish and chill in the fridge until set.

day seventeen

Mayo
The Ceide Fields and Downpatrick Head

One of the most exciting prehistoric discoveries of recent years in Ireland, indeed anywhere in western Europe, has been the Ceide Fields (pronounced kay-jeh), high on a wind-swept headland in the northwest corner of Mayo about 30 miles from the busy town of Ballina. Five thousand years ago, before the Pyramids in Egypt were built, there was a sizeable population of farmers here who grew crops, raised cattle and fished from the sea 350 feet below them. Their land was fertile, their community organized, their lives peaceful. Now the farms are gone, and this whole area is covered in up to 12 feet of blanket bog. All you can see as you drive across it is mile after mile of brown and purple bog-covered hills, sometimes patterned with sunshine, often misty with rain driven by the tireless wind from the sea. In the 1930s, the remains of the settlement were first discovered and slowly the area is being excavated. Walking round the site and the visitors' centre is like being on one long glorious prehistoric detective trail. When you leave the Ceide Fields, follow the coast road and signs to Downpatrick Head, huge dark cliffs like fingers pointing out to sea with the waves of the Atlantic crashing against them. It is a brisk and bracing walk with views that can only be described as breathtaking—if you have any left to take after the power of the wind!

Getting there

From Ballina, there are excellent signposts directing you the 30 miles or so to the Ceide Fields. It is a beautiful route which takes you towards Killala and Bally-castle and then around a high coast road to the Ceide Fields themselves. If you leave Ballina early then there is time for you to visit two ruins which lie very close

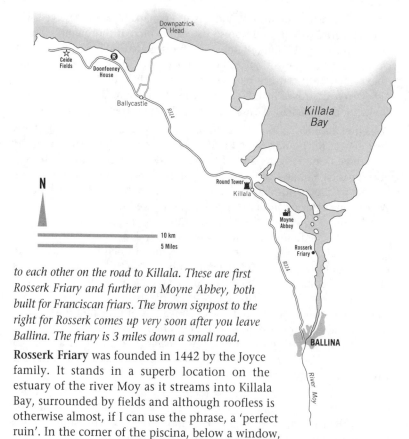

to each other on the road to Killala. These are first Rosserk Friary and further on Moyne Abbey, both built for Franciscan friars. The brown signpost to the right for Rosserk comes up very soon after you leave Ballina. The friary is 3 miles down a small road.

Rosserk Friary was founded in 1442 by the Joyce family. It stands in a superb location on the estuary of the river Moy as it streams into Killala Bay, surrounded by fields and although roofless is otherwise almost, if I can use the phrase, a 'perfect ruin'. In the corner of the piscina, below a window, are two carvings of angels, one carrying a hammer, the other three nails—representations of the instruments of the Passion. There is also a little stone carving of a round tower. When you get to Killala you will see the same round tower, but full-size. The stone staircases, which are still sound, lead up to where the monks would have had their dormitories. You can still see the layout of the rooms with their imposing fireplaces.

To get to **Moyne Abbey**, you do not have to go back to the main road. Retrace your steps to the first T-junction, where there is a cottage on the right and a 'Yield Right of Way' sign, and turn right. Moyne Abbey is about a mile and a half down this road on the right, its huge bell tower visible from some distance away. To get to it, you climb over a stile and walk perhaps quarter of a mile past a farmyard and fields. Architecturally, it looks like a larger version of Rosserk, and it is also remarkably well preserved. The staircases are in good condition so you can explore it thoroughly. Moyne was founded by the Burke family and consecrated in 1462. If you look closely at the plasterwork near the west door you will see an unusual and unexpected 16th-century representation of a ship. Both the Friary and Abbey were destroyed in 1590 by Sir Richard Bingham, Queen Elizabeth I's Governor of Connacht, whose violent deeds so incensed Grace O'Malley.

You enter another period of Irish history when you arrive at **Killala**. It was near here at Kilcummin Strand that in 1798 the French General Humbert with three French frigates and 1100 men landed and, en route south, very quickly took Killala itself and then Ballina. Their aim was to join the United Irishmen, formed the previous year by the Belfast Protestant, Wolfe Tone, whose colleagues had been influenced strongly by the French Revolution of 1789. The French gave arms, clothing and ammunition to the locals, issued bulletins which were headed 'Liberty, Equality, Fraternity, Union!' and called on the Irish to join their French friends to liberate Ireland from the English. The bulletins ended: 'The Irish Republic! Such is our shout! Let us march! Our hearts are devoted to you! Our glory is your happiness!' Alas! like so many episodes in Irish history, Humbert's efforts were in vain. He was joined by no Irish leaders of note and those locals who did rally to him seem to have been more of an embarrassment than a help. The English regrouped after early setbacks, and Humbert was forced to surrender. The French were treated courteously as prisoners of war; their Irish colleagues were hanged as traitors.

Killala itself is a pretty little town above its small harbour. It has two notable monuments: one is a 12th-century round tower, the other the spire of the Church of Ireland Cathedral of St Patrick. The cathedral was built in 1680 on the site believed to have been where St Patrick in AD 434 or 435 had built a small chapel.

From Killala, the road heads for the town of Ballycastle. As you come into it, you can see the great majestic cliffs of Downpatrick Head looming over the Atlantic—but that is for the afternoon. Once through Ballycastle, you have little if anything between you and the five miles to the Ceide Fields except a vast landscape. On one side is a huge view of the sea, on the other, rolling brown and purple blanket bog, covering the hills for mile after mile. Gradually in the distance you begin to make out a little blob on the side of a distant hill. As you draw nearer, the blob becomes a mound with a sort of pyramid-shaped greenhouse on top. This is the visitors' centre for the **Ceide Fields**. I must admit, the first time I saw this I had reservations: what was that 'thing' on the sky-line spoiling—or was it spoiling—the view? It is so incongruous, so different in this empty landscape, that I like it. It is also highly functional providing, like an ancient round tower or monument, a commanding view over the whole neighbourhood just as our ancestors might have made for their own protection. Look again at the empty landscape of unremitting blanket bog and imagine instead a network of green fields and golden crops, broken by a regular pattern of dry-stone walls and scattered homesteads—pretty much what you see in many parts of Ireland. What is unique about the Ceide Fields is that this is just what existed here 5000 years ago. What is now often a wet, grey, windswept and soggy landscape was once flourishing farmland, and the pattern of those fields and homes exists beneath its protective covering of bog, undisturbed for thousands of years.

The site is set spectacularly on the cliffs, hundreds of feet above the sea. There is a car park at the Ceide Fields and from there a short walk to the visitors' centre. The building nestles into the hillside, with the curious glass observation gallery perched on top. Inside, it is a model of what every such centre should be like. There is an excellent film which explains what you are going to see, and an exhibition hall dominated by a huge Scots pine, thousands of years old, which has survived because until 50 years ago it was buried by the blanketing bog. There is also a café.

While you are waiting for the film to start, look round the displays. There is the model of a cross-section through the bog, illustrations of flora and fauna from 5000 years ago, and some excellent life-size tableaux illustrating what life was like for farmers then: a little boy grinds corn between two stones, an old woman lies in a rough wooden bed, covered in sheepskins, and there is a simple wooden plough. All around clear and well-written boards explain the site: the flora and fauna, the climate, and the bog—how it was formed and how it preserved the site so effectively.

From now on, put yourself entirely in the hands of the centre's guides: they are trained, informative and most helpful. The tours of the excavated parts of the site leave every half hour or so from inside the visitors' centre. Work continues on various projects all the time under the organization of the Office of Public Works, and across the site you can see the flags which mark the areas currently under examination. What you actually see is a huge area of bog, with stretches of exposed white stones marching, as it were, up the hillside.

The Ceide Fields were discovered quite by chance. Over the years, the bog had been cut down for fuel and, in places where it had been cut right back to the soil, long lines of stones were revealed which disappeared again under the bog. In the 1930s the local schoolmaster, Patrick Caulfield, became convinced that these finds were of enormous significance, and though they excited great interest, nothing much was done until the 1970s. The prime mover then and now was Patrick's son, the archaeologist Seamus Caulfield. With teams of students, he began walking up and down the soggy bog, investigating every square foot of hillside, prodding down six, 10, even 12 feet with long rods to find the path of the walls which were then marked with flags. Through his energy and total faith in the importance of the site, funds were raised to create the visitors' centre, and to ensure continued exploration.

What has so far been uncovered and mapped over 18 summers of excavations are at least 75 kilometres of stone walls, 50 to 60 house sites and the remains of 10 huge court tombs. The nearest of these is some 500 yards away from the visitors' centre on private land and therefore it is not possible to view it. The total settlement covers a huge area of valley and hillside and more is being discovered with each summer of work. This must have been home to a very substantial population. These were not the first inhabitants of Ireland; before them came hunters and fishermen. The men and women who made their homes in and around the Ceide Fields were the first real farmers. They cleared the land, raised cattle and sheep and were the first residents of Ireland to settle in one place all the year round.

Why they chose to settle here we do not know. The land was covered in forests of hazel, pine and oak, which they had to clear with stone axes (metal was a thousand years or so into the future) and it is believed from the lack of charcoal in the ground that they did not burn the trees. The land they were left with was good farmland, where they grew wheat and barley which they tilled with a wooden plough, drawn by a cow as there were then no horses in Ireland. What they also had to do was divide their land up into fields. The walls are about three feet thick and three feet high and around a quarter of a million tons of stones went into building them. The stones were not quarried, but lifted off the land where they had been deposited by the last Ice Age. It must have taken a great band of men, women and probably children to build those walls: some of the stones, which are nearly all sandstone, are pretty hefty. Originally they would have been brown or black in colour; the brilliant whiteness that you see now is due to bleaching by acid in the bog.

The house sites are scattered across the hillsides, and so far one house has been found on each strip of land, not in clusters for safety. The questions that everyone wanted to ask the guide when we went round the site were why on earth did these people leave if they lived such peaceful, prosperous lives, and why were their farms blanketed by bog? The answer apparently is because the climate changed. Five thousand years ago, the temperature was about 2°C warmer than today. Rainfall was about the same and grass grew all the year round. As the temperature dropped, grass grew instead for 10 or 11 months, while less of the rain evaporated and more was absorbed by the ground. As time passed the land grew gradually wetter and the soil became poorer and poorer. The farmers began to move away, probably inland to more sheltered parts. And all you need to encourage blanket bog to grow is a fairly moderate climate with at least 50 inches of rain every year—easily exceeded here. Why the climate itself changed we do not know. I suppose it is always possible, if we are to accept the current theories of global warming, that in time this bogland could revert to agricultural land once more. Even now you can see the occasional green field in this area where the bog has been artificially drained. And if you are wondering how archaeologists know that the climate changed, it is all there in the bog.

Bog is 90 per cent water, and holding all that water together here is about 5000 layers of dead plants, dust particles and pollen. Because the bog is so acid, there is no oxygen, no micro-organisms, no bacteria in it. In ordinary soil, plants grow, die, rot and so re-fertilize the soil. In bog, plants die but they do not rot away; they just build up layer upon layer of dead plants. For archaeologists it is the perfect time capsule. They know what the climate was like by analyzing the pollen grains from the different plants found in the bog at different levels, last year, 100 years ago, and 5000 years ago.

Towards the end of the tour, you can have a go at a little archaeology. Using one of the long thin metal rods the archaeologists use, the guides show you how to plunge it into the springy bog. It is a very strange feeling when you strike a buried wall many feet down to know that you have discovered something last touched by man some 5000 years ago.

When your tour of the outside site is over, come back into the centre and climb up the stairs to the very top of the glass observation tower. Here you have a complete panorama of the Ceide Fields, Ballycastle, Downpatrick Head on one side and out and over the Atlantic, while to the distant northeast is Donegal and the fishing port of Killybegs.

When you leave the Ceide Fields, turn right and head back towards Downpatrick Head. Your first stop, however, is lunch at Doonfeeney House, conveniently placed pretty well midway between the two.

Lunch at Doonfeeney House

Doonfeeney House Restaurant, Doonfeeney, Ballycastle, Co.Mayo
℗ *(096) 43092*

Open daily for lunches (at bar) and for dinner all year. Sandwiches: about IR£1.20; poached salmon: IR£4.50

Doonfeeney House must be one of the best placed pub-restaurants in Ireland. Just five minutes or so by car from the Ceide Fields, and the same again from Downpatrick Head, the place stands as an oasis of good food and drink in this sea of bog. You cannot miss it: it stands right by the road and is painted a deep pink. Originally a farmhouse, it was bought by John and Pauline Busby about 10 years ago. To start with it was a restaurant only, with John, who is English, as the chef. Then they opened the bar as well, where they serve food at lunch time. John is now behind the bar and their daughter Aine is the chef. The restaurant, which attracts people from 40 or 50 miles away, is open only in the evenings. The Busbys come from Sutton Coldfield, not far from Birmingham, and the bar is very much the sort of place you would expect to find in the heart of England: dark wood tables and chairs and polished horse brasses on pretty well every available surface.

The bar snacks are just what you need after a morning at the Ceide Fields—generously filled sandwiches, light dishes and some tempting puds. Salmon and crab come from a little port about a mile away, and Aine's hot poached salmon and her crab claw salad are renowned locally. The generously sized mushroom omelette is served with buttered new potatoes and peas, or you could try the crispy skinned barbecued chicken leg. The sandwiches are splendidly filled with ham, cheese, salad or chicken and there is a choice of white or brown bread, soda bread or scones. For pudding there is meringue glacé, fruit pavlova or perhaps apple almond gateau, which is deliciously warm with lovely chunks of apple sprinkled with almonds and a layer of piping hot jam between the flaky pastry and the frangipani filling. A little thick cream melting into it made it perfect comfort food. This is a really welcoming place with reasonable prices.

From Doonfeeney, drive back into Ballycastle and follow the signs to the left for Downpatrick Head. After a bit the road forks. Take the left hand fork for the headland. Park the car where you can and walk.

This meeting of land and sea is awesome. **Downpatrick Head** juts out to sea and looks—no matter how far from it you are—enormous. At the far point of the Head, now cut off totally from it by the battering of waves over thousands of years, is a huge lump of cliff called Doonbristy, with a few yards of boiling sea between it and the headland. It has been compared to a slice of cake, but it is considerably more dramatic than that. This place is desolation and beauty. The walk up the Head is over green turf and, when I was last there, against a battling wind. It is the most exhilarating place. The cliffs here drop quickly more than 150 feet so be careful, though there is some necessary wire-netting to keep you back. The sea has cracked open huge holes in the rock and if the waves are violent enough, spray shoots up them. The largest of these, called Poulnachantinny, is in the middle of the headland. It was formed, so legend tells, when St Patrick, during a fight with the devil, hit him so hard with his crozier that the devil was knocked all the way through the rock into the cavern below. So violent was this fight that Doonbristy was also knocked off the end of the headland. At the bottom of Poulnachantinny is a tunnel, which runs from the cliff-face for about 200 yards or so and through which the sea surges. In 1798 during the French invasion in this neighbourhood, 75 people tried to hide here from the English, but all were drowned. A plaque to their memory has been erected in front of Poulnachantinny.

Just a few yards from the dizzying edge of the Head stands a statue of St Patrick, dated 1993.

Downpatrick Head

As you drive away from Downpatrick Head across the blanket bog with its ancient secrets, you wonder how many other settlements might lie buried here in the west of Ireland. Anywhere, we were told, where there is low-land blanket bog—in Mayo, Donegal, or Sligo—traces of the same field walls may be found at some time in the future. The next day takes us to Sligo, the second smallest county in Ireland but one of great beauty, history and culture. It is forever associated with the Nobel Prize-winning Irish poet and dramatist, William Butler Yeats, and his brother Jack, the painter.

Apple Almond Gateau
from Doonfeeney House

Ingredients:

5oz/150g shortcrust pastry (you can buy it readymade)

1 tablespoon jam—apricot, blackcurrant or your favourite flavour

2 eggs (size 2)

4oz/100g castor sugar

4oz/100g soft butter

2oz/50g plain white flour

2oz/50g ground almonds

1 teaspoon almond oil or essence

2 large Bramley cooking apples

2oz/50g flaked almonds

Method:

Roll out the pastry and line a greased 8-inch flan case with it. Spread the jam over the pastry. To make the frangipani, mix together in a large bowl the eggs, sugar, butter, flour, ground almonds and almond oil or essence. When well mixed together, spread it over the jam. Peel and slice the apples and arrange them on top of the frangipani mix. Sprinkle the flaked almonds over the apple. Bake in a pre-heated moderate oven, gas mark 4, 350°F, 180°C for about 40 minutes. Test with a skewer to see if it is done—if it comes out clean, the gateau is ready, otherwise give it just a few more minutes. Serve warm with cream, ice cream or on its own.

day eighteen

Sligo
Knocknarea, Queen Maeve's Cairn and Rosses Point

Before you enter the county of Sligo, make two purchases: the collected works of the poet William Butler Yeats, and some form of representation of the paintings of his younger brother Jack—a catalogue from an exhibition will do. From the time they were children, the brothers stayed here and both have immortalized in their work the scenery, the light, the faces and the grandeur of Sligo. Much of it still looks as it did then, a century or so ago: a small county with huge golden beaches, strangely shaped mountains and haunting prehistoric remains. Dominating the county town of Sligo— surprisingly large for such a small county—is the 2000-foot Knocknarea, the 'Hill of the Kings', in Irish *Ard na Riaghadh*, crowned with a great stone mound called Queen Maeve's Cairn, which not only has extraordinary legends attached to it, but also conceals a 5000-year-old tomb, as yet unexcavated. The 45-minute walk to the top is worth every step for the spectacular views. Afterwards, drive to Rosses Point with its two beaches where the young W.B. Yeats would walk with his uncle, who, it is said, was possessed of psychic powers. There is also a championship golf course here.

Getting there

From Mayo, the most direct road to Sligo is the N59 from Ballina. With the towering Ox mountains to your right, you head through the town of Dromore West to Skreen and Ballisodare into Sligo town. The views over Sligo Bay from this road are magnificent—wide golden stretches of sand, the blue of the mountains, and the Atlantic surf rolling in, which makes this one of the most popular places for surfers and windsurfers in Ireland.

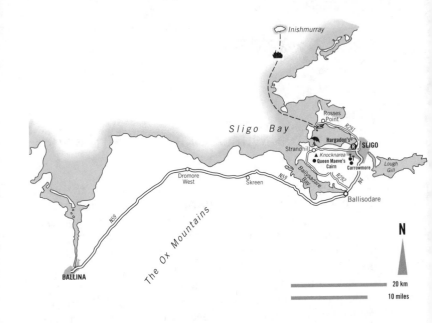

The road to **Knocknarea** is the R292 heading west out of Sligo town. After about three miles you pass Strandhill, a magnificent beach but where there has been too much modern development. As the huge green and dark grey mass of Knocknarea gets closer, you will need to look out for a little road marked 'Glen'. It is easily missed, so be careful. Turn up this road, which begins to wind up Knocknarea through farmland. The views just get better and better, even if it is raining. When you run out of road, leave your car in the car park at the foot of the path to the summit. A sign has been erected there which reads: 'Knocknarea. Queen Medhbh, goddess and mythical queen of Connacht, is said to be buried under this great stone mound on top of the hill of Knocknarea. The mound may contain a passage grave like that known at New Grange, and was probably erected in about 2500 BC.' I love the blending in Ireland of myth and fact and that the Celtic legend should have given to the queen a grave some thousands of years older than she was! Queen Maeve is principally famous in Irish mythology for her challenge to Ulster over ownership of a bull that resulted in a great battle. This story, which you can find in a variety of splendid translations, is recorded in one of the great poems in the Irish language, *Tain Bo Cualigne*, The Cattle Raid of Cooley. The poem was written by monks in the 12th century though its origins are probably much earlier. It was in such legends from Sligo that **W.B. Yeats** found so much inspiration.

The volume he produced in 1899 called the *Wind Among the Reeds* is one of his early great works, the first poem of which is called 'The Hosting of the Sidhe' (pronounced Shee). It begins:

> *The host is riding from Knocknarea*
> *and over the grave of Clooth-na Bare;*
> *Caoilte tossing his burning hair,*
> *And Niamh calling:* Away, come away:
> Empty your heart of its mortal dream.

It was the plan of W.B. Yeats and others who felt as he did, notably, for example, Lady Gregory of Coole near Kinvara, to preserve and spread the best traditions of Irish myth and culture based on, and deep-rooted in, Celtic myths—the so-called Celtic twilight. Nowhere inspired him more than Sligo, as it did his painter brother Jack, whose work is greatly influenced by his early life here. **Jack Yeats** is one of the greatest artists Ireland has ever produced and an outstanding and transcendental contributor to 20th-century painting. In the 1920s and 1930s, when Jack struggled as a painter, his work could be bought for a few pounds: these days those lucky enough to own a Yeats need have no financial worries—except perhaps the insurance costs!

Your immediate concern, however, as you start to climb Knocknarea is the state of the path: the climb is not a difficult one, but the walk is part stone and after rain also part mud. It was raining the last time I walked it and in places what should have been the path was a very pleasant gurgling stream. But I cannot emphasize enough how stunning the views are: that patchwork quilt of Irish green-grassed countryside, the solemn sheep meandering their way from one tuft of juicy grass to the next, deep purple and brown moorland replacing the grass, and then the summit. There you may well feel like Alexander Selkirk (the original Robinson Crusoe) as for a moment you can pretend to be monarch of all you survey.

Queen Maeve's Cairn on the summit is a large flat-topped edifice of stones, more than 70 feet high and an astonishing 600 feet in circumference. This massive structure is said to be built of more than 40,000 stones and is actually a passage tomb built by Stone Age farmers about 2500 BC. The site has never been excavated. When we visited the extraordinary Stone Age cemetery at Carrowmore, we were told Maeve's Cairn could be in danger of collapse because too many visitors insist on climbing up the stones, in spite of a notice telling them not to. You are urged instead to replace as many stones as you can on the cairn—indeed parties of school children have been organized to replace slipped stones—but your help is vital too. What you see on the summit now is the massive cairn, surrounded by satellite graves, very much as its architects planned it. If further deterioration of the cairn is caused by thoughtless visitors, it will, unhappily, have to be fenced off.

Round huts and kitchen middens of a similar date to the cairn have been found on the slopes of Knocknarea. The view from the summit is one of the finest in Ireland: a sweep of mountain and plain stretching from Mayo in the southwest through Sligo and upwards to the northeast and north into Donegal. Closer, as you look down on the beaches and sea beneath you, you can enjoy the intricacies of Sligo Bay, look back towards Sligo town and, shining in the distance, Lough Gill. In turn, the cairn on Knocknarea can be clearly seen, as surely it was designed to be, from far away. There is a clear, uninterrupted view of the cairn from the prehistoric cemetery at Carrowmore to the southeast, almost as if the sites were umbilically linked.

Before you leave the summit of Knocknarea, look almost directly due north towards the bottom lefthand corner of Donegal as it would be on a map, and you will see a small island. This is **Inishmurray**, Inish Mhuire or Mary's Island. It is quite a way out to sea, but if you have a day in hand and fine weather it is well worth a visit. But a note of warning: Inishmurray is not like, say, Inishbofin or the Aran Islands. There is no regular ferry service but a good reliable boat service provided by the Lomax family in Mullaghmore, whom you must contact if you want to visit the island. There is no pier and you have to skip from the ferry boat onto the rocks. This is not as difficult as it sounds and, as the owners of the boat have told me, in good conditions they have had men and women, boys and girls from 8 to 80 doing the trip. The boat and its crew stay with you for the four or five hours you are there and have a signal system in case the weather turns and you have to leave ahead of schedule. Your reward for getting to Inishmurray is that there is an almost perfectly maintained monastery, St Molaise's, with a vast 14-foot wall surrounding it, a ruined church and a small beehive hut which used to be the school-house for the inhabitants, the last of whom left in 1947.

This is one of the best-preserved monasteries in Ireland and was founded sometime in the 6th century but destroyed in early Viking raids probably about 807. There are crosses dotted all over the island which served as Stations of the Cross, but just to prove Christians had a sense of fury too, there are what are believed to be 'cursing stones', used to cast evil on one's enemies. The original wooden statue of the founder of the Abbey St Molaise is in the National Museum in Dublin.

Inishmurray is an extra day in itself, not really an adventure to be undertaken after climbing Knocknarea. What you should do when you come off the mountain is drive back to Sligo town for lunch.

Lunch at Hargadon's Pub, Sligo

Hargadon's Pub, 4/5 O'Connell Street, Sligo
✆ (071) 70933

Open daily for lunch except Sundays. No evening meals. Soups: about £IR1.30; hot dishes: about £IR3.75; open sandwiches and vegetarian dishes: about £IR3.00; puddings: around £IR1.50.

I love the word quintessential, but it is not exactly the sort of word you can find a use for every day. In relation to Hargadon's, however, you can use it happily, for this is, without doubt, the quintessential Irish pub. There has been a pub on this site in O'Connell Street since at least 1868, but it was bought by the Hargadon family in 1908 and has been run by them ever since. In many small Irish towns you will still find grocers' shops which sell everything from carrots to toothpaste to car spanners, and at the back of the shop, as if it were the most normal thing in the world, you find a bar. The front of Hargadon's still has all the wooden fittings and the splendid pot-bellied stove of the original grocer's shop of a century ago, though the groceries went long ago. The wooden shelves run at an angle, there are large stoneware flasks and jars and painstakingly collected bottles of brown ale of a suitable age, and rows of little drawers which once held coffee, tea and spices. The original counter is still here, complete with till drawer with its compartments carved out of wood, though instead of waiting in front of the counter to be served, you now sit at it to drink your pint. Time and chance have created this place. For the last ten years it has been run by Pat and Mary Leigh-Doyle. He was, as he describes himself, an unemployed bacon-curer from Wexford when his wife's family asked him to come and take over the pub. When Mary's grandfather died, no-one else in the family was really interested in taking it on and the pub was in dire straits. Since then it has been transformed into a bustling, busy place.

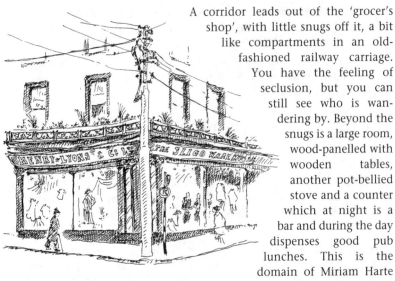

A corridor leads out of the 'grocer's shop', with little snugs off it, a bit like compartments in an old-fashioned railway carriage. You have the feeling of seclusion, but you can still see who is wandering by. Beyond the snugs is a large room, wood-panelled with wooden tables, another pot-bellied stove and a counter which at night is a bar and during the day dispenses good pub lunches. This is the domain of Miriam Harte and Joe Grogan, who run the food side of Hargadon's. Food in fact dominates their lives. Everything here is prepared fresh on the day, and from 7.00am they are in the small kitchen, from where in high season they can expect to serve 200 meals a day, from coffee and home-baked scones at 10.30am, through lunch, to the last sandwich at 5.00pm. That is the day job, as they also run a restaurant a few miles away at Strandhill.

At Hargadon's they serve soups with home-made brown bread, a range of sandwiches, open and closed, two or three hot dishes and always a vegetarian dish. Among Miriam's soups are tomato and basil, thick and warming beef and carrot soup, or perhaps leek and potato.

The hot dishes might include beef in Guinness, mussels in seafood sauce and pork in apples and cider, while for vegetarians Miriam cooks a range of quiches—spinach and mushroom, courgette and cheese or tomato and broccoli—and there might also be vegetable lasagne or home-made pizza.

The open sandwiches are more like salads. Thick slices of good moist ham are accompanied by a couple of slices of Miriam's brown bread, with coleslaw, sweetcorn, lettuce and tomato, or you might prefer cheddar cheese, smoked salmon or chicken. Puddings include apple and raisin sponge, chocolate biscuit pie or Bailey's cheesecake.

Prices are reasonable, the food is well prepared, and there is plenty of it.

After lunch, head for the seaside village of Rosses Point. It is well-sign-posted in Sligo town, and within a few minutes you are on the coast road with a concentration of houses on your right and the bay glistening into view on your lefthand side.

Rosses Point belongs to my childhood—when we were not in Galway or the Isle of Man. What a sheer paradise it is for children and adults. Like most of the beaches in the west of Ireland, it is very clean, unpolluted and clear: a delight with its crisp sand, bracing breeze and Atlantic waves crashing into Sligo Bay. And it is combined with one of the finest golf courses imaginable, where championships are regularly played and to which the golfing equivalent of a Croagh Patrick pilgrimage is made by both Irish sportsmen and foreign tourists. There is a tradition here which seems to take place all the year round: that of walking in the late after-noon along the strand. In all weathers you will find people just simply taking the air and the sea breeze along as many of the miles of strand as they have energy for. If you take this walk when the sun is setting the whole place seems to take on an extraordinary golden glow. I know people become excited about the sunset over Galway Bay, which may or may not be connected with the fact that there is a famous song about it, but here in Sligo there is a luminosity about the light at sunset which is unparalleled. As a teenager coming here on holiday, I would sit and gaze as sunset turned to night and the moon rose, with a head full of Yeats whom we were then studying at school:

> *Where the wave of moonlight glosses*
> *The dim grey sands with light,*
> *Far off by furthest Rosses*
> *We foot it all the night,*

Curragh

Weaving olden dances,
Mingling hands and mingling glances
Till the moon has taken flight...

and the refrain which haunts even now:

Come away, O human child!
To the waters and the wild
With a faery, hand in hand,
For the world's more full of weeping than you
...can understand.

'The Stolen Child'

Honey-baked Ham
from Hargadon's Pub

Ingredients:

Serves 6–8

4lb/1.75kg cured ham
3oz/75g brown sugar
3 tablespoons honey
20 (approx) cloves
½ pint/300ml cider

Method:

Steep the ham in cold water overnight, drain well then put it into a large saucepan and cover with fresh cold water. Bring it to the boil, then turn the heat down and simmer gently for 1 hour. At the end of the cooking time, turn the heat off and leave the ham to cool in the liquor for 4 hours. Take the ham out, and reserve one pint of the cooking liquor. Remove the outside layer of skin leaving a nice layer of fat. Put the ham into a deep roasting tin and pour over it the cider and the pint of cooking liquor. Mix together the sugar and honey and spread it generously over the ham. Stud with cloves. Bake for about an hour in a pre-heated oven gas mark 5, 375°F, 190°C, basting occasionally. Take it out of the oven and allow the ham to rest for at least 20 minutes before cutting it.

day nineteen

Sligo
Carrowmore and Carrowkeel—
The Day of the Dead

Today has nothing to do with crucifixes, garlic, young
maidens or even moonlight. Quite simply, Sligo contains
two of the most remarkable Neolithic cemeteries in Ireland.
One, at Carrowmore, contains 45 tombs and is the largest—
and one of the oldest—in the country. The other, at
Carrowkeel, is set dramatically on top of a mountain and
you will be forgiven for spending as much time looking
over one of the finest views in all Ireland as examining the
dozen or so passage graves. At the end of this day spent
contemplating memorials to mortality, dinner is at a
restaurant set splendidly on a hillside, overlooking Lough
Arrow and across to Carrowkeel.

Getting there

*Carrowmore lies about three miles to the west of Sligo town. Take the R292, and
follow the signs. The road goes through farmland of green fields fenced off from
the road and you are suddenly aware of huge stones in the middle of these fields.
The visitors' centre is just off the road, with a car park nearby. You are now in an
area where all around you are the astonishing remains of a Stone Age cemetery.*

Carrowmore is the second largest Stone Age cemetery in Europe, after
Carnac in France. The site is awesome: huge rounded stones many thousands of years old surrounded by farmland, with the occasional cow
wandering past. The burial grounds are spread over half a dozen fields or
more and the excavated chambers contained some cremated remains
which the experts say date back as early as 3000 BC. Here there are stone
circles, passage graves and dolmens, of which 45 remain. The area was
mapped in the 18th century, which is how it is known there were originally more than 200 tombs. Since then, many of the tombs have been

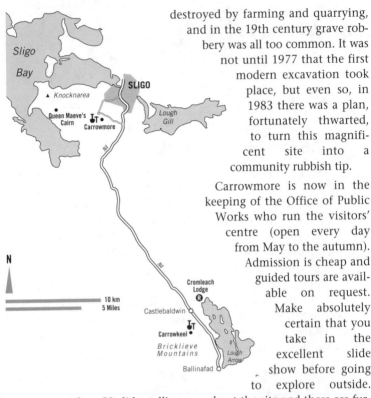

destroyed by farming and quarrying, and in the 19th century grave robbery was all too common. It was not until 1977 that the first modern excavation took place, but even so, in 1983 there was a plan, fortunately thwarted, to turn this magnificent site into a community rubbish tip.

Carrowmore is now in the keeping of the Office of Public Works who run the visitors' centre (open every day from May to the autumn). Admission is cheap and guided tours are available on request. Make absolutely certain that you take in the excellent slide show before going to explore outside.

There are more than 50 slides telling you about the site and there are further explanatory leaflets available. A team of Swedish archaeologists is excavating the site, after a lapse of 12 years, during the summer and when weather permits. The guided tour is essential, as the site is so diffuse and it is easy to miss some of the most interesting monuments, such as the largest of the passage graves into which, if you are small and agile (and probably under 12), it is possible to crawl.

However, if you are here during the six months of the year or so when the visitors' centre is closed, a word of warning. By each monument is a substantial, carefully engraved concrete slab, in English and Gaelic, telling you not, as you might expect, what it is you are looking at, but simply announcing that the OPW is responsible for its upkeep. When you are struggling through a muddy field in the rain, your guide book becoming soggy, it might have crossed some bureaucrat's mind that a little information about each monument would be of rather greater interest to the visitor than an OPW name-tag, especially as most slabs are easily big enough to include essential information as well. On enquiry, we were told that the lack of information was because the OPW wanted to keep the site as natural-looking as possible.

The site is about one and a half miles long and half a mile wide, and you are very aware in the distance of Maeve's Cairn on Knocknarea watching over it all. It is thought that the original structure of every tomb here was a dolmen with a huge capstone and burial chamber surrounded by a stone circle, but over the years one or the other has been removed, so you find stone circles on their own and dolmen on their own. One of the mysteries of Carrowmore is how they moved the huge stones. They are mainly made from granite and come from the Ox mountains about 14 miles away. Most may well have been deposited here by glaciers in the Ice Age, so they may have been lying within a radius of just a few miles. As to how the dolmens were constructed, it is thought that the standing stones were heaved into place, with just about one-third of the stone visible above ground. Earth and stones would then be built to form a ramp up which the capstone was pushed into place. An experiment was done to see if this were possible, and just six people managed to push a capstone into place, though I do not know how long it took.

Radiocarbon-dating has put one of the graves here as early as 3800 BC, although most date from 3000 BC and some of the tombs have also been used for later burials. Remains were cremated before burial, and personal belongings buried with the dead. Ornaments such as antler hairpins, necklaces made of beads and pendants of semi-precious stones have been found. Some of the finds have been extraordinary, remnants of rituals of which there is no explanation. In one of the tombs the bodies, which are believed to have been of girls whose ages were between 18 and 22, were buried with a piece of the skull of an older male and, nearby, unopened oysters. Not all the tombs have been excavated and, of those that have been in recent years, a quarter of each tomb is left undisturbed for future archaeologists. After excavation, everything is replaced exactly as it was, and once the grass has grown back you would not know that archaeologists had been at work.

There is, of course, a Celtic legend attached to Carrowmore. The site is believed to be that of the Battle of Northern Moytura fought during the age of early Irish mythology probably between the *Tuatha de Danann*, the people of the Goddess Danu, and invaders called the Formorians. Later

still when the Milesians arrived in Ireland, the once all-conquering *Tuatha de Danann* were banished to this magical world of underground burial sites, rather like Greeks being sent to the underworld. Interestingly enough it was the early Christian monks writing in the 5th and 6th centuries who first wrote down these pagan pantheistic myths. At first recorded in fragment form, by the 12th century completed works were the order of the day and in the Book of Invasions there are accounts of battles such as that of Moytura.

On the highest point in Carrowmore are the remains of the largest tomb, tomb 51. It is the only example of a cairn in Carrowmore and is believed to have been similar in size and shape to Maeve's Cairn. All the other tombs at Carrowmore radiate out from it. It probably has some central importance, but what it is is not yet known. Over the centuries the stones have been completely removed, and the tomb was opened by grave robbers in the last 200 to 300 years. All that remains is a large flat stone and entrance way. It is known locally as 'the giant's grave'. The big slab of limestone weighs about 12 tonnes and it is under this that slight people can crawl into the chamber below. You cannot stand up; if you want to do that, you must climb up to the passage graves on Carrowkeel.

This tomb is also very important because in the last couple of years a carving has been found on its front edge—the first indication that any of the tombs were decorated. It was found by chance by a tourist visiting Carrowmore on a wet day. She thought she saw a pattern of arcs and circles, and infra-red photographs proved her right. The pattern can only be seen when the tomb is wet, and then with great difficulty.

At **Carrowkeel**, many of the cairns still look intact, though some of them were subjected to some rather botched archaeological excavations in 1911. Their continued existence must be due to the fact that they are perched over 1000 feet up in the Bricklieve mountains.

To get to Carrowkeel, you go back towards Sligo town and follow the signs for the main Dublin road, the N4. It is a good fast road and after about 20 minutes you will see the signs for Carrowkeel when you reach the village of Castlebaldwin. There is a little information centre here which has some useful leaflets detailing what you are about to see. This is a very different place of burial to Carrowmore.

Turn right near the information centre onto a little road which winds up through farmland to what then becomes a combination of bog and moorland. The road then veers to the right and deteriorates rather fast, tarmac becoming gravel and asphalt and then a track. When you reach a farm gate, the track on the other side is close-packed stone and goes straight up the hillside. It is wild terrain, with little gorse bushes and moss-covered rocks. The road bends to the left and climbs steeply, then dips and climbs again. You know you are in the right place because there is a signpost for Carrowkeel, just as a staggering panorama of Sligo—probably the whole of Sligo—opens out in front of you. The road continues upwards, again just a track, and then you are at the site. There is space here to leave your car, but if the weather is good it might be better to leave it further down the mountain and walk the last half mile or so. This is not a site that caters for tourists. It is a hill-top for the prehistoric dead, a place of great beauty that superficially at least looks scarcely touched.

There are more than a dozen passage graves here, covered in mounds of stone. Over the centuries, peat covered and helped to preserve them. In 1911 the tombs were crudely excavated in a way that brings pain to modern archaeologists. The earlier archaeologists believed this to be a Bronze Age site; indeed there is a sign at the site to that effect. That no Bronze Age artefacts were found, only pottery, did not worry them—they simply argued that bronze was too valuable a resource to put in a grave. However, radiocarbon-dating has shown that the tombs are Stone Age, not Bronze Age, but detailed excavation is necessary before more is known. Some have collapsed internally, but one or two you can crawl into. According to the experts they are among the most elaborate ever planned.

The central cairn, known as cairn K, may have been designed as some form of solar calendar or clock since it catches the rays of the rising sun on the longest day of the year. Nearby there is a limestone plateau where you can see the remains of about 50 Stone Age huts, probably owned by the farmers who buried their dead in the nearby graves.

Crawling inside one of these cairns is an eerie experience. You move forward on hands and knees for a few feet, then the chamber opens up and it is easy to stand. The cairn I went into had two smaller chambers opening off it. Light filters dimly in through the opening, enough to see a beehive-shaped roof made of even-sized stones, with larger stones round the base of the walls. What was under my feet I did not wish to think about, nor the weight of the rock above my head. The experience, however, was unforgettable, and so was the view as I wriggled out. The position of the site itself is extraordinary. From here there are commanding views over the whole sweep of Sligo and down into Connacht. Without interruption you can see perhaps a dozen counties of Ireland. Below you there are three lakes in view, each more magical than the next: Lough Arrow, Lough Kee and Lough Gara. The belief that in death the body should have a good view is one that lasted a long time in pre-Christian society.

Take great care on the way down. You must return the way you came; the other side of Carrowkeel is not traversible by vehicles or indeed on foot by any other than the expert climber. Stick to the approved ways and you will have a great time.

Dinner at Cromleach Lodge

Cromleach Lodge Country House, Ballindoon, Boyle, Co.Sligo
© (071) 65155
Open daily for dinner February–October. Set dinner: IR£29.50.

As you are coming down from Carrowkeel, look across Lough Arrow. Half-way up the opposite hillside is a long low, slightly odd-looking modern building with a black slate roof, lots of windows and a conservatory in front. I am *almost* moved to say that I am not sure whether the view from Cromleach Lodge which looks directly up to the cairns of Carrowkeel is the better, or the view from Carrowkeel down to Cromleach Lodge when you know the sort of dinner awaiting you there!

It is a small hotel, with just 10 large and very comfortable rooms and a restaurant which quite simply serves some of the best food in Ireland. It is owned and run by Christy and Moira Tighe who, with no background or training in either food or hotel management, have yet created this gastronomic gem. Fifteen or so years ago, they both worked in telephones, she as a telephonist, he as a technician. They lived in a bungalow on the site and started to do bed and breakfast. When the first of their two children was born, Moira, who loved cooking, left telephones and they began seriously to consider opening a restaurant.

It began in a small way. They took the roof off the bungalow and moved the front wall forward to create the restaurant. Moira started with simple dishes cooked well, and for the first two years as the restaurant progressed she researched, tasted, tested and developed her own style. Inspiration came from a restaurant in Dublin called Whites, now long gone, and from reading a select few of the great contemporary chefs. Her food is French-orientated, but the style and presentation are all her own.

At the beginning, with no training, it was difficult to know what and how much to buy. Soups and sauces she made in advance, but nothing else would be cooked until the order came. Another major problem was finding suppliers for oils, chocolates, even fish such as John Dory, turbot or sea bass. They travelled and talked and asked advice. To start with, it was trial and error, but what Moira was looking for—and found—was excellence and consistency. All the vegetables and meat are organic, including venison and quail. Fish comes from a supplier north in Donegal, as no trawlers sail from Sligo these days. Cheeses come from good suppliers in Sligo and from Cork, as does the wonderful, creamy yoghurt.

To start with they still had rooms, but the quality of Moira's food was, they thought, fast overtaking the quality of the accommodation. For a year they operated just as a restaurant, and then they extended to build a hotel as luxurious as the food. The gleaming kitchen she uses now is not much bigger than the original bungalow kitchen, and the units are still the ones she had fitted 18 years ago. That is why, as you are walking into the hotel, you can smile at Moira as the kitchen is in the front! The pastry kitchen which produces sublime and award-winning desserts is in what was one of the children's bedrooms. She has five *sous-chefs*, all trained by herself. They are sent off on courses to learn basic skills, but they are not taught what she considers absolutely essential, and that is how to taste, so she does that herself. Consistency and tasting are her watchwords and the food she provides is some of the best I have eaten anywhere.

Drinks are taken in the bar or in a non-smoking drawing room. There are three and a half small dining rooms—the half is a gallery—all with wonderful views over Lough Arrow and all non-smoking. There is a great sense of intimacy and comfort, with elegant and stylish plates and silverware. There is a five-course dinner menu, with plenty of choice, and if you are staying here you are offered a six-course gourmet menu for the same price. You might start with a tartlet of quail's breasts on a bed of creamed lentils, a 'sausage' of chicken mousse and crab meat on a carrot and Sauternes sauce, or a small, light, baked goat's cheese soufflé on a hazelnut vinaigrette. We started with paupiettes of lemon sole with crab meat and ginger. Not only did it taste amazing, with the richness of the sole and crab meat perfectly contrasted with the hint of ginger and crispness of lightly cooked slivers of leek and a touch of fresh mint, but it looked stunning. It was a picture in white and pink, with the lime green leeks and deep green mint surrounded by fronds of herbs and tiny lemon-coloured petals. I know this is food I am talking about, but the skill, artistry and attention to detail which give such flair to each of Moira's dishes is something which many restaurants today find too labour-intensive and, as they might put it, not cost-effective.

You might follow this with a wonderful light celery cream soup—frothy, smooth and tasting of freshly cut celery—or perhaps a tossed salad with toasted pumpkin seeds or sun-dried tomatoes. For the main course there might be pan-fried escalope of veal on a grain mustard sauce, fillet of beef with a tartlet of mushroom and blue cheese sauce, poached turbot on a julienne of vegetables, or perhaps fillet of Sligo lamb with rosemary and Irish Mist and a parsnip purée. My lamb was pink, perfectly tender and surrounded by a marvellously intense sauce. The parsnip purée too had a wonderful texture and depth of flavour.

And then the puds. It is very difficult to know where to start with these. They are sublime, and even if you normally skip straight to coffee you should allow yourself to be tempted. The dessert menu is headed 'Tonight's Delights' and I would not argue with that for a second. There is strawberry and passion fruit mousse gateau, a terrine of dark and white chocolate and pistachio nuts, a parfait of tropical fruits wrapped in an exquisite parcel of the finest pastry, 'tied' with ribbons of chocolate and finished with a tiny flower of raspberry *coulis*. We had a selection of three, which included a florentina cornet of marinated tropical fruits. The crisp cone was filled with a creamy parfait and the tropical fruits, jewel-like and fresh, spilled brilliantly over the plate. In the centre of each plate was a flower, the outline drawn in the finest line of chocolate, each petal filled with a different flavoured *coulis*, passion fruit, peach and raspberry.

Coffee comes with a selection of little chocolates.

The service is friendly and faultless (young David Tighe, learning the business in his school holidays, deserves a special mention) and children over the age of seven are welcomed in the dining room. The set dinner was simply one of those rare meals you will long remember.

There is one other reason for visiting Cromleach, which if you arrive in daylight you should try to see, and that is a huge dolmen, just 10 minutes' walk away behind the hotel. Local people call it the Labby, which means bed, in this case that of the legendary Celtic lovers Diarmuid and Grainne. It is actually a portal tomb, unexcavated, and somewhere around 3000 to 5000 years old. Unusually, instead of standing proudly on a hill, it is hidden deep in a valley, its massive 70-ton roof stone now covered in a haze of purple heather. It is a splendid thing and the walk is very pleasant.

Loin of Sligo Lamb Scented with Rosemary and Irish Mist and Parsnip Purée
from Cromleach Lodge

Serves 6

Lamb from Sligo and Irish Mist liqueur are what Moira Tighe uses at Cromleach, but any good butcher will supply you with loin of lamb, and Madeira can be happily substituted for Irish Mist.

Parsnip Purée

Ingredients:

>1lb/450g parsnips
>¼ pint/150ml chicken or vegetable stock
>¼ pint/150ml fresh double cream
>Salt and freshly ground black pepper

Method:

Clean and chop the parsnips. In a saucepan bring the cream and stock to the boil, add the parsnips and season. Simmer until the parsnip is very tender. Allow to cool, then blend until completely smooth.

Loin of Lamb

Ask your butcher to bone out two loins of young lamb, approximately 3lbs each on the bone, so you have two strip loins and the bones.

To make the stock:

> Bones from the loins of lamb
>
> 1 bouquet garni and 2 cloves garlic
>
> 6 large tomatoes or 1 tin chopped tomatoes
>
> 4oz/100g each of carrots, leeks and celery, washed and trimmed

Method:

Trim the bones of all excess fat and brown in a hot oven for about 30 minutes. Heat a little oil in a saucepan and brown the carrots, leeks, celery and the garlic. Add the bones and enough cold water to cover. Add the bouquet garni and tomatoes. Bring to the boil and simmer for 3 hours, occasionally skimming off any fat which may form on the top. Strain the stock to remove bones and vegetables, and then strain again through a fine sieve or muslin.

To make the sauce:

> 1 sprig fresh rosemary
>
> 2 cloves garlic, crushed
>
> 1floz/25ml Irish Mist liqueur (or Madeira)
>
> salt and freshly ground black pepper
>
> 1floz/25ml fresh double cream

Method:

Bring the strained stock to the boil, add the fresh rosemary and crushed garlic, and then simmer until it has reduced to a third of its original volume. Strain and add the Irish Mist liqueur (or Madeira). Season and simmer gently for approximately 5 minutes. Just before serving stir in the cream and keep warm.

To cook the lamb:

Preheat the oven to gas mark 3, 325°F, 160°C, or 150°C for fan-assisted ovens.

Season the lamb with salt and black pepper and in a very hot pan, oiled with a knob of butter, seal the meat all over. Put it in the oven and cook for just 5 minutes if you like it pink, 8–10 minutes for medium to well done. To serve, remove the fat, cut the lamb into slices and arrange on warm plates. Pour the sauce around the meat and garnish with a quenelle of the parsnip purée.

day twenty

Sligo
Homage to W.B. Yeats

I do not suppose there is an area of Ireland more identified with one great writer than Sligo is with W.B. Yeats. True, Joyce, Synge and Shaw are very much identified with Dublin but they share the glory. Yeats, W.B., and his brother, the artist Jack, have a cultural stranglehold on Sligo that is at one and the same time unbreakable and ultimately so rewarding for the traveller that I think you will really feel after today in Sligo that not only do you know the county, you know the poet too.

Armed with that book of poems I suggested you buy (*see* 'Knocknarea, Queen Maeve's Cairn and Rosses Point', Day 18), you can pay homage to the poet where he is buried 'Under bare Benbulben's head' in Drumcliffe churchyard. You will see 'Where the wandering water gushes/From the hills above Glen-Car'. Just as W.B. did, you will be able to visit a place of memories and enjoy the 'light of evening, Lissadell'. And you will be able to see what we know Yeats had in mind that famous day in London when, walking down Fleet Street feeling very homesick, he saw in a shop-window display a jet of water which was keeping a little plastic ball permanently in the air. At that moment Yeats began to remember lake water, and was inspired to write: 'I will arise and go now, and go to Innishfree', the famous Lake Isle of Inishfree, a little island in Lough Gill. And you can if you like stand where Yeats did 'among a crowd in Dromahair'.

I suggest that today your route takes you from Sligo to Dromahair, then Manorhamilton and along to Glencar lake and waterfall, to Yeats's grave at Drumcliffe and, hopefully in the setting evening or late afternoon sun, to the house and grounds at Lissadell.

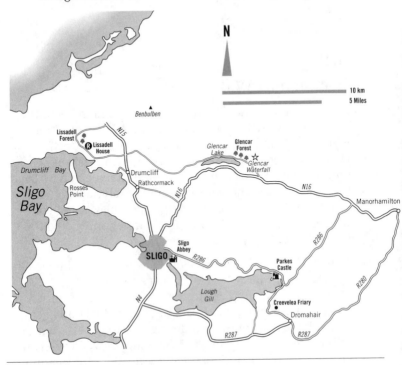

Getting there

It is not hard in Sligo to go in search of Yeats. All you do is leave Sligo town in pretty nearly any direction, following the brown and white signs marked simply 'Yeats Country'. Head south from Sligo town on the N4 (the Collooney road) following the signs for Dromahair.

Although just over the county border in Leitrim, Dromahair is so much part of a day enjoying Yeats country that I am including it here. A quiet little town, its name means 'the ridge of the air demons', and it appears in the opening lines of 'The Man Who Dreamed of Faeryland':

> He stood among a crowd at Dromahair;
> His heart hung all upon a silken dress,
> And he had known at last some tenderness,
> Before earth took him to her stony care.

On the road to Dromahair you will soon see a signpost for Dooney Rock. If you are so minded and have the time—it will not take long—pull off the road, park in the tiny car park and wander through rustling pine and silver birch to the edge of Lough Gill. It is a lovely sight on a fine summer's afternoon and you will begin to understand very quickly how such an area was a poet's inspiration.

When you have finished here, rejoin the main road and towards the bottom of Lough Gill you will come to another set of signposts (Sligo has to be one of the best signposted counties in Ireland). The road straight ahead will eventually take you to Parkes Castle just before Dromahair itself, but first turn left and follow the signs for the **Lake Isle of Inishfree**. The road is a dead end with a car park, and a few yards further on you can walk down to the water's edge—which, with 'lake water lapping with low sounds by the shore', is the inspiration for one of Yeats's best-known poems. It is a tiny island, covered in trees, with a boat moored by it. Who indeed would not wish to live in a 'bee-loud glade', on this dreaming lake, surrounded by green woods and friendly hills? There is something in the gentleness of these surroundings which seems to breathe peace and tranquillity and share them with the casual visitor.

An added bonus along the road to the lake's edge is the changing scenery, but by now you have probably come to take that as normal in the west of Ireland. When you have drunk deep of the view of the lake, go back and take the signs for **Dromahair** itself and very shortly you will enter this neat and quiet little hamlet with its few pubs, a couple of hotels, post office and local shops. What you are looking for now is **Creevelea Friary**, and though access to it is possible from the road leading to the village it is much easier to park in Dromahair and take the path which leads directly to the ruins.

With luck you will meet the soft-spoken and knowledgeable Tom Laughlin, who has been caretaker here for more than 60 years and who knows every stone and brick of the abbey. It was founded in or around 1508 by O'Rourke, Prince of Breffni, and his wife Margaret. Creevelea was the last friary established in Ireland before the suppression of the monasteries so it occupies a unique spot in Irish history. Its first community was brought from an abbey in Donegal but in 1536 Creevelea was accidentally destroyed by fire; since that date neatly coincides with the Dissolution, however, you have to ask just how much of an accident this may have been! The Franciscans, whatever the reasons for the loss of their monastery, were dispersed, not to return until 1642, but a few years later in 1650 they were expelled and the friary fell into decline physically. But like Rosserk and Moyne Abbeys in Mayo, this really is a very fine ruin. Tom Laughlin will take you round, gently explaining the sights available. He will unlock an iron grill to let you climb the almost perfectly preserved stairs from the ruined nave up to the very top of the tower. Here you can see down to the church, which is still used as a graveyard to this day and, in the distance, Leitrim and of course Sligo. Incidentally, half-way up the staircase there is a hole in the wall, known slightly off-puttingly as the 'Lepers' Squint'. Whether it refers to leprosy as such or other diseases is uncertain, but the fact appears to be that sick clerics would drag their beds to the wall and through this tiny 'window' could view and listen to the religious services down below.

Notice particularly at ground level among the tombstones one dated 1721, which for some inexplicable reason has perfect carvings of the four suits of cards; you can easily make out the diamond, spade, club and heart.

The stonework in the windows is unusually shaped, almost like tongues of flame, and well-preserved. Three sides of the cloisters are still intact, and make sure Tom shows you the delightful engraving on one of the columns of St Francis talking to the birds.

Just north of Dromahair is **Parkes Castle**, a 17th-century manor house which has a visitors' centre and an audio-visual display which will bring you up to speed on many of the historic and prehistoric sites in the area.

From here, your next stop is **Glencar** with its tumbling, 50-foot waterfall. Leave Parkes Castle, retrace your steps slightly and take the signs for Manorhamilton on the R286, until you reach a T-junction where you turn left for Glencar and the waterfall. A good rule of thumb here is that you will be going in the right direction so long as you can see Benbulben—flat, long and sparkling in the sunshine or glowering in the swirling mist, but in any event towering over everything in the immediate vicinity.

The lake of Glencar lies in a wooded valley of probably more than 20 intense shades of green. As you approach Glencar all the road signs make a point of reminding you that you are in Leitrim—and this is their bit of Yeats! The scenery is spectacular and locals are right to boast: here are huge hills on either side with the lake itself on your left as you drive. At one moment the lake is sun-splashed and inviting; the next, with a cloud passing over the water, dark and secret.

After a few hundred yards there is a car park on your left and you cross the road to walk to the falls. A long time ago when I first visited Glencar you scrambled through grass and stone to reach them, but now it is a well-paved path through woodland with the river tumbling down towards you. As you round a bend, suddenly there it is—a huge rock face, 80, perhaps 90-feet high, confronting you with water thumping and cascading over it. Here, 'Where the wandering water gushes/From the hills above Glen-car' is temptation for 'The Stolen Child', danced away by the fairies: 'Come away, O human child!/To the waters and the wild/With a faery, hand in hand...'. Here is faeryland indeed, this green valley with its rush of water. The pool below the falls must be very, very deep, because as the water flows away it does so slowly and into shallow nooks and crannies, the very 'pools among the rushes that scarce could bathe a star' of which Yeats wrote.

From Glencar continue on the road, heading away from the waterfall. After about a mile there is a turning on your left which you should take. On your right now there is Benbulben and to your left Maeve's Cairn visible on the top of Knocknarea. Shortly afterwards you join the Sligo road (N16) and after a mile you should turn off right to Rathcormack. At the end of this road turn left and you are only a mile or so away from **Drumcliffe** and Yeats's grave. Very soon you see the tower of the little church on your righthand side, peering up through the trees. The church is small but well worth a visit, but the Mecca is the limestone slab marking the poet's grave. He lies facing Benbulben and his own words need no addition from anyone, for he accurately penned his own epitaph to remind us of his attitude to human existence:

Drumcliffe church

> *Cast a cold eye,*
> *On life, on death,*
> *Horseman, pass by!*

In the past I have spent many an hour just sitting in the quiet of this graveyard reading from Yeats's poems or prose or perhaps a snatch of his many dramas. Not for any other reason than simply to revel in the genius of the man in the setting where his inspiration was at its height and his writings at their best. If however you just want to visit the graveyard, be photographed by the head-stone and then, like the horseman, pass by, a half an hour or so will do. Above you all the time you will be conscious of the presence of Benbulben.

Benbulben dominates the skyline in Sligo in much the same way as Croagh Patrick does in west Mayo. Completely flat-topped, it stands like a huge plateau sloping quite quickly at one end towards the sea and tapering off to foothills at the other. In many ways it has always reminded me a bit of another famous Irish mountain, the flat-topped MacArt's Fort which towers over the city of Belfast. Recent excavations near Benbulben have unearthed traces of ancient settlements, and there are flowers growing here which will excite the botanist since they are more common to alpine regions of Europe. Incidentally, the International Yeats Summer School held annually in Sligo since 1959 regularly makes pilgrimages here, but there is a steady stream of visitors the year round and no tour bus worthy of the name would dare not stop.

Tea at the Old Stables Tea House, Drumcliffe

Old Stables Tea House and Craft Shop, Drumcliffe, Co.Sligo

A slice of cake: 90p–IR£1; sandwiches: IR£1.30 (open ones are about IR£2.75); seafood: IR£3.95; tea for one: 50p; coffee: 70p

As if you needed one, there is a perfectly valid reason for staying a little longer at Drumcliffe, and that is to have tea in the small stone building right by the churchyard. Afternoon tea for me is nearly as big a treat as breakfast in bed—who has the time these days to sit down in those fleeting hours between lunch and dinner? But this is what holidays are about.

For the last seven years, Jill Barber has owned, run and baked at the Old Stables, serving tea to those who have come to pay homage at Yeats's grave and to those who may have just had the pleasure of discovering who he was and what he wrote. She also provides food for the mind in the excellent selection of books she has on sale. Obviously a large number are about Yeats and his circle but there are general works on Ireland too. There are also T-shirts with Yeats portrayed on the front, pottery, post-cards and little gifts.

The Old Stables is small and comfortable and if the weather is fine you can eat outside. On the walls are pictures of Yeats and miniature landscape paintings. The tables and chairs are pine, the tablecloths red and white gingham. Although primarily a tea place, you can also have garlic mussels, crab claws with garlic mayonnaise and fresh prawns. There is a wide variety of sandwiches, sausage rolls and of course cakes, all baked by Jill. Guinness cake is about the most popular. It is really porter cake, but she changed the name after deciding life was just too short to answer all the queries as to what porter cake was. It is a golden brown cake, rich, fruity and spicy, with delectable pieces of angelica, peel, cherries and lots of raisins, and it is served here with butter. And there are lots more: carrot cake with a light cream cheese topping, rich chocolate cake with a rum butter filling, chocolate chip muffins, and deliciously fresh and jamless sugar ring doughnuts. The scones, plain or fruity, are light and warm and served with jam made by Jill's mother-in-law. Cheesecakes are strawberry or raspberry flavoured or with Irish whiskey, while the chocolate crispies made from melted Mars Bars, rice crispies, syrup and butter disappear as fast as she can make them. And on top of all that, there is a range of bis-cuits and ice creams.

The cakes are on display at the counter where you order, but in the time we were there, as one cake was finished, yet another kind took its place, so ask what they have.

Leave the churchyard and turn right onto the main road heading for **Lissadell**. Watch out on your left for the signs for the house and very shortly you will enter the estate itself. After a short drive up a narrow track full of potholes, with open fields on one side and the ubiquitous Highland spruce on the other, you come to a sort of tunnel of trees, and as you drive out of it there stands the beautiful, elegant grey stone house. It belonged, indeed it does still, to the Gore-Booths. It was built in the 19th century by Sir Robert, who, during the famine, mortgaged the house to raise money for the starving.

The first thing you notice about this house are the huge windows. And what did Yeats write in his poem, 'In Memory of Eva Gore-Booth and Con Markiewicz', but the opening lines which go:

> *The light of evening, Lissadell,*
> *Great windows open to the south,*
> *Two girls in silk kimonos, both*
> *Beautiful, one a gazelle.*

And there before you are the windows, the two girls—sisters—you can but dream about. Eva was a poet and Constance Gore-Booth became Markiewicz when she married a Polish count. Not quite in keeping with the family's traditions, she became an ardent Irish republican, was condemned to death for her part in the 1916 uprising but was reprieved. In 1918, she became the first woman ever to be elected to the British Parliament, but refused to take her seat as did all the members representing Sinn Fein. Instead she became the first minister for Labour in the new Parliament in Dublin, the Dail. The house is open during the high tourist season but even if you do not go in, try and time your visit for the late afternoon: seeing the setting sun as you leave the grounds and head back for the main road is a wondrous experience.

You drive away by a different road, marked exit. It too is a track through a tunnel of trees, but then suddenly you burst out onto the shores of Sligo Bay. Stop where you can, and just listen. All you can hear is the gentle ploppy murmur of the water as it shrugs itself against the shore. Look up and beyond the bay to the drift of misty hills following one another until they merge with the sky. It is the most extraordinarily beautiful setting. Of all the counties in the west of Ireland, Sligo is the one that makes you feel most as if time is standing still. Sometimes clichés are true! The combination here of evening sunlight falling across the water and the greens and purples and golds of the surrounding hills make the type of spectacular landscape that the other great Yeats, Jack, poured so wonderfully into his paintings. Here you can witness at first hand the combination of forces that not only give us so much joy as we observe them, but are reproduced in word and painting so majestically that they never need be far from us.

As you drive round the shores of the bay, the road turns and takes you back through the woods and so on to the main road and the short drive to Sligo town. **Sligo** is the gateway historically, and indeed to this day, between Connacht and Ulster, and is situated on the river Garavogue which could be forded here. A castle was built in the town in 1245 by Maurice Fitzgerald, an Anglo-Norman, who was probably the first to spot the town's strategic importance. Sligo Abbey remains the only really medieval survivor. It was built by Fitzgerald for the Dominicans in 1252 and in 1414 was burned to the ground when a candle fell over and started a huge fire. Restored, it was again destroyed in 1641 but the legend goes that the abbey's great silver bell was saved by worshippers who decided the

safest place for it was in Lough Gill. It is said—and some still believe it—that the bell peals from under the water but can be heard only by those who are free from sin.

After your pursuit of Yeats today, here in the town you can see original work by both Jack and W.B. The Sligo Art Gallery, for example, has works by their father John, a well-known painter, works by Jack himself and other paintings by prominent Irish painters.

As for W.B., there is the summer school, the Yeats Visitors' Centre with the family's Sligo connections illustrated by an audio-visual exhibition, and the Sligo County Museum, which houses a section devoted to him. It has a complete collection of Yeats's poems from 1889 to 1936, some unpublished letters and other writings. The citation for his Nobel Prize for Literature in 1928 is also here, though not the wonderful story of his reply to the legendary Bertie Smyllie who, as editor of the *Irish Times*, saw the news of Yeats's prize coming into the office late one evening. Catching up with Yeats, who was walking through Dublin from the Abbey Theatre to his home in Sandymount, a suburb along the shores of Dublin Bay, Smyllie grabbed Yeats by the arm and excitedly gushed: 'Will, Willie, you've won the Nobel Prize for Literature.' Yeats looked down at Smyllie, quietly adjusted his bow tie, thought for a moment and then asked: 'How much, Smyllie, how much?'

Guinness or Porter Cake
from the Old Stables Tea House

Ingredients:

4oz/100g margarine or butter

8oz/225g sultanas

4oz/100g raisins

4oz/100g mixed peel and cherries

¼ pint/150ml Guinness or stout

4oz/100g brown sugar

8oz/225g plain flour

½ level teaspoon each of baking soda, cinnamon, mixed spice, nutmeg and ground cloves

2 eggs, beaten

2oz/50g flaked almonds

Method:

Lightly grease a 2lb/900g loaf tin and line it with greaseproof paper. Pre-heat the oven to gas mark 2, 300°F, 150°C, or 140°C for fan-assisted ovens.

In a heavy-based saucepan, melt the butter or margarine slowly and add the sultanas, raisins, mixed peel and cherries, Guinness or stout and the brown sugar. Bring to the boil, reduce heat and allow to simmer for 10–15 minutes, stirring occasionally. Remove from the heat and allow to cool until almost cold. Stir in sieved flour, baking powder and all the spices and the beaten eggs. Mix it all together well and spread into the prepared loaf tin. Sprinkle some flaked almonds on top and bake for one hour. Test the centre of the cake with a skewer. If it comes out clean, the cake is done, otherwise give it a few more minutes and test again. Allow the cake to cool, and, if you can bear to, leave it for two days before eating. It is delicious on its own or with butter, as it is served in the Old Stables.